On both sides of the Atlantic, V.S. Pritchett has been acclaimed as one of the great masters of the short story. He is also distinguished as a critic and a traveller. He was born in Suffolk in 1900, and left school at the age of sixteen to work in the leather trade in London. In the twenties in Paris he worked as a shop assistant and a shellac salesman and took to journalism, first the Irish Civil War and later, in Spain. His first book, *Marching Spain*, the account of a long walk from Badajoz to Vigo, was published in 1928 and since then travel has been his recreation, inspiring evocations of places and peoples in *The Spanish Temper*, *Foreign Faces*, *London Perceived*, *Dublin* and *New York Proclaimed*. The author of biographies of Balzac and Turgenev, he gave the Clark Lectures on George Meredith in 1969. For many years he was a director of and contributor to the *New Statesman*. He is President of the Society of Authors and is a foreign honorary member of the American Academy of Arts and Sciences. He contributes regularly to the *New Yorker* and the *New York Review of Books*. His critical works include *The Living Novel*, *The Myth Makers* and *The Tale Bearers*. His two volumes of autobiography, *A Cab at the Door* and *Midnight Oil* are well known in Great Britain and abroad. His novels include *Nothing Like Leather*, *Mr Beluncle* and *Dead Man Leading*: the last will shortly reappear in the Oxford Classics. The first volume of his *Collected Stories* appeared in 1982 and *More Collected Stories* in 1983. V.S. Pritchett is married and lives in London.

THE OTHER SIDE
OF A FRONTIER

A V.S. Pritchett Reader

ROBIN CLARK LTD.
London

For Dorothy

Published by Robin Clark Ltd.
A member of the Namara Group
27/29 Goodge Street
London WIP IFD

Typeset by A.K.M. Associates, Southall, Greater London
Reproduced, printed and bound in Great Britain by
Hazell Watson & Viney Limited, Member of the BPCC Group,
Aylesbury, Bucks

British Library Cataloguing in Publication Data

Pritchett, V.S.
  The other side of a frontier:
  a V.S. Pritchett reader.
  I. Title
  828'.91208   PR6031.R7

  ISBN 0-86072-075-6

Contents

For myself that is what a writer is — a man living on the other side of a frontier.

V.S. Pritchett
A Cab at the Door

Preface

I am glad to have become a portable writer in my old age because I was a perpetual reader of pocket collections when I was a boy, with a book bulging in one coat pocket and a notebook in the other. The present selection, from my writings in book form, starts in the thirties and approaches the present year. In the twenties when I left London to scratch a living in Paris, Dublin, Madrid and briefly in the United States, I went in order to learn how to write short stories, novels and reviews. Travel and reading foreign literature helped to give me the foreign eye I sought, that sense a writer has that he is living with one foot over a frontier in everything he does. I have preferred in this book to present myself specifically as a traveller in passages from *The Spanish Temper*, chiefly because Spain woke me up and changed me at a time of personal crisis, rather than in my essays on London, Dublin and New York. I have written five novels, two of them in print: *Dead Man Leading* and *Mr Beluncle*, but it is difficult to extract convenient passages from a novel. On the other hand there are nine complete stories and early scenes from my autobiographies and a good deal of my criticism. In the last analysis it is clear that I am not scholarly, that language rather than the arguments of the Schools has entranced me. I have in short been a nomadic critic, nomadic at home and abroad, one who writes as a means of discovery, perhaps one whose eye is directed at the quintessential nature of the writers he examines, and on the skills which have brought their scenes and people to life.

V.S. Pritchett

Acknowledgements

V.S. Pritchett and the publishers wish to express their grateful thanks to Mrs Norah Smallwood for her invaluable help in the selection of this book.

All the author's works are in copyright, and were originally published in volume form in the United Kingdom by Chatto & Windus as detailed below:

'The Sailor' from *It May Never Happen and Other Stories* (Chatto & Windus, London, 1945)

'Things as They Are' from *Collected Stories* (Chatto & Windus, London, 1956)

'Sense of Humour' from *You Make Your Own Life* (Chatto & Windus, London, 1938)

'The Wheelbarrow', 'The Fall', 'When My Girl Comes Home' from *When My Girl Comes Home* (Chatto & Windus, London, 1938)

'A Debt of Honour' from *Blind Love and Other Stories* (Chatto & Windus, London, 1969)

'The Diver', 'Did You Invite Me?' from *The Camberwell Beauty and Other Stories* (Chatto & Windus, London, 1974)

Chapters One, Two, Six and Nine from *A Cab at the Door* (Chatto & Windus, London, 1968)

Chapters Two, Three, and Four from *Midnight Oil* (Chatto & Windus, London, 1971)

Chapters One and Six from *The Spanish Temper* (Chatto & Windus, London, 1954)

'Samuel Pepys' from *The Tale Bearers* (Chatto & Windus, London, 1980)

'Jonathan Swift' from *The Tale Bearers* (Chatto & Windus, London, 1980)

'Boswell's London' from *Books in General* (Chatto & Windus, London, 1953)

'The Carlyles' from *Books in General* (Chatto & Windus, London, 1953)

Clarissa from *The Living Novel* (Chatto & Windus, London, 1966)

'The Shocking Surgeon' from *The Living Novel* (Chatto & Windus, London, 1966)

Tristram Shandy from *Books in General* (Chatto & Windus, London, 1953)

Excerpts from Chapters One and Two from *George Meredith and English Comedy*, The Clark Lectures of 1969 (Chatto & Windus, London, 1970)

'Stendhal' from *The Myth Makers* (Chatto & Windus, London, 1979)

'Poor Relations' from *The Living Novel* (Chatto & Windus, London, 1966)

'Flaubert' from *The Myth Makers* (Chatto & Windus, London, 1979)

'Maupassant' from *Books in General* (Chatto & Windus, London, 1953)

'Turgenev' (original title 'The Russian Day') from *The Living Novel* (Chatto & Windus, London, 1966)

'The Hypocrite' from *The Living Novel* (Chatto & Windus, London, 1966)

'The Great Absentee' from *The Living Novel* (Chatto & Windus, London, 1966)

'The Minor Dostoevsky' from *The Living Novel* (Chatto & Windus, London, 1966)

'An Irish Ghost' from *The Living Novel* (Chatto & Windus, London, 1966)

'Galdos' from *Books in General* (Chatto & Windus, London, 1953)

'Henry James' from *The Tale Bearers* (Chatto & Windus, London, 1980)

'An Emigré' from *Books in General* (Chatto & Windus, London, 1953)

'Kafka' from *The Myth Makers* (Chatto & Windus, London, 1979)

'An Irish Oblomov' from *The Working Novelist* (Chatto & Windus, London, 1965)

'Graham Greene' from *The Tale Bearers* (Chatto & Windus, London, 1980)

'The Art of Koestler' from *Books in General* (Chatto & Windus,

London, 1953)

'Saul Bellow' from *The Tale Bearers* (Chatto & Windus, London, 1980)

'Márquez' from *The Myth Makers* (Chatto & Windus, London, 1979)

Excerpts from Chapters One, Nine, Eleven and Thirteen from *The Gentle Barbarian*: the Life and Work of Turgenev (Chatto & Windus, London, 1977)

Chapter Six: 'Bankruptcy and Genius' and Chapter Fifteen 'The Price of a Dream Achieved' from *Balzac* (Chatto & Windus, London, 1973)

All reproduced by permission of the Publisher Chatto and Windus.

The publishers are indebted to the following for permission to quote from their publications: W.H. Allen & Co. Ltd. and Grossman Publishers, Inc. (Marceau, *Balzac and His World*); Editions Gallimard, Felicier Marceau, *Balzac and His World*; © Editions Gallimard 1955; The Bodley Head Ltd. (*The Unpublished Correspondence of Honoré de Balzac and Madame Zulma Carraud*); Cassell & Co. Ltd. (Zweig, *Balzac*); Macdonald & Co. Ltd. (*Les Illusions Perdues*. Published as *Lost Illusions* by Alfred A. Knopf, Inc. in the USA and Canada); and Penguin Books Ltd. (*The Chouans*). The quotation from *My Past and Thoughts* (Herzen) is from the edition revised by H. Higgins, published by Chatto & Windus Ltd. and Alfred A. Knopf, Inc., 1968. Maurois, *Prometheus: the Life of Balzac* is © 1965 in the translation by the Bodley Head Ltd., reprinted by Harper & Row, publishers, Inc.; Penguin Books Ltd. for permission to reprint brief excerpts from pages 94, 97, 105, 126, 142, 165, 169, 189, 220, 271 and 291 of *Fathers and Sons* by Ivan Turgenev, translated by Rosemary Edmonds (Penguin Classics, 1965). Copyright © 1965 by Rosemary Edmonds.

Select Bibliography

MARCHING SPAIN. J.M. Dent & Sons, London, 1928
CLAIRE DRUMMER. Ernest Benn, London, 1929
THE SPANISH VIRGIN AND OTHER STORIES. Ernest Benn, London, 1930
SHIRLEY SANZ. Victor Gollancz, London, 1932
NOTHING LIKE LEATHER. Chatto & Windus, London, 1935
DEAD MAN LEADING. Chatto & Windus, London, 1937
THIS ENGLAND. New Statesman & Nation, London, 1937
YOU MAKE YOUR OWN LIFE. Chatto & Windus, London, 1938
IN MY GOOD BOOKS. Chatto & Windus, London, 1942
IT MAY NEVER HAPPEN AND OTHER STORIES. Chatto & Windus, London, 1945
THE LIVING NOVEL. Chatto & Windus, London, 1946
TURNSTILE ONE. A LITERARY MISCELLANY FROM THE NEW STATESMAN AND NATION. New Statesman and Nation, London, 1948
WHY DO I WRITE? AN EXCHANGE OF VIEWS BETWEEN ELIZABETH BOWEN, GRAHAM GREENE & V.S. PRITCHETT
MR. BELUNCLE. Chatto & Windus, London, 1951
BOOKS IN GENERAL. Chatto & Windus, London, 1953
THE SPANISH TEMPER. Chatto & Windus, London, 1954
COLLECTED STORIES. Chatto & Windus, London, 1956
WHEN MY GIRL COMES HOME. Chatto & Windus, London 1961
LONDON PERCEIVED. Chatto & Windus; William Heinemann, London, 1962
THE KEY TO MY HEART. Chatto & Windus, London, 1963
FOREIGN FACES. Chatto & Windus, London, 1964
NEW YORK PROCLAIMED. Chatto & Windus; William

Heinemann, London, 1965

THE WORKING NOVELIST. Chatto & Windus, London, 1965

THE SAINT AND OTHER STORIES. Penguin Books in association with Chatto & Windus, London, 1966

DUBLIN. A PORTRAIT. Bodley Head, London, 1967

A CAB AT THE DOOR. AN AUTOBIOGRAPHY. Chatto & Windus, London, 1968

BLIND LOVE, AND OTHER STORIES. Chatto & Windus, London, 1969

GEORGE MEREDITH AND ENGLISH COMEDY. Chatto & Windus, London, 1970

MIDNIGHT OIL. Chatto & Windus, London, 1971; Penguin Books, London, 1974

BALZAC. A BIOGRAPHY. Chatto & Windus, London, 1974

THE CAMBERWELL BEAUTY. Chatto & Windus, London, 1974

THE GENTLE BARBARIAN: the Life and Work of Turgenev. Chatto & Windus, London, 1977

THE MYTH MAKERS. Chatto & Windus, London, 1979

THE TALE BEARERS. Chatto & Windus, London, 1980

ON THE EDGE OF THE CLIFF. Chitto & Windus, London, 1980

COLLECTED STORIES. Chatto & Windus, London, 1982

COLLECTED STORIES. Chatto & Windus, London, 1983

I · OTHER LIVES:
THE SHORT STORIES

The Sailor

He was lifting his knees high and putting his hand up when I first saw him, as if, crossing the road through that stinging rain, he were breaking through the bead curtain of a Pernambuco bar. I knew he was going to stop me. This part of the Euston Road is a beat of the men who want a cup of tea or their fare to a job in Luton or some outlying town.

'Beg pardon, chum,' he said in an anxious hot-potato voice. 'Is that Whitechapel?'

He pointed to the traffic clogged in the rain farther down where the electric signs were printing off the advertisements and daubing them on the wet road. Coatless, with a smudged trilby hat on the back of his head so that a curl of boot-polish black hair glistered with raindrops over his forehead, he stood there squeezing the water in his boots and looking at me, from his bilious eyes, like a man drowning and screaming for help in two feet of water and wondering why the crowd is laughing.

'That's St Pancras,' I said.

'Oh, Gawd,' he said, putting his hand to his jaw like a man with toothache. 'I'm all messed up.' And he moved on at once, gaping at the lights ahead.

'Here, wait,' I said. 'Which part of Whitechapel do you want? Where have you come from?'

'Surrey Docks,' he said. 'They said it was near Surrey Docks, see, but they put me wrong. I bin on the road since ten this morning.'

'Acton,' he read a bus sign aloud, recalling the bottom of the day's misery. 'I bin there,' and, fascinated, watched the bus out of sight.

The man's worried mouth dropped open. He was sodden. His clothes were black with damp. The smell of it came off him. The rain stained from the shoulders of his suit past the armpits over the ribs to the waist. It spread from dark blobs over his knees to his thighs. He was a greasy-looking man, once fat, and the fat had gone down unevenly like a deflating bladder. He was calming as I spoke to him.

A sailor, of course, and lost. Hopelessly, blindly lost. I calculated that he must have wandered twenty miles that day, exhausting a genius for misdirection.

'Here,' I said. 'You're soaked. Come and have a drink.'

There was a public house nearby. He looked away at once.

'I never touch it,' he said. 'It's temptation.'

I think it was that word which convinced me the sailor was my kind of man. I am, on the whole, glad to say that I am a puritan and the word 'temptation' went home, painfully, pleasurably, excitingly and intimately familiar. A most stimulating and austerely gregarious word, it indicates either the irresistible hypocrite or the fellow struggler with sin. I couldn't let him go after that.

Presently we were in a café drinking acrid Indian tea.

'Off a ship?' I said.

He looked at me as if I were a magician who could read his soul.

'Thank Gawd I stopped you,' he said. 'I kep' stopping people all day and they messed me up, but you been straight.'

He gave me his papers, his discharge paper, his pension form, official letters, as he said this, like a child handing himself over. Albert Edward Thompson, they said, cook, born '96, invalided out of the service two years before. So he was not just off a ship.

'They're clean,' he said suspiciously when I asked him about this. 'I got ulcers, riddled with ulcers for fourteen years.'

He had no job and that worried him, because it was the winter. He had ganged on the road, worked in a circus, had been a waiter in an Italian restaurant. But what worried him much more was getting to Whitechapel. He made it sound to me as though for two years he had been threshing about the country, dished by one job and another, in a less and less successful attempt to get there.

'What job are you going to do?' I said.

'I don't know,' he said.

'It's a bad time,' I said.

'I fall on my feet,' he said, 'like I done with you.'

We sat opposite to each other at the table. He stared with his appalled eyeballs at the people in the café. He was scared of them and they looked scared too. He looked as though he was going to give a yell and spring at them; in fact, he was likelier to have gone

4

down on his knees to them and to have started sobbing. They couldn't know this. And then he and I looked at each other and the look discovered that we were the only two decent, trustworthy men in a seedy and grabbing world. Within the next two hours I had given him a job. I was chum no longer, but 'sir'. 'Chum' was anarchy and the name of any twisty bleeder you knocked up against, but 'sir', for Thompson (out of the naval nursery), was hierarchy, order, payday, and peace.

I was living alone in the country in those days. I had no one to look after me. I gave Albert Thompson some money; I took him to Whitechapel and wrote down the directions for his journey to my house.

The bungalow where I lived was small and stood just under the brow of a hill. The country was high and stony there. The roads broke up into lanes, the lanes sank into woods, and cottages were few. The oak woods were naked and as green as canker. They stood like old men, and below them were sweet plantations of larch where the clockwork pheasants went off like toys in the rainy afternoons. At night you heard a farm dog bark like a pistol and the oceanic sound of the trees and sometimes, over an hour and a half's walk away, the whistle of a train. But that was all. The few people looked as though they had grown out of the land, sticks and stones in cloth; they were old people chiefly. In the one or two bigger houses they were childless. It was derelict country; frost with its teeth fast in the ground, the wind running finer than sand through a changeless sky or the solitary dribble of water in the butts and the rain legging it over the grass – that was all one heard or saw there.

'Gawd!' said Thompson when he got there. 'I thought I'd never strike the place.' Pale, coatless again in the wet, his hat tipped back from a face puddingy and martyred, he came up the hill with the dancing step of a man treading on nails. He had been lost again. He had travelled by the wrong train, even by the wrong line, he had assumed that, as in towns, it was safest to follow the crowd. But country crowds soon scatter. He had been following people – it sounded to me – to half the cottages for miles around.

'Then I come to the Common,' he said. 'I didn't like the look of that. I kept round it.'

At last some girl had shown him the way.

I calmed him down. We got to my house and I took him to his room. He sat down on the bed and told me the story again. He took off his boots and socks and looked at his blistered feet, murmuring to them as if they were a pair of orphans. There was a woman in the train with a kid, he said, and to amuse the kid he had taken out his jackknife. The woman called the guard.

After we had eaten and I had settled in, I went for a walk that afternoon. The pleasure of life in the country for me is in its monotony. One understands how much of living is habit, a long war to which people, plants and animals have settled down. In the country one expects nothing of people; they are themselves, not bringers of gifts. In towns one asks too little or too much of them.

The drizzle had stopped when I went out, the afternoon was warmer and inert, and the dull stench of cattle hung over the grass. On my way down the hill I passed the bungalow that was my nearest neighbour. I could see the roof as pink as a slice of salt ham, from the top of my garden. The bungalow was ten years old. A chicken man had built it. Now the woodwork was splitting and shrinking, the garden was rank, two or three larches, which the rabbits had been at, showed above the dead grass, and there was a rosebush. The bush had one frozen and worm-eaten flower which would stick there half the winter. The history of the bungalow was written in the tin bath by the side door. The bath was full of gin, beer, and whisky bottles discarded after the weekend parties of many tenants. People took the place forever and then, after a month or two, it changed hands. A businessman, sentimental about the country, an invalid social worker, a couple with a motor bicycle, an inseparable pair of schoolteachers with big legs and jumping jumpers; and now there was a woman I hardly saw, a colonel's daughter, but the place was said to belong to a man in the Northampton boot trade.

A gramophone was playing when I walked by. Whenever I passed, the colonel's daughter was either playing the gramophone or digging in the garden. She was a small girl in her late twenties, with a big knowledgeable-looking head under tobacco-brown curls, and the garden fork was nearly as big as herself. Her gardening never lasted long. It consisted usually in digging up a piece of the matted lawn in order to bury tins; but she went at it intensely, drawing back the fork until her hair fell over her face and the sweat stood on her brow. She always had a cigarette in her mouth, and every now and then the carnation skin of her face, with its warm, dark-blue eyes, would be distorted and turned crimson by violent bronchial coughing. When this stopped she would straighten up, the delicacy came back to her skin, and she would say: 'Oh, Christ. Oh, bloody hell,' and you noticed at the end of every speech the fine right eyebrow would rise a little, and the lid of the eye below it would quiver. This wink, the limpid wink of the colonel's daughter, you noticed it at once. You wondered what it meant and planned to find out. It was as startling and enticing as a fish rising, and you discovered when you went after it that the colonel's daughter was the hardest-drinking and most blasphemous piece of apparent childish innocence you had ever seen. Old men in pubs gripped their sticks, went scarlet, and said someone ought to take her drawers down and give her a tanning. I got a sort of fame from being a neighbour of the colonel's daughter. 'Who's that piece we saw down the road?' people asked.

'Her father's in the Army.'

'Not,' two or three of them said, for this kind of wit spreads like measles, 'the Salvation Army.' They said I was a dirty dog. But I hardly knew the colonel's daughter. Across a field she would wave, utter her obscenity, perform her wink, and edge off on her slight legs. Her legs were not very good. But if we met face to face on the road she became embarrassed and nervous; this was one of her dodges. 'Still alone?' she said.

'Yes. And you?'

'Yes. What do you do about sex?'

'I haven't got any.'

'Oh, God, I wish I'd met you before.'

When I had friends she would come to the house. She daren't come there when I was alone, she said. Every night, she said, she locked and bolted up at six. Then the wink – if it was a wink. The men laughed. She did not want to be raped, she said. Their wives froze and some curled up as if they had got the blight and put their hands hard on their husbands' arms. But the few times she came to the house when I was alone, the colonel's daughter stood by the door, the full length of the room away, with a guilty look on her face.

When I came back from my walk the gramophone had stopped. The colonel's daughter was standing at the door of her bungalow with her sleeves rolled up, a pail of water beside her, and a scrubbing brush in her hand.

'Hullo,' she said awkwardly.

'Hullo,' I said.

'I see you've got the Navy down here. I didn't know you were that way.'

'I thought you would have guessed that straight away,' I said.

'I found him on the Common crying this morning. You've broken his heart.' Suddenly she was taken by a fit of coughing.

'Well,' she said, 'every day brings forth something.'

When I got to the gate of my bungalow I saw that at any rate if Thompson could do nothing else he could bring forth smoke. It was travelling in thick brown funnel puffs from the short chimney of the kitchen. The smoke came out with such dense streaming energy that the house looked like a destroyer racing full steam ahead into the wave of hills. I went down the path to the kitchen and looked inside. There was Thompson, with not only his sleeves rolled up but his trousers also, and he was shovelling coal into the kitchener with the garden spade, the face of the fire was roaring yellow, the water was throbbing and sighing in the boiler, the pipes were singing through the house.

'Bunkering,' Thompson said.

I went into the sitting-room. I thought I had come into the wrong house. The paint had been scrubbed, the floors polished like decks, the reflections of the firelight danced in them, the windows gleamed, and the room was glittering with polished metal. Doorknobs, keyholes, fire-irons, window-catches, were polished; metal that I had no idea existed flashed with life.

'What time is supper piped – er, ordered,' said Thompson, appearing in his stockinged feet. His big round eyes started out of their dyspeptic shadows and became enthusiastic when I told him the hour.

A change came over my life after this. Before Thompson everything had been disorganized and wearying. He drove my papers and clothes back to their proper places. He brought the zest and routine of the Royal Navy into my life. He kept to his stockinged feet out of tenderness for those orphans, a kind of repentance for what he had done to them; he was collarless and he served food with a splash as if he allowed for the house to give a pitch or a roll that didn't come off. His thumbs left their marks on the plates. But he was punctual. He lived for 'orders'. 'All ready sir,' he said, planking down the dish and looking up at the clock at the same moment. Burned, perhaps, spilling over the side, invisible beneath Bisto – but on time!

The secret of happiness is to find a congenial monotony. My own housekeeping had suffered from the imagination. Thompson put an end to this tiring chase of the ideal. 'What's orders for lunch, sir?'

'Do you a nice fried chop and chips?' he said. That was settled. He went away, but soon he came back

'What pudding's ordered, sir?' That stumped both of us, or it stumped me. Thompson watched me to time his own suggestion.

'Do you a nice spotted dick?' So it was. We had this on the second day and the third, we changed on the fourth, but on the fifth we came back to it. Then Thompson's mind gave a leap.

'Do you grilled chop, chips, spotted dick *and custard*?' he said. That became almost our fixed menu. There were bouts of blancmange, but spotted dick came back.

Thompson had been sinking towards semi-starvation, I to the insidious Oblomovism of the country. Now we were reformed and happy.

'I always fall on my feet,' he said, 'like I done with you.' It was his refrain.

The winter dripped like a tap, the fog hardly left our hill. Winter in England has the colourless, steaming look of a fried-fish-shop window. But we were stoking huge fires, we bunkered, the garden spade went through coal by the hundredweight. We began to talk a more tangy dialect. Things were not put away; they were 'stowed'. String appeared in strange knots to make things 'fast', plants were 'lashed' in the dying garden, washing was 'hoist' on the lines, floors were 'swabbed'. The kitchen became the 'galley'. The postman came 'alongside', all meals were 'piped', and at bedtime we 'piped down'. At night, hearing the wind bump in the chimneys and slop like ocean surf in the woods, looking out at the leather darkness, I had the sensation that we were creeping down the Mersey in a fog or lumping about in the Atlantic swell off Ushant.

I was happy. But was Thompson happy? He seemed to be. In the mornings we were both working, but in the afternoons there was little more to do. He sat on a low chair with his knees close to the bars of the range or on the edge of his bed, darning his clothes. (He lived in a peculiar muddle of his own and he was dirty in his own quarters.) In the evenings he did the same and sometimes we talked. He told me about his life. There was nothing in it at all. It was buried under a mumble of obscurity. His memories were mainly of people who hadn't 'behaved right', a dejecting moral wilderness with Thompson mooching about in it, disappointed with human nature. He didn't stay to talk with me much. He preferred the kitchen, where, the oil lamp smoking, the range smoking, and himself smoking, he sat chewing it all over, gazing into the fire.

'You can go out, you know,' I said, 'whenever you want. Do what you like.'

'I'm OK,' he said.

'See some of the people,' I said. Thompson said he'd just as lief stand by.

Everyone knows his own business best. But I was interested one night when I heard the sound of voices in the kitchen. Someone had come in. The voices went on and on other nights. Who was it? The milker from the farm probably or the cowman who cleaned out cesspits by lantern light at night and talked with nostalgia about burying bodies during the war. 'If there hadn't been a war,' this man used to say, 'I wouldn't have seen nothing. It was an education.'

I listened. Slow in question, slow in answer, the monotonous voices came. The woodcutter, the postman? I went into the kitchen to see who the profound and interminable crony was.

There was no one. There was only Thompson in the kitchen. Sitting close to the fire with all windows closed, a shallow, stupefied, oil-haired head in his own fug, Thompson was spelling out a story from a *Wild West Magazine*. It was old and dirty and his coal-blackened finger was moving from word to word.

So far Thompson had refused to go out of the house except as far as the coal-shed, but I was determined after this discovery that he should go out. I waited until payday.

'Here's your money,' I said. 'Take the afternoon off.'

Thompson stepped back from the money.

'You keep it,' he said, in a panic. 'You keep it for me.'

'You may need it,' I said. 'For a glass of beer or cigarettes or something.'

'If I have it I'll lose it,' he said. 'They'll pinch it.'

'Who?' I said.

'People,' Thompson said. I could not persuade him.

'All right, I'll keep it for you,' I said.

'Yes,' he said eagerly. 'If I want a bob I'll ask you. Money's temptation,' he said.

'Well, anyway,' I said, 'take the afternoon off. It's the first sunny afternoon we've had. I'll tell you where to go. Turn to the right in the lane . . .'

'I don't like them lanes,' said Thompson, looking suspiciously out of the window. 'I'll stay by you.'

'Well, take a couple of hours,' I said. 'We all need fresh air.'

He looked at me as if I had suggested he should poison himself; indeed as if I were going to do the poisoning.

'What if I do an hour?' he began to bargain.

'No, the afternoon,' I said.

'Do you half an hour?' he pleaded.

'All right, I don't want to force you,' I said. 'This is a free country. Go for an hour.'

It was like an auction.

'Tell you what,' he said, looking shifty. 'I'll do you twenty minutes.' He thought he had tricked me, but I went back into the kitchen and drove him to it. I had given him an overcoat and shoes, and it was this appeal to his vanity that got him. Out he went for his twenty minutes. He was going straight down the lane to where it met the main road and then straight back; it would take a smart walker about twelve minutes on a winter's day.

When an hour passed, I was pleased with myself. But when four hours had gone by and darkness came, I began to wonder. I went out to the gate. The land and the night had become one thing. I had just gone in again when I heard loud voices and saw the swing of a lamp. There came Thompson with a labourer. The labourer, a little bandy man known as Fleas, stood like a bent bush with a sodden sack on his shoulders, snuffling in the darkness, and he grinned at me with the malevolence of the land.

'He got astray,' he said, handing Thompson over.

'Gawd,' exclaimed Thompson, exhausted. His face was the familiar pale suety agony. He was full of explanations. He was sweating like a scared horse and nearly hysterical. He'd been on the wrong course. He didn't know where to steer. One thing looked like another. Roads and lanes, woods and fields, mixed themselves together.

'Woods I seen,' he said in horror. 'And that Common! It played me up proper.'

'But you weren't anywhere near the Common,' I said.

'Then what was it?' he said.

That night he sat by the fire with his head in his hands.

'I got a mood,' he said.

The next morning cigarette smoke blew past my window and I heard coughing. The colonel's daughter was at the kitchen door talking to Thompson. 'Cheero,' I heard her say and then she came to my door and pushed it open. She stood there gravely and her eye winked. She was wearing a yellow jersey and looked as neat as a bird.

'You're a swine,' she said.

'What have I done?'

'Raping women on the Common,' she said. 'Deserting your old friends, aren't you?'

'It's been too wet on the Common,' I said.

'Not for me,' she said. 'I'm always hopeful. I came across last night. There was the minister's wife screaming in the middle of it. I sat on her head and calmed her down, and she said a man had been chasing her. "Stop screaming," I said. "You flatter yourself, dear." It was getting dark and I carried her shopping bag and umbrella for her and took her to her house. I often go and see her in the evenings. I've got to do something, haven't I? I can't stick alone in that bungalow all day and all night. We sit and talk about her son in China. When you're old you'll be lonely too.'

'What happened on the Common?'

'I think I'm drunk,' said the colonel's daughter, 'but I believe I've been drunk since breakfast. Well, where was I? I'm losing my memory too. Well, we hadn't gone five minutes before I heard someone panting like a dog behind us and jumping over bushes. Old Mrs Stour started screaming again. "Stand still," I said, and I looked and then a man came out of a tree about ten yards away. "What the hell do you want?" I said. A noise came back like a sheep. "Ma'am, ma'am, ma'am, ma'am," it said.'

'So that's where Thompson was,' I said.

'I thought it was you,' the colonel's daughter said. ' "There's a woman set about me with a stick on the Common," he said. "I didn't touch her, I was only following her," he said. "I reckoned if I followed her I'd get home." '

When they got to the wood, Thompson wouldn't go into it and she had to take his hand; that was a mistake. He took his hand away and moved off. So she grabbed his coat. He struggled after this, she chased him into the thicket and told him not to be a fool but he got away and disappeared, running on to the Common.

'You're a damn swine,' the colonel's daughter said to me. 'How would you like to be put down in the middle of the sea?'

She walked away. I watched her go up the path and lean on the gate opposite to stroke the nose of a horse. She climbed into the field and the horses, like hairy yokels, went off. I heard her calling them, but they did not come.

When she was out of sight, the door opened behind me and Thompson came in.

'Beg pardon, sir,' he said. 'That young lady, sir. She's been round my kitchen door.'

'Yes,' I said.

He gaped at me and then burst out: 'I didn't touch her, straight I didn't. I didn't lay a finger on her.'

'She didn't say you did. She was trying to help you.'

He calmed down. 'Yes, sir,' he said.

When he came back into the room to lay the table I could see he was trying to catch my eye.

'Sir,' he said at last, standing at attention. 'Beg pardon, sir, the young lady . . .'

His mouth was opening and shutting, trying to shape a sentence.

'The young lady – she'd had a couple, sir,' he said in a rush.

'Oh,' I said, 'don't worry about that. She often has.'

'It's ruination, sir,' said Thompson evangelically.

She did not come to the house again for many days, but when she came I heard him lock both kitchen doors.

Orders at the one extreme, temptation at the other, were the good and evil of Thompson's life. I no longer suggested that he go out. I invented errands and ordered him to go. I wanted, in that unfortunate way one has, to do good to Thompson. I wanted him to be free and happy. At first he saw that I was not used to giving orders and he tried to dodge. His ulcers were bad, he said. Once or twice he went about barefoot, saying the sole was off one of his boots. But when he saw I meant what I said, he went. I used to watch him go, tilted forward on his toes in his half-running walk, like someone throwing himself blindly upon the mercy of the world. When he came back he was excited. He had the look of someone stupefied by incomprehensible success. It is the feeling a landsman has when he steps off a boat after a voyage. You feel giddy, canny, surprised at your survival after crossing that bridge of deep, loose water. You boast. So did Thompson – morally.

'There was a couple of tramps on the road,' Thompson said. 'I steered clear. I never talked to them,' he said.

'Someone asked me who I was working for.' He described the man. 'I never told him,' he said shrewdly. 'I just said "A gentleman." Meaning you,' he said.

There was a man in an allotment who had asked him for a light and wanted to know his business.

'I told him I didn't smoke,' said Thompson. 'You see my meaning – you don't know what it's leading up to. There warn't no harm, but that's how temptation starts.'

What was temptation? Almost everything was temptation to Thompson. Pubs, cinemas, allotments, chicken-runs, tobacconists – in these, everywhere, the tempter might be. Temptation, like Othello's jealousy, was the air itself.

'I expect you'd like to go to church,' I said. He seemed that kind.

'I got nothing *against* religion,' Thompson said. 'But best keep clear. They see you in church and the next thing they're after you.'

'Who?' I asked.

'People,' he said. 'It's not like a ship.'

I was like him, he said, I kept myself to myself. I kept out of temptation's way. He was glad I was like that, he said.

It was a shock to me that while I observed Thompson, Thompson observed me. At the same time one prides oneself, the moment one's character is defined by someone else, on defeating the definition. I kept myself to myself? I avoided temptation? That was all Thompson knew! There was the colonel's daughter. I might not see her very often; she might be loud, likeable, dreary or alarming by turns, but she was Temptation itself. How did he know I wasn't tempted? Thompson's remark made me thrill. I began to see rather more of the colonel's daughter.

And so I discovered how misleading he had been about his habits and how, where temptation was concerned, he made a difference between profession and practice. So strong was Thompson's feeling about temptation that he was drawn at once to every tempter he saw. He stopped them on the road and was soon talking about it. The postman was told. The shopkeepers heard all his business and mine. He hurried after tramps, he detained cyclists, he sat down on the banks with road-makers and ditchers, telling them the dangers of drink, the caution to be kept before strangers. And after he had done this he always ended by telling them he kept himself to himself, avoided drink, ignored women, and, patting his breast pocket, said that was where he kept his money and his papers. He behaved to them exactly as he had behaved with me two months before in the Euston Road. The colonel's daughter told me. She picked up all the news in that district.

'He's a decent, friendly soul,' muttered the colonel's daughter thickly. 'You're a prig. Keep your hair on. You can't help it. I expect you're decent, too, but you're like all my bloody so-called friends.'

'Oh,' I said hopefully, 'are prigs your special line?'

I found out, too, why Thompson was always late when he came home from his errands. I had always accepted that he was lost. And so he was in a way, but he was lost through wandering about with people, following them to their doorsteps, drifting to their allotments, backyards, and all the time telling them, as he clung to their company, about the dangers of human intercourse. 'I never speak to nobody' – it was untrue, but it was not a lie. It was simply a delusion.

'He lives in two worlds at once,' I said to the colonel's daughter one morning. I had sent Thompson to the town to buy the usual chops, and I was sitting in her bungalow. This was the first time I had ever been in it. The walls were of varnished matchboarding like the inside of a gospel hall, and the room was heated by a paraffin stove which smelled like armpits. There were two rexine-covered chairs, a rug, and a table in the room. She was sorting out gramophone records as I talked and the records she did not like she dropped to the floor and broke. She was listening very little to what I said but walked to the gramophone, put on a record, stopped it after a few turns, and then, switching if off, threw the record away.

'Oh, you know a hell of a lot, don't you?' she said. 'I don't say you're not an interesting man but you don't get on with it, do you?'

'How old are you? Twenty-five?' I said.

Her sulking, ironical expression went. She was astonished.

'Good God!' she exclaimed with a smile of sincerity. 'Don't be a damn fool.' Then she frowned. 'Or are you being professionally clever?'

'Here,' she said. 'I was damn pretty when I was twenty-five. I'm thirty-nine. I've still got a good figure.'

'I would have put you at twenty-seven at the most,' I said truthfully.

She walked towards me. I was sitting on the armchair and she stood very close. She had never been as close to me before. I had thought her eyes were dark-blue, but now I saw they were green and grey, with a moist lascivious haze in them and yet dead and clock-like, like a cat's on a sunless day. And the skin, which had seemed fresh to me, I saw in its truth for the first time. It was clouded and flushed, clouded with that thickened pimpled ruddiness which the skin of heavy drinkers has and which in middle age becomes bloated and mottled. I felt: This is why she has always stood the length of the room away before.

She saw what was in my mind and she sat down on the chair opposite me. The eye winked.

'Keep control of yourself,' she said. 'I came down here for a rest and now you've started coming round.'

'Only in the mornings,' I said.

She laughed. She went to a bookshelf and took down a bottle of whisky and poured out half a tumblerful.

'This is what you've done coming in here, early bird,' she said. 'Exciting me on an empty stomach. I haven't touched it for ten days. I had a letter this morning. From my old man.'

'Your father?'

I had always tried to imagine the colonel. She gave a shout of cheerful laughter and it ended in coughing till tears came to her eyes.

'That's rich. God, that's rich. Keen observer of women! No, from my husband, darling. He's not my husband, damn him, of course, but when you've lived with someone for ten years and he pays the rent and keeps you, he is your husband, isn't he? Or ought to be. Ten years is a long time and his family thought he ought to be married. He thought so too. So he picked up a rich American girl and pushed me down here to take it easy in the country. I'm on the dole like your sailor boy. Well, I said, if he felt that way, he'd better have his head. In six months he'll tire of the new bitch. So I left him alone. I didn't want to spoil his fun. Well, now, he writes me, he wants to bring his fiancée down because she's heard so much about me and adores the country . . .'

I was going to say something indignant.

'He's nice too,' she said casually. 'He sells gas heaters. You'd like him all the same. But blast that bloody woman,' she said, raising her cool voice. 'She's turned him into a snob. I'm just his whore now.

'Don't look so embarrassed,' she said. 'I'm not going to cry.

'For ten years,' she said, 'I read books, I learned French, educated myself, learned to say "How d'you do?" instead of "Pleased to meet you," and look down my nose at everything in his sort of way. And I let him go about saying my father was in the Army too, but they were such bloody fools they thought he must be a colonel. They'd never heard of sergeant majors having children. Even my old man, bless his heart' – she smiled affectionately – 'thought or let himself think as they did. I was a damn silly little snob.'

'I don't know him,' I said. 'But he doesn't sound much good to me.'

'That's where you're wrong,' she said sharply. 'Just weak, poor kid, that's all. You don't know what it is to be ashamed your mother's a housemaid. I got over it – but he didn't, that's all.'

She paused and the wink gave its signal.

'This is more embarrassing than I thought,' she said.

'I am very sorry,' I said. 'Actually I am in favour of snobbery, it is a sign of character. It's a bad thing to have, but it's a bad thing not to have had. You can't help having the diseases of your time.'

'There you go,' she said.

The suffering of others is incredible. When it is obscure it seems like a lie; when it is garish and raw, it is like boasting. It is a challenge to oneself. I got up from my chair and went towards her. I was going to kiss her.

'You are the sentimental type,' she said.

So I didn't kiss her.

Then we heard someone passing the bungalow and she went to the window. Thompson was going by. The lock of black hair was curling over his sweating forehead and he gave a hesitant staggering look at the bungalow. There was a lump of fear on his face.

'He'd better not know where you've been,' she said. She moved her lips to be kissed, but I walked out.

I was glad of the steady sense of the fresh grey air when I got outside. I was angry and depressed. I stood at the window of my house. Thompson came in and was very talkative. He'd been lost, of course. He'd seen people. He'd seen fields. He'd heard trees. He'd seen roads. I hardly listened. I was used to the jerky wobbling voice. I caught the words 'legion' and 'temptation', and thought he was quoting from the Bible. Presently I realized he was talking about the British Legion. The postman had asked him to go to a meeting of the British Legion that night. How simple other people's problems are! Yet 'No' Thompson was saying. He was not going to the British Legion. It was temptation.

I ought to have made love to her and kissed her, I was thinking. She was right, I was a prig.

'You go,' I said to Thompson, 'if you want to. You'd enjoy it.'

But how disgusting, obvious, stupid, to have made love to her then, I thought.

'Do as you like,' I said.

'I'm best alongside you,' said Thompson.

'You can't always be by me,' I said. 'In a month, perhaps less, as you know, I'll be leaving here and you'll have to go.'

'Yes,' he said. 'You tol' me. You been straight. I'll be straight with you. I won't go to the Legion.'

We ate our meal and I read.

'In every branch of our spiritual and material civilization we seem to have reached a turning point,' I read. 'This spirit shows itself not only in the actual state of public affairs . . .'

Well, I thought, I can ask her over tonight, I needn't be a fool twice. I went out for an hour. When I returned, Thompson was fighting Temptation hard. If he went to the Legion how would he get back? No, best not. He took the Legion on in its strength. (She is a type, I thought.) At four he was still at it. At five he asked me for his money. (Well, we are all types, I was thinking.) Very shortly he brought the money back and asked me to keep his pension papers. At half past six I realized this meant that Thompson was losing and the Legion and all its devils winning. (What is a prig, anyway?) He was looking out at the night. Yet, just when I thought he had lost, he had won. There was the familiar sound of the Wild West monologue in the kitchen. It was half past eight. The Legion was defeated.

I was disappointed in Thompson. Really, not to have had more guts than that! Restlessly I looked out of the window. There was a full moon spinning on the tail of a dying wind. Under the moonlight the fields were like wide-awake faces, the woods like womanish heads of hair upon them. I put on my hat and coat and went out. I was astonished by the circle of stars. They were as distinct as figures on a clock. I took out my watch and compared the small time in my hand with the wide time above. Then I walked on. There was a sour smell at the end of the wood, where, no doubt, a dead rabbit or pigeon was rotting.

I came out of the wood onto the metalled road. Suddenly my heart began to beat quickly as I hurried down the road, but it was a long way round now. I cut across fields. There was a cottage and a family were listening to a dance-band on the wireless. A man was going the rounds of his chickens. There was a wheelbarrow and there were spades and steel bars where a water mill was being built.

Then I crossed the last fields and saw the bungalow. My heart throbbed heavily and I felt all my blood slow down and my limbs grow heavy. It was only when I got to the road that I saw there were no lights in the bungalow. The colonel's daughter, the sergeant's daughter, had gone to bed early like a child. While I stood I heard men's voices singing across the fields. It must have gone ten o'clock and people were coming out of the public house. In all the villages of England, at this hour, loud-voiced groups were breaking up and dispersing into the lanes.

I got to my house and lit a candle. The fire was low. I was exhausted and happy to be in my house among my own things, as if I had got into my own skin again. There was no light in the kitchen. Thompson had gone to bed. I grinned at the thought of the struggles of poor Thompson. I picked up a book and read. I could hear still the sound of that shouting and singing. The beer was sour and flat in this part of the country, but it made people sing.

The singing voices came nearer. I put down the book. An argument was going on in the lane. I listened. The argument was nearing the cottage. The words got louder. They were going on at my gate. I heard the gate go and the argument was on my path. Suddenly – there could be no doubt – people were coming to the door. I stood up, I could recognize no voice. Loud singing, stumbling feet, then bang! The door broke open and crashed against the wall. Tottering, drunk, with their arms round each other, Thompson and the colonel's daughter nearly fell into the room.

Thompson stared at me with terror.

'Stand up, sailor,' said the colonel's daughter, clinging to him.

'He was lonely,' she said unsteadily to me. 'We've been playing gramophone records. Sing,' she said.

Thompson was still staring.

'Don't look at him. Sing,' she said. Then she gave a low laugh and they fell bolt upright on the sofa like prim, dishevelled dolls.

A look of wild love of all the world came into Thompson's eyes and he smiled as I had never seen him smile before. He suddenly opened his twitching mouth and bawled:

> 'You've robbed every tailor,
> And you've skinned every sailor,

But you won't go walking Paradise Street no more.'

'Go on. That's not all,' the colonel's daughter cried and sang: 'Go on – something – something, deep and rugged shore.'.

She put her arms round his neck and kissed him. He gaped at her with panic and looked at her skirt. It was undone.

He pointed at her leg in consternation. The sight sobered him. He pulled away his arms and rushed out of the room. He did not come back. She looked at me and giggled. Her eyes were warm and shining. She picked leaves off her skirt.

'Where's he gone? Where's he gone?' she kept asking.

'He's gone to bed,' I said.

She started a fit of coughing. It strained her throat. Her eyes were dilated like an animal's caught in a trap, and she held her hand to her chest.

'I wish,' she cried hysterically, pointing at me in the middle of her coughing, 'I wish you could see your bloody face.'

She got up and called out: 'Thompson! Thompson!' And when he did not answer she sang out: 'Down by the deep and rugged shore – ore-ore-ore.'

'What's the idea?' I said.

'I want Thompson,' she said. 'He's the only man up here.'

Then she began to cry. She marched out to his room, but it was locked. She was wandering through the other rooms calling him and then she went away, away up the path. She went calling him all the way down to her bungalow.

In the morning Thompson appeared as usual. He brought the breakfast. He came in for 'orders'. Grilled chop, did I think? And what about spotted dick? He seemed no worse. He behaved as though nothing had happened. There was no guilty look in his eyes and no apprehension. He made no apology. Lunch passed, teatime, and the day. I finished my work and went into the kitchen.

'Tell me,' I said, 'about last night.'

Thompson was peeling potatoes. He used to do this into a bucket on the floor, as if he were peeling for a whole crew. He put down the clasp-knife and stood up. He looked worried.

'That was a terrible thing,' Thompson said, as if it was something he had read about in the papers. 'Terrible, sir. A young lady like that, sir. To come over here for me, an educated lady like that. Someone oughter teach her a lesson. Coming over and saying she wanted to play some music. I was took clean off my guard. It wasn't right,' said Thompson. 'Whichever way you look at it, it wasn't right. I told her she'd messed me up.'

'I'm not blaming you. I want to know.'

'And she waited till you was out,' Thompson said. 'That's not straight. She may class herself as an educated young lady, but do you know what I reckon she is? I reckon she's a jane.'

I went down to the bungalow. I was beginning to laugh now. She was in the garden digging. Her sleeves were rolled up and she was sweating over the fork. The beds were thick with leaves and dead plants. I stood there watching her. She looked at me nervously for a moment. 'I'm making the garden tidy,' she said. 'For Monday. When the bitch comes down.'

She was shy and awkward. I walked on and, looking back, saw her go into the house. It was the last I ever saw of her. When I came back, the fork she had been using was stuck in the flower bed where she had left it. She went to London that night and did not return.

'Thank Gawd,' Thompson said.

There was a change in Thompson after this and there was a change in me. Perhaps the change came because the dirty February days were going, the air softer and the year moving. I was leaving soon. Thompson mentioned temptation no more. Now he went out every day. The postman was his friend. They used to go to the pub. He asked for his money. In the public house the labourers sat around muttering in a language Thompson didn't understand. He stood them drinks. At his first pint he would start singing. They encouraged him. He stood them more drinks. The postman ordered them for him and then tapped him on the pocket book. They emptied his pockets every night. They despised him and even brought complaints to me about him after they had emptied his pockets.

Thompson came back across the Common alone, wild, enthusiastic, and moaning with suspicion by turns. The next day he would have a mood. All the countryside for ten miles round knew the sailor. He became famous.

Our last week came. He quietened down.

'What are you going to do?' I asked.

'I'll stay by you.'

'You can't,' I said. 'I'll be going abroad.'

'You needn't pay me,' he said. 'I'll stay by you.' It was hard to make him understand he could not stay with me. He was depressed.

'Get me out of here safe,' he pleaded at last. 'Come with me to the station.' He could not go on his own because all the people he knew would be after him. He had told them he was going. He had told them I was saving his pension and his last fortnight's pay. They would come creeping out of cottage doors and ditches for him. So I packed his things and got a taxi to call for us. How slowly we had lived and moved in these fields and lanes! Now we broke through it all with a rush as the car dropped down the hill and the air blew in at the window. As we passed the bungalow with the sun on its empty windows, I saw the fork standing in the neglected bed. Then we swept on. Thompson sat back in the car so that no one should see him, but I leaned forward to see everything for the last time and forget it.

We got to the town. As the taxi slowed down in the streets, people looked out of shops, doors; a potman nodded from the pub.

'Whatcha, Jack,' the voices called.

The police, the fishmonger, boys going to school, dozens of people waved to him. I might have been riding with royalty. At the station a large woman sweeping down the steps of the bank straightened up and gave a shout.

'Hi, Jacko!' she called, bending double, went into shrieks of laughter and called across to a friend at a first-floor window. It was a triumph. But Thompson ignored them all. He sat back out of sight.

'Thank Gawd I've got you,' he said. 'They skin you of everything.'

We sat in the train. It was a two-hour journey.

'Once I strike Whitechapel,' he said in the voice of one naming Singapore, 'I'll be OK.' He said this several times, averting his face from the passing horror of the green fields.

'Don't you worry,' he said. 'Don't fret yourself for me. Don't you worry.' His optimism increased as mine dwindled as we got nearer London. By the time we reached London he was almost shouting. 'I'll fall on my feet, don't you worry. I'll send you my address.'

We stood on the kerb and I watched him walk off into the yellow rain and the clogged, grunting, and mewing traffic. He stepped right into it without looking. Taxis braked to avoid him. He was going to walk to Whitechapel. He reckoned it was safer.

Things as They Are

Two middle-class women were talking at half past eleven in the morning in the empty bar of a suburban public house in a decaying district. It was a thundery and smoky morning in the summer and the traffic fumes did not rise from the street.

'Please, Frederick,' said Mrs Forster, a *rentier* who spoke in a small, scented Edwardian voice. 'Two more large gins. What were you saying, Margaret?'

'The heat last night, Jill. I tossed and I turned. I couldn't sleep – and when I can't sleep I scratch,' said Margaret in her wronged voice. She was a barmaid and this was her day off.

Mrs Forster drank and nodded.

'I think,' said Margaret, 'I mean I don't mean anything rude, but I had a flea.'

Mrs Forster put her grey head a little on one side and nodded again graciously under a flowered hat, like royalty.

'A flea, dear?' she said fondly.

Margaret's square mouth buckled after her next drink and her eyes seemed to be clambering frantically, like a pair of blatant prisoners behind her heavy glasses. Envy, wrong, accusation, were her life. Her black hair looked as though it had once belonged to an employer.

'I mean,' she began to shout against her will, and Frederick, the elderly barman, moved away from her. 'I mean I wouldn't have mentioned it if you hadn't mentioned it.'

Mrs Forster raised her beautiful arms doubtfully and touched her grey hair at the back and she smiled again.

'I mean when you mentioned when you had one yesterday you said,' said Margaret.

'Oh,' said Mrs Forster, too polite to differ.

'Yes, dear, don't you remember, we were in here – I mean, Frederick! Were we in here yesterday morning, Frederick,

Mrs Forster and me . . .'

Frederick stood upright, handsome, old, and stupid.

'He's deaf, the fool, that's why he left the stage,' Margaret said, glaring at him, knowing that he heard. 'Jill, yesterday? Try and remember. You came in for a Guinness. I was having a small port, I mean, or were you on gin?'

'Oh, gin,' said Mrs Forster in her shocked, soft, distinguished way, recognizing a word.

'That was it, then,' said Margaret, shaking an iron chin up and down four times. 'It might have hopped.'

'Hopped,' nodded Mrs Forster pleasantly.

'I mean, fleas hop. I don't mean anything vulgar.' Margaret spread her hard, long bare arms and knocked her glass. 'Distances,' she said. 'From one place to another place. A flea travels. From here, at this end of the bar, I don't say to the end, but along or across, I mean it could.'

'Yes,' said Mrs Forster with agreeable interest.

'Or from a person. I mean, a flea might jump on you – or on me, it might jump from someone else, and then off that person, it depends if they are with someone. It might come off a bus or a tram.' Margaret's long arms described these movements and then she brought them back to her lap. 'It was a large one,' she said. 'A brute.'

'Oh, large?' said Mrs Forster sympathetically.

'Not large – I mean it must have been large, I could tell by the bites, I know a small flea, I mean we all do – don't mind my mentioning it – I had big bites all up my leg,' said Margaret, stretching out a long, strong leg. Seeing no bites there, she pulled her tight serge skirt up with annoyance over her knee and up her thigh until, halted by the sight of her suspender, she looked angrily at Frederick and furtively at Mrs Forster and pulled her skirt down and held it down.

'Big as pennies, horrible pink lumps, red, Jill,' argued Margaret. 'I couldn't sleep. Scratching doesn't make it any better. It wasn't a London flea, that I know, Jill. I know a London flea, I mean you know a London flea, an ordinary one, small beastly things, I hate them, but this must have been some great black foreign brute, Indian! Frederick! You've seen one of those things?'

Frederick went with a small business of finger-flicking to the curtains at the back of the bar, peeped through as if for his cue. All bars were empty.

'Never,' he said contemptuously when he came back, and turning his back on the ladies, hummed at the shelves of bottles.

'It's easy,' Margaret began to shout once more, swallowing her gin, shouting at her legs, which kept slipping off the rail of the stool and enraged her by jerking her body, 'I mean, for them to travel. They get on ships. I mean those ships have been in the tropics, I don't say India necessarily, it might be in Egypt or Jamaica, a flea could hop off a native onto some sailor in the docks.'

'You mean, dear, it came up from the docks by bus,' said Mrs Forster. 'You caught it on a bus?'

'No, Jill,' said Margaret. 'I mean some sailor brought it up.'

'Sailor,' murmured Mrs Forster, going pale.

'Ted,' said Margaret, accusing. 'From Calcutta. Ted could have brought it off his ship.'

Mrs Forster's head became fixed and still. She gazed mistily at Margaret and swayed. She finished her drink and steadied herself by looking into the bottom of the glass and waited for two more drops to come. Then she raised her small chin and trembled. She held a cigarette at the end of her thumb and her finger as if it were a stick of crayon and she were writing a message in blue smoke in the air. Her eyes closed sleepily, her lips sucked, pouted, and two tears rolled down her cheeks. She opened her large handbag and from the mess of letters, bills, money, keys, purses, and powder inside she took a small handkerchief and dabbed her eyes.

'Ah!' said Margaret, trying to get her arm to Mrs Forster, but failing to reach her because her foot slipped on the rail again, so that she kicked herself. 'Ah, Jill! I only mentioned it, I didn't mean anything, I mean when you said you had one, I said to myself: "That's it, it's an Indian. Ted's brought it out of the ship's hold." I didn't mean to bring up Ted, Jill. There's nothing funny about it, sailors do.'

Mrs Forster's cheeks and neck fattened amorously as she mewed and quietly cried and held her handkerchief tight.

'Here,' said Margaret, mastering her. 'Chin-chin, Jill, drink up, it will do you good. Don't cry. Here, you've finished it. Frederick, two more,' she said, sliding towards Mrs Forster and resting one breast on the bar.

Mrs Forster straightened herself with dignity and stopped crying.

'He broke my heart,' said Mrs Forster, panting. 'I always found one in the bed after his leave was over.'

'He couldn't help it,' said Margaret.

'Oh, no,' said Mrs Forster.

'It's the life sailors live,' said Margaret. 'And don't you forget, are you listening, Jill? Listen to me. Look at me and listen. You're among friends, Jill. He's gone, Jill, like you might say, out of your life.'

'Yes,' said Mrs Forster, nodding again, repeating a lesson. 'Out of my life.'

'And good riddance, too, Jill.'

'Riddance,' murmured Mrs Forster.

'Jill,' shouted Margaret. 'You've got a warm heart, that's what it is, as warm as Venus. I could never marry again after what I've been through, not whatever you paid me, not however much money it was you gave me, but you're not like me, your heart is too warm. You're too trusting.'

'Trusting,' Mrs Forster repeated softly, squeezing her eyelids.

'I tell you what it was,' Margaret said. 'You were in love, Jill,' said Margaret, greedy in the mouth. 'Can you hear me?'

'Yes, dear.'

'That's what I said. It was love. You loved him and you married him.'

Margaret pulled herself up the bar and sat upright, looking with surprise at the breast that had rested there. She looked at her glass, she looked at Mrs Forster's; she picked up the glass and put it down. 'It was a beautiful dream, Jill, you had your beautiful dream and I say this from the bottom of my heart, I hope you will have a beautiful memory.'

'Two months,' sighed Mrs Forster, and her eyes opened amorously in a grey glister and then sleepily half closed.

'But now, Jill, it's over. You've woke up, woken up. I mean, you're seeing things as they are.'

The silence seemed to the two ladies to stand in a lump between them. Margaret looked into her empty glass again. Frederick lit a cigarette he had made, and his powdered face split up into twitches as he took the first draw and then put the cigarette economically on the counter. He went through his repertory of small coughs and then, raising his statesman-like head, he listened to the traffic passing and hummed.

Mrs Forster let her expensive fur slip back from her fine shoulders and looked at the rings on her small hands.

'I loved him, Margaret,' she said. 'I really did love him.'

'We know you loved him. I mean, it was love,' said Margaret. 'It's nothing to do with the age you are. Life's never over. It was love. You're a terrible woman, Jill.'

'Oh, Margaret,' said Mrs Forster with a discreet glee, 'I know I am.'

'He was your fourth,' said Margaret.

'Don't, Margaret,' giggled Mrs Forster.

'No, no, I'm not criticizing. I never criticize. Live and let live. It wasn't a fancy, Jill, you loved him with all your heart.'

Jill raised her chin in a lady-like way.

'But I won't be hit,' she whispered. 'At my age I allow no one to strike me. I am fifty-seven, Margaret, I'm not a girl.'

'That's what we all said,' said Margaret. 'You were headstrong.'

'Oh, Margaret!' said Mrs Forster, delighted.

'Oh, yes, yes, you wouldn't listen, not you. You wouldn't listen to me. I brought him up to the Chequers, or was it the Westmoreland? – no, it was the George – and I thought to myself, I know your type, young man – you see, Jill, I've had experience – out for what he could get – well, honest, didn't I tell you?'

'His face was very brown.'

'Brown! Would you believe me? No, you wouldn't. I can see him. He came up here the night of the dance. He took his coat off. Well, we all sweat.'

'But,' sighed Mrs Forster, 'he had white arms.'

'Couldn't keep his hands to himself. Put it away, pack it up, I said. He didn't care. He was after Mrs Klebs and she went potty on him till Mrs Sinclair came and then that Mr Baum interfered. That sort lives for trouble. All of them mad on him – I bet Frederick could tell a tale, but he won't. Trust Frederick,' she said with a look of hate at the barman, 'upstairs in the billiard room, I shan't forget it. Torpedoed twice, he said. I mean Ted said: he torpedoed one or two. What happened to him that night?'

'Someone made him comfortable, I am sure,' said Mrs Forster, always anxious about lonely strangers.

'And you were quite rude with me, Jill, I don't mean rude, you couldn't be rude, it isn't in you, but we almost came to words . . .'

'What did you say, Margaret?' said Mrs Forster from a dream.

'I said at your age, fifty-seven, I said you can't marry a boy of twenty-six.'

Mrs Forster sighed.

'Frederick. Freddy, dear. Two more,' said Mrs Forster.

Margaret took her glass, and while she was finishing it Frederick held his hand out for it, insultingly rubbing his fingers.

'Hah!' said Margaret, blowing out her breath as the gin burned her. 'You bowled over him, I mean you bowled him over, a boy of twenty-six. Sailors are scamps.'

'Not,' said Mrs Forster, reaching to trim the back of her hair again and tipping her flowered hat forward on her forehead and austerely letting it remain like that. 'Not,' she said, getting stuck at the word.

'Not what?' said Margaret. 'Not a scamp? I say he was. I said at the time, I still say it, a rotten little scamp.'

'Not,' said Mrs Forster.

'A scamp,' said Margaret.

'Not. Not with a belt,' said Mrs Forster. 'I will not be hit with a belt.'

'My husband,' began Margaret.

'I will not, Margaret,' said Mrs Forster. 'Never. Never. Never with a belt.'

'Not hit, struck,' Mrs Forster said, defying Margaret.

'It was a plot, you could see it a mile off, it would make you laugh, a lousy, rotten plot,' Margaret let fly, swallowing her drink. 'He was after your house and your money. If he wasn't, what did he want to get his mother in for, a big three-storey house like yours, in a fine residential position? Just what he'd like, a little rat like that . . .'

Mrs Forster began a long laugh to herself.

'My grandfather,' she giggled.

'What?' said Margaret.

'Owns the house. Not owns. Owned, I say, the house,' said Mrs Forster, tapping the bar.

'Frederick,' said Mrs Forster. 'Did my grandfather own the house?'

'Uh?' said Frederick, giving his cuff links a shake. 'Which house?'

'My house over there,' said Mrs Forster, pointing to the door.

'I know he owned the house, dear,' Margaret said. 'Frederick knows.'

'Let me ask Frederick,' said Mrs Forster. 'Frederick, you knew my grandfather.'

'Uh?' said Frederick, leaning to listen.

'He's as deaf as a wall,' Margaret said.

Frederick walked away to the curtain at the back of the bar and peeped through it. Nervously he came back, glancing at his handsome face in the mirror; he chose an expression of stupidity and disdain, but he spoke with a quiet rage.

'I remember this street,' he raged, 'when you could hardly get across it for the carriages and the footmen and the maids in their lace caps and aprons. You never saw a lady in a place like this.'

He turned his back on them and walked again secretively to the curtain, peeped again, and came back stiffly on feet skewed sideways by the gravity of the gout and put the tips of his old, well-manicured fingers on the bar for them to admire.

'Now,' he said, giving a socially shocked glance over the windows that were still half boarded after the bombing, 'all tenements, flats, rooms, walls falling down, balconies dropping off, bombed out, and rotting,' he said. He sneered at Margaret. 'Not the same people. Slums. Riff-raff now. Mrs Forster's father was the last of the old school.'

'My grandfather,' said Mrs Forster.

'He was a gentleman,' said Frederick.

Frederick walked to the curtains.

'Horrible,' he muttered loudly, timing his exit.

There was a silence until he came back. The two women looked at the enormous empty public house, with its high cracked and dirty ceilings, its dusty walls unpainted for twenty years. Its top floor had been on fire. Its windows had gone, three or four times.

Frederick mopped up scornfully between the glasses of gin on the counter.

'That's what I mean,' said Margaret, her tongue swelling up, her mouth side-slipping. 'If you'd given the key to his mother, where would you have been? They'd have shut you out of your own house and what's the good of the police? All the scum have come to the top since the war. You were too innocent and we saved you. Jill, well, I mean if we hadn't all got together, the whole crowd, where were you? He was going to get into the house and then one night when you'd been over at the George or the Chequers or over here and you'd had one or two . . .'

Jill looked proudly and fondly at her glass, crinkled her childish eyes.

'Oh,' said Jill in a little naughty-faced protest.

'I mean, I don't mean plastered,' said Margaret, bewildered by the sound of her own voice and moving out her hand to bring it back.

'Not stinking, Jill, excuse me. I mean we sometimes have two or three. Don't we?' Margaret appealed to the barman.

'Uh?' said Frederick coldly. 'Where was this?'

'Oh, don't be stupid,' said Margaret, turning round suddenly and knocking her glass over, which Frederick picked up and took away. 'What was I saying, Jill?'

A beautiful still smile, like a butterfly opening on an old flower, came onto Mrs Forster's face.

'Margaret,' she confided. 'I don't know.'

'I know,' said Margaret, waving her heavy bare arm. 'You'd have been signing papers. He'd have stripped you. He might have murdered you like that case last Sunday in the papers. A well-to-do woman like you. The common little rat. Bringing his fleas.'

'He–was–not–common,' said Mrs Forster, sitting upright suddenly, and her hat fell over her nose, giving her an appearance of dashing distinction.

'He was off a ship,' said Margaret.

'He was an officer.'

'He *said* he was an officer,' said Margaret, struggling with her corsets.

Mrs Forster got down from her stool and held with one hand to the bar. She laughed quietly.

'He – ' she began.

'What?' asked Margaret.

'I shan't tell you,' said Mrs Forster. 'Come here.'

Margaret leaned towards her.

'No, come here, stand here,' said Mrs Forster.

Margaret stood up, also holding to the bar, and Mrs Forster put her hands to Margaret's neck and pulled her head down and began to laugh in Margaret's ear. She was whispering.

'What?' shouted Margaret. 'I can't hear. What is it?'

Mrs Forster laughed with a roar in Margaret's ear.

'He – he – was a man, Margaret,' she whispered. She pushed her away.

'You know what I mean, Margaret,' she said in a stern clear voice. 'You do, don't you? Come here again, I'll tell you.'

'I heard you.'

'No, come here again, closer. I'll tell you. Where are you?'

Mrs Forster whispered again and then drew back.

'A man,' she said boldly.

'And you're a woman, Jill.'

'A man!' said Mrs Forster. 'Everything, Margaret. You know – everything. But not with a belt. I won't be struck.' Mrs Forster reached for her glass.

'*Vive la France!*' she said, holding up her glass, drank, and banged it down. 'Well, I threw him out.'

A lament broke from Margaret. She had suddenly remembered one of *her* husbands. She had had two.

'He went off to his work and I was waiting for him at six. He didn't come back. I'd no money in the house, that was seventeen years ago, and Joyce was two, and he never even wrote. I went through his pockets and gave his coats a shake, wedding rings poured out of them. What do you get for it? Your own daughter won't speak to you, ashamed to bring her friends to the house. "You're always drunk," she says. To her own mother. Drunk!' said Margaret. 'I might have one or perhaps two. What does a girl like that know!'

With a soft, quick crumpling, a soft thump and a long sigh, Mrs Forster went to the floor and full-length lay there with a beautiful smile on her face, and a fierce noise of pleasure came from her white face. Her hat rolled off, her bag fell down, open, and spilling with a loud noise.

'Eh,' said Frederick, coming round from behind the counter.

'Passed out again. Get her up, get her up quick,' said Margaret. 'Her bag, her money.

'Lift her on the side,' she said. 'I will take her legs.'

They carried Mrs Forster to the broken leather settee and laid her down there. 'Here's her bag,' Margaret wrangled. 'It's all there.'

'And the one in your hand,' said Frederick, looking at the pound note in Margaret's hand.

And then the crowd came in: Mrs Klebs, Mrs Sinclair, Mr Baum, the one they called Pudding, who had fallen down the area at Christmas, and a lot more.

'What's this?' they said. 'Not again? Frederick, what's this?'

'They came in here,' Frederick said in a temper. 'Ladies, talking about love.'

Sense of Humour

It started one Saturday. I was working new ground and I decided I'd stay at the hotel the weekend and put in an appearance at church.

'All alone?' asked the girl at the cash desk.

It had been raining since ten o'clock.

'Mr Good has gone,' she said. 'And Mr Straker. He usually stays with us. But he's gone.'

'That's where they make their mistake,' I said. 'They think they know everything because they've been on the road all their lives.'

'You're a stranger here, aren't you?' she said.

'I am,' I said. 'And so are you.'

'How do you know that?'

'Obvious,' I said. 'Way you speak.'

'Let's have a light,' she said.

'So's I can see you,' I said.

That was how it started. The rain was pouring down on the glass roof of the office.

She'd a cup of tea steaming on the register. I said I'd have one, too. What's it going to be and I'll tell them, she said, but I said just a cup of tea.

'I'm TT,' I said. 'Too many soakers on the road as it is.'

I was staying there the weekend so as to be sharp on the job on Monday morning. What's more, it pays in these small towns to turn up at church on Sundays, Presbyterians in the morning, Methodists in the evening. Say 'Good morning' and 'Good evening' to them. 'Ah!' they say. 'Churchgoer! Pleased to see that! TT too.' Makes them have a second look at your lines in the morning. 'Did you like our service, Mr -er-er?' 'Humphrey's my name.' 'Mr Humphrey.' See? It pays.

'Come into the office, Mr Humphrey,' she said, bringing me a cup. 'Listen to that rain.'

I went inside.

'Sugar?' she said.

'Three,' I said. We settled to a very pleasant chat. She told me all about herself, and we got on next to families.

'My father was on the railway,' she said.

' "The engine gave a squeal," ' I said. ' "The driver took out his pocket-knife and scraped him off the wheel." '

'That's it,' she said. 'And what is your father's business? You said he had a business.'

'Undertaker,' I said.

'Undertaker?' she said.

'Why not?' I said. 'Good business. Seasonable like everything else. High-class undertaker,' I said.

She was looking at me all the time wondering what to say, and suddenly she went into fits of laughter.

'Undertaker,' she said, covering her face with her hands and went on laughing.

'Here,' I said, 'what's up?'

'Undertaker!' She laughed and laughed. Struck me as being a pretty thin joke.

'Don't mind me,' she said. 'I'm Irish.'

'Oh, I see,' I said. 'That's it, is it? Got a sense of humour.'

Then the bell rang and a woman called out 'Muriel! Muriel!' and there was a motorbike making a row at the front door.

'All right,' the girl called out. 'Excuse me a moment, Mr Humphrey,' she said. 'Don't think me rude. That's my boyfriend. He wants the bird turning up like this.'

She went out, but there was her boyfriend looking over the window ledge into the office. He had come in. He had a cape on, soaked with rain, and the rain was in beads in his hair. It was fair hair. It stood up on end. He'd been economizing on the brilliantine. He didn't wear a hat. He gave me a look and I gave him a look. I didn't like the look of him. And he didn't like the look of me. A smell of oil and petrol and rain and mackintosh came off him. He had a big mouth with thick lips. They were very red. I recognized him at once as the son of the man who ran the Kounty Garage. I saw this chap when I put my car away. The firm's car. Locked up, because of the samples. Took me ten minutes to ram the idea into his head. He looked as though he'd never heard of samples. Slow – you know the way they are in the provinces. Slow on the job.

'Oh, Colin,' says she. 'What do you want?'

'Nothing,' the chap said. 'I came in to see you.'

'To see me?'

'Just to see you.'

'You came in this morning.'

'That's right,' he said. He went red. 'You was busy,' he said.

'Well, I'm busy now,' she said.

He bit his tongue and licked his big lips over and took a look at me. Then he started grinning.

'I got the new bike, Muriel,' he said. 'I've got it outside. It's just come down from the works,' he said.

'The laddie wants you to look at his bike,' I said. So she went out and had a look at it.

When she came back she had got rid of him.

'Listen to that rain,' she said. 'Lord, I'm fed up with this line,' she said.

'What line?' I said. 'The hotel line?'

'Yes,' she said. 'I'm fed right up to the back teeth with it.'

'And you've got good teeth,' I said.

'There's not the class of person there used to be in it,' she said. 'All our family have got good teeth.'

'Not the class?'

'I've been in it five years and there's not the same class at all. You never meet any fellows.'

'Well,' said I, 'if they're like that half-wit at the garage, they're nothing to be stuck on. And you've met me.'

I said it to her like that.

'Oh,' says she. 'It isn't as bad as that yet.'

It was cold in the office. She used to sit all day in her overcoat. She was a smart girl with a big friendly chin and a second one coming, and her forehead and nose were covered with freckles. She had copper-coloured hair too. She got her shoes through the trade from Duke's traveller and her clothes, too, off the Hollenborough mantle man. I told her I could do her better stockings than the ones she'd got on. She got a good reduction on everything. Twenty-five or thirty-three and a third. She had her expenses cut right back. I took her to the pictures that night in the car. I made Colin get the car out for me.

'That boy wanted me to go on the back of his bike. On a night like this,' she said.

'Oh,' she said, when we got to the pictures. 'Two shilling's too much. Let's go into the one-and-sixes at the side and we can nip across into the two-shillings when the lights go down.

'Fancy your father being an undertaker,' she said in the middle of the show. And she started laughing as she had laughed before.

She had her head head screwed on all right. She said:

'Some girls have no pride once the lights go down.'

Every time I went to that town I took a box of something. Samples, mostly, they didn't cost me anything.

'Don't thank me,' I said. 'Thank the firm.'

Every time I took her out I pulled the blinds in the back seat of the car to hide the samples. That chap Colin used to give us oil and petrol. He used to give me a funny look. Fishy sort of small eyes he'd got. Always looking miserable. Then we would go off. Sunday was her free day. Not that driving's any holiday for me. And, of course, the firm paid. She used to take me down to see her family for the day. Start in the morning, and taking it you had dinner and tea there, a day's outing cost us nothing. Her father was something on the railway, retired. He had a long stocking somewhere, but her sister, the one that was married, had had her share already.

He had a tumour after his wife died and they just played upon the old man's feelings. It wasn't right. She wouldn't go near her sister and I don't blame her, taking the money like that. Just played upon the old man's feelings.

Every time I was up there Colin used to come in looking for her.

'Oh, Colin,' I used to say. 'Done my car yet?' He knew where he got off with me.

'No, now, I can't, Colin. I tell you I'm going out with Mr Humphrey,' she used to say to him. I heard her.

'He keeps on badgering me,' she said to me.

'You leave him to me,' I said.

'No, he's all right,' she said.

'You let me know if there's any trouble with Colin,' I said. 'Seems to be a harum-scarum sort of half-wit to me,' I said.

'And he spends every penny he makes,' she said.

Well, we know that sort of thing is all right while it lasts, I told her, but the trouble is that it doesn't last.

We were always meeting Colin on the road. I took no notice of it first of all and then I grew suspicious and awkward at always meeting him. He had a new motor bicycle. It was an Indian, a scarlet thing that he used to fly over the moor with, flat out. Muriel and I used to go out over the moor to Ingley Wood in the firm's

Morris – I had a customer out that way.

'May as well do a bit of business while you're about it,' I said.

'About what?' she said.

'Ah-ha!' I said. 'That's what Colin wants to know,' I said.

Sure enough, coming back we'd hear him popping and backfiring close behind us, and I put out my hand to stop him and keep him following us, biting our dirt.

'I see his little game,' I said. 'Following us.'

So I saw to it that he did follow. We could hear him banging away behind us, and the traffic is thick on the Ingley road in the afternoon.

'Oh, let him pass,' Muriel said. 'I can't stand those dirty things banging in my ears.'

I waved him on and past he flew with his scarf flying out, blazing red into the traffic. 'We're doing fifty-eight ourselves,' she said, leaning across to look.

'Powerful buses those,' I said. 'Any fool can do it if he's got the power. Watch me step on it.'

But we did not catch Colin. Half an hour later he passed us coming back. Cut right in between us and a lorry – I had to brake hard. I damn nearly killed him. His ears were red with the wind. He didn't wear a hat. I got after him as soon as I could, but I couldn't touch him.

Nearly every weekend I was in that town seeing my girl, that fellow was hanging round. He came into the bar on Saturday nights, he poked his head into the office on Sunday mornings. It was a sure bet that if we went out in the car he would pass us on the road. Every time we would hear that scarlet thing roar by like a horse-stinger. It didn't matter where we were. He passed us on the main road, he met us down the side roads. There was a little cliff under oak trees at May Ponds, she said, where the view was pretty. And there, soon after we got there, was Colin on the other side of the water, watching us. Once we found him sitting on his bike, just as though he were waiting for us.

'You been here in a car?' I said.

'No, motorbike,' she said, and blushed. 'Cars can't follow in these tracks.'

She knew a lot of places in that country. Some of the roads weren't roads at all and were bad for tyres and I didn't want the firm's car scratched by bushes, but you would have thought Colin could read what was in her mind. For nine times out of ten he was there. It got on my nerves. It was a red, roaring, powerful thing and he opened it full out.

'I'm going to speak to Colin,' I said. 'I won't have him annoying you.'

'He's not annoying me,' she said. 'I've got a sense of humour.'

'Here, Colin,' I said one evening when I put the car away. 'What's the idea?'

He was taking off his overalls. He pretended he did not know what I was talking about. He had a way of rolling his eyeballs, as if they had got wet and loose in his head, while he was speaking to me, and you never knew if it was sweat or oil on his face. It was always pale, with high colour on his cheeks and very red lips.

'Miss MacFarlane doesn't like being followed,' I said.

He dropped his jaw and gaped at me. I could not tell whether he was being very surprised or very shy. I used to call him 'Marbles' because when he spoke he seemed to have a lot of marbles in his mouth.

Then he said he never went to the places we went to, except by accident. He wasn't following us, he said, but we were following him. We never let him alone, he said. Everywhere he went, he said, we were there. Take last Saturday, he said, we were following him for miles down the bypass, he said. 'But you passed us first and then sat down in front,' I said. 'I went to Ingley Wood,' he said. 'And you followed me there.' No, we didn't, I said, Miss MacFarlane decided to go there.

He said he did not want to complain, but fair was fair. 'I suppose you know,' he said, 'that you have taken my girl off me. Well, you can leave *me* alone, can't you?'

'Here,' I said. 'One minute! Not so fast! You said I've taken Miss MacFarlane off you. Well, she was never your girl. She only knew you in a friendly way.'

'She was my girl' was all he said.

He was pouring oil into my engine. He had some cotton wool in one hand and the can in the other. He wiped up the green oil that had overflowed, screwed on the cap, pulled down the bonnet, and whistled to himself.

I went back to Muriel and told her what Colin had said.

'I don't like trouble,' I said.

'Don't you worry,' she said. 'I had to have someone to go to all these places with before you came. Couldn't stick in here all day Sunday.'

'Ah,' I said. 'That's it, is it? You've been to all these places with him?'

'Yes,' she said. 'And he keeps on going to them. He's sloppy about me.'

'Good God,' I said. 'Sentimental memories.'

I felt sorry for that fellow. He knew it was hopeless, but he loved her. I suppose he couldn't help himself. Well, it takes all sorts to make a world, as my mother used to say. If we were all alike it wouldn't do. Some men can't save money. It just runs through their fingers. He couldn't save money, so he lost her. I suppose all he thought of was love.

I could have been friends with that fellow. As it was, I put a lot of business his way. I didn't want him to get the wrong idea about me. We're all human after all.

We didn't have any more trouble with Colin after this until Bank Holiday. I was going to take her to see my family. The old man's getting a bit past it now and has given up living over the shop. He's living out on the Barnum Road, beyond the tram stop. We were going down in the firm's car, as per usual, but something went wrong with the mag and Colin had not got it right for the holiday. I was wild about this. What's the use of a garage who can't do a rush job for the holidays! What's the use of being an old customer if they're going to let you down! I went for Colin bald-headed.

'You knew I wanted it,' I said. 'It's no use trying to put me off with a tale about the stuff not coming down from the works. I've heard that one before.'

I told him he'd got to let me have another car, because he'd let me down. I told him I wouldn't pay his account. I said I'd take my business away from him. But there wasn't a car to be had in the town because of the holiday. I could have knocked the fellow down. After the way I'd sent business to him.

Then I saw through his little game. He knew Muriel and I were going to my people and he had done this to stop it. The moment I saw this I let him know that it would take more than him to stop me doing what I wanted.

I said: 'Right. I shall take the amount of Miss MacFarlane's train fare and my own from the account at the end of the month.'

I said: 'You may run a garage, but you don't run the railway service.'

I was damned angry going by train. I felt quite lost on the railway after having a car. It was crowded with trippers too. It was slow – stopping at all the stations. The people come in, they tread all over your feet, they make you squeeze up till you're crammed against the window, and the women stick out their elbows and fidget. And then the expense! A return for two runs you into just over a couple of quid. I could have murdered Colin.

We got there at last. We walked up from the tram stop. Mother was at the window and let us in.

'This is Miss MacFarlane,' I said.

And Mother said: 'Oh, pleased to meet you. We've heard a lot about you.

'Oh,' Mother said to me, giving me a kiss, 'are you tired? You haven't had your tea, have you? Sit down. Have this chair, dear. It's more comfortable.'

'Well, my boy,' my father said.

'Want a wash,' my father said. 'We've got a washbasin downstairs,' he said. 'I used not to mind about washing upstairs before. Now I couldn't do without it. Funny how your ideas change as you get older.

'How's business?' he said.

'Mustn't grumble,' I said. 'How's yours?'

'You knew,' he said, 'we took off the horses: except for one or two of the older families we have got motors now.'

But he'd told me that the last time I was there. I'd been at him for years about motor hearses.

'You've forgotten I used to drive them,' I said.

'Bless me, so you did,' he said.

He took me up to my room. He showed me everything he had done to the house. 'Your mother likes it,' he said. 'The traffic's company for her. You know what your mother is for company.'

Then he gives me a funny look.

'Who's the girl?' he says.

My mother came in then and said: 'She's pretty, Arthur.'

'Of course she's pretty,' I said. 'She's Irish.'

'Oh,' said the old man. 'Irish! She's got a sense of humour, eh?'

'She wouldn't be marrying me if she hadn't,' I said. And then I gave *them* a look.

'Marrying her, did you say?' exclaimed my father.

'Any objection?' I said.

'Now, Ernest dear,' said my mother. 'Leave the boy alone. Come down while I pop the kettle on.'

She was terribly excited.

'Miss MacFarlane,' the old man said.

'No sugar, thank you, Mrs Humphrey. I beg your pardon, Mr Humphrey?'

'The Glen Hotel at Swansea, I don't suppose you know that?' my father said. 'I wondered if you did, being in the catering line.'

'It doesn't follow she knows every hotel,' my mother said.

'Forty years ago,' the old man said, 'I was staying at the Glen in Swansea and the headwaiter – '

'Oh, no, not that one. I'm sure Miss MacFarlane doesn't want to hear that one,' my mother said.

'How's business with you, Mr Humphrey?' said Muriel. 'We passed a large cemetery near the station.'

'Dad's Ledger,' I said.

'The whole business has changed so that you wouldn't know it, in my lifetime,' said my father. 'Silver fittings have gone clean out. Everyone wants simplicity nowadays. Restraint. Dignity,' my father said.

'Prices did it,' my father said.

'The war,' he said.

'You couldn't get the wood,' he said.

'Take ordinary mahogany, just an ordinary piece of mahogany. Or teak,' he said. 'Take teak. Or walnut.'

'You can certainly see the world go by in this room,' I said to my mother.

'It never stops,' she said.

Now it was all bicycles over the new concrete road from the gun factory. Then traction engines and cars. They came up over the hill where the AA man stands and choked up around the tram stop. It was mostly holiday traffic. Everything with a wheel on it was out.

'On this stretch,' my father told me, 'they get three accidents a week.' There was an ambulance station at the crossroads.

We had hardly finished talking about this – in fact, the old man was still saying that something ought to be done – when the telephone rang.

'Name of MacFarlane?' the voice said on the wire.

'No. Humphrey,' my father said. 'There is a Miss MacFarlane here.'

'There's a man named Colin Mitchell lying seriously injured in an accident at the Cottage Hospital, gave me the name of MacFarlane as his nearest relative.'

That was the police. On to it at once. That fellow Colin had followed us down the road.

Cry, I never heard a girl cry as Muriel cried when we came back from the hospital. He had died in the ambulance. Cutting in, the old game he used to play on me. Clean off the saddle and under the Birmingham bus. The blood was everywhere, they said. People were still looking at it when we went by. Head on. What a mess! Don't let's talk about it.

She wanted to see him, but they said no. There wasn't anything recognizable to see. She put her arms around my neck and cried, 'Colin, Colin,' as if I were Colin, and clung to me. I was feeling sick myself. I held her tight and I kissed her and I thought: Holiday ruined.

Damn fool man, I thought. Poor devil, I thought.

'I knew he'd do something like this.'

'There, there,' I said to her. 'Don't think about Colin.'

Didn't she love me, I said, and not Colin? Hadn't she got me? She said yes, she had. And she loved me. But 'Oh, Colin! Oh, Colin!' she cried. 'And Colin's mother,' she cried. 'Oh, it's terrible.' She cried and cried.

We put her to bed and I sat with her, and my mother kept coming in.

'Leave her to me,' I said. 'I understand her.'

Before they went to bed they both came in and looked at her. She lay sobbing with her head in the pillow.

I could quite understand her being upset. Colin was a decent fellow. He was always doing things for her. He mended her electric lamp and he riveted the stem of a wine glass so that you couldn't see the break. He used to make things for her. He was very good with his hands.

She lay on her side with her face burning and feverish with misery and crying, scalded by the salt, and her lips shrivelled up. I put my arm under her neck and I stroked her forehead. She groaned. Sometimes she shivered and sometimes she clung to me, crying: 'Oh, Colin! Colin!'

My arm ached with the cramp and I had a crick in my back, sitting in the awkward way I was on the bed. It was late. There was nothing to do but to ache and sit watching her and thinking. It is funny the way your mind drifts. When I was kissing her and watching her I was thinking out who I'd show our new Autumn range to first. Her hand held my wrist tight, and when I kissed her I got her tears on my lips. They burned and stung. Her neck and shoulders were soft and I could feel her breath hot out of her nostrils on the back of my hand. Ever noticed how hot a woman's breath gets when she's crying? I drew out my hand and lay down beside her and 'Oh, Colin, Colin,' she sobbed, turning over and clinging to me. And so I lay there, listening to the traffic, staring at the ceiling, and shivering whenever the picture of Colin shooting right off that damned red thing into the bus came into my mind – until I did not hear the traffic any more, or see the ceiling any more, or think any more, but a change happened – I don't know when. This Colin thing seemed to have knocked the bottom out of everything and I had a funny feeling we were going down and down and down in a lift. And the further we went, the hotter and softer she got. Perhaps it was when I found with my hands that she had very big breasts. But it was like being on the mail steamer and feeling engines start under your feet, thumping louder and louder. You can feel it in every vein of your body. Her mouth opened and her voice was blind and husky. Colin, Colin, Colin, she said, and her fingers were hooked into me. I got out and turned the key in the door.

In the morning I left her sleeping. It did not matter to me what my father might have heard in the night, but still I wondered. She would hardly let me touch her before that. I told her I was sorry, but she shut me up. I was afraid of her. I was afraid of mentioning Colin. I wanted to go out of the house there and then and tell someone everything. Did she love Colin all the time? Did she think I was Colin? And every time I thought of that poor devil covered over with a white sheet in the hospital mortuary, a kind of picture of her and me under the sheets with love came into my mind. I couldn't separate the two things. Just as though it had all come from Colin.

I'd rather not talk any more about that. I never talked to Muriel about it. I waited for her to say something, but she didn't. She didn't say a word.

The next day was a bad day. It was grey and hot and the air smelt of oil fumes from the road. There's always a mess to clear up when things like this happen. I had to see to it. I had the job of ringing up the boy's mother. But I got round that, thank God, by ringing up the garage and getting them to go round and see the old lady. My father is useless when things are like this. I was the whole morning on the phone: to the hospital, the police, the coroner – and he stood fussing beside me, jerking up and down like a fat indiarubber ball.

I found my mother washing up at the sink and she said: 'That poor boy's mother! I can't stop thinking of her.'

Then my father comes in and says – just as though I was a customer: 'Of course if Mrs Mitchell desires it we can have the remains of the deceased conveyed to his house by one of the new specially sprung motor hearses and can, if necessary, make all the funeral arrangements.'

I could have hit him because Muriel came into the room when he was saying this. But she stood there as if nothing had happened.

'It's the least we can do for poor Mrs Mitchell,' she said. There were small creases of shadow under her eyes, which shone with a strong light I had never seen before. She walked as if she were really still in that room with me, asleep. God, I loved that girl! God, I wanted to get all this over, this damned Colin business that had come right into the middle of everything like this, and I wanted to get married right away. I wanted to be alone with her. That's what Colin did for me.

'Yes,' I said. 'We must do the right thing by Colin.'

'We are sometimes asked for long-distance estimates,' my father said.

'It will be a little something,' my mother said.

'Dad and I will talk it over,' I said.

'Come into the office,' my father said. 'It occurred to me that it would be nice to do the right thing by this friend of yours.'

We talked it over. We went into the cost of it. There was the return journey to reckon. We worked it out that it would come no dearer to old Mrs Mitchell than if she took the train and buried the boy here. That is to say, my father said, if I drove it.

'It would look nice,' my father said. 'Saves money and it would look a bit friendly,' my father said. 'You've done it before.'

'Well,' I said. 'I suppose I can get a refund on my return ticket from the railway.'

But it was not as simple as it looked, because Muriel wanted to come. She wanted to drive back with me and the hearse. My mother was very worried about this. It might upset Muriel, she thought. Father thought it might not look nice to see a young girl sitting by the coffin of a grown man.

'It must be dignified,' my father said. 'You see, if she was there, it might look as though she were just doing it for the ride – like these young women on bakers' vans.'

My father took me out into the hall to tell me this because he did not want her to hear. But she would not have it. She wanted to come back with Colin.

'Colin loved me. It is my duty to him,' she said. 'Besides,' she said suddenly, in her full open voice – it had seemed to be closed and carved and broken and small – 'I've never been in a hearse before.'

'And it will save her fare too,' I said to my father.

That night I went again to her room. She was awake. I said I was sorry to disturb her, but I would go at once only I wanted to see if she was all right. She said, in the closed voice again, that she was all right.

'Are you sure?' I said.

She did not answer. I was worried. I went over to the bed.

'What is the matter? Tell me what is the matter,' I said.

For a long time she was silent. I held her hand, I stroked her head. She was lying stiff in the bed. She would not answer. I dropped my hand to her small white shoulder. She stirred and drew up her legs and half turned and said, 'I was thinking of Colin. Where is he?' she asked.

'They've brought him round. He's lying downstairs.'

'In the front room?'

'Yes, ready for the morning. Now be a sensible girl and go back by train.'

'No, no,' she said. 'I want to go with Colin. Poor Colin. He loved me and I didn't love him.' And she drew my hands down to her breasts.

'Colin loved me,' she whispered.

'Not like this,' I whispered.

It was a warm grey morning like all the others when we took Colin back. They had fixed the coffin in before Muriel came out. She came down wearing the bright-blue hat she had got off Dormer's millinery man and she kissed my mother and father goodbye. They were very sorry for her. 'Look after her, Arthur,' my mother said. Muriel got in beside me without a glance behind her at the coffin. I started the engine. They smiled at us. My father raised his hat, but whether it was to Muriel and me or to Colin, or to the three of us, I do not know. He was not, you see, wearing his top hat. I'll say this for the old boy, thirty years in the trade have taught him tact.

After leaving my father's house you have to go down to the tram terminus before you get on the bypass. There was always one or two drivers, conductors, or inspectors there, doing up their tickets, or changing over the trolley arms. When we passed I saw two of them drop their jaw, stick their pencils in their ears, and raise their hats. I was so surprised by this that I nearly raised mine in acknowledgement, forgetting that we had the coffin behind. I had not driven one of my father's hearses for years.

Hearses are funny things to drive. They are well-sprung, smooth-running cars, with quiet engines, and if you are used to driving a smaller car, before you know where you are, you are speeding. You know you ought to go slow, say twenty-five to thirty maximum, and it's hard to keep it down. You can return empty at seventy if you like. It's like driving a fire engine. Go fast out and come back slow – only the other way round. Open out in the country, but slow down past houses. That's what it means. My father was very particular about this.

Muriel and I didn't speak very much at first. We sat listening to the engine and the occasional jerk of the coffin behind when we went over a pothole. We passed the place where poor Colin – but I didn't say anything to Muriel, and she, if she noticed – which I doubt – did not say anything to me. We went through Cox Hill, Wammering, and Yodley Mount, flat country, don't care for it myself. 'There's a wonderful lot of building going on,' Muriel said at last.

'You won't know these places in five years,' I said.

But my mind kept drifting away from the road and the green fields and the dullness, and back to Colin – five days before, he had come down this way. I expected to see that Indian coming flying straight out of every corner. But it was all bent and bust up properly now. I saw the damned thing.

He had been up to his old game, following us, and that had put the end to following. But not quite; he was following us now, behind us in the coffin. Then my mind drifted off that and I thought of those nights at my parents' house, and Muriel. You never know what a woman is going to be like. I thought, too, that it had put my calculations out. I mean, supposing she had a baby. You see I had reckoned on waiting eighteen months or so. I would have eight hundred then. But if we had to get married at once, we should have to cut right down. Then I kept thinking it was funny her saying 'Colin!' like that in the night; it was funny it made her feel that way about me, and how it made me feel when she called me Colin. I'd never thought of her in that way, in what you might call the 'Colin' way.

I looked at her and she looked at me and she smiled but still we did not say very much, but the smiles kept coming to both of us. The light-railway bridge at Dootheby took me by surprise and I thought the coffin gave a jump as we took it.

'Colin's still watching us,' I nearly said.

There were tears in her eyes.

'What was the matter with Colin?' I said. 'Nice chap, I thought. Why didn't you marry him?'

'Yes,' she said. 'He was a nice boy. But he'd no sense of humour.

'And I wanted to get out of that town,' she said.

'I'm not going to stay there, at that hotel,' she said.

'I want to get away,' she said. 'I've had enough.'

She had a way of getting angry with the air, like that. 'You've got to take me away,' she said. We were passing slowly into Muster, there was a tram ahead and people thick on the narrow pavements, dodging out into the road. But when we got into the Market Square, where they were standing round, they saw the coffin. They began to raise their hats. Suddenly she laughed. 'It's like being the King and Queen,' she said.

'They're raising their hats,' she said.

'Not all of them,' I said.

She squeezed my hand and I had to keep her from jumping about like a child on the seat as we went through.

'There they go.'

'Boys always do,' I said.

'And another.

'Let's see what the policeman does.'

She started to laugh, but I shut her up. 'Keep your sense of humour to yourself,' I said.

Through all those towns that run into one another as you might say, we caught it. We went through, as she said, like royalty. So many years since I drove a hearse, I'd forgotten what it was like.

I was proud of her, I was proud of Colin, and I was proud of myself. And after what had happened, I mean on the last two nights, it was like a wedding. And although we knew it was for Colin, it was for us too, because Colin was with both of us. It was like this all the way.

'Look at that man there. Why doesn't he raise his hat? People ought to show respect for the dead,' she said.

The Wheelbarrow

'Robert,' Miss Freshwater's niece called down from the window of the dismantled bedroom, 'when you have finished that, would you mind coming upstairs a minute? I want you to move a trunk.'

And when Evans waved back from the far side of the rumpled lawn where he was standing by the bonfire, she closed the window to keep out the smoke of slow-burning rubbish – old carpeting, clothes, magazines, papers, boxes – which hung about the waists of the fir trees and blew towards the house. For three days the fire had been burning, and Evans, red-armed in his shirt-sleeves and sweating along the seams of his brow, was prodding it with a garden fork. A sudden silly tongue of yellow flame wagged out: some inflammable piece of family history – who knew what? Perhaps one of her aunt's absurd summer hats or a shocking year of her father's daydream accountancy was having its last fling. She saw Evans pick up a bit of paper from the outskirts of the fire and read it. What was it? Miss Freshwater's niece drew back her lips and opened her mouth expectantly. At this stage all family privacy had gone. Thirty, forty, fifty years of life were going up in smoke.

Evans took up the wheelbarrow and swaggered back with it across the lawn towards the house, sometimes tipping it a little to one side to see how the rubber-tyred wheel was running and to admire it. Miss Freshwater's niece smiled. With his curly black hair, his sun-reddened face, and his vacant blue eyes, and the faint white scar or chip on the side of his nose, he looked like some hard-living, hard-bitten doll. 'Burn this? This lot to go?' was his cry. He was an impassioned and natural destroyer. She could not have found a better man. 'Without you, Robert,' she said on the first day and with real feeling, 'I could never have faced it.'

It was pure luck getting him, but, lazy, smiling and drifting, she always fell on her feet. She had stepped off the morning train from London at the beginning of the week and had stood on the kerb in the station yard, waiting for one of the two or three taxi drivers who were talking there to take notice of her. Suddenly Evans drove in fast from the street outside, pulled up beside her, pushed her in, and drove off. It was like an abduction. The other taxi drivers shouted at him in the bad language of law-abiding men, but Evans slowly moved his hand up and down, palm downwards, silently and insultingly telling them to shut up and keep their hair on. He looked very pious as he did this. It made her laugh out loud.

'They are manner-less,' he said in a low, rebuking voice, giving each syllable its clear value as if he were speaking the phrase of a poem. 'I am sorry I did not ask you where you want me to take you.'

They were going in the wrong direction, and he had to swing round the street. She now saw him glance at her in the mirror and his doll's eyes quickly changed from shrewd pleasure to vacancy: she was a capture.

'This is not the first time you are here, I suppose?' he said.

'I was born here,' she said. 'I haven't been here for twenty-five years – well, perhaps just for a day a few years ago. It has changed. All this building!'

She liked friendly conversations.

They were driving up the long hill out of the town towards her aunt's house. Once there had been woodland here, but now, like a red hard sea flowing in to obliterate her memory, thousands of sharp villas replaced the trees in angular waves.

'Yes,' he said simply. 'There is money everywhere.'

The car hummed up the long, concrete hill. The villas gave way to ribbons of shacks and bungalows. The gardens were buzzing with June flowers. He pointed out a bungalow that had a small grocery shop in the lean-to at the side, a yard where a couple of old cars stood, and a petrol pump. That was his place, he said. And then, beyond that, were the latest municipal housing estates built close to the Green, which was only half a mile from her aunt's house. As they passed, she saw a white marquee on the Green and a big sagging white banner with the words 'Gospel Mission' daubed on it.

'I see the Gospellers still keep it up,' she said. For it was all bad land outside the town, a place for squatters, poor craftsmen, smallholders, little men with little sheds, who in their flinty way had had for generations the habit of breaking out into little religious sects.

'Oh, yes,' said Evans in a soft voice, shocked that she could doubt it. 'There are great openings. There is a mighty coming to the Lord. I toil in the vineyard myself. You are Miss Freshwater's niece?' he said. 'She was a toiler too. She was a giantess for the Lord.'

She saw she had been reckless in laughing. She saw she was known. It was as if he had knowingly captured her.

'You don't come from these parts, do you?' she said.

'I am from Wales,' he said. 'I came here from the mines. I ob-jected to the starvation.'

They arrived at the ugly yellow house. It could hardly be seen through the overgrown laurels and fir trees which in some places fingered the dirty windows. He steadied her as she got out, for she had put on weight in the last year or so, and while she opened her bag to find some money, he walked to the gate and looked in.

'It was left to you in the will, I suppose?' he said.

'Yes,' she said. She was a woman always glad to confide. 'I've come down to clear up the rubbish before the sale. Do you know anyone here who would give me a hand?'

'There are many,' he pronounced. 'They are too handy.' It was like a line from an anthem. He went ahead, opened the gate, and led the way in, and when she opened the front door, splitting it away from the cobwebs, he went in with her, walking into the stale, sun-yellowed rooms. He looked up the worn carpet of the stairs. He looked at the ceilings, measuring the size of everything.

'It will fetch a high price,' he said in a sorrowful voice and then, looking over her figure like a farmer at the market, in case she might go with the property, he added enthusiasm to his sorrow.

'The highest!' he said. 'Does this door go to the back?' She lost him for a while. When she found him he was outside, at the back of the house, looking into sheds. He had opened the door of one that contained gardening tools and there he was, gazing. He was looking at a new green metal wheelbarrow with a red wheel and a rubber tyre and he had even pulled it out. He pushed it back, and when he saw her he said accusingly:

'This door has no lock. I do not like to see a door without a lock. I will bring one this afternoon.'

It was how she knew he had appointed himself.

'But who will do your taxi work?'

'My son will do that,' he said.

From that moment he owned her and the house.

'There will be a lot of toil in this vineyard,' she said to him maliciously and wished she had not said it; but Evans's eyes lost their vacancy again and quickened and sparkled. He gave a shout of laughter.

'Oh, boy, there will!' he said, admiring her. And he went off. She walked from room to room opening windows, and from an upper one she saw distantly the white sheet of the Gospel tent through the fir trees. She could settle to nothing.

It was an ugly house of large mean rooms, the landings dark, the stairs steep. The furniture might have come out of old-fashioned hotels and had the helpless look of objects too large, ill-met commercially, and too gregarious. After her mother's death, her father had moved his things into his sister's house. Taste had not been a strong point in the family. The books, mainly sermons, were her grandfather's; his son had lived on a hoard of engineering textbooks and magazines. The sister read chiefly the Bible and the rest of her time changed her clothes, having the notion that she might be going out.

What paralysed Miss Freshwater's niece was the emptiness of the place. She had expected to disturb ghosts if she opened a drawer. She had expected to remember herself. Instead, as she waited for Evans to come on the first day she had the sensation of being ignored. Nothing watched in the shadows, nothing blinked in the beams of sunlight slanting across the room. The room she had slept in meant nothing. To fit memories into it was a task so awkward and artificial that she gave up trying. Several times she went to the window, waiting for Evans to walk in at the gate and for the destruction to begin.

When he did come he seized the idea at once. All files marked 'A.H.F.' – that was her father – were 'rubbish'.

'Thorpe?' he said. 'A.H.F., more A.H.F.! Burn it?' He was off with his first load to lay the foundation to the fire.

'And get this carpet up. We shall trip on it: it is torn,' she said. He ripped the carpet off the stairs. He tossed the doormats, which were worn into holes, outside. By the barrowload out went the magazines. Every now and then some object took his eye – a leather strap, a bowl, a pipe rack – which he put into a little heap of other perquisites at the back door.

But to burn was his passion, to push the wheelbarrow his joy. He swaggered with it. He unloaded it carefully at the fire, not putting it down too near or roughly tipping it. He often tried one or two different grips on the handles before he started off. Once, she saw him stop in the middle of the lawn and turn it upside down and look it over carefully and make the wheel spin. Something wrong? No, he lovingly wiped the wheel with a handful of grass, got an oilcan from his pocket, and gave the wheel a squirt. Then he righted the wheelbarrow and came on with it round the house, singing in a low and satisfied voice. A hymn, it sounded like. And at the end of the day, when she took him a cup a tea and they stood chatting, his passion satisfied for the time being, he had a good look at her. His eye was on the brooch she was carelessly wearing to fasten her green overall. He came closer and put his hand to the brooch and lifted it.

'Those are pearls, I shouldn't wonder?' he said.

'Yes,' she said. He stepped nimbly away, for he was as quick as a flea.

'It is beautiful,' he said, considering the brooch and herself together. 'You would not buy it for fifty pounds, nor even a hundred, I suppose. A present I expect?' And before she could answer, he said gravely: 'Half past five! I will lock the sheds. Are you sleeping here? My wife would go off her head, alone in the house. When I'm at the mission, she's insane!'

Evans stared at Miss Freshwater's niece, waiting for a response to his drama. She did not know what to do, so she laughed. Evans gave a shout of laughter too. It shook the close black curls of his hair and the scar on the side of his nose went white.

'I have the key,' he said seriously, and went off.

'Robert!' Miss Freshwater's niece opened the window and called again. 'Can you come now? I can't get on.'

Evans was on his way once more to the house. He stamped quickly up the bare stairs.

'I'm in here,' she called. 'If you can get in!'

There was a heap of old brown paper knee-high at the door. Some of the drawers of a chest had been taken out, others were half open; a wardrobe's doors were open wide. There were shoes, boxes, and clothes piled on the bed, which was stripped. She had a green scarf in a turban round her head, and none of her fair hair could be seen. Her face, with its strong bones and pale skin marked by dirty fingers, looked hard, humorous, and naked. Her strong lips were dry and pale with dust.

They understood each other. At first he had bossed her, but she had fought back on the second day and they were equals now. She spoke to him as if they were in a conspiracy together, deciding what should be 'saved' and what could be 'cast into the flames'. She used those words purposely, as a dig of malice at him. She was taller than he. She couldn't get over the fact that he preached every night at the mission and she had fallen into the habit of tempting him by some movement of arm or body, when she caught him looking at her. Her aunt had used the word 'inconvenient', when her niece was young, to describe the girl's weakness for dawdling about with gardeners, chauffeurs, errand boys. Miss Freshwater's niece had lost the sense of the 'convenient' very early in life.

'I've started upstairs now,' she said to Evans. 'It's worse than downstairs. Look at it.'

Evans came a step further into the room and slowly looked round, nodding his head.

She leaned a little forward, her hands together, eagerly waiting for him to laugh so that they could laugh together.

'She never threw away a scrap of paper. Not even paper bags. Look at this,' she said.

He waded into the heap and peeped into a brown paper bag. It contained a bun, as hard as stone.

'Biscuits too,' she said. 'Wrapped up! Like a larder. They must have been here for years. In the top drawer.'

Evans did not laugh.

'She feared starvation,' he said. 'Old people are hungry. They are greedy. My grandmother nibbled like a little rat, all day. And in the night too. They wake up in the night and they are afraid. They eat for comfort. The mice did not get in, I hope,' he said, going to look in the drawer.

'She was eighty-four,' she said.

'My grandmother was ninety,' he said. 'My father's mother. She liked to hear a mouse. It was company, she said.'

'I think my aunt must have been fond of moths,' she said. 'They came out in clouds from that wardrobe. Look at all those dresses. I can hardly bear to touch them.'

She shook a couple of dresses in the wardrobe and then took them out. 'There you are, did you see it? There goes one.'

She held up an old-fashioned silk dress.

'Not worn for twenty years, you can see by the fashion. There!' She gave the dress a pull. 'Did you hear? Perished. Rotten. They are all like that. You can't give them away. They'd fall off you.'

She threw the dresses on the floor and he picked up one and he saw where moths had eaten it.

'It is wicked,' he said. 'All that money gone to waste.'

'Where moth and dust doth corrupt,' she mocked him, and took an armful of the clothes and threw them on the floor. 'Why did she buy them if she did not want them? And all those hats we had to burn? You haven't seen anything yet. Look at this.'

On the bed was lying a pile of enormous lace-up corsets. Evans considered them.

'The men had patience,' he said.

'Oh, she was not married,' she said.

He nodded.

'That is how all the property comes to you, I suppose,' he said. There was a shrewd flash in his blue eyes and she knew he had been gazing at her all this time and not at the clothes; but even as she caught his look the dissembling, still, vacant light slid back into it.

'Shoes!' she said with excitement. 'Do you want any shoes?' A large number of shoes of all kinds, little worn or not worn at all, were rowed in pairs on the bed and some had been thrown into a box as well.

'Fifty-one pairs I counted,' she said. 'She never went out but she went on ordering them. There's a piece of paper in each pair. Have a look. Read it. What does it say?'

He took a piece of paper out of a shoe.

' "Comfortable for the evening," ' he read out. He took another. ' "For wet weather." Did it rain indoors?'

She took one and read out: ' "With my blue dress"! Can you imagine? "Sound walking pair." ' She laughed, but he interrupted her.

'In Wales they lacked them,' he said. 'In the bad times they were going barefoot. My sisters shared a pair for dances.'

'What shall I do with them?' she asked. 'Someone could wear them.'

'There are good times now. They have the money,' he said, snubbing her. 'They buy new.'

'I mean – anyone,' she said. 'They are too big for me. I'll show you.'

She sat down on a packing case and slipped her foot into a silver evening shoe.

'You can see, my feet are lost in them,' she said.

'You have small feet,' he said. 'In Wales the men would be chasing you.'

'After chapel, I've no doubt,' she said. 'Up the mountain – what was the name of it? You told me.'

'It has the best view in Wales. But those who go up it never see it,' he laughed. 'Try this pair,' he said, kneeling down and lifting her foot. 'Ah no, I see. But look at those legs, boy!'

Miss Freshwater's niece got up.

'What size does your wife take?' she asked.

'I don't know,' he said, very pleased with himself. 'Where is this trunk you said we had to move?'

'Out in the landing cupboard. I'll show you. I can't move it.'

She led the way to the landing and bent down to tug at it.

'You must not do that,' he said, putting his hands on her waist and moving her out of the way. He heaved at the trunk and tipped it on end. She wanted it, she said, in the light, where she could see.

'Here on the chest,' she said.

He lifted it up and planked it down on the chest.

'Phew!' he said. 'You have a small waist for a married woman. Soft. My wife is a giantess, she weighs thirteen stone. And yet you're big, too, oh, yes, you are. But you have light bones. With her, now, it is the bones that weigh. Shall we open it?'

She sat down on a chair and felt in her pocket for a mirror.

'Why didn't you tell me I looked such a sight?' she said, wiping her face. 'Yes, open it.'

The trunk was made of black leather, it was cracked, peeling, stained, and squashed by use. Dimly printed on it was her father's fading name in white, large letters. The trunk had been pitched and bumped and slithered out of ships' holds and trains, all over the world. Its lid, now out of the true, no longer met the lock and it was closed by a strap. It had lain ripening and decaying in attics and lofts for half a lifetime.

'What is in it?' she called, without looking from her mirror.

'Clothes,' he said. 'Books. A pair of skates. Did the old lady go skating?'

He pulled out a Chinese hat. There was a pigtail attached to it and he held it up.

'Ah,' he called. 'This is the job.' He put the hat on his head and pulled out a mandarin coat.

Miss Freshwater's niece stared and then she flushed.

'Where did you get that?' she cried, jumping up, taking the hat from his head and snatching the coat. 'They're mine! Where were they?'

She pushed him aside and pulled one or two things from the trunk.

'They're mine!' she accused him. 'All mine.'

She aged as she looked at him. A photograph fell to the floor as she lifted up a book. ' "To darling Laura," ' she read out. 'Tennyson.'

'Who is this?' he said, picking up the photograph.

She did not hear. She was pulling out a cold, sequined evening dress that shrank almost to nothing as she picked it up.

'Good God,' she said and dropped it with horror. For under the dress was an album. 'Where,' she said, sharply possessive, 'did you put the skates?' She opened the album. She looked at a road deep in snow leading to a hotel with eaves a yard wide. She had spent her honeymoon there.

'Kitzbühel,' she said. 'Oh, no!'

She looked fiercely at him to drive him away. The house, so anonymous, so absurd, so meaningless and ghostless, had suddenly got her. There was a choke of cold wonder in her throat.

She turned on him. 'Can't you clear up all that paper in the room?' She did not want to be seen by him.

Evans went to the door of the bedroom and, after a glance inside, came back. He was not going to leave her. He picked up the book of poems, glanced at a page or two, and then dropped it back in the trunk.

'Everyone knows,' he said scornfully, 'that the Welsh are the founders of all the poetry of Europe.'

She did not hear him. Her face had drained of waking light. She had entered blindly into a dream in which she could hardly drag herself along. She was looking painfully through the album, rocking her head slowly from side to side, her mouth opening a little and closing on the point of speech, a shoulder rising as if she had been hurt, and her back moving and swaying as she felt the clasp of the past like hands on her. She was looking at ten forgotten years of her life, her own life, not her family's, and she did not laugh when she saw the skirts too long, the top-heavy hats hiding the faces, her face too full and fat, her plainness so sullen, her prettiness too open-mouthed and loud, her look too grossly sly. In this one, sitting at the café table by the lake when she was nineteen, she looked masterful and at least forty. In this garden picture she was theatrically fancying herself as an ancient Greek in what looked like a nightgown! One of her big toes, she noticed, turned up comically in the sandal she was wearing. Here on a rock by the sea, in a bathing dress, she had got thin again – that was her marriage – and look at her hair! This picture of the girl in skis, sharp-faced, the eyes narrowed – who was that? Herself – yet how could she have looked like that! But she smiled a little at last at the people she had forgotten. This man with the crinkled fair hair, a German – how mad she had been about him. But what pierced her was that in each picture of herself she was just out of reach, flashing and yet dead; and that really it was the things that burned in the light of permanence – the chairs, the tables, the trees, the car outside the café, the motor launch on the lake. These blinked and glittered. They had lasted and were ageless, untouched by time, and she was not. She put the album back into the trunk and pulled out an old tweed coat and skirt. Under it was an exercise book with the word 'Diary' written on it in a hand more weakly rounded than the hand she wrote today. Part of a letter fell out of the diary, the second page, it seemed, of a letter of her own. She read it.

'. . . the job at any rate,' she read. 'For a whole week he's forgotten his chest, his foot, his stomach. He's not dying any more!!! He conde (crossed out) congratulates himself and says it just shows how doctors are all fools. Inner self-confidence is what I need, he tells me!! It means giving up the flat and that's what I keep thinking – Oxford will be much more difficult for you and me. Women, he says, aren't happy unless they're sacrificing themselves. Darling, he doesn't know: it's the thought of You that keeps . . .'

She turned over the page. Nothing. She looked through the diary. Nothing. She felt sick and then saw Evans had not gone and was watching her. She quickly put the letter back into the diary.

'Ah,' she said nervously. 'I didn't know you were here. I'll show you something.' She laughed unnaturally and opened the album until she found the most ludicrous and abashing picture in the book, one that would humiliate her entirely. 'Here, look at this.'

There was a see-saw in the foreground surrounded by raucously laughing people wearing paper hats and looking as though they had been dipped in glycerine: she was astride at the higher end of the see-saw, kicking her legs, and on the lower end was a fat young man in a pierrot costume. On her short, fuzzy, fair hair was a paper hat. She showed the picture to Evans and picked out the terrible sequin dress from the trunk.

'That's the dress!' she said, pointing to the picture. 'I was engaged to him. Isn't it terrible?' And she dropped the dress back again. It felt cold and slippery, almost wet. 'I didn't marry him.'

Evans scowled.

'You were naked,' he said with disgust.

'I remember now. I left it all here. I kept that dress for years. I'll have to go through it all.' And she pulled down the lid.

'This photograph fell out,' he said.

It was the picture of another young man.

'Is this your husband?' Evans asked, studying the man.

'My husband is dead,' she said sharply. 'That is a friend.' And she threw the picture back into the trunk. She realized now that Evans had been holding her arm a long time. She stepped away from him abruptly. The careless friendliness, the sense of conspiracy she had felt while they worked together, had gone. She drew away and said, in the hostile voice of unnecessary explanation:

'I mean,' she said, 'my husband died a few years ago. We were divorced. I mustn't waste any more time.'

'My wife would not condescend to that,' he said.

'She has no reason, I am sure,' said Miss Freshwater's niece severely, and returned to the bedroom.

'Now! We can't waste time like this. You'd better begin with what is on the bed. And when you've cleared it you can put the kettle on.'

When Evans had gone downstairs with his load, she went to the landing and glared at the trunk. Her fists were clenched; she wished it was alive and that she could hit it. Glancing over the banisters to be sure she was alone, she opened it again, took out the photograph and the letter from her diary and put them in her handbag. She thought she was going to be sick or faint, for the past was drumming, like a train coming nearer and nearer, in her head.

'My God,' she said. And when she saw her head in its turban and her face hardened by shock and grief in her aunt's absurd dressing-table mirror, she exclaimed with real horror. She was crying. 'What a mess,' she said and pulled the scarf off her head. Her fair, thick hair hung around her face untidily. Not once, in all those photographs, had a face so wolfish with bitterness and without laughter looked back at her.

'I'm taking the tea out,' Evans called from below.

'I'm just coming,' she called back and hurriedly tried to arrange her hair and then, because she had cried a little, she put on her glasses. Evans gave a keen look at the change in her when she got downstairs and walked through the hall to the door.

He had put the tray on the grass near a yew hedge in the hot corner at the side of the house and was standing a few yards away drinking his tea. In the last two days he had never drunk his tea near her but had chatted from a distance.

In her glasses and with her hair girlishly brushed back, Miss Freshwater's niece looked cold, tall, and grand, like a headmistress.

'I hope we shan't get any more smoke here,' she said. 'Sit down. You look too restless.'

She was very firm, nodding to the exact place on the lawn on which she required him to sit. Taken aback, Evans sat precisely in that place. She sat on the grass and poured herself a cup of tea.

'How many souls came to Jesus last night?' she asked in her lady-like voice. Evans got up and squatted cheerfully but watchfully on his heels.

'Seventeen,' he said.

'That's not very good,' she said. 'Do you think you could save mine?'

'Oh, yes,' he said keenly.

'You look like a frog,' she said, mocking. He had told her miners always squat in this way after work. 'It's too late,' she went on. 'Twenty years too late. Have you always been with the mission?'

'No,' he said.

'What was it? Were you converted, did you see the light?' she mocked, like a teacher.

'I had a vision,' he said seriously.

'A vision!' she laughed. She waved her hand. 'What do you mean – you mean, you – well, where? Up in the sky or something?'

'No,' he said. 'It was down the mine.'

'What happened?'

He put down his cup and he moved it away to give himself more room. He squatted there, she thought, not like a frog at all, but like an imp or a devil, very grave and carven-faced. She noticed now how wide his mouth was and how widely it opened and how far the lips drew back when he spoke in his declamatory voice. He stared a long time waiting for her to stop fidgeting. Then he began.

'I was a drunkard,' he declaimed, relishing each syllable separately. 'I was a liar. I was a hypocrite. I went with women. And married women, too!' His voice rose. 'I was a fornicator. I was an adulterer. Always at the races, too, gambling: it was senseless. There was no sin the Devil did not lead me into; I was like a fool. I was the most noteworthy sinner in the valley; everyone spoke of it.

But I did not know the Lord was lying in wait for me.'

'Yes, but what happened?' she said.

He got to his feet and gazed down at her and she was compelled to look up at him.

'I will tell you,' he said. 'It was a miracle.' He changed his manner, and after looking round the garden, he said in a hushing and secretive voice:

'There was a disaster in the mine,' he said. 'It was in June. I was twenty-three and I was down working and I was thinking of the sunlight and the hills and the evening. There was a young girl called Alys Davies, you know, two or three had been after her and I was thinking I would take her up the rock, that is a quiet place, only an old mountain ram would see you – '

'You were in the mine,' she said. 'You are getting too excited about this Alys Jones – '

'Davies,' he said with a quick grin. 'Don't worry about her. She is married now.' He went back to his solemn voice.

'And suddenly,' he said, 'there was a fall, a terrible fall of rock like thunder and all the men shouting. It was at eleven in the morning when we stopped work for our tea. There were three men in there working with me and they had just gone off. I was trapped alone.'

'Were you hurt?' she said anxiously.

'It was a miracle, not a stone touched me. I was in a little black cave. It was like a tomb. I was in that place alone for twelve hours. I could hear them working to get at me, but after the first fall there was a second and then I thought I was finished. I could hear nothing.'

'What did you do? I would have gone out of my mind,' she said. 'Is that how you got the scar on your nose?'

'That was in a fight,' he said, off-hand. 'Madness is a terrible thing. I stared into the blackness and I tried to think of one thing to stop my mind wandering but I could not at first for the fear, it was chasing and jumping like a mad dog in my head. I prayed, and the more I prayed, the more it chased and jumped. And then suddenly it stopped. I saw in my mind a picture. I saw the mantelpiece at home and on it a photograph of my family – my father and mother, my four sisters and my brother. And we had an aunt and uncle just married; it was a wedding photograph. I could see it clearly as if I had been in my home. They were standing there looking at me and I kept looking at them and thinking about them. I held on to them.

I kept everything else out of my mind; wherever I looked that picture was before my eyes. It was like a vision. It saved me.'

'I have heard people say they hear voices,' said Miss Freshwater's niece, kindly now.

'Oh, no! They were speechless!' said Evans. 'Not a word! I spoke to them,' he said. 'Out loud. I promised God in front of all my family that I would cleanse my soul if I got out.'

Evans stood blazing in his trance and then he picked up his cup from the grass and took it to her.

'May I please have some more tea?' he said.

'Of course,' she said. 'Sit down.'

He considered where he should sit and then put himself beside her.

'When I saw you looking at your photographs,' he said, 'I thought: She is down the mine.'

'I have never been down a mine in my life. I don't know why. We lived near one once when I was in the north,' she evaded.

'The mine of the past,' he said. 'The dark mine of the past.'

'I can see why you are a preacher, Robert.' She smiled. 'It's funny how one cannot get one's family out of one's head. I could feel mine inside me for years – but not now.'

She had entirely stopped mocking him.

'I can't say they ever saved me,' she said. 'I think they nearly ruined me. Look at that ugly house and all that rubbish. Did you ever see anything like their furniture? When I was a girl I used to think: Suppose I got to look like that sideboard! And then money was all they ever talked about – and good and nice people, and nice people always had money. It was like that in those days; thank God that has gone. Perhaps it hasn't. I decided to get away from it and I got married. They ought to have stopped me – all I wanted to do was to get away – but they thought my husband had money, too. He just had debts and a bad stomach. When he spent all my money, he just got ill to punish me . . . You don't know anything about life when you're young, and when you are old it's too late . . .

'That's a commonplace remark,' she went on, putting her cup on the tray and reaching for his. 'My mother used to make it.' She picked up her scarf and began to tie it on her head, but as she was tying it Evans quickly reached for it and pulled it off. His hand held the nape of her neck gently.

'You are not old,' he shouted, laughing and sparkling. 'Your hair is golden, not a grey one in it, boy.'

'Robert, give me that scarf. It is to keep out the dust,' she said, blushing. She reached for the scarf and he caught her wrist.

'When I saw you standing at the station on Monday, I said: "Now, there is a woman! Look at the way she stands, a golden woman, that is the first I have seen in this town, she must be a stranger," ' he said.

'You know all the others, I expect,' she said, with amusement.

'Oh, indeed, yes I do! All of them!' he said. 'I would not look at them twice.'

His other hand slipped from her neck to her waist.

'I can trust myself with them, but not with you,' he said, lowering his voice and speaking down to her neck. 'In an empty house,' he whispered, nodding to the house, letting go of her hand and stroking her knee.

'I am far past that sort of thing,' said Miss Freshwater's niece, choosing a lugubrious tone. She removed his arm from her waist. And she stood up, adroitly picking up the tray, and from behind that defence, she looked round the garden. Evans sprang up, but instead of coming near her, he jumped a few yards away and squatted on his heels, grinning at her confidently.

'You look like the Devil,' she said.

He had placed himself between her and the way to the house.

'It is quiet in the garden, too,' he said with a wink. And then she saw the wheelbarrow, which he had left near the fire.

'That barrow ought to go well in the sale,' she said. 'It is almost new. How much do you think it will fetch?'

Evans stood up at once and his grin went. An evasive light, almost the light of tears, came into his hot blue eyes and he stared at her with an alarm that drove everything else out of his head.

'They'll put it with the tools, you will not get much for it.'

'I think every man in the town will be after it,' she said, with malice.

'What price did you want for it?' he said, uncertain of her.

'I don't know what they cost,' she said carelessly and walked past him very slowly back to the house, maddening him by her walk. He followed her very quickly, and when she turned, still carrying the tray, to face him in the doorway, she caught his agitation.

'I will take the tray to the kitchen,' he said politely.

'No,' she said, 'I will do that. I want you to go upstairs and fetch down all those shoes. And the trunk. It can all go.'

And she turned and walked through the house to the kitchen. He hesitated for a long time; at last she heard him go upstairs and she pottered in the kitchen, where the china and pans were stacked on the table, waiting for him to come down. He was a very long time. He came down with the empty trunk.

'It can all go. Burn it all. It's no good to anyone, damp and rotten. I've put aside what I want,' she said.

He looked at her sullenly. He was startled by her manner and by the vehemence of her face, for she had put on the scarf and her face looked strong-boned, naked, and ruthless. She was startled herself.

His sullenness went; he returned to his old excitement and hurried the barrow to the fire and she stood at the door impatiently waiting for the blaze. When he saw her waiting he came back.

'There it goes,' he said with admiration.

The reflection of the flame danced in points of light in her eyes; her mouth was set, hard and bitter. Presently the flame dropped and greenish smoke came out thickly.

'Ah!' she gasped. Her body relaxed and she smiled at Evans, tempting him again.

'I've been thinking about the barrow,' she said. 'When we've finished up here, I'll make you a present of it. I would like to give it to you, if you have a use for it?'

She could see the struggle going on inside him as he boldly looked at her; and she saw his boldness pass into a small shrug of independent pride and the pride into pretence and dissembling.

'I don't know,' he said, 'that I have a use – well, I'll take it off you. I'll put the shoes in it, it will save bringing the car.' He could not repress his eagerness any longer. 'I'll put the shoes into it this evening. Thank you.' He paused. 'Thank you, ma'am,' he said.

It was the first time he had called her 'ma'am'. The word was like a blow. The affair was over. It was, she realized, a dismissal.

An hour later she heard him rumbling the barrow down the path to the gate. The next day he did not come. He had finished with her. He sent his son up for his money.

It took Miss Freshwater's niece two more days to finish her work at the house. The heavy jobs had been done, except for putting the drawers back into the chests. She could have done with Evans's help there, and for the sweeping, which made her hot, but she was glad to be alone because she got on more quickly with the work. She hummed and even sang as she worked, feeling light and astonishingly happy. Once or twice, when she saw the white sheet of the mission tent distantly through the trees, she smiled.

'He got what he wanted! And I'm evidently not as old as I look.'

The last hours buzzed by and she spun out the time, reluctant to go. She dawdled, locking the sheds, the windows and doors, until there was nothing more to keep her. She brought down a light suitcase in which she had put the few things she wanted to take away and she sat in the dining-room, now as bare as an office, to go through her money. After the destruction she was having a fit of economy and it had occurred to her that instead of taking a taxi to the station, she would walk down to the bus stop on the Green. She knew that the happiness she felt was not ebbing, but had changed to a feeling she had not had for many years – the feeling of expectancy – and as this settled in her, she put her money and her papers back into her bag. There was a last grain of rubbish here: with scarcely a glance at them, she tore up the photograph and the unfinished letter she had found in the trunk.

I owe Evans a lot, she thought.

Nothing retained her now.

She picked up her case. She left the house and walked down the road in the strong shade of the firs and the broad shade of the oak trees, whose leaves hardened with public contentment in the long evening light. When she got to the open Green, children were playing round the Gospel tent and, in twos and threes, people were walking from the houses across the grass towards it. She had twenty minutes to wait until her bus arrived. She heard the sound of singing coming from the tent. She wondered if Evans would be there.

I might give him the pleasure of seeing what he missed, she thought.

She strolled across to the tent.

A youth who had watered his hair and given it a twirl with a comb was standing in his best clothes at the entrance to the tent.

'Come to Jesu! Come to Jesu!' he said to her as she peeped inside.

'I'm just looking for someone,' she said politely.

The singing had stopped when she looked in, but the worshippers were still standing. They were packed in the white light of the tent and the hot smell of grass and somewhere at the far end, invisible, a man was shouting like a cheap jack selling something at an auction. He stopped suddenly and a high, powerful, country voice whined out alone: 'Ow in the vale . . .' and the congregation joined in for another long verse.

'Is Mr Evans here tonight?' she asked the youth.

'Yes,' he said. 'He's witnessing every night.'

'Where is he? I don't see him.'

The verse came to an end and once more a voice began talking at the other end of the tent. It was a woman's voice, high and incomprehensible and sharp. The hymn began again and then spluttered into an explosive roar that swept across the Green.

'They've fixed it. The loudspeaker!' the youth exclaimed. Miss Freshwater's niece stepped back. The noises thumped. Sadly she looked at her watch and began to walk back to the bus stop. When she was about ten yards from the tent, the loudspeaker gave a high whistle and then, as if God had cleared his throat, spoke out with a gross and miraculous clearness.

'Friends,' it said, sweeping right across the Green until it struck the furthest houses and the trees. 'My friends . . .'

The word seemed to grind her and everyone else to nothing, to mill them all into the common dust.

'When I came to this place,' it bellowed, 'the serpent . . .' – an explosion of noise followed, but the voice cleared again –' . . . heart. No bigger than a speck it was at first, as tiny as a speck of coal grit in your eye . . .'

Miss Freshwater's niece stopped. Was it Evans's voice? A motor coach went by on the road and drowned the next words, and then she heard, spreading into an absurd public roar:

'I was a liar. I was an adulterer. Oh my friends, I was a slave of the strange woman the Bible tells about, the whore of Babylon, in her palace where moth and dust . . .' Detonations again.

But it was Evans's voice. She waited and the enormously magnified voice burst through.

'And then by the great mercy of the Lord I heard a voice cry out: "Robert Evans, what are you doing, boy? Come out of it . . ."' But the voice exploded into meaningless concussions, suddenly resuming:

' . . . and burned the adulteress in the everlasting fire, my friends – and all her property.'

The hymn started up again.

'Well, not quite all, Robert,' said Miss Freshwater's niece pleasantly aloud, and a child eating an ice cream near her watched her walk across to the bus stop.

The Fall

It was the evening of the annual dinner. More than two hundred accountants were at that hour changing into evening clothes, in the flats, villas, and hotel rooms of a large, wet, Midland city. At the Royal was Charles Peacock, slender in his shirt, balancing on one leg and gazing with frowns of affection in the wardrobe mirror at the other leg as he pulled his trouser on; and then with a smile of farewell as the second went in. Buttoned up, relieved of nakedness, he visited other mirrors – the one at the dressing table, the two in the bathroom, assembling the scattered aspects of the unsettled being called Peacock 'doing', as he was apt to say, 'not so badly' in this city that smelt of coal and where thirty-eight years ago he had been born. When he left his room there were mirrors in the hotel lift and down below in the foyer and outside in the street. Certain shop windows were favourable and assuring. The love affair was taken up again at the Assembly rooms by the mirrors in the tiled corridor leading towards the bullocky noise of two hundred-odd chartered accountants in black ties, taking their drinks under the chandeliers that seemed to weep above their heads.

Crowds or occasions frightened Peacock. They engaged him, at first sight, in the fundamental battle of his life: the struggle against nakedness, the panic of grabbing for clothes and becoming someone. An acquaintance in a Scottish firm was standing near the door of the packed room as Peacock went in.

'Hullo, laddie,' Peacock said, fitting himself out with a Scottish accent as he went into the crowded, chocolate-coloured buffet.

'What's to do?' he said, passing on to a Yorkshireman.

'Are you well now?' he said in his Irish voice. And, gaining confidence, 'Whatcha cock!' to a man up from London, until he was shaking hands in the crowd with the President himself, who was leaning on a stick and had his foot in plaster.

'I hope this is not serious, sir,' said Peacock in his best southern

65

English, nodding at the foot.

'Bloody serious,' said the President, sticking out his peppery beard. 'I caught my foot in a grating. Some damn fools here think I've got gout.'

No one who saw Peacock in his office, in boardrooms, on committees, at meetings, knew the exhausting number of rough sketches that had to be made before the naked Peacock could become Peacock dressed for his part. Now, having spoken to several human beings, the fragments called Peacock closed up. And he had one more trick up his sleeve if he panicked again; he could drop into music-hall Negro.

Peacock got a drink at the buffet table and pushed his way to a solitary island of carpet two feet square, in the guffawing corral. He was looking at the back of the President's neck. Almost at once the President, on the crest of a successful joke he had told, turned round with appetite.

'Hah!' he shouted. 'Hah! Here's friend Peacock again.' Why 'again' thought Peacock.

The President looked Peacock over.

'I saw your brother this afternoon,' shouted the President. The President's injured foot could be said to have made his voice sound like a hilarious smash. Peacock's drink jumped and splashed his hand. The President winked at his friends.

'Hah!' said the President. 'That gave our friend Peacock a scare!'

'At the Odeon,' explained a kinder man.

'Is Shelmerdine Peacock your brother? The actor?' another said, astonished, looking at Peacock from head to foot.

'Shelmerdine Peacock was born and bred in this city,' said the President fervently.

'I saw him in *Waste*,' someone said. And others recalled him in *The Gun Runner* and *Doctor Zut*.

Four or five men stood gazing at Peacock with admiration, waiting for him to speak.

'Where is he now?' said the President, stepping forward, beard first. 'In Hollywood? Have you seen him lately?'

They all moved forward to hear about the famous man.

Peacock looked to the right – he wanted to do this properly – but there was no mirror in that direction; he looked to the left, but there was no mirror there. He lowered his head gravely and then looked up, shaking his head sorrowfully. He brought out the old reliable Negro voice.

'The last time I saw l'il ole brudder Shel,' he said, 'he was being thrown out of the Orchid Room. He was calling the waiters "goatherds".'

Peacock looked up at them all and stood, collected, assembled, whole at last, among their shouts of laughter. One man who did not laugh and who asked what the Orchid Room was, was put in his place. And in a moment a voice bawled from the door: 'Gentlemen. Dinner is served.' The crowd moved through two anterooms into the great hall, where, from their portraits on the wall, mayors, presidents, and justices looked down with the complacent rosiness of those who have dined and died. It was gratifying to Peacock that the President rested his arm on his shoulder for a few steps as they went into the hall.

Shel often cropped up in Peacock's life, especially in clubs and at dinners. It was pleasing. There was always praise; there were always questions. He had seen the posters about Shel's film during the week on his way to his office. They pleased, but they also troubled. Peacock stood at his place at table in the great hall and paused to look round, in case there was one more glance of vicarious fame to be collected. He was enjoying one of those pauses of self-possession in which, for a few seconds, he could feel the sensations Shel must feel when he stepped before the curtain to receive the applause of some great audience in London or New York. Then Peacock sat down. More than two hundred soup spoons scraped.

'Sherry, sir,' said the waiter.

Peacock sipped.

He meant no harm to Shel, of course. But in a city like this, with Shel appearing in a big picture, with his name fifteen feet long on the hoardings, talked about by girls in offices, the universal instinct of family disparagement was naturally tickled into life. The President might laugh and the crowd admire, but it was not always agreeable for the family to have Shel roaming loose – and often very loose – in the world. One had to assert the modesty, the anonymity of the ordinary assiduous Peacocks. One way of doing this was to add a touch or two to famous scandals: to enlarge the drunken scrimmages and add to the divorces and the breaches of contract, increase the overdoses taken by flighty girls. One was entitled to a little rake-off – an accountant's charges – from the fame that so often annoyed. One was entitled, above all, because one loved Shel.

'Hock, sir?' said the waiter.

Peacock drank. Yes, he loved Shel. Peacock put down his glass, and the man opposite him spoke across the table, a man with an amused mouth, who turned his sallow face sideways so that one had the impression of being enquired into under a loose lock of black hair by one sharp, serious eye only.

'An actor's life is a struggle,' the man said. Peacock recognized him: it was the man who had not laughed at his story and who had asked what the Orchid Room was, in a voice that had a sad and puncturing feeling for information sought for its own sake.

Peacock knew this kind of admirer of Shel's and feared him. They were not content to admire, they wanted to advance into intimacy, and collect facts on behalf of some general view of life's mysteriousness. As an accountant Peacock rejected mystery.

'I don't think l'il ole brudder Shel has struggled much,' said Peacock, wagging his head from side to side carelessly.

'I mean he has to dedicate himself,' said the man.

Peacock looked back mistrustfully.

'I remember some interview he gave about his school days – in this city,' said the man. 'It interested me. I do the books for the Hippodrome.'

Peacock stopped wagging his head from side to side. He was alert. What Shel had said about his early life had been damned tactless.

'Shel had a good time,' said Peacock sharply. 'He always got his own way.'

Peacock put on his face of stone. He dared the man to say out loud, in that company, three simple English words. He dared him. The man smiled and did not say them.

'Volnay, sir,' said the waiter as the pheasant was brought. Peacock drank.

'Fried-fish shop,' Peacock said to himself as he drank. Those were the words. 'Shel could have kept his mouth shut about that. I'm not a snob, but why mention it? Why, after they were all doing well, bring ridicule upon the family? Who not say simply: "Shop"? Why not say, if he had to, "Fishmonger"? Why mention frying? Why add: "*Bankrupt* fried-fish shop"?'

It was swinish, disloyal, ungrateful. Bankrupt – all right; but some of that money, Peacock said, hectoring the pheasant on his plate, paid for Shel's years at the Dramatic school. It was unforgivable.

Peacock looked across at the man opposite, but the man had turned to talk to a neighbour. Peacock finished his glass and chatted with the man sitting to his right, but he felt like telling the whole table a few facts about dedication.

'Dedication,' he would have said. 'Let us take a look at the figures. An example of Shel's dedication in those fried-fish-shop days he is so fond of remembering to make fools of us. Saturday afternoon. Father asleep in the back room. Shel says: "Come down the High Street with me, Tom. I want to get a record." Classical, of course. Usual swindle. If we get into the shop he won't have the money and will try and borrow from me. "No," I say, "I haven't got any money." "Well, let's get out of this stink of lard and fish." He wears me down. He wore us all down, the whole family. He would be sixteen, two years older than me. And so we go out and at once I know there is going to be trouble. "I saw the Devil in Cramer's," he says. We go down the High Street to Cramer's – it's a music shop – and he goes up to the girl to ask if they sell bicycle pumps or rubber heels. When the girl says no, he makes a terrible face at her and shouts out "Bah." At Hook's, the stationer's, he stands at the door and calls to the girl at the cash desk: "You've got the Devil in here. I've reported it," and slams the door. We go on to Bond's, the grocer's, and he pretends to be sick when he sees the bacon. Goes out. "Rehearsing," he says. The Bonds are friends of Father's. There is a row. Shel swears he was never anywhere near the place and goes back the following Saturday and falls flat on the floor in front of the Bond daughter, groaning: "I've been poisoned. I'm dying. Water! Water! Falls flat on his back . . ." '

'Caught his foot in a grating, he told me, and fell,' the man opposite was saying. 'Isn't that what he told you, Peacock?'

Peacock's imaginary speech came suddenly to an end. The man was smiling as if he had heard every word.

'Who?' said Peacock.

'The President,' said the man. 'My friend, Mr McAlister, is asking me what happened to the President. Did he fall in the street?'

Peacock collected himself quickly and to hide his nakedness became Scottish.

'Ay, mon.' He nodded across the table. 'A wee bit of a tumble in the street.'

Peacock took up his glass and drank.

'He's a heavy man to fall,' said the man called McAlister.

'He carries a lot of weight,' said his neighbour. Peacock eyed him. The impression was growing that this man knew too much, too quietly. It struck him that the man was one of those who ask what they know already, a deep unbelieving man. They have to be crushed.

'Weight makes no difference,' said Peacock firmly.

'It's weight and distance,' said the Scotsman. 'Look at children.'

Peacock felt a smile coming over his body from the feet upwards.

'Weight and distance make no difference,' Peacock repeated.

'How can you say that?'

An enormous voice, hanging brutally on the air like a sergeant's, suddenly shouted in the hall. It was odd to see the men in the portraits on the wall still sitting down after the voice sounded. It was the voice of the toastmaster.

'Gen-tle-men!' it shouted. 'I ask you. To rise to. The toast of Her Maj-es-ty. The Queen.'

Two hundred or more accountants pushed back their chairs and stood up.

'The Queen,' they growled. And one or two, Peacock among them, fervently added: 'God bless her,' and drained his glass.

Two hundred or more accountants sat down. It was the moment Peacock loved. And he loved the Queen.

'Port or brandy, sir?' the waiter asked.

'Brandy,' said Peacock.

'You were saying that weight and distance make no difference. How do you make that out?' the sidelong man opposite said in a sympathetic and curious voice that came softly and lazily out.

Peacock felt the brandy burn. The question floated by, answerable if seized as it went and yet, suddenly, unanswerable for the moment. Peacock stared at the question keenly as if it were a fly that he was waiting to swat when it came round again. Ah, there it came. Now! But no, it had gone by once more. It was answerable. He knew the answer. Peacock smiled, loosely biding his time. He felt the flame of authority, of absolute knowledge burn in him.

There was a hammering at the President's table, there was hand-clapping. The President was on his feet and his beard had begun to move up and down.

'I'll tell you later,' said Peacock curtly across the table. The interest went out of the man's eye.

'Once more,' the President's beard was saying, and it seemed sometimes that he had two beards: 'Honour,' said one beard; 'privilege,' said the other, 'old friends,' said both beards together. 'Speeches . . . brief . . . reminded of story . . . shortest marriage service in the world . . . Tennessee . . .'

'Hah! Hah! Hah!' shouted a pack of wolves, hyenas, hounds in dinner jackets.

Peacock looked across at the unbeliever who sat opposite. The interest in weight and distance had died away in his face.

'Englishman . . . Irishman . . . Scotsman . . . train . . . Englishman said . . . Scotsman said . . . Och, says Paddy . . .'

'Hah! Hah! Hah!' from the pack.

Over the carnations in the silver-plated vases on the table, over the heads of the diners, the cigar smoke was rising sweetly and the first-level indigo shafts of it were tipping across the middle air and turning the portraits of the past masters into daydreams. Peacock gazed at it. Then a bell rang in his ear, so loudly that he looked shyly to see if anyone else had heard it. The voice of Shel was on some line of his memory, a voice richer, more insinuating than the toastmaster's or the President's, a voice utterly flooring.

'Abel?' Shel was saying. 'Is that you, Abel? This is Cain speaking. How's the smoke? Is it still going up straight to heaven? Not blowing about all over the place? . . .'

The man opposite caught Peacock's eye for a second, as if he too had heard the voice, and then turned his head away. And just at the very moment when once more Peacock could have answered that question about the effect of weight and distance, the man opposite stood up; all the accountants stood up. Peacock was the last. There was another toast to drink. And immediately there was more hammering and another speaker. Peacock's opportunity was lost. The man opposite had moved his chair back from the table and was sitting sideways to the table, listening, his interest in Peacock gone for good.

Peacock became lonely. Sulkily he played with matchsticks and arranged them in patterns on the tablecloth. There was a point at annual dinners when he always did this. It was at that point when one saw the function had become fixed by a flash photograph in the gloss of celebration and when everyone looked sickly and old. Eyes became hollow, temples sank, teeth loosened. Shortly the diners would be carried out in coffins. One waited restlessly for the thing to be over. Ten years of life went by and then, it seemed, there were no more speeches. There was some business talk in groups; then twos and threes left the table. Others filed off into a large chamber next door. Peacock's neighbours got up. He, who feared occasions, feared even more their dissolution. It was like that frightening ten minutes in a theatre when the audience slowly moves out, leaving a hollow stage and row after row, always increasing, of empty seats behind them. In a panic Peacock got up. He was losing all acquaintance. He had even let the man opposite slip away, for that man was walking down the hall with some friends. Peacock hurried down his side of the long table to meet them at the bottom, and when he got there he turned and barred their way.

'What we were talking about,' he said. 'It's an art. Simply a matter of letting the breath go, relaxing the muscles. Any actor can do it. It's the first thing they learn.'

'I'm out of my depth,' said the Scotsman.

'Falling,' said Peacock. 'The stage fall.' He looked at them with dignity, then he let the expression die on his face. He fell quietly full length to the floor. Before they could speak he was up on his feet.

'My brother weighs two hundred and twenty pounds,' he said with condescension to the man opposite. 'The ordinary person falls and breaks an arm or a foot because he doesn't know. It's an art.'

His eyes conveyed that if the Peacocks had kept a fried-fish shop years ago, they had an art.

'Simple,' said Peacock. And down he went, thump, on the carpet again, and lying at their feet he said:

'Painless. Nothing broken. Not a bruise. I said "an art". Really one might call it a science. Do you see how I'm lying?'

'What's happened to Peacock?' said two or three men joining the group.

'He's showing us the stage fall.'

'Nothing,' said Peacock, getting up and brushing his coat-sleeve and smoothing back his hair. 'It is just a stage trick.'

'I wouldn't do it,' said a large man, patting his stomach.

'I've just been telling them – weight is nothing. Look.' Peacock fell down and got up at once.

'You turn. You crumple. You can go flat on your back. I mean, that is what it looks like,' he said.

And Peacock fell.

'Shel and I used to practise it in the bedroom. Father thought the ceiling was coming down,' he said.

'Good God, has Peacock passed out?' A group standing by the fireplace in the hall called across. Peacock got up and, brushing his jacket again, walked up to them. The group he had left watched him. There was a thump.

'He's done it again,' the man opposite said.

'Once more. There he goes. Look, he's going to show the President. He's going after him. No, he's missed him. The old boy has slipped out of the door.'

Peacock was staring with annoyance at the door. He looked at other groups of twos and threes.

'What was the casualty over there?' someone said to him as he walked past.

Peacock went over to them and explained.

'Like judo,' said a man.

'No!' said Peacock indignantly, even grandly. And in Shel's manner. Anyone who had seen Shelmerdine Peacock affronted knew what he looked like. That large white face trod on you. 'Nothing to do with judo. This is the theatre . . .'

'Shelmerdine Peacock's brother,' a man whispered to a friend.

'Is that so?'

'It's in the blood,' someone said.

To the man who had said 'judo', Peacock said: 'No throwing, no wrestling, no somersaulting or fancy tricks. That is not theatre. Just . . . simply . . .' said Peacock. And crumpling, as Shel might have done in *Macbeth* or *Hamlet*, or like some gangster shot in the stomach, Peacock once more let his body go down with the cynicism of the skilful corpse. This time he did not get up at once. He looked up at their knees, their waists, at their goggling faces, saw under their double chins and under their hairy eyebrows. He grinned at their absurdity. He saw that he held them. They were obliged to look at him. Shel must always have had this sensation of hundreds of astonished eyes watching him lie, waiting for him to move. Their gaze would never leave the body. He never felt at a loss, never felt more completely himself. Even the air was better at carpet level; it was certainly cooler and he was glad of that. Then he saw two pairs of feet advancing from another group. He saw two faces peep over the shoulders of the others, and heard one of them say:

'It's Peacock – still at it.'

He saw the two pairs of boots and trousers go off. Peacock got to his feet at once and resentfully stared after them. He knew something, as they went, that Shel must have known: the desperation, the contempt for the audience that is thinning out. He was still brushing his sleeve and trousers legs when he saw everyone moving away out of the hall. Peacock moved after them into the chamber.

A voice spoke behind him. It was the quiet, intimate voice of the man with the loose lock of black hair who had sat opposite him.

'You need a drink,' the man said.

They were standing in the chamber, where the buffet table was. The man had gone into the chamber and, clearly, he had waited for Peacock. A question was going round as fast as a catherine wheel in Peacock's head and there was no need to ask it: it must be so blindingly obvious. He looked for someone to put it to, on the quiet, but there were only three men at the buffet table with their backs turned to him. Why (the question ran) at the end of a bloody good dinner is one always left with some awful drunk, a man you've never liked – an unbeliever?

Peacock mopped his face. The unbeliever was having a short, disgusting laugh with the men at the bar and now was coming back with a glass of whisky.

'Sit down. You must be tired,' said the unbeliever.

They sat down. The man spoke of the dinner and the speeches. Peacock did not listen. He had just noticed a door leading into a small anteroom and he was wondering how he could get into it.

'There was one thing I don't quite get,' the man said: 'perhaps it was the quickness of the hand deceiving the eye. I should say "feet". What I mean is – do you first take a step, I mean like in dancing? I mean is the art of falling really a paradox – I mean the art of keeping your balance all the time?'

The word 'paradox' sounded offensive to Peacock.

The man looked too damn clever, in Peacock's opinion, and didn't sit still. Wearily Peacock got up.

'Hold my drink,' he said. 'You are standing like this, or facing sideways – on a level floor, of course. On a slope like this . . .'

The man nodded.

'I mean – well, now, watch carefully. Are you watching?'

'Yes,' said the man.

'Look at my feet,' said Peacock.

'No,' said the man hastily, putting out a free hand and catching

Peacock by the arm. 'I see what you mean. I was just interested in the theory.'

Peacock halted. He was offended. He shook the man's arm off.

'Nothing theoretical about it,' he said, and, shaking his sleeves, added: 'No paradox.'

'No,' said the man, standing up and grabbing Peacock so that he could not fall. 'I've got the idea.' He looked at his watch. 'Which way are you going? Can I give you a lift?'

Peacock was greatly offended. To be turned down! He nodded to the door of the anteroom. 'Thanks,' he said. 'The President's waiting for me.'

'The President's gone,' said the man. 'Oh well, good night.' And he went away. Peacock watched him go. Even the men at the bar had gone. He was alone.

'But thanks,' he called after him. 'Thanks.'

Cautiously Peacock sketched a course into the anteroom. It was a small, high room, quite empty and yet, one would have said, packed with voices, chattering, laughing, and mixed with music along the panelled walls, but chiefly coming from behind the heavy green velvet curtains that were drawn across the window at one end. There were no mirrors, but Peacock had no need of them. The effect was ornate – gilded pillars at the corners, a small chandelier rising and falling gracefully from a carven ceiling. On the wall hung what at first sight seemed to be two large oil paintings of queens of England, but on going closer, Peacock saw there was only one oil painting – of Queen Victoria. Peacock considered it. The opportunity was enormous. Loyally, his face went blank. He swayed, loyally fell, and loyally got to his feet. The Queen might or might not have clapped her little hands. So encouraged, he fell again and got up. She was still sitting there.

'Shel,' said Peacock aloud to the Queen, 'has often acted before royalty. He's in Hollywood now, having left me to settle all his tax affairs. Hundreds of documents. All lies, of course. And there is this case for alimony going on. He's had four wives,' he said to Queen Victoria. 'That's the side of theatre life I couldn't stand, even when we were boys. I could see it coming. But – watch me,' he said.

And delightfully he crumpled, the perfect backwards spin. Leaning up on his elbow from where he was lying, he waited for her to speak.

She did not speak, but two or three other queens joined her, all

75

crowding and gossiping together, as Peacock got up. The royal box! It was full. Cars hooting outside the window behind the velvet curtains had the effect of an orchestra and then, inevitably, those heavy green curtains were drawn up. A dark, packed, and restless auditorium opened itself to him. There was dense applause.

Peacock stepped forward in awe and wholeness. Not to fall, not to fall, this time, he murmured. To bow. One must bow and bow and bow and not fall, to the applause. He set out. It was a strangely long uphill journey towards the footlights, and not until he got there did it occur to him that he did not know how to bow. Shel had never taught him. Indeed, at the first attempt the floor came up and hit him in the face.

When My Girl Comes Home

She was kissing them all, hugging them, her arms bare in her summer dress, laughing and taking in a big draught of breath after every kiss, nearly knocking old Mrs Draper off her feet, almost wrestling with Mrs Fulmino, who was large and tall. Then Hilda broke off to give another foreign-sounding laugh and plunged at Jack Draper ('the baby') and his wife, at Mr Fulmino, who cried out: 'What, again?' and at Constance, who did not like emotion; and after every kiss, Hilda drew back, getting her breath and making this sound like 'Hah!'

'Who is this?' she said, looking at me.

'Harry Fraser,' Mr Fulmino said. 'You remember Harry?'

'You worked at the grocer's,' she said. 'I remember you.'

'No,' I said, 'that was my brother.'

'This is the little one,' said Mrs Fulmino.

'Who won the scholarship,' said Constance.

'We couldn't have done anything without him,' said Mr Fulmino, expanding with extravagance as he always did about everything. 'He wrote to the War Office, the Red Cross, the Prisoners of War, the American government, all the letters. He's going to be our head librarian.'

Mr Fulmino loved whatever had not happened yet. His forecasts were always wrong. I left the library years ago and never fulfilled the future he had planned for me. Obviously Hilda did not remember me. Thirteen years before, when she married Mr Singh and left home, I was no more than a boy.

'Well, I'll kiss him too,' she said. 'And another for your brother.'

That was the first bad thing to happen, the first of many signs of how her life had had no contact with ourselves.

'He was killed in the war, dear,' said Mrs Fulmino.

'She couldn't know,' said Constance.

'I'm sorry,' said Hilda.

We all stood silent, and Hilda turned to hold on to her mother, little Mrs Johnson, whose face was coquettish with tears and who came up only to Hilda's shoulder. The old lady was bewildered. She was trembling as though she were going to shake to pieces like a tree in the autumn. Hilda stood still, touching her tinted brown hair, which was done in a tight, high style and still unloosened, despite all the hugs and kissings. Her arms looked as dry as sand, her breasts were full in her green, flowered dress, and she was gazing over our heads now from large yellow eyes that had almost closed into two blind, blissful curving lines. Her eyebrows seemed to be lacquered. How Oriental she looked on that first day! She was looking above our heads at old Mrs Draper's shabby room and going over the odd things she remembered, and while she stood like that, the women were studying her clothes. A boy's memory is all wrong. Naturally, when I was a boy I had thought of her as tall. She was really short. But I did remember her bold nose: it was like her mother's and old Mrs Draper's; those two were sisters. Otherwise I wouldn't have known her. And that is what Mr Fulmino said when we were all silent and incredulous again. We had Hilda back. Not just 'back', either, but 'back from the dead', reborn.

'She was in the last coach of the train, wasn't she, Mother?' Mr Fulmino said to Mrs Johnson. He called her 'Mother' for the occasion, celebrating her joy.

'Yes,' said Mrs Johnson. 'Yes.' Her voice scraped and trembled.

'In the last coach, next to the van. We went right up the platform, we thought we'd missed her, didn't we? She was,' he exclaimed with acquisitive pride, 'in the first class.'

'Like you missed me coming from Penzance,' said Mrs Fulmino, smelling powerfully and going that thundery violet colour which old wrongs gave her.

'Posh!' said Hilda. And we all smiled in a sickly way.

'Don't you ever do it again, my girl! Don't you ever do it again,' said her mother, old Mrs Johnson, clinging to her daughter's arm and shaking it as if it were a bell rope.

'I was keeping an eye on my luggage,' Hilda said, laughing.

Ah! That was a point! There was not only Hilda, there was her luggage. Some of it was in the room, but the bigger things were outside on the landing, piled up, looking very new, with the fantastic labels of hotels in Tokyo, San Francisco, and New York on it, and a beautiful jewel box in white leather on top like a crown. Old Mrs Draper did not like the luggage being outside the room in case it was in the way of the people upstairs. Constance went out and fetched the jewel box in. We had all seen it. We were as astonished by all these cases as we were by Hilda herself. After thirteen years, six of them war, we recognized that the poor ruined woman we had prepared for had not arrived. She shone with money. Later on, one after the other of us, except old Mrs Draper, who could not walk far, went out and looked at the luggage and came back to study Hilda in a new way.

We had all had a shock. She had been nearly two years coming home from Tokyo. Before that there was the occupation; before that the war itself. Before that there were the years in Bombay and Singapore, when she was married to an Indian they always called Mr Singh. All those years were lost to us. None of us had been to India. What happened there to Mr Singh? We knew he had died – but how? Even if we had known, we couldn't have imagined it. None of us had been to Singapore, none of us to Japan. People from streets like Hincham Street do go to such places: it is not past belief. Knock on the doors of half the houses in London and you will find people with relations all over the world. But none of *us* had. Mention these places to us, we look at our grey skies and see boiling sun. Our one certainty about Hilda was what, in fact, the newspaper said the next day, with her photograph and the headline: A MOTHER'S FAITH. FOUR YEARS IN JAPANESE TORTURE CAMP. LONDON GIRL'S ORDEAL. Hilda was a terrible item of news, a gash in our lives, and we looked for the signs of it on her body, in the way she stood, in the lines on her face, as if we were expecting a scream from her mouth like the screams we were told Bill Williams gave out at night in his sleep, after he had been flown back home when the war ended. We had had to wait and wait for Hilda. At one time – there was a postcard from Hawaii – she was pinned like a butterfly in the middle of the Pacific Ocean; soon after there was a letter from Tokyo saying she couldn't get a passage. Confusing. She was travelling backwards. Letters from Tokyo were still coming after her letters from San Francisco.

We were still standing, waiting for Constance to bring in the teapot, for the tea was already laid. The trolley buses go down Hincham Street. It is a mere one hundred and fifty yards of a few little houses and a few little shops, which has a sudden charmed importance because the main road has petered out at our end by the Lord Nelson and an enormous public lavatory, and the trolley buses have to run down Hincham Street before picking up the main road again, after a sharp turn at the convent. Hincham Street is less a street than an interval, a disheartened connection. While we stood in one of those silences that follow excitement, a trolley bus came by and Hilda exclaimed:

'You've still got the old trams. Bump! Bump! Bump!' Hilda was ecstatic about the sound. 'Do you remember I used to be frightened the spark from the pole would set the lace curtains on fire when I was little?'

For as the buses turned, the trolley arms would come swooping with two or three loud bumps and a spit of blue electricity, almost hitting Mrs Draper's sitting-room window, which was on the first floor.

'It's trolleys now, my girl,' said old Mrs Draper, whose voice was like the voice of time itself chewing away at life. 'The trams went years ago, before the war.'

Old Mrs Draper had sat down in her chair again by the fire that always burned winter and summer in this room; she could not stand for long. It was the first remark that had given us any sense of what was bewildering all of us: the passing of time, the growing of a soft girl into a grown, hard-hipped woman. For old Mrs Draper's mind was detached from events round her and moved only among the signal facts and conclusions of history.

Presently we were, as the saying is, 'at our teas'. Mr Fulmino, less puzzled than the rest of us, expanded in his chair with the contentment of one who had personally operated a deeply British miracle. It was he who had got Hilda home.

'We've got all the correspondence, haven't we, Harry?' he said. 'We kept it – the War Office, Red Cross, Prisoner of War Commission – everything, Hilda. I'll show it to you.'

His task had transformed him and his language. Identification, registration, accommodation, communication, rehabilitation, hospitalization, administration, investigation, transportation – well, we had all dreamt of Hilda in our different ways.

'They always said the same thing,' Mrs Fulmino said reproachfully. 'No one of the name of Mrs Singh on the lists.'

'I wrote to Bombay,' said Mr Fulmino.

'He wrote to Singapore,' said Mrs Fulmino.

Mr Fulmino drank some tea, wiped his lips, and became geography. 'All British subjects were rounded up, they said,'

Mrs Fulmino said.

We nodded. We had made our stand, of course, on the law. Mrs Fulmino was authority.

'But Hilda was married to an Indian,' said Constance.

We glanced with a tolerance we did not usually feel for Constance. She was always trying to drag politics in.

'She's a British subject by birth,' said Mrs Fulmino firmly.

'Mum,' Hilda whispered, squeezing her mother's arm hard, and then looked up to listen, as if she were listening to talk about a faraway stranger. 'I was in Tokyo when the war started,' she said. 'Not Singapore.'

'Oh, Tokyo,' exclaimed Mr Fulmino, feeling in his waistcoat for a pencil to make a note of it and, suddenly, realizing that his note-taking days were over.

'Whatever the girl has done she has been punished for it,' came old Mrs Draper's mournful voice from the chair by the fire; but in the clatter no one heard her, except old Mrs Johnson, who squeezed her daughter's arm and said:

'My girl is a jewel.'

Still, Hilda's words surprised us. We had worked it out that after she and Mr Singh were married and went to Bombay, he had heard of a better job in the state railway medical service and had gone to Singapore, where the war had caught her. Mrs Fulmino looked affronted. If Mr Fulmino expanded into geography and the language of state – he worked for the Borough Council – Mrs Fulmino liked a fact to be a fact.

'We got the postcards,' said Mrs Fulmino, sticking to chronology.

'Hawaii,' Mr Fulmino said. 'How'd you get there? Swim, I suppose.' He added: 'A sweet spot, it looks. Suit us for a holiday – palms.'

'Coconuts,' said young Jack Draper, who worked in a pipe factory, speaking for the first time.

'Be quiet,' said his wife.

'It's an American base now,' said Constance with her politically sugared smile.

We hesitated but let her observation pass. It was simple to ignore her. We were so happy.

'I suppose they paid your fare,' said Jack Draper's wife, a north-country woman.

'Accommodation, transportation,' said Mr Fulmino, 'food, clothing. Everything. Financed by the international commission.'

This remark made old Mrs Johnson cry a little. In those years none of us had deeply believed that Hilda was alive. The silence was too long; too much time had gone by. Others had come home by the thousand with stories of thousands who had died. Only old Mrs Johnson had been convinced that Hilda was safe. The landlord at the Lord Nelson, the butcher, anyone who met old Mrs Johnson as she walked by like a poor, decent ghost with her sewing bundles, in those last two years, all said in war-staled voices:

'It's a mother's faith, that's what it is. A mother's faith's a funny thing.'

She would walk along with a cough, like someone driving tacks. Her chest had sunk and under her brown coat her shoulder blades seemed to have sharpened into a single hump. Her faith gave her a bright, yet also a sly, dishonest look.

'I'm taking this sewing up to Mrs Tracy's. She wants it in a hurry,' she might say.

'You ought to rest, Mrs Johnson, like the doctor said.'

'I want a bit of money for when my girl comes home,' she said. 'She'll want feeding up.'

And she would look round, perhaps, for a clock, in case she ought by this time to have put a pot on the stove.

She had been too ill, in hospital, during the war, to speak about what might have happened to Hilda. Her own pain and fear of dying deafened her to what could be guessed. Mrs Johnson's faith had been born out of pain, out of the inability – within her prison of aching bones and crushed breathing – to identify herself with her daughter. Her faith grew out of her very self-centredness. And when she came out from the post office every week, where she put her savings, she looked demure, holy, and secretive. If people were too kind and too sympathetic with her, she shuffled and looked mockingly. Seven hospitals, she said, had not killed *her*.

Now, when she heard Mr Fulmino's words about the fare, the clothes, the food, the expense of it all, she was troubled. What had she worked for – even at one time scrubbing in a canteen – but to save Hilda from a charity so vast in its humiliation, from so blank a herding mercy. Hilda was hers, not theirs. Hilda kept her arm on her mother's waist, and while Mr Fulmino carried on with the marvels of international organization (which moved Mrs Fulmino to say hungrily: 'It takes a war to bring it out'), Hilda ignored them and whispered to comfort her mother. At last the old lady dried her eyes and smiled at her daughter. The smile grew to a small laugh; she gave a proud jerk to her head, conveying that she and her Hil were not going to kotow in gratitude to anyone, and Hilda at last said out loud to her mother what no doubt she had been whispering.

'He wouldn't let me pay anything, Mum. Faulkner, his name was. Very highly educated. He came from California. We had a fancy-dress dance on the ship and he made me go as a geisha . . . He gave me these . . .' And she raised her hand to show her mother the bracelets on it.

Mrs Johnson laughed wickedly. 'Did he . . .? Was he . . .?' said Mrs Johnson.

'No. Well, I don't know,' said Hilda. 'But I kept his address.'

Mrs Johnson smiled round at all of us, to show that in spite of all, being the poorest in the family and the ones that had suffered most, she and Hilda knew how to look after themselves.

This was the moment when there was that knock on the door. Everyone was startled and looked at it.

'A knock!' said Mr Fulmino.

'A knock, Constance,' said young Mrs Draper, who had busy north-country ears.

'A knock,' several said.

Old Mrs Draper made one of her fundamental utterances again, one of her growls from the belly of the history of human indignation.

'We are,' she said, 'in the middle of our teas. Constance, go and see and tell them.'

But before Constance got to the door, two young men, one with a camera, came right into the room, without asking. Some of us lowered our heads and then, just as one young man said 'I'm from the *News*,' the other clicked his camera.

Jack Draper said, nearly choking: 'He's taken a snap of us eating.'

While we were all staring at them, old Mrs Draper chewed out grandly: 'Who may they be?'

But Hilda stood up and got her mother to her feet, too. 'Stand up, all of us,' she said eagerly. 'It's for the papers.'

It was the Press. We were in confusion. Mrs Fulmino pushed Mr Fulmino forward towards the reporter and then pulled him back. The reporter stood asking questions and everyone answered at once. The photographer kept on taking photographs and, when he was not doing that, started picking up vases and putting them down and one moment was trying the drawer of a little table by the window. They pushed Hilda and her mother into a corner and took a picture of them, Hilda calling to us all to 'come in' and Mr Fulmino explaining to the reporters. Then they went, leaving a cigarette burning on one of old Mrs Draper's lace doilies under the fern and two more butts on the floor. 'What did they say? What did they say?' we all asked one another, but no one could remember. We were all talking at once, arguing about who had heard the knock first. Young Mrs Draper said her tea was spoiled, and Constance opened the window to let the cigarette smoke out and then got the kettle. Mr Fulmino put his hand on his wife's knee because she was upset, and she shook it off. When we had calmed down, Hilda said:

'The young one was a nice-looking boy, wasn't he, Mum?' and Mr Fulmino, who almost never voiced the common opinion about anything but who had perhaps noticed how the eyes of all the women went larger at this remark, laughed loudly and said:

'We've got the old Hilda back!'

I mention this because of the item in the papers next day: A MOTHER'S FAITH. FOUR YEARS IN JAPANESE TORTURE CAMP. LONDON GIRL'S ORDEAL.

Wonderful, as Mr Fulmino said.

To be truthful, I felt uncomfortable at old Mrs Draper's. They were not my family. I had been dragged there by Mr Fulmino, and by a look now and then from young Mrs Draper and from Constance, I had the feeling that they thought it was indecent for me to be there when I had only been going with Iris, Mr Fulmino's daughter, for two or three months. I had to be tolerated as one more example of Mr Fulmino's uncontrollable gift — the gift for colonizing.

Mr Fulmino had shot up from nothing during the war. It had given him personality. He was a short, talkative, heavy man of forty-five with a wet gold tooth and glossy black hair that streamlined back across his head from an arrow point, getting thin in front. His eyes were anxious, overworked, and puddled; indeed, of you had not known him you would have thought he had had a couple of black eyes that had never got right. He bowled along as he walked, like someone absorbed by fondness for his own body. He had been in many things before he got to work for the council – the Army (but not a fighting soldier) in the war, in auctions, and at the bar of a club. He was very active, confiding and enquiring.

When I first met him I was working at the counter of the public library, during the war, and one day he came over from the council offices and said importantly: 'Friend, we've got a bit of a headache. We've got an enquiry from the War Office. Have you got anything about Malaya – with maps?'

In the next breath he was deflating himself.

'It's a personal thing. They never tell you anything. I've got a niece out there.'

Honesty made him sound underhand. His manner suggested that his niece was a secret fortification somewhere east of Suez. Soon he was showing me the questionnaire from the Red Cross. Then he was telling me that his wife, like the rest of the Drapers, was very handsome – 'A lovely woman' in more ways, his manner suggested, than one – but that since Hilda had gone, she had become a different woman. The transition from handsome to different was, he suggested, a catastrophe that he was obliged to share with the public. He would come in from fire-watching, he said, and find her demented. In bed, he would add. He and I found ourselves fire-watching together, and from that time he started facetiously calling me 'my secretary'.

'I asked my secretary to get the sand and shovel out,' he would say about our correspondence, 'and he wrote the letter.'

So I was half a stranger at Hilda's homecoming. I looked round the room or out at the shops opposite, and when I looked back at the family several times I caught Hilda's eyes wandering too. She also was out of it. I studied her. I hadn't expected her to come back in rags, as old Mrs Draper had, but it was a surprise to see she was the best-dressed woman in the room and the only one who looked as if she had ever been to a hairdresser. And there was another way in which I could not match her with the person Mr Fulmino and I had conjured up. When we thought of everything that must have happened to her, it was strange to see that her strong face was smooth and blank. Except for the few minutes of arrival and the time the reporters came, her face was vacant and plain. It was as vacant as a stone that had been smoothed for centuries in the sand of some hot country. It was the face of someone to whom nothing had happened; or perhaps so much had happened to her that each event wiped out what had happened before. I was disturbed by something in her – the lack of history, I think. We were worm-eaten by it. And that suddenly brought her back to me as she had been when she was a schoolgirl and when my older brother got into trouble for chasing after her. She was now sharper in the shoulders and elbows, no longer the swollen schoolgirl, but, even as a girl, her face had had the same quality of having been fixed and unchangeable between its high cheekbones. It was disturbing, in a face so anonymous, to see the eyes move, especially since she blinked very little; and if she smiled it was less a smile than an alteration of the two lines at the corners of her lips.

The party did not settle down quite in the same way after the reporters had been, and there was talk of not tiring Hilda after her long journey. The family would all be meeting tomorrow, the Sunday, as they always did, when young Mrs Jack Draper brought her children. Jack Draper was thinking of the pub, which was open now, and asking if anyone was going over. And then something happened. Hilda walked over to the window to Mr Fulmino and said, just as if she had not been there at the time:

'Ted, what did that man from the *News* ask you – about the food?'

'No,' said Mr Fulmino, widening to a splendid chance of not giving the facts. 'No – he said something about starving the prisoners. I was telling him that in my opinion the deterioration in conditions was inevitable after the disorganization in the camps resulting from air operations . . .'

'Oh, I thought you said we starved. We had enough.'

'What?' said Mr Fulmino.

'Bill Williams must have been in one of those labour camps,' bowl of rice a day. Rice!' said Mrs Fulmino. 'And torture.'

'Bill Williams must have been in one of those labour camps,' said Hilda. 'Being Japanese, I was all right.'

'Japanese!' said Mrs Fulmino. 'You?'

'Shinji was a Japanese,' said Hilda. 'He was in the Army.'

'You married a Japanese!' said Mrs Fulmino, marching forward.

'That's why I was put in the American camp, when they came. They questioned everyone, not only me. That's what I said to the reporter. It wasn't the food, it was the questions. What was his regiment? When did you hear from him? What was his number? They kept on. Didn't they, Mum?'

She turned to her mother, who had taken the chance to cut herself another piece of cake and was about to slip it into her handkerchief, I think, to carry to her own room. We were all flabbergasted. A trolley bus went by and took a swipe at the wall.

Young Mrs Draper murmured something, and her young husband, Jack, hearing his wife, said loudly:

'Hilda married a Nip!'

And he looked at Hilda with astonishment. He had very blue eyes.

'You weren't a prisoner!' said Mrs Fulmino.

'Not of the Japanese,' said Hilda. 'They couldn't touch me. My husband was Japanese.'

'I'm not stupid. I can hear,' said young Mrs Draper to her husband. She was a plainspoken woman from the Yorkshire coalfields, one of a family of twelve.

'I've nowt to say about who you married, but where is he? Haven't you brought him?' she said.

'You were married to Mr Singh,' said Mrs Fulmino.

'They're both dead,' said Hilda, her vacant yellow eyes becoming suddenly brilliant like a cat's at night. An animal sound, like the noise of an old dog at a bone, came out of old Mrs Draper by the fire.

'Two,' she moaned.

No more than that. Simply, again: 'Two'.

Hilda was holding her handbag and she lifted it in both hands and covered her bosom with it. Perhaps she thought we were going to hit her. Perhaps she was going to open the bag and get out something extraordinary – documents, letters, or a handkerchief to weep into. But no – she held it there very tight. It was an American handbag; we hadn't seen one like that before, cream-coloured, like the luggage. Old Mrs Johnson hesitated at the table, tipped the piece of cake back out of her handkerchief onto a plate, and stepped to Hilda's side and stood, very straight for once, beside her, the old blue lips very still.

'Ted,' accused Hilda. 'Didn't you get my letters? Mother' – she stepped away from her mother – 'didn't you tell them?'

'What, dear?' said old Mrs Johnson.

'About Shinji. I wrote you. Did Mum tell you?' Hilda appealed to us and now looked fiercely at her mother.

Mrs Johnson smiled and retired into her look of faith and modesty. She feigned deafness.

'I put it all in the post office,' she said. 'Every week,' she said. ' "Until my girl comes home," I said. "She'll need it." '

'Mother!' said Hilda, giving the old lady a small shake. 'I wrote to you. I told you. Didn't you tell them?'

'What did Hilda say?' said Mr Fulmino gently, bending down to the old lady.

'Sh! Don't worry her. She's had enough for today. What did you tell the papers, Ted?' said Mrs Fulmino, turning on her husband. 'You can't ever keep your big mouth shut, can you? You never let me see the correspondence.'

'I married Shinji when the war came up,' Hilda said.

And then old Mrs Draper spoke from her armchair by the fire. She had her bad leg propped up on a hassock.

'Two,' said Mrs Draper savagely again.

Mr Fulmino, in his defeat, lost his nerve and let slip a remark quite casually, as he thought, under his voice, but everyone heard it – a remark that Mrs Fulmino was to remind him of in months to come.

'She strikes like a clock,' he said.

We were stupefied by Mr Fulmino's remark. Perhaps it was a relief.

'Mr Fraser!' Hilda said to me. And now her vacant face had become dramatic and she stepped towards me, appealing outside the family. 'You knew, you and Ted knew. You've got all the letters . . .'

If ever a man looked like the captain going down with his ship and suddenly conscious, at the last heroic moment, that he is not on a ship at all, but standing on nothing and had hopelessly blundered, it was Mr Fulmino. But we didn't go down, either of us. For suddenly old Mrs Johnson couldn't stand straight any longer, her head wagged and drooped forward, and but for a chair, she would have fallen to the ground.

'Quick! Constance! Open the window,' Mrs Fulmino said. Hilda was on her knees by her mother.

'Are you there, Hilly?' said her mother.

'Yes, I'm here, Mum,' said Hilda. 'Get some water – some brandy.' They took the old lady next door to the little room Hilda was sharing with her that night.

'What I can't fathom is your aunt not telling me, keeping it to herself,' said Mr Fulmino to his wife as we walked home that evening from Mrs Draper's, and we had said goodbye to Jack Draper and his wife.

He was not hurt by Mrs Johnson's secretiveness but by an extraordinary failure of co-operation.

It was unwise of him to criticize Mrs Fulmino's family.

'Don't be so smug,' said Mrs Fulmino. 'What's it got to do with you? She was keeping it from Gran: you know Gran's tongue. She's her sister.' They called old Mrs Draper 'Gran' or 'Grandma' sometimes.

But when Mr Fulmino got home he asked me in so that we could search the correspondence together. Almost at once we discovered his blunder. There it was in the letter saying a Mrs Singh or Shinji Kobayashi had been identified.

'Shinji!' exclaimed Mrs Fulmino, putting her big index finger on the page. 'There you are, plain as dirt.'

'Singh,' said Mr Fulmino. 'Singh, Shinji, the same name. Some Indians write Singh, some Shinji.'

'And what is Kobayashi? Indian too? Don't be a fool.'

'It's the family name or Christian name of Singh,' said Mr Fulmino, doing the best he could.

'Singh, Shinji, Shinji, Singh,' he murmured to himself, and he walked about trying to convince himself by incantation and hypnosis. He lashed himself with Kobayashi. He remembered the names of other Indians, Indian cities, mentioned the Ganges and the Himalayas; had a brief, brilliant couple of minutes when he argued that Shinji was Hindu for Singh. Mrs Fulmino watched him with the detachment of one waiting for a bluebottle to settle so that she could swat it.

'*You* thought Kobayashi was Indian, didn't you, Harry?' he appealed to me. I did my best.

'I thought,' I said weakly, 'it was the address.'

'Ah, the address!' Mr Fulmino clutched at this, but he knew he was done for. Mrs Fulmino struck. .

'And what about the Sunday papers, the man from the *News*?' she said. 'You open your big mouth too soon.'

'Christ!' said Mr Fulmino. It was the sound of a man who has gone to the floor.

I will come to that matter of the papers later on. It is not very important.

When we went to bed that night we must all have known in our different ways that we had been disturbed in a very long dream. We had been living on inner visions for years. It was an effect of the long war. England had been a prison. Even the sky was closed, and, like convicts, we had been driven to dwelling on fancies in our dreary minds. In the cinema the camera sucks some person forward into an enormous close-up and holds a face three yards wide, filling the whole screen, all holes and pores, like some sucking octopus that might eat up an audience many rows at a time. I don't say these pictures aren't beautiful sometimes, but afterwards I get the horrors. Hilda had been a close-up like this for us when she was lost and far away. For myself, I could hardly remember Hilda. She was a collection of fragments of my childhood and I suppose I had expected a girl to return.

My father and mother looked down on the Drapers and the Johnsons. Hincham Street was 'dirty', and my mother once whispered that Mr Johnson had worked 'on the line', as if that were a smell. I remember the old man's huge, crinkled, white beard when I was a child. It was horribly soft and like pubic hair. So I had always thought of Hilda as a railway girl, in and out of tunnels, signal boxes, and main-line stations, and when my older brother was 'chasing' her, as they said, I admired him. I listened to the quarrels that went on in our family: how she had gone to the convent school and the nuns had complained about her; and was it she or some other girl who went for car rides with a married man who waited round the corner of Hincham Street for her? The sinister phrase 'The nuns have been to see her mother' stuck in my memory. It astonished me to see Hilda alive, calm, fat, and walking after that, as composed as a railway engine. When I grew up and Mr Fulmino came to the library, I was drawn into his search because she brought back those days with my brother, those clouts on the head from some friend of his, saying: 'Buzz off. Little pigs have big ears,' when my brother and he were whispering about her.

To Mrs Fulmino, a woman whose feelings were in her rolling arms, flying out from one extreme to another as she talked, as if she were doing exercises, Hilda appeared in her wedding clothes and all the sexuality of an open flower, standing beside her young Indian husband, who was about to become a doctor. There was trouble about the wedding, for Mr Singh spoke a glittering and palatial English – the beautiful English a snake might speak, it seemed to the family – that made a few pockmarks on his face somehow more noticeable. Old Mrs Draper alone, against all evidence – Mr Singh had had a red racing car – stuck to it that he was 'a common Lascar off a ship'. Mrs Fulmino had been terrified of Mr Singh, she often conveyed, and had 'refused to be in a room alone with him'. Or 'How can she let him touch her?' she would murmur, thinking about that, above all. Then whatever vision was in her mind would jump forward to Hilda captured, raped, tortured, murdered in front of her eyes. Mrs Fulmino's mind was voluptuous. When I first went to Mr Fulmino's house and met Iris and we talked about Hilda, Mrs Fulmino once or twice left the room and he lowered his voice. 'The wife's upset,' he said. 'She's easily upset.'

We had not all been under a spell. Not young Jack Draper or his wife, for example. Jack Draper had fought in the war, and whereas we thought of the war as something done to us and our side, Jack thought of it as something done to everybody. I remember what he said to his wife before the Fulminos and I said good night to them on the Saturday Hilda came home.

'It's a shame,' said Jack, 'she couldn't bring the Nip with her.'

'He was killed,' said his wife.

'That's what I mean,' said Jack. 'It's a bleeding shame she couldn't.'

We walked on and then young Mrs Draper said, in her flat, northern, laconic voice:

'Well, Jack, for all the to-do, you might just as well have gone to your fishing.'

For Jack had made a sacrifice in coming to welcome Hilda. He went fishing up the Thames on Saturdays. The war for him was something that spoiled fishing. In the Normandy landing he had thought mostly of that. He dreamt of the time when his two boys would be old enough to fish. It was what he had had children for.

'There's always Sunday,' said his wife, tempting him. Jack nodded. She knew he would not fall. He was the youngest of old Mrs Draper's family, the baby, as they said. He never missed old Mrs Draper's Sundays.

It was a good thing he did not, a good thing for all of us that we didn't miss, for we would have missed Hilda's second announcement.

Young Mrs Draper provoked it. These Sunday visits to Hincham Street were a ritual in the family. It was a duty to old Mrs Draper. We went there for our tea. She provided, though Constance prepared for it as if we were a school, for she kept house there. We recognized our obligation by paying sixpence into the green pot on the chiffonier when we left. The custom had started in the bad times when money was short; but now this money was regarded as capital, and Jack Draper used to joke and say: 'Who are you going to leave the green pot to, Mum?' Some of Hilda's luggage had been moved by the afternoon into her mother's little room at the back, and how those two could sleep in a bed so small was a question raised by Mrs Fulmino, whose nights with Mr Fulmino required room for struggle, as I know, for this colonizing man often dropped hints about how she swung her legs over in the night.

'Have you unpacked yet, Hilda?' Mrs Fulmino was asking.

'Unpacked!' said Constance. 'Where would she put all that?'

'I've been lazy,' said Hilda. 'I've just hung up a few things because of the creases.'

'Things do crease,' said Mrs Fulmino.

'Bill Williams said he would drop in later,' said Constance.

'That man suffered,' said Mrs Fulmino, with meaning.

'He heard you were back,' said Constance.

Hilda had told us about Shinji. Jack Draper listened with wonder. Shinji had been in the jute business, and when the war came he was called up to the Army. He was in Stores. Jack scratched with delight when he heard this. 'Same as I tried to work it,' Jack said. Shinji had been killed in an air raid. Jack's wife said, to change the subject, she liked that idea, the idea of Jack 'working' anything; he always let everyone climb up on his shoulders. 'First man to get wounded. I knew he would be,' she said. 'He never looks where he's going.'

'Is that the Bill Williams who worked for Ryan, the builder?' said Hilda.

'He lives in the Culverwell Road,' young Mrs Draper said.

Old Mrs Draper, speaking from the bowels of history, said: 'He got that Sellers girl into trouble.'

'Yes,' exclaimed Hilda, 'I remember.'

'It was proved in court that he didn't,' said Constance briskly to Hilda. 'You weren't here.'

We were all silent. One could hear only the sounds of our cups on the saucers and Mrs Fulmino's murmur: 'More bread and butter?' Constance's face had its neat, pink, enamelled smile, and one saw the truthful blue of her small eyes become purer in colour. Iris was next to me and she said afterwards something I hadn't noticed, that Constance hated Hilda. It is one of the difficulties I have in writing, that, all along, I was slow to see what was really happening, not having a woman's eye or ear. And being young. Old Mrs Draper spoke again, her mind moving from the past to the present with that suddenness old people have.

'If Bill Williams is coming, he knows the way,' she said.

Hilda understood that remark, for she smiled and Constance flushed. (Of course, I see it now: two women in a house! Constance had ruled old Mrs Draper and Mrs Johnson for years and her money had made a big difference.) They knew that one could, as the saying is, 'trust Gran to put her oar in'.

Again, young Mrs Draper changed the subject. She was a nimble, tarry-haired woman, impatient of fancies, excitements, and disasters. She liked things flat and factual. While the family gaped at Hilda's clothes and luggage, young Mrs Draper had reckoned up the cost of them. She was not avaricious or mean, but she knew that money is money. You know that if you have done without. So she went straight into the important question, being (as she would say) not like people in the south, double-faced Wesleyans, but honest, plain, and straight out with it, what are they ashamed of? Jack, her husband, was frightened by her bluntness, and had the nervous habit of folding his arms across his chest and scratching fast under his armpits when his wife spoke out about the money; some view of the river, with his bait and line and the evening flies, came into his panicking mind. Mr Fulmino once said that Jack scratched because the happiest moments of his life, the moments of escape, had been passed in clouds of gnats.

'I suppose, Hilda, you'll be thinking of what you're going to do?' young Mrs Draper said. 'Did they give you a pension?'

I was stroking Iris's knee but she stopped me, alerted like the rest of them. The word 'pension' is a very powerful word. In this neighbourhood one could divide the world into those who had pensions and those who hadn't. The phrase 'the old pensioner' was one of envy, abuse and admiration. My father, for example, spoke contemptuously of pensioners. Old Mrs Draper's husband had had a pension, but my father would never have one. As a librarian, Mr Fulmino pointed out, I would have a pension and thereby I had overcome the first obstacle in being allowed to go out with his daughter.

'No,' said Hilda, 'nothing.'

'But he was your husband, you said,' said Constance.

'He was in the Army, you say,' said young Mrs Draper.

'Inflation,' said Mr Fulmino grandly. 'The financial situation.'

He was stopped.

'Then,' said young Mrs Draper, 'you'll have to go to work.'

'My girl won't want for money,' said old Mrs Johnson, sitting beside her daughter as she had done the day before.

'No,' said young Mrs Draper, 'that she won't while you're alive, Mrs Johnson. We all know that, and the way you slaved for her. But Hilda wants to look after you, I'm sure.'

It was, of course, the question in everyone's mind. Did all those clothes and cases mean money or was it all show? That is what we all wanted to know. We would not have raised it at that time and in that way. It wasn't our way; we would have drifted into finding out – Hilda was scarcely home. But young Mrs Draper had been brought up hard, she said, twelve mouths to feed.

'*I'm* looking after *you*, Mum,' said Hilda, smiling at her mother.

Mrs Johnson was like a wizened little girl gazing up at a taller sister.

'I'll take you to Monte Carlo, Mum,' Hilda said.

The old lady tittered. We all laughed loudly. Hilda laughed with us.

'That gambling place!' the old lady giggled.

'That's it,' laughed Hilda. 'Break the bank.'

'Is it across water?' said the old lady, playing up. 'I couldn't go on a boat. I was so sick at Southend when I was a girl.'

'Then we'll fly.'

'Oh!' the old lady screeched. 'Don't, Hil – I'll have a fit.'

'The man who broke the bank at Monte Carlo,' Mr Fulmino sang. 'You might find a boyfriend, Mrs Johnson.'

Young Mrs Draper did not laugh at this game; she still wanted to know; but she did smile. She was worried by laughter. Constance did not laugh but she showed her pretty white teeth.

'Oh, she's got one for me,' said Mrs Johnson. 'So she says.'

'Of course I have. Haven't I, Harry?' said Hilda, talking across the table to me.

'Me? What?' I said, completely startled.

'You can't take Harry,' said Iris, half frightened. Until then I did not know that Iris was interested in me.

'Did you post the letter?' said Hilda to me.

'What letter?' said Iris to me. 'Did she give you a letter?'

Now, there is a thing I ought to have mentioned! I had forgotten all about the letter. When we were leaving the evening before, Hilda had called me quietly to the door and said:

'Please post this for me. Tonight.'

'Hilda gave me a letter to post,' I said.

'You did post it?' Hilda said.

'Yes,' I said.

She looked contentedly round at everyone.

'I wrote to Mr Gloster, the gentleman I told you about, on the boat. He's in Paris. He's coming over at the end of the week to get a car. He's taking Mother and me to France. Mr Gloster, Mum, I told you. No, not Mr Faulkner. That was the other boat. He was in San Francisco.'

'Oh,' said Mrs Johnson, a very long 'oh', and wriggling like a child listening to a story. She was beginning to look pale, as she had the evening before when she had her turn.

'France!' said Constance in a peremptory voice.

'Who is Mr Gloster? You never said anything,' said Mrs Fulmino.

'What about the currency regulations?' said Mr Fulmino.

Young Mrs Draper said: 'France! He must have money.'

'Dollars,' said Hilda to Mr Fulmino.

Dollars! There was a word!

'The almighty dollar,' said Constance, in the cleansed and uncorrupted voice of one who has mentioned one of the Commandments. Constance had principles; we had the confusion of our passions.

And from sixteen years or more back in time, or perhaps it was from some point in history hundreds of years back and forgotten, old Mrs Draper said: 'And is this Indian married?'

Hilda, to whom no events, I believe, had ever happened, replied: 'Mr Gloster's an American, Gran.'

'He wants to marry her,' said old Mrs Johnson proudly.

'If I'll have him!' said Hilda.

'Well, he can't if you won't have him, can he, Hilda?' said Mrs Fulmino.

'Gloster. G-L-O-S-T-E-R?' asked Mr Fulmino.

'Is he in a good job?' asked young Mrs Draper.

Hilda pointed to a brooch on her blouse. 'He gave me this,' she said.

She spoke in her harsh voice and with a movement of her face which in anyone else one would have called excited, but in her it had a disturbing lack of meaning. It was as if Hilda had been hooked into the air by invisible wires and was then swept out into the air and back to Japan, thousands of miles away again, and while she was on her way, she turned and knocked us flat with the next item.

'He's a writer,' she said. 'He's going to write a book about me. He's very interested in me . . .'

Mrs Johnson nodded.

'He's coming to fetch us, Mum and me, and take us to France to write this book. He's going to write my life.'

Her life! Here was a woman who had, on top of everything else, a life.

'Coming *here*?' said Mrs Fulmino with a grinding look at old Mrs Draper and then at Constance, trying to catch their eyes and failing; in despair she looked at the shabby room, to see what must be put straight, or needed cleaning or painting. Nothing had been done to it for years, for Constance, teaching at her school all day and very clean in her person, let things go in the house, and young Mrs Draper said old Mrs Draper smelt. All the command in Mrs Fulmino's face collapsed as rapidly, on her own, she looked at the carpets, the lino, the curtains.

'What's he putting in this book?' said young Mrs Draper cannily.

'Yes,' said Jack Draper, backing up his wife.

'What I tell him,' Hilda said.

'What she tells him,' said old Mrs Johnson, sparkling. Constance looked thoughtfully at Hilda.

'Is it a biography?' Constance asked coldly. There were times when we respected Constance and forgot to murmur 'Go back to Russia' every time she spoke. I knew what a biography was and so did Mr Fulmino, but no one else did.

'It's going to be made into a film,' Hilda replied.

'A film,' cried Iris.

Constance gleamed.

'You watch for American propaganda,' said Constance. There you are, you see: Constance was back on it!

'Oh, it's about me,' said Hilda. 'My experiences.'

'Very interesting,' said Mr Fulmino, preparing to take over. 'A Hollywood production, I bet. Publication first and then they go into production.' He spread his legs.

None of us had believed or understood what we heard, but we looked at Mr Fulmino with gratitude for making the world steady again.

Jack Draper's eyes filled with tears because a question was working in him but he could not get it out.

'Will you be in this film?' asked Iris.

'I'll wait till he's written it,' said Hilda with that lack of interest we had often noticed in her after she had made some dramatic statement.

Mrs Fulmino breathed out heavily with relief and after that her body seemed to become larger. She touched her hair at the back and straightened her dress, as if preparing to offer herself for the part. She said, indeed:

'I used to act at school.'

'She's still good at it,' said Mr Fulmino with daring to Jack Draper, who always appreciated Mr Fulmino but, seeing the danger of the moment, hugged himself and scratched excitedly under both armpits, laughing.

'You shouldn't have let this Mr Gloster go,' said Constance.

Hilda was startled by this remark and looked lost. Then she shrugged her shoulders and gave a low laugh, as if to herself.

Mr Fulmino's joke had eased our bewilderment. Hilda had been our dream, but now she was home she changed as fast as dreams change. She was now, as we looked at her, more remote to us than she had been all the years when she was away. The idea was so far beyond us. It was like some story of a bomb explosion or an elopement or a picture of bathing girls one sees in the newspapers – unreal and, in a way, insulting to being alive in the ordinary daily sense of the word. Or she was like a picture one sees in an art gallery which makes you feel sad because it is painted.

After tea, when Hilda took her mother to the lavatory, Constance beckoned to Iris and let her peep into the room Hilda was sharing, and young Mrs Draper, not to be kept out of things, followed. They were back in half a minute.

'Six evening dresses,' Iris said to me.

'She said it was Mr Faulkner who gave her the luggage, not this one who was going to get her into pictures,' said Mrs Fulmino.

'Mr Gloster, you mean,' said Constance.

Young Mrs Draper was watching the door, listening for Hilda's return.

'Ssh,' she said at the sound of footsteps on the stairs, and to look at us – the men on one side of the room and the women on the other, silent, standing at attention, facing each other – we looked like soldiers.

'Oh,' said Constance. The steps we had heard were not Hilda's. It was Bill Williams who came in.

'Good afternoon, one and all,' he said. The words came from the corner of a mouth that had slipped down at one side. Constance drew herself up; her eyes softened. She had exact, small, round breasts. Looking round, he said to Constance: 'Where is she?'

Constance lowered her head when she spoke to him, though she held it up shining, admiring him, when he spoke to us, as if she were displaying him to us.

'She'll be here in a minute,' she said. 'She's going into films.'

'I'll take a seat in the two-and-fourpennies,' said Bill Williams, and he sat down at his ease and lit a cigarette.

Bill Williams was a very tall, sick-faced man who stooped his shoulders as if he were used to ducking under doors. His dry black hair, not oiled like Mr Fulmino's, bushed over his forehead, and he had the shoulders, arms, and hands of a lorry driver. In fact, he drove a light van for a textile firm. His hazel eyes were always watching and wandering, and we used to say he looked as though he was going to snaffle something, but that may simply have been due to the restlessness of a man with a poor stomach. Laziness, cunning, and aches and pains were suggested by him. He was a man taking his time. His eyebrows grew thick and the way one brow was raised, combined with the side slip of his mouth, made him look like some shrewd man about to pick up a faulty rifle, hit the bull's-eye five times running at a fair, and moan afterwards. He glanced a good deal at Constance. He was afraid of his manners before her, we thought, because he was a rough type.

'Put it here,' said Constance, bringing him an ashtray. That was what he was waiting for, for he did not look at her again.

Bill Williams brought discomfort with him whenever he came on Sundays, and we were always happier when he failed to come. If there was anything private to say, we tried to get it over before he came. How a woman like Constance, a true, clean, settled schoolteacher who even spoke in the clear, practical, and superior manner of someone used to the voice of reason, who kept her nails so beautifully, could have taken up with him baffled us. He was very often at Mrs Draper's in the week, eating with them, and Constance, who was thirty-five, quarrelled like a girl when she was getting things ready for him. Mrs Fulmino could not bear the way he ate, with his elbows out and his face close to the plate. The only good thing about the affair was that, for once, Constance was overruled.

'Listen to her,' Bill Williams would say with a nod of his head. 'A rank-red Communist. Tell us about Holy Russia, Connie.'

'Constance is my name, not Connie,' she said.

Their bickering made us die. But we respected Constance even when she was a trial. She had been twice to Russia before the war, and though we argued violently with her, especially Mr Fulmino, who tried to take over Russia and populate it with explanations, we always boasted that she'd been there, to other people.

'On delegations,' Mr Fulmino would say.

But we could *not* boast that she had taken up with Bill Williams. He had been a hero when he came back from Japan, but he had never kept a job since, he was rough, and his lazy, zigzagging habits in his work made even Constance impatient. He had for her the fascination a teacher feels for a bad pupil. Lately their love affair had been going better because he was working outside London and sometimes he worked at weekends; this added to the sense of something vague and secretive in his life that had attracted Constance. For there was much that was secret in her, or so she liked to hint; it was political. Again, it was the secretiveness of those who like power; she was the schoolmistress who has the threat of inside knowledge locked up in the cupboard. Once Mrs Fulmino went purple and said to her husband (who told me; he always told me such things) that she believed Constance had lately started sleeping with Bill Williams. That was because Constance had once said to her:

'Bill and I are individuals.'

Mrs Fulmino had a row with Iris after this and stopped me seeing her for a month.

Hilda came back into the room alone. Bill Williams let his mouth slip sideways and spoke a strange word to her, saying jauntily to us: 'That's Japanese.'

Hilda wasn't surprised. She replied with a whole sentence in Japanese.

'That means – ' Bill Williams was beaten, but he passed it off. 'Well, I'd best not tell them what it means,' he said.

'East meets East,' Mr Fulmino said.

'It means,' said Hilda, 'you were on the other side of the fence, but now the gate is open.'

Bill Williams studied her inch by inch. He scratched his head.

'Straight?' he said.

'Yes,' she said.

'Stone me, it was bloody closed when we were there,' said Bill Williams offensively, but then said: 'They fed her well, didn't they, Constance? Sit down.' Hilda sat down beside him.

'Connie!' he called. 'Seen these? Just the job, eh?' He was nodding at Hilda's stockings. Nylons. 'Now,' he said to Hilda, looking closely at her. 'Where were you? It got a bit rough at the finish, didn't it?'

Jack Draper came close to them to hear, hoping that Hilda would say something about what moved him the most: the enemy. Bill Williams gave him a wink and Hilda saw it. She looked placidly at Bill Williams, considering his face, his neck, his shoulders, and his hands, which were resting on his knees.

'I was okey doke,' she said.

Bill Williams dropped his mouth open and waggled the top of his tongue in a back tooth in his knowing manner. To our astonishment Hilda opened her mouth and gave a neat twist to her tongue in her cheek in the same way.

Bill Williams slapped his knee and, to cover his defeat in this little duel, said to all of us: 'This little girl's got yellow eyes.'

All the colour had gone from Connie's face as she watched the meeting.

'They say you're going to be in pictures,' said Bill Williams.

And then we had Hilda's story over again. Constance asked what papers Mr Gloster wrote for.

'I don't know. A big paper,' said Hilda.

'You ought to find out,' Constance said. 'I'll find out.'

'Um,' said Hilda with a nod of not being interested.

'I could give him some of my experience,' said Bill Williams. 'Couldn't I, Connie? Things I've told you – you could write a ruddy book.'

He looked with challenge at Hilda. He was a rival.

'Gawd!' he exclaimed. 'The things.'

We heard it again, how he was captured, where his battery was, the long march, Sergeant Harris who was hanged, Corporal Rowley bayoneted and left to die in the sun, the starvation, the work on the road that killed half of them. But there was one difference between this story and the ones he had told before. The sight of Hilda altered it.

'You had to get round the guards,' he said with a wink. 'If you used your loaf a bit, eh? Scrounge round, do a bit of trade. One or two had Japanese girls. Corporal Jones went back afterwards trying to trace his, wanted to marry her.'

Hilda listened and talked about places she had lived in, how she had worked in a factory.

'That's it,' said Bill Williams, 'you had to know your way round and talk a bit of the lingo.'

Jack Draper looked with affection and wonder at the talk, lowering his eyes as if her eyes caught his. Every word entered him. The heat! she said. The rain. The flowers. The telegraph poles! Jack nodded.

'They got telegraph poles.' He nodded to us.

You sleep on the floor. Shinji's mother, she mentioned. She could have skinned her. Jack, brought up among so many women, lost interest, but it revived when she talked of Shinji. You could see him mouthing his early marvelling sentence: 'She married a Nip,' but not saying it. She was confirming something he had often thought of in Normandy; the men on the other side were married too. A bloody marvel. Why hadn't she brought him home? He would have had a friend.

'Who looked after the garden when Shinji was called up?' he asked. 'Were they goldfish, ordinary goldfish, in the pond?'

Young Mrs Draper shook her head. 'Eh,' she said. 'If he'd known he'd have come over to change the water. Next time we have a war you just let him know.'

Mrs Fulmino, who was throbbing like a volcano, said: 'We better all go next time by the sound of it.'

At the end, Bill Williams said: 'I suppose you're going to be staying here.'

'No,' said Constance quickly, 'she isn't. She's going to France. When is it, Hilda? When is Mr Gloster coming?'

'Next week, I don't know,' said Hilda.

'You shouldn't have let him go!' laughed Bill Williams. 'Those French girls will get him in Paree.'

'That is what I have been saying,' said Constance. 'He gave her that brooch.'

'Oh ah! It's the stockings I'm looking at,' said Bill Williams. 'How did you get all that stuff through the customs? Twenty cases, Connie told me.'

'Twelve,' said Hilda.

Bill Williams did not move her at all. Presently she got up and started clearing away the tea things. I will say this for her: she didn't let herself be waited on.

Iris, Mr and Mrs Fulmino, and the young Drapers and their children and myself left Hincham Street together.

'You walk in front with the children, Iris,' said Mrs Fulmino. Then they turned on me. What was this letter, they wanted to know. Anyone would have thought by their questions that I ought to have opened it and read it.

'I just posted it at the corner.' I pointed to the pillar box. Mrs Fulmino stopped to look at the pillar box and I believe was turning over in her mind the possibility of getting inside it. Then she turned on her husband and said with contemptuous suspicion. 'Monte Carlo!' As if he had worked the whole thing in order to get there himself.

'Two dead,' she added in her mother's voice, the voice of one who would have been more than satisfied with the death of one.

'Not having a pension hasn't hurt her,' said Mrs Draper.

'Not a tear,' said Mrs Fulmino.

Jack and Mr Fulmino glanced at each other. It was a glance of surreptitious gratitude: tears – they had escaped that.

Mr Fulmino said: 'The Japanese don't cry.'

Mrs Fulmino stepped out, a bad sign; her temper was rising.

'Who was the letter to?' she asked me. 'Was the name Gloster?'

'I didn't look,' I said.

Mrs Fulmino looked at her husband and me and rolled her eyes. Another of our blunders!

'I don't believe it,' she said.

But Mrs Fulmino *did* believe it. We all believed and disbelieved everything at once. I said I would come to the report in the *News*. It was in thick lettering like mourning, with Hilda's picture: A MOTHER'S FAITH. FOUR YEARS IN JAPANESE TORTURE CAMP. LONDON GIRL'S ORDEAL.

And then an account of how Hilda had starved and suffered and been brainwashed by questioners. Even Hilda was awed when she read it, feeling herself drain away, perhaps, and being replaced by this fantasy; and for the rest of us, we had become used to living in a period when events reduced us to beings so trivial that we had no strong feeling of our own existence in relation to the world round us. We had been bashed first one way, then the other, by propaganda until we were indifferent. At one time people like my parents or old Mrs Draper could at least trust the sky and feel that it was certain, and before it they could have at least the importance of being something in the eye of heaven.

Constance read the newspaper report and it fulfilled her.

'Propaganda,' she said. 'Press lies.'

'All lies,' Mr Fulmino agreed with wonder. The notion that the untrue was as effective as the true opened to him vast areas to his powers. It was like a temptation.

It did not occur to us that we might be in a difficult situation in the neighbourhood when the truth came out until we heard Constance and Bill Williams had gone over to the Lord Nelson with the paper and Constance had said: 'You can't believe a word you read in the capitalist press.'

Alfred Levy, the proprietor and a strong Tory, agreed with her. But was Hilda criticized for marrying an enemy? The hatred of the Japanese was strong at this time. She was not. Constance may not have had the best motives for spreading the news, we said, but it did no harm at all. That habit of double vision affected everyone publicly. We lived in the true and the untrue, comfortably and without trouble. People picked up the paper, looked at her picture, and said: 'That's a shocking thing. A British subject,' and even when they knew, even from Hilda's own lips, the true story, they said, congratulating themselves on their cunning: 'The papers make it all up.'

Of course, we were all in that stage where the forces of life, the desire to live, were coming back, and although it was not yet openly expressed, we felt that curiosity about the enemy that ex-soldiers like Jack Draper felt when he wondered if some Japanese or some Germans were as fed up as he was on Saturdays by missing a day's fishing. When people shook Hilda's hand they felt they gave her life. I do not say there were not one or two mutterings afterwards, for people always went off from the Lord Nelson when it closed in a state of moralization: beer must talk; the louts singing and the couples saying this or that 'wasn't right'. But this gossip came to nothing because, sooner or later, it came to a closed door in everybody's conscience. There were the men who had shot off trigger fingers, who had got false medical certificates, deserters, ration frauds, black marketeers, the pilferers of Army stores. And the women said a woman is right to stand by her husband and, looking at Hilda's fine clothes, pointed out to their husbands that that kind of loyalty was sometimes rewarded.

Mrs Fulmino, indeed, asserted it ought to be – by law.

We had been waiting for Hilda; now, by a strange turn, we were waiting for Hilda's Mr Gloster. We waited for a fortnight and it ran on into three weeks. George Hartman Gloster. I looked up the name on our cards at the library, but we had no books of his. I looked up one or two catalogues. Still nothing. It was not surprising. He was an American who was not published in this country. Constance came in and looked too.

'It is one of those names the Americans don't list,' she said. Constance smiled with the cool air of keeping a world of meaningful secrets on ice.

'They don't list everything,' she said.

She brought Bill Williams with her. I don't think he had ever been in a public library before, because his knowing manner went and he was overawed. He said to me:

'Have you read all these books? Do you buy them second-hand? What's this lot worth?'

He was a man always on the look-out for a deal; it was typical of him that he had come with Constance in his firm's light-green van. It was not like Constance to travel in that way. 'Come on,' he said roughly.

The weather was hot; we had the sun blinds down in the library. We were in the middle of one of those brassy fortnights of the London summer when English life as we usually know it is at a standstill, and everyone changes. A new, grinning, healthy race, with long red necks sticking out of open shirts and blouses, appears, and the sun brings out the variety of faces and bodies. Constance might have been some trim nurse marching at the head of an official procession. People looked calm, happy, and open. There was hardly ever a cloud in the sky, the slate roofs looked like steel with the sun's rays hitting them, and the side streets were cool in sharp shadow. It was a pleasant time for walking, especially when the sky went whitish in the distances of the city in the evening and when the streets had a dry, pleasant smell and the glass of millions of windows had a motionless but not excluding stare. Even a tailor working late above a closed shop looked pleased to be going on working while everyone else was out, wearing out their clothes.

Iris and I used to go to the park on some evenings, and there every blade of grass had been wire-brushed by sunlight; the trees were heavy with still leaves, and when darkness came they gathered into soft black walls and their edges were cut out against the nail varnish of the city's night. During the day the park was crowded. All over the long sweeps of grass the couples were lying, their legs at careless angles, their bottoms restless as they turned to the horseplay of love in the open. Girls were leaning over the men rumpling their hair, men were tickling the girls' chins with stalks of grass. Occasionally they would knock the wind out of each other with plunging kisses; and every now and then a girl would sit up and straighten her skirt at the waist, narrowing her eyes in a pretence of looking at some refining sight in the distance, until she was pulled down again and, keeping her knees together, was caught again. Lying down, you smelt the grass and listened to the pleasant rumble of the distant traffic going round like a wheel that never stopped.

I was glad to know the Fulminos and to go out with Iris. We had both been gayer before we met each other, but seriousness, glumness, a sadness came over us when we became friends – that eager sadness that begins with thoughts of love. We encouraged and discouraged these thoughts in each other, yet were always hinting, and the sight of so much love round us turned us naturally away from it to think about it privately the more. She was a beautifully formed girl, as her mother must have once been, but slender. She had a wide laugh that shook the curls of her thick black hair. She was being trained at a typing school.

One day when I was sitting in the park and Iris was lying beside me, we had a quarrel. I asked her if there was any news of Mr Gloster – for she heard everything. She had said there was none and I said, sucking a piece of grass:

'That's what I would like to do. Go round the world. Anywhere. America, Africa, China.'

'A chance is a fine thing,' said Iris, daydreaming.

'I could get a job,' I said.

Iris sat up. 'Leave the library?' she said.

'Yes,' I said. 'If I stay there I won't see anything.' I saw Iris's face change and become very like her mother's. Mrs Fulmino could make her face go larger and her mouth go very small. Iris did not answer. I went on talking. I asked her what she thought. She still did not answer.

'Anything the matter?' She was sulking. Then she said, flashing at me:

'You're potty on that woman too. You all are. Dad is, Jack is –

and look at Bill Williams. Round at Hincham Street every day. He'll be having his breakfast there soon. Fascinated.'

'He goes to see Constance.'

'Have you seen Constance's face?' she jeered. 'Constance could kill her.'

'She came to the library.'

'Ah.' She turned to me. 'You didn't tell me that.'

'She came in for a book, I told you. For Mr Gloster's books. Bill Williams came with her.'

Iris's sulk changed into satisfaction at this piece of news.

'Mother says if Constance's going to marry a man like Mr Williams,' she said, 'she'll be a fool to let him out of her sight.

'I'll believe in Mr Gloster when I see him,' Iris said. It was, of course, what we were all thinking. We made up our quarrel and I took Iris home. Mrs Fulmino was dressed up, just putting the key in the door of her house. Iris was astonished to see her mother had been out and asked where she had been.

'Out,' said Mrs Fulmino. 'Have I got to stay in and cook and clean for you all day?'

Mrs Fulmino was even wearing gloves, as if she had been to church.

And she was wearing a new pair of shoes. Iris went pale at the sight of them. Mrs Fulmino put her gloves down on the sitting-room table and said:

'I've got a right to live, I suppose?'

We were silenced.

One thing we all agreed on while we waited for Mr Gloster was that Hilda had the money and knew how to spend it. The first time she asked the Fulminos and young Drapers to the cinema, Mrs Fulmino said to her husband:

'You go. I've got one of my heads.'

'Take Jack,' young Mrs Draper said. 'I've got the children.'

They were daring their husbands to go with her. But the second time, there was a party. Hilda took some of them down to Kew. She took old Mrs Johnson down to Southend – and who should they meet there but Bill Williams, who was delivering some goods there, spoiling their day, because old Mrs Johnson did not like his ways. And Hilda had given them all presents. And two or three nights a week she was out at the Lord Nelson.

It was a good time. If anyone asked: 'Have you heard from Mr Gloster yet?' Hilda answered that it was not time yet, and as a dig at Constance which we all admired, she said once: 'He has business at the American embassy.' And old Mrs Johnson held her head high and nodded.

At the end of three weeks we became restless. We noticed old Mrs Johnson looked poorly. She said she was tired. Old Mrs Draper became morose. She had been taught to call Mr Gloster by his correct name, but now she relapsed.

'Where is this Indian?' she uttered.

And another day, she said, without explanation:

'Three.'

'Three what, Gran?'

'There've been two, that's enough.'

No one liked this, but Mrs Johnson understood.

'Mr Gloster's very well, isn't he, Hil? You heard from him yesterday?' she said.

'I wasn't shown the letter,' said old Mrs Draper. 'We don't want a third.'

'We don't,' said Mrs Fulmino. With her joining in 'on Gran's side', the situation changed. Mrs Fulmino had a low voice and the sound of it often sank to the floor of any room she was in, travelling under chairs and tables, curling round your feet, and filling the place from the bottom as if it were a cistern. Even when the trolley bus went by, Mrs Fulmino's low voice prevailed. It was an undermining voice, breaking up one's uppermost thoughts and stirring up what was underneath them. It stirred us all now. Yes, we wanted to say, indeed, we wanted to shout, where is this Mr Gloster, why hasn't he come, did you invent him? He's alive, we hope? Or is he also, as Gran suggests, dead?

Even Mr Fulmino was worried. 'Have you got his address?' he asked.

'Yes, Uncle dear,' said Hilda. 'He'll be staying at the Savoy. He always does.'

Mr Fulmino had not taken out his notebook for a long time, but he did so now. He wrote down the name.

'Has he made a reservation?' said Mr Fulmino. 'I'll find out if he's booked.'

'He hasn't,' said Bill Williams. 'I had a job down there and I asked. Didn't I, Connie?'

Mrs Fulmino went a very dark colour; she wished she had been as cunning as Williams. Hilda was not offended, but a small smile clipped her lips as she glanced at Connie.

'I asked Bill to do it,' she said.

And then Hilda, in that harsh, lazy voice which she had always used for announcements:

'If he doesn't come by Wednesday you'll have to speak for me at your factory, Mr Williams. I don't know why he hasn't come, but I can't wait any more.'

'Bill can't get you a job. You have to register,' said Constance.

'Yes, she'll have to do that,' said Mr Fulmino.

'I'll fix it. Leave it to me,' said Bill Williams.

'I expect,' said young Mrs Draper, 'his business had kept him.' She was sorry for Hilda.

'Perhaps he's gone fishing,' said Jack Draper, laughing loudly in a kind way. No one joined in.

'Fishing for orders,' said Bill Williams.

Hilda shrugged her shoulders and then she made one of those remarks that Grandma Draper usually made: I suppose the gift really ran through the family.

'Perhaps it was a case,' she said, 'of ships that pass in the night.'

'Oh, no, dear,' said Mrs Johnson, trembling, 'not ships.' We went to the bus stop afterwards with the Fulminos and the Johnsons. Mrs Fulmino's calm had gone. She marched out first, her temper rising.

'Ships!' she said. 'When you think of what we went through during the war. Did you hear it? Straight out?'

'My brother Herbert's wife was like that. She's a widow. Take away the pension and they'll work like the rest of us. I had to.'

'Job! Work! I know what sort of work she's been doing. Frank, walk ahead with Iris.'

'Well,' said young Mrs Draper. 'She won't be able to go to work in those clothes and that's a fact.'

'All show,' said Mrs Fulmino triumphantly. 'And I'll tell you something else: she hasn't a penny. She's run through her poor mother's money.'

'Ay, I don't doubt,' said young Mrs Draper, who had often worked out how much the old lady had saved.

Mr Gloster did not come on Wednesday or on any day, but Hilda did not get a job either, not at once. And old Mrs Johnson did not go to Monte Carlo. She died. This was the third, we understood, that old Mrs Draper had foreseen.

Mrs Johnson died at half past eight in the morning just after

Constance had gone off to school, the last day of the term, and before old Mrs Draper had got up. Hilda was in the kitchen wearing her blue Japanese wrap when she heard her mother's shout, like a man selling papers, she said, and when Hilda rushed in, her mother was sitting up in bed. She gripped Hilda with the ferocity of the dying, as if all the strength of her whole life had come back and she was going to throw her daughter to the ground. Then she died. In an hour she looked like a white leaf that has been found after a lifetime pressed between the pages of a book and as delicate as a saint. The death was not only a shock; from the grief that spread from it staining all of us, I trace the ugly events that followed. Only the frail figure of old Mrs Johnson, with her faith and her sly smile, had protected us from them until then, and when she went, all defence went with her.

I need not describe her funeral: it was done by Bickerson's; Mr Fulmino arranged it. But one thing astonished us: not only our families but the whole neighbourhood was affected by the death of this woman who, in our carelessness, we thought could hardly be known to anyone. She had lived there all her life, of course, but people come and go in London; only a sluggish residue lay still; and I believe it was just because a large number of passing people knew just a little about her, because she was a fragment in their minds, that her death affected them. They recognized that they themselves were not people but fragments. People remembered her going into shops now and then, or going down to the bus stop, passing down a street. They remembered the bag of American cloth she used to carry containing her sewing; they spoke for a long time afterwards about this bag, more about it, indeed, than about herself. Bickerson's is a few doors from the Lord Nelson, so that when the hearse stood there covered with flowers, everyone noticed it, and although the old lady had not been in that public house for years since the death of her husband, all the customers came out to look. And they looked at Hilda sitting in her black in the car when the hearse moved slowly off, and all who knew her story must have felt that the dream was burying the dreamer. Hilda's face was dirty with grief and she did not turn her head to right or left as they drove off. I remember a small thing that happened when we were all together at old Mrs Draper's, after we had got her back with difficulty up the stairs.

'Bickerson's did it very well,' said Mr Fulmino, seeking to distract the old lady, who, swollen with sadness, was uncomfortable in her best clothes. 'They organize everything so well. They gave me this.'

He held up a small brass disc on a little chain. It was one of those identity discs people used to wear on their wrists in the war.

'She had never taken it off,' he said. It swung feebly on its chain. Suddenly, with a sound like a shout, Mr Fulmino broke into tears. His face caved in and he apologized.

'It's the feeling,' he said. 'You have the feeling. You feel.' And he looked at us with panic, astonished by this discovery of an unknown self, spongy with tears, that had burst out and against which he was helpless. Mrs Fulmino said gently: 'I expect Hilda would like to have it.'

'Yes, yes. It's for her,' he said, drying his eyes, and Hilda took it from him and carried it to her room. While she was there (and perhaps she was weeping, too), Mr Fulmino looked out from his handkerchief and said, still sobbing:

'I see that the luggage has gone.'

None of us had noticed this and we looked at Constance, who said in a whisper: 'She is leaving us. She has found a room of her own.' That knocked us back. 'Leaving!' we exclaimed. It told against Hilda, for although we talked of death being a release for the dead person, we did not like to think of it as a release for the living; grief ought to hold people together, and it seemed too brisk to have started a new life so soon. Constance alone looked pleased by this. We were whispering but stopped when we heard Hilda coming back.

Black had changed her. It set off her figure, and although crying had hardened her, the skin of her neck and her arms and the swell of her breasts seemed more living than they had before. She looked stronger in body perhaps because she was shaken in mind. She looked very real, very present, more alive than ourselves. She had not heard us whispering, but she said, to all of us, but particularly to Mr Fulmino:

'I have found a room for myself. Constance spoke to Bill Williams for me: he's good at getting things. He found me a place and he took the luggage round yesterday. I couldn't sleep in that bed alone any more.'

Her voice was shaky.

'She didn't take up much room. She was tiny and we managed. It was like sleeping with a little child.'

Hilda smiled and laughed a little.

'She used to kick like a kid.'

Ten minutes on the bus from Hincham Street and close to the centre of London is a dance hall called the Temple Rooms. It has two bands, a low gallery where you can sit, and a soft-drink bar. Quite a few West Indians go there, mainly students. It is a respectable place; it closes at eleven and there is never any trouble. Iris and I went there once or twice. One evening we were surprised to see Constance and Bill Williams dancing there. Iris pointed to them. The rest of the people were jiving, but Bill Williams and Constance were dancing in the old-fashioned way.

'Look at his feet!' Iris laughed.

Bill Williams was paying no attention to Constance, but looking round the room over her head as he stumbled along. He was tall.

'Fancy Auntie Constance!' said Iris. 'She's getting fed up because he won't listen.'

Constance Draper dancing! At her age! Thirty-eight!

'It's since the funeral,' said Mr Fulmino over our usual cup of tea. 'She was fond of the old lady. It's upset her.'

Even I knew Mr Fulmino was wrong about this. The madness of Constance dated from the time Bill Williams had taken Hilda's luggage round to her room and got her a job at the reception desk in the factory at Laxton. It dated from the time a week later when, standing at old Mrs Draper's early one evening, Constance had seen Hilda get out of Bill Williams's van. He had given her a lift home. It dated from words that passed between Hilda and Constance soon afterwards. Hilda said Williams hung round for her at the factory and wanted her to go to a dance. She did not want to go, she said, and here came the fatal sentences – both of her husbands had been educated men. Constance kept her temper but said coldly:

'Bill Williams is politically educated.'

Hilda had her vacant look. 'Not his hands aren't,' she said.

The next thing, Constance, who hardly went into a pub in her life, was in the Lord Nelson night after night, playing bar billiards with Bill Williams. She never let him out of her sight. She came out of school and instead of going home, marking papers, and getting a meal for herself and old Mrs Draper, she took the bus out to the factory and waited for him to come out. Sometimes he had left on some job by the time she got there and she came home, beside herself, questioning everybody. It had been her habit to come

111

twice a week to change her library books. Now she did not come. She stopped reading. At the Temple Rooms, when Iris and I saw her, she sat out holding hands with Bill Williams and rubbing her head into his shoulder, her eyes watching him the whole time. We went to speak to them and Constance asked:

'Is Hilda here tonight?'

'I haven't seen her.'

'She's a whore,' said Constance in a loud voice. We thought she was drunk.

It was a funny thing, Mr Fulmino said to me, to call a woman a whore. He spoke as one opposed to funny things.

'If they'd listened to me,' he said, 'I could have stopped all this trouble. I offered to get her a job in the council office, but' – he rolled his eyes – 'Mrs F. wouldn't have it, and while we were arguing about it, Bill Williams acted double quick. It's all because this Mr Gloster didn't turn up.'

Mr Fulmino spoke wistfully. He was, he conveyed, in the middle of a family battle; indeed, he had a genuine black eye the day we talked about this. Mrs Fulmino's emotions were in her arms.

This was a bad period for Mr Fulmino because he had committed a folly. He had chosen this moment to make a personal triumph. He had got himself promoted to a much better job at the council offices and one entitling him to a pension. He had become a genuine official. To have promoted a man who had the folly to bring home a rich whore with two names, so causing the robbery and death of her mother, and to have let her break Constance's heart was, in Mrs Fulmino's words, a crime. Naturally, Mr Fulmino regarded his mistakes as mere errors of routine and even part of his training for his new position.

'Oh, well,' he said when we finished our tea and got up to pay the bill. 'It's the British taxpayer that pays.' He was heading for politics. I have heard it said, years later, that if he had had a better start in life he would have gone to the top of the administration. It is a tragic calling.

If Hilda was sinister to Constance and Mrs Fulmino, she made a different impression on young Mrs Draper. To call a woman a whore was neither here nor there to her. Up north where she came from, people were saying that sort of thing all day long as they scrubbed floors or cleaned windows or did the washing. The word gave them energy and made things come up cleaner and whiter. Good money was earned hard; easy money went easy. To young

Mrs Draper, Hilda seemed 'a bit simple', but she had gone to work, she earned her living. Cut off from the rest of the Draper family, Hilda made friends with this couple. Hilda went with them on Saturdays to the zoo with the children. They were looking at a pair of monkeys. One of them was dozing and its companion was awake, pestering and annoying it. The children laughed. But when they moved on to another cage, Hilda said sulkily:

'That's one thing. Bill Williams won't be here. He pesters me all the time.'

'He won't if you don't let him,' said young Mrs Draper.

'I'm going to give my notice if he doesn't stop,' said Hilda. She hunched a shoulder and looked round at the animals.

'I can't understand a girl like Constance taking up with him. He's not on her level. And he's mean. He doesn't give her anything. I asked if he gave her that clip, but she said it was Gran's. Well, if a man doesn't give you anything he doesn't value you. I mean she's a well-read girl.'

'There's more ways than one of being stupid,' said young Mrs Draper.

'I wonder she doesn't see,' said Hilda. 'He's not delivering for the firm. When he's got the van out, he's doing something on the side. When I came home with him, there was stuff at the back. And he keeps on asking how much things cost. He offered to sell my bracelet.'

'You'd get a better price in a shop if you're in need,' said young Mrs Draper.

'She'd better not be with him if he gets stopped on the road,' said Jack, joining in. 'You wouldn't sell that. Your husband gave it to you.'

'No, Mr Faulkner,' said Hilda, pulling out her arm and admiring it.

Jack was silent and disappointed; then he cheered up. 'You ought to have married that earl you were always talking about when you were a girl. Do you remember?' he said.

'Earls – they're a lazy lot,' said young Mrs Draper.

'I did, Jack,' said Hilda. 'They were as good as earls, both of them.'

And to young Mrs Draper she said: 'They wouldn't let another man look at me. I felt like a woman with both of them.'

'I've nowt against that if you've got the time,' said young Mrs Draper. She saw that Hilda was glum.

'Let's go back and look at the giraffes. Perhaps Mr Faulkner will come for you now Mr Gloster hasn't,' young Mrs Draper said.

'They were friends,' said Hilda.

'Oh, they knew each other!' said young Mrs Draper. 'I thought you just . . . met them . . .'

'No, I didn't meet them together, but they were friends.'

'Yes. Jack had a friend, didn't you?' said Mrs Draper, remembering.

'That's right,' said Jack. He winked at Hilda. 'Neck and neck, it was.' And then he laughed outright.

'I remember something about Bill Williams. He came out with us one Saturday and you should have seen his face when we threw the fish back in the water.'

'We always throw them back,' said young Mrs Draper, taking her husband's arm, proudly.

'Wanted to sell them or something. Black-market perch!'

'He thinks I've got dollars,' said Hilda.

'No, fancy, Jack – Mr Gloster and Mr Faulkner being friends. Well, that's nice.'

And she looked sentimentally at Hilda.

'She's brooding,' young Mrs Draper said to Mrs Fulmino after this visit to the zoo. 'She won't say anything.' Mrs Fulmino said she had better not or *she* might say something. 'She knows what I think. I never thought much of Bill Williams, but he served his country. She didn't.'

'She earns her living,' said Mrs Draper.

'Like we all do,' said Mrs Fulmino. 'And it's not men, men, men all day long with you and me.'

'One's enough,' said young Mrs Draper, 'with two children round your feet.'

'She doesn't come near me,' said Mrs Fulmino.

'No,' Mr Fulmino said sadly, 'after all we've done.'

They used to laugh at me when I went dancing with Iris at the Temple Rooms. We had not been there for more than a month and Iris said:

'He can't stop staring at the band.'

She was right. The beams of the spotlights put red, green, violet, and orange tents on the hundreds of dancers. It was like the Arabian nights. When we got there, Ted Custer's band was already at it like cats on dustbins and tearing their guts out. The pianist had a very thin neck and kept wagging his head as if he were ga-ga; if his head had fallen off he would have caught it in one of his crazy hands and popped it on again without losing a note; the trumpet player had thick eyebrows that went higher and higher as he tried and failed to burst; the drummers looked doped; the saxophone went at it like a man in bed with a girl who had purposely left the door open. I remember them all, especially the thin-lipped man, very white-faced, with the double bass drawing his bow at knee level, to and fro, slowly, sinful. They all whispered, nodded, and rocked together, telling dirty stories until bang, bang, bang, the dancers went faster and faster, the row hit the ceiling or died out with the wheeze of a balloon. I was entranced.

'Don't look as though you're going to kill someone,' Iris said.

That shows how wrong people are. I was full of love and wanted to cry.

After four dances I went off to the soft-drink bar and there the first person I saw was Bill Williams. He was wearing a plum-coloured suit and a red and silver tie and he stood, with his dark hair, dusty-looking and spouting forward as if he had just got out of bed and was ducking his head on the way to the lavatory.

'All the family here?' he asked, looking all round.

'No,' I said. 'Just Iris and me.'

He went on looking round him.

'I thought you only came Saturdays,' he said suspiciously. He had a couple of friends with him, two men who became restless on their feet, as if they were dancing, when I came up.

'Oh,' said Bill Williams. Then he said, 'Nicky pokey doda – that's Japanese, pal, for "keep your mouth shut". Anyone say anything, you never see me. I'm at Laxton, get me? Bill Williams? He's on night shift. You must be barmy. Okay? Seeing you,' he said. 'No sign of Connie.'

And he walked off. His new friends went a step or two after him, dancing on their pointed shoes, and then stopped. They twizzled round, tapping their feet, looking all round the room until he had got to the carpeted stairs at the end of the hall. I got my squash, and when I turned round, the two men had gone also.

But before Bill Williams had got to the top of the stairs he turned round to look at the dancers in one corner. There was Hilda. She was dancing with a young West Indian. When I got back to our table she was very near.

I have said that Hilda's face was eventless. It was now in a tranced state, looking from side to side, to the floor, in the quick turns of the dance, swinging round, stepping back, stepping forward. The West Indian had a long jacket on. His knees were often nearly bent double as though he were going to do some trick of crawling towards her; then he recovered himself and turned his back as if he had never met her and was dancing with someone else. If Hilda's face was eventless, it was the event itself, it was the dance.

She saw us when the dance was over and came to our table breathlessly. She was astonished to see us. To me she said, 'And fancy you!' She did not laugh or even smile when she looked at me. I don't know how to describe her look. It was dead. It had no expression. It had nothing. Or rather, by the smallest twitch of a muscle, it became nothing. Her face had the nakedness of a body. She saw that I was deaf to what Iris was saying. Then she smiled, and in doing that, she covered herself.

'I am with friends over there' – we could not tell who the friends were – and then she leaned towards us and whispered:

'Bill Williams is here, too.'

Iris exclaimed.

'He's watching me,' Hilda said.

'I saw him,' I said. 'He's gone.'

Hilda stood up, frowning. 'Are you sure? Did you see him? How long ago?'

I said it was about five minutes before.

She stood as I remember her standing in Mrs Draper's room on the first day when she arrived and was kissing everyone. It was a peculiar stance because she usually stood so passively; a stance of action and, I now saw, a stance of plain fright. One leg was planted forward and bent at the knee like a runner at the start and one arm was raised and bent at the elbow, the elbow pushed out beyond her body. Her mouth was open and her deep-set yellow eyes seemed to darken and look tired.

'He was with some friends,' I said, and, looking back at the bar: 'They've gone now.'

'Hah!' It was the sound of a gasp of breath. Then suddenly the fright went and she shrugged her shoulders and talked and laughed to all of us. Soon she went over to her friends, the coloured man and a white couple; she must have got some money or the ticket for her handbag from one of them, for presently we saw her walking quickly to the cloakroom.

Iris went on dancing. We must have stayed another half an hour, and when we were leaving we were surprised to see Hilda waiting in the foyer. She said to me:

'His car has gone.'

'Whose?'

'Bill Williams's car.'

'Has he got a car?' Iris said.

'Oh, it's not his,' said Hilda. 'It's gone. That's something. Will you take me home? I don't want to go alone. They followed me here.'

She looked at all of us. She was frightened.

I said: 'Iris and I will take you on our way.'

'Don't make me late,' said Iris crossly. 'You know what Mum is.' I promised. 'Did you come with him?'

'No, with someone else,' Hilda said, looking nervously at the revolving glass door. 'Are you sure his friends went too? What did they look like?'

I tried to describe them.

'I've only seen the short one,' she said, frowning, 'somewhere.'

It was only a quarter of an hour's ride at that hour of the night. We walked out of the Temple Rooms and across the main road to the bus stop and waited under the lights that made our faces corpse-like. I have always liked the hard and sequined sheen of London streets at night, their empty-dockyard look. The cars came down them like rats. The red trolley bus came up at last, and when we got in, Hilda sat between us. The busload of people stared at her and I am not surprised. I have not said what she looked like – the hair built up high, her bright-green wrap and red dress. I don't know how you would describe such clothes. But the people were not staring at her clothes. They were staring at her eyebrows. I said before that her face was an extension of her nakedness. I say it again. Those eyebrows of hers were painted and looked like the only things she had on; they were like a pair of beetles with turned-up tails that had settled on her forehead. People laughed behind their hands and two or three youths at the front of the bus turned round and guffawed and jostled and whistled; but Hilda, remember, was not a girl of sixteen gone silly, but a woman, hard rather than soft in the face, and the effect was one of exposure, just as a mask has the effect of exposing. We did not talk, but when the trolley arm thumped two or three times at a street junction, Hilda said with a sigh: 'Bump! Bump! Bump!' She was thinking of her childhood in old Mrs Draper's room at Hincham Street. We got off the bus a quarter of a mile further on, and as she was stepping off, Hilda said, speaking of what was in her mind, I suppose, during the ride:

'Shinji had a gold wristwatch with a gold strap and a golden pen. They had gone when he was killed. They must have cost him a hundred pounds. Someone must have stolen them and sold them.

'I reported it,' Hilda said. 'I needed the money. That is what you had to do – sell. Everything. I had to eat.'

And the stare from her mask of a face stated something of her life that her strangeness had concealed from us. We walked up the street.

She went on talking about that watch and how particular Shinji was about his clothes, especially his shirts. All his collars had to be starched, she said. Those had gone too, she said. And his glasses. And his two gold rings. She walked very quickly between us. We got to the corner of her street. She stopped and looked down it.

'Bill Williams's van!' she said.

About thirty houses down the street we could indeed see a small van standing.

'He's waiting for me,' she said.

It was hard to know whether she was frightened or whether she was reckoning, but my heart jumped. She made us stand still and watch. 'My room's in the front,' she said. I crossed over to the other side of the street and then came back.

'The light is on,' I said.

'He's inside,' she said.

'Shall I go and see?' I said.

'Go,' said Iris to me.

Hilda held my wrist. 'No,' she said.

'There are two people, I think, in the front garden,' I said.

'I'm going home with you,' Hilda said to Iris decisively. She rushed off and we had to race after her. We crossed two or three streets to the Fulminos' house. Mrs Fulmino let us in.

'Now, now, Hilda, keep your hair on. Kill you? Why should he? This is England, this isn't China . . .'

Mr Fulmino's face showed his agony. His mouth collapsed, his eyes went hard. He looked frantic with appeal. Then he turned his back on us, marched into the parlour, and shouted as if he were calling across four lines of traffic:

'Turn the wireless off.'

We followed him into the room. Mrs Fulmino, in the suddenly silent room, looked like a fortress waiting for a flag to fall.

We all started talking at once.

'Can I stay with you tonight?' she said. 'Bill Williams has broken into my house. I can't go there. He'll kill me.' The flag fell.

'Japan,' said Mrs Fulmino, disposing of her husband with her first shot. Then she turned to Hilda; her voice was coldly rich and rumbling. 'You've always a home here, as you well know, Hilda,' she went on, giving a very unhomely sound to the word. 'And,' she said, glancing at her neat curtains, to anyone who might be in ambush outside the window, 'if anyone tries to kill you, they will have to kill' – she nodded to her husband – 'Ted and me first. What have you been doing?'

'I was down at the Temple. Not with Bill Williams,' said Hilda. 'He was watching me. He's always watching me.'

'Now, look here, Hilda, why should Bill Williams want to kill you? Have you encouraged him?'

'Don't be a fool,' shouted Mrs Fulmino.

'She knows what I mean. Listen to me, Hilda. What's going on between you and Bill Williams? Constance is upset, we all know.'

'Oh, keep your big mouth shut,' said Mrs Fulmino to her husband. 'Of course she's encouraged him. Hilda's a woman, isn't she? I encouraged *you*, didn't I?'

'I know how to look after myself,' said Hilda, 'but I don't like that van outside the house at this hour of night. I didn't speak to him at the dance.'

'Hilda's thinking of the police,' ventured Mr Fulmino.

'Police!' said Mrs Fulmino. 'Do you know what's in the van?'

'No,' said Hilda. 'And that's what I don't want to know. I don't want him on my doorstep. Or his friends. He had two with him. Harry saw them.'

Mrs Fulmino considered.

'I'm glad you've come to us. I wish you'd come to us in the first place,' she said. Then she commanded Mr Fulmino: 'You go up there at once with Harry,' she said, 'and tell that man to leave Hilda alone. Go on, now. I can't understand you' – she indicated me – 'running off like that, leaving a van there. If you don't go, I'll go myself. I'm not afraid of a paltry . . . a paltry . . . What does he call himself? You go up.'

Mrs Fulmino was as good a judge of the possibilities of an emotional situation as any woman on earth: this was her moment.

119

She wanted us out of the house and Hilda to herself.

We obeyed.

Mr Fulmino and I left the house. He looked tired. He was too tired to put on his jacket. He went out in his shirt-sleeves.

'Up and down we go, in and out, up and down,' said Mr Fulmino. 'First it's Constance, now it's Hilda. And the pubs are closed.'

'There you are, what did I tell you?' said Mr Fulmino when we got to Hilda's street. 'No van, no sign of it, is there? You're a witness. We'll go up and see, all the same.'

Mr Fulmino had been alarmed, but now his confidence came back. He gave me a wink and a nod when we got to the house.

'Leave it to me,' he said. 'You wait here.'

I heard him knock at the door and after a time knock again. Then I heard a woman's voice. He was talking a long time. He came away.

He was silent for a long time as we walked. At last he said:

'That beats all. I didn't say anything. I didn't say who I was. I didn't let on. I just asked to see Hilda. "Oh," says the landlady, "she's out." "Oh," I said, "that's a surprise." I didn't give a name. "Out, you say? When will she be back?" "I don't know," said the landlady, and this is it, Harry – "she's paid her rent and given her notice. She's leaving first thing in the morning," the landlady said. "They came for the luggage this evening." Harry,' said Mr Fulmino, 'did Hilda say anything about leaving?'

'No.'

'Bill Williams came for her luggage.'

We marched on. Or rather we went stealthily along like two men walking a steel wire of suspicion. We almost lost our balance when two cats ran across the street and set up howls in a garden, as if they were howling us down. Mr Fulmino stopped.

'Harry!' he said. 'She's playing us up. She's going off with Bill Williams.'

'But she's frightened of him. She said he was going to kill her.'

'I'm not surprised,' said Mr Fulmino. 'She's been playing him up. Who was she with at the dance hall? She's played everyone up. Of course she's frightened of him. You bet. I'm sorry for anyone getting mixed up with Bill Williams: he'll knock some sense into her. He's rough. So was her father.'

'Bill Williams might have just dropped by to have a word,' I said.

Mr Fulmino marched forward again.

'Funny word at half past eleven at night,' said Mr Fulmino. 'When I think of all that correspondence, all those forms – War Office, State Department, United Nations – we did, it's been a poor turnout. You might say' – he paused for an image sufficiently devastating – 'a waste of paper, a ruddy wanton waste of precious paper.'

We got back to his house. I have never mentioned I believe that it had an iron gate that howled and a clipped privet hedge like a moustache to the tiny garden.

We opened the gate, the gate howled, Mrs Fulmino's nose appeared at the curtains.

'Don't say a word,' said Mr Fulmino.

Tea – the room smelt of that, of course. Mrs Fulmino had made some while we were out. She looked as though she had eaten something, too. A titbit. They all looked sorry for Mr Fulmino and me. And Mrs Fulmino *had* had a titbit! In fact I know from Iris that the only thing Mrs Fulmino had got out of Hilda was the news that she had had a postcard from Mr Faulkner from Chicago. He was on the move.

'Well?' said Mrs Fulmino.

'It's all right, Hilda,' said Mr Fulmino coldly. 'They've gone.'

'There,' said Mrs Fulmino, patting Hilda's hand.

'Hilda,' said Mr Fulmino, 'I've been straight with you. I want you to be straight with me. What's going on between you and Bill Williams? . . .'

'Hilda's told me,' Mrs Fulmino said.

'I asked Hilda, not you,' said Mr Fulmino to his wife, who was so surprised that she went very white instead of her usual purple.

'Hilda, come on. You come round here saying he's going to kill you. Then they tell me you've given your notice up there.'

'She told me that. I think she's done the right thing,' Mrs Fulmino said.

'And did you tell her why you gave your notice?' asked Mr Fulmino.

'She's given her notice at the factory, too,' said Mrs Fulmino.

'Why?' said Mr Fulmino.

Hilda did not answer.

'You are going off with Bill Williams, aren't you?'

'Ted!' Hilda gave one of her rare laughs.

'What's this?' cried Mrs Fulmino. 'Have you been deceiving me?

Deceit I can't stand, Hilda.'

'Of course she is,' said Mr Fulmino. 'She's paid her rent. He's collected her luggage this evening. Where is it to be? Monte Carlo? Oh, it's all right, sit down.' Mr Fulmino waved Mrs Fulmino back. 'They had a row at the dance this evening.'

But Hilda was on her feet.

'My luggage?' she cried, holding her bag with both hands to her bosom as we had seen her do once before when she was cornered. 'Who has touched my luggage?'

I thought she was going to strike Mr Fulmino.

'The dirty thief. Who let him in? Who let him take it? Where's he gone?'

She was moving to the door. We were stupefied.

'Bill Williams!' she shouted. Her rage made those artificial eyebrows look comical, and I expected her to pick them off and throw them at us. 'Bill Williams, I'm talking about. Who let that bloody war hero in? That bitch up there . . .'

'Hilda,' said Mrs Fulmino. 'We don't want language.

'You fool,' said Mrs Fulmino in her lowest, most floor-sweeping voice to her husband. 'What have you been and done? You've let Bill Williams get away with all those cases, all her clothes, everything. You let that spiv strip her.'

'Go off with Bill Williams!' Hilda laughed. 'My husband was an officer.

'I knew he was after something. I thought it was dollars,' she said suddenly.

She came back from the door and sat down at the table and sobbed.

'Two hundred and fifty pounds he's got,' she sobbed. It was a sight to see Hilda weeping. We could not speak.

'It's all I had,' she said.

We watched Hilda. The painted eyebrows made the grimace of her weeping horrible. There was not one of us who was not shocked. There was in all of us a sympathy we knew how to express but it was halted – as by a fascination – with the sight of her ruin. We could not help contrasting her triumphant arrival with her state at this moment. It was as if we had at last got her with us as we had, months before, expected her to be. Perhaps she read our thoughts. She looked up at us and she had the expression of a person seeing for the first time. It was like an inspection.

'You're a mean lot, a mean respectable lot,' she said. 'I

remember you. I remember when I was a girl. What was it Mr Singh said? I can't remember – he was clever – oh well, leave it, leave it. When I saw that little room they put my mother in, I could have cried. No sun. No warmth in it. You just wanted someone to pity. I remember it. And your faces. The only thing that was nice was' – she sobbed and laughed for a moment – 'the bump, bump, bump, the trolley.' She said loudly: 'There's only one human being in the whole crew – Jack Draper. I don't wonder he sees more in fish.'

She looked at me scornfully. 'Your brother – he was nice,' she said. 'Round the park at night! That was love.'

'Hilda,' said Mrs Fulmino without anger. 'We've done our best for you. If we've made mistakes I hope you haven't. We haven't had your life. You talk about ships that pass in the night. I don't know what you mean, but I can tell you there are no ships in this house. Only Ted.'

'That's right,' said Mr Fulmino quietly too. 'You're overwrought.'

'Father,' said Mrs Fulmino, 'hadn't you better tell the police?'

'Yes, yes, dear,' agreed Mr Fulmino. 'We'd better get in touch with the authorities.'

'Police,' said Hilda, laughing in their faces. 'Oh, God. Don't worry about that. You've got one in every house in this country.'

She picked up her bag, still laughing, and went to the door.

'Police,' she was saying, 'that's ripe.'

'Hilda, you're not to go out in the street looking like that,' said Mrs Fulmino.

'I'd better go with her,' said Mr Fulmino.

'I'll go,' I said. They were glad to let me.

It is ten years since I walked with Hilda to her lodgings. I shall not forget it, and the warm, dead, rubbery city night. It is frightening to walk with a woman who has been robbed and wronged. Her eyes were half closed as though she was reckoning as she walked. I had to pull her back onto the pavement or she would have gone flat into a passing car. The only thing she said to me was:

'They took Shinji's rings as well.'

Her room was on the ground floor. It had a divan and a not very clean dark-green cover on it. A pair of shoes were sticking out from under it. There was a plain deal cupboard and she went straight to it. Two dresses were left. The rest were gone. She went to a table and opened the drawer. It was empty except for some letters.

I stood not knowing what to say. She seemed surprised to see me there still.

'He's cleared the lot,' she said vacantly. Then she seemed to realize that she was staring at me without seeing me, for she lowered her angry shoulders.

'We'll get them back,' I said.

'How?' she said, mocking me, but not unkindly.

'I will,' I said. 'Don't be upset.'

'You!' she said.

'Yes, I will,' I said.

I wanted to say more. I wanted to touch her. But I couldn't. The ruin had made her untouchable.

'What are you going to do?' I said.

'Don't worry about me,' she said. 'I'm okey doke. You're different from your brother. You don't remember those days. I told Mr Gloster about him. Come to that, Mr Faulker too. They took it naturally. That was a fault of Mr Singh' – she never called him by his Christian name – jealousy.'

She kicked off her shoes and sat down on the cheap divan and frowned at the noise it made and she laughed.

'One day in Bombay I got homesick and he asked me what I was thinking about, and I was green, I just said, "Sid Fraser's neck. It had a mole on it." You should have seen his face. He wouldn't talk to me for a week. It's a funny thing about those countries. Some people might rave about them, I didn't see anything to them.'

She got up.

'You go now,' she said, laughing. 'I must have been in love.'

I dreamt about Hilda's face all night, and in the morning I wouldn't have been surprised to see London had been burned out to a cinder. But the next night her face did not come and I had to think about it. Further and further it went, and became a little less every day, and I did not seem to notice when someone said Bill Williams had been picked up by the police, or when Constance had been found half dead with aspirins, and when, in both cases, Mr Fulmino told me he had to 'give assistance in the identification', for Hilda had gone. She left the day after I took her to her room. Where she went no one knew. We guessed. We imagined. Across water, I thought, getting further and further away, in very fine clothes and very beautiful. France, Mr Fulmino thought, or possibly Italy. Africa, even. New York, San Francisco, Tokyo, Bombay, Singapore. Where? Even one day six months after she had left, when he came to the library and showed me a postcard he had had from her, the first message, it did not say where she was and someone in the post office had pulled off the stamp. It was a picture of Hilda herself on a seat in a park, sitting with Mr Faulkner and Mr Gloster. You wouldn't recognize her.

But Mr Gloster's book came out. Oh yes. It wasn't about Japan or India or anything like that. It was about us.

A Debt of Honour

Mrs Thwaite got off the bus and turned the street corner, holding her key ready to get into her new flat. Every evening, for months now, she was eager to be home, to sniff the new paint and to stand looking at the place, wanting to put her arms around it. She ran up the stairs, let herself in and threw her old fur coat on the divan in the sitting-room, put the gas poker in the fire and drew the curtains which did not quite meet, as if – by her intention – they had been carelessly made so as to let a little of the shabby Square and a stare of the London night into the flat. Then she went into the bedroom to see to the bed she had left unmade all day; almost at once she was sitting on the edge of it laughing, and telephoning to dear Argo – as she called him – to ask him to guess what she had found: his wristwatch under the pillow! And in a lower voice: 'Oh, wasn't it lovely?'

She was swinging the wristwatch in her hand, Argo was saying he would be round, as usual, at half past seven, and just then the doorbell gave its ugly little buzz.

'Hold on a minute, darling. Someone at the door.'

When she got there, still dangling the watch, she saw a man with his hat in his hand standing there, a short figure with silver hair brushed straight back and wearing a silvery-grey overcoat. His face looked like a white blown-out paper bag. Long afterwards, she used to say he had the gleam of a simulacrum or a ghost. Then the paper bag burst and he showed his teeth in a smile. She instantly hid the watch in her hand. The teeth were unmistakable. They were not false teeth, but they looked false because they were not closely set; they were a squad of slight gaps, but the gaps were a little wider now than they had been nine years ago in her short married life. Her husband was standing there.

'Hullo, Phoebe,' he said, and with that he marched in past her across the little hall into the middle of the sitting-room. He was much shorter than she was. She was a very tall woman and instinctively she stooped (as she had always done with him) when she followed the gleam of his overcoat into the room.

He turned round and said at once, 'Nice place. Newly decorated. Frankly I didn't expect it in a neighbourhood like this.' He marked at once his disappointment with her. After nine years, he conveyed, she had gone downhill.

Mrs Thwaite could not speak. A long scream seemed to be frozen in her. The shock was that, but for his teeth, Charles Thwaite was unrecognizable. She might have been telling lies about him for years.

He had been a bland little dark-haired pastry-fed fellow from the North when they had first gone off together, her fur-coat collar sticking to the frost inside the window of the night train. What a winter that was! He was a printer but had given that up, a man full of spit when he talked and his black eyebrows going up like a pair of swallows. The kind of man who said, 'When I believe in a thing I put everything on it. Every penny in the bank, house, wife, children, shirt – everything.' Even in those days his face had been blown out. Under the eyebrows there were a pair of earnest eyes fixed in an upward look, the eyes of a chapel-going boy caught with a finger in the jam pot; under them were curious, almost burned scoops of brown shadow – trademarks of a fate, the stamp of something saleable, they had seemed to her. She could never stop wondering what it was.

But now, as she stood there with her hands clenched upon Argo's watch, and looking down at her husband she saw that age had efficiently smoothed him. The stains were like hard coins; his effect was metallic. He looked collected, brisk and dangerous. And she had forgotten how short he was, for her Argo was a tall man.

What came back to her in the instant of this meeting was the forgotten, indignant girlish feeling – which living with Argo had cured her of – that she was lanky and exposed. If she had been able to move from where she was standing, she would have made a grab at her coat in order to cover herself and especially to cover her legs. She had the sensation that she had become a joke once more.

For, to start with, her height had always been ridiculous. Men passing in the street turned to look up at her, startled and in dismay, and she was not a beauty; her features were too large. And jokes attract jokes; only stumpy little fellows – her husband was one of them – ever looked twice at her, and with a very trying ambition or imprudence puffing themselves out. She had had the timid impression that men were playing a game of hide-and-seek round her, as boys playing in the street sometimes did. This made her either stare crushingly over their heads or droop like a schoolgirl. In her early meetings with Charles she had got into the habit of finding a long low seat and at a distance from him where she could sit down, draw up her long legs, and listen, an equal on the same level. Being tall had turned her into a believer and listener, listening being a kind of apology; and she would look covertly down at her legs with a reproach that would change to a pout; for – when she had been with Charles – she was proud of the dashing ways in which her legs had rushed her into this love affair and marriage and had disorganized her life. Nowadays, even with Argo, she would look at her legs with fear, thinking they belonged to someone else or were a pair of fine but disobedient daughters. What they had done to her, carrying her into that story of disaster! But the story itself, of course, had attracted Argo, and she had come to feel that she had the grand distinction of being a woman to whom happiness and good luck were pettily irrelevant.

One Sunday Argo looked at his feet sticking out boastfully from the bottom of the bed and said, 'Don't talk nonsense. Nine years is a long time. Your husband may be dead.'

'Oh, no!' She still wanted her husband to be alive – and not for the sake of vengeance only.

'If he were, we could get married. Anyway, the law could presume death . . .' Argo went on.

She was happy with Argo after years of misery. But she wouldn't have *that*. She did not quite want to lose the gamble, the incompleteness – so breathlessly necessary to her – of her history.

History was standing there at ease, looking at the flat.

'I've given you a surprise,' her husband said.

'What do you want?' She could speak at last. 'I can't have you here. I have people coming.'

'May I take my coat off?' he said, and taking it off put it down beside hers on the divan.

'New?' he said, looking at hers.

At that her courage returned to her. 'That's the only thing you left me with,' she almost shouted and was ready to fly at him if he touched it. For in this frightened moment the coat, poor as it was, seemed to be her whole life – more than the office she worked in, more than Argo, more than her marriage. It was older than any of them. It was herself; it had known her longer than anything in the room.

Her husband turned away contemptuously, and while she unclenched her hands and put Argo's watch on the mantelpiece he sat down in an armchair. As his eyes stripped the room, he said, 'Very nice, very nice. Kitchen there, I suppose. Bedroom through the door. Is that rug Chinese? I'm glad you're comfortable. You haven't changed. I must say you're very beautiful. By the way, I think you've left the telephone off in the bedroom – I can hear it crackling. Put it back, will you? Naturally I want to say a few words to explain . . .'

'Say a few words' – how the phrase came back! There would be a lot of phrases.

She was determined not to sit down. The crackling of the telephone made her feel Argo was near.

An explanation! She wanted to demand it, rage for it, but she could not get the word out. She wanted to say, 'Why? I just want to know why you left me. Don't imagine that I care, but I have a right to know. Then go.'

'I found the address in the telephone book,' he said, noting how well the world was organized. Then he made his announcement. It was more; it was a pronouncement, made with the modesty of an enormous benefactor.

'I have come back to you,' he said.

'Argo, he's going to kill us,' she wanted to cry out, and moved behind her chair for protection. The chair, the whole room seemed to be sickening, sliding her into the past, out of the window, into the flat she and her husband had had – the flat at the top of the small hotel she had bought for them with her own money – to those terrible scenes, to the sight of him opening the drawers of her desk in the little office, to that morning when she had unlocked the safe and found all the money gone – eight hundred pounds. Two of her father's pictures as well – but he left the frames behind! – and with them the foreign girl in Number 7. She held the chair tightly to hold the drifting room still. There he sat and, by merely sitting, occupied more and more of the room until only the few inches where she stood belonged to her. Nothing in the room, the pictures, the tables, the curtains, chairs, not even the little blue pot on the mantelpiece with pencils in it, came to her help. She would have to pass him to shout from the window.

129

'You are a very beautiful woman,' he said in his praying, looking-skyward manner, but now the look was obsequious. 'You are the most beautiful woman I have ever known. You are the only woman I have been in love with.'

'You cannot break into my life like this,' she said. 'I have never been taken in by flattery.'

'You are my wife,' he said.

'I am certainly not,' she said. 'What is it you want?' And then she felt tears on her cheeks; ruinous tears, for this was the moment when he would get up and put his arms round her and she would be helpless. She tried to glare through her tears and did not know that this made her look brilliant, savage and frightening, indeed not helpless at all.

'I want *you*,' he said, without moving.

It was so wonderfully meaningless to hear him say this. Her tears stopped and she laughed loudly and did not know she was laughing. The laughter chased the fright out of her body. The joke restored her. That was the rock she stood on: a joke had been played on her when she was a child. She must put up with being a collection of jokes, but this joke was so preposterous that it drove all the others out. She could feel her laughter swallowing the little man up. It was wonderful also to see how her laughter took him aback and actually confused him so that he raised his chin and held up his hand to silence her. He had a small white hand. She remembered that this meant he was going to make a moral statement.

'I am a man who has sacrificed himself to women,' he said, pointing to this as one of his unanswerable historic benefactions.

Another of his sayings! How she longed for Argo to come in and hear it. Charles was a man who had always gone blandly back to first principles. Argo never quite believed the things she said about her marriage.

'"I am a man who has sacrificed myself to women" – it was one of the first things he said to me when I met him. It was that cold winter, the worst winter for seventeen years – I told you my coat stuck to the frosty window in the train – shall I tell you about it? You don't mind? There was an election. He was – you won't believe, but it is true, it was one of his "ideas" – standing for Parliament. Can you see him? He was standing as an Independent Republican – can you imagine it – in England, in the twentieth century! A gang of youths went round his meetings and sang

"Yankee Doodle" when he was speaking. Of course he didn't get in. He got two hundred and thirty-five votes. He lost his deposit. There was a row in the town. They were afraid he was splitting the vote. Splitting – he didn't even touch it! I was staying at the only hotel, a freezing-cold place. I had gone north to see my brother, who was in hospital. Charles was always rushing in and out of the hotel, telephoning to his wife in London, who was behaving very well – they were being divorced but she was holding the divorce up to stop the scandal – and to his mistress, who was very tiresome. You could hear what he was saying all over the hotel because the telephone box was in the hall and he came out of it one evening and knew that I had heard. I was sitting wrapped up because I couldn't get near the fire.

' "You look warm," he said, and then he looked back at the telephone box and said – well, that sentence. His set piece: "I've sacrificied myself to women." '

(What she did not tell Argo was that the remark was true. The scoundrel had 'sacrificed' himself to women and that this was what had attracted her. She really had wanted in her naive way to be the chief altar.)

'I told my brother when I went to the hospital. He said, "He certainly doesn't sacrifice himself to anything else." '

Now as he sat there in her flat and her laughter was warming her, Charles went one better.

'Everything I have done,' he said, 'I have done for you. Oh, yes, I have. You have been the cause and inspiration of it. You are the only woman who has influenced my mind. You changed my life. You were the making of me. When I went to South America . . .'

'Not South America!' she said. 'Really! Think of something better than that. Monte Carlo. Cape Town.'

'Buenos Aires first of all, then Chile – the women have beautiful voices there: it is the German and English influence,' he went on, taking no notice of her. 'Colombia – there's a culture that has collapsed. Bolivia, an extreme revolutionary situation, Ecuador, Indians in trilby hats looking like wood. I met the President. I've just come from Barranquilla. I flew.'

'With that girl?' she said. A bad slip. He'd be the first to note her jealousy and mock it.

'Of course not,' he said. He had a flat Yorkshire accent. 'I have always been interested, as you know, in the Republican experience. You remember the book you made me write?'

'You didn't write it!' she said.

It was fabulous, after nine years, to see again his blank, baby-like effrontery, to hear his humourless, energetic innocence. He wasn't joking: the scoundrel *was* seriously, very seriously interested in republics! In a moment, he would tell her that he had stolen eight hundred pounds from her and deserted her out of a pure, disinterested passion for a harem of republics in South America!

The dangerous thing was that he was manoeuvring her back to the time of their marriage. She could feel him re-creating their marriage, against all her resistance, so that the room was filling with it. She feared he would wait for some sign of weakness, and then leap at her; the little man was very strong. She saw that he was already undressing the years from her and taking her back to her naked folly and credulity; until, if she was not careful, he would bring her to the point of the old passion. The Republic – it was incredible to remember – he had caught her with it.

It was a shock to her to remember what she had been like in those days – for example, how for years she had nursed her mother and had no friends. Every day she pushed the old lady down the sea front in her chair. Men looked at her or rather stepped back in half-grinning astonishment at a young woman so lanky, so gauche and shy and craving. The sight of her scared them. When her mother died, she got away to London. She had a little money which she knew she must be careful with and tried to find a job. Living alone, she simply read. Her tallness made her crave, and since no man came near she craved for an idea.

So she was divided now between impatience and the memory he was rousing in her. She saw a half-empty room in that Town Hall in the North and him on the platform, uttering the fatal word, at the end of his speech. Republic – all men equal – equal height, perhaps that was the lure? – and so on: Republic. Quoted Plato even: 'Love the beloved Republic.' In a small industrial town, the war just over, snow frozen to black rock for six weeks on the pavements outside; and the small audience of men just back from the war, breaking up, drifting out, the gang of louts singing their 'Yankee Doodle'. She saw herself, exalted, turning in anger on the bored people around who were so rudely getting out and clattering their chairs; and gazing back at him, she signalled to him, 'Yes, yes, yes, the Republic!' And when he lost, she really felt *she* would be the Republic! She told Argo about this. 'How I hate that word now. I can't even bear to read it in the newspapers. I was mad,' she said. Argo could be very nasty sometimes. He said, 'I thought it was only men who went to bed with an idea.'

She had to admit, as she listened, that dear Argo knew little about women. She had had two triumphs in her marriage: she had won a short period of power over her husband by persuading him that if he thought so much about republics he ought to write a book about them. She put her money into a small London hotel and drove him off to the British Museum to write it. If she had thought, she would have seen it was the ideal place for picking up foreign girls; but never mind about that. The other triumph was more important. She had beaten those two women, his wife in London and his mistress who was there in the North working for him. She – and the winter – had frozen them out.

Her husband was now in San Tomás – was it? – and in the midst of the mulatto problem.

'Where did you get the money?' she said coldly.

'Money?' he said. 'I went back to the printing trade.'

It was the first hint of reproach. She had persuaded him to give up that trade. Once she had got him she had been going to turn him into a political thinker. She had always said grandly to her friends: 'He's in politics.' Now she noticed a little colour come to his face and that he was patting his small hand up and down on the arm of the chair in a dismissing way, as he had always done when money was mentioned. She had asked, she knew, the right question: indifference had made her intelligent.

'The heat was awful,' he was saying. 'When you go out into the street it is like a wall standing against you – I was glad you weren't there' – he had the nerve to say – 'it shuts you in. I used to change my clothes four or five times a day . . .'

'Expensive,' she said. 'I couldn't have afforded it.' He ignored this: no irony ever touched him.

'The only air-conditioned place was the casino and the cinema. The printing press was always breaking down. I was doing repairs half the time. I've not much use for casinos but I used to go there to cool off.'

He raised his eyes seriously in the manner of the schoolboy now licking the spoon – who was he raising them to? Some feared schoolmaster, preacher or father? – and she remembered with pleasure that this presaged the utterance of some solemn, earnestly believed untruth.

'I have never been a gambling man,' he said, 'as you know – but there the casino is packed every night. You have to get a permit, of course. Thousands change hands. I used to watch the tables and then go home along the shore road. I used to listen to the sea; you couldn't see the waves, except sometimes a flash of white, like Robin Hood's Bay on a rough night – remember, lass?' – dropping into broad Yorkshire – 'Listen to this. One night when I went to the casino I had a shock: I saw *you*. I could have sworn it was you. You were standing there by one of the tables with a man, some politician: I knew him, the cousin of a man who owned one of the local papers. It was you, tall, beautiful, even the way you do your hair. I shan't forget the look in your eyes when you saw me. I thought: My God. I didn't do the right thing by her. I took her money. I have been a swine. I'll get the money and go back to her. I'll go down on my knees and beg her to take me back. You don't know what remorse is.'

'Oh, so you've come to pay me back?' she said.

'I knew it wasn't you, but it showed how you've haunted my mind every night for the last nine years,' he said. 'I couldn't take my eyes off that woman. She was playing. I went close to her and I played. I followed her play and won. I kept winning. Her husband came and joined us and we were all winning and I thought all the time: This is for her. For her.'

'For whom?' asked Mrs Thwaite.

'For you.'

'Did you sleep with her?'

'You can't sleep with those women. I was sleeping with an Indian girl,' he said impatiently. 'Don't interrupt me. It was for you. And then we started losing. I borrowed from her husband – he was excited like me. We all were. I'm not hiding anything. I lost everything I had. More than I had. A very large sum. I was ruined. Well, people are rich there. There was a thunderstorm that night. I couldn't pay for a taxi. The rain came down in sheets and the lightning was dancing about over the water in the streets. The whole placed looked violet and yellow. I never saw anything like it. I wish you could have seen it. I stood there watching. You could see the sea, waves shooting up high, like hands. I thought, What have I done? What have I done to her?'

'Who?' she said.

'*You.* I thought, My God, suppose she is dead! I've never spent such a night in my life. At the door of the casino I heard that woman's voice. I thought it was yours. I went out. I went searching among the cars.'

'And she wasn't there?'

'I was drenched. I was out in it for half an hour. I didn't know what I was doing.'

'How did you pay back the money?' she said. '*Did* you pay it back?'

'Naturally,' he said with stupendous coldness. 'I had borrowed it from her husband. It was a debt of honour.'

'Oh, honour,' she said. 'And what about the lady?' It shocked her that she felt that not quite conquerable disloyalty of the body when he mentioned the woman.

She had long ago admitted to herself that jealousy had been the foundation of her love for him. At the first sight of him in that hotel in the North, she had seen him sitting with three or four people near the fire. There was a cheerful vulgar fellow with drink-pimpled skin – his agent, no doubt. There was an elderly man who looked at him with a noble pathos and two grey-haired women who watched him with mistrust. They were talking about the meeting in the Town Hall and one said, 'In this weather there'll be a poor turnout.' A very thin young woman in a cheap black coat came in from the street kicking snow off her shoes and carrying a roll of posters which were packed in wet newspaper. Her stockings were wet. He went up to her quickly, scowling (but smiling too), and after taking the posters, he led the wretched girl by the arm not to the fire, but to the street door, speaking in a loud official voice about canvassing in the morning; at the door, he lowered his voice and said, shadily and sharply and intimately, looking into her defiant eyes: 'I told you not to come here.'

An intrigue! She heard it. A flame of desire to be part of it, and of jealousy, went through her, a sudden hungry jealousy. She had never felt like this until then, not at any rate since she was a child. She felt she had been set alight.

Now, nine years later, she said, 'I don't know what you want. Why you're telling me this tale. It's all a lot of lies, I know. I never wanted to see you again, but now I'm glad you've come. Where are you staying? Give me your address. I want a divorce. I shall divorce you. It's not a question of what you want. It is what I want now.'

She was fighting for Argo and herself.

'Just a moment,' he said. 'I haven't come to talk about divorces.'

'You can't stay here,' she said. 'I won't have you here.'

'Let me speak,' he said. 'I haven't come here to quarrel.' And shyly – how extraordinary to see him shy, for once – 'I want your help. I know I must have made you suffer. You have something rare in a woman: integrity. You tell the truth.'

'I'm certainly not going to help you about anything,' she said.

'Divorce,' he said. 'Of course, I hadn't thought of that. It's natural, of course: I'm a Catholic, but still . . .'

'Yes?' she said.

He tapped one of his teeth with his finger thoughtfully.

'Let's get to the point. I'm in a little difficulty. Let me go on with what I was telling you. I've saved the printers a great deal of money – the firm in San Tomás. They were going to be forced to buy a new machine in New York, but I told them to wait, to let me work on it. That's what I've been doing. I've saved them thousands. These South Americans are no good at machinery. They just say, "Buy a new one" – like that. They've got piles of money.'

Perhaps he *has* come to pay me back? Is that the idea – buying me back? she wondered. The white hand went slowly up and down on the arm of the chair.

'What is it you really came here for?' she said reasonably. A full smile of pure, admiring pleasure made his white skin shine, a smile of polite tenderness and discreet thanks.

'I want twelve hundred pounds,' he said. 'I had to borrow it from the firm to pay that man – as I told you just now. I want it rather quickly. The accountants come in at the end of the month. I want you to lend it to me.'

He said this in a voice of stupefying kindness and seriousness, as if he were at last atoning for what he had done, unasked, in real friendship and generosity. It would, he gravely conveyed, be the most binding of ties. It would remind her of those happy days – ah, he too wished them to return! – when he had had money from her before. He conveyed that she would instinctively see the beauty of it – that he had come to her, the perfect woman, a second time; that she was, in truth, the only woman in his life, that of no one else would he ask such a thing.

And the strange part of it was that as she gasped at the preposterous suggestion and was about to turn on him a small thrill went through her. She was a prudent woman, if anything a shade mean about the little money left to her, but he brought back to her the sense of unreason and danger that had turned her head when she had first met him. He brought back to her the excitement of the fact that he was – as she knew – unbelievable. It enhanced some quality in her own character: she was the kind of woman to whom mad things happened. And she saw herself running to Argo with her astounded mouth open and telling him, telling everyone. And, for a few seconds, she admired her husband. Twelve hundred pounds! In nine years his price had gone up!

'You stole twelve hundred pounds?' she said. 'Fiddled the books?'

'Stole?' he said. 'I don't like to hear you use a word like that. I borrowed it. I told you. It was a debt of honour.'

'You must be mad to think I would be such a fool. I haven't got twelve hundred pence. I've never had such a sum in my life.'

Stole! Arrest! Prison! Perhaps he had already been in prison? Was that why he was so pale? She was not frightened, but his case seemed to taint herself.

'But you can raise it,' he said briskly, dismissing what she said.

'I work for my living. I go to my office every day. I've had to. Where do you think I could get the money?'

There was a silence filled by the enormity of that sum. He was proposing to come here, settle here, and tie that huge debt to her neck, like a boulder. Argo must turn him out. He must come and turn him out.

'I was very sorry to see – when was it? I saw an English paper over there – that your aunt had died,' he said in a changed and sorrowful voice. 'I think you *can* raise it,' he said suddenly, coolly threatening.

'Ah!' She woke up to it. '*Now* I see why you have come back to me. You thought I had just come into her money. You saw it in the paper and you came rushing back.'

'It was coming to you. I remember you telling me. And I am your husband.'

'Well, if you want to know, it did *not* come to me. When you left me, she blamed me, not you. But do you think even if I had, I would give it to you? She left it to her brother.'

'Your brother?' he said sharply.

'No, *her* brother,' she said triumphantly.

'Is that true?'

'Ask him.'

He took out a pocket notebook and turned over a page or two. 'The one in Newcastle?' he said. He had obviously been checking her family.

'You got nothing at all?' he said.

'No.' And this time she really did shout at him.

'I can't believe it,' he said curtly. 'I just can't believe you can have been such a damn fool.'

She could see he was affronted and injured. 'I offer you everything,' he seemed to say. 'And you give me nothing.'

There was a sneer on his papery face. The sneer, she knew, concealed desperation and she felt the beginnings of pity, but she knew now – what she had not known nine years ago – that this pity was dangerous to her; he would see it at once, and he would come towards her, grip her arm, press upon her, ignoring her mind but moving her body. He had a secret knowledge of her, for he had been the first to know that her body was wild.

She was frightened of herself. She had to get out of the room, but each room was a trap. The only hope was the most dangerous room: the bedroom. It had a telephone in it.

'Argo, Argo, please come. Hurry,' she was crying to herself. But her husband did not step towards her, he went over to the mantelpiece and he was looking at something on it. He picked up Argo's watch. She moved to snatch it from him, but he closed his hand. She actually touched his sleeve: touching him made her feel sick.

'Beginning all over again, I see,' he said. 'Does he live here?'

'That's my business.'

'Snug under the coat?' He laughed and let the watch dangle by its strap. She was blushing, and almost gasping, fearing he would now attack her.

But he did not.

'You realize, I hope, that you are committing adultery?' he said stiffly. 'I don't understand what has happened to you. You seem to have gone to pieces since I left you. I was surprised to see you living in a low-class district like this – what is he? Some clerk? You can't even manage your own money. Left it to her brother! How often I've told you – you never had any sense of reality. And by the way,' he went on angrily, 'if you had not left all your money in the safe, none of this would have happened. You should have paid it into the bank.'

'He is not a clerk,' she said. 'He's a professor in the university.'

He laughed. 'That's what you wanted me to be. You are just romantic. The printing trade was not good enough for the lady.'

'I didn't want you to be a professor.'

'Write about the Republic. What republic?' he jeered.

'It was your idea,' she said.

'Sitting in the British Museum, coming round to you for my money. I sacrificed myself to you. Why? I have always sacrificed myself to women. I loved you and you ruined me.'

'I don't believe you ever went to the museum,' she said, 'except to pick up girls.'

'To think of my wife committing adultery!' he exclaimed. And – she could not believe her luck – he put the watch back on the mantelpiece with disgust. He ran his fingers on the mantelpiece and saw dust on his fingers.

'You don't look after your things. There are cigarette burns on this mantelpiece. I don't like your pictures – one, two, three nudes. Indecent. I don't like that. I suppose that is how you see yourself.'

He mooched about the flat and pointed at the frayed lining of her coat on the divan.

'That ought to have gone to the furrier's,' he said. He stared at the coat and his temper quietened.

'It was a very cold winter, wasn't it?' he said. 'The worst winter for years. It cut down the canvassing, I couldn't get people to the polls. It wasn't that, though. Do you know what lost me that election? Your coat. That was a true thing Jenny said after you saw me tell her to keep out of the hotel. "We're up against those hard-faced Tory women in their mink." '

'It's not mink,' she said.

'Whatever it is. Of course she was suspicious. But that wasn't the trouble. She was just freezing cold. Her room was an icebox. She couldn't stand it. She was coughing even when we started. She went off.'

He suddenly laughed. 'She was frozen out. You had a fur coat, she hadn't. Your coat won. Fourteen Purser Street, do you remember? – it kept us warm, after she had gone?'

'She didn't go for a week,' she said. After all, she had sat her rival out. But Mrs Thwaite was watching for her opportunity. How to get past him and snatch back the watch? She saw her chance and grabbed it. He was taken by surprise and did not, as she feared he would, catch her arm.

'I feel sick,' she said and rushed with her handkerchief to her mouth to the bedroom.

She sat on the bed and heard the crackling of the telephone

receiver, which she had not replaced. She put it back and then took it off to dial Argo's number, looking in fear at the door she had left open.

'Darling, darling. Charles has come back. My husband, yes. Yes, he's here. I am frightened. He won't go. I can't get him out. Please come, he's horrible. What are we to do? No, if he sees you he will go. Call the police? How can I do that? He's my husband. He's in the sitting-room, he's moving about. I can hear him. Get a taxi. I'm afraid. I'm afraid of what he'll do. I can't tell you. Get him out? How can I? Oh, please, thank you, darling, thank you, I love you . . . He's horrible.'

She put down the telephone and moved away, standing with her back to the window. If he came into the bedroom she would open the window and jump out. But he did not. He seemed to be picking up things in the sitting-room. She went back boldly now. He had picked up her coat and was holding it by the shoulders.

'Get out. Put that down. Get out. I have my own life now. I never want to set eyes on you again. I'm going to divorce you. I have rung for help.' She was astonished by her own power and the firmness of her voice.

'Yes, I heard you,' he said. He had put his overcoat on again.

'And put my coat down!' she shouted again.

They stood outstaring each other. He was half smiling with passing admiration.

'No,' he said, 'I'll take it with me. A souvenir. Goodbye.'

She was flabbergasted to see him walk past her out of the room, open the door of the flat and go downstairs with her coat on his arm.

'Charles.' She ran to the door. 'Charles.' He went on.

'Charles, come back here.'

She was down at the street door, but already yards away, crossing the street. He looked not so much ridiculous as luxurious carrying the coat. She felt he was carrying her off too. She shouted again but not loudly, for she did not want people to stare at them in the street. She was about to run after him when she saw the blind man who lived further down come tapping towards her with his white stick. He slowed down, sensing disturbance. He paused like a judgement. And in her pause of indecision, she saw her husband get to the bus stop and instantly, as if he were in league with buses and had bribed one or got it by some magic, a bus floated up beside him and he was off on it.

He had taken the last thing she had, he had taken twenty years of her life with him. She watched the bus until it was out of sight.

She went back to the door and she climbed the stairs and got inside and looked at the room where he had stood; it seemed to her that it was stripped of everything, even of herself. It seemed to her that she was not there. 'Why are women so mad about furs?' he had once said to her. 'To keep warm? No, so that they can feel naked.' One of his 'sayings'. But that was what she felt as she sat waiting for Argo to come; her husband had taken her nakedness.

Argo found her sitting there. When she stopped crying in his arms he said, 'He won't come back. I'll get on to the police.'

'Oh, no.'

'He'll sell it. He was just after anything he could get. He might get fifty pounds for it.'

'He was very jealous. He used to try to make me say some man had given it to me.' She was proud of that. 'He's a funny man. He may not sell it.'

'You mean,' said Argo who, though placating, had his nasty side, 'he'll give it to one of his girlfriends?'

'No,' she said angrily. She was not going to have that! An old feeling, one she used to have, that there was something stupid about very tall men like Argo, came back to her.

In the night she lay awake, wondering where her husband was. Perhaps everything he said had been true: that he did love her more than any of the women he had known, that he did want to be forgiven, that she had been hard and was to blame from the beginning. He had remembered Purser Street. Perhaps he *had* been in South America. She wished she had had twelve hundred pounds to give him. She would never forgive herself if he was arrested. Then her thoughts changed and she fell into thinking in his melodramatic way: he had taken her youth, her naked youth, with him and left her an old woman. She got up in the night and went to her mirror to see how much grey there was in her hair. She was not very much younger than Charles. She went back cold to bed and put her arms round Argo.

'Love me. Love me,' she said.

She hated Argo for saying that her husband had given the coat to another woman.

In the morning she went to her office.

'Someone walked into my flat yesterday and stole my fur coat,' she said.

What a life, they said, that poor woman has had; something is always happening to her. It never ends. But they saw her eyes shining brilliantly within their gloom.

The Diver

In a side street on the Right Bank of the Seine where the river divides at the Île de la Cité, there is a yellow and red brick building shared by a firm of leather merchants. When I was twenty I worked there. The hours were long, the pay was low, and the place smelt of cigarettes and boots. I hated it. I had come to Paris to be a writer, but my money had run out and in this office I had to stick. How often I looked across the river, envying the free lives of the artists and writers on the other bank. Being English, I was the joke of the office. The sight of my fat pink innocent face and fair hair made everyone laugh; my accent was bad, for I could not pronounce a full 'o'; worst of all, like a fool, I not only admitted I hadn't got a mistress, but boasted about it. To the office boys this news was extravagant. It doubled them up. It was a favourite trick of theirs, and even of the salesman, a man called Claudel with whom I had to work, to call me to the street door at lunchtime and then, if any girl or woman passed, they would give me a punch and shout, 'How much to sleep with this one? Twenty? Forty? A hundred?' I put on a grin, but to tell the truth, a sheet of glass seemed to come down between me and any female I saw.

About one woman the lads did not play this game. She was a woman between thirty and forty, I suppose: Mme Chamson, who kept the menders and cleaners down the street. You could hear her heels as she came, half running, to see Claudel, with jackets and trousers of his on her arm. He had some arrangement with her for getting his suits cleaned and repaired on the cheap. In return – well, there was a lot of talk. She had sinfully tinted hair built up high over arching, exclaiming eyebrows, hard as varnish, and when she got near our door there was always a joke coming out of the side of her mouth. She would bounce into the office in her tight navy-blue skirt, call the boys and Claudel together, shake hands with them all, and tell them some tale which always ended, with a dirty glance round, in whispering. Then she stood back and shouted with laughter. I was never in this secret circle, and if I happened to grin she gave me a severe and offended look and marched out scowling. One day, when one of her tales was over, she called back from the door, 'Standing all day in that gallery with all those naked women, he comes home done for, finished.'

The office boys squeezed each other with pleasure. She was talking about her husband, who was an attendant at the Louvre, a small moist-looking fellow whom we sometimes saw with her, a man fond of fishing, whose breath smelt of white wine. Because of her arrangement with Claudel, and her stories, she was a very respected woman.

I did not like Mme Chamson: she looked to me like some predatory bird; but I could not take my eyes off her pushing bosom and her crooked mouth. I was afraid of her tongue. She caught on quickly to the fact that I was the office joke, but when they told her that on top of this I wanted to be a writer, any curiosity she had about me was finished. 'I could tell him a tale,' she said. For her I didn't exist. She didn't even bother to shake hands with me.

Streets and avenues in Paris are named after writers; there are statues to poets, novelists, and dramatists, making gestures to the birds, nurse-maids, and children in the gardens. How was it these men had become famous? How had they begun? For myself, it was impossible to begin. I walked about packed with stories, but when I sat in cafés or in my room with a pen in my hand and a bare sheet of paper before me, I could not touch it. I seemed to swell in the head, the chest, the arms and legs, as if I were trying to heave an enormous load onto the page and could not move. The portentous moment had not yet come. And there was another reason. The longer I worked in the leather trade and talked to the office boys, the typists there and Claudel, the more I acquired a double personality: when I left the office and walked to the Métro, I practised French to myself. In this bizarre language the stories inside me flared up, I was acting and speaking them as I walked, often in the subjunctive, but when I sat before my paper the English language closed its sullen mouth.

And what were these stories? Impossible to say. I would set off in the morning and see the grey, ill-painted buildings of the older quarters leaning together like people, their shutters thrown back, so that the open windows looked like black and empty eyes. In the mornings the bedding was thrown over the sills to air and hung out, wagging like tongues about what goes on in the night between men and women. The houses looked sunken-shouldered, exhausted, by what they told; and crowning the city was the church of Sacré-Coeur, very white, standing like some dry Byzantine bird, to my mind hollow-eyed and without conscience, presiding over the habits of the flesh and – to judge by what I read in newspapers – its crimes also; its murders, rapes, its shootings for jealousy and robbery. As my French improved, the secrets of Paris grew worse. It amazed me that the crowds I saw on the street had survived the night, and many indeed looked as sleepless as the houses.

After I had been a little more than a year in Paris – fourteen months, in fact – a drama broke the monotonous life of our office. A consignment of dressed skins had been sent to us from Rouen. It had been sent by barge – not the usual method in our business. The barge was an old one and was carrying a mixed cargo, and within a few hundred yards from our warehouse it was rammed and sunk one misty morning by a Dutch boat taking the wrong channel. The manager, the whole office, especially Claudel, who saw his commission go to the bottom, were outraged. Fortunately the barge had gone down slowly near the bank, close to us; the water was not too deep. A crane was brought down on another barge to the water's edge and soon, in an exciting week, a diver was let down to salvage what he could. Claudel and I had to go to the quay, and if a bale of our stuff came up, we had to get it into the warehouse and see what the damage was.

Anything to get out of the office. For me the diver was the hero of the week. He stood in his round helmet and suit on a wide tray of wood hanging from four chains, and then the motor spat, the chains rattled, and down he went with great dignity under the water. While the diver was underwater, Claudel would be reckoning his commission over again – would it be calculated only on the sale price or on what was saved? 'Five bales so far,' he would mutter fanatically. 'One and a half per cent.' His teeth and his eyes were agitated with changing figures. I, in imagination, was groping in the gloom of the riverbed with my hero. Then we'd step forward; the diver was coming up. Claudel would hold my arm as the man appeared with a tray of sodden bales and the brown water streaming off them. He would step off the plank onto the barge, where the crane was installed, and look like a swollen frog. A workman unscrewed his helmet, the visor was raised, and then we saw the young diver's rosy, cheerful face. A workman lit a cigarette and gave it to him, and out of the helmet came a long surprising jet of smoke. There was always a crowd watching from the quay wall, and when he did this, they all smiled and many laughed. 'See that?' they would say. 'He is having a puff.' And the diver grinned and waved to the crowd.

Our job was to grab the stuff. Claudel would check the numbers of the bales on his list. Then we saw them wheeled to our warehouse, dripping all the way, and there I had to hang up the skins on poles. It was like hanging up drowned animals – even, I thought, human beings.

On the Friday afternoon of that week, when everyone was tired and even the crowd looking down from the street wall had thinned to next to nothing, Claudel and I were still down on the quay waiting for the last load. The diver had come up. We were seeing him for the last time before the weekend. I was waiting to watch what I had not yet seen: how he got out of his suit. I walked down nearer at the quay's edge to get a good view. Claudel shouted to me to get on with the job, and as he shouted I heard a whizzing noise above my head and then felt a large, heavy slopping lump hit me on the shoulders. I turned round and, the next thing, I was flying in the air, arms outspread with wonder. Paris turned upside down. A second later, I crashed into cold darkness, water was running up my legs swallowing me. I had fallen into the river.

The wall of the quay was not high. In a couple of strokes I came up spitting mud and caught an iron ring on the quay wall. Two men pulled my hands. Everyone was laughing as I climbed out.

I stood there drenched and mud-smeared, with straw in my hair, pouring water into a puddle that came from me, getting larger and larger.

'Didn't you hear me shout?' said Claudel.

Laughing and arguing, two or three men led me to the shelter of the wall, where I began to wring out my jacket and shirt and squeeze the water out of my trousers. It was a warm day, and I stood in the sun and saw my trousers steam and heard my shoes squelch.

'Give him a hot rum,' someone said. Claudel was torn between looking after our few bales left on the quay and taking me across the street to a bar. But checking the numbers and muttering a few more figures to himself, he decided to enjoy the drama and go with me. He called out that we'd be back in a minute.

We got to the bar and Claudel saw to it that my arrival was a sensation. Always nagging at me in the office, he was now proud of me.

'He fell into the river. He nearly drowned. I warned him. I shouted. Didn't I?'

The one or two customers admired me. The barman brought me the rum. I could not get my hand into my pocket because it was wet.

'You pay me tomorrow,' said Claudel, putting a coin on the counter.

'Drink it quickly,' said the barman.

I was laughing and explaining now.

'One moment he was on dry land, the next he was flying in the air, then plonk in the water. Three elements,' said Claudel.

'Only fire is missing,' said the barman.

They argued about how many elements there were. A whole history of swimming feats, drowning stories, bodies found, murders in the Seine sprung up. Someone said the morgue used to be full of corpses. And then an argument started, as it sometimes did in this part of Paris, about the exact date at which the morgue was moved from the island. I joined in, but my teeth had begun to chatter.

'Another rum,' the barman said.

And then I felt a hand fingering my jacket and my trousers. It was the hand of Mme Chamson. She had been down at the quay once or twice during the week to have a word with Claudel. She had seen what had happened.

'He ought to go home and change into dry things at once,' she said in a firm voice. 'You ought to take him home.'

'I can't do that. We've left five bales on the quay,' said Claudel.

'He can't go back,' said Mme Chamson. 'He's shivering.'

I sneezed.

'You'll catch pneumonia,' she said. And to Claudel: 'You ought to have kept an eye on him. He might have drowned.'

She was very stern with him.

'Where do you live?' she said to me.

I told her.

'It will take you an hour,' she said.

Everyone was silent before the decisive voice of Mme Chamson.

'Come with me to the shop,' she ordered and pulled me brusquely by the arm. She led me out of the bar and said as we walked away, my boots squeaking and squelching, 'That man

147

thinks of nothing but money. Who'd pay for your funeral? Not he!'

Twice, as she got me, her prisoner, past the shops, she called out to people at their doors, 'They nearly let him drown.'

Three girls used to sit mending in the window of her shop and behind them was usually a man pressing clothes. But it was half past six now and the shop was closed. Everyone had gone. I was relieved. This place had disturbed me. When I first went to work for our firm Claudel had told me he could fix me up with one of the mending girls: if we shared a room it would halve our expenses and she could cook and look after my clothes. That was what started the office joke about my not having a mistress. When we got to the shop Mme Chamson led me down a passage, inside which was muggy with the smell of dozens of dresses and suits hanging there, into a dim parlour beyond. It looked out onto the smeared grey wall of a courtyard.

'Stay here,' said Mme Chamson, planting me by a sofa. 'Don't sit on it in those wet things. Take them off.'

I took off my jacket.

'No. Don't wring it. Give it to me. I'll get a towel.'

I started drying my hair.

'All of them,' she said.

Mme Chamson looked shorter in her room, her hair looked duller, her eyebrows less dramatic. I had never really seen her closely. She had become a plain, domestic woman; her mouth had straightened. There was not a joke in her. Her bosom filled with management. The rumour that she was Claudel's mistress was obviously an office tale.

'I'll see what I can find for you. You can't wear these.'

I waited for her to leave the room and then I took off my shirt and dried my chest, picking off the bits of straw from the river that had stuck to my skin. She came back.

'Off with your trousers, I said. Give them to me. What size are they?'

My head went into the towel. I pretended not to hear. I could not bring myself to undress before Mme Chamson. But while I hesitated she bent down and her sharp fingernails were at my belt.

'I'll do it,' I said anxiously.

Our hands touched and our fingers mixed as I unhitched my belt. Impatiently she began on my buttons, but I pushed her hands away.

She stood back, blank-faced and peremptory in her stare. It was the blankness of her face, her indifference to me, her ordinary womanliness, the touch of her practical fingers that left me without defence. She was not the ribald, coquettish, dangerous woman who came wagging her hips to our office, not one of my Paris fantasies of sex and danger. She was simply a woman. The realization of this was disastrous to me. An unbelievable change was throbbing in my body. It was uncontrollable. My eyes angrily, helplessly asked her to go away. She stood there implacably. I half turned, bending to conceal my enormity as I lowered my trousers, but as I lowered them inch by inch so the throbbing manifestation increased. I got my foot out of one leg but my shoe caught in the other. On one leg I tried to dance my other trouser leg off. The towel slipped and I glanced at her in red-faced angry appeal. My trouble was only too clear. I was stiff with terror. I was almost in tears.

The change in Mme Chamson was quick. From busy indifference she went to anger.

'Young man,' she said. 'Cover yourself. How dare you. What indecency. How dare you insult me!'

'I'm sorry. I couldn't help . . .' I said.

Mme Chamson's bosom became a bellows puffing outrage.

'What manners,' she said. 'I am not one of your tarts. I am a respectable woman. This is what I get for helping you. What would your parents say? If my husband were here!'

She had got my trousers in her hand. The shoe that had betrayed me now fell out of the leg to the floor.

She bent down coolly and picked it up.

'In any case,' she said, and now I saw for the first time this afternoon the strange twist of her mouth return to her as she nodded at my now concealing towel, 'that is nothing to boast about.'

My blush had gone. I was nearly fainting. I felt the curious, brainless stupidity that goes with the state nature had put me in. A miracle saved me. I sneezed and then sneezed again – the second time with force.

'What did I tell you!' said Mme Chamson, passing now to angry self-congratulation. She flounced out to the passage that led to the shop, and coming back with a pair of trousers she threw them at me and, red in the face, said, 'Try those. If they don't fit I don't know what you'll do. I'll get a shirt,' and she went past me to the door of the room beyond, saying, 'You can thank your lucky stars my husband has gone fishing.'

I heard her muttering as she opened drawers. She did not return. There was silence.

In the airless little salon, looking out (as if it were a cell in which I was caught) on the stained smeared grey wall of the courtyard, the silence lengthened. It began to seem that Mme Chamson had shut herself away in her disgust and was going to have no more to do with me. I saw a chance of getting out, but she had taken away my wet clothes. I pulled on the pair of trousers she had thrown; they were too long but I could tuck them in. I should look an even bigger fool if I went out in the street dressed only in these. What was Mme Chamson doing? Was she torturing me? Fortunately my impromptu disorder had passed. I stood listening. I studied the mantelpiece, where I saw what I supposed was a photograph of Mme Chamson as a girl in the veil of her first communion. Presently I heard a voice. 'Young man,' she called harshly, 'do you expect me to wait on you. Come and fetch your things.'

Putting on a polite and apologetic look, I went to the inner door which led into a short passage only a yard long. She was not there.

'In here,' she said curtly.

I pushed the next door open. This room was dim also, and the first thing I saw was the end of a bed and in the corner a chair with a dark skirt on it and a stocking hanging from the arm, and on the floor a pair of shoes, one of them on its side. Then suddenly I saw at the end of the bed a pair of bare feet. I looked at the toes; how had they got there? And then I saw: without a stitch of clothing on her, Mme Chamson – but could this naked body be she? – was lying on the bed, her chin propped on her hand, her lips parted as they always were when she came in on the point of laughing to the office, but now with no sound coming from them; her eyes, generally wide open, were now half closed, watching me with the stillness of some large white cat. I looked away and then I saw two other large brown eyes gazing at me, two other faces: her breasts. It was the first time in my life I had ever seen a naked woman, and it astonished me to see the rise of a haunch, the slope of her belly and the black hair like a moustache beneath it. Mme Chamson's face was always strongly made up with some almost orange colour, and it astonished me to see how white her body was from the neck down – not the white of statues, but some sallow colour of white and shadow, marked at the waist by the tightness of the clothes she

150

had taken off. I had thought of her as old, but she was not: her body was young and idle.

The sight of her transfixed me. It did not stir me. I simply stood there gaping. My heart seemed to have stopped. I wanted to rush from the room, but I could not. She was so very near. My horror must have been on my face, but she seemed not to notice that, but simply stared at me. There was a small movement of her lips and I dreaded that she was going to laugh, but she did not; slowly she closed her lips and said at last between her teeth in a voice low and mocking: 'Is this the first time you have seen a woman?'

And after she said this a sad look came into her face.

I could not answer.

She lay on her back and put out her hand and smiled fully. 'Well?' she said. And she moved her hips.

'I,' I began, but I could not go on. All the fantasies of my walks about Paris as I practised French rushed into my head. This was the secret of all those open windows of Paris, of the vulture-like head of Sacré-Coeur looking down on it. In a room like this, with a wardrobe in the corner and with clothes thrown on a chair, was enacted – what? Everything – but above all, to my panicking mind, the crimes I read about in the newspapers. I was desperate as her hand went out.

'You have never seen a woman before?' she said again.

I moved a little and out of reach of her hand I said fiercely, 'Yes, I have.' I was amazed at myself.

'Ah!' she said, and when I did not answer, she laughed. 'Where was that? Who was she?'

It was her laughter, so dreaded by me, that released something in me. I said something terrible. The talk of the morgue at the bar jumped into my head.

I said coldly, 'She was dead. In London.'

'Oh my God,' said Mme Chamson, sitting up and pulling at the coverlet, but it was caught and she could only cover her feet.

It was her turn to be frightened. Across my brain, newspaper headlines were tapping out.

'She was murdered,' I said. I hesitated. I was playing for time. Then it came out. 'She was strangled.'

'Oh, no!' she said, and she pulled the coverlet violently up with both hands until she had got some of it to her breast.

'I saw her,' I said. 'On her bed.'

'You *saw* her. *How* did you see her?' she said. 'Where was this?'

Suddenly the story sprang out of me, it unrolled as I spoke.

It was in London, I said. In our street. The woman was a neighbour of ours, we knew her well. She used to pass our window every morning on her way up from the bank.

'She was robbed,' said Mme Chamson. Her mouth buckled with horror.

I saw I had caught her.

'Yes,' I said. 'She kept a shop.'

'Oh my God, my God,' said Mme Chamson, looking at the door behind me, then anxiously round the room.

It was a sweetshop, I said, where we bought our papers too.

'Killed in her shop,' groaned Mme Chamson. 'Where was her husband?'

'No,' I said, 'in her bedroom at the back. Her husband was out at work all day and this man must have been watching for him to go. Well, we knew he did. He was the laundryman. He used to go in there twice a week. She'd been carrying on with him. She was lying there with her head on one side and a scarf twisted round her neck.'

Mme Chamson dropped the coverlet and hid her face in her hands, then she lowered them and said suspiciously, 'But how did *you* see her like this?'

'Well,' I said, 'it happened like this. My little sister had been whining after breakfast and wouldn't eat anything and Mother said, "That kid will drive me out of my mind. Go up to Mrs Blake's" – that was her name – "and get her a bar of chocolate, milk chocolate, no nuts, she only spits them out." And Mother said, "You may as well tell her we don't want any papers after Friday because we're going to Brighton. Wait, I haven't finished yet – here, take this money and pay the bill. Don't forget that, you forgot last year, and the papers were littering up my hall. We owe for a month." '

Mme Chamson nodded at this detail. She had forgotten she was naked. She was the shopkeeper and she glanced again at the door as if listening for some customer to come in.

'I went up to the shop and there was no one there when I got in – '

'A woman alone!' said Mme Chamson.

'So I called, "Mrs Blake," but there was no answer. I went to the inner door and called up a small flight of stairs, "Mrs Blake" – Mother had been on at me as I said, about paying the bill. So I went up.'

'You went up?' said Mme Chamson, shocked.

'I'd often been up there with Mother, once when she was ill. We knew the family. Well – there she was. As I said, lying on the bed, naked, strangled, dead.'

Mme Chamson gazed at me. She looked me slowly up and down from my hair, then my face and then down my body to my feet. I had come barefooted into the room. And then she looked at my bare arms, until she came to my hands. She gazed at these as if she had never seen hands before. I rubbed them on my trousers, for she confused me.

'Is this true?' she accused me.

'Yes,' I said, 'I opened the door and there – ' ·

'How old were you?'

I hadn't thought of that, but I quickly decided.

'Twelve,' I said.

Mme Chamson gave a deep sigh. She had been sitting taut, holding her breath. It was a sigh in which I could detect just a twinge of disappointment. I felt my story had lost its hold.

'I ran home,' I said quickly, 'and said to my mother, "Someone has killed Mrs Blake." Mother didn't believe me. She couldn't realize it. I had to tell her again and again. "Go and see for yourself," I said.'

'Naturally,' said Mme Chamson. 'You were only a child.'

'We rang the police,' I said.

At the word 'police' Mme Chamson groaned peacefully.

'There is a woman in the laundry,' she said, 'who was in the hospital with eight stitches in her head. She had been struck with an iron. But that was her husband. The police did nothing. But what does my husband do? He stands in the Louvre all day. Then he goes fishing, like this evening. Anyone,' she said vehemently to me, 'could break in here.'

She was looking through me into some imagined scene and it was a long time before she came out of it. Then she saw her own bare shoulder and, pouting, she said slowly, 'Is it true you were only twelve?'

'Yes.'

She studied me for a long time.

'You poor boy,' she said. 'Your poor mother.'

And she put her hand to my arm and let her hand slide down it gently to my wrist; then she put out her other hand to my other arm and took that hand, too, as the coverlet slipped a little from her. She looked at my hands and lowered her head. Then she looked up slyly at me.

'*You* didn't do it, did you?' she said.

'No,' I said indignantly, pulling back my hands, but she held on to them. My story vanished from my head.

'It is a bad memory,' she said. She looked to me once more as she had looked when I had first come into her salon soaking wet – a soft, ordinary, decent woman. My blood began to throb.

'You must forget about it,' she said. And then, after a long pause, she pulled me to her. I was done for, lying on the bed.

'Ah,' she laughed, pulling at my trousers. 'The diver's come up again. Forget. Forget.'

And there was no more laughter. Once, in the height of our struggle, I caught sight of her eyes: the pupils had disappeared and there were only the blind whites and she cried out, 'Kill me. Kill me,' from her twisted mouth.

Afterwards we lay talking. She asked me if it was true I was going to be a writer, and when I said yes, she said, 'You want talent for that. Stay where you are. It's a good firm. Claudel has been there for twelve years. And now get up. My little husband will be back.'

She got off the bed. Quickly she gave me a complete suit belonging to one of her customers, a grey one, the jacket rather tight.

'It suits you,' she said. 'Get a grey one next time.'

I was looking at myself in a mirror when her husband came in, carrying his fishing rod and basket. He did not seem surprised. She picked up my sodden clothes and rushed angrily at him. 'Look at these. Soaked. That fool Claudel let this boy fall in the river. He brought him here.'

Her husband simply stared.

'And where have you been? Leaving me alone like this,' she carried on. 'Anyone could break in. This boy saw a woman strangled in her bed in London. She had a shop. Isn't that it? A man came in and murdered her. What d'you say to that?'

Her husband stepped back and looked with appeal at me.

'Did you catch anything?' she said to him, still accusing.

'No,' said her husband.

'Well, not like me,' she said, mocking me. 'I caught this one.'

'Will you have a drop of something?' said her husband.

'No, he won't,' said Mme Chamson. 'He'd better go straight home to bed.'

So we shook hands. M Chamson let me out through the shop door while Mme Chamson called down the passage to me, 'Bring the suit back tomorrow. It belongs to a customer.'

Everything was changed for me after this. At the office I was a hero.

'Is it true that you saw a murder?' the office boys said.

And when Mme Chamson came along and I gave her back the suit, she said, 'Ah, here he is – my fish.'

And then boldly: 'When are you coming to collect your things?'

And then she went over to whisper to Claudel and ran out.

'You know what she said just now,' said Claudel to me, looking very shrewd. 'She said, "I am afraid of that young Englishman. Have you seen his hands?" '

Did You Invite Me?

Rachel first met Gilbert at David and Sarah's, or it may have been at Richard and Phoebe's – she could not remember – but she did remember that he stood like a touchy exclamation mark and talked in a shotgun manner about his dog. His talk jumped, so that she got confused: the dog was his wife's dog but was he talking about his dog or his wife? He blinked very fast when he talked of either. Then she remembered what David (or maybe Richard) had told her. His wife was dead. Rachel had a dog, too, but Gilbert was not interested.

The bond between all of them was that they owned small white stuccoed houses, not quite alike – hers alone, for example, had Gothic churchy windows, which, she felt, gave her point – on different sides of the park. Another bond was that they had reached middle life and said nothing about it, except that Gilbert sharply pretended to be younger than the rest of them in order to remind them they had arrived at that time when one year passes into the next unnoticed, leaving among the dregs an insinuation that they had not done what they intended. When this thought struck them they would all – if they had the time – look out of their sedate windows at the park, the tame and once princely oasis where the trees looked womanish on the island in the lake or marched in grave married processions along the avenues in the late summer, or in the winter were starkly widowed. They could watch the weekend crowds or the solitary walkers on the public grass, see the duck flying over in the evenings, hear the keeper's whistle and his shout 'All out!' when the gates of the park closed an hour after sunset; and at night, hearing the animals at the zoo, they could send out silent cries of their own upon the place and evoke their ghosts.

But not Gilbert. His cry would be a howl and audible, a joint howl of himself and this dog he talked about. Rachel had never seen a man so howling naked. Something must be done about him, she thought every time she met him. Two years ago, Sonia, his famous and chancy wife, had died – 'on the stage', the headlines in the London newspapers said, which was nearly true – and his eyes were red-rimmed as if she had died yesterday, his angry face was raw with drink or the unjust marks of guilt and grief. He was a tall man, all bones, and even his wrists coming out of a jacket that was too short in the sleeve seemed to be crying. He had also the look of a man who had decided not to buy another suit in his life, to let cloth go on gleaming with its private malice. It was well known – for he boasted of it himself – that his wife had been much older than he, that they had quarrelled continually, and that he still adored her.

Rachel had been naked, too, in her time when, six or seven years before, she had divorced her husband. Gilbert is 'in the middle of it', she thought. She had been 'through it' and had 'come out of it', and was not hurt or lonely any more and had crowded her life with public troubles. She was married to a newspaper column.

'Something really *must* be done about him,' she at last said out loud to David and Sarah as she tried to follow Gilbert's conversation that was full of traps and false exit lines. For his part, he sniffed when he spoke to them of Rachel.

'Very attractive woman. Very boring. All women are boring. Sonia was a terrible bore sometimes, carrying on, silly cow. What of it? You may have remarked it: I'm a bore. I must go. Thank you, Sarah and David, for inviting me and offering me your friendship. You did invite me, didn't you? You did? I'm glad. I have no friends. The friends Sonia and I invited to the house were hers, not mine. Old codgers. I must go home and feed her dog.'

They watched him go off stiffly, a forty-year-old.

An outsider he was, of course, because of loss. One feels the east wind – she knew that. But it was clear – as she decided to add him to her worries – that he must always have been that. He behaved mechanically, click, click, click, like a puppet or an orphan, homelessness being his vanity. This came out when David had asked Gilbert about his father and mother in her presence. From David's glances at his wife, Rachel knew they had heard what he said many times before. Out came his shot, the long lashes of his childish eyes blinking fast: 'Never met the people.'

He was showing contempt for a wound. He was born' in Singapore, he said. One gathered the birth had no connection with either father or mother. She tried to be intelligent about the city.

'Never saw the place,' he said. The father became a prisoner of the Japanese: the mother took him to India. Rachel tried to be intelligent about India.

'Don't remember it,' he said.

'The old girl', his mother, sent him home to schools and holiday schools. He spent his boyhood in camps and dormitories, his Army life in Nissen huts. He was twenty when he really 'met' his parents. At the sight of him they separated for good.

No further answers. Life had been doled out to him like spoonfuls of medicine, one at a time; he returned the compliment by doing the same and then erected silences like packs of cards, watching people wait for them to fall down.

How, Rachel asked, did the raw young man come to be married to Sonia, an actress at the top of the tree, fifteen years older than he? 'The old girl knew her,' he said; she was his mother's friend. Rachel worried away at it. She saw, correctly, a dramatic woman with a clever mouth, a surrogate mother – but a mother astute in acting the part among her scores of grand and famous friends. Rachel had one or two famous friends too, but he snubbed her with an automatic phrase: 'Never met him.' Or: 'Never met her.'

And then Rachel, again correctly, saw him standing in the doorway of Sonia's drawing-room or bringing drinks perhaps to the crowd, like an uncouth son; those wrists were the wrists of a growing boy who silently jeered at the guests. She heard Sonia dressing him down for his Nissen-hut language and his bad manners – which, however, she encouraged. This was her third marriage and it had to be original. That was the heart of the Gilbert problem: Sonia had invented him; he had no innate right to be what he appeared to be.

So Rachel, who happened to be writing an article on broken homes, asked him to come round and have a drink. He walked across the park from his house to hers. At the door he spoke his usual phrase, 'Thank you for inviting me. You did invite me, didn't you? Well, I thank you. We live on opposite sides of the park. Very convenient. Not too near.'

He came in.

'Your house is white and your dog is white,' he said.

Rachel owned a dog. A very white fox terrier came barking at him on a high, glassy note, showing a ratter's teeth. Rachel was wearing a long pale-blue dress from her throat to the tips of her shoes and led him into the sitting-room. He sank into a soft silky sofa with his knees together and politely inspected her as an interesting collection of bones.

'Shall I ever get up from this?' he said, patting the sofa. 'Silly question. Yes, I shall, of course. I have come, shortly I shall go.' He was mocking someone's manners. Perhaps hers. The fox terrier, which had followed him into the small and sunny room, sniffed long at Gilbert's shoes and his trouser legs and stiffened when he stroked its head. The dog growled.

'Pretty head,' he said. 'I like dogs' heads.' He was staring at Rachel's head. Her hair was smooth, neat and fair.

'I remarked his feet on the hall floor, tick, tick, tick. Your hall must be tiled. Mine is carpeted.'

'Don't be so aggressive, Sam,' said Rachel gravely to the dog.

'Leave him alone,' said Gilbert. 'He can smell Tom, Sonia's bull terrier. That's who you can smell, isn't it? He can smell an enemy.'

'Sam is a problem,' she said. 'Everyone in the street hates you, Sam, don't they? When you get in the garden you bark and bark, people open their windows and shout at you. You chase cats, you killed the Gregory boy's rabbit and bit the Jackson child. You drive the doctor mad. He throws flowerpots at you.'

'Stop nagging the poor animal,' said Gilbert. And to the dog he said, 'Good for you. Be a nuisance. Be yourself. Everyone needs an enemy. Absolutely.'

And he said to himself, She hasn't forgiven her husband. In her long dress she had the composure of the completely smoothed-over person who might well have nothing on underneath. Gilbert appreciated this, but she became prudish and argumentative.

'Why do you say "absolutely",' she said, seeing a distracting point for discussion here. 'Isn't that relative?'

'No,' said Gilbert with enjoyment. He loved a row. 'I've got an enemy at my office. Nasty little creepy fellow. He wants my job. He watches me. There's a new job going – promotion – and he thinks I want it. So he watches. He sits on the other side of the room and is peeing himself with anxiety every time I move. Peeing himself, yes. If I leave the room he goes to the door to see if I'm going to the director's office. If I do he sweats. He makes an excuse to go to the director to see if he can find out what we've been talking about. When I am working on a scheme he comes over to look at it. If I'm working out costs he stares with agony at the layout and the figures. "Is that Jameson's?" He can't contain himself. "No, I'm doing my income tax," I tell him. He's very shocked at my doing that in office hours and goes away relieved. He'll report that to the director. Then a suspicion strikes him when he is halfway back to his desk and he turns round and comes over again panting. He doesn't believe me. "I'm turning inches into centimetres," I say. He still doesn't believe me. Poor silly bugger.' He laughed.

'Wasn't that rather cruel?' she said. 'Why centimetres?'

'Why not? He wants the French job. Boring little man. Boring office. Yes.'

Gilbert constructed one of his long silences. Rachel saw skyscrapers, pagodas, the Eiffel Tower, and this little man creeping up them like an ant. After a while Gilbert went on and the vision collapsed. 'He was the only one who came from the office to Sonia's funeral. He brought his wife – never met her before – and she cried. The only person who did. Yes. He'd never missed a show Sonia was in.'

'So he isn't an enemy. Doesn't that prove my point?' she said solemnly. Gilbert ignored this.

'They'd never met poor Sonia,' he said. And he blinked very fast.

'I never met your wife either, you know,' said Rachel earnestly. She hoped he would describe her; but he described her doctors, the lawyers that assemble after death.

'What a farce,' he said. 'She had a stroke in the theatre. Her words came out backwards. I wrote to her two husbands. Only one replied. The theatre sent her to hospital in an ambulance – the damn fools. If you go to hospital you die of pneumonia, bloody hospital won't give you enough pillows, you lie flat and you can't get your breath. What a farce. Her brother came and talked, one of those fat men. Never liked the fellow.'

She said how terrible it must have been. 'Did she recover her speech? They sometimes do.'

'Asked,' he said, 'for the dog. Called it God.'

He got up suddenly from the sofa.

'There! I got up. I am standing on my feet. I am a bore,' he said. 'I shall go.'

As he left the room the terrier came sniffing at his heels.

'Country dogs. Good ratters. Ought to be on a farm.'

She plunged into a confidence to make him stay longer.

'He used to be a country dog. My husband bought him for me when we lived in the country. I know' – she luxuriated in a worry –

'how important environment is to animals and I was going to let him stay, but when you are living alone in a city like London – well, there are a lot of burglaries here.'

'Why did you divorce your husband?' he asked as he opened the front door. 'I shouldn't have asked. Bad manners. I apologize. I was rude. Sonia was always on to me about that.'

'He went off with a girl at his office,' she said staunchly.

'Silly man,' said Gilbert, looking at the dog. 'Thank you. Goodbye. Do we shake hands? You invited me, now it is my turn to invite you. That is the right thing, of course it is. We must do the right thing. I shall.'

Weeks passed before Gilbert invited Rachel. There were difficulties. Whatever he decided by day was destroyed at night. At night Sonia would seem to come flying out of the park saying the house had belonged to her. She had paid for it. She enumerated the furniture item by item. She had the slow, languid walk of her stage appearances as she went suspiciously from room to room, asking what he had done with her fur coats and where her shoes were. 'You've given them to some woman.' She said he had a woman in the house. He said he asked only David and Sarah; she said she didn't trust Sarah. He pleaded he had kept the dog. When he said that, her ghost vanished saying he starved the poor thing. One night he said to her, 'I'm going to ask Rachel, but you'll be there.' 'I damn well will,' she said. And this became such a dogma that when at last he asked Rachel to come, he disliked her.

His house was not as sedate as hers, which had been repainted that year – his not. His windows seemed to him – and to her – to sob. There was grit on the frames. When he opened the door to her she noted the brass knocker had not been polished and inside there was the immediate cold odour of old food. The hall and walls echoed their voices and the air was very still. In the sitting-room the seats of the chairs, one could see, had not been sat on for a long time, there was dust on the theatrical wallpaper. Hearing her, Sonia's dog, Tom, came scrabbling downstairs and rushed into the room hysterically at both of them, skidding on rugs, snuffling, snorting, whimpering, and made at once for her skirts, got under her legs, and was driven off onto a sofa of green silk, rather like hers, but now frayed where the dog's claws had caught.

'Off the sofa, Tom,' said Gilbert. The dog ignored this and snuffled from its squat nose and gazed from wet eyes that were like enormous marbles. Gilbert picked up a rubber bone and threw it to the dog. Down it came and the racing round the room began again. Rachel held her glass in the air for safety's sake and the dog jumped at it and made her spill whisky on her dress. In this confusion they tried to talk.

'Sonia liked being photographed with Tom,' he said.

'I only saw her on the stage once. She was very beautiful,' she said. 'It must have been twelve years ago. Gielgud and another actor called Slade were in it. Was it Slade? Oh, dear! My memory!'

'Her second husband,' he said.

He picked up the dog's rubber bone. The dog rushed to him and seized it. Man and dog pulled at the bone.

'You want it. You won't get it,' said Gilbert while she seemed to hear her husband say: 'Why can't you keep your mouth shut if you can't remember things?' And Gilbert, grinning in his struggle with the dog, said, 'Sonia always had Tom to sleep on our bed. He still does. Won't leave it. He's on it even when I come back from the office.'

'He sleeps with you?' she said with a shudder.

'I come home. I want someone to talk to.'

'What d'you do with him when you go to your office?' The dog pulled and snorted.

'The woman who comes in and cleans looks after the dog,' he said. And went on: 'Your house has three storeys, mine has two, otherwise the same. I've got a basement full of rubbish. I was going to turn it into a flat but Sonia got worse. Futile. Yes, life is futile. Why not sell the damn place. No point. No point in anything. I go to the office, come back, feed the dog, and get drunk. Why not? Why go on? Why do *you* go on? Just habit. No sense in it.'

'You *do* go on,' she said.

'The dog,' he said.

I must find some people for him to meet. He can't live like this, she thought. It is ghastly.

When she left he stood on the doorstep and said, 'My house. Your house. They're worth four times what we gave for them. There it is.'

She decided to invite him to dinner to meet some people – but whom could she ask? He was prickly. She knew dozens of people, but as she thought of them there seemed, for the first time, to be something wrong with all of them. In the end she invited no one to meet him.

On a diet, silly cow, he thought when she came to the door, but he fell back on his usual phrase as he looked about the empty room. 'Did you invite me? Or shall I go away? You *did* invite me. Thank you. Thank you.'

'I've been in Vienna with the Fladgates. She is a singer. Friends of David and Sarah.'

'Fladgates? Never heard of the people,' he said. 'Sonia insulted someone in Vienna. I was drunk. Sonia never drank anything – that made her insults worse. Did your husband drink?'

'Indeed not.'

He sat down on the sofa. The evening – Sonia's time. He expected Sonia to fly in and sit there watching this woman with all her 'problems' hidden chastely except for one foot which tipped up and down in her shoe under her long dress. But to his surprise Sonia did not come. The terrier sat at Rachel's feet.

'How is your enemy?' she said as they drank. 'The man in the office.'

'He and his wife asked me to dinner,' he said.

'That's kind,' she said.

'People are kind,' he said. 'I've remarked that.'

'Does he still watch you?'

'Yes. You know what it was? He thinks I drink too much. He thinks I've got a bottle in my desk. It wasn't the job that was worrying him. We are wrong about people. I am. You are. Everyone is.'

When they went into dinner, candles were on the table.

Bloody silly having candles, he said to himself. And when she came in with the soup, he said, 'We had candles. Poor Sonia threw them out of the window once. She had to do it in a play.'

The soup was iced and white and there was something in it that he could not make out. But no salt. That's it, he thought, no salt in this woman. Writing about politics and things all day and forgets the salt. The next course was white too, something chopped or minced with something peculiar, goodness knew what. It got into his teeth. Minced newsprint, he thought.

'Poor Sonia couldn't cook at all,' he said, pushing his food about, proud of Sonia. 'She put dishes on the floor near the stove, terrible muddle, and rushed back to hear what people were saying and then an awful bloody stink came from the kitchen. I used to go down and the potatoes had burned dry and Tom had cleared the plates. Bloody starvation. No dinner.'

'Oh no!' she said.

'I live on chops now. Yes,' he said. 'One, sometimes two, every day, say ten a week. Am I being a bore? Shall I go?'

Rachel had a face that had been set for years in the same concerned expression. That expression now fell to pieces from her forehead to her throat. Against her will she laughed. The laugh shook her and was loud; she felt herself being whirled into a helpless state from the toes upward. Her blood whirled too.

'You laughed!' he shouted. 'You did not protest! You did not write an article. You laughed. I could see your teeth. Very good. I've never seen you laugh before.'

And the dog barked at them.

'She laughed,' he shouted at the dog.

She went out to make coffee, very annoyed at being trapped into laughing. While he waited, the dog sat undecided, ears pricked, listening for her and watching him like a sentry.

'Rats,' whispered Gilbert to the dog. It stood up sharply.

'Poor bastard. What a life,' he said.

The dog barked angrily at him, and when she came in he said, 'I told your dog he ought to be on a farm.'

'You said that before,' she said. 'Let us have coffee next door.' They moved into the next room and she sat on the sofa while she poured the coffee.

'Now *you* are sitting on the sofa. I'm in this armchair,' he said, thinking of life tactically. 'Sonia moved about too. I used to watch her going into a room. Where will she sit next? Damned if I ever got it right. The same in restaurants. Let us sit here, she'd say, and then when the waiter came to her chair, she'd say, "No, not here. Over there." Never knew where she was going to settle. Like a fly. She wanted attention. Of course. That was it. Quite right.'

'Well,' she said coldly, 'she was an actress.'

'Nothing to do with it,' he said. 'Woman.'

'Nonsense,' she said, hating to be called a woman, and thought, It's my turn now.

'My husband,' she said, 'travelled the whole time. Moscow, Germany, Copenhagen, South Africa, but when he got home he was never still, posing to the animals on the farm, showing off to barns, fences, talking French and German to birds, pretending to be a country gentleman.'

'Let the poor man alone,' he said. 'Is he still alive?'

'I told you,' she said. 'I won't bore you with it all.'

She was astonished to find herself using his word and that the full story of her husband and herself she had planned to tell and which she had told so many people suddenly lost interest for her. And yet, anyway, she thought, why shouldn't I tell this man about it? So she started, but she made a muddle of it. She got lost in the details. The evening, she saw, was a failure. He yawned.

If there was one thing Rachel could honestly say, it was that she had not thought of her husband for years. She had not forgotten, but he had become a generality in the busyness of her life. But now, after the evening when Gilbert came to dinner, her husband came to life and plagued her. If an aeroplane came down whistling across the wide London sky, she saw him sitting in it – back from Moscow, Cape Town, Copenhagen – descending not upon her, but on another woman. If she took the dog for a run in the park, the cuddling couples on the grass became him and that young girl; if babies screamed in their prams they were his children; if a man threw a ball it was he; if men in white flannels were playing cricket, she wondered if he was among them. She imagined sudden, cold meetings and ran through tirades of hot dialogue. One day she saw a procession of dogs tails up and panting, following a bitch, with a foolish grin of wet teeth in their jaws, and Sam rushed after them; she went red in the face shouting at him. And yet she had gone to the park in order to calm herself and to be alone. The worst thing that could happen would be to meet Gilbert, the cause of this, but like all malevolent causes, he never showed his face. She had wished to do her duty and be sorry for him, but not for him to become a man. She feared she might be on the point of talking about this to a woman, not a woman she knew well – that would be disastrous – but, say, to some woman or girl sitting alone on a park seat or some woman in a shop: a confidence she would regret all her life. She was touchy in these days and had a row with the doctor who threw flowerpots at her dog. She petted the animal. 'Your head is handsome,' she said, stroking its head, 'but why did you go after that silly bitch?' The dog adored her when she said this. 'You're vain,' she said to it.

Gilbert *did* go to the park, but only on Saturdays, when the crowds came. He liked seeing the picnics, the litter on the grass; he stood still with pleasure when babies screamed or ice cream dripped. He grinned at boys throwing water from drinking fountains and families trudging, drunks lying asleep, and fat girls lying on top of their young men and tickling their faces with grass. The place is a damn bedroom. Why not? Where else can they go?

Lucky, boring people. I've got a bedroom and no one in it.

One Saturday, after three days of rain, he took his dog there and – would you believe it? – there the whole crowd was again, still at it, on the wet grass. The trouble with Sonia was that she thought the park was vulgar and would never go there – went once and never again, hadn't brought the right shoes.

He remarked this to his dog as he let it off its leash. The animal scampered round him in wide circles; came back to him and then raced off again in circles getting wider and wider until it saw a man with string in his hand trying to fly a kite. The kite was flopping on the ground, rose twenty or thirty feet in the air and then dived again. The dog rushed at the kite, but the man got it up again, higher this time. Gilbert walked towards the man. 'Poor devil, can't get it up,' he said as he walked. He got near the man and watched his struggles.

Then the kite shot up high and Gilbert watched it waving there until suddenly it swept away higher still. Gilbert said, 'Good for him.' The boredom of the grey afternoon was sweet. He lit a cigarette and threw the empty packet on the grass and then he found he had lost sight of the dog. When he saw it again it was racing in a straight line towards a group of trees by the lake. It was racing towards another dog. A few yards away from the dog it stopped and pranced. The dog was a terrier and stopped dead, then came forward. They stood sniffing at each other's tails and then jumped round muzzle to muzzle. They were growling, the terrier barked, and then the two dogs flew at each other's necks. Their play had turned to a war, their jaws were at each other's necks and ears. Gilbert saw at once it was Rachel's dog, indeed Rachel was running up shouting, 'Sam! Sam!' The fight was savage and Tom had his teeth in.

'Stop them!' Rachel was shouting. 'Stop them! They'll kill each other. He's got him by the throat.'

And then she saw Gilbert. 'You!'

Gilbert was enjoying the fight. He looked round and picked up a stick that had fallen from a tree.

'Stop them,' she shouted.

'Get yours by the collar, I'll get mine,' he shouted at her.

'I can't. Sam! Sam! They're bleeding.'

She was dancing about in terror, trying to catch Sam by the legs.

'Not by the legs. By the collar, like this, woman,' he shouted. 'Don't put your arms round him, you idiot. Like

166

this. Stop dancing about.'

He caught Tom by the collar and lifted him as both dogs hung on to each other.

'You're strangling him. I can't, I can't,' she said. Gilbert brought his stick down hard on the muzzles of the dogs, just as she was trying to grasp Sam again.

'You'll kill them.'

He brought the stick down hard again. The dogs yelped with pain and separated.

'Get the leash on,' he said, 'you fool.'

Somehow she managed it and the two dogs now strained to get at each other. The terrier's white neck and body were spotted with blood, and smears of it were on her hands.

Gilbert wiped their spit off his sleeve.

They pulled their dogs apart and she stared at him. It infuriated her that he was laughing at her with pure pleasure. In their stares they saw each other clearly and as they had never seen each other before. To him, in her short skirt and her shoes muddied by the wet grass, her hair disordered and the blood risen to her pale face, she was a woman. The grass had changed her. To her he was not a pitiable arrangement of widower's tricks, but a man on his own. And the park itself changed him in her eyes: in the park he, like everyone else there, seemed to be human. The dogs gave one more heave to get at each other.

'Lie down, Sam,' Gilbert shouted.

She lifted her chin and was free to hate him for shouting at her animal.

'Look after yours. He's dangerous,' she called back, angered by the friendliness of his face.

'Damn silly dogs enjoyed it. Good for them. Are you all right? Go up to the kiosk and get a drink – if I may, I'll follow you up – see you're all right.'

'No, no,' she put out a loud moan – far too loud. 'He's bleeding. I'll take him home,' and she turned to look at the park. 'What a mess people make.' And now, walking away, shouted a final accusation: 'I didn't know you brought your dog here.'

He watched her go. She turned away and dragged the struggling terrier over the grass uphill from the lake. He watched her walking unsteadily.

Very attractive figure, he thought. Silly cow. Better go home and ring her up.

He turned and on the way back to his house he could still see her dancing about on the grass and shouting. He went over the scene again and repeated his conclusion. 'She's got legs. Never saw them before. A woman. Must be. Full of life.' She was still dancing about as he put a bowl of water down for the dog. It drank noisily and he gave it another bowl and then he washed the dog's neck and looked at its ear. 'Nothing much wrong with you,' he said. He fed the animal, and soon it jumped on the sofa and was instantly snorting, whimpering and shaking into sleep.

'I must ring her up, yes, that is what I must do.'

But a neighbour answered and said Rachel had gone to the vet and had come back in a terrible state and had gone to bed with one of her migraines.

'Don't bother her,' he said. 'I just rang to ask how the dog was.'

Rachel was not in bed. She was standing beside the neighbour, and when the call was over she said, 'What did he say?'

'He asked about the dog.'

'Is that all?'

'Yes.'

This flabbergasted her.

In the middle of the night she woke up, and when her stupefaction passed she damn well wished he was there so that she could say, 'It didn't occur to you to apologize. I don't like being called a fool. You assume too much. Don't think I care a damn about *your* dog.' She was annoyed to feel a shudder pass through her. She got out of bed, and looking out of her window at the black trees, saw herself racing across the park to his house and pulling that dog of his off his bed. The things she said! The language she used! She kicked the dog out of the room and it went howling downstairs. She went back to bed weak and surprised at herself because, before she realized it, Sam became Tom in her hand. She lay there stiff, awake, alone. Which dog had she kicked? Sam or Tom?

In his house Gilbert locked up, poured himself a strong whisky, then a second, then a third. Uncertain of whom he was addressing, Rachel or Sonia, he said, 'Silly cow,' and blundered drunkish to bed. He woke up at five very cold. No dog. The bed was empty. He got out of bed and went downstairs. For the first time since Sonia had died the dog was asleep on the sofa. He had forgotten to leave his door open.

In the morning he was startled to hear Sonia's voice saying to him in her stage voice, 'Send her some flowers. Ask her to dinner.'

So he sent the flowers, and when Rachel rang to thank him he asked her to dinner – at a restaurant.

'Your house. My house,' he said. 'Two dogs.'

There was a long silence and he could her breath bristling.

'Yes, I think it has to be somewhere else,' she said. And added, 'As you say, we have a problem.'

And after this dinner and the next, she said, 'There are so many problems. I don't really know you.'

They talked all summer, and people who came regularly to the restaurant made up stories about them and were quite put out when in October they stopped coming. All the proprietor had heard was that they had sold their houses – in fact he knew what they'd got for them. The proprietor had bought Sonia's dog. There was a terrier, too, he said, but he didn't know what had happened to that.

II · AUTOBIOGRAPHIES

A Cab at the Door

Chapter 1

In our family, as far as we are concerned, we were born and what happened before that is myth. Go back two generations and the names and lives of our forbears vanish into the common grass. All we could get out of Mother was that her grandfather had once taken a horse to Dublin; and sometimes in my father's expansive histories, *his* grandfather had owned trawlers in Hull, but when an abashed regard for fact, uncommon in my father, touched him in his eighties, he told us that this ancestor, a decayed seaman, was last seen gutting herrings at a bench in the fishmarket of that city. The only certainty is that I come from a set of story tellers and moralists and that neither party cared much for the precise. The story tellers were for ever changing the tale and the moralists tampering with it in order to put it in an edifying light. On my mother's side they were all pagans, and she a rootless London pagan, a fog-worshipper, brought up on the folk-lore of the North London streets; on my father's side they were harsh, lonely, God-ridden sea or country people who had been settled along the Yorkshire coasts or among its moors and fells for hundreds of years. There is enough in the differences between North and South to explain the battles and uncertainties of a lifetime. 'How I got into you lot, I don't know,' my mother used to say on and off all her life, looking at us with fear, as if my father and not herself had given birth to us. She was there, she conveyed, because she had been captured. It made her unbelieving and sly.

A good many shots must have been fired during the courtship of my parents and many more when I was born in lodgings over a toy shop in the middle of Ipswich at the end of 1900. Why Ipswich? My parents had no connexion with the town. The moment could not have been worse. Queen Victoria was dying and my mother, young and cheerful though she was, identified herself, as the decent

London poor do, with all the females of the Royal Family, especially with their pregnancies and funerals. She was a natural Victorian; the past with all its sadness meant more to her than the hopes of the new century. I was to be called Victoria, but now surgery had to be done on the name, and quickly too, for my father's father, a Congregationalist Minister in Repton, was pressing for me to be called Marcus Aurelius. The real trouble was more serious.

On my birth certificate my father's trade is written 'Stationer (master)'. An ambitious young man, he had given up his job as a shop assistant in Kentish Town and had opened a small newsagents and stationers in the Rushmere district of Ipswich. He did not know the city and had gone there because he thought he had a superb 'opening'. He did not know the trade but he had found 'premises' – a word that was sacramental to him all his life. He spoke of 'premises' as others speak of the New Jerusalem. He had no capital. He was only twenty-two; the venture was modest, almost pastoral; but he had smelled the Edwardian boom and it enlarged a flaw that had – I have been told – even then become noticeable in his character. One of nature's salesmen, he was even more one of nature's buyers. He looked at the measly little shop, stripped it and put in counters, cabinets and shelves ('You know your father, dear'). The suspicious Suffolk folk hated this modern splash and saw that we had spent so much on fittings that we had nothing left for stock. The bright little shop stood as a warning to all in a crafty neighbourhood. Few customers came. The new paint smelled of sin to them. At the age of twenty-two my young father was affronted and flabbergasted to find after a few months that he was bankrupt, or if not legally bankrupt, penniless and pursued.

There is a picture of him a year or two before this time. He is thin, jaunty, with thick oily black hair, a waxed moustache, and eyes caught between a hard, brash stare and a twinkle. He would be quick to take a pencil out and snap down your order. He wears a watch and chain. Not for long: he will soon pawn them – as he had done before – and my mother's engagement ring too, escape from the premises, put her into those rooms over the toy shop. Once I am born, the young Micawber packs us off to his father's manse in Yorkshire, while he goes indignantly back to London to get a 'berth'. The fact that he has gone bust means nothing to him at all. He goes to the nearest Wesleyan Church – for he has already left the Congregationalists – and sings his debts away in a few stentorian hymns. And so I, dressed in silk finery and wrapped in a white shawl, go screaming up to Yorkshire to meet my forbears.

Our journey to the Manse at Repton is miserable. Love in a nice little shop had been – and remained for life – my mother's ideal. Now, though a cheeky Cockney girl, she was wretched, frightened and ashamed. ('We never owed a penny; us girls were brought up straight.') She was a slight and tiny fair-headed young woman with a sulky seductive look. In the train a sailor pulled out a jackknife and tossed it about: she called the guard. The sailor said he was only doing it to stop the kid crying. The arrival at the Manse was awful. My grandmother was confirmed in her opinion – she had given it bluntly and within earshot, when my father had first taken my mother there, wearing her London clothes – that her favourite son had been trapped and ruined by a common shop-girl of whom she said:

'I lay she's nowt but a London harlot.'

She said she'd take the baby.

'She tried to snatch you away from me, Vic dear, and said she'd bring you up herself,' my mother often told me.

Mary Helen, my father's mother, was a great one for coveting a dress, a brooch, a ring, a bag, even a baby from any woman. As for choice of words – this bonnie little white-haired woman with a smile that glistered sweetly like the icing of one of her fancy cakes, fed her mind on love stories in the religious weeklies and the language of fornication, adultery, harlotry and concubinage taken from the Bible, sharpened by the blunt talk of the Yorkshire villages. Harlots was her general name for the women of her husband's congregations who bought new hats. The old lady assumed that my mother, like any country girl, had come to leave me and would return next day to London to take up her profession again.

In the early days of my boyhood I spent long periods at the Manse. I have little memory of Repton, beyond the large stone pantry smelling of my grandmother's bread and the pans of milk; and of the grating over the cellar where my grandfather used to growl up at me from the damp, saying in his enormous and enjoyable voice:

'I'm the grisly bear.'

My grandmother had always lived in small Yorkshire towns or villages. Her maiden name was Sawdon and she came from a place of that name near the moors inland from Whitby; it is a purely

Scandinavian part of England – and she was the youngest, prettiest and most exacting of three daughters of a tailor in Kirbymoorside, in the godly Pickering valley near by. My father was born there and spoke of seeing the old man sitting cross-legged and sewing on the table in the window of his shop. Grandma was vain of her clothes and her figure. She usually wore a dark blue-and-white spotted dress. She had pale-blue eyes deeply inset, a babyish and avid look, and the drooping little mouth of a spoiled child. Her passion for her husband and her two sons was absolute; she thought of nothing else and me she pampered. With outsiders she was permanently 'right vexed' or 'disgoosted'.

Her 'Willyum', my grandfather, was let out of her sight as little as possible. The minister had the hard northern vanity also, but it differed from hers. He was a shortish, stout, hard-bellied and muscular man with a strong frightening face, iron-grey hair and looked like a sergeant major who did not drink. He was a man of authority with a deep, curt sarcastic voice used to command. When I was a child I had the impression that he was God and the Ten Commandments bound together by his dog-collar. He was proud of his life story.

Gradually I learned that he was the youngest son of a fishing family in Hull – his father was a trawler seaman – and that all his brothers had been drowned between Hull and the Dogger Bank. His mother had picked him up and taken him inland to Bradford, away from ships, and had brought him up there in great poverty. He had known what it was to 'clem'. He grew up and worked on the roads for a time; then ran off and joined the Army, (this would have been in the sixties) and since only the hungry or the riff-raff did this, he must have been in a poor way. He chose the artillery. This led to an event of which he boasted.

There is a strain of truculence and insubordination running through our family: at any moment, all of us, though peaceable enough, are liable to stick our chins out and take our superiors down a peg or two if our pride is touched. We utter a sarcastic jibe especially at the wrong moment and are often tempted to cut off our noses to spite our faces, in a manner very satisfying to ourselves and very puzzling to amiable people. My grandfather was kindly enough, but one noticed that, at certain moments, he would raise one fine eyebrow dangerously, the eyes would widen into a fixed stare, the pupils would go small and look as hard as marbles, and the sharp arc of white would widen above them, as a horse's eye does when it is bolting. This is the moment of cold flat contradiction; also the moment of wit. And there is a grin at the startled face of the listener.

This must have been the expression on my grandfather's face one day when his battery was stationed outside some seaside place, I believe, on the Mersey. They were at artillery target practice, firing out to sea, and the safety of passing vessels was regulated by a flag signal. It is quite in my grandfather's character that he fired his gun when the flag was up and contrary to orders and sent what he used to tell me was a 'cannon ball' through the mainsail of a passing pleasure yacht. There was a rasp of glee in his voice when he stressed the word 'pleasure'. He told me this story more than once when I was a child, sitting with him under a plum tree and eyeing the lovely Victoria plums in his garden at Sedbergh on the Fells – to which he moved after Repton. The yacht, of course, belonged to a rich man who made a fuss and my grandfather was arrested and court-martialled. He was dismissed from the Army. The moral was that you could never get a fair deal from the officer class; he could, he conveyed, have wiped the floor with any of them. The tale would end with him getting a stick for me – I was about five at the time – and putting me through military drill. We had the movements of 'Ready! Present: Fire!' and, more alarming, the 'Prepare to Receive Cavalry'. Down on one knee I went in the manner of the first lines of the British squares, with the stick waiting to bayonet the impending charge of Lancers on their horses. He had a loud, resonant voice and, being a fairish actor, could evoke the gallop of horses and spears instantly. The peaceful minister concealed a very violent man, and religion had made him live well below his physical strength and natural vitality. He then gave me a Victoria plum and moralized. He pointed out that war was wicked — on wickedness he was an expert – and that to become a soldier was the lowest thing in life, though he was proud of knowing what lowness was. And, he would add, that his wicked younger son – my father's brother – had brought sorrow on them all by running off to be a soldier in turn. The news had turned my grandmother's hair white – 'in a night' of course. And, my grandfather said, they had got their savings together and gone off to York to buy the boy out at once for £25. I did not understand, at the time, but this episode was traumatic for them. My grandfather never earned more than £150 a year in his life and, when he died, all he left was £70 in Co-op tickets which were kept in a tea-caddy on the kitchen mantelpiece. That £25 must have drawn blood.

How and why did my grandfather, uneducated and living by manual labour, become a Congregationalist Minister? In the middle of the nineteenth century, and especially in the industrial north where the wealth was made, the pessimism and anarchy of the early industrial times had passed. Even Manchester – the world's byword for poverty and revolutionary class-hatred – was becoming respectable. The idea of self-improvement was being dinned into the industrious poor; ambition was put into their heads by the dissenting churches, religion of this kind became a revolutionary force, for if it countered the political revolutionaries, it put a sense of moral cause into the hands of the ambitious. The teachings of Carlyle – the gospel of work – and later of Ruskin had their effect on hundreds of thousands of men like my grandfather. Snobbery and the Bible are dynamic in English life; respectability or – to be kinder – self-respect is the indispensable engine of British revolution or reform; and classes are getting just a little better off. As you rose socially so – see the novels of George Eliot – you rose in virtue. There is no doubt also that among Protestants, the tendency to break up into sects comes from a nagging desire to be distinctive and superior, spiritually and socially, to one's neighbours.

After he was thrown out of the Army, my grandfather got a job as a bricklayer. It is a chancy and travelling trade and he went from town to town. He did most of his travelling on foot; thirty or forty miles a day was nothing to him. Eventually he appeared in Kirbymoorside. By this time religion must have been strong in him. It sounds as though the court martial had given him a sense of injustice: he had been in the wrong; all the more reason to reverse the verdict and assert that by the higher law of God's justice he was in the right. The more wrong, the more right, the Old Testament offering its eloquent and ferocious aid.

It was easy to become a preacher in those days; gospel halls and missions were everywhere; the greater the number of sects, the greater the opportunities for argument. Soon he was at it in the evenings, after he had put down the hod. Yet to have got religion would not have been enough. I think that what impelled and gave him a rough distinction was his commanding manner and the knowledge that he had a fine voice. He was a good singer, he loved the precise utterance of words. He loved language. All we ever knew was that a pious, spinster lady in Kirbymoorside, heard him and was impressed by his militant looks, his strength and his voice. She got him off the builder's ladder and arranged for him to be sent to a theological college in Nottingham.

But the flesh – and ambition – were as strong as the spirit in Grandfather. He was courting the tailor's daughter and perhaps as a common workman he would not have got her. So at nineteen or twenty, on his prospects, he married her and went off with her to Nottingham as a student, and in a year was a father. He had only a small grant to live on. He got odd jobs. He told me he learned his Latin, Greek and Hebrew travelling on the Nottingham trains. He saved pennies, for it was part of the arrangement that he should pay back the cost of his education at so much a year in five years. My father had unhappy memories of a hungry childhood, and one of great severity. But once his training was over Grandfather triumphed. At twenty-two – the family legend is – he 'filled the Free Trade Hall in Manchester' with his harsh, denouncing sermons.

Why was it, then, that after this success he was to be found in Bradford and then – getting smaller and smaller – in the little towns of the moors and the fells? It may have been that all his energy had been spent in getting out of the working class and becoming a middle-class man.

Chapter 2

Perhaps Granda – as we always called him – was tired of hearing other women decried by his wife in the Manse; he was kind to my mother and liked her good sense and common London ways. She thought him a hard man, too God-fearing for her, but decent.

'I belong to the poor old Church of England, say what you like about it,' she used to say to us.

When I was about seven, just before my youngest brother was born, I used to go up to her bedroom in the afternoons at a house we had in Ealing and worry her to let me go and work on the building site opposite our house. I had studied the builders and could tell her exactly how building was done. You dig a trench, you put the bricks in.

'Go on, Mum. Why can't I? Let me,' the perpetual song of small boys. She told me bits about my grandfather. I stood fidgeting at her dressing-table. Once I picked up a hand mirror with a crack in it. 'Put that down.' She snatched it – she was a fanatical snatcher – and said, 'I don't want another seven years' bad luck. I've had my troubles. Gran had her troubles, too.'

> Needles and pins,
> Needles and pins,
> When a man marries
> His trouble begins.

'Give me that brush.'

She was brushing out her long straight hair and she looked like a funny witch with a narrow forehead. I hated, but with fascination, to see her dressing and undressing. Those bloomers! That corset!

She was always talking about her troubles. 'Things you don't know about.' Then she would laugh and sing a music-hall song.

> At Trinity Church I met me doom
> Now we live in a top back room
> Up to me eyes in debt for rent
> That's what he done for me.

'Go on, Mum.'

'That's enough. Look at my hair. I can't do anything with it. You have a go, Vic.'

So I brushed her hair.

'Your dad fell in love with my hair,' she said. 'But it's fine, thin, look at it. You can't do anything with it. My poor sister Fanny had such long hair she could sit on hers. So can Ada. Ada's is thick.'

'Mum, can't I go out to the builders?'

At this time she did her fair hair on top in a tea-cake-like shape which was full of hair pins. She had salty, greyish-green eyes – 'Green eyes jealousy' she used to say. 'That's me. I'm a wicked girl' – a longish nose, a talkative, half-sulky mouth not quite straight and quick-tempered elbows, one with a large mole on it. She was lively, sexy and sharp-spoken in the London way and very changeable, moody and, in the long run, not to be trusted.

Mother had grown up in the London jungle, in the needy streets of Kentish Town, Finsbury Park and off the Seven Sisters Road. Her father came from Bedfordshire. He had been a stable boy and gardener who went up to London to be coachman and gardener to a tea-merchant who lived in Highgate. I never saw this grandfather, he died when she was a girl. From his picture he was a tall noble-looking young fellow, with a beard that spread wide over his chest like a fine mist, fond of canaries, dogs, horses and chrysanthemums and tomatoes – said to be fatal to him because they gave him cancer. 'It grew all over him like a tree, from those blessed pips.' He was a touchy servant. One day, the tea-merchant's lady said to her maid: 'Put my jewellery away, the window cleaner's coming.' Grandfather Martin said to the maid: 'Take my watch, too, if there are dishonest people about.' This was meant as a reproach to his mistress. Death walked in and out of the Martin family in dramatic ways. My grandfather drove the carriage to the tea-merchant's office to pick him up one evening, and found his employer dead at his desk. He carried the body out to the carriage, propped it in a respectable attitude inside and drove him home to his wife. Soon after, Grandfather died too.

The Martins were left without a penny. Gran, his widow, had been a pert little barmaid in an Oxford public house – she had relations in the fish business in Uxbridge – and now she was left with three daughters in North London. There was Fanny, the eldest and laughing girl, the 'cure'; she was so funny as to be 'chronic'. There was Ada, funny, coquettish but more demure. These two girls were apprenticed to a well-known City shop called Spiers and Ponds when they were fourteen. My mother, the youngest and the pet, was to be kept at home to work in the house, for Gran had taken in lodgers. But Fanny sickened; she was a gay consumptive. There was a cab rank opposite their house and Fanny trained the parrot to say 'Walk up. Walk up,' at which the dozing cabbies would wake up, whip up their horses, because they thought the leading cab had been hired. Fanny, who read *Little Meg's Children* and *East Lynne* to her sisters, making them weep voluptuously, herself became a fading Victorian heroine. She died, saying as her last words, 'Oh! Illuminations.' She had entered heaven.

Ada worked in the china department at Spiers and Ponds and eventually married another 'cure', a young man called Frank Tilly who was in gents' tailoring at a shop called Daniels in Kentish Town. He had the waxen look of the young Chatterton and waving long dark hair. 'Poor Frank' was a consumptive too; he married Ada and before the year was out he died. They had emigrated to South Africa, he collapsed in Cape Town, took the next ship back, and died at sea in the middle of 'the worst storm for forty years'. The Union Jack floated over his body at the burial, while Ada prayed in the storm saying 'Oh God, let the ship go down.' She was pregnant.

. So Gran had seen three deaths and poverty too, in a few years. Her relations helped her – the fishmonger at Uxbridge, Louis, her cousin, a poor dressmaker, a skeleton figure out of a Gissing novel; Emmy, a lady's maid, brother Gil who whipped up the fish cart. Gran's grief had made her a savage little figure, terrifying to be with, for she had a prickly, bearded chin and the sour smell of stout, port, cheese and onions was on her breath. She would sit in her bonnet, with the veil that covered her face raised to her wicked red nose, swallowing her quart of stout, and the crumbs of the bread catching on to her veil. She looked like a damp and injured beetle. Her temper was violent for her knuckles were swollen with gout and rheumatism. She was embattled in pain. Worse was to happen to her in the end, years later, for Ada's gay little girl, Hilda Tilly, was to grow up and die also of consumption in her twenties. I was grateful to Gran for one thing. One day in Ipswich she pulled me off the outside WC when I was six or seven and was screaming with terror. I thought I was falling in. The neighbours called her.

But Gran had one fantastic stroke of luck and, in fact, it was a good deal responsible for my existence. One morning she traipsed off, grousing to herself as usual, to the butcher's. 'I've got something for you, Mrs Martin,' said the butcher pulling out a piece of blood-stained newspaper. It contained the Missing Money column. There the lawyers appealed for the relatives of a Mr Hawes. Sure enough it was Gran's brother who had died in Australia and Gran inherited a small sum of money. She was able to buy a house in Medina Road and take more lodgers. One of them was an actor, the other a young man who had lately become shopwalker in Daniels. He was to be my father.

It struck me a few years ago that I was born into a family of pets and favourites. Granda, a Pritchett, a youngest son, a pet, saved from the sea; Grandma Pritchett, the youngest pet daughter of the tailor; Father a pet also, for his brother showed early signs of being a distress; and Mother, the youngest pet of her sad family. It was ominous.

For at the age of seventeen, three years later than her sisters, my mother was sent as an apprentice to work in this large draper's shop. At Daniels Mother was put into the millinery and there my father saw her. He saw her fair hair. She looked – he told me – like a goddess in her mutton-chop sleeves and so desirable with her tiny waist. ('Eighteen inches,' she would put in.) She was so quick with the customers, he said, so clever with trimmings! She could put an ugly hat on a grumbling woman, give a twist, snatch a feather or a bunch of cherries and so dazzle the customer with chatter and her smiles.

As for my father, Mother was astonished by him.

'He was so clean, dear. You never saw anything so clean.' The poorly paid shop assistant fed in the basement, slept in the attics and went out to get drunk when the shop closed.

'Eight to eight, weekdays, eleven o'clock Saturday nights,' Mother would say. 'Old Daniels was a beast.'

They worked in the cold draughts and the poisonous, head-aching smell of gaslight.

'He was high up in Masonry and a Wesleyan,' my father would say, correcting my mother's temper.

'So clean,' my mother would go on, 'and so particular about his clothes – you know your father. Always the silk hat and spats. Countrified though. I could tell that. Rosy cheeks. He might have got some bad girl if he hadn't had me.'

She was in awe of him; he kept his nails perfect and there was a pleasant smell of Pears' soap and cachous about him and his teeth were white. He cleaned them – as his mother did – with soot or salt.

At this period my father – who was eventually to become very fat indeed, going up to eighteen stone in his time – was a slender young man. He looked grave, his fine brown eyes seemed to burn, and he could change from the effusive to the canny hard look of the brisk young Yorkshireman out for the 'brass'. But there was sometimes a hollow-eyed and haunted look on his face. The fact is – and this is what he told my dumbstruck mother when they talked together – he had had a wretched childhood. My grandfather, so benevolent to me, had been a harsh, indeed a savage, father.

I had seen the minister in his easy country days, idling with his small congregations of country folk, talking of Carlyle and Ruskin and English history. My father had known him as the disciplinarian not long out of the Army, living from hand to mouth in industrial towns, sending his children off to school hungry. They were forbidden to sit down at meals: it would make them soft. He made them stand rigid at the table in silence while they ate their food. His sons were in barracks. My father and his brother were not allowed out of the house after six in the evening, not even when they were grown up. What schools they went to was never made clear to me by my father. He evaded the subject, either out of shame or because he hated being definite about anything. I know he had a French lesson for he had learned by heart the phrase '*Trois hommes voyageaient en France*'. Education was expensive and my grandfather, who used to talk at large about the beauties of education, seems to have been able to give little to his two sons. He lived – as my father was to do – in a dream. At fourteen my father had gone to work as a grocer's errand boy and then worked behind the counter. At sixteen or so, he seems to have had an interesting friendship with a young doctor in the village. This – in view of what I shall tell later about my father – was important. The boy was eager to become a doctor or surgeon which would have been far beyond my grandfather's means. One evening he went to the doctor's surgery and watched him dress a man's poisoned thumb. The sight of pus and blood was too much: my father fainted. This led to delay in getting home. He arrived there after dark just before eight in the evening, to find my grandfather waiting with a carriage whip in his hand. Whipping was common in the family, but now my father was nearly a man. My grandfather roared at him for disobeying orders, accused him of drinking or going after women – a scene which was to be re-enacted by Father in his turn and for similar reasons, when my brother Cyril and I were in our late teens – and when Father answered back he was struck across the face and the back by the whip, two or three hard blows. That was enough: hatred had been growing for years. Father went up to his room and in the middle of the night climbed out of his bedroom window, hid in the railway station and went off to York next morning to stay with an uncle. Then he went to London. He had a cousin, Sawdon, in the rag trade: after short jobs in the drapery, Father arrived in glory in Kentish Town.

'I could tell,' said my mother, feeling sorry for him as well as being in awe, 'he had never met a girl before. And his mother standing there, doing nothing, seeing her son horse-whipped – I could have limbed the old . . .'

Mother was an expert in leaving her sentences unfinished.

Daniels was a Wellsian establishment. It was a good 'crib' or berth and the workers were scared of losing it. From Mother's account of it, it was the leading humorous establishment in North London. 'What us girls used to get up to. The nerve we had, dodging across the street, under the horses' heads, playing tricks on your poor father, he looked so stuck up till you got to know him, putting fly papers on old Daniels's chair ... Oh, I was a young limb. One day I tipped a whole pile of hat boxes, the white cardboard ones dear, on top of your dad. Us girls were always giggling round corners. Frank' – this was Ada's young man – 'was a cruel mimic. Everything was in farthings in those days and poor Mr Thomas could not pronounce his "th's". Frank used to go up to him and say, large as life, "What's the price of this, Mr Thomas? Free free farvings?" and Old Thomas would go wild and say "I'll free free farvings you with a fump." '

My mother's laugh was always near hysteria. She would sit on her chair by the fire with a long skirt pulled up over her knees to the elastic of her grey bloomers and rock back and forth as she talked. And when she came to the comic point she would spread her excited fingers over her face and stare through the gaps at us and go into fits until her untidy hair started to come through.

Frank's other gift was to say people's names backwards. This kept the shop 'rocking'. Ecirtaeb Nitram was my mother's name. My father's, which was difficult, became Retlaw Tetchirp.

'Dad didn't like it, you know he's proud.'

Father was certainly easily offended. He soon told her something that alarmed her: he was not going to stay at Daniels at the end of the year. 'My name's Walker,' he said. He was going out 'on the road'. He was going to get a job with a 'good comm. and A1 expenses'. Mother cunningly persuaded him to come and lodge at her mother's house: he noticed that she was a flirt and playing him up with one of the other assistants, so he moved so as to keep possession of her.

He had a shock when he met Gran. There had been no drink at the Manse. At Medina Road someone was always going round to the off-licence. And Gran was not very clean. She could not cook as well as his mother and he complained that London water was hard and did not get the dirt out of the pores of one's skin. He sent his shirts and underclothes back to Yorkshire to be washed and starched or ironed by his mother. Whatever you liked to say about his relations in Yorkshire, he pointed out, they were not servants, they didn't kotow; they didn't keep pubs and they were all out to improve their position. The Martins were stagnant and, like all southerners, they were all servile smiles and lies to your face. When he was in a rage with Mother in the years to come I am sorry to say that he would shout: 'I raised you from the gutter' and, with a glance of appeal to us, would say, 'You can't make a silk purse out of a sow's ear.'

These insults were no more than Yorkshire plain-speaking. All his relatives talked cheerfully like this to one another. As a Cockney Mother had a tongue, too. She would mock Father's piety with phrases like 'two-faced Wesleyans' and 'Hallelujah, keep your hands off'.

Gran Martin, of course, hated Father. She called him only by his surname for years. Father did not hide his feelings that the Martin family needed cleaning up. Morally, in particular, for he was soon taking my mother on Sundays to hear the famous preachers at the City Temple. Spurgeon and others. He loved their dramatic manner. One of these preachers told how, when he was coming into the City Temple that morning, he heard two young sparks debating whether to go in or not. 'Damn it, what odds,' said one and went in. My father admired his remark. He quoted it for years. He wanted religion to smarten up and get snappy. He liked the evangelical singing and sang well for he had been trained in one of the excellent Yorkshire choirs. But he sang mainly hymns, his favourite being 'Tell Me the Old, Old Story' which came so richly from him that it brought us nearly to tears when we were very young. He knew how much preachers were paid. 'Big men' he would say. He liked 'big men'. It was the age when the Victorian Grand Old Man or Great Men were beginning to be succeeded by the Big, like Selfridge and the new race of great shopkeepers in London, Manchester and Chicago. He did not really distinguish between the big shopkeepers and the popular Nonconformist preachers, who had also broken with the theology of the Victorian age: for suddenly money was about, commerce was expanding, there was a chance for the lower middle class. They would have a slice of the money the middles had sat so obdurately on for so long. The difference between 'goods' and 'the good' was fading. My father took to smoking cigars and my mother, hunching her pretty shoulders a little before his self-confident ambition, also sparkled and admired. He always ended by saying how hungry he was. Oysters – a poor man's food in those days – were pretty cheap. My father's later size was due to early hunger. He ate to make up for the craving of his childhood. He became cheerfully gluttonous. He talked for hours about food as much as he did about religion. Sixty years later when he died his last coherent words were: 'That woman meant well but she did not give me enough to eat.' He was speaking of his landlady. It was untrue. The hunger of his boyhood grew and grew as he neared death.

Beatrice Martin's idea of pleasure was Hampstead Heath Fair and the music halls. My father could not stand a dirty joke; and he mildly complained that in any music hall she was the first in the audience to see the joke and give her hysterical laugh so that voices from the gallery shouted admiringly at her and egged her on.

So my father and mother courted in Finsbury Park and Parliament Hill, went boating out on the Thames, rioted with the mob on Mafeking Night, he carrying her on his shoulder round Trafalgar Square while she waved a Union Jack. He walked out, as he had promised, from Daniels and got another berth; then the minister married them and they set off for Ipswich and bankruptcy, where Gran and Mother's sister, Ada, later widowed, appeared too. The battle between North and South was on.

. . .

Chapter 6

We were off again, of course. The year's soft and lazy affair with my birthplace had passed. We had scarcely heard the word God at all for a twelvemonth in this pagan holiday. We had made two or three more visits to our Aunt Ada's. I see her, on one of them, duck-breasted, wearing a fanciful dress and under a large Edwardian hat, raising her lorgnette to the one or two nudes in a local picture exhibition and te-he-he-ing in her bird-like way to me, telling me to come over and admire. Mother would have gone pink and pushed me out of the gallery. Uncle, a believer in practical education, sent my brother and me up the vertical ladder of one of the towers of his waterworks on Rushmere Common and instructed us in the digging of artesian wells and the economics of diesel power. There was an election that year and a crowd of us went into town singing:

> Vote, vote, vote for Mr Churchman
> Kick old Goddard in the eye.

At Felixstowe we saw the sea for the first time. It seemed like a wide-eyed face pressing against our faces and tingling in our hair. Mother talked of ships going down on the Goodwin sands and shouted from the shingle: 'Don't go in deeper.' An hotel caught fire.

In Yorkshire and in Suffolk there had been peace. No one spoke about money or the struggle for existence; there was none of our family talk about 'getting on'; there was no anxiety. My brother and I had the freedom of country life; we need not 'get on' at all. These influences slowly made me feel that although I was not as clever as many boys at school, I was clever enough and egotistical enough to be able to do what I liked with my life, and that my mind was already deciding what this should be. Money would have nothing to do with it. Just as I could feel myself grow and urge myself to grow more, so I felt that the important thing was to be alone – alone in the street, in the fells or on the Suffolk commons. And always walking and moving away.

My aunt's pictures gave me a hint of how this would be possible: not her gravy-coloured Academy landscapes, but the water-colours of Barlow Woods. This gentleman was alive. He was also young. He was witty, my aunt said. He sat down alone in a field by the Orwell and painted the trees by the water, the tide ebbing from the silvered mud banks. I liked painting and I wondered, when I walked to the lane where Gainsborough had painted his elms, whether some of that influence would fall upon me. The thought of being a writer had not occurred to me. I did feel that I could choose some studious kind of life but the barriers to knowledge seemed to me far too great. I would not have to read or know, to be a painter. A picture took one instantly through a door into another world, one like our own, but silent. There were no raised voices. There were no rows. And there, alive, was Barlow Woods creating these scenes. I never saw him. Whether he was a good painter or a poor one, I do not know. But, unlike ours at home, his pictures were done in real paint. In Ipswich, in that peaceful interregnum of my boyhood, the idea of being a painter began to dawdle in my mind.

But we left.

There is a short tunnel on the south side of Ipswich station and we all came out of it in a cloud of smoke and steam, with the solemn knowledge that we were now heading for London's aching skies. We had one glimpse of the blue spear of sea in the Stour estuary and of the sailing boats of Manningtree – except for those days at Felixstowe we were sea-starved children and often went into moans of self-pity because of this. We had said our last Suffolk 'Farewell, boa' to the lazy and forgotten country of slow-talking Suffolk people who had been stunned by the east wind. We got two shillings and some cultural advice each from Uncle: not bad.

We arrived on a dull May day, in London, at the pleasant suburb of Dulwich. The centre of Dulwich is still a Georgian village of fine houses and stately trees. There was the College and the old College chapel; and near it the small and famous Art Gallery. Everywhere one saw notice-boards reading Alleyn's College of God's Gift. College boys in their blue striped caps were in the streets. Ruskin, always dogging me, had often visited the Gallery; Browning had walked in the woods that overhung the village; and the Crystal Palace, built for the exhibition of 1851 and moved to Sydenham Hill, dominated all with its strange glass towers and its lolloping glass dome, like a sad and empty conservatory. From the Parade, at the top, one could see the dome of St Paul's only a few miles away, and a distant slit of the Thames.

We noticed that the family fortunes had gone up a little when we got to Dulwich. Our destination was not the sedate part of the district but on the outskirts at the Norwood end. We found ourselves in a rather taller villa than usual in a street where dozens of houses were to let, for this was the period of the Edwardian housing slump. Father was indignant at the rent: 16s. a week. He was often in arrears with it. But the house had one distinctive feature – he proudly pointed out – dark-blue fireproof paper in its front room.

But the London air was mottled with worry. We had come back to a father who had changed his character. The merry, bouncing fellow with the waxed moustaches and the cigar, the genial carver of the commercial rooms, the singer of bits of Kathleen Mavourneen had shaved off his moustache, and had been replaced by a man whose naked face was stern. In the past year he also had experienced freedom – freedom from us. He had been living in a comfortable furnished flat and had had leisure to remake his own life. He had found another self. We had come back and this new self was trapped in a situation he could not get out of. He stared at us and the corners of his mouth drooped: he saw the ineluctable. When I was eighteen he once said bitterly: 'I'm warning you. Don't make my mistake. I married too young, before I knew my own mind.' I hated him then and even more for saying this. At Dulwich it was plain that he had passed through some crisis and not a simple one. The idea of righteousness was very powerful in him, despite his unreliability; it was this idea, I believe, that began to corrupt him. An emotional struggle – I would guess – and then righteousness killed his heart. His gaiety vanished. Self-punished, he slowly drifted into punishing us. How else to account for his black moods?

But his losses had their gains – perhaps after all the will meant more than the heart to him. One short-term gain for him was his new religion which, since Mother rejected it, he kept to himself. We knew nothing about it, but we knew it existed. He was determined to keep *that*, a romantic compensation and counsellor which corrupted him very quickly. Or, perhaps he corrupted it. He once told me more about his conversion. Mother was wrong in saying that Cousin Dick's peculiar recovery from chronic dyspepsia was the main cause. The decisive thing – and the decisive would always be personal for him – was the death of a friend of Cousin Dick's. This man was dying of tuberculosis but believed that he could be cured by Christian Science treatment. The worse he got, the more he believed; and just before he died he declared that he knew it was 'the Truth' and made my father swear to stick to it. It was this tragic failure, arriving at a moment when I think Father himself felt he was in a desperate situation, that converted my father.

The second gain was remarkable. He had refused to give in to bad luck in his business and now he had at last succeeded. In that year while he was alone in Dulwich and with the help of the clever woman who had got him back from Liverpool in the nick of time, he at last realized his dream. And this time it was no deception. He had got out of the despised retail trade; he had left the jaunty and vulgar world of the commercial traveller and out of that came one remarkable change, one that separated us from him, as if there had been a real divorce. His name had changed. Until now, he had been Walter S. Pritchett; now the Walter was dropped. His second name appeared. He was Sawdon Pritchett, a name so sonorous, so official, so like a public meeting that we went off into corners and sniggered at it. He would, all the same, lower his eyes with his touching modesty when he said it. He pulled out a card to establish his new name with us. There it was:

Sawdon Pritchett Ltd.,
Art Needlework Manufacturers,
Offices and Showrooms Newgate Street.

'Opposite the Old Bailey,' he pointed out.

When will you pay me
Said the Bells of Old Bailey,
When I grow rich
Said the bells of Shoreditch

Mother sang. Ominously too.

He took us to his office. Pigeons laid their eggs on the dirty balcony of his floor of the building. The crowds queued outside the Courts for the murder trials and down below, on the wood-blocked streets, scavenger boys in white coats dashed in and out of the traffic with brushes and wide pans to sweep up the horse manure. My brother and I envied their dangerous and busy life and their wide-brimmed hats.

Father's elevation and dignity had a silencing effect on our home. The words, Managing Director, put him in a trance. He told us that we now had many privileges; first we were the children of a Managing Director, living in a refined neighbourhood among neighbours who would study our manners. We had also the privilege of living within a couple of hundred yards of a remarkable family and an even more remarkable woman, the secretary to the Company whose brother, high in financial circles, played tennis at a most exclusive club. My father doubted if this family would feel able to know us immediately, but if by some generous condescension they did, we would remember to have our hands and shoes clean, brush our hair, raise our caps and never sit down until told to do so. Father's face had lost its roundness. It had become square, naked and authoritative. It also looked pained; as if he were feeling a strange, imposed constraint.

Mother supported him vigorously; in fact, as we soon saw, with unnatural vigour. It was irony on her part. Our debt to this family and to this lady was total, she said. The lady appeared almost before Father finished speaking, which took my father and mother aback, my mother's hair (as usual) being not quite in a state for receiving another woman. And we were taken aback too. We had expected perhaps another operatic Mrs Murdo in red velvet;

instead a tall, beautiful young woman with burning brown eyes, and black hair, came in. Her eyelashes fluttered. She had alluring lips and, on the upper lip, a few black hairs at the corners which, before the fashion changed, made women sensually disturbing. Her voice was a shade mannish, low and practical, she was slender and wore a business-like coat and skirt with a white blouse. She struck us as elegant, even fashionable. To our delight she teasingly addressed our father as 'Father' which made him blush. She even called him 'Sawdon'; it was as if she had called him Lord. She put us so much at our ease that we loved her at once and got boisterous; my father deferred to her and so did my mother who also blushed.

One of her first questions to me was: when was I going to sit for a scholarship to the College? This was startling to me and I looked for help to my father.

'When he is ready,' said my father. 'I do not want him to imagine that just because his father has his own business he has only to sit about waiting for everything to fall into his lap.'

'Which school are you going to send him to?' she turned to my mother.

'I really don't know,' said my mother.

'We are considering the matter,' said my father in his board-room manner. 'It may be this or that. It may be the College, though we shouldn't limit ourselves to that. There may be other, better schools, than the College.'

My father's evasions stopped. Certainty appeared and a look of polite but firm rebuke came to his face. He liked the gaiety of the lady but he was not going to allow her to lead the way in his family or anywhere else. The matter was raised to a graver, higher and crushing tribune.

'He will go where the Divine Mind wishes him to go, for he is a reflection of the Divine Mind, as Mrs Eddy says.'

This puzzling remark lifted me into a region I had never heard of before; my head seemed to stretch painfully. I thought someone had put on me a hat that came down over my ears.

My mother looked appealingly and mistrustfully at the lady. 'Are you in this too?' she seemed to signal anxiously, but what she said was: 'I never had much education myself.'

'We were brought up very poor but my parents were careful. We had to earn our living early, my brother and I. We worked hard and went to evening classes. Father made us get our diplomas,' said the refined lady in her precise way. 'My brother qualified as an accountant.'

My spirits fell. After the gaieties of Ipswich we were once more caught by the doctrine of hard work and bleak merit. Mother's neck wobbled in a pained way as if she had been shot, but was too lady-like to mention it.

'If I may offer a thought there,' said my father, for he had not quite lost touch with the charms of an easy life. 'What these boys need, what we all need, is the Truth.'

'Stick to the point,' said my mother, desperately blinking at him.

'I'm sure you've been too busy to think about it yet,' said the lady tactfully, but Mother did not take it as tact, and gave her one of her looks.

'Why don't you do something about it, making a fool of me in front of that woman?' my mother shouted at my father when the lady went. 'And why don't you get those boys to a school?'

Father pointed out that now my mother had a friend and we all had a friend and that soon our general tone would be raised by this fortunate contact. This did not happen. In the years to come my mother kept herself apart from this family.

'Who was her father? Only a man on the railway and the mother takes lodgers. Why are we beholden to her?' Mother said. For many years the lady was known to us only as 'Miss H'.

There was my father sitting in that office with 'that woman' all the week; Mother said: why didn't he stay with her if she was so wonderful. We know she put up the money. How did she get it? Cheese paring. My mother was not going to cheapen herself by visiting them. She might not be educated but she knew the difference between sixpence and a shilling and had been brought up straight. We were shocked. Mother was jealous. There were two women: Mrs Eddy and this lady, Miss H.

And why had we got to be so polite to her? The Business, that's what it was, Mother said. The Business. Our father had ceased to be our father. He now became 'the Business'. It was a shadow in our fireproof room.

And then this woman, Miss H, was a woman and women are woman-like, Mother said. Not that she had any doubts about Father, for she knew he was true, but if women don't get one thing, they go for another. They don't let go.

As for Father being true, this is as certain as anything can be. He really hated women. He despised them. They existed to be his servants, for his mother – as my mother said – had waited on him hand and foot. Of course he charmed women; they liked talking to him, he appealed to their masochism. If they fought back or showed any signs of taking charge of him, his face went cold. His favourite gesture was to hold up his hand, palm upwards and wag it insultingly up and down, silently telling them to shut up. Their role was to listen to him and he had a lot to say. But once let them discuss, differ or suggest another idea, and the hand went up, playfully at first but, if they persisted, he was blunt with them. He described these incidents to us often. His phrase was 'I put her in her place'. It was unlucky that he had not met Mrs Eddy. She was dead. It was unlucky also that in his trade most of the workers were women. It must be said that several of these, who admired his vitality, loved him all their lives. Perhaps Miss H the bookkeeper did; Mother scornfully thought so.

At Dulwich the question of schools became grandiose for my brother and me. We were the sons of a Managing Director: our value rose. Prospectuses came in from half the great Public Schools of England. Eton and Harrow were dismissed easily; it was astonishing how many boys from such schools uttered false cheques in the course of a decade and got into the papers. We saw ourselves at Dulwich College, swaggering arm in arm like the College prefects in their tasselled hats. We walked behind them listening with awe to their astonishing man-of-the-world talk about girls. We caught drawling hints of musical plays and lavish disputes about whether the Indian Civil Service or the Army were to be preferred. One day we heard a youth pity another whose father was in a Line regiment. These snobberies had – I now see – the effect of gin upon our unaccustomed fancies. We began to live double lives. I read the prospectuses eagerly. At these schools one was away from home, and that I longed for. But I saw the fatal difficulty: I knew no Latin. For twopence cadged off my mother I bought a second-hand Latin Primer. I decided to teach myself and enter paradise.

I was defeated on the very first page. There was a sentence that ran: 'Inflection is a change in the form of a word.' There was no dictionary in the house. Mother had never heard of the word 'inflection' nor had Father. But I had heard of 'form'. But how could a word have form? It wasn't a thing like a table, or a vase. I drew a pencil line carefully following the shapes of the letters round a word or two; that led nowhere. I skipped to '*mensa*' but what on earth did 'by with or from a table' mean? I'd never heard anyone say it. Mother hadn't either. As for the verb '*sum*' mentioned idolatrously by my grandfather when I was five or six, I couldn't find it in the book.

One morning there was a click at the letter-box and Mother said, in a panic: 'What was that?'

'Someone at the door,' we said, but all stood still, knowing that this was a dangerous moment.

'Stay here,' said my mother. 'Vic, open the kitchen door and peep up the hall.' I peeped. No person stood beyond the coloured glass of the front door, which threw a sad and bloody light on the passage, but a letter was on the linoleum.

'A letter,' I said.

'Wait,' she said, drying her hands on her apron; then all advanced towards the letter. My mother stopped about a yard away looking cautiously at it. Then she made a dart at it and picked it up. It was only a circular.

'It give me a turn,' said Mother, whose English had deteriorated in the last year.

It was a circular begging on behalf of Treloar's Home for Crippled Children and contained pictures of the school rooms, and workshops, the dormitories, the playgrounds by the sea in the south of England where these children lived. I envied them. How lucky to be a cripple. If only, in some game of football in the Park, I could get my leg broken, go on crutches and, helped on to a train, go to this place. The thought was luxurious. For an hour or two I tried limping.

Then, with the suddenness with which everything happened to us, Father having gone off at seven to be at his workroom before the 'hands' got there to see they did not cheat him of his time, Mother put the two youngest children with the next-door neighbour and marched my brother and me for a mile and a half, muttering to herself, to Rosendale Road School, near Herne Hill.

'I've brought these two boys,' she said, giving us a push, to a dapper little man in a tail-coat and who looked like a frosted pen-nib. His name was Timms.

What Mr Timms said I don't know, but I was aware of what I looked like. Mother had a hard time making both ends meet and, on a day like this, wanted us to be dressed in something respectable. The day before she put the sewing-machine on the dining-room table, took out a paper pattern and set about making

195

me some trousers. She made many of her own dresses and a lot of our clothes; indeed, if she was making a dress for herself or my sister, I was often the model. I had to stand up while she pinned patterns all over me. She was often puzzled by the strips of pattern that were left over. If only she had her cousin Emmy or better still Cousin Louie, the dressmaker, she would say; for it was a fate with her often to cut out, say, two left sleeves, or to be short of a quarter of a yard on the length. She knitted our stockings and never learned how to turn a heel, so that a double heel often hung over the backs of our boots: jerseys for us she never finished; but for herself – for she did not want to make victims of *us* – she would knit recklessly on while I read the instructions to her, and turn out narrow tubes of wool that she would stretch, laughing till she cried, to her knees. She had to pay for the material for her dressmaking out of the housekeeping money and she would raid any free material in sight. I have described her attacks on our curtains. Her own bloomers were a byword: for in gay moments she would haul up her long skirts above her knees and show my father – who was always shocked – what could be done with a chair cover or something robust of that kind. 'You want me in the business instead of "that woman",' she'd say.

For she had a vengeful streak in her, and looking at our father, the impressive Managing Director, and counting his suits and knowing how she couldn't get a penny out of him for our clothes, she attacked his wardrobe. She found a pair of striped trousers of the kind worn with morning dress. Just the thing for me. Out came the scissors. Slicing the enormous trousers roughly at the knees she saw that my brother and I could get into them both at once. She was upset by our laughter. She now slashed at the trousers again and narrowed them to my size. The insoluble difficulty was the fly buttons; these she pulled round to the side of one leg; cutting and then tacking her way up the middle while they were on me at the final try-on, she sewed me up totally in front.

'I won't be able to *go*, Mum,' I said.

She was flabbergasted, but in her careless way, she snipped a couple of stitches in her tacking.

These were the trousers I was wearing as I stood before Mr Timms, very pleased by Father's fashionable stripes and willing to show any boy who was interested the original touch of having Savile Row fly buttons down the side of one leg. What I feared was happening; the hole was lengthening in front. I could feel an alarming draught. I dared not look down. I hoped Mr Timms would not look down, as my mother chatted on and on about our family. Nothing happened. I went to my classroom; at playtime I dared not run, for fear the tacking would go. When I pulled the thread to tighten it I was left with a length of thread hanging down from the vulnerable part. When I went home after school the thread went altogether and I had to cover myself with my hand.

So my first day at Rosendale Road School began. Wearing my father's classy cut-downs I knew the distinction of our family and its awkward difference from the families of all the other children. No one else had a Managing Director's trousers on. No one else had (I was sure) our dark adventures. We were a race apart; abnormal but proud of our stripes, longing for the normality we saw around us.

I was eleven. Between the age of ten and fourteen a boy reaches a first maturity and wholeness as a person; it is broken up by adolescence and not remade until many years later. That eager period between ten and fourteen is the one in which one can learn anything. Even in the times when most children had no schooling at all, they could be experts in a trade: the children who went up chimneys, worked in cotton mills, pushed coster barrows may have been sick, exhausted and ill-fed, but they were at a temporary height of their intelligence and powers. This is the delightful phase of boyhood, all curiosity, energy and spirit.

I was ready for a decisive experience, if it came. It did come. At Rosendale Road School I decided to become a writer. The decision did not drop out of the sky and was not the result of intellectual effort. It began in the classroom and was settled in the school lavatory. It came, of course, because of a personal influence: the influence of a schoolmaster called Bartlett. There were and are good and bad elementary schools in London. They are nearly as much created by their districts and their children as by their teachers. The children at Rosendale Road, which was a large school, were a mixture of working class and lower middles with a few foreigners and colonials – Germans, Portuguese, Australians, French and one or two Indians. It was a mixed school. We sat next to girls in class and the class was fifty or sixty strong. We had overgrown louts from Peabody's Buildings and little titches, the sons of coalmen, teachers, railwaymen, factory workers, sailors, soldiers, draughtsmen, printers, policemen, shop assistants and clerks and salesmen. The Germans were the children of people in the pharmaceutical trades; they had been better educated than we were and had more pocket money. One dark satanically handsome boy owned a 'phonograph' and claimed to be a direct descendant of Sir Francis Drake and did romantic pictures of galleons. At fourteen the girls would leave school, work in offices, in factories like my father's or become waitresses or domestic servants.

In most schools such a crowd was kept in order by the cane. Girls got it as much as the boys and snivelled afterwards. To talk in class was a crime, to leave one's desk inconceivable. Discipline was meant to encourage subservience, and to squash rebellion – very undesirable in children who would grow up to obey orders from their betters. No child here would enter the ruling classes unless he was very gifted and won scholarship after scholarship. A great many boys from these schools did so and did rise to high places; but they had to slave and crush part of their lives, to machine themselves so that they became brain alone. They ground away at their lessons, and, for all their boyhood and youth and perhaps all their lives, they were in the ingenious torture chamber of the examination halls. They were brilliant, of course, and some when they grew up tended to be obsequious to the ruling class and ruthless to the rest, if they were not tired out. Among them were many who were emotionally infantile.

A reaction against this fierce system of education had set in at the turn of the century. Socialism and the scientific revolution – which Wells has described – had moved many people. New private schools for the well-off were beginning to break with the traditions of the nineteenth century and a little of the happy influence seeped down to ourselves. Mr Bartlett represented it. The Education Officer had instructed Mr Timms to give Mr Bartlett a free hand for a year or so and to introduce something like the Dalton or tutorial system into our class. The other teachers hated him and it; we either made so much noise that the rest of the school could hardly get on with their work, or were so silent that teachers would look over the frosted glass of the door to see if we had gone off for a holiday.

Mr Bartlett was a stumpy, heavy-shouldered young man with a broad swarthy face, large brown eyes and a lock of black hair wagging romantically over his forehead. He looked like a boxer, lazy in his movements and his right arm hung back as he walked to the blackboard as though he was going to swing a blow at it. He wore a loose tweed jacket with baggy pockets in which he stuck books, chalks and pencils and, by some magnetism he could silence a class almost without a word. He never used the cane. Since we could make as much noise as we liked, he got silence easily when he wanted it. Manners scarcely existed among us except as a scraping and snivelling; he introduced us to refinements we had never heard of and his one punishment took the form of an additional and excruciating lesson in this subject. He would make us write a formal letter of apology. We would make a dozen attempts before he was satisfied. And, when, at last, we thought it was done he would point out that it was still incomplete. It must be put in an envelope, properly addressed: not to Mr Bartlett, not to Mr W.W. Bartlett, not as I did, to Mr W.W. Bartlett Esquire, but to the esquire without the mister. It often took us a whole day and giving up all the pleasant lessons the rest were doing, to work out the phrasing of these letters of shame.

At Rosendale Road I said goodbye to Stephen and Matilda and the capes and rivers of England, the dreary sing-song. We were no longer foredoomed servants but found our freedom. Mr Bartlett's methods were spacious. A history lesson might go on for days; if it was about early Britain and old downland encampments he would bring us wild flowers from the Wiltshire tumuli. He set up his easel and his Whatman boards and painted pictures to illustrate his lesson. Sometimes he changed to pastels. And we could go out and watch him and talk about what he was doing. He made us illustrate our work and we were soon turning out 'Bartletts' by the dozen. He set us tasks in threes or fours; we were allowed to talk to each other, to wander about for consultations: we acted short scenes from books at a sudden order.

For myself the lessons on literature and especially poetry were the revelation. No textbooks. Our first lessons were from Ford Madox Ford's *English Review* which was publishing some of the best young writers of the time. We discussed Bridges and Masefield. Children who seemed stupid were suddenly able to detect a fine image or line and disentangle it from the ordinary. A sea poem of Davidson's, a forgotten Georgian, remains in my mind to this day: the evocation of the sea rolling on the single on the coast between Romney and Hythe:

> The beach with all its organ stops
> Pealing again prolongs the roar

Bartlett dug out one of James Russell Lowell's poems, *The Vision of Sir Launfal*, though why he chose that dim poem I do not know; we went on to Tennyson, never learning by heart. Bartlett must have been formed in the late days of pre-Raphaelitism, for he introduced us to a form of writing then called half-print. He scrapped the school pens, made us use broad nibs and turn out stories written as near to the medieval script as possible. (This and German script, four years later, ruined my handwriting for ever.) We had a magazine and a newspaper.

Many of Bartlett's methods are now commonplace in English schools; in 1911 they were revolutionary. For myself, the sugar-bag-blue cover of the *English Review* was decisive. One had thought literature was in books written by dead people who had been oppressively over-educated. Here was writing by people who were alive and probably writing at this moment. They were as alive as Barlow Woods. The author was not remote; he was almost among us. He lived as we did; he was often poor. And there was another aspect; in Ipswich I had been drawn to painting and now in poems and stories I saw pictures growing out of the print. Bartlett's picture of the *Hispaniola* lying beached in the Caribbean, on the clean-swept sand, its poop, round house, mainsails and fore-tops easily identified, had grown out of the flat print words of *Treasure Island*. Bartlett was a good painter in water-colour. When we read *Kidnapped* he made us paint the Scottish moors. We laughed over *Tom Sawyer* and *Huckleberry Finn*. The art of writing became a manual craft as attractive – to a boy – as the making of elderberry pipes or carpentering. My imagination woke up. I now saw my grandfather's talk of Great Men in a new light. They were not a lot of dead Jehovahs far away; they were not even 'Great'; they were men. I went up to dirty second-hand bookshops in Norwood where I had found the Latin grammar; now, as often as I could cadge the penny off my mother, I went up there and out of the dusty boxes I bought paperbacks called *The Penny Poets*. One could have a complete edition of *Paradise Regained* (but not, for some reason, *Paradise Lost*) or Wordsworth's *Prelude*, the *Thanatopsis* (but what on earth was that?) of William Cullen Bryant, the poems of Cowper and Coleridge. To encourage my mother to open her purse or to reward her with a present, I bought penny sheets of second-hand music for her. I was piqued by her laughter.

'This old stuff,' she said, sitting down at the piano.

'The Seventh Royal Fusiliers'.

'The gallant Fusiliers, they march their way to glory,' I sang out.

'You're flat,' she said. 'Where did you get it?'

I had found a collection of the worst patriotic songs of the Crimean War, full of soldierly pathos. The music sheets were very dirty and they smelled of hair oil, tea and stale rooms.

That I understood very little of what I read did not really matter to me (Washington Irving's *Life of Columbus* was as awful as the dictionary because of the long words.) I was caught by the passion for print as an alcoholic is caught by the bottle. There was a small case of books at home, usually kept in the backroom which was called my father's study. Why he had to have a study we could not see. There was an armchair, a gate-legged table, a small rug, piles of business magazines usually left in their wrappers; the floorboards were still bare as indeed were our stairs; Father had temporarily suppressed his weakness for buying on credit. I had not dared often to look much at his books. It is true I had read *Marriage on Two Hundred a Year*, because after all the quarrels in our house, marriage was a subject on which I had special knowledge. From the age of seven I often offered my parents bits of advice on how to live. I knew what the rent was and what housekeeping cost. I had also read *Paper Bag Cookery* – one of Father's fads – because I wanted to try it. Now I saw *The Meditations of Marcus Aurelius* in leather: it defeated me. Wordsworth and Milton at least wrote in short lines with wide margins. I moved on to a book by Hall Caine called *The Bondman*. It appeared to be about a marriage and I noticed that the men and women talked in the dangerous adult language which I associated with *The Bad Girl of the Family*. *The Bondman* also suggested a doom – the sort of doom my mother sang about which was connected with Trinity Church and owing the rent.

Hall Caine was too thundery for me. I moved to Marie Corelli and there I found a book of newspaper articles called *Free Opinions*. The type was large. The words were easy, rather contemptibly so. I read and then stopped in anger. Marie Corelli had insulted me. She was against popular education, against schools, against Public Libraries and said that common people like us made the books dirty because we never washed, and that we infected them with disease. I had never been inside a Public Library but I now decided to go to one. Mr Bartlett had advised us to get notebooks to write down any thoughts we had about what we read. I got out mine and I wrote my first lines of English prose: hard thoughts about Marie Corelli.

This exhausted me and the rest of the notebook was slowly filled with copied extracts from my authors. I had a look at *In Tune with the Infinite*. I moved on to my father's single-volume, India-paper edition of *Shakespeare's Complete Works* and started at the beginning with the *Rape of Lucrece* and the sonnets and continued slowly through the plays during the coming year. For relief I took up Marie Corelli's *Master Christian* which I found more moving than Shakespeare and more intelligible than *Thanatopsis*.

On the lowest shelf of my father's bookcase were several new ornate and large volumes of a series called the International Library of Famous Literature. They were bound in red and had gold lettering. They had never been opened and we were forbidden to touch them. I think Father must have had the job of selling the series, on commission, at one time. I started to look at them. There were photographs of busts of Sophocles and Shakespeare. There were photographs of Dickens, Thomas Hardy, of Sir James Barrie and Sir Edmund Gosse in deep, starched wing collars, of Kipling rooting like a dog at his desk and of G.K. Chesterton with his walking-stick. There was Tolstoy behind his beard. The volumes contained long extracts from the works of these writers. I found at once a chapter from Hardy's *Under the Greenwood Tree*; and discovered a lasting taste for the wry and ironical. I moved on to *Longinus on the Sublime* and could not understand it. I was gripped by Tolstoy and a chapter from *Don Quixote*. In the next two or three years I read the whole of the International Library on the quiet. These volumes converted me to prose. I had never really enjoyed poetry for it was concerned with inner experience and I was very much an extrovert and I fancy I have remained so; the moodiness and melancholy which fell on me in Dulwich and have been with me ever since, must have come from the disappointments of an active and romantic nature; the forms of Protestantism among which I was brought up taught one to think of life rigidly in terms of right and wrong and that is not likely to fertilize the sensibilities or the poetic imagination. The poet, above all, abandons the will; people like ourselves who were nearly all will, burned up the inner life, had no sense of its daring serenity and were either rapt by our active dramas or tormented by them; but in prose I found the common experience and the solid worlds where judgements were made and which one could firmly tread.

An extract from *Oliver Twist* made me ask for a copy for Christmas. I put it in our one green armchair and knelt there reading it in a state of hot horror. It seized me because it was about London and the fears of the London streets. There were big boys at school who could grow up to be the Artful Dodger; many of us could have been Oliver; but the decisive thing must have been that Dickens had the excited mind, the terrors, the comic sense of a boy and one who can never have grown emotionally older than a boy is at the age of ten. One saw people going about the streets of London who could have been any of his characters; and right and wrong were meat to him. In all of Dickens, as I went from book to book, I saw myself and my life in London. In Thackeray I found the gentler life of better-off people and the irony I now loved. To have been the young man in *The Virginians*, to have travelled as he did and to find oneself among affectionate genial and cultivated families who enjoyed their fortunes, instead of struggling for them, must be heaven. And I had seen enough in our family to be on the way to acquiring a taste for disillusion.

My mother's tales about her childhood made the world seem like a novel to me and with her I looked back and rather feared or despised the present. The present was a chaos and a dissipation and it was humiliating to see that the boys who lived for the minute and for the latest craze or adventure, were the most intelligent and clear-headed. Their families were not claustrophobic, the sons were not prigs, as I was. There was a boy with a Japanese look to him – he had eyes like apple pips – who had introduced me to Wells's *Time Machine*. He went a step further and offered me his greatest treasures: dozens of tattered numbers of those famous stories of school life, the *Gem* and the *Magnet*. The crude illustrations, the dirty conditions of the papers, indicated that they were pulp and sin. One page and I was entranced. I gobbled these stories as if I were eating pie or stuffing. To hell with poor self-pitying fellows like Oliver Twist; here were the cheerful rich. I craved for Greyfriars, that absurd Public School, as I craved for pudding. There the boys wore top hats and tail-coats – Arthur Augustus D'Arcy, the toff, wore a monocle – they had feasts in their 'studies'; they sent a pie containing a boot to the bounder of the Remove; they rioted; they never did a stroke of work. They 'strolled' round 'the Quad' and rich uncles tipped them a 'fivah' which they spent on more food. Sometimes a shady foreign language master was seen to be in touch with a German spy. Very rarely did a girl appear in these tales.

The Japanese-looking boy was called Nott. He had a friend called Howard, the son of a compositor. The *Gem* and the *Magnet* united us. We called ourselves by Greyfriars' names and jumped about shouting words like 'Garoo'. We punned on our names. When anything went wrong we said, in chorus: 'How-'ard! Is it Nott?' And doubled with laughter dozens of times a day and as we 'strolled' arm in arm on the way home from school.

I knew this reading was sin and I counteracted by reading a short life of the poet Wordsworth. There was a rustic summer-house at the end of our back garden. It had stained glass windows. Driving my brothers and sisters out, I claimed it as my retreat and cell. When they kicked up too much noise I sat up on the thatched roof of the house where, when life at Grasmere bored me, I had a good view of what other boys were doing in their gardens. I forgot about prose and said I was going to be a poet and 'Dirty Poet' became the family name for me. Sedbergh is not far from the Lake Country: destiny pointed to my connexion with Wordsworth. We had a common experience of Lakes and Fells. His lyrical poems seemed too simple and girlish to me: I saw myself writing a new *Prelude* or *Excursion*. Also the line 'Getting and spending we lay waste our powers' struck home at our family. I read that Wordsworth had been Poet Laureate: this was the ideal. To my usual nightly prayers that the house should not catch fire and that no burglar should break in, I added a line urging God to make me Poet Laureate 'before I am twenty-one'. This prayer lasted until I was sixteen.

One day Mr Bartlett made this possibility seem nearer. He got us to put together a literary magazine. Nott and Howard efficiently produced a pair of thrillers, one set among the opium dens of Hong Kong. I got to work on a long poem. Finding – to my surprise – that Wordsworth was not a stirring model, I moved to Coleridge's *Cristabel*. My first line thrilled me. It ran: 'Diana, goddess of the spectre moon'. I turned in fifty or sixty lines of coagulated romantic images in this manner and waited for the startled applause, especially from Mr Bartlett. There was silence. There was embarrassment. Nott and Howard were stunned by the poem. Ginger Reed, a little red-haired Cockney flea, skinny, ill and lively, who skipped around cheeking me in the streets and clattering the hobnails of his brother's boots that were too heavy for his thin legs – Ginger Reed tore the poem to bits line by line:

why call a 'bird' Diana? Why 'spectre' – was the 'bird' dead? Metaphor and simile, I said. Stale, he said. I was very small, but he was smaller and people in Herne Hill might have been surprised to know that one urchin pestering another at a street corner were on the point of fighting about a poem, while a pale child with owlish glasses called Donald stood there as a kind of doleful referee. The thing to do was to wait for Bartlett, but he would not speak. At last I was driven to ask his opinion as he walked in the school yard.

'Too many long words,' he said. And no more.

I was wretched. A gulf opened between myself and Coleridge.

To me, my Diana was a burst of genius. I have never had the sensation since.

I went home and sitting in our attic on a tin trunk, which I called my desk, I gave up poetry for prose once again and started on my first novel. My father had sensibly given us the *Children's Encyclopaedia* and in that I had found some more Washington Irving, simplified and abridged from his book about the legends of the Alhambra. The thought of that ethereal Moorish girl rising from the fountain entranced me. Here was a subject: the story of that girl who rises and is caught in the wars of the Moors and the Spaniards. There was more than a boyish interest in war in this choice of subject. Nasty wars had been boiling up in Edwardian Europe. We had had an illustrated history of the Boer War at home; and in the illustrated papers there had been dramatic pictures of contemporary wars in Greece and the Balkans, pictures of destroyed muddy towns and fleeing people. The Balkan wars seeped into my novel. When I was short of invention – I could never make the Moorish girl do anything except wave her languorous arms – I put in a battle scene, usually a tragic defeat, ending with my stock device: a lament by the Moorish women looking on the battlefield for their dead. Laments had an intimate appeal; my mother lamented often in these days. Day after day I wrote, until my novel reached about 130 pages, and I showed some of it to my friends.

'How-'ard is it Nott?' they said, tactfully advising me to cut out the laments. I kept the MS from Ginger Reed. He was spiteful in these months. He always came top in arithmetic and was leaving school to become a van boy: stunted, he was older than the rest of us, we discovered. He was over fourteen and he jeered bitterly at us. We were rich, he said. We had opportunities, he jeered, as he ate his bread and dripping (his breakfast) as he danced about us in the school yard.

Then two bad things happened and their effect was to poison my life and was lasting. It took me many years to recover from them. Father discovered I was reading the *Gem* and the *Magnet*. To think that a son of a Managing Director of a Limited Company which had just paid off its debentures, a son who was always putting on the airs of a Professor, and always full of Mr Bartlett This and Mr Bartlett That: who had been brought up in the shadow of his grandfather's utterances about John Ruskin and possibly even deceived himself that he was John Ruskin, should bring such muck into the house.

We were sitting at tea. It was Sunday. The family looked at the criminal and not without pleasure. I had tried to force books on them. I had cornered them and made them listen to my poem and my novel. I had read *Thanatopsis* at them. I had made them play schools which they hated. I had hit out at the words Dirty Poet and had allowed no one near the tin trunk and, in fact, had put an onion in a jar of water on it, as a piece of Nature Study, to mark the intellectual claims on the spot. Naturally they couldn't help being a little pleased. My mother, always capricious, liable to treachery and perhaps glad not to be the centre of a quarrel herself for once, betrayed me also.

'He reads them all day. Dozens of them. Dirty things.'

'Where are they? Bring them down,' said my father. I went upstairs and came back with about twenty or thirty grubby *Gem*s and *Magnet*s.

'Good godfathers,' said my father, not touching the pile, for he hated dust and dirt. 'I give you your Saturday penny and this is what you're doing with it. Wasting the money I earn. I suppose you think you're so superior because you have a father who has his own business and you spend right and left on muck like this.'

'I borrowed them. A boy lent them to me.'

'A man is known by the company he keeps,' said my father. And getting up, his face greenish with disgust, he threw the lot in the fireplace and set fire to them.

'Walt, Walt, you'll have the soot down,' screamed my mother. 'You know we haven't had the sweep.'

But father liked a blaze. What could I say to Howard and Nott?

'Why do you read that muck when you could be reading John Ruskin?'

'We haven't got any of Ruskins's books.'

'He writes poetry. He wants to be a poet,' said my brother Cyril.

'He's writing a book, all over the table instead of his homework,' said my mother.

'No, upstairs.'

'Don't contradict your mother. What's this? So you are writing a book? I hope it will improve us. What is it? Where is it?'

'Upstairs,' the traitors chimed. 'Shall we go and get it?'

'No,' I shouted.

'Go and get it.'

'Oh, if he doesn't want us to see it . . .' my mother began.

'I suppose a boy would want his own father to see it,' said my father. Anger put me on the point of tears. Very easily I cried when Father reprimanded me.

I brought the manuscript and gave it to my father.

'The Alhambra – remember we used to go to the Alhambra, Beat?' he said.

'It's the Alhambra in Spain,' I said scornfully.

'Oh, superior!' said my father. 'Let's have a look at it.'

And, to my misery, he began reading aloud. He had scarcely read ten lines before he came across the following line:

'She adjusted her robe with ostentatious care. She omited to wear a cloak.'

'Ostentatious,' exclaimed my father. 'That's a big word – what does it mean?'

'I don't know,' I sulked.

'You wrote a word and you don't know what it means?'

'It means sort of proud, showing off . . .' I could not go on. The tears broke out and I sobbed helplessly. I had got the word from Marie Corelli.

'Ostentatious,' said my father. 'I never heard of it. And what's this? "Omited". I thought they taught you to spell.'

'Omitted,' I sobbed.

'Don't bully the boy,' said my mother. I tried to rescue myself in the Howard-Nott manner.

'O mite I have done better,' I blubbered.

'O-mite, omit – it's a pun,' I said and sent up a howl.

It ended, as trouble usually did in our house, with a monologue from Father saying that he had always dreamed – for a father always dreams – that having founded a business, he might have a son who – if he were worthy of it – might conceivably be invited to come into it, a privilege hundreds of young men less fortunately placed would give their eyes for. Only this week he had had an applicant. A young man who thought just because he was his father's son (his father being something big in the trade and making two or three thousand a year), he could just walk into anything. A matter on which Father instantly put him right, for he might have been to Eton and Harrow, but that meant nothing. For my father's business was God's business. Unlike other businesses, it was directed by the Divine Mind. 'And by the way,' Father said, 'I always look at a man's boots when he applies for a job.' My father's voice became warmer and more benign as he expanded on the subject of the Divine Mind, who was his manager, and we drifted into other fields. My mother's mind, less divine, wandered.

I took my novel back. I put it inside the tin trunk. Blackened by hatred, I did not touch it again. I hated my father. And one morning in the winter the hatred became intense or rather I decided I could never talk to him again about what went on in my mind.

It was an early morning of London fog. The room was dark and we had lit the gas. I was reading Shakespeare in bed. I had by now reached *Measure for Measure* when my father came in.

'Get out of bed you lazy hound,' he said. 'What are you reading?' He took the book and started reading himself and was perhaps startled by Claudio's proposal.

'Poetry,' he said. Then very seriously and quietly said: 'Do you really want to be a poet?'

'Yes I do.'

He went red with temper.

'If that's what you want,' he shouted, 'I have nothing more to say to you. I won't allow it. Get that idea out of your head at once.'

Why my father raged against my literary tastes I never really knew. He had been very poor, of course, and really feared I would 'starve in a garret'. He wanted – in fancy only – to found a dynasty in business; and he heard no word of money in writing poetry. At this time he had many anxieties and the family, from my mother down, exasperated and tormented him. He was a perfectionist. He was also an egoist who had identified himself – as indeed I was doing – with an ideal state of things. And then there comes a time when a man of strong vitality finds it hard to bear the physical sight of his growing sons. He found it harder and harder; and he was to be even more severe with my brothers and my sister, especially Cyril who adored him. We were at the beginning of a very long war; these were the first rumblings. One by one, we fell into secrecy. In self-preservation we told him lies.

He was behaving exactly to us as his own father had behaved to him; there was a strain of gritty, north-country contempt and sarcasm in all of us.

. . .

Chapter 9

I was rushing downstairs at school because I was late for the parade of the Cadet Corps which I hated, when one of my puttees came undone. I tripped and fell down the full flight of stairs. A hot pain shot into my foot and I fainted. A master came to help me and told me it was nothing; my ankle was not broken, but I had sprained it badly. A boy wheeled me on the cross-bar of his bike to West Dulwich station and then took me home. I bathed the foot and Mother put a cold compress on it, and I lay, aching but happy in the thought of a week or so's holiday from Mr Callaghan.

My father was home on one of his visits that evening and called me into his study. I said I could not get upstairs. 'You can get up easily,' he said. I put on a great act in getting up the stairs.

We rarely went into his study for it was uninteresting. We were used to the small bookcase, the sacred gate-legged table with an art needlework runner on it, the engraving of Daniel in the Lions' Den, and a fading photograph of the Mother Church of the Christian Scientists in Boston. There were piles of unopened American periodicals on the table and a small collection of morocco-bound books. Father rarely used the room himself.

'Now,' he said. 'I want you to understand there are no accidents in God's kingdom. You think you have sprained your ankle, but it says in the Bible that we are all the children of God, made in his image and likeness. How can you believe that a good omnipotent God would let one of his children sprain his ankle?'

The argument floored me.

'I suppose not,' I said. 'But . . .'

'I have purposely not told you anything about this, but I expect you have heard I am a Christian Scientist. I have no wish to force my religion on you and perhaps you prefer to believe what your mother believes, but I will tell you about it and then you can make

209

your mind up. Christian Science can heal your so-called sprained ankle this very moment. In fact is is healed now, for nothing has happened to it. That is simply a mistake.'

My father then explained to me the doctrine of Christian Science. If I agreed that God was Good and Infinite and Omnipotent and had created Man in his image and likeness then there was no place where evil could possibly exist. Evil was an illusion, generated by the five senses. They were unreliable.

'Your eyes tell you that railway lines meet in the distance, but that is an illusion; they do not meet. You believe you can see a swollen ankle, but God can't see a swollen ankle, and nor can you, in reality, for since you are made in his image and likeness, you can only see what He sees.'

My father said that if I wished he would demonstrate this to me by treating me in the Christian Science way, at once. I agreed. He closed his eyes and began the process I afterwards understood as 'knowing the Truth' about me.

I was very moved. I had often hated my father but this first moment of intimacy with him was good. I felt that I was going to be cut off from him no longer. And that there would be other good results. If what he said was true, the quarrels would stop in the house, we would see more of him, he would take us to his Christian Science church, we would have some friends, for we were not allowed to have friends to the house. Anyway, in Bromley, we knew no one except the organist next door.

His eyes opened. He said:

'You are healed. I want you to walk to school tomorrow. You'll find in the morning that you can.'

And then he slipped one of the periodicals on his desk out of its wrapper and said I could read it. It was the *Christian Science Sentinel* and it contained not only articles, but a number of testimonies of healing of all kinds of diseases. He opened another wrapper. It contained a newspaper, the *Christian Science Monitor*. I discovered it had a literary page. I resented being sent back to school but I was impressed by being taken into my father's confidence and of hearing about his religion properly – for until then we had no real notion of what it was and why he made the startling statements he often shouted in our home.

I woke up next morning and my ankle was still bad. He made me walk to the station and then walk to school from West Dulwich. I was in great pain. In a few days it gradually got better – which is not surprising for doctors recommend walking on a sprained foot. At the end of the week my father said I had had a startling proof of the truth of Christian Science teaching. I did not think I had but I set about reading the works of Mrs Eddy. There was a great deal I could not understand but the fundamental teaching was that life was a dream – how many writers had said that! The novelty, the dramatic and beneficent nature of the doctrine, exalted me, the hatred, sins and defeats of my life seemed to melt before my eyes.

'You believe what your father does?' my mother asked, peering suspiciously at me.

'I do,' I said and explained to her. She had lost an ally.

'I can't fathom it,' said my mother. 'I keep on having these whitlows. It's cruel. Look at it.' She held up her poisoned thumb.

Underlying my conversion to Christian Science was a desire for friends and the fact that this church had a Sunday School to which one could go until the age of twenty, was a strong attraction. The Sunday School met in a pretty house, the church services were held in a light and pleasant hall. The sect was cheerful and business-like: the notion of original sin had vanished, so had guilt. We were all good. It is true that evil was said to be an illusion caused by malicious animal magnetism, a mysterious yet unreal force that did its best to influence the mind and particularly 'worked through sex' whatever that meant. But the evil was not in ourselves. One became as guiltless as any atheist, and I have never since been able to regard the doctrine of original sin as anything more than an intellectual convenience, though it is more than forty years since I went into a Christian Science church.

It is natural to have religious emotions in adolescence and – except for the very few who have a religious vocation – it is well for it to be short. The influence of Christian Science on my father's life and upon us was eventually dulling and even tragic; for although doctors now speak with mild tolerance of the usefulness of its belief in the influence of the mind upon the body and are amiably amused by their patients who dabble with both medicine and faith, in order to be on the safe side, the occasional healings or even the many tragic failures to heal are not the important aspect of this religion. The real objection is to the impoverishment of mind, the fear of knowledge and living that Christian Science continuously insinuates; the futility of its total argument and its complacency. It operates like a leucotomy that puts the patient into an amiable stupor. A debased form of New England Transcendentalism,

Christian Science spread easily in New England in the general pessimism that followed the Civil War; it was one of the symptoms of the decay of the vigorous New England culture. William James treated it gently in his *Varieties of Religious Experience* because of his psychological curiosity; but he understood it was an enfeebled form of Emersonian metaphysics; and, in fact, my interest in it was sustained by the discovery of Emerson's writings. How clearly now one sees the sage, drifting as he grows older, in two directions at once; up into the thin upper air of a beautiful but nebulous metaphysical persuasion and down into the cult of success. The heirs of the Transcendentalists were businessmen; they blandly denied the reality of matter in order to justify themselves in raking in more and more of it.

To England, Christian Science was brought by one or two aristocratic ladies, heirs of that small evangelical movement which had caught the consciences of the upper classes in the eighteenth century. The new religion was a resource for those who could not face late-Victorian doubts: the mixture of religion (without theology) and of supposed science smoothed over the troubles caused by Darwin and Huxley; its optimism accorded with the continuously growing wealth in England. The religion appealed to the ambitious lower middle class and also to the insensitive and organizational among the blander uppers. It solved so many problems of public conscience: there were nice women who would go down to the slums, watch a hospital train packed with wounded go by at Bromley station, look at processions of unemployed, close their eyes, 'Know the Truth' and go away convinced that they had helped to 'heal' the situation. Their complacency was naive and sentimental; they were indignant if you suggested that they had closed their minds to reality, for they regarded themselves as 'true' revolutionaries, and indeed had to put up with a lot of ridicule and attack. This stimulated them. Most of them had belonged to the traditional churches and were glad to be free of the tragic implication of the Christian myth and its cult of suffering. There was something Quakerish about them. It is characteristic that they had a daily newspaper which reported no crime, no accounts of disaster – though the war was a problem – in which the general tone was liberal and which for years had some of the best foreign correspondents in daily journals; its literary pages were un-adventurous, but many good English and American writers contributed to them. The gap between the tone of this paper and the material of their purely religious papers was great: the difference between literacy and amateur moralizing.

Most of all, I was attracted by this newspaper: the *Christian Science Monitor*. To one as little educated as I was, it was an educator, for it was imbued with that unembarrassed seriousness about learning things which gives American life its tedium but also a moral charm. In Europe the standards have been high for the few, the path of education has been made severe. If we learn, if we express ourselves in the arts, we are expected to be trained by obstruction and to emerge on our own and to be as exclusive, in our turn, as our mentors; willingness and general goodwill are – or have been until very lately – despised. There were, in fact, better popular educators in England than in America, but a paper like the *Monitor* made my interests sound easier. In reality the gaps in the *Monitor* – as I came to know when later on I wrote for it – were preposterous. It was good about foreign politics because no Christian Scientist and no American – at that time – was very interested in them.

I thought of Christian Scientists as living in a dramatic and liberating illumination. It was natural that I should be attracted to this religion. Its idealism and novelty appealed to one who had scarcely ever been to church but had lived in a house filled with religious echoes and disputes. I had been brought up as a Christian without being taught very much of what Christianity was. It was nothing but words. This new religion was *taught* to me. Father had a natural attraction to all quacks and to any crank – outside the political – who was mellifluous.

But how was it that I, with all my literary pretensions, did not see that Mrs Eddy was a loose thinker and a very bad writer; that scarcely one of her sentences followed from its predecessor, that she blocked in long strings of big words like Soul, Principle, Substance, God, Good when in doubt; that her books were a rambling collection of assertions and jumbled quotations from the Bible? How was it – after all the jokes at school about 'artful alliteration's awful aid', I could stand a phrase like 'Meekly our Master Met the Mockery' . . . and many more like it? Or not laugh out loud at 'Thou art right, oh immortal Shakespeare' whom she showed no signs of having read except in a book of quotations? It is astonishing how faith makes one shut one's eyes; or how willingly the intelligence takes a holiday from intelligence. Why, at least, did the language of the King James's Bible not preserve me?

213

The answer to that is simple: *that* language appeared to me not of this world, a spiritual utterance and not a language at all. After all, why had I swallowed the Bible and believed that the Israelites were superior in spirit, history and culture to the Greeks, the Medes and Persians, peoples far more gifted and enlightened?

Fortunately, nature asserted itself. I was soon leading a double life. I believed, yet did not believe, very comfortably, at the same time. The believing part of me was the simple idealist: also the insubordinate youth was vain of belonging to a sect that was often ridiculed. It appealed to my vanity to belong to a peculiar minority and I did not notice that we were a mild and tepid group who had cut off our noses to spite our faces. More than the nose: I was to discover among my co-religionaries that we had become as dim as eunuchs.

What began to save us was our family egotism. From our mother we had inherited an eye and ear for comedy, from our grandfather and father, a gift for irony and sarcasm.

All sects have their jargon and Father, eager as an advertising man is for slogans, had picked them all up and lived by them. We soon saw that we were supposed to go through the fundamental process of 'knowing the Truth' about this or that person or situation. For example, the truth about a burglar was that he was not a burglar but a child of God, who had seemingly taken to burglary because he had failed to see that he had 'abundance' already, for did not the Scriptures say: 'Day by day, the manna fell.' Or, rather, a hymn said that. A phrase that infuriated Mother. If I 'knew the Truth' about Mr Callaghan, that child of God, he would stop insulting my English; or if I knew the Truth about my father's violent opposition to our inviting friends to the house, or to my desire to be a writer, he would stop these tyrannies. I tried it, but was haunted by the danger that I was transforming Mr Callaghan and my father, without their permission. Suppose they, or indeed I, became transfigured, would it not be unnerving? I was handing out dangerous haloes. It seemed far too risky to know the Truth about oneself. But many of the good people – though mostly the bossy ones – in the church that met at the Town Hall were knowing the Truth about each other left and right. And even more, they were enjoined to 'voice' it when it was opportune; it was constantly opportune and rarely complimentary. Father 'voiced' very often to a Mrs E, who 'voiced' back. Not to 'know the Truth' was a certain way of 'letting Error into consciousness' – I have since discovered that this, like the word 'problem', is a common Americanism: perhaps, after all, Christian Science is a normal product of the middle-class American ethos. One of the ways of 'letting Error in' was to 'outline' the desire we were 'working', i.e. praying for. It was right to 'work', say, for a better job; but it was 'outlining' to say what precise job you wanted. Father never 'outlined' that he wanted £15 to pay the quarter's rent and stop a writ being served: he worked for 'supply', i.e. the infinitude of God's blessings, a fatal thing for his character; he would always have been better off with the Finite. Instead of 'outlining' you let God's will 'unfold'. Hence the delays in sending us to school, the refusal to take a family holiday: and eventually, Father took to allowing his manufacturing and sales to 'unfold' and sat in his office, gazing at estate agents' offers in a dream that at last became stagnant, then corrupting and finally pernicious. Still, when something did 'unfold' one had 'made one's demonstration', i.e. demonstrated the truth of Christian Science. If anything went wrong in the lives of any of the church members – Mr X was still stone deaf, Mr Y losing his job, Mrs X still walking on a club foot – Father would snort that they 'had not made their demonstration'. We had a sad example in our own home: Mother – in refusing to have anything to do with this religion, and becoming more and more a worn-out nervous wreck – was obviously not going to make her demonstration. But what could you do, Father would ask? It's no good casting your pearls before swine. We let a great deal of Error in, in our home.

Sunday was the worst day for Error. It began early with my brother and me standing in the scullery and cleaning the boots and shoes of the family. We did the younger children's first, then our own and then moved on to a long display of Father's. This was an anxious task for, when they were done, we would have to take them up to his bedroom where he examined them, pair by pair, and often sent us back to do them again. He was vigilant for specks of cunningly disguised mud; and he always turned the boots over to see if we had blackened and polished the instep between heel and sole.

This was a preparation for his rising and dressing, a long business. Once or twice he was asked to take the collection at the church and then he was in a state only to be compared with that of an actor on a first night. His lotions and perfumes made the air heady, as he changed from shirt to shirt and went through his collars minutely examining them. Mother would send us up to spy to see 'how your father's getting on'. At last, on these occasions, he appeared downstairs, in a tail-coat, a waistcoat discreetly outlined by a white, piqué under-waistcoat, and a pair of trousers of astounding and tigerish stripes. He wored a winged collar, a silk stock, a pearl tie-pin and a buttonhole. On his feet were spats.

'Beat,' he would call, in the voice of one getting ready for sacrifice, 'brush me.'

Mother, dressed anyhow, came out of the kitchen, and going down on her knees would brush him, working upwards to the summit. He stood there like some exotic, tropical plant that perhaps needed watering.

It was our duty to go to church with him and not to the Sunday School, on these special Sundays. On the way, except to mutter words like 'Keep your feet up', once or twice, he scarcely spoke, from fear of spoiling his entrance at our tabernacle. He so outshone the other sidesmen that they backed away and he walked up and down the aisle between the chairs with all the polish and *savoir-faire* of the perfect shopwalker. Sniggers – we were annoyed to hear – came from one or two of our friends, and ladies nodded ironically to each other.

'The guv'nor,' Cyril muttered, 'has overdone it.'

He had. Yet, if anyone of that crowd appeared to be the image and likeness of the Divine Mind, we felt, that man was our father. We kept our eye on him, our excess of glory, as Mrs Norman (the first reader) read out the first words of a passage from the King James's Bible and the second reader (Mr Gordon) responded with what were called the 'correlative passages' from Mrs Eddy which had little or no relation to the Biblical passage, and which were of impenetrable verbosity. They held our attention for a while because, I now suppose, they appealed to that self-satisfaction which is born out of straining to find meaning in the meaningless.

After the service everyone chatted happily. Father stood apart as a rule, on the look-out for Error, and as the congregation was mostly female, there was a good deal of it about, from his point of view; but generally his view, and mine, was that we had had a refreshing contact with the Absolute. We walked home, but the voyage down from the Absolute to the Relative is tricky. Mother would be in her usual state of fighting with the kitchen stove.

'Walt, look at this brute. Look at the smoke.'

'Letting Error in,' muttered Cyril.

Mother spoke of the stove as of a horse kicking up its legs.

'Push the damper,' said Father.

'You expect me to slave ...' Mother began. She was a talented wrecker of Sundays. Father changed his clothes and from this moment the day went to pieces.

Why, I asked, did this happen? Why did Eternal Harmony vanish so quickly? Mrs Norman and others would have said we were being 'handled' by malicious animal magnetism; others, 'higher up in the movement' would have said we were being 'handled by Rome', for it was well known to advanced students that the Roman Catholic priesthood sent out spells of witchcraft especially upon Christian Scientists; many a 'problem' was made difficult because the jealous Jesuits – highly trained in these things – were sending out anti-prayers to frustrate us. Having escaped from the dead hand of theology, we found ourselves eager for magic and superstition. This disturbed me, but Mrs Norman told me not to worry about that now and asked me kindly how 'the writing was getting on'.

'Desire is prayer' are the opening words of *Science and Health with a Key to the Scriptures*. I was nearing my sixteenth birthday: I was desire in person, frantic, stiff with it. To sit in our Sunday School faced by several pretty girls was an ordeal. I could not take my eyes off the breasts of Mrs Murstein, our teacher, a Rubens-like woman who wore her blouses so low, in the fashion of the time, that the tops of those rumbustious globes were easily seen, indeed positively offered. Her rich lips, her faint moustache, her forty-year-old but innocent doll-like eyes destroyed me as she explained to us that the true meaning of 'to commit adultery' was the 'mixing of incompatible elements' – an example was adulterated food. I had read fortunately a popular book that told me masturbation would *not* affect my health or drive me mad; but my burdened state was too much for my modesty. At Alleyn's, someone would pass the word along that 'old Johnson' was playing pocket billiards and so was Fatty Brown; the whole of Remove B was as stiff as monkeys. Cook, the new French master, made jokes about it, which was a relief. But, at that age, one cannot get it out of one's head that one is, if not unique, at least visible in this villainous and muscle-bound state. I hated to go into shops where girls were working because of it; yet I could not stop myself trying to catch up with girls in the street. In Sunday School I sublimated.

'Still, still with Thee when purple morning breaketh,' we sang the hymn, but as fast as I sublimated, so the sublimation increased the desire and, as I sang, I was in bed with Holy Eileen or Doris or Isabel singing in the row in front. I dared not look up from my hymn-book at the pretty girls and my eyes sought out plain and ugly ones; but the disadvantage of this was that the pretty girls looked coldly innocent and the plain ones were more eager to respond. One could only cling to Mrs Eddy's mixture of sentimentality about 'trysting' and her severe teaching – and St Paul's – that sexual intercourse was something to 'overcome' in the interests of something higher. One clung. One believed. Yet every instinct told me that the doctrine was ludicrous; and the result of it was that my desires were perverted in their fantasy. Dreams of sadism, of terrible sexual sacrifices on altars, of torture by machines, haunted my pious head; so that when I hear of some maniac tried for crimes of sexual perversion I think there, but for the Grace of God, go I. But it is not by the Grace of the Christian Science God or any other, that I have escaped.

Certainly fear of scandal or disease were responsible for my chastity for many years. I might dream otherwise, but chastity was a pride. The possibility of becoming an artist of some kind seemed small, but it also seemed to depend on it. I should lose command of my whole self if I lost it, and that would be the end of the force that made me want to be an artist. At school, when the boys said they had girls, I knew they wanted to settle down in little villas where they lived, in jobs like their fathers' jobs, marry, have children. The thought repelled me. To go from family life into family life again, seemed to me tragic; for myself, a death. To be alone – I told my mother – was the idea; to be unhappy was not inevitable. But there was one infallible resource: literature and art.

Mother looked mockingly at me; I could see the alarm and the humour move over her face, and then her expression settle into something stonily accusing.

'I never heard anything like it in me natural. You are going to be a very wicked man,' she said. And covered it up with: 'I can't make head or tail of any of you.'

I found many things to interest me in Christian Science. It introduced me to Emerson, Thoreau, Hawthorne. I was rather snobbishly shocked to see Mrs Eddy had admired Whittier, a namby-pamby poet. To keep me occupied the following year Father made me translate a Christian Science pamphlet into German; the smattering of German metaphysical terms interested me. The religion sounded better in German. I had a bad month with the origin of evil, because, to my dismay, I defeated several older members of our church in my enquiries and arguments. There was alarm about my doubts: I was handed on from eminence to eminence, and eventually to a visiting Christian Science lecturer. The young are surprisingly decent and tactful; I agreed with what was said, but I did not believe a word of it. Any fool could see this error and I was a worse fool than most, but I let the matter slide. There were more important things than the question of the origin of evil on my mind.

A more serious concern for me was the attitude of my co-religionaries to literature and the arts. Clearly art prolonged the errors of the senses, the greater the art, the greater the error. The word 'death' for example, was never used by Christian Scientists; one 'passed on' for one never, in fact, died. Similarly descriptions of battles, illness, 'inharmony' etc., were banned or had, at any rate, to be so framed in 'Suffer it to be so now' as to be emasculated. Insofar as Shakespeare or Homer approached Christian Science beliefs they were considered good, yet sadly lacking. It was disappointing to see that Christian Scientists were quick to 'give up' things – they gave up sex, and wrecked their marriages on this account, and it was notoriously a menopause religion; they gave up politics; they gave up art but, oddly, they did not give up business.

Mr Graves gave up music; he looked back lingeringly at his passion for Beethoven. He would play a little but reflect that it was hard to see which part of the music came from the Divine Mind and which from Mortal Mind. Mr Hotchkiss, the lawyer with big feet, occasionally took a glass of wine, but he had given up reading Russian novels: there was something fleshy in Tolstoy; a Miss Humphrey had given up the National Gallery; for though the pictures (she said) were works of genius, it was waste of time now to consider anything but the images in the mind of God. There was almost unanimous feeling against a couple called Fitzgerald who had not yet given up socialism. Many sympathized with a Mrs Merton, a lady of large, low duck-like breast which she bore before her like a personal tragedy: her husband played in amateur theatricals and wanted to leave the bank where he worked and go on the stage. So far nothing had 'unfolded' and Mrs Merton conveyed to her friends the reason for this. So did he to me: he was one of those lost middle-aged men who confide in everyone.

'Victor, I know what's holding me up. I'm carnal.'

Also he was a chain-smoker. Everyone was sorry for Mrs Merton because she had a carnal husband.

It seemed to me that if I approached the Divine Mind on the subject of literature, I would have to give it up or – and this is what generally happened in our religion – I would be allowed to start and then I would find I had risen above it and leave it. However, Father came down from London one day and said that in Hollywood many actresses were Christian Scientists. That was a long way off; in England people took a less cheery attitude to the religion.

Such was my state of confusion in the autumn of 1916. I went to my room at the top of the house in the evenings to read Macaulay and to see if I could get a sight of the large lady lodger in the house opposite, undressing. I gazed at my own naked body in a mirror and could, at mere thought, make my organ stand upright; how surprising I looked. What was the Divine Mind going to do with this? I tried to write but could think of no subject. I sat in the laburnum tree at the bottom of the garden, feeling the lift of its boughs in the wind, imagining I was flying or sailing. More than once in that tree I shut my eyes and tried to divest myself of my mortal senses and mind and, in a few empty seconds, waited to be filled with the Divine as the mystics, I discovered years afterwards, tried to experience a unity with God. Sometimes I seemed on the point of this union, when a car hooted or my mother called and I came sulkily down. I did not know then that my methods were dubious: I ought to have felt conviction of sin, I ought to have mortified my body; alas I liked my body. But one afternoon in the laburnum tree, where I had taken Molière's *L'Avare* to read, I *did* have a convincing experience. The pleasure of finding that French was getting easier to read, the pleasure in the sparkle of words in that comedy, suddenly made me hear a voice. The voice said: 'You are a sceptic.' It was my own voice, but speaking as I had never heard it before. I closed the book, climbed down the tree and stood on the lawn longing for the sensation to remain, for someone to tell it to. Even as I longed, the beautiful sensation faded; but I had had it and I felt older.

An event – innocent in appearance – soon showed that I had been 'letting Error in' on a serious scale. It was announced that Grandfather and Grandmother Pritchett were coming down from Yorkshire to stay. Mother set about cleaning the house from top to bottom, for she knew the old lady would open every cupboard of it. The larder was cleared, for Grandma would bring two large boxes, one containing a week's baking of her best bread, cakes and pastries; the other a couple of geese from Appleton. Mother prepared two stewed rabbits – no other meat being available in wartime – and my brother betted that he would be given the heads, because she disliked him. So prepared, we waited for the three o'clock train, when my father (who had slipped away from his aircraft factory) brought his parents down. They did not arrive. Nor at four. Nor at five. We had no telephone and could not ring up my father to ask for news. Not until eight o'clock did they arrive. Into the house walked Grandmother, white-faced, in pain, holding one hand to her chest, and leaning on my father's arm. After her came Grandfather, his right arm in a sling and his head and hand bandaged, and one eye blackened. Once a soldier, he now marched in wounded like a true soldier. The train they had travelled in from Manchester had come off the rails and their coach had struck a bridge. They were scarcely in the house before a reporter came to interview them. The next day we were proud to see for the first time Granda's name in the papers.

Manchester Express Derailed. Minister Injured.

It is to misunderstand our family to think that this drama passed off entirely in anxious questions, affection and condolences; within half an hour Grandmother, Grandfather and Father were shouting in angry argument across the table, about God and 'that Eddy woman'. Grandma, for once, was on her daughter-in-law's side and she said she doubted but what Father wouldn't drive Beatty 'to go elsewhere'. She was appeased by serving the rabbit. 'Eh, Cyril, ah'd forgotten you,' she said, when we were all served except him. And she gave him the head of one of the rabbits.

After the meal talk became serious, about trade, the war, and so on, while Grandmother told how Father had given her the best handbag in his showroom and said, 'Has he given you one?' 'Yes,' said my mother and went to get it and showed her. The old lady was upset.

'Eh, Walter, you gave Beatty a better handbag than you gave your own mother.'

'Here, take it,' said Mother.

'Eh, ah think ah will,' said the old lady. And did so.

Grandfather said:

'How old's Victor? Fifteen? And still at school?'

I gazed expectantly at the man who I thought was a friend to my hopes.

'Put him to work,' said my grandfather.

So one is betrayed. I could not believe it. Everything I hoped for collapsed in that minute. Tears came to my eyes.

'There's three more mouths to feed,' my grandfather said. 'You must start earning.'

How was I to face the boys I knew, boys to whom I had boasted and before whom I had unwisely glittered? How was I to face Mr Callaghan? Where was the School Prize for French? To despair was now added shame. If Ginger could have seen me then what a triumph for him.

In fact, at school, everyone envied me and Callaghan said:

'Just as well. You haven't done much good here. What are you going into?'

'The leather trade.' For so it had been decided.

Callaghan gave one of his delighted sniffs.

'Nothing like leather,' he said over his shoulder, as he waltzed out of the room under his rusty gown.

My boyhood was over.

Despite his literary inclinations, V.S. Pritchett left school at sixteen, and went into the leather trade. Although he was initially dispirited by the mechanical repetition of the work, the encouragement to become a writer in fact came from people in the trade. But this ambition was achieved only when, following long illness, he emigrated to Paris; he lived there for two years earning his living as a shellac salesman, photographer's assistant, and finally as a freelance writer.

We take up the second volume of his autobiography in Paris, at the moment of transformation: as the youth Victor Sawdon Pritchett becomes the professional writer and critic V.S. Pritchett.

Midnight Oil

Chapter 2

Now I could speak two kinds of French fairly well. The first was polite. On my free Sunday afternoons I used to sit on a hard upholstered chair and have conversations about literature with a severe and very old French lady in Auteuil. She was a friend of my landlady's priest and approved only of the greatest writers – Racine and Corneille – who were correct in style and in morals. She pulled me up at every sentence and I had to be wary of the grammar and pronunciation I had picked up from Pierre and the Breton at the shop. A mild phrase like '*Sans blague*' annoyed her. My afternoons with the old lady were painfully polished exercises.

My desire to appear to be French took an extravagant turn. For a long time Pierre and I had admired each other's footwear. He wanted me to send to England for some shoes like mine. I admired his boots.

'Let's swap,' I said.

We measured our feet and, one evening in the shop, we swapped. He wore boots laced to the top from the small, black patent toecaps. The boots had yellowish uppers that looked like a pair of old banana skins and very high, small, black heels. Tipping forward in his boots – which pinched a bit – I was forced out of my natural rushing walk into a small mincing step. I was very much struck by this when I saw myself in the mirrors of shops. The next thing was to get a wide-brimmed black hat with a round crown of the Bohemian kind worn by the photographers. On a youth as short as I was, these hats looked like umbrellas. I could not afford them. I settled for one with a high crown, pinched in the middle at the top, black and with a wide-ish brim. It made me look tall – more hat than suit. A pipe was the next thing. I would pass a shop in the Boulevard St Michel where there was a pipe with a ten-inch stem. I used to visit this pipe nearly every day, yearning for it. At last I got paid for one of the articles I had written and bought the pipe. I filled it with rough French tobacco which blazed up like dry hay, and I was soon sick in the street. This long pipe was impossible out of doors, for it was easily jogged down my throat if someone bumped into me; and it nearly dragged my teeth out. I returned to cigarettes: Gauloises or an English cigarette called Pirate which blistered my tongue. I smoked all day long, except in the shop. I took to doubling and trebling the usual amount of coffee I drank because Balzac had done this. On my way to the shop I passed his house in the Rue Raynouard which reminded me of this; and there was another reason for drinking more coffee. I wanted to get a dark complexion. I had seen a man of thirty-five or so sitting on the terrace of a café; a tired, cynical boulevardier who had the dark olive look I wanted. His hair was receding. I cut a chunk of hair on the left side of my head to get this superb effect of a dissolute life.

I began to go to cheap cabarets. There were two popular places in Montmartre called Le Ciel and L'Enfer. In L'Enfer one was greeted by a smelly young wit dressed as the devil who mocked each customer. I slipped in behind two middle-aged women and so escaped his joke. But to the ladies he shouted:

'*Oh, voilà deux nourisses de Saint-Germain-en-laye-en-lait.*' This joke came out every time I went there. I picked up a lot of songs and swapped them with Pierre.

'You can see M Schwep has a mistress,' said the Breton.

'I have,' I said.

'Where does she live?'

'In my quarter. Auteuil.'

'That is chic.'

They were awed.

'Is she English?'

'Yes.'

'Ah,' said the Breton, giving me a slap. 'You come from Great Britain. I come from Little Britain. We understand each other. You're cunning; you've kept it very quiet.'

I had invented this, of course.

That summer, the Bohemian crowd in Montparnasse had thinned. They put on fisherman's shirts in fisherman blue, or loud red and white checks and went off to the South of France. I could not afford such a journey, but in September when my fortnight's holiday came, I took the train to Rouen. My brother came over from London with a friend. I had longed to sleep *à la belle étoile* in the manner of Stevenson. I warned my brother and his friend of this, but they arrived in Rouen wearing bowler hats, without knapsacks, ground-sheets or blankets. The hats disgusted me; I made them leave them in the railway cloakroom. A heavy lunch, beginning with oysters, and washed down with cheap wine, put us in a better temper. The friend wanted to get to Paris, but we forced him to walk northward. We were aiming for Dieppe. An hour or two after leaving Rouen clouds piled up, then a heavy rain came on as we got to a large forest where we sheltered. We sat under trees eating bread and sausage and then pressed on into the forest. Soon the wet darkness came, the footpaths confused us, and we had to find our way by striking matches that went out almost as soon as they were struck. The expedition was losing its high literary quality and soon sank to the coarse level of *Three Men in a Boat*; for when we decided to lie down for the night my ground-sheet and blanket had to serve for the three of us.

So our night passed in a vulgar struggle with the blanket: now my brother pulled it his way, and the other youth pulled it off both of us. The rain, spouting through the trees, came down on us in lumps. At about three in the morning we could stand this no longer. We got up, and finding a path we groped mile after mile, until daylight when at the edge of the forest we could smell apples. We were among the Normandy orchards and dogs barked at us. But no one was about. The rain stopped, the sun came out and we found a lane and staggered along it. We fell asleep as we walked, like drunks; we had to hold one another up. Eventually we gave in and lay down on a wet grass bank by the roadside.

Two hours later we woke up; we found we had rolled off the bank and were sleeping in the road. One of Maupassant's peasants croaking along with a wagon had to stop to get by us. He did not say much. I was shabby, but the respectable clothes of my brother and his friend, though mud-spattered, must have saved us from suspicion. The fine rain came on again. We went through a sodden cornfield to a river where we got out of our clothes and stood naked among the boulders waist-deep in rushing cold water; then we wrang out our clothes, dried ourselves on our shirts, and went on to a village. No villagers were about, but there were carters at the inn: we wisely drank a lot of cognac. My companions wanted to stay, but I was fiercely for the road; we found another village inn kept by a decent couple. Seeing an advertisement for a drink called *Amourette*, we plumped for that. The landlady dried our clothes and gave us a huge meal with two bottles of Normandy cider. Strong as Devonshire cider is, Normandy cider is much stronger; it flowed into us as innocently as lemonade and suddenly made us incapable. The man and his wife couldn't stop laughing at us and the end of it was that we slept in a bed that night.

The roads of Normandy are exposed, hedgeless and boring. We slept out again, in a field and once in a barn. Outside Dieppe we visited a castle from tower to dungeon; in the town we guzzled, but slept out on a cliff outside. I tried to make coffee on a methylated spirit stove and when we lay down we spent a cold night watching the lights of the fishing boats in the Channel. Then, for several days, we walked back to Rouen by some roundabout route through some pretty places. I enjoyed this journey, as a young animal does, but except for games of billiards with village people in the inns and a dance with some railway workers and their girls, the expedition was not up to the standard of Borrow, Stevenson and Belloc. There were no heroic invocations or poetic jollities; only grunts and wondering if our money would hold out. Jerome K. Jerome, as I say, haunted it. It worried me that as a traveller I was evidently tame. I also saw that to travel well, one must travel alone.

The secret of happiness (they say) is to live in the imagination. I had many imaginary lives, building up every day and dissolving at night. I lay in bed reading, occasionally putting a date on the page of say *Le Père Goriot* and wondered what I should be doing in years incredibly far ahead – say 1930 or 1940. A strange woman with large dark eyes and wearing a long red velvet robe used to console me sexually. I fancy she must have been an idealized version of that disturbing second-hand-clothes dealer my family had taken us to see in the Edgware Road when I was a boy. She had worn red velvet too. Late one night, having waited in a café near the Etoile for the orchestra to get round again to the Danse Macabre by Saint-Saens, I walked up the Avenue Hoche. Two girls jumped out at me and one called out:

'*Où allez vous, M le Marquis? Où couchez vous?*'

'*Chez la Marquise,*' I said, shooting up into High Society, this being near the Avenue Hoche. What wit! I was a marquis.

And I *had* found a marquise, a young girl. At any rate, her mother was having a quarrel with a Baroness, an Italian-American. This girl was training in Paris to be an actress. I met her at the time of my acquaintance with Ralph Shaw: and my tales about him went down well with her mother who was very snobbish. ('Who were his people?' she kept speculating.) Our meeting had a headlong, unreal quality that lasted throughout our friendship. I had not been near the Christian Scientists for some time (one or two complained that my breath almost knocked them down with the smell of wine) and I found they had moved their meeting place because their numbers had trebled. The new meeting place was a fashionable night-club off the Champs Elysées, which was closed on Sundays. Two or three of the few men in the congregation used to go there at eight in the morning to remove the tables and the bottles, open the windows to get out the smell of wine and stale tobacco, and turn about twenty *Gravures Libertines* to the wall. On the platform where the band had played the night before, the Readers now read from Mrs Eddy and the Bible, in that curious game of swapping texts which dissenting Protestants play.

Here I saw a graceful, but militant, well-tailored woman with straw-coloured hair come in with a girl so strange and exquisite that my eyes filled with tears. Her body was slight, but she had a fine forehead and black hair that had the soft gleam of oil in its waves. Her long eyelashes hung over large blue eyes and she had very heavy short eyebrows. She wore a big bow in her hair so that the effect was of being half girl, half heavy-headed, thin-legged butterfly, rather than anything human; yet the artifice was not complete. Her lips and her round chin could hardly keep still for amusement. As the two passed where I was sitting I could see the maddening dark hair of her armpits under her sleeveless summer dress and there was a breath of musky scent that put me in a frantic state. It melted into sadness for I had the sensation (when she sat down two or three rows in front of me and I gazed at every move of her shoulders) that she had passed into an unattainable foreign distance. The older woman – her mother, I was to find out – could not have been more than thirty-seven. She was a pretty woman, with a small decided chin and the proud collected eyes of a cat, and all through the service she kept turning to look at her daughter's hair and her face, as if the girl were some adored doll. Afterwards, a middle-aged Italian was talking to them and gazing as intently as I was at the daughter and the mother looked at him mockingly as if she were saying: 'Yes, of course, you have fallen for her. Everyone does. Isn't she dazzling? I invented her. You're not dangerous. But she is. She's mine.' And, indicating the rest of us with a nod, 'How she shows up these awful people.'

I went away desperate. I had heard the mother's voice: they were rich, inaccessible English.

The next Sunday I went again in order to suffer. But, after the service the mother was caught up in a conversation with a grand and sullen-looking woman, and the daughter was alone. I was impelled by a force I did not know existed in me. I worked my way through the chairs to her. We looked at each other. I smiled. She smiled. I knocked over a chair. She laughed. We started talking fast. She had a low warm voice and everything that came spitting out of me made her laugh more. I had an inspiration. I pointed to the pictures with their backs turned towards us.

'I wonder what's on the other side of these pictures. Shall we try to see?'

'Oh yes.' Enthusiasm!

'Come along.' I dared her. 'I'll turn one round.'

'Please!' she said.

We made our way to the wall. I reached for a picture. It was very large and I could not turn it more than a few inches; a heap of dust fell into my eyes.

'You see!' she said. 'You must not get so excited. You *are* funny.' Funny: the word haunted my efforts with girls. I was in love. And – I could not believe it – we instantly seemed to be living in each other's eyes.

Her watchful mother came smiling towards us and I put on my best behaviour.

'We wanted to look at the pictures.'

'And he got covered in dust,' the girl said.

We walked out of the building, talking. I was determined not to let them go. They had heard about this church from 'the Baroness' the mother said. They had come, the mother said, to have a word with her. She asked me questions in an unusual, drawling voice, looking me up and down. I was wearing my French hat, but I had put on my best suit.

'Where are you having lunch?' the mother said, suddenly. 'Are you free today?'

It was a miracle. We walked into the Champs Elysées and once she turned to her daughter and murmured:

'The Baroness was impossible,' she said.

'Poor Mummy,' the girl said in a sorrowful voice and slowly shook her curls. And to me:

'The Baroness is dreadful.'

I was in the middle of a play.

'We come from Mexico,' the mother said in a grand, drawling voice. The Baroness: Mexico: High Society.

We went off to a flat they had rented in the Rue Notre Dame des Champs that looked down on the Bal Bullier.

'I have brought Judy to Paris because she is going on the stage. It is possible, of course, nowadays, for *ladies* to go on the stage,' Mrs Lang drawled on.

'I am going to be a writer,' I said.

The girl clapped her hands.

'You will write plays for me!' she said.

The mother smiled at me.

'Isn't she a child?' she laughed.

By four o'clock that afternoon, in the impetuous laughing way of strangers who meet outside their own country, we had told one another what is called 'everything' about ourselves. It was in fact a meeting not of three people, but of six – ourselves and our fictions. I have said that it was like being in a play, but really it was more like being in a puppet show. The girl was her mother's doll.

'You shall be cousins,' said the mother when she had questioned me about my family. (I had, I must admit, moved them up in the world.) 'He must be part of the family, mustn't he? You must call me Tia, that is Spanish for Aunt. Jolly good pals.'

There was a man-to-man touch about Mrs Lang.

'Oh yes,' cried the girl to her mother. 'He's like your pony, that wicked pony of yours who took you to assignations.'

'Really Judy!' said Mrs Lang. 'Assignations – what a word!'

'Oh, but he did! It used to stand under Mummy's window waiting for her to climb down and dash off to marvellous parties.'

Mrs Lang said fondly: 'You can't remember. You were only six in Puebla.'

'It was the only way she could get out,' said the girl.

I saw Mrs Lang galloping across the landscape, in the moonlight, to some hacienda. It was a thrilling sight.

'Married to that brute' – the brute was her elderly husband – 'when I was sixteen, it was the only way. Her grandmother was

Spanish – look at her hair,' said Mrs Lang in her off-hand way.

Whenever I saw Mrs Lang after this I imagined her on a wild horse. Her life seemed to come out of a novel. The 'brute' had been shot in the Revolution – 'a good thing too' – and here she was fighting to get her money (for he had a big estate) out of the Mexican government. They had refused to hand it over; but now, after years, they had promised to pay up and so she had come to Paris. I was captivated by Mrs Lang, especially by her strange straw-like hair, her cold eyes and her lazy laughing manner. I could see her sitting in her Mexican house, which had once been a convent. She gets up and sticks a hat pin into a scorpion (or was it a tarantula?) that is going to drop on Judy's bed. Some nights a dozen hat pins impale the bodies on the wall. In the morning the maid collects them. I saw Mrs Lang get a revolver out from under her pillow and shoot at the hand of a thief that comes stealthily round the handle of the door one night. Was it a thief or was it the ghost of a nun? Mrs Lang was open-minded but she was (she said) a devilish good shot.

I left the house at five and walked down to the Boulevard Saint Germain, then along the river, all the way to Auteuil, but I seemed to float. What I had so often dreamed had magically happened. I was in love, and although Judy and I had done nothing but laugh together, surely she was in love too? I was to meet them the next evening at a small restaurant. No one was happier than I to be able to lend Mrs Lang fifteen francs towards paying the bill: she had foolishly left her purse in her other handbag. This evening Mrs Lang told me that Judy was engaged to be married – engaged since the age of twelve: but the marriage would not take place until she became an actress.

'They'll give their eyes for her,' the mother said. 'The moment the lights go up . . .'

'Glorious lights, Puck!' Judy exclaimed. That was the name they gave me: they hated Victor as much as I did.

'She will make a fortune.'

'Oh yes! And you will be famous and write a play and I will act in it,' she said again.

Engaged! For a second time I was jealous, but dismissed it. We had years before us.

So began – what? A love affair? Hardly. The sketch or outline of a love affair. A fantasy. I could never quite bring myself to believe

Judy was human. But when the Breton at the shop had asked if I had a mistress and I had said 'Yes' it was Judy I was thinking of. After leaving the shop I would hurry up to the flat and would hear of her dangerous career. She was seeing theatre managers in Montmartre, of all places; or she was having tea with that Italian; or considering posing as a model – 'but only for the face', Mrs Lang said. How reckless the rich English were. And then Judy's talk was a mixture of mischief and the unbelievable. She would say, 'Monsieur began to get – you know? Hot? He looked awfully hot.' Or Monsieur wanted to make 'assignations' or was 'a bit *gallant*'. And to me: 'Your heart is like one of those hotels, you know?' And the mother said proudly, 'Isn't she dreadful?'

Where was I? Hadn't I read this somewhere – in Wilde? Was she an *ingénue*? Now, when I think of our chats and our walks, I understand that Mrs Lang and her daughter were both acting Edwardian roles. The mother could have appeared in any of the plays of the period.

The comedy of it all excited me and my vanity was flattered when men turned to look at Judy as we walked down the street. I discovered I was a natural flirt – as the word then was – and since the word 'gallant' was a favourite of Mrs Lang's, I was as gallant as anything with her daughter. A new faculty: what a pleasure it is to discover that when one is young and coming out of one's shell. And there was a darker side to this: I feared the accusations, the solemnities, the jealousies of adult love. I was 'in love' with a girl who was really a child, though she was older than I. Was I child, too? The doubt was wounding.

Paris had put a spell on me. Mrs Lang and Judy were part of that spell. Mrs Lang often had to go and see someone or other about her Mexican affairs (she said), and Judy and I were left in the evenings or on Saturday or Sunday afternoons to ourselves. We wandered along the Seine, laughing and inventing fantasies. One afternoon we went out to Saint-Cloud and sat in the park. The girl started collecting snails from the grass and we put a wall of stones round them.

'Look at our children,' she said.

She said this at the moment when I was wondering whether to break the spell and kiss her. There are *voyeurs* in Saint-Cloud on Saturdays. I could hear one crawling on his hands and knees nearer and nearer to us. I got up in a temper and found the man.

'How dare you spy on us!' I said.

A sullen man stood up.

'Who is spying? I have as much right to be here as you.' My imagination and temper went up in the air together.

'I shall report you to the British Ambassador for molesting his daughter.'

'Go on!' sneered the man.

I can't think what made me say such an absurd thing. I advanced upon him and he walked backwards from me swearing. I watched him till he went off.

'What was he doing?' Judy said.

'They spy on lovers.'

It was the nearest I came to saying I loved her.

'Whatever for?' she laughed. 'You were very funny.'

We went back to my room. This agitated me. The sight of the big double bed was like something large and human, and we behaved very respectfully before it. She looked at herself in the big mirror and for long afterwards I used to remember her face reflected in it. I had bought some cherries and we threw them into the branches of the tree in the yard so that they looked as if they were growing there. Madame Chapin came in. She was delighted my 'cousin' was so pretty: and often asked about her eagerly. I had gone up in Madame Chapin's estimation and she became almost fond.

What puzzled me was that the desire I had felt for Judy when I first met her would vanish when she was present; it was only when she was away that it returned.

I was now – mysteriously to me – the chief acknowledged, imaginary lover of Judy among her friends, who were mostly students, and I had no rivals. It was agreed that we were both extraordinary and I certainly played on that. There was only one critical figure: this was a tall Danish girl who took an austere interest in Judy and me. She had straight hair and greenish eyes and was writing a philosophical thesis. She was the daughter of a sea captain. Those greenish eyes gazed at Judy and then at me greedily. One weekend we all went off to Fontainebleau together, taking a cheerful English youth with us. We walked through the forest, but he and I walked faster than they and so the girls were far behind most of the day. We stayed in a cheap hotel. The moon came up, the nightingales belled all night and I could not sleep. I shared my room with the young man who made a whistling noise when he slept. The girls were next door. I longed to be with Judy and lay tortured by the moonlight and the nightingales. The next day the girls were always together and I was jealous. Judy had to go home when we got to Paris and I did not go with her. I was left with the Dane.

'I thought you always went with Judy.'

'Not always,' I said.

'I think you should have gone with her,' she said. 'She is unhappy.'

I could guess the cause of Judy's unhappiness: the habits of the adventurous Mrs Lang. The Mexican stories were true, but the Mexican money was a dream. The puzzle was to know whether Judy understood that her beauty was being used by her mother; knowing that it attracted us all, the gambler took to borrowing money from everyone Judy met. The Baroness had been at the beginning of this career. Now I, who had had a struggle with an overwhelming father, saw Judy in a similar case. The Danish girl soon told me the rest.

'We both love Judy,' she said. 'We ought to tell her. She must get away from her mother.'

'I am not in love with Judy,' I said.

And I wasn't. The nightingales singing all night had sung it all away.

'Judy is sleep-walking and so are you,' said the girl.

So love turned into fascination. Mrs Lang, keeping up a fight for her dream, forgot about Mexico and took a job as a governess. Judy went from family to family looking after children. When she had time off I would go to fetch her. I felt great tenderness for her, but she would not speak of her troubles. Then, in a bad crisis in their affairs – for Mrs Lang quarrelled with her employers, usually about some slight to 'an English lady' – they moved to (of all places) the Avenue Hoche, my marquis street.

I went there and a butler at the front door sent me to the servants' quarters. There, in the ironing-room and treated with the contempt the French keep for the inferiors, the mother and daughter were living. We went out to a cab drivers' restaurant. The following week the mother went to work with a family in Dieppe, leaving Judy with me. I was living in her daydream; she was living in mine and, taking my opportunity, the disciple of Belloc and W.J. Locke made her walk most of the way to Triel down the Seine. It was a hot, happy day. I remember the smell of hay and drinking wine and eating lunch under a tree. I remember I fell asleep for I was woken up by Judy laughing at me. We traipsed on to an hotel at Triel and there I wanted to stay with her; but we were tired, I had just enough money left to take us back to Paris by train. So I said nothing. In fact, having been paid for two of my articles and having, unfortunately, boasted to Mrs Lang about it, the clever lady had soon got most of it out of me.

The next week a message commanded Judy to join her mother in Dieppe. I saw Judy off at the Gare Saint Lazare. We were not sad. We still seemed to be living in each other's eyes. At twenty one is light-hearted. It had all been gayer than love. A lesson, too: altogether Mrs Lang had had from me what seemed the enormous sum of £10.

Chapter 3

Now when I look back on the tragic figure of Mr Shaves I see he was not a born banker. He shared a corner of the bank with three other men. The other clerks looked like repressed rips, especially when they talked to women at the counter. Shaves was an indigestible pudding of suppressed virtues. The other clerks wore black or dark-grey suits; he wore either a cocoa-brown or grey one with holiday stripes on it. There was a buttonhole in his jacket. His glossy, buttery hair frisked in curls of grey at the ears, he had a smoker's stained moustache; and very often he sat sideways at his desk lost in the sheer wonder of gazing at his trouser legs, his coloured socks and his shoes. Only by an effort of will, recollecting his duty, would he suddenly sit straight at his work. Then he put on an absurdly mean expression.

Shaves was short and had puddled impudent eyes; he looked vulgar. His powerful voice had made the worst of American and English speech. I learned my first American phrases from him, leading from 'Whad d'ya know?' on to 'I'm through' and 'I can't make it'. Hollywood made them current in England eventually. He was a rumbustious English patriot who saw himself, after twenty-five years in the United States, fighting a dogged one-man war against that country.

'Jesus,' he would say, 'you can have Paris and New York. I'm through with them. I can't take them.'

The bank was a 'whore-shop'. In twenty-five years he had picked up every cliché going in suburban America. When he cashed my first cheque, he said:

'You're a writer? You come from Bromley? Whad d'ya know! I was born in Lewisham.'

He spread his arms: I thought he was going to embrace me. He had found what he was longing for, an ally.

'This'll interest you,' he said and from the counter he took a circular. On it was printed 'The Boulevard Players Present *Fanny's First Play* by George Bernard Shaw'. Among the cast of players was Basil Chavasse.

'I'm playing Gilbey,' he said. 'Ever seen it? That's my stage name.'

'No,' I said.

He was indignant: then he lit up. In the next quarter of an hour he ran through his favourite scenes. One I was to hear time and time again:

'Remember how it goes – Gilbey says:

' "We've done what we can for the boy. Short of letting him get into temptation of all sorts he can do what he likes. What more does he want?" And Doris comes back with "Well, he wants *me*!" Can you beat it?'

In the middle of this, Basil Shaves had passed my cheque, collected the money himself and gave it to me.

'He's a Britisher,' he called around to the office.

He asked me to come and see the Shaves family in Neuilly.

The Shaves lived in a small villa, built in a mixture of red brick, yellow brick and dotted with tiles; it looked like a coloured crossword puzzle. There was a high noisy iron gate with spikes on top – French suburbanites fortify themselves – and as we crossed the pebbled stretch to the steps between dusty shrubs, Mr Shaves said:

'See that? No grass. You never see a decent lawn outside of England.'

There were two very young children. Mrs Shaves was a short woman with a heavy blob of white hair and a duck-like bosom which she seemed to carry about as if it were a personal tragedy. She made a soft noise like a carpet sweeper when she walked. There was a slender fair-haired daughter with her mother's pretty blue eyes and delicate voice, a child of nine. There was also a son with exactly her boyish pouting lips. The family gathered protectively round the husband and father. They laughed as he darted at once to a piano in the sitting-room the first time I went there, banged out a tune, and wagging his head from side to side, started to sing. His voice had some quality that brought home the London streets. He swung round on the piano stool and called to me:

'Pagliacci – know it?'

Mrs Shaves said: 'Basil's father was a singer.'

'Chavasse, Cecil Chavasse, Metropolitan Opera House, New York.'

He had told me this when we had first met.

'Victor is too young,' she said tenderly.

Shaves was annoyed that I was too young. His mean look came on for a moment.

'Basil's father. Chavasse was the stage name,' his wife said.

'Berlin, Vienna, Brussels, New York, all over America. Australia. Italian opera,' said Basil Shaves.

One of those marital interludes of competitive story-telling began.

'It was after the Australian tour that he brought Basil and the family from London to New York,' Mrs Shaves said complacently.

'I was twelve.'

'All the famous singers used to come to my father's house.'

Mrs Shaves said: 'That is how Basil and I met.'

The Paris furniture, she took care to explain, was not theirs. All her best French furniture was at her sister's in New York.

'Her father was a connoisseur,' said Mr Shaves, admiring her family.

'My mother was French,' Mrs Shaves said, in a distinguished way.

'Yeah,' said Mr Shaves. There was a reverent pause and then Mr Shaves switched back to his father.

'Cecil Chavasse,' he said. 'A tragedy.'

'A tragedy,' said Mrs Shaves in a firm voice.

'After the Australian tour he was billed to sing in Chicago. It was in December. Jesus, can it be cold in Chicago! The inside of his coat froze. He got laryngitis, his voice went. He couldn't sing. The voice went like that.'

'They got a specialist from Vienna,' said Mrs Shaves, in her refined hoot.

'It went on for months,' said Mr Shaves. 'He never sang again.'

'At the height of his career,' said Mrs Shaves. 'That's the trouble with the theatre. A little thing – and you're finished. At fifty-one.

'It was terrible for Basil,' said Mrs Shaves. 'He was only sixteen. At that age you are impressionable. And for the family – his mother and two sisters.'

'Father always lived,' said Mr Shaves. 'We were at the Waldorf – suddenly, not a cent. He was a spender. Champagne dinners, open house, and,' Mr Shaves lowered his voice, 'there were women. We were down to living in a couple of cheap rooms in Brooklyn,' Mr Shaves said.

Mrs Shaves shook her head sadly.

'They put me into the bank. I wanted to be an actor,' said Mr Shaves. 'The Rooters were looking after my mother. Her sister,' he jerked a proud thumb at his wife, and said with awe, 'married a Rooter.'

I was lost.

'Bankers. Own the bank,' he said. Mr Shave's awe increased and he gazed at his wife.

In all the time I knew Mr Shaves his astonishment, his pride and his despair at having pretty well married into the Rooters always came out. He had married above himself. Mrs Shaves was high above him – socially, intellectually, morally: *she* could have married a Rooter, too, instead of an unsuccessful clerk. He had ruined her.

We sat down to a meal. When Mrs Shaves brought the casserole to the table and steam rose from it, Mr Shaves said:

'Victor understands what I mean. He's a writer. I ought to have left the bank. I'm an actor.'

He looked at the food as if it were part of a plot against him.

'I ought to have starved,' he said. He was accusing us of preventing the starvation of an artist. The children lowered their eyes and giggled.

After dinner Mr Shaves went to the piano, singing out a few lines from an aria and then changing to another and another.

'Do you sing?' he called to me. 'Come on. I'll find something.'

'I can't sing.'

'You've never tried. Here, how about this? Cutts of the Cruiser What-not. Know it?'

'Oh Basil, please not that. Haven't you a French folk song? I'm sure Victor would like that,' said Mrs Shaves.

Mr Shaves stuck a finger in an ear, burrowing there, in thought.

'Basil,' said Mrs Shaves.

He pulled his finger out of his ear. He had vulgar habits.

'Come on, all of you.' And he banged out a tune and sang:

> I'm Cutts of the Cruiser What-not
> A cruetty salt of the sea . . .

He paused. 'That's good – a cruetty salt.'

> When homeward bound
> My old ship runs aground
> I love it – I shriek with glee.

Soon he forced all of us, except Mrs Shaves, to sing it.

When I left Mrs Shaves said to me: 'I'm so glad Basil has found a friend.'

A tussle was going on in the Shaves family. It had begun in 1914 in New York when the war broke out. Firmly kept away from the theatre by his wife and his relations, he now saw his chance. He became violently patriotic, went off to Canada and got himself into the Army; he expected to be sent to London. Instead he was sent to the weariest of the campaigns in that war: the stalemate in Salonika. His age was even then against him: something in his appearance, the moustache, no doubt, suggested Bairnsfather's Old Bill in the shell-hole, but Shaves was an old Bill in the regimental kitchens throughout this war. When the war was over he went back to New York and the bank. He got his wife to pull strings with her relations and to get his transfer to London. No American in 1919 wanted to go to London. They couldn't believe him. They sent him to Paris. His wife may have had a hand in this: Paris was far from Shaftesbury Avenue. Mr Shaves admiringly agreed but set about getting his transfer to London. Mrs Shaves thought his part with the Boulevard Players would divert him from this. On the contrary, it aroused his desire to throw up everything for the stage. How complex are human manoeuvres: to get Mrs Shaves out of Paris he conveyed to her that he was exposed to moral danger there. Paris was a sink, the office was a brothel. Once I stayed the night in their house and when we went off to our jobs in the morning it was touching to see his wife and his children standing on the doorstep to see him off. Their smiles were anxious, protective and wistful, as they saw the breadwinner light up his cigarette and under the halo of smoke go bravely out, his shoulders wagging, to face the sins and temptations of the wicked city.

These things came out in my occasional walks with him when I ran into him on the Boulevard.

A walk with Mr Shaves was always embarrassing. Once out of the bank he looked like a tourist doing 'gay Paree', with a foolish smile on his face. He waltzed along, humming a tune out of one side of his mouth. His cigarette holder went up and down according to his moods. What I dreaded was that he would stop walking; for when a thought struck him he would start to sing – as he thought – quietly. 'La, da di da, la la,' a bit of Italian opera; if it was a favourite bit, he would go on far more loudly, making a sweep with his arms. 'La di da di plonk, plonk, plonk da-a-a-a-' in some finale and utter his common phrase: '*Figaro* – know it?' Or '*Tosca* – get it?' We would continue our saunter. But sometimes he stopped with indignation: his moral nature gave him his mean expression.

'See that? No, there. That waiter looking at that woman – mentally undressing her. Victor, that's what I can't stand about this place. I've got to get my transfer.'

Yet if a pretty girl passed us, his face would become dreamy:

'Look at those breasts,' he would say.

But if the girl happened to look at him he would put on a stern look; if she looked at me, he would say, warning me:

'They're brazen.'

Outside a newspaper kiosk near the Palais Royal when, in a fit of showing off, I had stopped to buy *Le Crapouillot*, a gossipy paper about the arts and the theatre – he started spouting his favourite lines from *Fanny's First Play*, the ones about the cockatoo. He was running over the scene with Knox. I have looked them up.

My Uncle Phil was a teetotaller. My father used to say to me Rob, he says, don't you ever have a weakness. If you find one getting hold of you, make a merit of it, he says, your Uncle Phil doesn't like spirits but he makes a merit of it and is Chairman of the Blue Ribbon Committee. I do like spirits; and I make a merit of it, and I'm the King Cockatoo of the Convivial Cockatoos. Never put yourself in the wrong.

He came out strongly with the last lines:

'Convivial Cockatoos, Victor! Can you beat it?'

A load of tourists were going into the hotel there. One or two looked cross because they thought he was shouting at them.

'What I've got to show is the change in Gilbey's character,' he said and he walked worrying under the arcades of the Rue de Rivoli.

The bond between us, as he saw it, was that we were fellow artists, both at the beginnings of our careers.

I did not see much of him and then, in August, when so many shops and restaurants put up their iron shutters that the streets look blind, and when the Seine has its white August gleam, Mrs Shaves's sister, the genuine Rooter, came over from New York, looking like something out of a bazaar. She soon put on the fashionable tawny, orange make-up and became parrot-like – Mrs Shaves never had more than a dab of powder on her face – and took the family off to Brittany, leaving Mr Shaves behind. I saw him sagging in the Café de la Paix. He was lost without them all. This brought out his confessional side. One Saturday afternoon we walked together. A walk with Mr Shaves was like walking with someone undressed. We paused in fascination at Maxim's. What wickedness went on there! Up the Champs Elysées we strolled under the trees. We came to a stop at a café opposite Fouquet's where we sat and where his look alternated between the showy and the agonized. The quickness of his fantasy and its sudden extinction gave one the impression that he was shady. He was not. He was tormented. Enthusiastically tormented. There was his enthusiasm for the affection of the two sisters. He sunned himself in it, congratulating himself on being adjacent to it.

'I have a lovely family,' he said.

But a cloud came over the sun. The sister-in-law had taken the whole family to Fouquet's to dinner the night before their holiday.

'I ought to have starved. Father starved when he was young.' This theme returned.

'I ought not to have gone into the bank.' This lead on to 'ruin'.

'I could not ruin them.'

Looking for money in his wallet he found a photograph.

'She' – he showed me his wife's picture; she was a slender young woman at that time – 'could have had anything she wanted. I have ruined them already.'

There was remorse in this but out came the sun again, and his foot wagged faster and he hissed a tune and rolled his head from one side to the other, in time with it, happily. It was, I gathered, a kind of coup to have 'ruined' someone who was almost a Rooter, a liberation.

He said: 'The Thousand Islands – ever heard of them? You haven't head of the Thousand Islands? Well, whad d'ya know! On the St Lawrence – that's where we spent our honeymoon. It took me six months to break the hymen. It all dates back to that – then the war – I was away. I came back. She wants something higher, Victor. She says I'm holding her back from God. Her sister's the same. That's my problem – I can't make it. I'm not pure, Victor!'

He looked at me with dreadful appeal.

'I sometimes undress and look at myself in the mirror. I get a funny pleasure out of looking at myself.'

'Tolstoy used to do that,' I said.

'What – Tolstoy the writer?' said Mr Shaves, amazed.

'Yes.'

'Well, whad d'ya know!'

He became furtive. 'You know – the way my hair grows, everything about my body – interests me. I sometimes sit in a bus and imagine everybody there without a stitch on – nude. No kidding. I enjoy it. You say Tolstoy was like that?'

He sat like some steaming nudist beside me. He had put on weight in the last month or two, he said, his chest was over-developing; it worried him. Do men get like women? It was funny the pleasure you get from scratching your backside, almost like going to bed with a woman. That was why the Rooters got him into the bank: he'd got into a small touring company going to Detroit when he was sixteen and a girl in the company was very kind to him. The company was broke and she let him lie beside her, naked, in her room. No, he never touched her. They just looked at each other. Innocent. But the family found out and got him back to New York; he was too obviously following in father's footsteps.

Mr Shaves, in confessions like these, would seem to swell. He was the Flesh, a man encumbered by his physical person. He saw the very pores of his skin through a kind of sensual magnifying glass: I often saw him hold up his hand and look at it with secretive wonder. Even in his walk, the roll of his gait, one could see he was bewildered by the obligation of carrying this warm throbbing load of flesh and tissues around, singing to himself as he went (I suppose), to distract his mind from it.

I sometimes saw Basil Shaves sitting at lunch-time with friends in one of the cafés on the Boulevard des Italiens. He had the gift of admiring his friends. He was casting himself for their lives. One day he called to me as I passed. I went to his table.

'This is Victor, he's a writer,' he said.

I met a tall talkative Englishman, with sandy sidewhiskers, a military type; and a silent burly Frenchman. They said they were in the shellac trade. The Frenchman asked me, in French, what I was doing. Fatal question to a young man like me: I told him, at length.

'Tell him about that office boy, and Mac. Go on,' said Shaves. 'Tell him about your father,' Shaves said. I had an audience. The listening Englishman said to the Frenchman: 'Just what we want, don't you think?' And to me: 'Do you want a job?'

The Frenchman nodded. At the end of half an hour I found myself in the shellac trade at double my salary, employed as a commercial traveller. The minds of businessmen – as Walter Bagehot says – live in a sort of twilight: the Englishman had taken me on because he had read Maupassant; the Frenchman because I had never played Rugby football. He had been one of the first to introduce Rugby football to France.

The Englishman had been a Staff Officer during the war. He was a bookish man, a connoisseur of pictures and would-be Bohemian. His voice was icy and excitable. The Frenchman was dour and quiet.

The office – I was glad to find – was far from the despised Grands Boulevards, in the old Temple quarter on the edge of the Marais and the old bourgeois Paris of Balzac. It was in a small seventeenth-century building in the Rue Vieille du Temple. The staff were a grumpy French virgin who had been educated in an English convent and who soon needled me about the looseness of English morals; and a sad French salesman called Leger, an anxious, penny-counting man with a large family. He and the typist believed I was the son of a rich Englishman who had put money into the business and despised me. They were shocked by my light-headedness. He and the typist had a facility for hackneyed quotations. They talked like a French edition of the *Reader's Digest*. When I told Leger about my writings he said – but with sinister overtones:

'*Le journalisme mène à tout.*'

The girl said, with disapproval:

'I see you are a follower of Montaigne rather than Pascal.' She said that the English boss was going too far in discounting bills and putting unsold goods down to a varnish maker who had some connection with the firm; and by her look I saw she thought I was in the manoeuvre. Her tale was nonsense. The girl was in love with the boss who could not bear her. She tried to interest him by putting on a sulky look and saying men were always pinching her breasts in the Métro. I tried to smile away her sulks first of all; then I tried to dazzle. Another failure. I fell back on bickering; she liked that.

The job in the shellac and glue trade was very suited to me. It was more interesting than work at the photographer's. I was out of the office all day, calling on ironmongers, paint makers, furniture shops and sealing-wax factories, all over Paris and the suburbs. The glue buyers would hold my sample of glue up to the light, they they would give it a lick as if it were toffee. 'Yes, very good, but we've got plenty.' I never sold any glue, but we had interesting conversations. I always carried a book with me; some wanted to know what it was, and it was surprising among these tradesmen to find how many had views on Balzac, Hugo, Dickens and so on. I had a pleasant afternoon with a sealing-wax man, chatting about *Manon Lescaut*, a tale that put me in an erotic daze; he bought nothing, but twelve years later, when I was a known writer, I came across my old boss in London. He had given up shellac in the 1929 crash and was running three pubs near Leicester Square, and told me that the sealing-wax man had become one of the firm's best customers. I don't think this was true: my boss had the romantic belief in his own intuitions. I scarcely tried at all, for I was writing on or two more sketches and thinking of nothing else. The typist and Leger were scornful when I came back without orders every day.

The opportunity to go, with a purpose, into innumerable streets and corners of Paris, particularly in the old part where the big middle-class houses had been chopped into rooms for tailors, printers, cabinet makers and all the petty trades – had for me the excitement of real travel. And, since I carried with me my little rustling samples of shellac, I felt I had a working right to be there. I strongly wanted to belong to his world of small trades. A man who made varnish became a human being to me. I would admire the way he fingered the flakes of shellac or studied my opal gum. My boss was an enthusiast and was sure that I was just the bright young man the business needed; so did the French Rugby player.

They took me out to smart restaurants. In spite of the story of my violent difficulties with my father – for I was always talking about this – the boss, I found, had convinced himself that, handled the right way, my father would buy me a partnership in the firm: he saw money in me. Nothing could possibly have made me present my father as a man willing to pour out money on his son: rather the reverse. Like so many Englishmen, like myself indeed, the boss was a daydreamer. Carried away by what I told him, he instinctively reversed it to suit his dream. In time he saw there was no hope in me and he became doubtful. He was a hard-working man and was surprised that I would not work on Sundays.

Presently there was a disaster. Leger, the salesman, had had a temporary triumph. He had sold a large quantity of copal gum and he sat working out his commission to the last centime.

But the copal (it turned out), was adulterated with gravel and quantities of cinder and dust; there was a row. The stuff – tons of it – was returned to the yard of the varnish manufacturer near St Denis to be sorted. The salesman, who was nearly out of his mind, was told to sort the stuff and I had to work with him.

The week was hot. It was a long way to the factory, which was in a street that might have been painted by Utrillo. Leger told me to get there at seven in the morning. He was eager to get the job done. I managed to arrive on the first morning at half past seven, but the following days I found it hard to wake up and I was an hour or more late. The tons of gum were stacked in a yard against a wall and looked like a heap of grey marbles. Our task was to shovel the gum and pass it through sieves: a cindery dust fell through and often left large stones which we had to throw out. We sieved and shovelled until six or seven every evening. The dust choked us, sweat choked us and, all the time, Leger was muttering about the swindle and groaning about his commission which diminished with every shovelful. He groaned about his wife and family and the recklessness of the boss and sneered when I came late: 'You don't care. Your father's a rich man.' The drains of the neighbourhood had gone wrong and gangs were digging up the road for half a mile and the air was sour with the stink of cess. At midday we went to a rough restaurant where the roadworkers crowded in. We sat down at long tables. The labourers shouted and swore, swallowed their food and then, having drunk a bottle of wine apiece, fell asleep, some of them with their faces in their plates. They looked a savage lot, most of them, naked to the waist. There was one from

Marseilles who bawled out the sailors' word for red wine: *Encore du pousse-au-crime.*

Back to work we went in the long afternoons. At the end of the day, Leger and I stripped off our filthy shirts and went to the pump in the yard. I pumped water over Leger's back and he pumped it over mine. One or two women from the factory came to jeer at us.

After a week of this the heap wasn't much smaller. We got careless.

'Leave the stones in,' shouted Leger in a rage.

We got used to the jeering girls. Leger uttered a few well-known proverbs about women – not relevant to our situation. There were two or three more women every day and they came nearer to us. Their jeers became dirtier.

'Want to push your trunk upstairs?' a big one shouted at Leger.

'Whore,' shouted Leger.

It was a mistake. He had just stripped and was under the pump. The big woman strode forward, got a quick grip of his trousers at the back and pulled them down his thin, hairy legs, to his ankles. The women screamed with laughter. Leger thought I had done this and, blinded by water, grabbed a bucketful out of the trough and emptied it on me.

It soaked me and, seeing my state, one of the girls copied the big one, pounced on me from behind and the fat one pulled down my trousers too.

'Look at his little toy,' the big one called out.

The owner of the factory had heard the shouts and found Leger and me trying to pull our sodden trousers up. The women ran off.

Leger behaved badly about this. He was getting his revenge. We sat streaming and soaking in the bus back into Paris, which was crowded with workers.

'They pulled his trousers off,' he called out, indicating me to the passengers in the bus every now and then, as new passengers got in.

Worse, he told the boss, and said I had started the water-throwing. He said he would rather finish the job himself. I was always late.

'What indecency,' the typist hissed at me in the office. 'Like all the English. I know what the English girls at the convent were like. I've seen it with my own eyes.'

The boss had lost money on this transaction and saw that after all these months I had sold little. He said he would give me one more chance. He was buying a consignment of ostrich feathers and

I was to sell them in the Faubourg St Honoré.

I felt insulted and mystified by this new job. Everything connected with the dress trade depressed me. I liked the dirtier occupations. But feathers! A world of women! The milliners and dressmakers, I found, always seemed to be at the top of high buildings. Some stout or waspish woman would either shut the door in my face or tell me no one used ostrich feathers any more now. One said cuttingly, 'Go to the Folies Bergère.' I gave up trying. Leger was sarcastic and so was the girl. The boss had forgotten his loss and had had a sudden success with shellac. 'Nothing as usual?' he said, with a short laugh, to me. A distant look came on to his face. He wondered why on earth I was there. I was sacked. He gave up ostrich feathers, too – the final insult.

I left the office frightened by my situation, but also in a temper. I trudged glumly a good deal of the way to the Boulevard St Germain where the lights were brighter, and suddenly I realized I was free. I had a month's money in my pocket. I felt the abandon of the workless. My sexual instincts, distracted by the anxieties of having to earn my living, came undeniably alive. I made a reckless decision and the sight of Sacré-Coeur on its hill had a curious part in it. I have told how, when I first arrived in Paris, it seemed like some evil and exotic bird regarding the city with cynical eye and frightening. Now it frightened me no longer: I felt it connived with me. The erection symbolized one thing only and blatantly. I found myself looking into the windows of pharmacies. I was working up courage to buy a packet of contraceptives.

The bother was that I knew only the slang words for these objects. My first attempt was at a small shop of the shabby kind. The assistant came to the counter, but I was unable to speak to him because of his face. He had a red nose with white pimples on it; he looked sly and horrible; his condition (I imagined) being the result of some sexual disease. I quickly changed my mind and asked for a headache cachet and when I got outside I threw it into the street. I walked on looking for a larger, less unpleasantly intimate shop. The next shop had several women in it. I moved on. At last, after passing and repassing the door and making a cautious study of the assistants in a larger shop, I went in. They wore white coats and looked like an impersonal priesthood. But when one of the men asked me what I wanted my aggressiveness turned to nervousness. The French language became jumbled up in my head and vanished. I stammered out 'French letters'. The young assistant was puzzled. I tried one or two more slang names in a voice that was scarcely a murmur. The assistant was mystified. Another and older assistant came up and said, 'What is it for?' In the state I was in I could not tell him, except in a way that was meaningless. He listened and then suddenly he said: 'In the second drawer.'

A package was brought out and carefully wrapped up. I rushed out of the shop.

The experience exhausted me and indeed my sexual desires. I took the packet home and put it in my wardrobe. Slowly a strange feeling of power, of being at last at one with the world, came over me; indeed it was so strong that I forgot the packet itself and never thought of taking it out with me. It was a sort of hidden capital. Its immediate efect was to make me start writing again and to think of living by writing only.

Chapter 4

From the beginning my efforts succeeded. I wrote an account of the walk to Orleans; also a portrait of one of the *bouquinistes* on the quays. I went to see the old man and his wife in their attic in the Rue de Seine. These articles were accepted, soon published and paid for. I went on to an article about Chartres. This also was accepted. Although I wrote each one three or four times, I found them easy to write and, for a while, was proud of them.

When I read memoirs about the Paris of the Steins, Sylvia Beach, Joyce, Hemingway and Scott Fitzgerald, I am cast down. I was there. I may have passed them in the street; I had simply never heard of them. Nor had I any notion of what they were trying to do. I had really carried my isolation in England with me. One evening I did see a number of young people walking up the Boulevard Montparnasse with a thick, blue-covered book, like a telephone directory. They went to the *Dôme*, the *Coupole* or the *Rotonde* and sat there reading. I asked a young Irishman who I sat next to at the *Dôme* what the book was. He was dressed in green and wore a cowboy hat. He was surprised to be asked such a question. The book, he said, was *Ulysses*; for years 'everyone' had been waiting for this great moment. He allowed me to read the first page; its adjectives and images annoyed and flustered me. (In fact it was a good five years before I could bring myself to read the book.) I did not know that I was living at the centre of a literary revolution. I was an outsider, and younger than the writers and painters who were becoming important; and if I *had* known, I would still have been under the delusion that before I could know anything about modern literature I must catch up with the old. When I did hear of Tristan Tzara and Dada, I was angry because he was smashing up a culture just as I was becoming acquainted with it. The only artist of importance I talked to was the sculptor, Zadkine. He took me to his studio for half an hour and I stood there in a crowd of primitive African totem poles, twelve feet high. I was speechless and came away lost.

There was a great difference between the American crowd who swamped the Left Bank at this time and the handful of Europeans; the French avoided this international circus. The Americans belonged to the generation who, for the first time in their history, had made a mass exodus from the United States. Always alert for the new thing, they arrived in gangs, dressed up in gaudy shirts and played the Bohemian part. They had a lot of money and took over cafés and restaurants and hotels. They drank heavily and brawled, which shocked the French. They boasted they had bought Europe. But one or two of them were sensitive and seriously encouraging. If I said I was 'trying to write' they enthusiastically announced to their friends that I was 'the writer'.

I became friends with an American painter and his wife. He was a frowning slow-thinking man of forty whose face was sullen with inner struggles that he could not get out except in sentences like: 'What a painter wants is a place near a good whore-shop – like Van Go or Says-Ann,' or in blasts of boasting. His hair stuck up in spikes and his blue eyes seemed to be bursting with tears he could not shed: he was of German origin and very sentimental. The sight of me brought out the worst in him. Europe was finished. The Americans had won the war. Europe was shit – a favourite word. America was the largest, the richest, the only country that believed in democracy and peace. The English accent was sissy. We were all homosexuals. What was wrong with us was our servile class system: there were no class differences in America.

He was a living proof of the opposite. He had married a Virginian of superior family. He boasted of this and he resented it at once. The unsure, the ugly part of American character – I have often found – is very near the surface. But he was decent and had the American virtue of seeing everything as a possibility. He was laborious and slow, but when his wife said I was a promising writer that was enough, I was *doing* something. One day, he said with awe and almost affection:

'Hold it. You just said an epigram.'

His wife was long-nosed, ugly and bony, but very intelligent and attractive. She thought and spoke the things her husband could not get out. He said that my writing needed an illustrator. He would do sketches to illustrate my articles and he'd see if the *Monitor* would run a series. He knew the paper. The editor was coming to Paris. The editor arrived. I met him as he was leaving his hotel. He paused on the steps. He was a gay fellow with a white beard.

'I like your stuff. I'll take ten more with those drawings.'

I walked away. Ten. Guaranteed. I was a commissioned writer, not an amateur any longer. No more leather, photography, shellac and glue. The dread that I had no talent at all, a dread that kept me awake at night, left me. The hotel was in the Faubourg St Honoré, the scene of my wretched attempt to sell ostrich feathers. I looked into the windows of jewellers, hosiers, tailors, perfumeries; wealth seemed to coat me. I went to an expensive shop that sold luxurious stationery, tooled blotting pads and so on. I went in and ordered a hundred engraved visiting cards, taking care in choosing the print. Afterwards I went to the Café Weber and ordered a bock.

Now my life as a professional writer, and the last six months I was to spend in Paris, began. It is true that if I had moved among cleverer and more instructed people I would not have been so late in developing an original imagination. And there is always the danger that people who work hard become blinded by work itself and, by a paradox, lazy-minded.

Since I no longer had to be at a shop or office between eight and nine, I lay in bed until eleven o'clock in the morning. I was, I suppose, making up for years of doing work I did not like. I lay in that wide and lumpy bed at Mme Chapin's until I was woken by the siren at the Fire Station near by. Then the life-long panic of the writer's life began. A whole day free, yet eaten by the anxiety of having to write something; the day of false starts, torn up paper – how I grew to love tearing up paper. And then there was the reaction against the task: to write little sketches of places, how feeble! How could it be important to go to Amiens, to Pontoise, to the stamp market on the Champs Elysées? I was nothing but a hack. And then I had no 'adventures' – an old complaint. In trains people talked of little but the price of food, the cost of living, or told stories about their illnesses and families. A writer ought, I felt, to know about 'low' society, but 'low life' is as hard to discover as High Society is. The *Monitor* certainly would not publish anything about the whores prancing about the hotels of Les Halles, with their red dresses, slit up to the thigh, and their hard voices shouting at the draymen below. If I nosed my way up to a *clochard* who had kipped down on one of those iron plates on the pavement where the warmth from the central heating comes through, near the Gare d'Austerlitz, I never got much more than a grunt out of him. The paper would not like that, unless I made him a picturesque character amusing to tourists. And Americans in 1920 loved the picturesque. I began to get the suspicion that I was hired to leave half of life out. Perhaps my discontent was spotted by the editors, who are no fools in matters like this. My first two articles appeared at length: the others were cut to little more than a dozen lines of caption for the pictures.

When I wrote my articles I showed one or two of them to the Danish girl who had been Judy's friend. It had been a joke between Judy and me to call her Hester, for she had a slow, considering manner which (we thought mischievously) went with her height. To our surprise she liked the name. It made her stern and truthful face soften with a yielding pleasure. I used to meet her at a café near the Palais Royal, because she often went shopping on the Right Bank. Her dissertation was done and she was waiting for her parents to take her to the South of France and then home. Hester read and spoke English exactingly well. She was taller than I and this, and her seriousness, made me show off to her; but when we sat down, on the same eye level, we were friends and she stopped snubbing me. In fact, she had the Danish gaiety with other people, but doubtfully with me. She had a good head, a straight nose and long, narrow hips and big bones. But girls turned into something else when I looked at them. In Hester's face I saw libraries and lecture halls and the philosopher Malebranche – I had not heard of him up till then and have never heard of him since – on whom she had written her dissertation. I also saw mountains and fjords, though there are none in Denmark which, she crossly told me many times, was flat. I could even see her father, the sea captain, to whom I gave a fair beard; twice she had been to Canada in his ship.

How healthy, free and confident she was: I was half angry with her for this. I cannot think why, but I was especially angry because her father was a sea captain. I felt a strong desire to get her off the sea. The sea made me sick. Only the pink inside of her long mouth when she laughed – which was not often – saved her, in my eyes. It reminded me that she was a girl.

I cannot remember our conversations. She told me, of course, about Malebranche; that has gone too; but I remember attacking him. She said: 'Why do you exaggerate?' or:

'That is superficial, isn't it?' or:

'I read what you wrote. Your writing is unequal. You will have to learn to say what you think.' or:

'Be careful. You will lose your integrity.' or:

'I don't understand your attitude.'

These phrases stick in my mind. She also quoted Shakespeare to me. 'To thine own self be true . . .' Suppose, I argued, the self was criminal or amoral? I was divided between admiration and awe of her. She said I lacked moral seriousness. I cultivated the lack of it with her. Look how I had treated Judy! Hester was very moved when she mentioned Judy and especially about that time at Fontainebleau. Nothing would convince her that Judy and I had not been lovers and when she said this, there was a change in Hester's face: her eyes became large and greedy.

I gazed at her and thought of the package in my room.

On 14 July she agreed, to my surprise, to come with me to the general dancing and soda-water-squirting along the Boulevard St Michel. She squirted soda water at me: that was an advance. A party of us danced in the streets. She had unfortunately brought her professor's son to whom I recklessly said something about Racine. He snubbed me. I puzzled Hester by dancing with a pretty Hungarian girl who could not speak French, English or German, so we had to make gestures that Hester assumed were intimate; and they were, because words were not obstructing us. I still see the sadness in her eyes when, in the end, I took Hester to her lodgings. Hester was silent; she did not believe the story that the girl and I had no language in common. When we got to the professor's house, I made an excited gesture and asked Hester to come to my room. My landlady was away. But, either because I shouted this, or she was too tall, she appeared not to hear me. We shook hands and I left. I trudged back, all the way through Grenelle, and got to bed tired out.

The next day in the streets, people looked pale and ill. In the bar near my room the barman had not shaved and a woman was trying to put her hair to rights by a mirror.

Once more Hester and I met at the Palais Royal. The Hungarian girl was on her mind. Her next remark was baffling: she insisted Judy had told her I had slept with her.

'Tell me the truth,' she said.

'But it is the truth,' I said. 'I haven't.'

And then I saw what had happened. I gave a yell of laughter at Judy's fanciful mind. Of course! I had fallen asleep under that tree on the hot day of the walk to Triel. Hester was put out.

'Babes in the wood,' she said.

She did not like being laughed at.

To talk about love is to make love: Hester and I were nervous of each other. I kept tapping the ash of my cigarette into an ash tray as we talked.

'I wish you'd stop that,' she said and put the ash tray out of reach, but I touched her hand as she did this. She took her hand away quickly. The marble-topped table between us seemed to become six feet wider and to heave like the sea. In the pit of my stomach I could almost hear the voice of a man choking and trying to speak and recasting the same question again and again.

Then Hester said that if what I said about Judy wasn't true, I had slept with the French girl at the shellac office. The voice in the pit of my stomach came blurting to the surface.

'I haven't slept with any girls,' I said.

'I don't believe you.'

I recast my sentence in negative form. I could think of no other.

'I wish I had slept with *you*, but you're going away . . .' There, I had got it out at last. I was startled to see Hester's pink face go dead white. A lot of words must have come out of me after that for I saw a satisfied look on her face.

'I have often wondered about you,' she said. 'I don't do that for the asking. I'm engaged to be married.'

I got up. 'I've got to go,' I said coldly, because I'd given myself away. I called the waiter and paid him.

'No. You can't go like that,' she said. 'We must talk.'

'Goodbye,' I said. She got up too. I went to the door. She called to me. I did not turn round but went blindly out, bumping into some man who was coming in. Once in the street, the strange thing is that I felt hysterically happy. The glass case in which I had been living was smashed. I raced down the street and got into the Métro. I only feared she might be following me. When I got home my larynx ached as if my voice had ripped it.

I decided not to see Hester again; the more I reflected on what I had said and her reply, the less clearly I remembered it all; and even now, my memory must have made the incident bleaker than it was. I suppose I am drastic because what I am really remembering is the uncouth figure I cut; also, I had fallen back into my defensive habit of expecting disappointment and unconsciously preparing for it. This has some connection with the idealizing of women, picked up from Victorian novels and punishing myself for it. And then, conceit is all the stronger in a young man who is afraid of love. I was sulking.

For two or three days I tried to work. Then I gave up and went to Montparnasse. There as I walked up the street from the station I heard a sound well known to me. A man was spitting and hawking a little way ahead of me. I knew him a little. He was a thin middle-aged American and a terrible bore. My desire for punishment must have been strong, for I hurried to catch him up. At other times I had often turned down side streets to avoid him.

Percy was a journalist who wrote fashion articles for American papers. As a bore he belonged to the race of the soft-voiced interminable and insidious, who catch you with a note of sympathy and then shoulder you into walls or trap you in doorways.

Like the air, Percy was always moving from one place to another; and, again like the air, he was invisible until you suddenly saw his face looking down into yours, a pale face stamped by pock marks that might have been the off-prints of faded conversations.

He stopped now at once when he saw me. After twenty minutes he said: 'Do you want to come along to the hotel? I'm meeting Fraser there.' I did not know who Fraser was, but I was so low that I went.

Percy was distinct from everyone else in this gaudy quarter by his quality of being the Invisible Man, for he wore a dim grey office-going suit, a stained trilby hat and walked in rapid vanishing little steps. He usually had the remains of a cigar on his lips. He lived in a poor hotel room at the corner of the Rue de la Gaieté. It was an hotel used as a rendezvous for lovers. He was bound to go into a long tale of his running war with the manager about the noises of fornication in the night. Percy had the Calvinist's obsession with the 'whore house', though he was a pious man who played the organ for the American Methodists on Sundays: an extension of his own monotone. He was an old Radical who hadn't been in the United States for twenty years and he had been a reporter in one of the Balkans wars. I think of him as one of those lost eighteenth-century Utopians who stray from country to country but who have caught from Longfellow Hiawatha's mania for detail. In Greece he had been imprisoned; and he brought to Paris that fear of foreign police which is so often buried in the guilt that haunts expatriates. Yet Percy was a saint of kinds, a soft touch for all 'the boys and girls' of the quarter. Broken painters, girls who could not pay the rent, always went to him. He was always doling out small sums of money. If any painter was carried off drunk or starving by the police, Percy was down at the station to rescue him at once. The only work of art he admired was 'The God Damn Great Cock', which the admirers of Wilde had erected over his grave in *Père Lachaise*. He was sad because the French police had covered it with a tarpaulin.

We skipped along to Percy's hotel and climbed to the top floor.

Percy spat once or twice into his washbasin in his small room. He was reminiscing about Trotsky. Shortly Fraser turned up, a red-faced and suspicious little Cockney mechanic.

'Aren't we going to do anything?' said the Cockney, uneasy about my being there.

'He'll watch us,' said Percy.

'We do it most Saturdays,' the Cockney said.

They got out a light round table and a pile of manuscript in single-spaced typing for me to study while they got going. Table turning was their bond. They were chasing spirits on the other side. They were secret agents between the living and the dead.

'We've had Hamlet three weeks running. You couldn't stop him,' said Percy. 'There it is.' He handed me a bundle of manuscript.

They put their hands on the table. They waited and waited. It was a grey day and rain came on.

'Nothing there,' said the Cockney.

'Ah, there's something,' said Percy. 'He's trying. Maybe it's Hamlet again. Perhaps he didn't finish. Is that you, Hamlet?'

No answering knocks came.

'Hostile presence,' said the Cockney, indicating me.

'Perhaps I'd better go,' I said.

'No,' said Percy. 'They're about.' He got up, made another spit into the washbasin and picked up the papers. 'We've had Julius Caesar. We had Bismarck. George Washington.' One or two Greeks had poured out their monologues.

'Perhaps they want you to join in,' Percy said to me. So we all sat with our fingers on the table. Occasionally there was a slight move, but nothing happened. I thought of my great Uncle Arthur, the cabinet maker, in York, who had upset the Bible-reading branch of my Yorkshire family by getting through to Burton, the author of his secret Bible, *The Anatomy of Melancholy*, with a signalman who was a friend of his in that city.

'They get like that,' said Percy. 'They get sulky or something.' We had to give up the séance. We passed the rest of the afternoon listening to Percy who read us pages and pages of literary material from the other world. Occasionally a fretful woman would turn up in the complaining notes of all the speakers who seemed to live in another version of Montparnasse. I think this woman was his mother. We were listening to a minced up instalment of Percy's autobiography.

When I got back to my room there was a note under my door. It said:

'Where have you been? I called this afternoon. I am terribly worried. I have some news I want to tell you, Hes.'

Victory, of course. I do not propose to tell in all its detail what happened between Hester and myself in my room when she came to it. Our encounter was helped because I had only one chair in which she sat for a short time and dabbed a few softening and attractive tears from her eyes. The thought thundered in my head that I was on the point of holding in my arms the serene author of a dissertation on Malebranche, a philosopher (she had told me), who had written a book entitled *De la recherche de la Vérité*. There was a bit of rational protest when we had got to the hooks and buttons. I excused myself and took my package into Madame Chapin's kitchen. I opened it and made a terrible discovery. The priests of the pharmacy, either out of cynicism or malice, had sold me a box containing twenty pills for the liver. I searched for hope in the 'directions', in four languages. I read the list of chemical content. I had not taken a pill of any kind for years and had no notion of what any medicine outside of a cough mixture was designed to do. I knew little about contraception. It occurred to me that these pills must be the things the French used, perhaps having esoteric knowledge of the action of the liver upon the sexual organs, and in a sudden fit of faith and superstition I swallowed one, indeed to make sure, swallowed two. Recklessly I went back to Hester, but the sight of her pulling a garment over her head and the long white back of a living woman who was an image no longer, brought me to my senses and made me tell her of the disaster. She did not understand and half-undressed and sitting on the bed asked to see the package. She read the directions carefully.

'Is there something the matter with your liver?' she said.

'No, it's not that,' I said and had to explain again. She said in her advisory voice, that she never trusted things like that.

She said: 'You must take it back to the shop. You must get your money back.'

'I couldn't. I've taken two.'

'Well it's their mistake,' she said, and pulled the garment back over her head. The Sorbonne, the lecture halls, the libraries, the imaginary fjords of Denmark vanished as I looked at her and all I can say is that, after some grapplings and false rammings, during which she talked fractiously, nineteen to the dozen, down went Malebranche and the captain of the ship. I looked down at her and saw two tears on her smiling face.

We went out and walked tenderly by the river where the lights were going down like spears into the water. Hester suddenly stopped. For the first time I heard her laugh out loud. She stood there laughing her head off, she was nearly doubled up with laughter and clung tottering to my arm. She could not stop.

'And you took two of them!' she said. 'I've just seen what you were trying to tell me.' And off she went again. Passing people were astonished by her. She recovered.

'I'm sorry. Why are you looking so sad?'

I wasn't sad. To make up for her laughter she said very seriously:

'You may not realize it, but your ideas have influenced me a lot.'

My ideas! What ideas? I had only one: terror that she would be pregnant. The philosopher Malebranche returned to reassure me. She had one or two young men, it seemed, in Denmark who were interested in him and her; and she said she knew how to look after herself. We sat closely in a restaurant and twice during the meal she put down her knife and fork and laughed like a Viking. People said: 'Americans!'

In the next five days, which were all we had, I said she must break her engagement. She frowned at me tenderly. Her parents arrived: the captain came to the surface. They were taking her for a spree. The captain had a tuft of fair hair on his chin (I saw), when we all met at the professor's and it made me gaze at Hester. Her small tuft had been fair, too. But the captain, who did not speak French, cottoned on to me and said roguishly that if only they had time, he would have asked me to show him Paris.

'I will write,' said Hester in the dark hall of the professor's flat. We shook hands. Her hands were long. It was awful leaving her. But I noticed as I went away how every man, woman or child I saw seemed more real to me. The whole of Paris ceased to be a dream and came alive. I had so often heard or read of the disgust and guilt of sexual love; I realized I had never believed these tales and now never believed them again. But often as I walked about I would look at the faces of women hoping I would see something of hers, and at every corner for a long time I had the illusion that only a minute before she might have turned down there.

I went on a wet day to Amiens and wrote about it, but slowly luck turned against me. My money was running out. Mrs Lang's promise to pay me back came to nothing and I could not get payment for my articles. There was – I heard – a lawsuit going on in the holy city of Boston: I knew nothing of the delicacies of the religion, but it seemed that the Divine Mind had split in two and – in the general phrase – someone had let Error in. Both parties were accusing each other of witchcraft, a common accusation among the congregations as I was soon to find out. In practical terms, the *Monitor*'s funds were frozen. Fortunately Madame Chapin stayed on in Tours and I could skip paying the rent.

I was back in my fear that I should have to leave Paris and go home. I was saved by one more cheque from a London review, but after that things went very wrong. A time came when I had to sell back my books, first one at a time, then two at a time: for two volumes I could get a cheap meal. So two by two, the row on my mantelpiece got shorter and shorter.

I wrote to Hester, but the letters became fewer. At last one came from Cape Town. She was going to be married. She had emigrated. And then I heard no more. Geography, that I loved so much, had swallowed her up.

I went on selling my books: off went Balzac and Boileau,

Maupassant, Vigny and Hugo, to be converted into soup, *noix d'agneau*, a *cassoulet*, ham sandwiches. I was soon down to an anthology of comic verse and Rabelais. I stuck to that; it was expensive.

Poverty makes one morose, envious and lethargic. I had a special hatred for small vans delivering food. I grazed off the menus outside restaurants. People eating there struck me as sordid and dogs as unnecessary. I developed lingering habits if I met an acquaintance to see if I could cadge a meal. I was far too proud to borrow from some of the Christian Scientists I knew, but from whom I had drifted away; and my father's habits, as I have said, had given me a fear of debt.

Madame Chapin came back. I evaded her. The good woman said nothing but, noticing that I did not go out in the evenings and sat eating a sandwich only, she got into the habit of bringing me a bowl of soup and invented a tale that she had brought back some pâtés of Touraine. The thing that reassured her was to hear me typing; but I had nothing to type, and if I heard her coming from the kitchen to my room I would start typing anything that came into my head to deceive her.

I sold one of my suits, a grey one. At last I ate my last book. The injustice of being forced to this sacrifice made me give up my principles. I would have to borrow for my next meal. The enterprise made me brash, and I began to feel contempt – contempt for my victim, whoever he should be. I arrived outside the *Dôme* and there he was – Percy, of course. I hadn't seen him since the séance.

'Where have you been?' he said. 'I haven't seen you since 14 July. Fraser and I have been worrying about you.'

My grin was ravenous.

'Could you lend me two francs?' I said. I explained my dilemma. I joined the long list of his charities in the quarter. The saintly bore paid for my dinner and gave me two francs more.

When the benefits of this feed had passed off in the next two days I was tempted to become one of Percy's regular following of beggars. After all, the tradition of debt for writers was an honourable one. I could not humiliate myself to rich friends: only to Percy whom, in my heart, I despised. The old puritan pride which had stiffened me had become shady and hypocritical.

Soon I had only a few centimes left. Perhaps Mrs Lang or the paper would pay? Perhaps there would be a letter? I searched all my clothes and my room, even under the bed, looking for one more dropped coin, but there was none. In the next six days I ate half a small roll per day. Hunger excited my imagination. What would it be like to starve? I got interested in my sensations, in the rumblings in the empty cave inside me, in my giddiness and my dashing indifference to traffic – for I seemed to be flying when I crossed the street. I talked to myself loudly as I walked. To go out by day was tormenting, for one saw people who had eaten; it was better to go out late at night when no one much was about in my neighbourhood. One night I went out just to look in at the door of the nearest café bar. Rain had set in heavily. I had no coat and the cold rain thrilled me. More suffering! I just stood, letting myself get soaked. I had once been in this bar with a young pianist who used to play Coleridge Taylor to the sharp daughters of a French Protestant clergyman in Asnières – a scene from André Gide I recognized later in life – he puffed like a steam engine as he thumped out the piece: he had gone back to England but, in a mad way, I half expected him to come puffing out. Instead, a ludicrous thing happened: a tipsy young student went into the bar, casually picked up three hard-boiled eggs from the counter, dropped them one by one on the floor and marched out shouting:

'*Ils sont tous morts les amoureux.*'

The world had simply come to a grotesque end: I walked home down the Rue Raynouard, past Balzac's house. I thought of him scrambling through the trap door when his creditors came after him. I stopped outside two closed warehouse doors where I had once seen a procession of five rats run out and disappear into a hole further down. One could eat rats. I was fascinated by this idea. It was nearly midnight when I passed the lodge of the concierge whom I could see in bed, through his little window, and splashed across the courtyard to my room.

Madame Chapin had not gone to bed. She was waiting up for me: she had never done this before. There was enough light in the little dark passage for me to see there was a change in her, or, perhaps in my exhausted state every thing and every person looked unreal and half-dreamed. I could see her white nightgown under a black overcoat – it was a cold time of the year – and her hair was drawn back from her forehead which looked broader and paler, showing two fine lines across it, and the hair was let down in two long plaits at the back. She looked severe instead of placid; the plaits made her look like a fierce schoolgirl and her voice had changed. We always addressed each other as Monsieur and Madame.

'Monsieur, I must speak to you.'

Then she saw I was soaked with rain; it was squelching out of my boots and on to the floor she so often polished.

'Look at my floor. Get your shoes off,' she said sharply. She pushed into my room ahead of me and lit my lamp.

'And look at you! Your jacket! Your trousers!' Sharp fingers gave a pull to my shirt.

'And your shirt! Get them off.' She opened the wardrobe.

'Where is your other suit?' she turned and accused.

I had, of course, sold it.

'At the cleaners,' I said.

'Get your pyjamas,' she said, and picking up my boots, as I took my jacket off and my belt, she left the room with a prim and huffy look I had never seen before. It was strange (I thought afterwards) that Madame Chapin, who came into my room every Sunday when I had nothing on and had to grab for a towel, seemed to think now there was something unspeakable about seeing me undress. A new, threatening formality had come between us. I was afraid of her and got into my pyjamas and dressing-gown – the one my mother had given me on my twenty-first birthday. Now Madame Chapin came back.

'Where are your books?' she said, looking at the empty mantelpiece. 'And your typewriter?'

'There!' I pointed to the side of the wardrobe. I had hung on to that.

'Ah!' she said. If that had gone I think she would have screamed. The sight of it calmed her down. She said, as I stood there, dazed, 'You have always been frank with me. You are not like my Pole. I have a right to know – are you leaving me?'

Oh dear, the rent! But she did not mention it.

'If you are leaving me, I have the right to a month's notice.' When she said 'the right' her eyes became bright with anxiety and I, in my weakness, could not stop grimacing as if I had St Vitus's Dance; instead of a sentence a noise that was like a yawn came out of me.

Well, what was it? Had I been drinking? Drinking! My voice squealed when I said I hadn't.

'Get into bed,' she said. 'You are ill. Oh, my God.'

And out of the room she went again. I heard her groaning in the kitchen; it was a relief to hear her return to her familiar lamenting voice. Presently she came back into the room with a bowl of soup.

'Sit up and eat that.'

'You can't deceive me,' she said. 'I've seen it for a long time. What has been happening to you? I've seen you've not been eating. God, if your poor mother knew.'

. She watched every spoonful go into my mouth. I was slowly able to stop grimacing. She went to get a glass of wine.

'I'm not afraid to give you this. It is good wine from my village.'

I drank it and when she stood questioning me in the next half hour I was liable either to mumble or to shout. It was a struggle, for her eyes didn't stop staring. The rent, I thought, was in her eyes.

'I'm waiting for my money to pay the rent,' I said. 'There has been a delay.'

I had to stop my tears when I said this, but she was evidently lost in suspicion.

'Where is that beautiful suit?' she said again.

In wine out came the truth.

'I sold it,' I said.

'You sold it! And the money for that beautiful story?' She was terrifying.

'Which one?' I was confused.

'The one I showed to the father.'

'I lent it to a friend,' I managed to get that out.

Madame Chapin suddenly looked older.

'Oh no you didn't,' she said. 'I know young men. You are like my Pole. Oh God, you threw it away to sleep with some *fille*.'

'I didn't,' I said.

I didn't realize I had shouted the words. The shout made Madame Chapin straighten and step back.

'I've seen the sheets,' she said and the beginnings of mockery ran along her lips.

'You poor young man,' she said. 'I suppose you gave it to your pretty cousin.'

'No. I lent money to her mother!' Then, thinking this would be an advantage, I told her the whole story. Out came the Mexican Revolution, the wild rides to the hacienda, the pistol, the dreadful husband. Madame Chapin was caught and carried away by it. As I got to the end she was turning to the mirror over the mantelpiece and looking at herself; then she remembered me and said:

'The rich! That's what those rich women are like. They are worse then kept women. At least *they* give something for their money!' And added: 'Her mother!'

I thought I made it better by confessing that Mrs Lang was not my aunt.

'That,' said Madame Chapin drily, 'I knew well, young man.'

There was no more to say and she came to the bedside to ask me if I wanted more soup and took the bowl, and that would have been the end of it. But the bugle went off at the barracks, clearer and harder as if it were in the room itself, because of the wet night. You could picture the man with his chest out and his cheeks swelling. Madame Chapin gave a jump and dropped the soup bowl on the floor.

'Oh my God!' she cried out, and put her hand to her breast. She stood there trembling. She leaned against the wall. 'My heart!' she said weakly and panting. Suddenly she snatched my hand and pulled it under her coat to her breast.

'Feel my heart. I am choking. Can you feel it?'

Her heart was indeed thumping, but I could feel her breast. Her hand was holding mine hard there. Her breast was not like Hester's, the small breast of a young woman.

Madame Chapin hesitated and took a long breath.

'Soldiers. That filthy war,' she said sadly, pushing my hand away. And then, sighing, she picked up the bowl from the floor. She considered me.

'In the morning I will lend you five francs,' she said in a tender voice. 'Get something to eat before I come back from work,' she said.

She came in the morning and put five francs on my table and left.

All day I could feel the roundness of Madame Chapin's breast, but I forgot it in the afternoon because a miracle happened. I had eaten, and then I went along the Boulevard des Italiens looking into the cafés where Mr Shaves often sat after lunch with his friends. He knew many people in business and in the theatre and he had said once or twice that he'd keep his ears open for news of a job I could do. He was there looking bumptious and pleased, his cigarette holder sticking up in the air under a lilac halo of smoke. His socks, which were in blue and yellow stripes, showed at the ankles and joined in his joy of life. When he saw me his smiles went.

'Where have you been?' he said. 'People have been asking at the Church.'

I didn't tell him much. He didn't appear to listen. One of his friends said to me: 'You've lost weight. I wish I could.'

I joined them nervously and I saw in Mr Shaves the mean, shrewd look of his that usually followed his loud laughs. He said that when his wife came back in a week's time they'd ask me to a meal. He kept staring at those boots of mine that had belonged to Pierre; they were worn down and shabby beside his and when I left I felt he was watching me. I did not realize that Mr Shaves was regarding me in a daydream of envy; that, in a sense, he wanted worn-out boots like mine. I took the Métro back to Auteuil; with food inside me I was wondering if I could write an article on starvation.

Madame Chapin was out, but there was a letter on the floor. It contained francs to the amount of £15, a large sum in those days. They came from the young Jewish abstract painter – the one who was no longer an abstract painter – who said he and his wife were concerned that I had not been paid for my writing and I needn't hurry about repaying the money. It came out eventually that Madame Chapin had been up the street to talk to the old lady with whom I sometimes had my excruciating French conversations on Sundays; this woman knew the painter; and that Mr Shaves had telephoned to the painter also and said I looked in a bad way. I went up to Montparnasse, ate an expensive meal, including the largest plate of *crêpes provençales* I have ever seen; nowadays, they would kill me. I paid Percy back the money I had borrowed. He was so astonished that he lost his power of monologue and went off with disappointment in his face, discerning perhaps that I had showed signs of ceasing to be one of his clientèle. He had the Bohemian's scorn.

I went back to Madame Chapin's. She was in her long black overall once more. She looked older than she had the night before when she had held my hand against her breast. I paid her rent and we resumed our formal conversations, I thanking her for her kindness and she saying that she had always had confidence in me.

This experience must have exhausted me, because I tired of Paris. The enchantment had gone. Basil Shaves's play came on at last after three postponements. I went to see it with Mrs Shaves and her children. There was a large audience in one of the Paris Salles. From the moment the rigged-up curtain rose and Basil came bounding on and shouting at Mrs Gilbey: 'Here's a nice thing. This is a b . . .' Basil Shaves was a success. All his vulgar mannerisms were there: his habit of boring his finger into his ear, his scratching of his armpit, the wagging of his shoes when he sat admiring the shape of his leg, the looks of hurt, meanness, absurdity jumped into his face; he looked outraged yet cunning, virtuous yet dubious. The casting was perfect. Basil Shaves was there to the life and yet was morally and physically, Gilbey. He was so pleased with himself in the part that, like all amateurs, he could not help glancing at the audience halfway through his longer speeches; but that look was one of wonder at himself.

There were good notices in the English papers and one in a French paper. He and the woman who played Doris – I had met her once with some of her friends in the Café de la Paix, a thin, dark woman with intense worried eyes, were the stars. 'A tragedy,' he had said to me at the time. 'Married a French actor who left her with two children.' This scandal of the theatre made him regard her as a very superior woman. 'Can you imagine it, in an office like ours? The men round her like flies. Why not another slice off a cut loaf?' Mr Shaves could be very crude.

It was not long after this that Mr Shaves sent me a note saying there was a job for me if I would take it. An English company he had mentioned at least six months before was coming to play Shakespeare. Hébertot had taken them on. The great Hébertot! I went to see him. He received me as if I had come from an embassy. He was nervous of not getting an audience. The job was to canvass the English and American colony and sell blocks of tickets. The good thing about it was the high pay which could be collected every evening at the box office. I took on the job.

My last efforts as a salesman were as poor in their results as my earlier ones had been. Happily Hébertot did not notice this for a long time. I bought books again and a green velour hat with a wide brim. It was in a shop window and I used to visit it every day dreading it would be sold, until I could risk the expense. The hat was my religion, I decided that I would go to London and see if I could get the money I was owed or if I could get a job as a Paris correspondent; I knew that it would be stupid to stay in Paris. I had met too many Frenchified Englishmen. For two years I had lived thoughtlessly from day to day. I could not go on like this. Still – clinging to a last hope that I still might see more of the world – I left my luggage behind with Madame Chapin and went back to London.

Before I left I heard bad news of Mr Shaves. It came from a man who worked with him at the bank. The husband of the woman who played Doris, and who had been acting in America, had come back with some large scheme for starting a new show in Paris. Mr Shaves had always been fascinated by this man whom he had never met: he had 'ruined his family'. The sight of a ruiner, coming at the same time when Shaves himself had shown that he could act, must have turned his head. As easily, as dreamily, as he had cashed my first cheque, he cashed a couple of large ones for this man. American banks do not forgive the wandering mind. Shaves was sacked. I saw him at his café.

'I have ruined them,' he said. 'The bank has fired me.'

'I heard,' I said.

I can only describe his appearance as haggard, but ecstatic.

'I've got my chance,' he said. 'We're going to London, too.'

What did I get out of my two years in Paris? Freedom above all, and the love of it has never left me. Self-confidence, too. I had rebelled successfully. I could stand on my own feet. I had another language, so I could now become two persons. I had had a large amount of time for reading; it was a small capital. I had learned to be absurd, was willing to see what happened to me. Above all, I had had pleasure, a thing suspected by the calculating, constrained and anxious lower middle class from which I came; to whom, all the same, I owed the habit of working hard. I was in the simplest way happy. My only dread was that I would be forced back into the world I came from.

And what did I get from France itself? I have known French people far better, their character, their literature, their arts, since that time and have even written about them. It has been hard not to smuggle in some of this later knowledge here. What I gained, lastingly, was a sense of the importance of the *way* in which things are done, a thrift of the mind. I also began to see my own country – a very powerful one at that time – from abroad; and I felt the beginning of a passion, hopeless in the long run, but very nourishing, for identifying myself with people who were not my own and whose lives were governed by ideas alien to mine.

III · TRAVEL

The Spanish Temper

Chapter 1

I make these notes during those two hours of impatience which begin in the early morning when the electric train clatters out of Biarritz Ville. One is hungry and queasy, one has slept badly and begins smoking nervously and too soon. In the corridor no one wants to talk after this night. Women are patching up their faces, combing their hair, men stand outside rubbing the night's growth of beard. The lavatory smells. One watches the long shadows of the rising sun in the pines; one sees the dust, the dewy greenness, the dry, heavily tiled houses, the fruitful green of a kind climate, a candid sky, and the sedate life. Yesterday's sun is still warm in these villa towns of terra-cotta. Here one would be glad to have a doll's house and count one's pension and *rentes* thirty times a day like a Frenchman and rest one's nervous northern mind in conversation consisting largely of abstract nouns, to parcel out one's sous, one's pleasures and permissions.

But the prolonged sight of France annoys; one is impatient for the drama of the frontier and for the violent contrasts, the discontent and indifference of Spain. One is anxious to fill out that famous text of Galdós, so often quoted from the *Episodios Nacionales*: 'O Spain, how thou art the same into whatsoever part of thy history one may look! And there is no disguise to cover thee, for wherever thou appearest, thou art recognized at once from a hundred miles away, one half of thy face – fiesta; and the other misery; one hand bearing laurels and the other scratching thy leprous sores.'

To know what we are up against we ought to go to Spain by aeroplane and fly to the centre of it. Beneath us England is packed with little houses, if the earth is visible at all through the haze; France lies clearly like green linoleum broken into a small busy pattern, a place of thriving little fields; but, cross the dark blot of the Pyrenees, and Spain is reddish brown, yellow, and black, like some dusty bull restive in the rock and the sand and (we would guess) uninhabited. The river-beds are wide and bleached and dry. After Switzerland this is the highest country in Europe. The centre is a tableland torn open by gorges, and on the table the mountain ranges are spaciously disposed. There is little green, except on the seabord; or rather the green is the dark gloss of ilex, olive, and pine, which from the height at which we are flying appear in lake-like and purple blobs. For the most part we are looking down at steppe which is iced in the long winter and cindery like a furnace floor in the short summer. Fortified desert – and yet the animal image returns again and again in this metalled and rocky scene, for occasionally some peak will give a sudden upward thrust, like the twist of a bull's horns, at the wings of the plane. Flying over Spain, we wonder at the torture that time has put upon the earth's crust and how human beings can live there. In Soria, the terrible province, below the wicked mountains of Aragón I remember picking up an old woman who had fallen off her donkey and carrying her to the side of the road and wiping the blood off her nose. She was a figure carved in wood, as light as a husk. It was like having starvation in one's hands.

But it is better, I think, to go the slow way to Spain and to feel the break with Europe at the land frontiers. It is true that at Irún one is not in Spain but in the Basque provinces, among people of mysterious race and language who are an anomaly in Europe; and that, at the other end of the Pyrenees, one is in Catalonia, where the people are really Provençal, speak their own tongue, and scornfully alter the Spanish proverb, 'Africa begins at the Pyrenees,' into 'African begins at the Ebro.' But the stamp of Spain is on these provinces and the Spanish stain runs over the frontiers. One finds it in Montpellier; on the Atlantic side it reaches into Biarritz, Saint-Jean-de-Luz, and Bayonne. And in these towns one meets something profoundly and disturbingly Spanish which goes down to the roots of the Spanish nature: one meets the exiles. For long before the Europe of the 1930s or the Russia of the early nineteenth century, Spain is the great producer of exiles, a country unable to tolerate its own people. The Moors, the Jews, the Protestants, the reformers – out with them; and out, at different periods, with the liberals, the atheists, the priests, the kings, the presidents, the generals, the socialists, the anarchists, fascists, and communists; out with the Right, out with the Left, out with every government. The fact recalls that cruel roar of abuse that goes up in the ring when the bullfighter misses a trick; out with him. Hendaye and Bayonne are there to remind us that before the dictatorships and police states and witch-hunters of contemporary history, Spain has been imperial in the trade of producing exiles. And the exiles go out over the bridge at Hendaye into France, the country that has tolerated all, and at the windows of the French hotel the new exile stands, looking across the bight of sea at the gloomy belfries of his native country, hears their harsh bells across the water, and hates the France which has given him sanctuary. He is proud of his hatred, sinks into fatalism, apathy, intrigue, quarrels with all the other exiles, and says with pride: 'We are the impossible people.'

Hendaye: the train dies in the customs. One gets a whiff of Spanish impossibility here. A young Spaniard is at the carriage window talking to a friend who is on the platform. The friend is not allowed on the platform; what mightn't he be smuggling? The gendarme tells him to go. The Spaniard notes this and says what he has to say to his friend. It is a simple matter.

'If you go over to see them on Wednesday tell them I have arrived and will come at the end of the week.' But if a bossy French gendarme thinks that is how a Spaniard proceeds, he is wrong. The simple idea comes out in this fashion:

'Suppose you see them, tell them I am here, but if not, not; you may not actually see them, but talk to them, on the telephone perhaps, or send a message by someone else and if not on Wednesday, well then Tuesday or Monday, if you have the car you could run over and choose your day and say you saw me, you met me on the station, and I said, if you had some means of sending them a message or you saw them, that I might come over, on Friday, say, or Saturday at the end of the week, say Sunday. Or not. If I come there I come, but if not, we shall see, so that supposing you see them . . .' Two Spaniards can keep up this kind of thing for an hour; one has only to read their newspapers to see they are wrapped in a cocoon of prolixity. The French gendarme repeats that the Spaniard must leave. The Spaniard on the platform turns his whole body, not merely his head, and looks without rancour at the gendarme. The Spaniard is considering a most difficult notion – the existence of a personality other than his own. He turns back, for he has failed to be aware of anything more than a blur of opposition. It is not resented. Simply, he is incapable of doing more than one thing at a time. Turning to the speaker in the train, he goes over the same idea from his point of view, in the same detail, adding personal provisos and subclauses, until a kind of impenetrable web has been woven round both parties. They are aware of nothing but their individual selves, and the very detail of their talk is a method of defeating any awareness of each other. They are lost in the sound of their own humming, monotonous egos and only a bullet could wake them out of it. Spanish prolixity, the passion for self-perpetuating detail, is noticeable even in some of their considerable writers – in the novels of Galdós, for example, in the passage I have quoted there are three images to describe 'disguise' – and it creates a soft impermeable world of its own. Yet they have a laconic language, the third-person form of address is abrupt and economical, their poetry even at its most decorative is compressed in its phrases and cut down to the lapidary and proverbial, and they can be as reserved and silent as the English; and yet when, in their habit of going to extremes, they settle down to talk, one feels one is watching someone knitting, so fine is the detail, so repetitious the method. The fact is that they are people of excess: excessive in silence and reserve, excessive in speech when they suddenly fly into it. It is absurd, of course, to generalize about a nation from the sight of two people on a railway platform; but we are travellers – let us correct one generalization by adding a great many more. There will be time to reflect on the variety of human nature, and the sameness of its types, afterwards. Let us consider the other Spaniards on the train.

It was easy to pick them out from the French when they got on the train in Paris; not quite so easy to pick them out from the Italians. The Spanish men were better dressed than other nationals, and this was true of all classes. Their clothes fitted them at the waist and the shoulders, they carried themselves with reserve and dignity. Their gestures were restrained, their farewells were quiet and manly, they did not talk much and what they said was dry, composed, and indifferent. They behaved with ease as people who live by custom do; and they gave an impression of an aristocratic detachment. This is true of all classes from the rich to the poor, who have the same speech and the same manners. There are no class accents in Spain worth mentioning; there are only the regional variants of speech. This man is an Andalusian, this is a Gallego; you can only guess his class from his clothes. One is markedly among gentlemen, and even the '*señorito*', the bouncing little mister, falls back on that when he has exhausted his tricks. The word 'gentleman' is not altogether complimentary, for it implies a continual conventional restraint on part of the human personality, and it carries a narrow connotation of class. In this narrow sense a Spaniard cannot be a 'gentleman', for though he has a sense of fitness in his quiescent mood, he is unrestrained when he wakes up. His conduct is ruled by his personal pride, not by his category; and it is natural for him to be proud. His pride may be a nuisance, but it fits him and it cannot be removed. He is, he has always been, a hidalgo – *a hijo de algo* – a person of some consideration. And upon this consideration, however impalpable it may be, the very beggar in the streets reposes. A point not to forget is that in the sixteenth and seventeenth centuries the Spaniards were the master-race of the world, the founders of the first great empire to succeed the Roman Empire, more permanent in their conquests and administration than the French, who followed them, successful where the Germans have never yet succeeded, the true predecessors of the British empire-makers of the eighteenth and nineteenth centuries. The Spaniards in the train had the simplicity of people who had once had the imperial role. One could suppose them to be looking back on it with philosophical resignation. The place of those who have ceased to rule is to teach.

There was no conceit or vanity in these travellers. The nervous pushing bustle of the European was not in them. The quick vanity and sharp-mindedness of the French, their speed in isolating and abstracting a problem, were not there. Nor were the naïve vivacity and affectibility which electrify the agreeable Italians. These races care to attract or please continuously; the Spaniard cares very little and leaves us to discover him. He gives us time to breathe by his very negligence, '*Nada* – nothing,' he says restfully before every subject that is broached.

They stood in the corridor of the train and they gazed at the fields of France. These fields are richer and better cultivated than a good deal of – though not all – the Spanish land. The Spaniard does not deny this, though he will think of the province of olives in Jaén, the *vega* of Granada, the vines of Rioja and Valdepeñas, and the long rich cultivations of Valencia and say, with that exaggeration which is natural to local pride, that these are 'the richest places in the whole world'; and about Valencia he will be right. But Spain on the whole is a poor country, and he does not deny it. He is simply not interested in what is outside of Spain; because he has no feeling for the foreign thing and even regards its existence as inimical and an affront. He turns his back. His lack of curiosity amounts to a religion.

When I first crossed the frontier at Irún nearly thirty years ago, I remembered listening to a declamation by a Spaniard against his own country. At the time I thought the protest was a sign of some specific political unrest, but I have heard that speech dozens of times since. Again and again: 'It is one of the evils of Spain. We are decadent, priest-ridden, backward, barbarous, corrupt, ungovernable,' etc., etc. Spain is either hell or heaven, a place for fury or ecstasy. Like Russians in the nineteenth century, the Spaniards are in the habit of breaking into denunciations of their country, and between 1898 and 1936 these denunciations culminated in a puritan renaissance. There had been two savage civil wars in that century and, among intellectuals, these wars presented themselves as a conflict between reactionary Catholicism and liberal Catholicism, between Africa and Europe, tradition and progress. In the writings of Ganivet, in Ortega y Gasset, Unamuno, the early Azorín, in Maeztu, in Ayala and Baroja – a brilliant school which has had no successors and which was contemporary with the effective efforts of Giner de los Ríos to create an educated minority – the examination of the Spanish sickness was made without rhetoric. Wherever one finds a superior mind in Spain it is certain to have been formed by this tragic generation, many of whom died of broken hearts in the Civil War, were executed, or are in exile. Possibly some of these train travellers have been influenced by them, possibly they are hostile or indifferent; if we are to find some common ground on which they stand we shall have to look beyond the accidents of opinion. That common ground is not their nationality.

For the Spaniards are not Spaniards first, if they are Spaniards in the end. The peninsula is a piece of rocky geography. It is the subject of Spanish rhetoric, the occasion for their talk about Spanishness, for chauvinism and rebellion – and they know from experience in every generation how those things end: they end in *nada*, nothing, resignation. The ground these travellers rest their lives on is something smaller than Spain. They are rooted in their region, even nowadays, after the Civil War, which has mixed up the population and broken so many ardently maintained barriers. They are Basques, Catalans, Galicians, Castilians, Andalusians, Valencians, Murcians, and so on, before they are Spaniards, and before they are men of these regions they are men of some town or village; and in that place, small or large, they think perfection lies – even the self-castigating people of Murcia, who say of themselves: 'Between earth and sky nothing good in Murcia.' One thinks of that little play of the Quintero brothers called *The Lady from Alfaqueque*: a lady in this lost little Andalusian town, who was so in love with it that she could be cajoled and swindled into any folly by anyone who said he came from that place. I remember a woman in Madrid who had spent the last ten years in political exile saying: 'We had a much better life abroad when we were in exile, but I could never forget the water of Madrid and the craving for the taste of it became a torture.'

This provinciality of the Spaniard is his true ground and passion. And with it runs a psychological parallel. His town is not like any other town. It is the only town. And he too is not like any other human being; he is indeed the only human being. If he is brought to the test, there is only himself in the world, himself and, at the other extreme, the Universe. For ourselves, the Westerners, there is something else besides man and the ultimate, or universal; there is civilization or what Spaniards call despairingly '*ambiente*'; and it is their continual argument that nothing can be done in Spain because of this 'lack of *ambiente*' or lack of a favourable atmosphere; how can anything as mundane as a 'favourable atmosphere' exist where people do not feel related to each other, but only to some remote personal extremity? The pious belong to God, not even to the city of God, but to some deeply felt invisible figure; the impious to some individual vision. In the end they are anarchists.

Irún. Holiday-makers on the French side of the river that divides the two sides of the Basque country watched the fighting begin the Civil War here and saw men swim the river to safety. The town Irún is famous in the history of Pyrenean smuggling. There have been two traditional kinds of smuggling on this frontier: the mule loaded with tobacco coming over the mountain paths at night, and the smuggling organized by high-up officials from Madrid, which is part of the bribery system that never dies in Spain. It is described in the Galdós novel *La de Bringas*. In all classes the personal approach through 'influence' is preferred to the direct one; without 'influence' one cannot 'get in'. A foreign official told me that after many years living in Spain he had come to the conclusion that there are two kinds of Spaniards, those who have 'influence' and those too poor to have any; for the former, life is 'normal', for the latter it is hell. The pursuit of 'influence' is partly due to economic causes. In poor countries a job of some slight importance is a phenomenon and attracts a court of parasites. The fortunate slave at the desk is besieged by a crowd of less fortunate slaves; the fortunate slave himself is the unfortunate slave of one more fortunate. Like the Russian bureaucracy in Gogol's time, the Spanish is a huge collection of poor men. One has only to buy a motor-car or make a contract to be surrounded by people consumed by the anxiety to 'facilitate' the deal, register the papers, put the thing through with the right officials, for a small commission. The affair would be lost in the ordinary and proper channels. Weeks and months would go by and nothing would happen. Fatal to take the normal course; indispensable to have an introduction in the right quarter. Watch the fortunate Spaniard at the railway office. Discreetly he inquires about a ticket, does not boldly ask for it. A significant rubbing together of thumb and forefinger takes place, a furtive flicker comes into the eyes. A little personal deal is starting: unfortunate Spaniards without 'influence' will not get the seat, but he will. It is an unjust system but one unjust flea has other unjust fleas on his back; the method introduces elaboration, sociability, a sea of acquaintance, into ordinary action: 'I will give you a card to my uncle, who will arrange everything.' Everyone in Spain, down to the extremely poor, to whom so little is possible, is writing for someone else, for a 'combination', or arrangement, of some kind, and since time is no object, they make a lot of friends. If time *is* an object, if it *is* a matter of life and death, then a black figure which all Spaniards understand rises up and interposes her immovable hand – the great croupier, Fate. '*Ay, señor, que triste es la vida.*'

The railway station at Irún is as shabby as it was thirty years ago. The place is glum, thinly painted, and grubby. The eye notices how many ordinary things – things like pipes, trolleys, door handles – are broken. The grass grows out of the rusting tracks, the decaying old-fashioned coaches and wagons rot in the sidings, the woodwork exposed to a destructive climate. The railways were half ruined by the Civil War, but, except for the electric trains of the Basque provinces, they were always shabby and went from bad to worse as one travelled southwards or got off the main lines. After France this material deterioration is sudden except in one respect; in the last two years the Spaniards have built a new train, called the Talgo, which runs three days a week to Madrid and has shortened the thirteen-hour journey across Castile by two or three hours. This Talgo is a luxury, Pullman train, low in build like the London tube coaches, and each coach has a concertina-like section in the middle which enables it to bend at the alarming mountain curves in the Basque mountains. Its motion is, however, violent. One cracks one's head, or bruises one's stomach against the handrails; but it is a change from the slow, dusty, bumping caravan of coaches that crawl to Madrid on other days of the week. Spanish locomotives are always breaking down. There is still not a complete double track from the frontier to Madrid, or from Madrid to Seville.

Nothing else has changed at Irún. One has heard Spanish garrulity; now one meets for the first time Spanish silence, disdain, and reserve on their own soil. Those superb Spanish customs officers, young, handsome, wearing the tropical uniforms of naval officers, stroll up and down in a quiet ecstasy of satisfaction, talking and handsomely ignoring the crowd. Their leisure is lovely to gaze at. The inferior officers who examine your luggage wearing white gloves – it is possible to refuse examination until the gloves are put on, but I have never seen a Spanish customs official without them – are poor devils and they get to work suspiciously and tragically. They fumble with listless dignity in the midst of some private wretchedness. The tragedy is the habit of work perhaps. They have the melancholy of people who go through this monotonous life with nothing on their minds, and not very much – at the present cost of living – in their stomachs. They look as though they are thinking of some other world, and possibly about death. More likely, until something dramatic happens, they are extinct. Our suitcases might be coffins.

Sombreness is so much the dominant aspect of these people that one is puzzled to know how the notion of a romantic and coloured Spain has come about.

What shall we declare at the customs? Almost everything will be opprobrious to them. We are English – and we have Gibraltar. We defeated the Germans and Italians; the Franco government supported them actively, and has in a large number of ways copied their régime. We are not Christians. By that the official means we are not Roman Catholics; if you are a Protestant you are not a Christian. You are, for him and historically speaking, a Moor, or a Jew. Or if we are Roman Catholics, Spanish Catholics will be quick to point out improprieties in our Catholicism. And then suppose you are on the Right politically, that will not help you. Are you a Carlist from Navarre, a descendant of those who supported the pretender to the Spanish throne in the two civil wars of the nineteenth century and who professed feudalism in politics and the ultramontane in religion? Or are you a monarchist, an old conservative, a clerical, a supporter of the Jesuits or the Army; are you *for* the Church *without* the Jesuits, or for Franco's Falange, which Franco himself does not much care for or, at any rate, plays down so that he can keep his balance between them, the higher Army officers, and the bishops? The Pope can be left out of it; the Spanish Catholics have always treated as equals with the Italian Pope. Or do you declare you are on the Left? Well, privately the customs officer is on the Left, or half his relations are. If you are on the Left you are a Red. But what kind of Red? Are you an old liberal republican, liberal monarchist, liberal anticlerical? One of several kinds of socialist? Which kind of anarchist? Which kind of Communist – Trotskyite, Titoist, Leninist, Stalinist? Though against the Church, are you a non-practising Catholic? A mystic? An atheist, a new atheist? The Spaniards are not allowed by government decree to discuss Party politics; there is only one Party. They do, of course, discuss them, but without much energy: that energy was exhausted in the Civil War, but the political look burns in the sad eye, a spark inviting to be blown on. And we have not exhausted the parties: for where do you stand on Basque and Catalan autonomy? Are you a centralist or a federalist?

These silent questions are rhetorical, for, as I say, no political questions may be publicly discussed in Spain today. There is only one Party, General Franco does not like it and has forbidden public discussions. So exhausted is the nation by the Civil War that people have little desire to talk about politics. They have fallen back on a few jokes. And suppose that, hoping to curry favour, you declared that you were in favour of the state of vertical syndicates, the military conquest of Gibraltar and Portugal, the renewal of the Spanish Empire, the ecclesiastical control of all ideas, and a return to the glories of Ferdinand and Isabel there would be an appalled suspicious silence. People would step back a yard or two from you and say: 'Yes, yes, of course,' and leave you firmly alone in your abnormal orthodoxy. For you would have declared something no Spaniard can possibly think: that the Spanish government is good.

But one does not make any of the foregoing declarations. One declares simply that, being a foreigner, one is inevitably the enemy; occasionally, in remote places, I have had showers of stones thrown at me when I walked into a village. I have been asked also whether I was a Portuguese jewel-smuggler in a place outside Badajoz. And, crossing the Tagus once, whether I was a Frenchman 'making plans' – the tradition of the Napoleonic invasion still alive, handed down from father to son for a hundred and fifty years. And many times if I was a Christian, suggesting as I have said, not that I was an atheist, but a Moor or a Jew.

I do not mean that enmity means open hostility; one meets that open suspicious antagonism in France and Italy, but not in Spain, where manly welcome and maternal kindness, simple and generous, are always given to the traveller without desire for reward or wish to exploit. The poorer and simpler the people, the more sincere the welcome. In some lonely inn, a *venta* of Extremadura, where there are never beds to sleep in, but men sleep on the floor in the outer stables, while their mules and donkeys sleep inside, just as they did in the time of Cervantes, they will ask you if you have brought your sack and your straw, and if you have not brought them, they will get them for you. The suspicion common in industrial society, the rudeness of prosperous people, have not touched the Spaniards; one is treated like an equal among equals. There is never avarice. One sits before the hearth, the brushwood blazes up, the iron pan splutters on the fire, and conversation goes on as it has always gone on. The enmity I speak of is part historical inheritance and part an unbridgeable difference of type. A very large number of the beliefs of people brought up in modern, urban, industrial civilization make no contact even with the urban Spaniard. As for the historical inheritance, an Englishman thinks of the life-and-death struggle with Spain in the Elizabethan age. Spain threatened our life as a nation, our Protestant faith, the idea of freedom on which, for economic and spiritual reasons, our life during the last four hundred years has prospered. A Dutchman would make the same reflection. To Protestants, Spain was what Protestants have hated most: the totalitarian enemy. To Spanish Catholics, the Protestant attack upon the Church was their supreme stimulus to action in the Counter-Reformation. They were the first people in Europe to put into practice ideals which liberal societies have always resisted: the ferocious doctrine of racial purity or '*limpieza*', revived by the Nazis; the paralysing idea of ideological rightness, the party line, supervised by the Inquisition, which, for all the excuses that are made on its behalf, remains the notorious model of contemporary persecution in Russia and in America. It was a Spaniard who founded the first order of Commissars in Europe, the Society of Jesus. Time has softened, abolished, or transformed these things in Spain; but they were, in spirit, models which the enemies of liberal civilization have copied. The Spanish mind invented them and made them intolerably powerful. They represent something which is permanent, still potential, if not always powerful in Spanish life. One may be a foreign Catholic and still be on one's guard against them; many great Spaniards have fought their country's tendency and suffered from its authoritarianism.

Spanish fanaticism has sown fanaticism on the other side of its frontiers. It has its comedies. How many foreigners, especially the English-speaking countries, are Ruskinians about Spain. In his autobiography *Et Praeterita*, Ruskin describes his own ludicrous meeting with the daughters of his father's Spanish partner in the sherry trade, the Domeqs. He behaved with all the gaucheness and absurdity of a Protestant youth.

' . . . my own shyness and unpresentableness were further stiffened, or rather sanded by a patriotic and Protestant conceit, which was tempered neither by politeness nor sympathy . . . I endeavoured to entertain my Spanish-born, Paris-bred and Catholic-hearted mistress with my views upon the subjects of the Spanish Armada, the Battle of Waterloo and the doctrine of Transubstantiation.'

The young ladies from Jérez de la Frontera would have only noticed his 'shyness'; shyness is incomprehensible to anyone born in Spain.

On their side, the Spaniards might reply, and many have: We are not an industrialized society, but look at the sickness of industrial man! We have little social conscience, but look at the self-mutilation of countries that have it. If we are medieval, the latest communities, and, most of all, the Communist, indicate a return to a medieval conception of society. Whom would you sooner have, the Commissars or the Jesuits? We have digested all that long ago, Spanish scepticism is inseparable from Spanish faith, and though we have a large population of illiterate serfs, we have not a population of industrial slaves. We present to you a people who have rejected the modern world and have preserved freedoms that you have lost. We have preserved personality.

This silent dialogue in the Customs House is a dialogue of half-truths. It indicates only one thing: we have already been infected by the Spanish compulsion to see things in black and white. We are entering the country of '*todo o nada*' – all or nothing.

And change is slow. In the Customs House at Irún there is still that finger-marked hole in the station wall through which you push your passport; still that thin, sallow-faced man with the sick eyes, the shrunken chest, the poor bureaucrat's jacket, writing slowly in the large useless book, in silence. Thirty, twenty, fifteen, two years ago he was there. He wears a black shirt now, a dirty white shirt no longer – that is the only difference. He sits like a prisoner. His hand can only do one thing at a time. It is impossible for him to write in his book, blot his paper, and hand you your passport in a single continuous action. He certainly cannot hold passport in one hand and pen in the other. Each action is separate and he does not speak.

The Talgo fills up at San Sebastian with rich Madrid people returning from their summer holidays. There are dressed-up children in the care of nurses. Everyone very well dressed. In the whole journey, little conversation. A Brazilian like a little dragonfly tries to make people talk by extravagant South American means. He stands up in the passageway, but has few words of Spanish and only a phrase or two of atrocious French. So he suddenly begins snapping his thumbs above his head and dancing.

'Carmen Miranda,' he sings out.

People turn their heads.

'Spain,' he says. 'Dance.

'Ta rara! Tarra,' he sings dramatically.

People turn away and look understandingly at one another. 'Brazilian,' they say. Two distinguished Spanish ladies resume reading their two books on Court Life in the Reign of Louis XIV.

'Spain', sings out the Brazilian. 'Bullfights.' He begins to play an imaginary bull. The performance is a failure. This is the most decorous train in Europe. He sits down behind me and taps me on the shoulder.

'Commercial traveller?' he says.

'Almost,' I say. 'Journalist.'

'Me, the same. Novelist. Forty-seven novels. How many?'

'Three or four,' I say.

'Come and see me at the Ritz.' (He was unknown at the Ritz.) This happy little waterfly had a demure wife who laughed quietly into her handkerchief all the time, in her pleasure with this exquisite husband. But the middle-class Spaniards – no. ('One does not know what class of person,' etc., etc.) Anyway, it was impossible to talk to him, but one could have sung, I suppose.

The train drops through the Basque provinces into the province of Alava. It is Welsh-looking country of grey hills, glossy woods, and sparkling, brawling brown trout streams. The haycocks are small in the steep fields, the villages are neat and are packed round their churches. One sees the pelota court, and sometimes the game is played by the church wall. Pelota is a fast game, and the great players are a delight to watch as they hit the white ball and send it in a lovely long flight and with an entrancing snap to the wall. It is a game that brings out the character of the players and, although the Basques are reserved in most things, they show their feelings of rage, disgust, resentment, and shame when they fail in a stroke. Their audience does the same. Sometimes an excited shout of praise comes from the spectators, often shouts of bitter mockery, which are answered by glares of hatred from the silent player. There is loud betting on the games. The bookmakers stand shouting the odds on the side of the court and throw their betting slips in balls to the audience. There is pandemonium, cigarette smoke, the beautiful leaping and running of the white-trousered players, the tremendous swing of the shoulders as the arm flies back for the full force of the stroke.

The Basques are the oldest settled race in Europe. They are locked in their language. Are they a pocket of the original Iberians caught in the mountains? No one knows. Their language is like the code of a secret society and has been very useful to them in smuggling. Racial generalizations are pleasant to make but they rarely fit the case. One would suppose, for example, that the French and the Spanish Basques are alike, but in fact the French Basques are a poor and backward race of peasants and fishermen; the Spanish Basques are prosperous and those in the cities are active, well off, and progressive in the material sense. To a northerner they are more 'progressive' than the people of Barcelona. When we notice that deterioration at Irún, what we are really looking at is not the Basque provinces, but the negligent stain of bureaucratic Spain seeping up by the railway from Castile.

The traditional fanaticism of the Spanish Catholic is the expression of a people who are naturally prone to scepticism: they go from one extreme to the other. Spanish atheism is as violent and intolerant as Spanish piety. The Basques have a different character. Their Catholicism is solid in all classes and is not in the least fanatical. They have little religious superstition and have little regard – perhaps because they are poor in imagination and poetry – for the image-loving and decorative forms of Catholicism. Their religion is plain; their faith is immovable – *Qui dit Basque, dit Catholique* – and is married to the sense of tradition which rules them. In this they have the integration of primitive societies. That is to say their religion is racial and dispenses with both the aggressive and the mystical feeling of other kinds of Catholicism. In the Spanish Civil War the Basque Catholics fought for their autonomy beside the Republicans – the so-called 'Reds', who were commonly anticlerical, when they were not irreligious – presumably because the Basques knew their religion could not be endangered. The Basque Christianity is closer to the Old Testament than to the New and is even a little Protestant in its plain, practical simplicity. The Basque novelist Pío Baroja, who speaks of himself as an anarchist and an atheist, goes as far as to question both the traditionalism and the religiosity of his people. He recalls the testimony of medieval missionaries who found the Basques at that time completely pagan, and Ortega y Gasset has pointed out that in the Basque language there was no word for God. For this conception the Basques used a circumlocution: *el señor de lo alto*, the feudal lord higher up, the chief or the laird, a simple idea springing from their tribal organization and not from the religious imagination. The religious spirit of the Basques is exemplified by Saint Ignatius de Loyola, the founder of the Jesuit order. Whatever may have been the visionary experiences of the saint, he thought of his mission in the practical terms of soldiery: the militant company obeying orders from someone 'higher up'. Elsewhere in Spain the Church has become separated from the people, in the Basque provinces it is united with them.

The Basques, like the Asturians and the people of Navarre, live in one of the satisfied areas of Spain – those coastal provinces of mild climate where the rainfall is regular and plentiful. They are either farmers on the family community system in which the property belongs to the family and the head of the family council decides on his successors among his children, or they are sharecroppers – and the success of this system lies in the liberal and reasonable spirit in which it has been worked. Yet every statement one makes about Spain has to be modified immediately. Navarre is a Basque province that has lost its language, and the Navarrese, shut up in their mountains, are in fact fanatical in religion and they are a main source of the ultramontane form of conservatism, called Carlism. Navarrese economy, too, is successful and prospers. But as the train travels south, the rainfall dwindles in Castile, the peasant farmer becomes poor; money, not crops, becomes the landowner's reward, the religious quarrel begins. We are among a different race of more dramatic, more egotistical, less reasonable men.

In the rest of Spain the Basque is thought of as insular, obstinate, reserved, and glum, a pedestrian and energetic fatalist, working in his fields, putting his steel-pointed goad into the oxen that plough his land, making the wines of his provinces, and smelting his iron ore; or he is thought of as a sardine fisherman and packer in those reeking little fishing towns of the coast where they stack the tins. These sea towns are clean, prim, dour places. There is a narrow gap between the headlands through which the Biscayan tide races into a scooped-out haven or lagoon – all harbours of the Bay of Biscay are like this from Pasajes, near the frontier, to the mountain-bound harbours of Corunna. It is a coast that smells of Atlantic fish, the sky is billowy white and blue, or the soft sea rain comes out of it. Basques who can afford it drive out of the grey, warm, glum days towards Alava and Castile, to breathe dry air and feel the sun, which reigns over the rest of Spain like a visible and ferocious god. There the Basque in his dark-blue beret, which sits square on his stolid forehead, is thought of as an oddity. His family is matriarchal. The breaking of the marriage bond is forbidden. Even the second marriages of widows or widowers are disliked. Rodney Gallop, in his scholarly book, *The Book of the Basques*, describes the wedding night of a widow. The mockery was kept up with the beating of tin cans, the ringing of bells, and blowing of horns until sunrise. This custom is called the *galarrotza* (night noise). It occurs, of course, in many peasant countries.

My own collection of Basques contains indeed one dour character: a man who ran a bar in France, one of the exiles. He was a municipal employee and fought against Franco in Bilbao. He was also obstinately determined to visit his family there and did so twice secretly. But money affairs cropped up. It was necessary to go to Bilbao openly. The matter proceeded in the usual manner of the peninsula. First his relatives used what 'influence' they could find, working through the relatives of relatives. He was told to come. This was above seven years ago and required courage, for at that time there were tens of thousands of political prisoners; but in addition to courage this man had the insurmountable Basque conscience. He fought (he told the authorities) because his conscience told him to do so; not necessarily for Basque autonomy, but simply because it was the duty of municipal employees to obey the lawful government. Such a conscience must have maddened and annoyed the Falange who had done just the opposite, but, for all their revengefulness and intolerance, the Spaniards recognize the man in their enemies, and when passions have fallen, maintain their dignity and seek for the *modus vivendi* in the same glance.

The other Basques I have known were Unamuno and Pío Baroja, the novelist. In Unamuno one saw the combativeness, the mischief, and pugnacious humour of the Basques. A brief light of unforgettable charm, delicacy, and drollery touches their set faces. In Pío Baroja it is the same. I sat in his dark flat in Madrid and listened to the gentle, tired, clear voice of the very old man talking very much in the diffident, terse way of his books, watched the shy, sharp smile that never becomes a laugh, and the sly naïve manner.

'But who else painted your portrait, Don Pío?'

'Many people. Picasso, I believe, did one once.'

'Picasso! Where is it?'

'Oh, I don't know. It may exist. Perhaps it got lost. It had no value.'

As evasive as a peasant, but say anything against the Pope or the Jesuits and he is joking at once. I asked about the puritanical Archbishop of Seville.

'Never trust a Spanish archbishop when he behaves like an Englishman,' Baroja says.

Baroja once signed the visitors' book in some place and where he was expected to add his profession, rank, or titles, wrote: 'A humble man and a tramp.'

He sat at his plain oak table in an upright chair, in needy clothes and the same blue beret on his grey hair – it seemed to me – that he had worn twenty years ago when I first saw him. His eyes were pale-blue, his face very white – one can imagine the baker's flour still on it, for he once ran a bakery with his brother. It is a sad sight, the old age of a writer who, in addition to the usual burdens, has to bear the affront of the Franco censorship, which refused to allow him to publish his book on the Civil War.

'They said it showed the Spanish character in a bad light. And that is true. We see now we are a nation of barbarians.'

Baroja and Unamuno were broken by the Civil War. Baroja has fallen into melancholy. Unamuno, who came out on Franco's side as a good many liberals did, heard of the atrocities and rushed out into the streets of Salamanca screaming curses on Franco, the Falange, and his country, and went out of his mind.

Baroja is an exceptional Basque in his hostility to the Church and in his anarchism; he has lived chiefly in Madrid. But he is thoroughly Basque in his obstinacy and his tenacity and his droll humour. Unamuno had the same obstinacy. His book *Del Sentimiento Trágico de la Vida – The Tragic Sense of Life* – is one of the most important works in the last fifty years of Spanish literature. He was the outstanding figure in the movement towards Europeanization, which began after the loss of Cuba in 1898, and he was all the more important because he embodied the ambiguity of the Spanish attitude to the modern world. The Basques live in a prosperous and liberal-minded community; the rhetorical exaggerations and the desuetude of the rest of Spain are alien to them. They are, in fact, 'modern' to a degree of modernity which not even the Catalans have attained. All the more, therefore, was Unamuno conscious of the need of Europe, all the more of the price. His life became a battleground for the quarrel between Reason and Faith, between the European consciousness and the medieval soul. *The Tragic Sense of Life* sets out the essence of a profound conflict in the Spanish mind on its opening page, where he describes the subject of his book: not man in the abstract, but 'the man of flesh and bone, who is born, suffers and dies – who, above all, dies and who does not wish to die'.

Unamuno's book is a search for the solution to the problem which cannot be solved: man's agonized desire to be assured of personal immortality. We cannot have this assurance, but out of the agony our soul must find its energy. With its pugnacious egoism, and its Quixotic quality, Unamuno's philosophy described the positive side of the Spanish spirit, and came closer to the positive side of the Spaniards in the Counter-Reformation than their reactionary successors have done. There is more than a touch of the Protestant preacher in Unamuno, and the great figures of the Counter-Reformation were, in fact, counter-protesters who had not yet dulled and hardened into an oligarchy. Unamuno's energy and truculence, his nonconformity before the Castilian mind and authority, were very Basque.

. . .

Chapter 6

There are two roads to the south: one straight across the tableland of La Mancha, with the sharp mountains burning and floating like crisp blue gas flame on the horizon; the other, the long way round, over the Gredos mountains into the sheep drives, the wilderness, the cork woods of Extremadura, where the great estates begin. The river Tagus lies green as a snake in its deep ravines in this country; in the oasis of Aranjuez it is muddy; at Toledo the river circles the town like some green viper in its gorge.

La Mancha is Don Quixote's country. Under a sun of brass it is greener than old Castile, for the short vines grow here mile after mile, the pony turns the waterwheel under the trees, and the villages and towns are white, single-storey places. Valdepeñas is a wine town; this wine and the heavier wines of Rioja in the north are the best-known wines of the country. There are no vintages and no châteaux. One takes the wine of the locality, some of it delicate, some of it tasting of the pine cask like the wines of Greece, some of it thin and sour. 'This is the best wine in the world,' people say. And they say the same of the water, which is generally pure, crystalline, and excellent. After Valdepeñas the soil reddens. The heat comes down on the earth like a crushing load, the people stare under the weight of the sun, the women fan themselves and sigh. We travel in the strong smell of the earth and its herbs, the scented smell of the soft-coal smoke, sweet human sweat, face powder, urine. In the towns the odours of olive oil, charcoal, and polish stand, almost like persons themselves, in the cold doorways of the hot streets. The olive groves begin, striping and furring the red hills for mile after mile, and in such wealth it is hard to understand Spanish poverty. We see those thin, crumpled-up monkey peasants, those lean and noble-looking people; we see the extraordinary division of Spain between them and the bland, unlined faces of the fat, who carry their bellies like terrestrial globes before them, whose chins appear like motor tyres under the jaws, whose small eyes have the innocence, the surprise, the resignation, and the malice of the obese. It is a country divided between those who eat well and those who do not, and when you talk about the next town to a countryman there is always the gesture of the fingers to the mouth: 'There they eat well.' Or, 'Here we do not eat.' And by 'well' they mean quantity. Since the war *no se come* – there is nothing to eat; how many scores of times I have heard those words! 'Eat' – it is the governing Spanish word; *mañana* is nowhere near it. We are always brought down to the fundamentals of life; he eats well; he does not; here I conducted my love affairs; there I have my family; my parents are dead; my parents are alive; life is sad; life is gay; I am alive; people manage to live. Rich people. Unfortunate people. Lucky and unlucky: the passing words of Spanish life display the primitive dichotomy of good and evil chance. One might be listening to the Bible.

Just as the Pancorbo Pass in the north takes one to the tableland, so the pass through the Sierre Morena drops one off it into the lower hills and plains of the south and Andalusia, out of the dry tingling air into an air that is softer and sweet as syrup. The mild winter and the early spring give a brief greenness to this country. By June the sun has scorched it up. The dry Spain, where the rainfall is poor, is fertile only by its slow rivers, but here the Guadalquivir crawls to Córdoba and Seville on its green plain. The cactus appear, like thick green cardboard on the roadside, and the spears of the aloes. Grey donkeys trot on the roads. The herds of little black goats tinkle on the wasteland and circle in the shade of the long avenues of eucalyptus. At Córdoba the green oranges are on the trees. Yet although the country looks soft and rich, this is the region of huge estates and casual, wretchedly paid labour. We are in the region of serfdom, the Spanish Russia of the nineteenth century. No people in Spain more gracious, none poorer than the peasantry of large areas of Andalusia; yet none more disposed, by traditional character, to finding the minimum that will support life.

Andalusia is what for a century or more the foreigner has understood to be Spain. It is the Spain of the romantic legend, as Castile is the Spain of the 'black legend', *la leyenda negra*. We see in our mind's eye the Córdoba hat of the Feria, the women with the high combs, the proud carriage, and the rose or carnation in their hair; we see the dangerous gypsy dancer, the long-toothed, narrow-hipped bullfighter, the figure of Don Juan. We see the cool tiled patios of Córdoba, Seville, and Granada, hear the lazy talking of the guitar, the electric crackle of castanets, as the twisting arms swing down. We are in the heart of the Moorish Kingdom and have one foot in the East. Flowers, singing, sunlight, black shade, and the rustle of water.

Is it like this? Shall we be deceived? No – as always in Spain, if we look at one face it is like this; the face turns and we see the opposite. Romantic Andalusia was an invention of the French, especially of Théophile Gautier, Mérimée, and, later, of Maurice Barrès; the country of *'Le sang, la volupté, et la mort,'* and in the enchantment of Holy Week in Seville these ideas easily catch the northern imagination. Nor must we underrate them: the French are more intelligent and imaginative than the Spaniards, and have simply prolonged certain Andalusian characteristics into a higher key and turned them into general ideas.

The traveller who goes by the Extremadura road into Andalusia, through Trujillo, where Cortés was born, and on to Plasencia, pretty Cáceres with its garrison, and Badajoz, has a sight of the real army that Castile sent out to attack the economy of southern Spain. He will see the survival of the *mesta*, the large migratory flocks of sheep slowly moving south or north according to the season. One sits under the cork trees of the wilderness talking to the shepherds. Spare, austere men, they wear tooled leather aprons over their trouser legs and carry the crook and the horn slung on their shoulders. Formed by the lonely life, they speak with majestic yet simple courtliness to strangers in a clear sagacious Castilian of complete purity. It is delivered slowly.

'Man! How are you? And how are your family? Is your wife well? Are your children well? I am glad. You are right to rest in the heat. If God does not want to send the rain, one may complain above, below, everywhere, but that will not make the rain come.'

'What do you think of life?'

'Nothing.'

'Nothing?'

'Nothing. When one eats well, good. When one eats badly – well, good too. One remains living until one is put into the ground. Then nothing, man – nothing.'

The white dust of the flocks clouds on the roads, and before the motor-car came in, whenever one saw a cloud of dust on the Castilian tracks it was made by the flocks of sheep. The flocks of the *mesta*, the great enemies of the dying farmer, and the enemies of Andalusia, were the sheep charged by Don Quixote when he thought they were an army led by hostile knights. In his madness, Don Quixote was right. When wool ousted silk as the profitable product – and the Arabs introduced the merino sheep into Spain – the famous wool monopoly of the *mesta* was founded in Castile, and Andalusian ruin was complete.

In his analysis of the condition of Andalusia in *The Spanish Labyrinth*, Gerald Brenan points out that until the coming of the industrial age the history of Spain can be dramatized as a struggle of the rich agricultural districts of Andalusia and the eastern or Mediterranean regions against semi-pastoral Castile. Córdoba, Seville, Málaga, and Almería – that now forgotten little Manchester frying in the heat of its pothole among the mountains of the coast – were rich industrial cities: the decline began when the cities of northern Europe, waking up from the Middle Ages, set up factories of their own. The semi-pastoral Spaniards of Castile were then able to conquer Andalusia and the south. It is the old story of trade and war. By the seventeenth century, huge tracts of once fertile country had reverted to wilderness. The Venetian ambassador observed the decline in the enormously rich province of Granada only thirty-four years after Granada was taken from the Moors in 1492. He wrote:

> Hidden among them [the waters, fruit, trees, wood] are the farms of the Moors, many in ruins, for the Moorish population is diminishing and it is they who kept everything in order; the Spaniards here, as in other parts of Spain, are not industrious and disdain work.

And Brenan enlarges on the political effects of this economic change:

> The shepherds wage a perpetual war on the agriculturalists, whom they regard as their inferiors, whilst both together feel a fierce envy of the city dwellers and cultivators of rich oases . . . Now this is a type of society which is not confined to Spain but appears wherever certain climatic conditions prevail. It is strongly developed in Persia and North Africa. One of its chief characteristics is its instability; it alternates violently between a centralized tyranny and an anarchic tribal or local life. With every bad drought or economic crisis there is either a revolution or a wave of religious exaltation, whilst at longer intervals there

are great upheavals in which all the energies of the country are poured out in a war of conquest, leaving it inert and exhausted afterwards . . . The famous orientalism of the Spaniards is not due to 'Arab blood', but to climate and geography.

In the seventeenth and eighteenth centuries there were attempts to deal with agriculture on collectivist lines – they were revived under the Spanish Republic of 1931 and abolished by General Franco – but the Napoleonic invasion put an end to reform. By the 1830s and '40s, the sale of the Church land and common lands led to a revival of capitalist agriculture; the land went out of the hands of the small owners into the hands of the large ones; the number of huge estates in Andalusia increased, falling mostly into the hands of a new rich class, who reduced the Andalusian peasant to the level of a labour force, miserably paid, controlled by the bailiffs, and kept down, when they protested, by the Civil Guard. There is a parallel in the condition of England during the industrial revolution. In Spain, likewise, the fortunes of the new middle class were made; a large class of absentee landlords was formed, and if one asks why one's friend X can spend all day sitting doing nothing in a café in Seville or Córdoba, or lie in bed all day in Madrid, to get up and talk and play cards with his friends all night, the answer is in the rush to buy the Church and common land cheap in the nineteenth century, and the profitable result.

Serfdom is behind the strength of the anarcho-syndicalist movement in Andalusia, the periodical riots, crop-burnings, the savage scenes of the Civil War, the fact that the only place in Spain where Communism, also, had a small hold was near Seville. After Córdoba one sees the palm huts or kraal-like villages of the peasants, the slums made of beaten-out petrol tins; the esparto grows where the crops ought to grow. And in this region 41 per cent of the land – and the best – is owned by the big estates, and farther south in Seville and Cádiz the figure rises to 58 per cent. The wages paid to the seasonal labourers are derisory and their conditions of life and work intolerable. The foreigner has only to stop and talk to any working man, especially in the south, to find himself suddenly surrounded by a dozen more and in the midst of a violent political meeting, though such discussions are forbidden under the Franco régime.

In Almería, last year, a group of ten fine fellows, naked to the waist, thin and lithe, put down their picks and rushed at me.

'Why do you come here? To look at our misery? Do people eat well in your country? Here we starve. How can one keep a wife and children on twelve pesetas a day?' (The wages seem to range from 12 to 18 pesetas; say, at the present exchange, about 15s. 0d. to £1 a week.)

They blow up with mocking rage. Their eyes look not with hostility but with astonished curiosity at one's respectable clothes. These men are well informed about conditions in other countries. They do not whine or threaten; in their excitability they do not lose human dignity or good manners. Unlike the Russian peasants who lived (or live) under the same conditions, the Spaniards are not soaked in drink, for they drink very little, and rarely spirits. (The *aguardiente* is the drink of the carters in the roadside taverns, not the drink of the ordinary worker.) Some show of providing social services has indeed been made by the Franco régime, but one of the first steps of Franco was to give back the land to the landlords who had been expropriated under the Republic; and no serious attempt has been made to deal with the terrible fundamental problem: how to support a huge and growing population by farming in a dry climate is the essence of it. The traveller is, of course, told that the condition of Andalusia is due to the idleness of the people in this soft climate, and it is true that in the towns one can see hordes of idle people. They belong to two groups: people content to live on their small rents and the large numbers of unemployed. Those who work are working hard.

When one eats the Andalusian *gazpacho*, that ice-cold soup of cucumber and tomatoes and peppers ground up in vinegar and oil, in the cool, darkened room of the pension in Seville or Córdoba, and after that the fish done in oil, the squids, the hakes and brill, and then the thin steaks or the chicken, one recalls that out in the palmetto kraals the poor man has eaten *gazpacho* alone; cold in the middle of the day, hot at night, and that the dish will be not much more than bread dipped into a dish of oil and vinegar.

The Andalusians are very different in general character from the Spaniards of Castile. They do not lisp the letter 'c' or 'z' in their speech; they drop out as many consonants as possible from their words and speak fast in shouting, headlong voices as if their mouths were full of marbles. They are very difficult to understand. They are gay, full of smiles and laughter in their talk, a frivolous and light-hearted people. They pride themselves on verbal wit and an allusiveness so fine and constant that the mind has to work at double speed to keep up with their fancifulness, their hyperbole, their mocking, and their sparkling conceit of themselves. Sedate Castilians regard the Andalusians as buffoons, without gravity or reserve; they are certainly nervous, naïve, easily happily, easily carried up and down by their feeling. They live in the minute. Their effervescence is delightful, their compliments are unending. Everyone seems to be a minor lyrical poet or a story teller. They are as quick as the Irish with a phrase. Only in Naples – a city long under Spanish dominion, whose dialect is full of Spanish turns of phrase – does one find something like the nature of the people of Seville. Yet Andalusia is also the home of the philosophers. The vice of these people who pride themselves on their gaiety and sparkle is avarice and stinginess. No one parts with a penny more reluctantly. Another weakness is for the cruel or dangerous practical joke; they love horseplay at the expense of strangers. Their religion is almost pagan, and they are less puritan than the Castilians in love. There are vestiges of the Moorish harem system in Andalusian life; it is not very uncommon to find men who have fathered two or three families and who solemnly go the rounds of them – a tolerated manner of living which is rare elsewhere in Spain, though – in true Spanish fashion – the habit is domestic, patriarchal, and connubial rather than licentious.

Deep personal reserve and formality combine, in the paradoxical Spanish fashion, with immediate easy familiarity, in most parts of Spain. In Andalusia the familiarity is more evident than the reserve. The servant slaps the fly on the master's shoulder, the people in the street call out to the image of the Virgin as it is borne down the street in the processions at Holy Week, as if she were a girl of the neighbourhood; no one can contain the amount of talk that is idling away inside him. One is surrounded by intimates who unbosom at once and pass off, forgetting you and what they said, in a moment.

One knows all the south, and Seville above all, by the slowness of the pace of people walking. Long before midday, when Easter has passed, the awnings are pulled over the streets like Sierpes, where no traffic is allowed to drive, and the cafés and clubs are packed with men. They are drinking sherry and eating prawns and shellfish. The women who regard themselves of any account rarely leave their homes till five in the afternoon, and the horse carriages, with their red-spoked wheels, are nearly as common as the taxis. One is back in the nineteenth century, though the new parts of Seville are modern enough.

293

In the Barrio Santa Cruz one walks streets that are hardly more than two yards wide, and the white-walled houses have the grille windows, the wrought-iron gates that lead into the cool courtyards where the ferns stand round the fountains. The privacy of these places is mysterious. They are houses made for a life lived in the shade or for the long conversations of the night, and as the year advances, in all of Spain, the long cool night reanimates people. It becomes a country where the whole population of the towns sits under the trees or slowly walks there in the strange solitude of Spaniards or in their loud, shouting, interminable conversations. These barred windows recall the pictures of the cloaked lover standing there and talking for hours to the young woman shut up within. I have not seen this happen for twenty years; the Civil War was a revolution.

Writing in the eighteenth century, Cadalso, a Spanish commentator on social customs, said that in general the Spaniards had an 'excessive propensity for love'. He was writing in a period of public licence, the time of the *cortejos* (or *cicebeos*), when, in imitation of the French, the stern duties of Spanish jealousy were relaxed at any rate in the smart circles of the great cities. The Spaniards have often been credited with this excessive propensity by romantically minded foreigners, and Seville is, after all, the city of Don Juan. Fashions in morals change very frequently and it would be absurd to generalize and invent a 'Spanish attitude to love'; but there is no doubt that the Andalusians have a gift for the poetical admiration of women and a considerable vanity in being thought pursuers and admirers. This warmth of temperament is an obligation to self-respect and is possibly a response to the segregation of women. Slowly this segregation is weakening, but even when segregation has ceased, its effect on manners still remains. Don Juan himself is a figure created in response to this separation of the sexes, and has also a sadistic side which perhaps comes from the excesses of the court of Philip IV in the seventeenth century, when some of the convents had fallen into disorder. The love affair with a nun, the murder of a wife whose honour had been perhaps innocently compromised, were popular fantasies of sexual violence. Spanish inhibition or love of extremity created these fantasies. The public scourgings of heretics, infidels, or penitents lasted well into the eighteenth century and indicate the tastes of a violent people.

Don Quixote, the deluded Castilian knight, and Don Juan, the inexhaustible and ruthless Andalusian lover, are the two great mythical figures which Spain has given to the world. Both are armed and warlike men; both are exemplars of the imagination attempting to impose itself upon reality. Don Quixote attempts to impose the vision of the romances of chivalry. He is defeated, and many serious readers have been tempted – as I have already said – to regard the tale as a tragic comment on the Spanish knightly adventure in the Counter-Reformation and the conquest of America. Don Quixote has been called the book that killed a nation by cutting away the illusion that was necessary to its life. The answer to this is that the decay had already begun by the time of Cervantes. Outside of Spain, Don Quixote is seen as an eccentric, a saint, a deluded idealist upon whom the sceptical realism of Sancho Panza makes the irreverent comment of reality. These elements can indeed be perceived in *Don Quixote*, but there is something subtler in the portrait. Don Quixote enacts not the tragedy of idealism or vision, but the condition of the imagination itself, which both illumines and darkens the mind. The story contains the mind's knowledge of its own hallucinatory nature. The great heights of the book are reached when the sly shafts of sanity light up the twilight of Don Quixote's mind, when he appears to know his own folly, but does so only to plunge deeper. Death alone can cure him, and the irony is that it is Sancho, the squire, who returns like a hero, for he at least has governed an island. Yet even he has been deceived: we have seen a parable not of the condition of Spain, but of the condition of human life. The extreme strains of the Spanish nature are celebrated in these two characters: the passionate tendency to fantasy, the fatal reaction into scepticism, realism, and cynicism.

Don Juan, on the other hand, is an example of the imagination imposing itself successfully upon reality, but failing to conquer death, for in the earliest play about Don Juan, by Tirso de Molina, where the character first appears, Don Juan goes down in the cold grip of the Comendador's stone hand, to eternal torment. In the romantic nineteenth-century play by Zorrilla, he is rescued for heaven by the pure love of Doña Inés. Because Don Juan always succeeds, he is not a character of any complexity, which Don Quixote is – indeed, he is hardly a character at all – but a universal daydream or myth. He expresses the male desire for inexhaustible sexual vitality, the female desire to be ravished against the will, reason, interest, or honour. He embodies an aspect of male anarchism and the desire for absolute power.

Although a Spanish playwright was the first to create Don Juan, modern Spanish critics deny – with strong reason – that he is a human being and that he is a Spaniard in any special sense at all. There is a paradox in this disowning of Don Juan, and it is interesting to examine it. The character of Don Juan has had a far greater development outside of Spain, in Mozart, in Molière, possibly in Richardson's Lovelace, obviously in Byron; but whenever the Italians, in their researches into the Italian theatre of Tirso's time, have claimed him, Spanish patriotism and scholarship are affronted. (See Ramiro de Maeztu's essay on the subject.) The second thing to notice is that if Spanish intellectuals have rejected Don Juan, the common people have not. The Don Juan they accept is not the original figure of Tirso de Molina, but the romantic, melodramatic, and Frenchified Don Juan of the nineteenth century invented by the dramatist Zorrilla. Zorrilla's *Don Juan Tenorio* is played every year on All Souls' Eve in most Spanish cities, and it has become a popular ritual rather like the annual reading of Dickens's *Christmas Carol* at Christmas in England. The packed audience knows the chief lines by heart. The famous moment when Don Juan describes how he nails up his truculent notice on the door of his house, saying: 'Here lives Don Juan Tenorio and if any man wants anything of him . . .' has become a proverbial satire of Spanish defiance. Don Juan's is an act which, in some form or other, every Spaniard dreams of performing, and in fact in his inner life is doing all the time. He is asserting the exclusive, dramatic rights of the human ego – myself before all other selves, unrepentantly. Yet, though the people respond to this aspect of Don Juan, the intellectual critics are right in pointing out that, even in Andalusia, Don Juan does not embody a specifically Spanish conception. There is little or no literature of gallantry in Spain; there is no book to compare with the *Liaisons dangereuses*. In the picaresque story of the Archpriest of Hita, either love is carnal or it is the love of the Virgin, and even the most decorous never think of disguising the carnality of love. As they see everything in black and white, the Stendhalian categories of love are a refinement they ignore or, indeed, reprehend. Whatever else he is, Don Juan is not an epicurean.

It is difficult to know when Don Juan is Spanish – for he was, at any rate, created a Spaniard – and when he is simply a universal wish. Tirso de Molina's play was written in the very early seventeenth century. It is called *El Burlador de Sevilla* – the mocker of Seville, not, it will be noted, the lover – for Don Juan is an Andalusian in his love of the preposterous fantasy, of laughing at his enemies, and of succeeding by boast and effrontery and trick. He is a picaresque character turned hero. In the first act of the play we see him in his typical situation. The scene is at night. Don Juan has entered the Duchess Isabel's room in the Royal Palace at Naples, and, persuading her in the dark that he is her betrothed, has seduced her. Not a very great feat: she had probably never seen her future husband. She longs to see her lover's face and moves to get a lamp. Don Juan stops her. She suspects at once and asks, in terror: 'What man are you?' Don Juan replies: 'A man without a name.' She cries for help, and when the King and the guards come in shouting: 'Who is there?' Don Juan answers dryly: 'A man and a woman – what else could it be?' Male and female: the world narrowed down to sex, to the primitive human situation. It is a sentence that smashes the elaborate Spanish marriage system at a blow. Man, woman, culminating in the sexal act; it is the basic meaning of so many of the Spanish dances, which are patterns not of romantic or gracious beguilement but of the phases of sexual challenge. There is as much hatred as there is love in these incitements, and they create the hallucination by which passion is built up and released. In this episode of Tirso's play, the most destructive and unflinching male who will stop at nothing has met the most difficult, the least accessible woman. Don Juan owes it to his honour to break the established codes of honour – to attack the royal Duchess, the friend's betrothed, the bride on her wedding day, the innocent girl who rescues him and saves his life, the novice in the convent. Speed, trickery – he wins easily by simple promise of marriage – the killing of any opponent, and the quick get-away sum up the process. 'I'll have her tonight' – once he has said that, his 'I' is committed. Nothing can be allowed to stand in the way of what he owes to his own pride. He is the national intransigence isolated.

The Don Juan of Tirso de Molina is a liar, a deceiver, a betrayer of friends, a brawler and murderer. He has one virtue: absolute fearlessness. What drives him on is pride and the idea of the greater difficulty. He claims total freedom and unlimited energy for enjoying it; no law of diminishing returns operates upon his desires. And he is good-humoured and a great mocker; his wit and recklessness fascinate his friends – Benavente, a contemporary dramatist, has shrewdly pointed out that Don Juan puts such a lasting spell upon the men to whom he boasts that the women hardly see him – as for the eternal punishment, that is 'a long way off'. He is not afraid of the dead and not respectful to sacred places: he pulls the stone beard of the Comendador's statue in the chapel, and it is he who has murdered the Comendador. Above all, he is a figure of the night. 'Why are you in my room at this hour of night!' exclaims one victim. 'These hours above all are my hours,' Don Juan replies.

Out of their context such satanic lines have an absurd ring, for we can only imagine an unreal, melodramatic figure speaking them. But, clearly, Don Juan is not a person, and in their context such lines are arresting. They are spoken not by a human being but by a demon, and those hours of darkness are, indeed, the kingdom of the carnal spirit.

In Tirso de Molina's play Don Juan does not love any woman. He merely possesses women. He is a ravisher – though by deceit, not by violence. His victims are left in tears and grief, for his promises are broken. We can indulge in speculations about the secret pleasure these women have in the irresistible, grief-dealing lover, but nothing in the play justifies us, and indeed Tirso accepts the common experience that the demands of the male ego are different from those of the female. In his long essay Ramiro de Maeztu makes the good point that there are two Don Juans: the Don Juan who appears north of the Pyrenees, who is the romantic rebel, the endless seeker of an ideal love, discarding because he has not found it; and the Don Juan of the south, who is not a lover, but an animal energy or will to power. The absence of northern idealism in love, according to this writer and, indeed, to many other Spanish commentators, is very Spanish; in place of idealism there is obsession, fantasy, passion, the desire to go to the limit. Even in the love of the divine Spouse, described by Spanish mystics (and this is the only Spanish literature which can be said to be exclusively concerned with the psychology of love), the ecstasy of ultimate union is reached by the established processes of our sensibility, and not by a sudden leap from the material to the spiritual world. If a spiritual world is imagined, it is not formless, bodiless, and metaphysical, but is conceived of in corporeal terms. Impossible for these realists to consider a union of souls which is not, by some magic of transubstantiation, a union of bodies. In the north, Don Juan is saved by the discovery of ideal love: in the south – he goes to hell in Tirso de Molina, and in Zorrilla's play he is saved by the chaste intercession of Doña Inés, which is a bow to

298

northern romantic sentiment. Doña Inés does succeed in awakening love in Don Juan, and in doing so turns him into a recognizable human being. The result is that he diminishes at once. But she has been able to do this because she is hardly more than a child, and may be considered as emotionally immature or unborn, as Don Juan is. She is, emotionally speaking, his similar and match. But in fact de Maeztu's generalizations about the northern and the southern Don Juan are not quite exact: Lovelace in Richardson's *Clarissa*, and Valmont in the *Liaisons dangereues*, are two hard militant Don Juans who seek no ideal woman. Their aim, like that of the Spanish Don Juan, is the destruction of the being they are seducing, and themselves are eventually destroyed in the personal hells they have been unconsciously preparing.

Don Juan is Spanish to the extent that he violently celebrates the implacable and unmovable '*Yo*' or '*I*' of Spanish individualism. Ganivet, who made an enquiry into the causes of Spanish decadence after the loss of Cuba in 1898, said the Spaniard was a man who carried on his passport the imaginary words 'This Spaniard is authorized to do whatever he wants.' Pride, courage, extremism, energy, anarchism are the Spanish substitutes for that idealism which is given to the Don Juan of the north. In Zorrilla's play, God agrees to make room for Don Juan, who, though supposedly repentant, is still shouting about his honour and is obviously going to be very troublesome in heaven.

Yet if Tirso's *Don Juan* had been simply a play about a man who runs after women, we can doubt if it would have had the myth-creating quality. The *Burlador* is really two plays in one: the story of Don Juan, the destroyer of women, is married to the old folk legend of the dead man invited to the feast. In some parts of Spain right up to the eighteenth century the peasants used to go to the churches on All Souls' Night to make prayers and offerings for the dead. As it was a feast day, they would often take their glasses of wine there and very soon were raising their glasses to the departed and inviting them mockingly to eat or drink. As in modern Mexico, the dead spirits were placated and kept off by comedy and mockery. Dr Marañón, who has written with scepticism about Don Juan, says that the religious and funereal elements in the play are the only truly Spanish things in it; the rest, he says, is simply an Italian Renaissance figure, a Borgia, or simply the gangster or condottiere. This argument is a counter-attack upon those who have seen Don Juan as an example of the spirit of the Spanish conquistador. Certainly the conquistadors were governed by a great idea and represent Spanish character at its most splendid; they were not intriguers and tricksters without religion. But by the early seventeenth century the figure of the conquistador was in decline, and Don Juan could be seen as a frustrated and decadent example of the type – an example, so familiar in Spain, of the man capable of great efforts of will, who recoils cynically upon himself. Another view is that Don Juan is the lawless man and rebel who rises to the top in periods of anarchy, corruption, and irreligion. He indeed first appeared in the reign of Velásquez's Philip IV, in that brilliant and licentious court, when the huge assertion of Spanish faith in the Counter-Reformation and the conquest of America was broken. Others see in him a sceptical attack on the accepted foundations of Spanish life; the powerful institution of the family, which breaks all lovers and which keeps the women shut away from the world; and an attack also on the cult of honour. In Tirso's time the cult of honour had reached a high point of intricacy and delicacy, and when Don Juan is shown tricking his friends, this has been regarded as a satire on men who professed honour like a religion and flagrantly ignored it in practice – a satire, in short, on the morals of 'young bloods'.

In recent years Don Juan has met his worst enemy – the psychologists. They find him to be not the mature and energetic man, but the infantile male, possibly homosexual, possibly almost impotent or with a neurotic fear of incapacity. He is fixed in the undifferentiated sexuality of adolescence. He is a myth created for those thousands of penniless lonely Spanish males who walk up and down the streets all night, who never see a woman outside their own homes, who are dominated by the all-powerful figure of the Spanish mother. Hundreds of these unstrenuous dreamers of love are supposed, in Madrid, to get their mild satisfactions from being crushed against the girls in the trams at the rush hour. The tramway lovers they are called: the Spanish tongue is ruthlessly satirical.

And who *was* Don Juan? Did he exist in real life? No one has ever found a model, but for a long time the figure of a celebrated Sevillano, Don Miguel de Mañara, was thought to be the original. His tomb lies in the Hospice for the Poor which he founded in Seville and bears the famous inscription: 'Here lie the ashes of the worst man the world has ever known.' Mañara's family had Corsican blood. He cannot be the original of Don Juan, for he was not born when the play was written; he is, however, an authentic Sevillian copyist of Don Juan. For the legend is that he saw the play and went home saying: 'Henceforth I shall be Don Juan.' He started on a career of quarrelling and murder in the street – Don Juan, of course, is a murderer more than a lover – and of seduction. After a terrible career he married, and the sudden death of his young wife turned him to religion. His remorse led the aristocrat to put himself at the service of the poor. In rags himself, he collected the vagabonds and starving from the street and took them to the Hospice that he had founded. He was also obsessed by the idea of death, for he collected the dead from the gallows and the streets, carrying the bodies himself and giving them Christian burial. It was a branch of that fierce, fanatical, and compulsive spirit of proselytism which had driven Spaniards to convert the Moorish remnant after the reconquest, and to save even their dead from the perils of hell. Mañara, like Don Juan, became the protagonist in a large number of gruesome death legends. He pursues a beautiful woman, through street after street in Seville at night, and not until she gets to her door does she allow him to overtake her; then she turns and lifts aside her veil and he sees not a face but a grinning skull. Or again a woman beckons to him from a balcony and when he mounts to her room, she has vanished; the room contains a body lying in its grave-clothes between candles. Or, walking the streets again, he meets men carrying a bier and asks them: 'Whose is that body? Who has died?' They answer: 'It is Don Miguel de Mañara.' The corpse is himself.

The Hospice in Seville contains two pictures by Valdés Leal which Mañara commissioned. One is a picture of richly dressed skeletons. A hand dangles a balance, and in one pan jewels are heaped and in the other, bones. On the velvet cloth cockroaches are crawling. The preoccupation with skeletons, skulls, and the dead in Spain recalls the similar preoccupation among the Mexican Indians. Spanish and Mexican Indian ferocity, cruelty, and regard for death were oddly matched in the conquest.

In his book on Don Juan, Dr Marañón has a far more plausible suggestion to offer those who search for an original figure in real life. His candidate is the Duke of Villamediana. He was a magnificent of Philip IV's court, a man of gorgeous apparel such as Velásquez painted, and supposed (until contemporary historical researches have proved it otherwise) to have been the lover of the Queen. He was a famous pursuer of women, immensely rich, a great gambler, an elegant poet, and a bullfighter, for bullfighting was originally an aristocratic sport – a knightly tourney between beautifully mounted riders and the bull. The court of Philip IV lived in a condition of scandal, and all Spain knew of Villamediana's career as an uncontrollable Renaissance figure. He was eventually assassinated, and it was generally thought by the King's order; but a curious fact has come out which has gone a certain way towards confirming the suspicions of the psychiatrists. Villamediana was not assassinated by the King's orders; he was not the lover of the Queen; he was killed by unknown men after he was found to be implicated in a homosexual scandal which touched a large portion of the court. Homosexuality exists in Spain but is much concealed; it is not as apparent as it is in Italy, England, Germany, or America.

The last Spanish play on Don Juan was written a year or two ago by Jacinto Benavente. Benavente is the last of a group of Spanish dramatists – Martínez Sierra and the Quintero brothers were the others – and he is now a very old man. His play was light and amusing and it suggested, as I said before, that the truth about Don Juan is that the women can never get near him, though they are longing to do so, because he is always surrounded by men who are fascinated by his stories and hope to learn a trick or two from an expert. A shrewd piece of observation – Spanish males will listen all night to the fantastic boasts and amusing inventions of a good talker who is telling of his own or someone else's adventures in love. Although he is represented as an energy in Tirso de Molina and Zorrilla, Don Juan is also unmistakably a traveller, a talker and story teller. The boasting match in Zorrilla's play is characteristic and important. We have to agree in the end that Don Juan is not a character but a wish.

It is tempting at this point to digress in a general way into the subject of the roles of the sexes in Spanish life and into the characteristics of Spanish love. To the northerner, Spain appears to be a male-dominated society in which the women have few rights or liberties and live in a state of complete subjection. He has only to meet a few educated women among either the intellectual classes of the Europeanized aristocracy to find that many of these women hold the same view. Married women live at certain legal disadvantages in relation to their husbands: the divorce laws which had a brief reign during the Republic from 1931 until 1936 have been repealed at the instance of the Church under General

Franco; birth control is forbidden – though not unknown – young women go out very little alone and are certainly not allowed the liberty which girls have in the rest of western Europe or America. Twenty-five years ago no nice young woman went to the cinema with a young man unless a duenna or another girl went too. This has changed, but the duenna still survives in disembodied form. The key to the Spanish love affair is the scene enacted every Sunday afternoon in the less frequented alleys of the parks in the big cities, and can be said to have its counterpart in the life of all classes. Seated on a chair with its back to a thick hedge is a young woman. Exactly in front of her sits the young man, his knees a respectful number of inches from hers. Occasionally his hand ventures towards her hands, there may be a fluttering touch of the tips of the fingers for a moment, but hers are expertly withdrawn; rarely is a hand held, almost never is an arm put round a waist or a kiss exchanged. If there is a kiss it will be upon the cheek, not the mouth – this is true, of course, in all Latin countries, where to kiss on the mouth publicly is considered an obscene act. It causes catcalls in the cinema. And then one observes that the lovers have brought with them a third chair. Nothing is on it, no one sits there. The chair is a piece of conventional stage furniture; it is meant to represent the imaginary duenna. To an extremely critical neighbour it can indicate that a chaperon had been there a minute ago or is in fact expected. The Spanish love affair requires this fiction.

Spain is the country of long engagements that go on for years. This is the custom and it arises chiefly because of economic difficulties. In order that its interest shall not be exhausted, the engagement is kept lively on the girl's part by all the devices of reproach, hurt feelings, feigned jealousy, coldness, coquetry, and reprobation, which are overcome by infinite small attentions, presents, punctiliousness – the whole armoury of the Victorian love affair. From the man the woman demands not passion but marriage; in the woman the man sees the future mother, the image of the mother who has dominated his life so far and who, until the end of her days, will be the ruling figure of his life. His future wife knows this and is not discountenanced. She will have the same role when her large family is born. Both parties will hope to have a very large family. Monogamy is the fixed principle, and although many Spanish men like, in the interest of *amour-propre*, to pretend otherwise, their attitude to sex is puritan and strict. They are deeply shocked by the enticements and behaviour of foreign women. It is a puritanism which is made emotional by the sense of honour and by continuous jealousy. These are a variable quantity from period to period in Spanish life, but in some degree they are always there.

Some Spanish writers have thought that the austerity of conventionality in Spanish love, its privacy too, contain a certain element of brutality or crudity. In times of notorious licence there is certainly something crude about the scandals of the convent, and the popular imagination runs easily to the thought of orgy. In any case, the classic Spanish attitude to love is maintained only by the preservation of the brothel and a very large population of prostitutes.

'And now,' says the complacent young girl at the window to her lover as he goes off, 'I suppose you are going off with one of the naughty women.' To preserve the conventional façade and the bourgeois Catholic morality, one has to have the imitation domestic world of the brothel. The great poverty of the masses in Spain has enormously increased prostitution, but Spaniards are not indignant about that. Passive, fatalistic, they accept the brothel and the prostitute as an ineluctable part of life, accept them with charity, pleasure, and indulgence.

The unabashed candour of the Spaniards, men and women, in their conversations about sexual love and the bodily passions is neither sensual nor obsessive. They talk without timidity or reserve. The common oaths or exclamations heard in any café or at any street corner are sexual. Everywhere, people swear by their private parts with a Rabelaisian freedom and laughter. In their speech nothing is hidden. And under the puritanism of behaviour is something primitive and animal. It does not occur to them to conceal their admiration or their desire as they turn in the street to gaze at the woman who catches their eye; and the women, who make absolutely no response, nevertheless are very gratified by this admiration. They pity those women of other countries where public admiration is restrained; they condemn the women of those countries where such an admiration has an open response. Formal, formal! How often, how many scores of times during the day, does one hear that almost military virtue in behaviour exalted! Preserve the formal, and after that – the whole mystery of private life, which no one can generalize about.

IV · CHARACTERS

Samuel Pepys
The Great Snail

It is obvious from the three opening volumes· that the new complete eleven-volume edition of Pepys's Diary is an excellent effort of Anglo-American scholarship. The omissions in earlier editions, whether from prudery, accident or fear of tedium, have been put back. The great difficulties of transcribing Pepys's shorthand with its curious half-words 'in clear' have been mastered as far as they can be; the innumerable notes are irresistible, and Robert Latham's introduction of 120 pages is by far the most searching and graceful essay available on the Diary in relation to Pepys himself and to history. It is particularly valuable to Pepys's methods. In short, full justice is done to the Great Snail of English diarizing.

The only serious rival to Pepys is Boswell, but Boswell is a snail without a shell. He trails through life unhoused and exclamatory, whereas Pepys is housed and *sotto voce*. Boswell is confessional before anything else, whereas, though he too tells all, Pepys is not; he records for the sensual pleasure of record. Boswell adores his damned soul to the point of tears and is in shameless, ramshackle pursuit of father-figures who will offer salvation. Unlike Pepys, he has above all a conceit of his own peculiar genius. Pepys had no notion of genius. Where Pepys is an eager careerist, struck by the wonder of it, Boswell has no career; he has only a carousel, and it is odd that the careerist has a more genuine sense of pleasure than the Calvinist libertine. Although both diarists are lapsed Puritans and owe something to the Puritan tradition of the diary as a training of conscience, Pepys writes without appealing to some private higher hope. He is as obsessional as Boswell, but to whom is the secretive Admiralty official talking as his shorthand flicks across the page? To no person, not even to himself, even when he adds a remorseful groan or two, after running his hand up the skirt of a servant girl or the wife of an officer who has come to bribe him for a job for her husband. Even the groan is record rather than adjuration. He is simply amazed that life exists in days, hours and minutes. He is transfixed by wonder at the quotidian of his bodily and working existence, as part of history. He is a man (as Arthur Bryant has said in his well-known Life, which must be read as a companion to the Diary) to whom the most common things were wonderful:

At night, writing in my Study, a mouse ran over my table, which I shut up fast under my shelfes upon my table till tomorrow. And so home and to bed.

No, he is not addressing a person. He is not even addressing God. It may be that he is addressing history, for he left the Diary to his college at Cambridge: yet the bequest may be due to his passion for preserving papers, for property, an act of vanity in administrative tidiness. No longing for immortality there. If he addressed anything, the future Fellow of the Royal Society was blamelessly addressing the new Curiosity, science itself. It was fashionable to be a Baconian, a virtuoso, to potter on the new outskirts of invention, to catalogue as the Victorian botanists did two centuries later; and this new itch for documentation does strongly influence the diarist as it also influences Defoe. The random private trait comes to life when it is a response to a consciousness of one's times.

Pepys was astutely aware that he was the success thrown up by a revolution which had got rid of its leaders and its dogma and now offered the technologist a fortune: in this he is very modern. The son of a tailor – outside the reactionary Guilds and therefore in the black market – to be shrewd and efficient enough to rise and become the friend of the King! To have erotic dreams about Lady Castlemayne, to become Head of the Navy – and rich! To be the all-powerful valet! Pepys has the essential and topical character of the hero of a picaresque novel like *Gil Blas*. His is the secrecy of the indispensable.

Yet as a careerist and an importance the little man who lets his hair go long is not a bore; he is large and various. His 'morning draught' at the tavern, his drunken evenings, his sing-songs, his playing of the lute, his dancing, his love of pretty well all women, his love of show, the theatre, silver plate; his martinet behaviour with his wife who leaves her clothes on the floor, but whom he adores – a myriad small interests keep him spry. One sees him boring holes into his office wall so that he can spy on his clerks, worried by playing the lute on Sundays, hitting his wife by accident when he wakes up in the morning, boxing his manservant's ears, being forced to leave the Abbey at the high moment of the Coronation because he is bursting to pee. He never misses a public occasion: there is an unmoved account of the execution of Sir Harry Vane. He stayed in London for the plague. His early life in the Admiralty has a low social note which the rising man begins to disapprove – how long a tradition lower-middle-class comedy has!

In the morning to my office, where after I had drunk my morning draught at Will's with Ethell and Mr Stevens, I went and told part of the excise money till 12 o'clock. And then called on my wife and took her to Mr Pierces, she in the way being exceedingly troubled with a pair of new pattens, and I vexed to go too slow, it being late. There when we came, we found Mrs Carrick very fine and one Mr Lucy, who called one another husband and wife; and after dinner a great deal of mad stir; there was pulling off Mrs Bride's and Mr Bridegroom's ribbons, with a great deal of fooling among them that I and my wife did not like; Mr Lucy and several other gentlemen coming in after dinner, swearing and singing as if they were mad; only he singing very handsomely.

Two years later, when he has cut down his oysters and his wine-drinking, moved into a grander house and doubled his time at the office, there is a memorable Sunday, beginning with church, sermon and an excellent anthem and symphony, the organ supported by wind instruments, until:

Thence to My Lord's, where nobody at home but a woman that let me in, and Sarah above, whither I went up to her and played and talked with her and, God forgive me, did feel her; which I am much ashamed of, but I did no more, though I had so much a mind to it that I spent in my breeches. After I had talked an hour or two with her, I went and gave Mr Hunt a short visit, he being at home alone. And thence walked homeward; and meeting Mr Pierce the Chyrurgeon, he took me into Somerset House and there carried me into the Queene-Mother's presence-chamber, where she was with our Queene sitting on her left hand . . . here I also saw Madame Castlemayne and, which pleased me most, Mr Crofts the King's bastard, a most pretty sparke of about 15 years old.

Then the King, the Duke and Duchess came in, 'such a sight as I could never almost have happened to see with so much ease and leisure'. The only thing that worried him on the way home was that he had promised his wife to be there before she got back. Yet he had not done this 'industriously' but by chance. There we have the Puritan, a bit of a cautious rake, a bit of a voyeur, a bit of a romantic snob; but, as he says, his great fault (which he will try and amend) is that he can never say 'No' to anyone. Enormous industry – starting work at four or five in the morning – and temptation are his fate: the Puritan syndrome.

The most absorbing historical part of these three early volumes concerns Pepys's modest, canny but courageous part in the crisis of getting Charles II over, seeing him crowned, and the religious manoeuvres as the Cromwellian revolution was liquidated. Such things in the Diary have been enormously important to historians and there is no more intimate guide to London life at the time. The city streets, taverns, theatres, courts, docks, the business of fitting out ships and paying for it, and political gossip live minutely in the pages. We simply follow in hundreds of journeys down streets or by water to Greenwich, because he is so busy. Why is he so alive, what has given this fat, slightly pompous and fussy little man an edge to his record? Obviously he worked at his desk longer than anyone else in the city, and because of that huge labour we know him. But what made him more than a recorder, and such a recorder? Vitality and curiosity, of course. Three other things are suggestive. First, he had nearly died of the stone when he was very young and he never stopped regarding himself as a miracle because he survived. Maybe – to judge by the case of Montaigne, which perhaps one should not do – the disease has something of the phenomenal in it that encourages a deep physical curiosity. Grave early danger stimulates the appetite for pleasure. Every minute is a gift: catching sight of Lady Castlemayne, 'I glutted myself with looking at her'. Then he was a linguist, which certainly diversifies personality and even offers disguises. The Puritan intensifies his secrecy and his pleasure in using dog-French, Spanish and Dutch in his erotic passages:

nuper ponendo mes mains in su des choses de son breast mais il faut que je leave it lest it bring me alcun major inconvenience.

Finally, in his indiscriminate dabbling in science there is not only his shorthand – the miraculous means of catching life as fast as it flows – but his microscope, which makes life stand still so that it can become as large as life is. Pepys's mind was genial because it was a microscope. By magnifying, the glass defeated time, it gave an overpowering vividness to memory. Take the example of the ship auction:

> Where pleasant to see how backward men at first to bid; and yet when the candle is going out, how they bawl and dispute afterwards who bid the most first.
> And here I observed one man cunninger than the rest, that was sure to bid the last man and to carry it; and enquiring the reason, he told me that just as the flame goes out the smoke descends, which is a thing I never observed before and by that he doth know the instant when to bid last – which is very pretty.

At night, under his own dying candle, Pepys systematically 'bid last'.

Mr Latham has gone deeply into Pepys's shorthand system and into his methods. His normal prose was the ornate style of the organization man of the period; in the Diary, as if sharing in the Royal Society's new programme for the prose of the new age, he used the plain, rapid, talking language. It catches the instant, saves time and catches time. But were there earlier notes and drafts? There is evidence that there were; that he wrote up the Diary from them days later. (It is known that his famous account of the Fire, which will appear in the later volumes, was done months after the event.) In other words – and this was to be true of Boswell also – the immediacy is in part the effect of revision. Good diaries are good because they are not left in a flabby state of nature, but have been worked on; they are not verbatim or documentary, they are works of art. And to become this they must be obsessional. This was tragically true for Pepys. After eight years he was threatened with blindness. He had to give up the Diary. True he could dictate, but how much he would have to leave out! The only thing was to get the clerk to leave a wide margin in which Pepys could add notes of his own, notes not suited to delicate ears.

'And so,' he ends,

I betake myself to the course which is almost as much as to see myself go into my grave; for which all the discomforts that will accompany my being blind, the good God prepare me.

The human microscope had given up. The snail retired to his official shell.

Jonathan Swift
The Infantilism of Genius

Those who have read Dr A.L. Rowse's little masterpiece of autobiography *A Cornish Childhood* will guess why that romantic and petulant historian had for over forty years hankered after writing a biographical portrait of Jonathan Swift. An outsider in the political acrimonies of the 1930s, an early 'Leftist' who has turned against 'Leftist liberal cant', Dr Rowse, in his new book, *Jonathan Swift*, portrays Swift as a fellow-recalcitrant whose ammunition is useful to his biographer in a one-man war against old appeasers and new fanatics: ex-Whig, high Tory, man of crusty commonsense – what could be closer to our combative Cornishman? It is indeed likely that Swift, who hated mankind as a generality but said he loved the individual Jack, William, and Tom, would have found our world third-rate and obscene beyond expression. It is conceivable that Swift would have raged against the appeasement of Hitler, the humbug of Baldwin's England, the errors of the American 'computerwar' in Vietnam, the belief in the educability of everyone, the political fancies of Laputa-like philosophers such as Bertrand Russell, and (of all petty things) even the Value Added Tax, which torments the British of today. (Probably the author of the *Drapier's Letters* would have hated that most.) But when Dr Rowse drags such matters into what is elsewhere a very lucid and moving study of the terrifying Dean of St Patrick's, he reduces him to the level of an irritable writer of letters to *The Times*. To take Swift out of his century is to cloud him and distract us from the incessant pride, passion, and imagination of our supreme satirist and his truly tragic person.

Although Swift struck nearly everyone – especially women – as the most dazzling, robust, and naturally open man, and one irresistible in his rudeness, he was deeply secretive and evasive. His practice of anonymity in his plain, ferocious writing was not simply a caution before the threats of imprisonment for libel; it

313

was meant to be a momentous underground game. His exhaustive biographers have found it impossible to make their minds up about the myths and gossip that surround his life – and not only because so much of it comes from Dublin, the most malicious city in Europe. One half hoped that Dr Rowse would start one of his well-known hares, but he does not: he ignores, for example, wild stories like the suggestion that Swift was Sir William Temple's bastard and the half brother of Stella (Esther Johnson) and confines himself to what the best scholars have suggested, sensibly and kindly weighing the possible against the probable. He bows to Harold Williams and follows Middleton Murry's much fuller and very feeling *Life*, although, unlike Murry, he regards Vanessa (Esther Vanhomrigh) as a devouring female egotist and an impossible plague. As he rather coarsely puts it, Vanessa was an instance of the unspeakable in pursuit of the uneatable. Whatever else may be said against the passionate Vanessa, she was not a fox-hunting girl.

It is agreed that Swift's humiliating failure as a very young man to persuade Jane Waring (Varina) to marry him set him violently against marriage for good, and that the words of his insulting farewell to her hardly suggest that he was impotent. If we are unlikely to know whether the tale of the secret marriage to Stella is true, it does seem very possible. Stella knew Vanessa was in pursuit; she could guess Swift had had his head turned. Stella's jealousy – and a very rational and Swift-like poem of hers expresses the feeling with extraordinary and painful detachment – may have made her insist upon a belated marriage in order to insure her position; Swift may very well have agreed to it as a secret trump card to play against Vanessa. We shall never be sure about Scott's tale that Vanessa found out and wrote to Stella, and that in a rage Swift rode out to confront Vanessa with the letter, threw it in her face, and never saw or wrote to her again. The scene is in character – supposing Swift to be a personage in one of Scott's novels. Dr Rowse makes much of the difference in social class between Stella and Vanessa. Once educated by Swift, Stella was well fitted to please in the retired life of clerical society in Ireland. But the gifted Vanessa belonged to fashionable society, which Swift adored, and in training her he made her much more intelligent than the usual run of fashionable women. The core of the comedy, which became a tragedy, is clear in Swift's private poem 'Cadenus and Vanessa', which she allowed to circulate after her death, as a vengeance. The insulting Dean was a practical feminist who in curing his two pupils of female silliness found that his Galateas had perfected their minds but retained their natures. Reason was not all. Stella and Vanessa were rival works of art who came only too powerfully to life when they were fighting for possession of him. His gift for intrigue and self-protection had failed him. What is truly horrible is that after their relatively early deaths, and for reasons of guilt, shame and probably a sexual repression we can only guess at, he became obsessed by the dreadful image of the female Yahoo and the scatological nightmares. Even here we must not be too sweeping. We know that the commonest sight of eighteenth-century streets was excrement; that society stank, and even elegant society was blunt in language; and that one or two men with a skin too few – Smollett, for example – may have revelled in dirt but also, like the scrupulous Dean, preached against it.

If Swift seemed a dull, cold, calculating man – as the bland and censorious Victorians thought – and something of a monster, he was pitiable. If he did not love, he was tender and craved tenderness and cleverness in women. As Dr Rowse says, everything in his life put him apart from other men. His father's death before he was born was surely one decisive factor. That he was kidnapped as a baby in Ireland and taken to England by his nurse, with whom he lived for three years, is strange. That his mother is shadowy and that he was sent away to school at Kilkenny – the best Ireland offered at that time – are pointers to an absolute loneliness. His uncle and cousins could claim connections, but only as poor and distant relations. By the time he was taken in by Sir William Temple at Moor Park, in England, the young egotist was formed. Temple became the father-figure to an uncouth boy who had stood on his own in the rough Anglo-Irish world – and what a rough lot the Cromwellian colonists must have been, freed as they were from their native English restraints, their liberty based on stolen land! What heady luck for a clever youth to go to a great English house like Moor Park and find a protector in one of the most cultivated and eminent men in English public life! It was a leap from barbarism to the graces of civilization. What a reinforcement for a poor boy's will to power and ambition! There was a price, of course, and one slowly learned: the great and powerful are wayward and lazy, especially when a difficult young man becomes importunate. Swift wanted spectacular advancement at once; with his eye on the main chance he was disappointed by queens, kings, lords and archbishops throughout his life. The touching thing is that Moor Park became a lasting dream of the good life. When, in a simple, practical way, he persuaded Stella and her companion, Miss Dingley – poor fellow relations – to settle in Dublin after Temple's death he was carrying an imaginary Moor Park in his head.

It strikes one that Swift is an instance of the infantilism of genius: he was a self-regarding child-egotist all his life. The will to instant power may not succeed, but intellectually it is devastating. In a rather schematic enquiry written in the thirties Mario M. Rossi and Joseph M. Hone have the following words about Swift's egotism which exactly convey his attitude to the great and to Stella and Vanessa:

> From Swift's assertion that he loathed humanity and yet loved Jack, William and Tom we are not to suppose that he loved them for what they were, nor indeed that he had even *knowledge* of them as they were. He loved them in so far as they surrendered to his whim, he loved them for being a sort of extension of himself, other bodies of his overlapping self. He disliked humanity because it was a number of extraneous selves; the egotist cannot identify himself with a mass. He identifies himself with individuals in so far as they are his servants.

In its drastic fashion this seems to be true; one has only to look at Swift's purely practical and self-protective attitude to Stella and Vanessa when emotionally they were in extremis, and indeed when they were dying. The two women loved him in their differing ways and were grateful to him. He was not cold, but – like a child – he was incapable of facing or understanding what *they* felt. And, like a child, he was an expert politician in playing where adults do not play. For example, the baby talk in the *Journal to Stella* so skilfully, to all appearance, addressed to Stella and Miss Dingley for respectability's ingenious sake, is not a lover's talk but a brilliant raillery which imitates Stella's lisping habit of speech with everyone when she was a backward child at Moor Park. It is a clever, affectionate, but daring mockery of her childhood, designed to keep her *in statu pupillari*. The baby talk – which he used with no other woman – is, so to say, a juvenile exercise in the art of philandering, at which he was notoriously expert.

Swift's hardness to Stella and Vanessa has often been described as mean, calculating and, at heart, frightened; but, as Dr Rowse can easily show, in Swift's relationship with everyone an exorbitant, ingrained pride – the pride of the solitary who will not give himself – is always there. As an unknown cleric, he forced the great Harley to walk halfway to meet him – not that Harley would notice: he would be either well-mannered or merely drunk in an aristocratic way. Such a pride looks almost insane; it was in fact the source of Swift's genius as a satirist. He did not simply hate; he drew upon all the minutiae that buried hatred makes vivid and effective. It is clear, plain, merry obloquy, as unremitting and unanswerable as a day's rain. What Dr Rowse does not go into – and a biography that makes us feel sympathy for a maimed character may not require this literary comment – is the curious influence of that new fashionable and scientific toy, the magnifying glass, on Swift's imagination. Perhaps that simple instrument played as great a part as pride when he came to assuage his passions in *Gulliver's Travels.* How monstrous or tiny it could make his disgusts or his fears, even his own ego. How right that the elderly child should have written a child's book.

I must say that for the first time in my reading, Dr Rowse has made the factional quarrelling of Queen Anne's London clear and even gripping. We are made to see it and feel it and want to be in it, for the moment, as Swift himself so avidly did. After all, he was trying to stop the slaughter of Marlborough's war. And Dr Rowse is even better on Swift's 'conversion' (if that is the word for it) to Ireland. Hated in Ireland, slandered in Ireland, he became eventually the spokesman for Irish (colonial) liberty – although he despised the Irish for their refusal to help themselves. In one way, little Dublin was just the place for the egotist so passionately and, above all, so pedantically concerned with his own liberty. The city was and is a place where one can exist as an irredeemable personality, giving and receiving blows and becoming notable as a protest at having been born – that splendid Irish grudge. Though Swift was elsewhere regarded as avaricious and as counting every penny, his continual and thoughtful charities in Dublin to those whose needs were real or bizarre made him at one with that charitable uncharitable city, a testy and at last a senile saint.

When one looks back on him again what strikes one is that he recorded the multitude of his daily acts pretty well as closely as Pepys did. He belongs to that very small number of famous people whose daily life is visible to us from hour to hour. That may be, as Rossi and Hone have said, because egotists of Swift's kind have instant passions but no lasting aim, grow tired when there is no one about and turn to telling us even about such silly things as how they get up in the morning.

So I'll rise, and bid you good morrow, my ladies both, good morrow. Come stand away, let me rise: Patrick, take away the candle. Is there a good fire? So – up a dazy.

It all comes as sweetly to him as handling a prime minister or terrorizing a duke. The terrible child will play his private games forever, until playing games drives him out his mind.

Boswell's London

The discovery of cache after cache of Boswell's manuscripts, journals and letters at Malahide and Fettercairn between 1925 and 1948 is one of the truly extraordinary events in the history of English letters. It gave us the original journal of the *Tour to the Hebrides*, before the war and now we have a totally new manuscript, appearing 180-odd years after it was written. This is the London journal which Boswell wrote in 1762 and 1763 when, twenty-three years old, he came to London to get a commission in the Guards, and, failing in that, met the man who was to be his god, his subject and his insurance of fame. What, we wonder, will be the state of our old editions of the *Life* of Johnson when the manuscripts yet to be seen are published? The *Life* has been a kind of lay scripture to the English, for it contains thought in our favourite, pragmatic form, that is to say, masticated by character. The book has been less a biography than a sort of parliamentary dialogue containing a thundering government and an adoring and obliging opposition. It will be strange if the proverbial and traditional characters are altered, though in the last generation the clownish Boswell has risen in esteem, and beyond Macaulay's derision. He has changed from the burr on the Doctor's coat-tails into an original blossom of the psychological hothouse.

Here we get on the dangerous ground of Plutarchian contrast. If Boswell created himself, we must never forget that Johnson made that possible. We lean to Boswell now because we have been bred on psychologists rather than philosophers, and love to see a man drowning in his own contradictions and self-exposures. The Doctor, who believed in Virtue, believed inevitably in repression, where we have been taught that it is immoral to hide anything. Boswell's very lack of foundation, his lack of judgement, are seen merely as the price he pays for the marvellous fluidity, transparency and curiosity of his nature. Dilapidation is his genius. Yet if

Boswell is a genius we cannot forget that the Doctor is a saint, a man of richer and more sombre texture than his parasite. He is a father-figure, but not in the mechanical fashion of psychological definition; he is a father-figure enlarged by the religious attribute of tragedy. It was the tragic apprehension that was above all necessary for the steadying of Boswell's fluctuating spirit and for the sustaining of his sympathetic fancy.

The marvel is that at the age of twenty-three Boswell was already turning his gifts upon himself in the *Journal.* Professor Pottle, his lively American editor, thinks that his detachment is more complete than that of Pepys or Rousseau. Boswell's picture of himself has indeed the accidental and unforeseeable quality of life which better organized, more sapient or more eloquent natures lose the moment they put pen to paper. Boswell's detachment comes from naïveté and humility. He was emotionally surprised by himself. To one who had been knocked off his balance by a severe Presbyterian upbringing the world is bound to be a surprising place. To those who have lived under intense pressure, what happens afterwards is a miracle and release is an historical event. If the will has been destroyed by a parent like Lord Auchinleck, it may be replaced by a shiftless melancholy, an abeyance of spirits, and, from that bewilderment, all life afterwards will seem an hallucination, when a high-blooded young man engages ingenuously with it.

There is an obscure period in Boswell's youth when he joined the Roman Catholic Church. We do not know whether passion, giddiness, his irrational fears, or his tendency to melancholy, moved him to this step. But native canniness got him out of the scrape which socially and materially would have been a disaster in that age, and we can be grateful that the confessional did not assuage what Puritan diarizing has preserved. For that confession contains more than an account of his sins; it contains his sillinesses, his vanities, moods, snobberies, the varying temperatures of his aspirations. 'I have a genius for Physick,' he says. For what did he not think he had genius? If only he could find out how to develop it! No symptom was too small when he studied the extraordinary illness, the remarkable fever, the very illusion of being a Self, James Boswell.

Exhibitionism? Vanity? The *Journal* was not private. It was posted every week to a friend, one of the inevitable devotions of the hero-worshipper. It is amazing that a young man should be an ass with such art, that judgement should not sprout anywhere. How rare to see a fool persisting in folly to the point of wisdom. One of the earliest comedies in the book is his lamentable affair with the actress Louisa. Calculation is at the bottom of it. Meanness runs through it, yet it is an exquisitely defenceless tale. In time he hoped to have a mistress who was a woman of fashion, but social inexperience and poverty – he is wonderfully stingy, a real hungry Scot of the period – held him back. As an actress Louisa could *cheaply* create the illusion of the woman of fashion. All this is innocently revealed later by introspection; at the beginning he is all fine feeling. To emphasize the fineness of the feeling, he astutely points out, in his first timid advances to Louisa, that love is above monetary considerations. Presently he begins to believe his own propaganda; he is in love and to the extent of lending the woman £2. In the seduction, his sexual powers at first disappoint and then suddenly surpass anything he (or Louisa) has ever heard of. The next time he has a shock. Love has vanished. He is an unstable character. Presently he discovers she has introduced him to the 'Signor Gonorrhoea'. Despair, rage, moral indignation – can he have left the path of Virtue? – hard bargainings with the surgeon, melancholy, the ridicule of friends, nothing to do but stay at home and read Hume's *History*. Philosophy calms him until the surgeon sends his bill. (In the matter of cash, the dissolving selves of Boswell always come together with certainty.) He writes to Louisa, points out what she has cost him, and asks for his £2 back, and says he is being generous. The doctor's bill was £5:

> Thus ended my intrigue with the fair Louisa which I flattered myself so much with and from which I expected at least a winter's safe copulation.

To be so transparent, thinking neither of the impression he makes upon himself nor of the figure he will cut before his friend, is possibly to be fatuous. But Boswell's fatuousness, which seems to arise from a lack of will or centre in his life, is inspired. Instead of will, Boswell had that mysterious ingredient of the soul, so admired in the age of sensibility: 'my genius', or, as we would say, his Id. On that point only is his *amour-propre* unyielding. Drowning in midstream, unable to reach the shore of Virtue and swept back into Vice and Folly, he clings to the straw of his 'genius' and spins round and round until, what is he but a frantic work of art?

'How well I write!' he exclaims, after flattering a peer in six lines of doggerel. How wonderfully 'facetious' he is with the Earl, how wonderful are 'the sallies of my luxuriant imagination'.

How easily and cleverly do I write just now! I am really pleased with myself, words come skipping to me like lambs upon Moffat Hill; and I turn my periods smoothly and imperceptibly like a skilful wheelright turning tops in a turning loom. There's a fancy! There's a simile.

Sheridan punctures him brutally, but Garrick comes along:

'Sir,' said he, 'you will be a great man. And when you are so, remember the year 1763. I want to contribute my part towards saving you. And pray, will you fix a day when I shall have the pleasure of treating you with tea.' I fixed the next day. 'Then Sir,' said he, 'the cups shall dance and the saucers skip.'

Like Moffat lambs, no doubt; fancy has been at work on Garrick's talk. Boswell continues innocently:

What he really meant by my being a great man I can understand. For really, to speak seriously, I think there is a blossom about me of something more distinguished than the generality of mankind.

If only it can be left to grow, instead of being chilled by 'my melancholy temper' and dishevelled by 'my imbecility of mind'. The extraordinary thing is that a man so asinine should be so right.

The words of a man fuddled by middle age? No, we have to remind ourselves, they are the words of a coxcomb of twenty-three. Hypochondria, as well as the prose manner of the time, has doubled his age. 'Taking care of oneself is amusing,' he says, filling his spoon with medicine. Life is an illness we must enjoy. In goes the thermometer at every instance. How is the genius for greatness? How is the fever for getting into the Guards, for chasing after English peers and avoiding the Scottish – if their accents are still bad – the fever for the theatre, for planning one's life, for wrecking the plan by the pursuit of 'monstrous' whores or by fanciful fornication on Westminster Bridge; the fever for wit; for being like Mr Addison; for a trip down the river; for lashings of beef; for cutting down his expenses and for freedom from error and infidelity in the eyes of Providence? Boswell goes round London with his biography hanging out of his mouth like the tongue of a panting dog, until the great climax comes. 'I am glad we have met,' says the Doctor, and the dog with the genius beneath the skin has found its master.

Boswell's picture of life in London drawing-rooms, coffee-houses, taverns and streets is wonderful. It is done by a man much alone – and such make the best observers – to whom every word heard is precious. Listening to the plays, listening to the ordinary talk at Child's, he makes his first experiment in that dramatic dialogue which later was to give the *Life* its crowning quality. His ear is humble at Child's:

> 1st citizen: Pray, doctor, what became of that patient of yours? Was not her skull fractured?
> Physician: Yes, to pieces. However, I got her cured.
> 2nd citizen: Good Lord!

Transparency is his gift of nature; affectability turns it into art; his industry, above all, fashions it. For Boswell stumbled soon upon the vital discovery that experience is three parts hallucination, when he made up his diary, not dryly on the spot but three or four days late. He had, as his present American editor shrewdly points out, a *little* foreknowledge. His 'genius' taught him to prepare the way for surprises which the reader could not know. It is one of his cunning strokes – he was not a regular theatre-goer for nothing – to repeat to Louisa, at the calamitous end of the affair, the words she had primly used at the beginning of it: 'Where there is no confidence, there is no bond.' And he is plotting, too, for that moment – surely handed to him by his Genius and not by Life – when she will send his £2 back in a plain envelope without a word. To illustrate, no doubt, his genius for stinginess. By the end, when the Doctor comes, the *Journal* overlaps the *Life*, but until then this is new Boswell, disordered and unbosomed.

The Carlyles

> The Universe, so far as sane conjecture can go, is one immeasurable swines' trough, consisting of solid and liquid, and other contrasts and kinds; – especially consisting of the attainable and unattainable, the latter in immensely greater quantities for most pigs.
>
> Moral evil is unattainability of Pig's wash; moral good attainability of ditto.

We are back in the Animal Farm of the Victorian Age, among the Pig Propositions of Carlyle's *Later Day Pamphlets*. We are at the stage before Orwell, before the unattainable has been made attainable by revolution and has been distributed. So the Victorians haunt us for we are still not out of the mess they were in. But what a difference of tone lies between Orwell and Carlyle! A stoical bitterness has succeeded to the rage of frustration. There is all the distance that lies between the Calvinist's pulpit version of disgust and doom, and the betrayal in the trench. What was literature, vision, or exhortation to Carlyle, we have had to see with our own eyes.

And history has been unkind to the preaching historian. We now pick up *Heroes & Hero Worship* gingerly: we have had to crush one or two dictator-heroes. Carlyle's ultimate contempt for the masses, his dream of an aristocracy of the wise, his call for a labour corps, take us back twenty years into Fascism. In England, where social injustice has been effectively attacked and constructively dealt with, the honour goes to the continuous, practical, rational efforts of the heirs of Bentham and Mill, and not to the mystics and supermen. Carlyle could describe the battlefields of the past, but he had no notion that war was the superman's chief export. He denied thinking might was right; but his statement that right is might 'in the long run' is comfortless; he certainly thought that might in the long run becomes right which was pleasant enough to believe in the long Victorian peace, but to our generation it seems to be one of those question-begging pieces of rhetoric which lead us straight to the concentration camp. It is not surprising that even at his most irascible and sadistic, Carlyle was pre-eminent among Victorian prophets: he embodied the energy and the pathos, the aggression and the guilt, of those who had exchanged belief in God for belief in themselves alone and, in many ways, Carlyle's attitude to religion is far more sympathetic than that of other apostates, for it was deeply tinctured by the tragic imagination and the sense of human pain. He never lost, as more optimistic or more accommodating figures did, the powerful morbidity of the Romantic movement into which, as a writer, he was born.

The Carlyle we have had in mind during the last thirty years or more is a very different character. We see a crabbed and complex person, a neurotic made for the problem-biography. Like Tolstoy, he is now almost more famous for the struggle of his married life, than for his doctrine; he is one of the keys to Puritan marriage. Turning to his work we see that his pungency, his incomparable physical portraiture and power of image-making, might have made him a supreme satirist, a writer as great as Swift, if he had lived a hundred years earlier – or perhaps in some more solid period ahead of us. His literary fame lies, for us, in his *Reminiscences* and above all in his letters. Carlyle is one of the supreme English letter-writers, and there is something tragically fitting in that – for there he was a great artist because he was no longer kicking against the pricks and was perfectly assimilated to life and his material. We must add, I think, that *Sartor Resartus* is a masterpiece of the grotesque; the strain of sanity, like the strain of simple religion and pure poetry, never dried up in him, and they worked together to make him a wonderful comic writer, one of the great clowns who are subtle with self-irony and who are untainted (on the whole, in a book like *Sartor*) by the poisons of satire.

But are we entering a new period when the kind of portrait we have just been looking at will require modification? Professor Willey, in his *Nineteenth Century Studies*, has enquired with sensibility and sympathy into the question of Carlyle's religion; and in a new, deeply considerate biography Mr Julian Symons has patiently gone into those social and political prophesyings which, most of all, had horrified liberal and what may be called Fabian thought. He has put himself into Carlyle's shoes and has related his life to his writings in a revealing and often delightful way – for Carlyle's pitiless, unsparing, almost photographic memory of his own life has preserved incomparable material for the biographer – and in tracing the course from Chartism to contempt for the masses, he has scrupulously looked at this from the point of view of Carlyle's own time. This is, for a change, a non-theoretical book about Carlyle; I mean that there are no dramatic theories about the notorious questions of his dyspepsia, his sexual deficiency, and there is no *parti pris* on the marriage to Jane Welsh. The human Carlyle is there in his incredible stoicism, bearishness, tenderness, pathos, in his generosity, his rages and his remorse; and to the intellect, when the exaggerations are washed away, are restored the force of his remarkable insights.

The main insight, on which Carlyle was to build both sane and – in his frustration – violent and sadistic conclusions, was into the power-basis of human societies. Mr Symons writes:

> In a time when most thinkers believed that the world could be changed by good will, he understood the basis of force upon which all modern societies rest. In a time when political economists thought that the industrial revolution must bring automatically increase in prosperity he realized that it would involve the overturning of established society. In a time of continual abstract arguments about the amount of liberty that might reasonably be allowed to human beings, he saw that liberties are obtained by one social class at the expense of another and that they are not abstract ideas but concrete realities.

It is inevitable to argue that Carlyle's cult of the hero sprang from his own pride, from the need to find a mystical father-surrogate and an alternative to the lost Biblical God of his childhood. It is impossible not to see that the individual who had been released from its classical chains by the Romantic movement, was moving, unchecked, towards megalomania. It is natural to smile when, famous at last after years of grind, loneliness and suffering, Carlyle began to believe in the wisdom of the aristocracy who had taken him up and whom he had once nicknamed Gigmanity and Imposture. But Mr Symons reminds us of the simplicity of Carlyle's character and the major cause of his social frustration. Looking at the condition of Victorian society he longed for action; looking at chaos he thought that it called for decisive authority. Dangerous talk. At bottom, it is clan talk. Carlyle's mind was formed in a society which still lived in the mental climate of the seventeenth century. One more imaginative, fanatical, dogmatic Scot had failed to understand English compromise, or our unprepossessing, semi-religious veneration of inertia. That we prefer worry to drama.

Carlyle, says Mr Symons, was a great magician who rubbed the wrong lamps. I have a suspicion that even in his Chartist days, when his voice rings most truly, Carlyle's effect was not political in the sense that he added to the practical or theoretical thought of politics. He added, rather, to that part of the inner life of people, to the imagination above all, which may take them to religious or political action. His objection to Bentham and Mill was fundamentally the poet's or the preacher's: they had ignored the soul, they had ignored the individual's need for a vision of his own drama and significance. The most satisfactory of Carlyle's revolutionary acts was the creation of his enraging prose which, as Mr Symons says, was an act of genius: nothing more calculated to break the smooth classical reign, than this Gothic and Gaelic confection. It takes us back to Sterne, Mr Symons says; but I think really it goes back to the language of another Puritan in whom the violent pressures of Puritanism had created an intense extravagance of fantasy: to the writing of Milton. I do not think Mr Symons makes enough of the Biblical strain. It is not the canting or whining of the dissenting tabernacles, or the uttering of magical passwords. It is a hybrid in which the Gaelic and Hebraic minds are joined. Energy, rather than the moral force of Milton, binds this writing which has all the Gaelic artifice, acting and love of decoration, all the intoxication of image with image, and the peculiar Gaelic cruelty. Carlyle was a Gaelic pagan with the Biblical rhythms thumping in his head and the German absurdities cavorting inside him 'in every conceivable sense'. Exhausting as we may find a style as consciously allusive as *Finnegan's Wake* is, we cannot but feel our imagination enlarged. Humility vanishes, acceptance goes, egoism expands. We live no longer in the prose in which it has pleased God to call us, but suddenly have the rights of our wild poetic intuition. We recognize our genius. In other words, we become human souls. Was that not at the heart of the tragic struggle of the poor peasant Calvinist: the struggle to become not a citizen but a human being in an iron age.

And the marriage of the Carlyles? Because sex is the predilection of the twentieth century, we have to turn to the late eighteenth century for the analysis of love, and to the Victorian Age for the specialists in marriage. We go, that is to say, to the professionals. For that is what the Tolstoys and the Carlyles are. No doubt enters their minds as to married monogamy being the only way and the most engrossing; their groans from the treadmill are part of their pleasure; they have the satisfaction of those who have chosen a Fate. Like Fundamentalists they live by the Book. Deeply they suspect any attempt to ameliorate this or that condition of their married life. When Geraldine Jewsbury wrote a novel which argued for the 'right' of a woman for freedom to choose her love but within marriage, both the Carlyles were indignant at the 'indecency' of the notion. Were they any different, one must ask, from the lovers of the eighteenth century, the figures of the *Liaisons Dangereuses*, of *Manon Lescaut*, or *Adolphe*, who held on just as tenaciously to the pain of their free condition; or from ourselves who cling to the privileged wounds of sexual aberration. The professional knows that part of the satisfaction is in the struggle, in the price to be paid daily. If the Tolstoys paid with their reason, and the Carlyles with their health, that is the compulsion of extremists. Their tragic genius enables us to appreciate, at its full worth, the mere talent for marriage of, say, the Brownings; just as the strategy of the *Liaisons Dangereuses* illumines the talent for the naval warfare of love in Jane Austen; just as Lawrence is the turbulent prophet of the sexual bliss, which has become free for all at any clinic.

What was it that bound the Carlyles, the most touching of unhappy and clinging couples? Sincere love and long affection, admiration, too; but that says all and nothing. Getting her blow in first, as usual, Jane Welsh said that habit was stronger in her husband than the passions. And she herself had, or came to have, short patience with them in other people. The pitiful side of her story is well known; its sexual misery is guessed at but not certainly known; but it has always been clear that she was not the downtrodden Victorian wife. The Carlyle marriage was a marriage between equals. On the negative side, difficulty must have been a bond between these arduous Scots; Scottishness, also, with its dry appreciation of the angers and humours of domestic recollection. The couple would be just a little tough about the miseries created by bad nerves, bad health, bad temper. On the positive side, the bond was surely their tongues; they had a common taste for satire, malice, exaggeration and everything that was singular, a zest for scorn and the damaging, picturesque images it could be expressed in. At their worst moments, in the absences brought about by their disagreements or their health, each could be tantalized by the thought that the other was seeing, saying, thinking or writing exaggerations of the most intimidating piquancy. Each would be feeling the hypnotic challenges of the other's wit.

There is a quality here that makes both of them arresting. Mrs Carlyle is one of the best letter-writers of the nineteenth century. He writes large and she writes small, but she rules her page, as certainly as he does his, like a circus master. Her exaggeration is conscious, too; it is not the helpless, personal hyperbole of a bosom too full. She was always fashioned by the subtle, disguising whalebone of common sense. She picks her subject and electrifies her brain. It is all irony. Why did she not, with her Jane Austenish tongue, become a novelist? Here, it is instructive to compare her with that disturbing gusher, Geraldine Jewsbury, of whom she said:

> her speech is so extremely insincere that I feel in our dialogues we are always acting in a play, and we are not to get either money or praise for it, and not being an amateur of play-acting, I prefer good honest *silence* . . . she is as sharp as a meat axe – but as narrow.

With all her quick, fantastic interest in people, Mrs Carlyle did not become a novelist and the gusher did. Mrs Carlyle was too interested in hitting people off, and in keeping on top herself, for the novelist's life; she totally lacked that Messiah-producing and soulful inner glumness of the pregnant artist; or the inner silence which a Jane Austen had.

The good letter-writer has to be an egotist with a jumping mind. Even at nineteen Jane Welsh was the born boss of the notepad:

> *Allons ma chère!* – let us talk of the 'goosish' man, my quondam lover.
>
> He came; arrived at the George Inn at eleven o'clock at night, twelve hours after he received my answer to his letter; slept there 'the more soundly' according to his statement 'than was to have been expected, all the circumstances of the case being considered'

and in the morning sent a few nonsensical lines to announce his nonsensical arrival . . . In a day or two after his return . . . there came a quantity of music from him. (*Pour parenthese*, I shall send you a sheet of it, having another copy of 'Home Sweet Home' beside.)

If Carlyle howled like a dervish, and went lamenting about his house like the Wandering Jew, when the cocks crowed or the dogs barked in the Chelsea gardens or the piano played next door, Mrs Carlyle had a tongue. It missed nothing. One evening, the impossible Mrs Leigh Hunt 'behaved smoothly, looked devilish and was drunkish'. Plain drunk would have been more amiable. When Mr Leigh Hunt, after the same party, went downstairs and gave a lady a couple of handsome smacks as he left and whispered 'God bless you, Miss Hunter,' Mrs Carlyle, with her 'wonted glegness', heard! Poor Mr Severn, so devoted to his wife, goes off to Italy alone with the sting that 'people who are so devoted to their wives are apt from mere habit, to get devoted to other people's'. What a power, 'beside a fund of vitality' Mr Sterling had of 'getting up a sentiment about anything or nothing'. And Geraldine, the never-spared, gets a letter with the immortal beginning: 'Dearest Geraldine, I am sending you two men.' The only way to get even with a lady as sharp as this was to use her own methods and make her laugh at herself; and this happily she could do. A young Charles Buller who had been snubbed by her on the sound Annandale ground that he was an expert philanderer and unkind to his parents, was not going to be put down. For two days she held out against him without a smile – and her face with its fine but sullen brow, its full-orbed eyes and hard mouth could look formidable – until a brilliantly silly idea occurred to him. They were all standing in the hall watching the rain fall on the Norfolk garden when the young man exclaimed, 'I will shoot a hollyhock' and did so at once, bringing her the trophy with all the solemnity (the learned and topical lady writes) of Mr Petrucci in the character of Heraclitus. She was obliged to laugh, 'to the disgrace of her originality'. The immoral Mr Buller had subdued a fantastic satirist, by a fantastic act.

Mrs Carlyle was the most amusing woman in London. Everyone with any brains came to her house. She astonished Tennyson by allowing him to smoke; she gave Mazzini many a dressing down. D'Orsay called twice: 'at first sight his beauty is that of the rather

330

disgusting sort which seems to be like genius of no sex'. But he had wit and sense on the first occasion; they had diminished by the second. No longer dressed like a humming bird, he had cleverly subdued his finery to the recognition that five years had made a difference to his figure. She was quite aware, in spite of a flutter of pretence, that people like seeing her as much as they like seeing her husband; and when Carlyle was beguiled to Bath House by Lady Ashburton, there was a lively salon in Cheyne Row to put against it. And put against it it was. With the acid relish of inner loneliness, she was a great deal out and about observing the human comedy. The born letter-writer sees incident or absurdity in the smallest things and picks out what will divert the reader. This was written for the scornful preacher in Carlyle:

A Mrs Darbyshire, whom you saw once, came the night before last to stay while I stayed. She seems a sensible *gentlewoman* enough – a Unitarian *without the* Doctrines. But I could not comprehend at first why she had been brought, till at last Mrs Paulet gave me to understand that she was there to use up Miss Newton. 'Not,' she said, 'that my sister is an illiberal person, though she believes in Christ, and *all that sort of thing.* She is quite easy to live with; but it will be pleasanter for herself as well as for us that she should have somebody to talk to of her own sort – a Catholic or Unitarian, she doesn't mind which.' After this initiation I could hardly look with gravity on these two shaking heads into one another's faces and bum-bumming away on *religious* topics, as they flatter themselves.

And she was capable of folly. There was the wonderful party when Dickens did his marvellous conjuring tricks, where the crackers went bang and the champagne flowed. She had been green, bilious and ill with her terrible nerves when she left Cheyne Row, but here in the uproar, she was suddenly cured. She talked mad nonsense to Thackeray; and at the climax Forster

seized me *round the waist*, whirled me into the thick of it and *made* me dance!!! Like a person in the treadmill who must move forward or be crushed to death! Once I cried out, 'For the love of heaven let me go; you are going to dash my brains out against the folding doors!' to which he answered, 'Your brains! Who cares about their brains here? Let them go.'

There were other lettings go of the brain. Obviously, taken in by Geraldine Jewsbury, she had let herself go too far for a moment or two. She was on the verge of a 'crush'. There was the Father Matthew episode, a pure case of hero-worship, when she rushed to his meeting in the East End, and, climbing on the platform, fell flat at the priest's feet. She gripped his hands, burst into tears and after a few choking words gave him a memento of herself, and went home sick and mad with exaltation. After her husband, the Father was 'the best man of modern times'. But here the ironist returned: 'Had you any idea your wife was such a fool?' And there was the sobering reflection that 'the Father got through the thing admirably'.

There must have been a good deal of 'getting through the thing' at Cheyne Row. It was, for all its ready sociability, a fort, with the old warrior upstairs, bloody and unbowed, and herself the sentinel below. They had, in this marriage, the belligerence and tenderness of soldiers. Her letters amuse like a novel because they catch the hour-to-hour life, the alarms and domesticity of this peculiar garrison. We are spared the hysteria of a Countess Tolstoy, for Jane Welsh and her husband were stoics; when the woe, the illness, the insomnia, the loneliness, the jealousy come through, and the wary hardness that followed their insoluble differences, it comes through a mind capable of some self-criticism. Strangely, it is not the *suffering* that moves one – only by an effort can one sympathize with neurotic or imaginary suffering, for one is always aware of how strong and relentless the neurotics are – rather, the happiness, the devotion, the love and the deep deposit of friendship that accumulate in a marriage, and the exquisite pain of the passage of time, that bring tears to the eyes. How quickly the early excitement goes; how warmly the devotion expands; how strong the ties between the contestants become. The Carlyle marriage becomes an archetype of the marriage of genius. We owe to Mrs Carlyle an intimate picture of a remarkable man caught, as in the Laocoon, by his own gifts; not once is there any attempt at that reckless, destructive criticism of his work, which animal jealousy and mania aroused in a woman like the Countess Tolstoy, unless the journals Mrs Carlyle destroyed contained such outbursts.

If both the Carlyles had a terrible power of speech – when one regards them from the Marriage Council point of view – they took a comic pride in the dramatic effect of their silences. Carlyle said hers was terrifying: and he would know, for he has given us a notion of his own when he speaks of resting on 'the iron pillar of silence and despair'. Mrs Carlyle dened she was a jealous woman when Geraldine Jewsbury was invited to stay, but the over-quickness of her denial, her clever turning of jealousy into what she could claim was ordinary worldly percipience about the effect of pushing young women on distinguished men, give her away. She was an exceedingly jealous woman. Carlyle, similarly, appears not to be a jealous man: she had far more men (and women) in varying states of passion for her, than he had women. He never objected. *His* jealousy was directed outside the home, at other writers. We owe to him the most brilliant, destructive, ill-tempered portraits of the chief figures of his time: Lamb sodden with gin, Godwin vacuously playing cards, Emerson thin as a reed and with a head like a starved cockerel's. He could pretend that these caricatures were quintessences caught by an infallible artist in the godly or the grotesque, and not the jealousy of a tormented egotist. Her caprice must be matched by his manias; his determination to hold the floor, by her determination to manage the table. It was sufficient to give either of them a present or to offer money, to insult them. If he saw through every other writer she saw through every woman, especially every married woman, the moment they opened their mouths. If she made a dead set at the husband of every woman who came into the room, especially if he were famous, Carlyle, just as possessive as a prophet, took possession of every major aspect of the fate of England.

There was fire in both of them. There was also porridge – the curious, flat, short-tasting gift for finding nourishment in daily, domestic ironies which, when one looks back on the lame attempts to describe love in Scottish novels, appears to be its sentimental substitute. How the Carlyle marriage recalls those domestic scenes (so often placed in the sculleries, kitchens, and backyards) of the novels of Scott and Stevenson, where scolding, clatter, a gift of tongues, retort and counter-attack are the language of love, and raised from squalor by the wanton bellicosity of the Gaelic imagination.

The archetypal marriages – and the Carlyles' was the archetype of the wedding of wit and genius – owe their position to the outspokenness of the parties. The Tolstoy diaries! The Carlyle letters! Can human happiness survive so much forthrightness? The Carlyles were saved because they admired each other's wit. Their worst agonies seem not to have come from their common hypochondria, her jealousy or his monstrous selfishness, but from not getting letters from each other on the day they were expected when they were separated. It is the most moving thing about them: their craving for the other's voice. But behind her skill and humour, behind her simplicity, behind the habit of a certain obdurate competition with each other lay something one can only call primitive. Like some couple out of a novel by D.H. Lawrence – some anti-phallic couple one must say and Carlyle, oddly, uses the word – they had built, open-eyed, a contest of essences and prides.

V · A CROWD OF FICTIONS

THE ENGLISH GENIUS

Clarissa

The modern reader of Richardson's *Clarissa* emerges from his experience exhausted, exalted and bewildered. The book is, I fancy, the longest novel in the English language; it is the one most crowded with circumstantial detail; it is written in the most dilatory of narrative manners, i.e. in the form of letters. It is a tale perceived through a microscope; it is a monstrosity, a minute and inordinate act of prolonged procrastination. And the author himself is a monster. That a man like Samuel Richardson should write one of the great European novels is one of those humiliating frolics in the incidence of genius. The smug, juicy, pedestrian little printer from Derbyshire, more or less unlettered, sits down at the age of fifty and instructs young girls in the art of managing their virtue to the best advantage. Yet, ridiculous as *Pamela* is, her creator disarms criticism by a totally new ingredient in the novel: he knows how to make the reader weep. And, stung by the taunts of the educated writers of his time, Richardson calmly rises far above *Pamela* when he comes to the story of Clarissa Harlowe; he sets the whole continent weeping. Rousseau and even Goethe bow to him and take out their handkerchiefs; the vogue of sensibility, the first shoots of the Romantic movement, spring from the pool of Richardson's pious tears like the grateful and delicate trees of an oasis. Yet there he is, plump, prosaic, the most middling of middling men, and so domestically fussy that even his gift of weeping hardly guarantees that he will be a major figure. Is there not some other strain in this dull and prodigiously painstaking little man? There is. Samuel Richardson was mad.

I do not mean that Richardson was a lunatic. I do not mean he was mad as Swift was mad. At first sight, an immeasurable smugness, an endlessly pettifogging normality seem to be the outer skin of Richardson's character. We know, as I have already said, that from his youth he was an industrious and timid young man who was, for some reason or other, used by young women who wanted their love letters written. Profoundly sentimental, he sat like some pious old cook in her kitchen, giving advice to the kitchen maids, and when he came to write novels he was merely continuing this practical office. He lived vicariously like some sedentary lawyer who has to argue the disasters of other people's lives letter by letter, but who himself never partakes. Genteel, he is, nevertheless, knowing; prim and cosy, he is, nevertheless, the victim of that powerful cult of the will, duty and conscience by which Puritanism turned life and its human relations into an incessant war. There is no love in Puritanism; there is a struggle for power. Who will win the daily battle of scruple and conscience – Pamela or the young squire; Clarissa or Lovelace? And yet what is urging Richardson to this battle of wills? What is it that the Puritan cannot get out of his mind, so that it is a mania and obsession? It is sex. Richardson is mad about sex.

His is the madness of Paul Pry and Peeping Tom. I said just now that *Clarissa* is a novel written under the microscope; really it is a novel written about the world as one sees it through the keyhole. Prurient and obsessed by sex, the prim Richardson creeps on tip-toe nearer and nearer, inch by inch, to that vantage point; he beckons us on, pausing to make every kind of pious protestation, and then nearer and nearer he creeps again, delaying, arguing with us in whispers, working us up until we catch the obsession too. What are we going to do when we get there? The abduction, the seduction, the lawful deflowering of a virgin in marriage are not enough for him. Nothing short of the rape of Clarissa Harlowe by a man determined on destroying her can satisfy Richardson's phenomenal daydream with its infinite delays.

The principle of procrastinated rape is said to be the ruling one in all the great best-sellers. It was in Richardson's genius that he was able to elevate the inner conflict of the passions and the will to an abstract level, so that the struggle of Clarissa and Lovelace becomes a universal battle-piece; and, in doing this, Richardson was able to paint it with the highly finished realism of the Dutch painters. At the beginning one might simply be reading yet another novel of intrigue, which just goes on and on; and but for the incredible suspense in the narrative I think many readers must have given up *Clarissa* by the end of the first volume. It is not until the third and fourth volumes are searched, when Richardson transposes his intrigue into the sustained and weeping music, the romantic tragedy of Clarissa's rape and long preparation for death, that we get his measure. She dies piously, yet like a Shakespearean conferring greatness upon all around her by the starkness of her defeat. At the beginning we are not prepared for this greatness in Clarissa; even in that last volume we are often uncertain of her real stature. It is not easy for virginity to become Virtue. Would she be anything without Lovelace? And yet, we know, she is the crown upon Lovelace's head. He too becomes tragic under her judgement as she becomes tragic by his act. These two reflect glory upon each other, like saint and devil. But in the first volume there is no difficulty about deciding who is the greater as a character or as an abstract conception. Lovelace has her beaten hands down. A practical and languid correspondence wakes up when he takes pen in hand. Anna Howe, the 'pert' friend, makes circles round her. Arabella, with her nose out of joint, is livelier comedy. The scheming brother, the gouty father with his paroxysms, the supplicating and fluttering mother, and the endearing uncles with their unendearing family solidarity, make a greater mark on our minds than the all-too-articulate Clarissa does. Our one hope is that witty Miss Howe is right when she teases Clarissa with maidenly self-deception. 'The frost piece', as Lovelace called her, looks exactly like one of those fascinating prudes whose minds are an alphabet that must be read backwards. But no; though she will enchant us when she is rattled, with cries like 'Oh, my Nancy, what shall I do with this Lovelace?' her course and her motives are clear to her; and we begin the slow and painful discovery of a virtue which finds no exhilaration except in scruple. We face an inexhaustible determination, and this is exhausting to contemplate, for Clarissa is as interested in the organization of human motives as Richardson himself; and he insinuates himself in her character so thoroughly, niggling away with his 'ifs' and his 'buts', that he overwhelms her, as Flaubert overwhelmed Madame Bovary.

Still this does not take from the drama of Clarissa's situation, and does, in fact, increase the suspense of it. If we skip – and of course we do, looking up the letters in the obliging synopsis – we do not, as in other novels, find ourselves caught out by an overlooked sub-plot; we are back in the main situation. Will the family relent? Will Lovelace abduct, marry, rape or reform? There's hardly a sub-plot worth mentioning in this huge novel. It follows the labyrinth of a single theme. And though we turn to

Anna Howe for glimpses of common sense, and for a wit to enliven the glum belligerents of what Lovelace – always a psychologist and nearly a Freudian – called 'the Harlowe dunghill' with its wills and deeds of settlement, we see in Clarissa's stand something more than a virtuous daughter bullied by her parents. She is a lawyer in family morals, and in Lovelace's too; but she is the first heroine in English fiction to stand against the family. Richardson called them 'the embattled phalanx', and in *Clarissa* he goes to the heart of the middle-class situation: money, accretion of estate, the rise in the world, the desire to found a family, in conflict with the individual soul. She and Lovelace complement each other here. She thinks her family ought not to do evil to her, yet takes their evil upon herself; she is not a rebel but is tricked and driven into becoming an outcast and at last a saint. Like Lovelace, she has asked too much, 'for people who allow nothing will be granted nothing; in other words, those who aim at carrying too many points will not be able to carry any'. Yes, and those who put up their price by the device of reluctance invite the violence of the robber. By setting such a price upon herself, Clarissa represents that extreme of puritanism which desires to be raped. Like Lovelace's, her sexuality is really violent, insatiable in its wish for destruction.

Lovelace is Richardson's extravagant triumph. How did such a burning and tormented human being come out of that tedious little printer's mind? In the English novel Lovelace is one of the few men of intellect who display an intellect which is their own and not patently an abstract of their author's intellectual interests. He is half-villain, half-god, a male drawn to the full, and he dominates English fiction. He is all the more male for the feminine strain in his character: his hatred of women, his love of intrigue, his personal vanity, his captiousness and lack of real humility. A very masculine novelist like Fielding is too much a moralist, and too confidently a man, to catch a strain like that. And how Lovelace can write! When Clarissa's letters drag, like sighing Sunday hymns, or nag at us in their blameless prose, like the Collect for the day, the letters of Lovelace crackle and blaze with both the fire and the inconsequence of life. His words fly back and forth, throwing out anecdotes and the characters of his friends, with wonderful transitions of mood. In one paragraph he is writing a set apostrophe to Clarissa, full of longing and halfway to repentance. He shakes the mood off like a man who is drunk with grief and throws off this description of his gouty old kinsman:

And here (pox of his fondness for me; it happens at a very bad time) he makes me sit hours together entertaining him with my rogueries (a pretty amusement for a sick man!) and yet, whenever he has the gout, he prays night and morning with his chaplain. But what must *his* notions of religion be, who, after he has nosed and mumbled over his responses, can give a sigh or groan of satisfaction, as if he thought he had made up with Heaven; and return with a new appetite to my stories? – encouraging them, by shaking his sides with laughing at them, and calling me a sad fellow, in such an accent as shows he takes no small delight in his kinsman.

The old peer has been a sinner in his day, and suffers for it now; a sneaking sinner, *sliding*, rather than *rushing* into vices, for fear of his reputation; or rather, for fear of detection, and positive proof; for this sort of fellow, Jack, has no real regard for reputation. Paying for what he never had, and never daring to rise to the joy of an enterprise at first hand, which bring him within view of a tilting or the honour of being considered as the principal man in a court of justice.

To see such a Trojan as this just dropping into the grave which I hoped ere this would have been dug, and filled up with him; crying out with pain and grunting with weakness; yet in the same moment crack his leathern face into a horrible laugh, and call a young sinner charming varlet, encoring him as formerly he used to do the Italian eunuchs; what a preposterous, what an unnatural adherence to old habits.

Or there is the awful description of that old procuress, Mrs Sinclair, a horror out of Rowlandson, who advances upon Clarissa on the night of the rape, when all Richardson's fascination with carnal horror breaks out. There is a double terror in it, because Lovelace himself is writing as if trying to drive evil out of his mind by a picture of evils still greater:

The old dragon straddled up to her, with her arms kemboed again, her eyebrows erect like the bristles upon a hog's back, and, scowling over her shortened nose, more than half hid her ferret eyes. Her mouth was distorted. She pouted out her blubber-lips, as if to bellow up wind and sputter into her horse-nostrils, and her chin was curdled, and more than usually prominent with passion.

The temperate, lawyer-like mind of Richardson does not prepare one for passages like this. When there is a matter-of-factness in the eighteenth century, one expects it to be as regular as Pope's couplets were. But Richardson is not consistent. In the sheer variety of their styles the letters in this novel are astonishing. The bovine uncles, the teasing parenthetical Miss Howe, the admonitory Belford, the curt Colonel Morden, heading for his duel, the climbing neurotic brother whose descendants were no doubt in the British Union of Fascists, all have their styles, and they are as distinctive as Lovelace's or Clarissa's. Richardson is the least flat, the most stereoscopic novelist of an age which ran the plain or formal statement to death in the end. Another point: he is a writer of indirect narrative. We are shown scenes at second hand, for the epistolary method requires it so; and we become used to a sort of memoranda of talk and action which will tire our inward eye because our judgement is called upon at the same time. So there are many reported scenes which are relative failures, for example, the early and rather confusing ones between Clarissa and her mother. One has a muddled impression of two hens flying up in the air at each other and scattering their feathers. Yet even in this kind of scene Richardson can, at times, write talk which is direct and put action wonderfully under our eye. The scene of the rape is tremendous in this respect; and so is the awful picture of the brothel when Mrs Sinclair breaks her leg and the harridans come out in their night attire; and there is the comic, savage picture of Lovelace defeating the attempt of his family to try him. But where Richardson shook off the slavery of his own method is shown at its best, I think, in Belford's letter describing the prison scene where the two prostitutes offer to bail Clarissa out:

'We are surprised at your indifference, Miss Harlowe. Will you not write to any of your friends?'
'No.'
'Why, you don't think of tarrying *here* always.'
'I shall not live always.'

Even in those few lines one sees Richardson advancing his inner narrative and, if one continues this conversation, one also sees him patiently and unerringly preserving character. One might almost say that prolix as it was, his method was economical, given his chosen end. The slowness comes from an excess of examination, not an excess of words. No prose has fewer redundancies.

We come to the death scene. The torment of Lovelace pacing his horse past the gate of the house he dare not enter, though Clarissa lies dying within, is not rhetorical. It is defiant as fits a being so saturnine, it is in the mind as becomes a man of intellect, it is the changeable, imploring, raging madness of a clever mind that has met its conqueror. Lovelace is a villain no man hates, because he is a man. He is candid, if he is vain. He can argue like Iago or debate like Hamlet, and in between send a purse of a few guineas to a rogue who has helped him to his present catastrophe. It is strange to think of him – the only Don Juan in English fiction and done to the last Freudian detail. Clarissa dies like a swan amid the formal melody of a prose into which Richardson fell without affectation.

> Her breath being very short, she desired another pillow. Having two before, this made her, in a manner, sit up in her bed; and she spoke then with more distinctness; and seeing us greatly concerned, forgot her own stutterings to comfort us; and a charming lecture she gave us, though a brief one, upon the happiness of a timely preparation, and upon the hazards of a late repentance, when the mind, as she observed, was so much weakened, as well as the body, as to render a poor soul hardly able to contend with its natural infirmities.

It is a strong test of the illusion that Richardson has cast upon us, that we think of Lovelace like a shadow cast upon Clarissa as she dies; and of Clarissa rather than of Lovelace when *he* appears. These lives are known by their absences; they are inextricable, tangled in the thousands of words they have spoken about each other, and are swept away at last into other people's words.

The Shocking Surgeon

The disappearance of illustrations from the English novel, and indeed the decline of the art of illustrating, is a loss to literary criticism. For one of the obligations of the critic is to possess himself of the eyes with which a novelist's contemporaries read him, and this the good illustrator helped him to do. Of course we never achieve this sight, but we can approach it. And how far off the mark we can be is shown by the shock that a good illustrator gives. Cruikshank, for example: he upsets all the weary pieties of realism that lie between us and a comprehension of Dickens; half the silly criticisms of Dickens need never have been written if Cruikshank had been studied as closely as the text. And Rowlandson: pick up an edition of Smollett that has Rowlandson's illustrations and see Smollett come into focus once more, so that his page is almost as fresh to us as it must have appeared to the eighteenth-century reader. It is true that outside this school of illustration the argument weakens; the wooden severity of late-Victorian realism was a lugubrious travesty of the text and one is glad that illustration has been dropped. The fact is that illustration was at its best when the English novel was also in its brash, vital, fantastic youth; when, though wigged in a judicious style, it had only a simple and crude concern with caricature, anecdote and the bad manners of society. Once the novel abandoned travel and developed plot and form, the English novel ceased to need the illustrator, or at any rate ceased to get the right one.

There are two pointers in the engravings which Rowlandson did for *Humphry Clinker*, pointers the reader of Smollett ought to follow. Look at the scrawny figure of that malign virgin, Tabitha Bramble, as she comes accusing into the room where her philanthropical brother has been caught with a lady; look at Humphry in the gaol, moaning out his grotesque Methodism to the felons; look at her ladyship, gluttonous, diseased and warty, tearing out her friend's hair. They are not human beings. They are lumps of animal horror or stupidity. To Rowlandson the human race are cattle or swine, a reeking fat-stock done up in ribbons or breeches, which has got into coffee-houses, beds and drawing-rooms. He was nauseated by the domesticity and the grossness of the eighteenth century's new rich. In fact, every eighteenth-century artist and writer jibbed at the filth of domestic life, at some time or other. These pictures of Rowlandson's (of Hogarth's too) show how urgent was the task of the reform of manners which the writers of the eighteenth century had set themselves, from Addison onwards. (The movement had been revived by William III, who, when he came from Holland, was horrified by the brutality of English life. He encouraged Defoe, especially, to write in the cause of reform.) The second point is that Rowlandson's people are portraits of Swift's Yahoos. In these pictures we see the nightmare lying behind the Augustan manner. The nightmare of the pox, the scurvy, delirium tremens, of obesity and gout, the nightmare of the insanitary streets, of the stairway which was a dunghill, of the sedate Georgian window which was a place for the emptying of chamber-pots; the nightmare of the suppurations that flowed into the waters at Bath, of the stenches that rose from the 'elegant' crowds at Assemblies; the nightmare of the lives of children flogged into stupidity – see the boyhood of *Peregrine Pickle* – so that, in Rowlandson and Hogarth, all the virtuous people look like lumps of suet; and, haunting this scene, the nightmare religion of Wesley. Smollett and Rowlandson run so closely together in the drawing of these things that one borrows from the other's brutality. Yet are they brutal? I do not know enough about Rowlandson to say, but I am pretty sure that Smollett, for all his obsession with the bladder and the backside, was not a brutal nor a filthy man. He enjoyed being the shocking surgeon who brings out horrors at the dinner-table; but because he was shocked himself. Smollett's sensibility is close to Swift's. There is enough proof of Smollett's intention in the reforms which followed his descriptions of the brutalities of naval life at his time in *Roderick Random*. And though there is a good deal of horseplay, battery and assault in his books, from the comic scene where Hawser Trunnion picks up a turkey from the table to beat an unwelcome visitor, to the one in *Roderick Random* where the hero and a friend tie up the schoolmaster and flog his naked backside with a rope, Smollett has strong views on the stupefying effects of flogging. These are clearly stated in *Peregrine Pickle*. It is true that Perry, after a period of beating, himself becomes the bully of the school, to Hawser Trunnion's great delight, but Trunnion's views are always presented as further fantastic aspects of a fantastic and maimed character. We see more of what Smollett was like in the portrait of Dr Bramble in *Humphry Clinker*. Generosity and goodness of heart go together with an impetuous temper and a good touch of hypochondria. He has a morbid nose which smells out every stench that Bath, Edinburgh and Harrogate can provide; and Smollett's own nose, in his book of travels in France and Italy, was as fastidious. Smollett may have enjoyed the brutality he described, but his protests and his hypochondria suggest that he felt the pleasure and the agony of the man who has a skin too few. His coarseness, like that of Joyce, is the coarseness of one whose senses were unprotected and whose nerves were exposed. Something is arrested in the growth of his robust mind; as a novelist he remains the portrayer of the outside, rarely able to get away from physical externals or to develop from that starting-point into anything but physical caricature.

A course of Smollett is hard for the modern reader to digest. The theatre advised and animated Fielding and gave him form and discipline. Smollett might have remained a ship's surgeon – and would probably have been a happier man. (Smollett figures in the elder Disraeli's gallery of literary calamities.) The difficulty of digestion is that he is raw and piquant meat; course follows course without abating, and one has a surfeit. One begins *Peregrine Pickle*, *Roderick Random*, *Humphry Clinker* or *Count Fathom*, exclaiming with pleasure at the physical zest and the racing speed of the narrative, but after a hundred and fifty pages one has had enough of the practical jokes, the heiresses and duellists, the cheats and the bawds. Our trouble is that the English novel changed direction after its early lessons with the French and Spanish picaresque writers. The novel of travel gave place to plot and developed character. The kind of thing that Smollett did in *Humphry Clinker* – which all the critics, except the unerring Hazlitt, over-praise – was turned into Young's *Tours* or Cobbett's *Rural Rides*.

One book of Smollett's can be recommended to the modern reader without reservations: the very original *Travels Through France and Italy*, the first ill-tempered, captious, disillusioned and vigorously personal travel book in modern literature. It is a tale of bad inns, illness, cheating customs officials, a thoroughly British book of grousings and manias – the aim of every Frenchman is to seduce your wife, or if not your wife, your sister, and if not your sister, your daughter, as a token of his esteem for you! – but packed with the irritable author and moments of fresh, unperturbed judgement. It annoyed Sterne and was meant to annoy him. Against Sterne's fancies stand Smollett's manias, and how well they stand. Elsewhere, in the novels, one thinks less of whole books than of scenes. *Peregrine Pickle* is not as vigorous in its strokes and movements as *Roderick Random*, but my favourite scenes come from the former book. Hawser Trunnion and his 'Garrison' are wonderful fantasies, which tumble upon the reader uproariously as if a party were going on upstairs and the ceiling had given way in the middle of it. Trunnion lying about his naval engagements, fooled by publicans, entrapped by women, and tacking across country to his wedding, is, as they say, 'a beauty and no mistake'. And his death – that is one of the great scenes of English literature, to be compared with that great death scene at the end of Dostoevsky's *The Possessed.* You can see, as you read, how Fielding's wittier and better-formed imagination would have improved this novel; though Smollett surpasses Fielding, I think, in female portraiture; his leading ladies have more spirit than Fielding's and can amuse themselves quite well without the help of the hero. *Roderick Random* is altogether more sardonic and violent; *Count Fathom* is more polished, an essay after the manner of *Jonathan Wild.* It contains two scenes which stand out – a robber scene, suggested, I suppose, by an early episode in *Gil Blas*, and an appalling chapter describing the Count's mother, who was a camp follower in Marlborough's wars and made a good living by cutting the throats of the wounded and robbing them. This is the kind of scene that reveals the exposed nerve in Smollett.

The physical realism of Smollett and his chamber-pot humour are one other link with Joyce and show how his mind may have had not dissimilar obsessions. Perhaps that is going rather far; but there is some hint of *Anna Livia* in the Welsh maid's letters in *Humphry Clinker.* Smollett extended the farce of punning and misspelling into new regions for his times:

Last Sunday in the parish crutch, if my own ars may be trusted, the clerk called the banes of marridge betwist Opaniah Lashme-heygo and Tapitha Bramble, spinster; he mought as well have called her inkle weaver, for she never spun a hank of yarn in her life. Young Squire Dollison and Miss Liddy make the second kipple and there might have been a turd, but times are changed for Mr Clinker.

Or:

Who would have thought that mistriss, after all the pains taken for the good of her prusias sole, would go for to throw away her poor body? that she would cast the heys of infection upon such a carrying crow as Lashmyhago, as old as Mathewsullin, as dry as a red herring, and as poor as a starved veezel . . . He's a profane scuffle, and as Mr Clinker says, no better than an imp-fiddle, continually playing upon the pyebill and the new burth.

That's going further than any Malaprop could go. It is more than the rollicking *double entendre* of Rowlandson's letterpress. It is a Scotsman making a Welsh woman play ducks and drakes with the English language. It is imaginative, festive and, like all Smollett's comedy, broad, bizarre and bold.

Tristram Shandy

A little of Sterne goes a long way – as long as nearly 200 years, for his flavour never dies in the English novel. It is true we cannot live on tears, fancy cakes and curry. But, take him out of the English tradition; point out that George Eliot, D.H. Lawrence, Conrad – the assembled moral genius of the English novel – ignore him; explain that he is not Henry James; despise him because he created 'characters', a form of dramatic person out of fashion for a generation or more – and still his insinuating touch of nature comes through. He is obvious in figures as different as Thackeray and Firbank; and *Ulysses* is sometimes thought of as the *Tristram Shandy* of our century. We see the releasing hand of Sterne in those instances where the English comic genius leaves the usual moral territory of satire or the physical world of knockabout, and finds a third region which is neither pure intellect, pure fantasy nor pure imagination and which is indeed an evasion of all three. To call this the eccentric strain explains nothing; it is well known that the English are eccentric. Sterne – it is better to say – is mad, using the word as we commonly do in England to avoid facing and judging people who themselves are engaged in not facing what they are really up to. Eccentricity is, in fact, practical madness. It is resorted to, Henry Adams said in his severe and shrewd New England way, by those who are up to something shameful or stupid or muddle-headed. And, in England, most of us are.

It is possible that the comedy, half artifice and half nature, which we extract from our 'madness' is fundamentally stupid; there is an excessive and stupid streak in Ben Jonson where this comedy abounds. All the same we have sometimes raised stupidity to the level of a fine art. The 'madness' of Sterne, the hostile critic might say, is a practical device for foisting upon the reader a brilliant but shameless egotism, an inexhaustible selfishness and a clever smirking insincerity. Compare his shamelessness with

Boswell's: the Scotsman is wanton, transparent and artless, haunted by the fear of the Presbyterian devil, whereas we can be sure the devil himself was afraid that the half-Irish Sterne would drag him into bad company. Boswell calculated nothing or, at any rate, nothing right, except his money. Sterne calculated eloquently. Constantly he reckoned up how much he was going to feel before he felt it; even calculated his words so subtly that he made a point of not ending half his sentences and preferred an innuendo to a fact. He relied on the reader's imagination. I notice that in the sympathetic and unprejudiced enquiry that Mr Peter Quennell made into Sterne's character in *Four Portraits* – and this contains the most illuminating study of Sterne that I know of – there is the suggestion that he was the first to use the word 'sentiment' in our imaginative literature and to found the modern meaning of the sentimental. I do not know whether this is so, but it ought to be. For Sterne was a sentimentalist, because his imagination was morbidly quick to impose the idea of a thing, its image-provoking words and its *ambiance* long before the feeling was evoked. He could talk his heart into beating. He could talk tears into his eyes. Or so we feel as we read him; never sure whether this sociable, good-natured, too impressionable man is sincere or not.

One can see Sterne's temperament at work in the account of the beginnings of the Widow Wadman's love of Uncle Toby. The widow's passion was not born until she had seen him among her things in her own house:

There is nothing in it out of doors and in broad daylight, where a woman has a power, physically speaking, of viewing a man in more lights than one – but here, for her soul, she can see him in no light without mixing something of her own goods and chattels along with him – till by reiterated acts of such combinations he gets foisted into her inventory –

This may be a universal truth about love, but down to the last *double entendre* – and, above all, because of it – the fancy encases the feeling as it did in the parallel circumstances of Sterne's courtship of his wife. His passion warmed when she let her lodgings to him in her absence.

'One solitary plate,' he wrote,

one knife, one fork, one glass! I have a thousand pensive penetrating looks at the chair thou hadst so often graced, in those quiet and sentimental repasts – then laid down my knife and fork, and took out my handkerchief, and clapped it across my face, and wept like a child.

Obviously one who felt so strongly for a chair could live very well alone in the comforts of his own imagination.

Alone: it is that word which rises at last to the mind after it has been dragged for miles at the heels of the bolting, gasping fancies and verbosities of *Tristram Shandy*. The gregarious, egotistical Sterne is alone; garrulously, festively and finally alone. If there is one thing he likes better – again, in literature as in life – than the accident of meeting, it is the agreement to part. One can put this down, at a guess, to his severance from his detested mother. In *Tristram Shandy* it is notable and important that all the characters are solitaries. Mr Shandy and his wife, Dr Slop, Uncle Toby and the Corporal live shut up in the madhouse of their own imaginations, oysters itching voluptuously upon the pearl within. Mr Shandy silences his brother with his philosophical systems and his cross-references, never sees a fact but he recedes from it into abstraction, and is determined that the palaverings of the search for Truth shall have one end only: that he gets his own way in his own home. The blameless Uncle Toby sits in his innocence, conducting his imaginary campaigns, short of speech and blinking at the world. Mrs Shandy hurriedly agrees with her husband; nobody knows what is on *her* mind. Dr Slop is shut up in the horror of his pendulous belly and Corporal Trim does what he's told, loves his master, but lives by his memories of his poor brother Tom in Lisbon. Habit rather than communication keeps them all happily together. They are bound by ennui, grey days and indolence. But, read the dialogue: it is a collection of monologues. True, Uncle Toby and the Corporal have occasional awkward interchanges, but the general impression is that no one answers serious questions and that they know one another far too well to listen. In family life there is nothing to do about the hard core of the human ego, but to accept it. The indecencies and the double meanings of Sterne, if anything, intensify the solitude; they provoke private reflection and erect barriers of silent lecherous satisfaction. How can the Widow discover where Uncle Toby was wounded, when he can only answer: 'In the siege of Namur.'

Sterne displays the egotist's universe: life is a personal dream.

Those who deny Sterne talent of the highest order and think of him as outside our tradition, must strip away half our tradition and character first. Sterne's discovery of the soliloquizing man, the life lived in fantasy, is the source of what is called the 'great character' in the English novel, a kind which only Russian fiction, with its own feeling for 'madness' in the nineteenth century, has enjoyed. *Tristram Shandy* is the inspiration of the solitaries of Dickens, the idea-ridden people in Peacock and many others in our literature; they are not literary theories but comic abstractions from a faculty of life. It must be admitted that Mr Shandy and Uncle Toby are both very stupid men; they are funny because Sterne is so much cleverer than either. He plays tunes on them. They are also bores – always the richest game for the comic instinct. If we compare them with other great bores, like Bouvard and Pécuchet, the Shandys have the advantage of not riding their hobby-horses to any purpose. They prove nothing either to us or to themselves but illustrate rather the vegetable inertia of the fanciful life and display the inhabiting of one's temperament as the most sensible thing to be engaged in. Every dog to his basket. Even in the torpor of their domesticity, the imagination can beguile.

The bother was that Sterne was a bore himself, as boring in his way as Mr Shandy is. That Irish loquacity which he got from his mother and his early years in Tipperary had deluded him. He has that terrible, professional, non-stop streak of the Irish. One feels, sometimes, that one has been cornered by some brilliant Irish drunk, one whose mind is incurably suggestible. Although we have a hypnotized picture of Uncle Toby's dubious fortifications they take on, in our minds after an hour or two, the heavy appearance of those surly battlements one sees during the migraine. *Tristram Shandy* must be the most put-down book in English literature. One can respond, of course, to the elaborate cunning of its counterpoint; there is method in the anarchy. But the book is a collection of fragments in which every fragment sticks: Mr Shandy fallen geometrically with grief in his bed; Uncle Toby dazed by the fire; the pipe stem snapping as the child is born upstairs; the ludicrous discussion about the landboat, with its foreshadowing of Peacock; Bridget putting Mrs Wadman to bed; Mr and Mrs Shandy on the 'bed of justice' with the inevitable chamber pot sticking out from under the vallance while they talk of putting young Tristram into breeches; the pretty picture of Brother Tom going into his sausage shop in Lisbon where there was a Negress driving off fleas with a feather.

Sterne has a genius for mosaic; for being any self he has decided to be; for living in the effeverscence of his nature. The sentimentalist is a cynic, naturally:

> Love, you see, is not so much a Sentiment as a Situation, into which a man enters, as my brother Toby would do, in a *corps* – no matter whether he loves the service or no – being once in it, he acts as he did . . .

Many have wondered at the feverish receptivity of his eye and some have seen the dread of death – for he was a consumptive – in his determination to look at each event through a microscope as if enlarging it would slow the course of time. That Sterne's sensibility to the passage of time was unusual is certain; he seemed to see each minute as it passed, and to be eager to hold it with a word. But others – of whom Mr Quennell is one – see in his minuteness the training of the painter. Every sight, every thought was a physical model. There can be no doubt that he broke into the stream of consciousness and was the first to splash about there – in rather shallow water; there can also be no doubt that he was never going to commit himself to anything deeper. It was enough that one thing led to another and that the sensibility was ready for the change. It was Sterne's wife, a woman heavily committed to housework and a bad temper, who, for a time, went out of her mind.

George Meredith and English Comedy

It seems to me that our comic tradition is fed by three main streams upon which Meredith drew. I think of them as the masculine, the feminine and the mythic or fantastic. The division is, of course, arbitrary. Sooner or later they will mingle, separate, mingle again. The masculine tradition, if you take this view, runs from Fielding, Scott, Jane Austen, Trollope, George Eliot and on to Kipling, Wells, Waugh, Ivy Compton-Burnett and Anthony Powell. A large number of brilliant minor figures belong to it. It is sanguine, sociable, positive, morally tough, believes in good sense, even in angered good sense and suspects sensibility. These novelists have paid their dues to society or a moral order. They are on the whole generous, though they have their acerbities. They are robust and hard-headed. They know that, in the long run, feeling must submit to intelligence. Masters like Jane Austen and Fielding also command a variety of comic styles. The undertone can be detected in Jane Austen, in the firm correction of Emma's character, or at the end of *Sense and Sensibility*, in which she is commenting on the complacency of a newly-married couple:

> One of the happiest couples in the world. They had in fact nothing to wish for, but the marriage of Colonel Brandon and Marianne – and rather better pasturage for the cows.

Compare this with the comment of a contemporary novelist, Anthony Powell, another aphorist:

> He also lacked that subjective, ruthless love of presiding over other people's difficulties which often makes basically heartless people adept at offering effective consolation.

Or again, sententiousness being natural to this kind of comedy:

Love had received one of those shattering jolts to which it is peculiarly vulnerable from extraneous circumstances.

Exercise – think of those long walks in Jane Austen's novels – and animal spirits, horseplay, good health have their parts especially in the *male* comic writing of the masculine school. And Fielding established it at that period of bluff settlement and confidence in the early eighteenth century. With him a conventional copy-book morality, dignified by epigram, had come in; later it would be made more subtle; it would appease if it did not satisfy. Those harsh, abstract, political seventeenth-century words like God, King or the State have been replaced by something called 'the World' and a very towny World it is. It is inhabited by 'men of the world' and 'women of discretion'. A certain dullness or triteness is relieved by the wild belief in Fortune, in extravagance of character and occasional glimpses of the madhouse. What does 'a man of the world' think? He does not think much, or rather he thinks as others do. He is intelligent, but not intellectual. He is a pragmatist. He respects something called 'the Way'. You follow 'the Way of the World' even when you try to reform or civilize 'the Way'. The title of Congreve's play points to the ruling preoccupation. And what do you *do*? You have adventures, you meet all classes of people, you conduct intrigues. It is a disturbed moral life. You will be observant of character in its *sociable* relationships. You will rarely see a man or woman alone in their privacy. You will be conscious of being an actor on the social scene and you will be given a certain consequential style, a public manner; its object, aided by the new cult of conversation, is to avoid any sight of the void or horror outside that cannot be governed. Hogarth thinks you can get people off gin by putting them on beer; only Swift, the half-colonial exile coming from savage Ireland, has a sense of the unsociable horror, only *he* conceives madness and misanthropy. Ireland had no rising middle class.

But suppose you reject the Way, the belief in habit and behaviour. Suppose you rely on your own mind and not on society's. Suppose you value your privacy, value imagination and sensibility more than common sense. Suppose you live not by clock time, but by the uncertain hours of your feeling. Suppose you live by your imagination or your fantasies. Suppose, with Gray, you think that all you have is your own 'pleasing anxious being' and are, perhaps, liable to fright, illness, egocentricity and sin. Then you will be with Sterne in the disorderly, talkative, fantasticating tradition. I call it the feminine, the affectable. It is wayward. Sterne dissolved the sense of order: he saw that we cannot do as we please but that we have a mind that does exactly as it pleases, moves back and forth in time. The 'I' is not a fixture; it dissolves every minute; its movements are as uncertain as the transparent jelly-fish as it washes back and forth in the current. Not action, but inaction, being washed along by the tide is the principle, astonished that we are a form of life. The Sterne or feminine trait in our comedy is discernible in Peacock, Dickens, bits of Thackeray, a lot of Meredith again, Lear, Carroll, Saki, Firbank, Virginia Woolf; in Joyce, of course, and in Beckett, in all the experiments and slackeners of social forms. I have seen Sterne described by a young critic, Alvarez, as 'cool' and 'poised' even existentialist and he is certainly, after being under a cloud, a reviving figure. For Sterne follows consciousness from sentence to sentence, image to image, wilfully, even in exhibitionist manner. He is receptive to sensation and believes in the mingling of meanings and in the oblique. His feminine strain is not consequential; if he is sententious this is only for the purpose of self-mockery; he may beat a sentimental bosom but his eye is always wandering, leading away his mind. He is a talker and very much a soliloquist. The characters in his novels do occasionally talk to each other, but they are always thinking of something else. They are self-obsessed. They live a good deal in the imagination. The speech they are interested in is the broken syntax of speech-in-the-mind and while that rambles on – not pointlessly, for Sterne is constructing a mosaic – Society, the great gregarious English burden with its call to presentable moral duty, melts away. It is replaced by an immense detail, seen as it might be under a magnifying glass that enlarges and makes everything seem to stand still. This is precisely the effect of trauma or fantasy upon us, for the magnifying glass has shown us at once a real object which is made dream-like by enlargement. Uncle Tony's fuss about the fortifications of Namur is the real fuss of a vegetative old soldier consumed by his memories; but by enlargement it is made to seem a symbol of an extreme modesty. It is to be noted that both Fielding and Sterne tell us when to laugh; but whereas Fielding in his authoritative way, stands back from his novel when he points the finger, Sterne directs from inside it. In fact, he intends that we shall laugh at him when we laugh at his characters. Both novelists digress in order to convey their opinions or the sensible drift of their work; but Fielding's digressions are mainly in his essayish pages, whereas, when Sterne digresses, the whole thing digresses with him. He is writing his novel backwards and very slowly backwards, the surprise lying in discovering what has already happened.

I have called the third strain in our comic tradition mythic or fantastic and this is so adjacent to Sterne's habit that I hesitate over the distinction. But it has to be made because the comedy of Dickens stands a great deal on its own because his genius belongs to a century of violent revolution. We shall find a good deal of Fielding and Sterne in Meredith and well-used. There is a little of Dickens, too, and it is nearly always poor copying and second-hand: the misunderstanding of the comic Dickens has already begun. In the last twenty years or so great stress has been put on the serious socially conscious Dickens, the poetic symbolist, the often melo-dramatic and violent enemy of social injustice; and the effect of this stress has been to make us treat his comedy as comic relief. (The comic writer never quite overcomes the classical reproof that comedy is an inferior form of writing.) I do not believe that Dickens can be split in two in this way: one part reformer, the other part original English humorist. He represents, for me, his century's powerful release of an important psychological force.

In Dickens's novels we are faced by a vast Gothic structure, a mixture of sprawling Parliament and sinister, often blood-and-thunder theatre. After the pragmatism of the eighteenth century, we have a myth-maker. No one believes in the Way of the World any longer. The Town has gone; it is replaced by the City and the swarm. The Town was a gambler and believed in Fortune. Money was not earned, it was won: an example, useful to comedy, was the abduction of heiresses. Debt was a luxury to be aimed at by the Town. In the City-dominated century, where money has to be earned, debt is an agony, a shame, a haunting nightmare that corrodes the next day. The first thing to say about the comedy of Dickens is that London, the city itself, becomes the chief character. Its fogs, its smoke, its noise, its courts, officers, bricks, slums and docks, its gentilities and its crimes, have a quasi-human body. London is seen as the sum of the fantasies and dreams of its inhabitants. It is a city of speeches and voices. The comedy will be in the fusion of the city's dream life and its realities. So will the committal to moral indignation. What we precisely find in this comedy is people's projection of their self-esteem, the attempt to disentangle the self from the ineluctable London situation; they take on the dramatic role of solitary pronouncers. All Dickens's characters, comic or not, issue personal pronouncements that magnify their inner life. Some are crude like Podsnap, others are subtle like Pecksniff or poetic like Micawber, unbelievable like Skimpole, aristocratic casuists like the father of the Marshalsea, glossy like the Veneerings. All are actors; quip or rhetoric is second nature to them. They are strange, even mad, because they speak as if they were the only persons in the world. They live by some private idea or fiction. Mrs Gamp lives in the fiction of the approval of her imaginary friend Mrs Harris. She, like the other important comic characters, is a self-made myth. Our comedy, Dickens seems to say, is not in our relations with others but in our relation with ourselves, our lives, our poetry, our genius; it is even our justification in what Mrs Gamp calls 'this wale', this vale of tears. A character like Pecksniff, may be inferior, as an analysis of hypocrisy, to Tartuffe or Iudushka in Shchedrin's *The Golovlyov Family*, but Dickens does perceive the ghastly fact that the hypocrite is a man who lives by words, destroys other people by words and himself by words that have lost all meaning; yet he is living in his imagination and by pronouncements. Pecksniff says, for example:

My feelings, Mrs Todgers, will not consent to be entirely smothered like the young children in the Tower. They are grown up and the more I press the bolster on them, the more they look round the corner of it.

The more closely one looks at that grotesque pronouncement, the more accurate it seems about the irrepressible nature of adult feeling. And yet, in those words he has drawn on his sense of himself as a walking history or legend.

This passage is one of the high moments of Dickens's comic art. But we must remember that, like Chekhov, he began his comic writing on the lowest rung of the ladder – the level of the humorist's brainwave and the odd 'character' made odder by caricature. But Dickens moved quickly away from the slapstick and arrived at his perception that the histrionic and self-made myth-makers are not simply odd 'characters' but are pretty well the norm in the myth city. Imitators of Dickens, in one respect, find that it is the easiest thing in the world, even today, to go out into a London street and pick up people who behave as funny 'characters' and as that they record them. But Dickens did far more than that: he saw that they were people whose inner life was hanging out, so to speak, on their tongues, outside their persons. To have the so-called Dickens character served up cold, without benefit of his own or the London or English sense of myth, is painful. And I am afraid that when we get to Meredith's *Evan Harrington* we shall have to say that he, like other novelists since, was cynically imitating. This is strange because fantasy is a most important part of Meredith's comedy.

There is one more thing to say about our comic tradition in the novel, before I return to Meredith. It has one serious defect: the lack of tragic irony. It is extraordinary when one thinks of the influence of *Don Quixote* on the English novelists how they have all – with gentlemanly or middle-class optimism, natural I suppose to an expansive culture which was dramatizing its satisfactions – how they all avoided the tragic conclusion. (The death of Hawser Trunnion in *Peregrine Pickle* is sometimes pointed to, but it is no more than touching.) The Russians, especially Dostoevsky, have gone deeper in comic writing than we have. One has to go back to Elizabethan drama – I think of the death of Falstaff – to see the comic cycle completed. The Elizabethans had not yet been caught by bourgeois sociability and cheerfulness.

· · ·

The price Meredith paid for the ease of his emancipation from religious doubt and social pessimism was, that he became far too back-slapping in his hearty paganism and in his easy and too personal flirtation with Darwinism and the idea of the survival of the fittest. He feels his characters must be, in some way, superb. But the positive influence of foreign education upon Meredith as a novelist was to make him look at character in a new way. When D.H. Lawrence (also a self-made foreigner in English life) attacked the traditional attitude to character in the English novel, he was enlarging a ground Meredith had already opened; there is a good deal of Meredith in Lawrence whether that influence was conscious or was simply in the air at the time. It is found in Lawrence's lyricism, but above all in the sardonic and reiterated stress on a single essence in all his characters.

Now Meredith has few 'characters' in the traditional sense, except in *Evan Harrington* and in one or two other places where he was imitating Dickens. (One original is Skepsey, the clerk and servant and fanatical boxer in *One of Our Conquerors*.) Both Meredith's belief in what he called Idea in comedy, and the fact that he was before everything a poet, made him see people as poetic or intellectual statements. They are essences or forces. Richard Feverel is Youth. Patterne is the Egoist. Victor Radnor is Power. But they are not allegorical; they are not humours. They have a living vehemence. They are psychological patterns. They are saturated in Meredith; their engine is his. They are driven along by him, by his beliefs, his mannerisms, his epigrams, his views about sentimentality, nature, blood and soul. They are individualities before they are persons. They are a species grafted on to him. They cannot escape him, just as – after the mining stories and *Sons and Lovers* – no one escapes Lawrence. They haven't a chance in *The Prussian Officer*, in *St Mawr* or *The Fox*. Of course Lawrence's intrusive person is more forceful and vital, more *inside*, than Meredith's. Meredith saw people from the outside; but Lawrence's incantations are as intrusive as Meredith's oratorical parades before the reader.

To the extent that he was freed of traditional character Meredith replaced it by another interest – psychological enquiry. He half-regretted this. He understood that he was sensitive to what he called 'the morbidities'. He wrote to a publisher:

Much of my strength lies in painting morbid emotion and exceptional positions ... My love is for epical subjects – not for cobwebs in a putrid corner, though I know the fascination of unravelling them.

The opposed directions of his talent, torn between epic and morbidity, Romance and anti-Romance, the poetic and the ironic, set up a central conflict. The device he used was to push forward his glittering and sceptical person. Several critics in the twenties – the astute young Mr Priestley was one – saw in Meredith a link with contemporary novelists, Lawrence and especially Virginia Woolf and E.M. Forster: with the personal voice, the pursuit of the mind's dramas of association, the feeling for image, and the emancipation from Mr Bennett and Mrs Brown. By the twenties the patronizing of Meredith had already begun, but the link is there. The personal conversational voice is clearly the mark of Meredith's immediate successors. It is evident in *The Longest Journey* and in

The Waves. And it is implicit in the doctrine of the supreme value of personal relationships and particularly in the Bloomsbury belief in extravagantly rational detachment.

By a paradox E.M. Forster's admirable account of Meredith's mastery of plot and contrivance shows (and perhaps unintentionally) the real link between Meredith and his successors in the next generation; but for the working writer, painfully learning to use tools that are new to him, these links are in technique, in the study of how things are done. Except for the reference to 'faking' which is gratuitous, for alas, all the most important novelists have faked somewhere or other, Mr Forster's remarks on Meredith as a technician are not only excellent in themselves, but describe certain things common to his own generation. Mr Forster says:

> A Meredithian plot is not a temple to the tragic or even to the Comic Muse, but rather resembles a series of kiosks most artfully placed among the wooded slopes which his people reached by their own impetus and from which they emerge with altered aspect. Incident springs out of character and alters that character. People and events are closely connected, and he does it by the means of these contrivances. They are often delightful, sometimes touching, always unexpected.

'Not a temple, but a series of kiosks' – how well that describes the Meredithian scene and how the art of moving from kiosk to kiosk, under personal impetus, caught on in the next generation!

But whether one thinks of Meredith as a Sultan among his kiosks or as a brilliant craftsman working in mosaic, it is obvious that he was unlucky in the commercial demands made upon the novelist in the nineteenth century. The novelist depended economically on serialization and on the demand for three volumes. All the Victorians padded outrageously, as Gissing said, at the rate of 4,000 words a day. This was no difficulty for the recklessly inventive. You simply sprawled as the new disorderly Victorian cities sprawled. But sprawling is dangerous to the novelist who is first a poet and then a wit. Six hundred pages of poetry and wit, in which every line and image is intense, in which there is an infinitude of small, separate visions, choke the mind and weary the eye.

To read some stretches of Meredith's prose is like living on a continuous diet of lobster and champagne: lobster done in every known sauce and champagne only too knowingly addressed as the Veuve. And yet the difficulties of his style have surely been exaggerated. Goodness knows, the modern reader has been brought up on difficult prose. He has been used to cracking images in his teeth like nuts. The later James and Proust are difficult writers. After Joyce, after the difficult poets, after all the unexplained, cinematic transitions of visual picture in the mind, surely Meredith's style ought to be easy. It is simply a matter of getting used to it. There *is* a difference between Meredith's difficulty and the kind we are used to. He is concerned with the actions of his characters or their description; he wishes to push forward; but cannot resist striking an attitude or going off at a tangent, so that in fact his narrative often stands still. He is like a walker, continually stopping to enthuse instead of getting on. And there are times when excess of brain turns him to vulgarity and when his prose scatters and disconnects what should be, and is intended to be, a harmonious flow.

. . .

As an avowed comedian in terms of poetic romance, Meredith thought of images, whether lyrical or comic, as promoters of dramatic movement. They are meant to give energy. The mind is made to gave a leap into fantasy and, with it, the scene is agitated. Meredith's prose was the imagination's revolt against the public prose of the main stream of novelists – the style that derived from what Scott called Big Bow Wow. It stands for the poet's impulse to work from inside. The image is the natural mode of consciousness; the image is meant, again and again, to catch a consciousness, as it passes from one feeling or experience to another. It is either a dramatic device or a form of gaiety or play. Meredith is rarely clumsy when he is, so to say, 'imaging out' young love and catching its changes. Landscape and seascape are used to describe aspects of love or other emotions. There is an important moment in the love duel between Willoughby Patterne and Clara Middleton when Clara is suddenly frightened just for a split second that Willoughby is going to give her the moral blackmailer's kiss. The moment is described in these words:

'You are cold, my love? You shivered.'
    'I am not cold,' said Clara. 'Someone, I suppose, was walking over my grave.'

The gulf of a caress hove in view like an enormous billow hollowing under the curled ridge.

She stooped to pick a buttercup; the monster swept by.

One must see these images in their context and then they no longer seem too large, outlandish or prolonged. They perfectly evoke and activate a feeling which is passing, brief but momentous. He is recording one of those tremors of association that the sensibility of a poet will infallibly hit upon.

Meredith is indeed a prose Browning and all the better for it. Take these lines from the *Flight of the Duchess*:

And what was the pitch of his mother's yellowness,
How she turned as a shark to snap the spare-rib
Clean off, sailors say, from a pearl-diving Carib,
When she heard, what she called the flight of the feloness

Compare that with Willoughby Patterne forced to give up Clara in *The Egoist*:

Laocoon of his own serpents, he struggled to a certain magnificence of attitude in the muscular net of constrictions he flung around himself. Clara must be given up. Oh bright Abominable! She must be given up: but not to one whose touch of her would be darts in the blood of the yielder, snakes in his bed; she must be given up to an extinguisher.

High stuff and not as concrete as Browning, but you *are* made to feel the bodily, physical shape of the feeling. It is in the nerves and muscles. The three obscure writers of the nineteenth century, Carlyle, Browning and Meredith, have the visual wit of those who stuck gargoyles and heraldic beasts on pseudo-medieval buildings, because the century's imaginative life was histrionic and loved the grotesque. The scene has to be itself and yet contain the imagination's energy. And what Browning wrote to Ruskin, in his defence of *his* own style, is pure Meredith:

You would have me paint it all plain out, which can't be; but by various artifices I try to make shifts with touches and bits of outline which succeed if they bear the conception from me to you. You ought, I think, to keep pace with the thought, tripping from ledge to ledge of my 'glaciers' as you call them, not poking your alpenstock into holes.

But, except in his lyrical passages, Meredith is perhaps a collector of styles rather than an innovator and he was not a success when, under the political influence of Carlyle, he also took over patches of his prose. The following is Carlyle who sees the image as action:

Let but Teufelsdröckh open his mouth, Heaschrecke's also unpuckered itself into a free doorway, besides his being all eye and ear, so that nothing might be lost and then, at every pause in the harangue, he gurgled out his pursy chuckle of a cough-laugh (for the machinery of laughter took some time to get in motion, and seemed crank or slack), or else his twanging nasal, Bravo! *Das glaub'ich.*

This is good Carlyle, and good Wyndham Lewis, too, twentyish stuff. But the effect of too much Carlyle was to make Meredith vulgar. An affecting scene between lover and mistress in *One of Our Conquerors* ends happily but in tears and Meredith comes galumphing in with this comment:

We cry to Women: Land ho! A land of palms after storms at sea, and at once they inundate us with a deluge of eye-water.

And Nataly, the weeping lady, is made to apologize to her lover:

I am like . . . the tearful woman whose professional apparatus was her soft heart and a cake of soap.

Instead of saying 'to steal a glance', he will call this 'the petty larceny of the optics'. This is not energizing Teuton but facetious English gentility. (On the other hand to describe parsons as 'the turncocks of one water company' is good.) Meredith writes in *The Amazing Marriage* – a passage that upset Edmund Gosse [the scene is a gambling table]:

He compared the creatures dabbling over the board to summer flies on butchers' meat, periodically scared by a cloth. More in the abstract they were snatching at a snap-dragon bowl.

It struck him that the gamblers had thronged in an invitation to drink the round of seed time and harvest at one gulp. Again they were desperate gleaners, hopping, skipping, bleeding, amid a whizz of scythe blades, for small wisps of booty. Nor was it long before the presidency of an ancient hoary Goat-Satan might be perceived, with skew-eyes, nursing a hoof on a tree.

Four attempts to find a metaphor for gambling when one alone is required: one for the commentator and a clumsy one at that. And they are all – unless in the mind of a farmer – inapt. Meredith has not only intruded personally, but his mind is not made up. It is all hit or miss. If images are meant to activate, too many images brawl. This passage stands still. We can cut out the butchers' meat and the snap-dragon bowl at once; they collide with the gleaning. The only good image in the passage is the skew-eye of the goat. How could Meredith, who took great care with his style, pass a paragraph like that?

The bother in those disastrous passages is that the mind is the mind of Meredith the artist showman, and that the final impression is one of great messy orchestral clash, ending in anti-climax. In *One of Our Conquerors*, a late novel in which one would have thought he would have learned his lesson, Meredith sets out on two or three panoramic scenes: the sight of London Bridge at the morning rush; and later, the sight of the crowd moving home westward at the end of the day. Both pieces are a hopeless mixture of the poetic and grotesque because they are not really made to mix. The workers have stopped work:

No longer mere concurrent atoms of the furnace of business (from coal dust to sparks rushing, as it were, on respiratory blasts of an enormous engine's centripetal energy) their step is leisurely to meet the rosy Dinner which is ever at see-saw with the God of light in his fall.

This sounds like, 'Sun down; Dinner up'. As for the sunset – and all Victorian writers and painters have a compulsion to describe sunsets – Meredith thinks of it in this way:

It is a Rape of the Sabines overhead from all quarters, either one of the winds brawnily larcenous; and London, smoking royally to the open skies, builds images of a dusty fray for possession of the portly dames. There is immensity, swinging motion, collision, dusky richness of colouring, to the sight; and to the mind idea.

Now this is not simply bad writing: it is ambitious bad writing. It is an outburst, for the rest of the novel is done in a plainish style. But if one reads this whole chapter called 'The London Walk Westward' one sees that Meredith did have a conscious, intelligent intention. He is staging London. He imagines a literary Rajah looking at the London scene with an Oriental eye who has the idea that Londoners march eastward for fuel and westward for food. The scene is a piece of theatre. He is explicit about this.

According to the Stage directions [he writes] the Rajah and His Minister *Enter a Gin Palace*. It is to witness a service that they have learned to appreciate as Anglicanly religious.

And there we have the key to this clumsy cleverness. Where have we read such things before? Meredith has taken them from the burlesque in Fielding. In Fielding it has dramatic effect. The artifice is clear. A classical mind controls it. In Meredith, German romantic grotesque has muddled it, and the cleverer he is the worse the muddle. The sunset hour may very well be London's sentimental hour, in which fancies are muddled; the stream of consciousness is probably pretty thick with stuff like this at that time of day; but for that reason it calls for a precise or selective describer.

There is no objection to Meredith putting his scenes on the stage. The tradition of Fielding, so strongly influenced by the theatre, is important to English comedy. One kind of comedy depends on seizing an incident or scene, setting it apart or aslant from its context – the fight between the women in the churchyard in *Tom Jones*, the rituals of the debtors in the Marshalsea scenes in *Little Dorrit*. The writer of comedy has to shape and form his scenes. Meredith is simply unsuccessful in staging crowds; he is effective in staging individual people.

The fact is that Meredith, the tailor and disciple of Teufelsdröckh, moves towards fantasy and abstraction the better to make his psychological point. The example of Sir Willoughby Patterne's leg shows him at work. There are two pages of it and it establishes Sir Willoughby's person, his character, and their effect on other people. For Meredith our ambience and what we suggest to the fancies of others is part of ourselves: we exist as histories, as poems in the minds of others:

> The leg of the born cavalier is before you: and obscure it as you will, dress it degenerately, there it is for the ladies who have eyes. You *see* it: or, you see *he* has it. Miss Isabel and Miss Eleanour disputed the incidence of the emphasis, but surely, though a slight difference of meaning may be heard, either will do: many, with a good show of reason, throw the accent on leg . . . Mrs Mountstuart signified that the leg is to be seen because it is a burning leg. There it is and it will shine through. He has the leg of Rochester, Buckingham, Dorset, Suckling; the leg that smiles, that winks, is obsequious to you, yet perforce of beauty self satisfied; that twinkles to a tender midway between imperiousness and seductiveness, audacity and discretion; between 'you shall worship *me*' and 'I am *devoted* to you' is your lord and slave alternatively. It is a leg of ebb and flow and high tide ripples.

(In that sentence we see Meredith as usual swapping into the wrong image. But he rescues himself and comes to the decisive point):

> Such a leg, when it has done with pretending to retire, will walk straight into hearts of women. Nothing so fatal to them.

Unmistakably, that leg is a sexual symbol. Meredith intends that. Patterne is as male, apparently, as Darcy was. The leg is not for the drawing-room alone. But Meredith quickly retreats from the unmannerly idea.

> A simple seeming word of this import is the triumph of the spiritual and where it passes for coin of value, the society has reached a high refinement: Arcadian by the aesthetic route.

There you have the late-Victorian pretender, rising above his insinuation.

There is a surprising passage of self-criticism in *Beauchamp's Career*, in the scene in which Beauchamp is explaining the difference between the Conservative and Liberal parties to Miss Halkett. It goes:

[Liberalism] stakes too much on the chance of gain. It is uncomfortably seated on half a dozen horses; and it has fed them, too, on varieties of corn.

Miss Halkett replies:

I know you wouldn't talk down to me but the use of imagery makes me feel that I am addressed as a primitive intelligence.

Beauchamp replies:

That's the fault of my trying at condensation, as the hieroglyphists put an animal for a paragraph. I am incorrigible you see.

Meredith *is* incorrigible and if he wearies one it is because he is the wit who always wins. Of course Beauchamp is not Meredith, but the important characters in Meredith are always extremists because they have to carry this thing he called Idea. He has another comment in *Diana of the Crossways* about Diana's writing, which reverts to the Arcadian argument I quoted just now. It obviously contains glances at his own prose. Diana had been hurt, therefore she plumped for metaphor. He writes in her defence and his own:

Metaphors were her refuge. Metaphorically she would allow her mind to distinguish the struggle she was undergoing, sinking under it. The banished of Eden had to put on metaphors, and the common use of them has helped largely to civilize us – the sluggish of intellect detest them, but our civilization is not much indebted to that major faction.

I have spoken at length about the excesses in Meredith's prose and have said that they show a mind that tends to disperse its gifts and to have difficulty in finding a common ground. But he does find it once he has settled in to his work, either in the well-known lyrical interludes – the river scene and storm scenes in *Richard Feverel* – and in his mastery of ironic narrative and commentary where his psychological curiosity subdues the actor. Then his inventiveness as a poet brings gaiety to a prose which is even more an essayist's than the prose of a novelist. And it is not so far from the agitated prose of those modern writers who seem to have sensed that the prose of the future will be heard and seen, and perhaps never read.

FRENCH MASTERS

Stendhal

An Early Outsider

Stendhal was one of those gamblers for whom the wheel of Fortune turned too late. Ignored by almost everyone except Mérimée and Balzac who considered that *La Chartreuse de Parme* was the most important French novel of their time, he declared, without a trace of self-pity, indeed confident in his blistering vanity, that the wheel would turn 100 years after his death. In fact in forty years the great egotist was justified by Zola. For Zola he was: 'a man composed of soul alone . . . One always feels him there, coldly attentive to the working of his machine. Each of his characters is a psychologist's experiment which he ventures to try on any man.' By the beginning of this century Henri Beyle – the figure hidden secretively behind more than 200 pseudonyms who had passed his life as a doubtfully combatant Napoleonic soldier in Italy and Russia, as a travelling and loitering journalist and plagiarizing high-class hack, as a dilettante, petty Consul, ugly and coarse in drawing-rooms, as a misfiring, theorizing lover and a novelist poor in invention who left his great novels abruptly unfinished – had become a cosmopolitan cult.

One important reason for this is that he knew the lasting force of that clear, plain, dry and caustic prose style: and knew that something curt and preposterous in one's style as a person will have its hour. At certain periods of crises in history and manners an intelligent man is forced to see that a change of style is being born. As a youth growing up in the French Revolution and with youth's need of a persona, he found himself divided between the eighteenth-century idea of 'the man of the world' and the first intimations of Romantic energy. One had to construct a new self. As an aspiring writer he was drawn to the art of his time: stage comedy – but he soon saw that this had become impossible. Stage comedy depended on a stable class system, fixed social values: these had gone with the Revolution and the post-Napoleonic world. He also saw that the novel was the new form to which the audience would respond but that it would impose a crude, impersonal omniscience and would be about 'other people' grouped in their acceptable categories: the novelist is drowned and effaced in other people, whereas he, Stendhal, secretive, addicted to masks and self-defence, was obsessed by his own intelligent private life, his need to begin constructing a Machiavellian and impervious self from the ground upwards. The egotist lay awake at night, tortured by the question: 'Who am I?' Even more important: 'What shall I make myself? What is my role? What are the correct tactics?' It is easy to understand why he is the precursor of Romanticism in *La Chartreuse de Parme* and why in *Le Rouge et le Noir* Julien Sorel foreshadows the large population of outsiders and the disaffected formed by the revolutions, wars, social crises, prisons and police states that have revived something of the climate and complacencies of the Napoleonic period. In a recent biography Joanna Richardson says that he was 'a provincial born outside of the Establishment, enjoying none of the privileges of birth, wealth or education. His sense of inequality and grievance led him bitterly to make amends. He despised authority, he professed to scorn the nobility and yet – like Julien Sorel – he wanted to conquer the nobility. He ridiculed the dignitaries of the Tuileries, and yet, with monotonous persistence, he tried to ensure himself a barony . . . all his life he was conscious of status.' Yet, of course, the desire to be either Sorel or Fabrice was a deeply imaginative conspiracy that sailed far beyond social or political considerations. The egotist's pursuit of personal happiness – *la chasse du bonheur* – led him to the Romantic idealization of solitude and reverie, the brief sublime moment.

The biographer of Stendhal is in competition with a perpetual autobiography – Stendhal has no other subject, in his novels, his letters, his exhaustive *Journal*, in the *Souvenirs d'Egotisme* and *La Vie de Henri Brulard.* He saw himself as a conspiracy. He was given to minute research into the moral history of his attitudes, so the biographer is left chiefly with the problem of deciding where, if ever, the candour ceased to be fantasy or petulance, where calculation in love was coxcombry, and where they were signs of a fatally split nature. There is no doubt that his celebrated hatred of his father and his sensual passion for his mother, who died when he was seven, reiterated the old Oedipus story, but it was political as well. Stendhal despised his father for being a bourgeois lawyer and a supporter of the Bourbons; very early the boy convinced himself that he was a putative aristocrat and yet at the same time a child of the French Revolution. He also despised his father for being a shrewd Dauphinois and a speculator in property, despised him even more for being unsuccessful in this, and resented the loss of a good deal of his inheritance. Stendhal was even jealous of his widowed father's grief, and went on to imagine, that on the mother's side, the family were of Italian origin and that they combined passionate Italian traits with the pride he oddly loved to call *espagnolisme*. Here, rather than in social snobbery, was the root of his aristocratic idea: he felt he belonged to the élite of another age and another country. Yet his truculence covered deep timidity. His temperament was lazy, but he read and worked like a diligent bourgeois. Only those who work, he said, were equipped for the true end of living – the study of the arts and pursuit of pleasure.

For one who thought himself born into the wrong class, Stendhal was lucky in 'the bastard', 'the Jesuit' (his father) who gave him a decent allowance and sent him to Paris to study. He was lucky also in family friends – the Darus, who took the conceited youth into their house. He refused to go to the Ecole Polytechnique, and they got him a job in the Ministry of War. Stendhal thrived on influence. In a few months, at the age of seventeen, he was commissioned an officer in Napoleon's reserve army in Italy. Italy transfigured him. Italy was freedom; hearing opera for the first time – 'the Scala transformed me'. A lifelong dislike of France – indeed, the pretence that he was not really French – began. He fell in love with Angela Pietragrua, a married woman – older than himself – whom he was too timid to approach; she fulfilled his need for the remote goddess. There were untouched remote goddesses to follow; there was also syphilis, caught in the brothels of Milan, which affected his health for the rest of his life. The only woman he was really devoted to for many years was one of his sisters, and in his letters to her a tutorial figure appears and one begins to see that he is constructing his own system of self-education and behaviour. The outsider is studying and acting out a role, creating a self from scratch; it is defiant, touching and a good deal absurd. In his love affairs – he was determined on seduction – the tactics, the search for a style, the analysis of his amorous campaigns have the fidgetiness of artificial comedy; he spent half of his youth putting obstacles in his own way, as Miss Richardson says. In the pursuit of these passions, he believed in the *coup de foudre*: when it occurred, he was paralysed and in tears; if he was encouraged, he fell into long storms of melancholy; if he was victorious, boredom arrived sooner or later, generally sooner. The perpetual cry of this adolescent, whether he is with Napoleon's army in Germany or Russia, whether he is back in Italy, is that he is bored to death. He is one of those who exhaust an experience before the experience occurs – the Romantic malady that becomes a pose and second nature. But if he did not succeed in creating an impenetrable new self and in becoming the superior man of sensibility, he had fitted himself to become a master of comedy in which scornful epigram and abrupt observation go off like rifle shots and leave the dry smell of gunpowder. Each sentence of his plain prose is a separate shock.

The later Romantics were too young for the Napoleonic glory, but in his harsh, sardonic way Stendhal had known it on the battlefield, though not as a fighting officer. From Smolensk he wrote in 1812, when he was twenty-nine:

> How man changes! My former thirst for seeing things is completely quenched, after seeing Milan and Italy, everything repels me by its coarseness . . . In this ocean of barbarity, there isn't a single sound that replies to my soul.

He was thinking of the music of Cimarosa and his love for Angela Pietragrua. When he watched Moscow burning, he had a toothache and read a few lines of *Virginie*, which revived him morally. He had taken the manuscript of his unfinished *Histoire de la Peinture en Italie* with him, read Mme du Deffand, pillaged a volume of Voltaire, whom he detested, and tried to think of the 'score of comedies' he would write 'between the ages of thirty-four and fifty-four' if only his father would die and leave him some money. He shows off to his correspondents, and rescues an early mistress who had married a Russian (she is very 'chilly'), but when the great fire starts he seems to keep his head and to display sang-froid – or so people reported. He was unconsciously collecting the material for the superb Waterloo chapter in

La Chartreuse de Parme, and one catches its accent. (He was not at Waterloo.) Of the beginning of the retreat he wrote in his diary, as one seeing the scene *staged* for his benefit:

> We broke through the lines, arguing with some of the King of Naples' carters. I later noticed that we were following the Tverskoï, or Tver Street. We left the city, illuminated by the finest fire in the world, which formed an immense pyramid which, like the prayers of the faithful, had its base on earth and its apex in heaven. [Very much like Stendhal's own nature.] The moon appeared above this atmosphere of flame and smoke. It was an imposing sight, but it would have been necessary to be alone or else surrounded by intelligent people in order to enjoy it. What has spoiled the Russian campaign for me is to have taken part in it with people who would have belittled the Colosseum or the Bay of Naples.

An aesthete's comment? Not entirely. It is an introspection we shall see transmuted when we find him examining the illusion of Napoleonic glory. Even before the grand scene the Stendhalian hero is a psychologist. History dished this outsider. He was the victim, he said, of the mediocrity that characterizes an age of transition.

There have been two revivals of interest in Stendhal in this century. In the twenties it was led by Francophiles who used it as a modish attack on the nineteenth century for its denigration of the eighteenth. Stendhal was useful, too, as a distant founder of the parricides' club which thrived after the 1914 war.

The hardness of his ego and his impudence were our admirations; and the 'enclosing reverie' no more than a charming Romantic nostalgia. Stendhal's curt, disabused and iconoclastic manner made the reader of Gide and Proust feel at home. But this movement fizzled out, though it persisted among Beylistes who had a delightful time taping Stendhal's mystifications, footnotes, vanishing tricks, love affairs and changes of address. In the thirties left-wingers and Catholics were frosty about Stendhal's politics and withering about his atheism: he gleamed like an arid Sahara. When the wheel is turned, in a second revival, we could feel ourselves to be in something like a Stendhalian situation. Existentialists found the self-inventing man sympathetic; practitioners of *le nouveau roman* looked to the novel without a centre.

In his *Stendhal: Notes on a Novelist*, Mr Robert Adams says:

Perhaps the most enchanting yet terrifying thing about the heroes of Stendhal is the sense that they define their own beings only provisionally and temporarily, in conflicts of thought and action, in negations; without enemies, they are almost without natures and wither away, like Fabrice, when deprived of danger. I think it is this vision of human nature which allies the novels of Stendhal with the great hollow, reverberant structures of Joyce, and the legerdemain card-houses of Gide; the fact that all systems of thought and feeling are tangential to the nature of their heroes is linked to the circumstances that their central natures are themselves a dark and hollow mystery. From this aspect there is no core or centre to the Stendhal fiction, as there is none to the fiction of Joyce: the more little anagrams and puzzles of correspondence one solves, the less one finds actually being asserted. What the novel means is its shape, its surface, its structure; the arcana of society, like those of thought, are simply emptiness which returns to the surface of light and the solitude of the cynical individual.

Another critic, Victor Brombert, writes in *Stendhal: Fiction and the Themes of Freedom*, that the self-inventing man is a lifelong pursuer of freedom:

Neither is it by coincidence that the greatest ecstasies of life take place behind austere and quasi-monastic walls. Ultimately it is freedom from all worldly ambitions, an almost spiritual elation, that Julien Sorel and Fabrice del Donga achieve . . . Freedom remains a prisoner's dream, and man's vocation is solitude.

This conclusion certainly fits with Stendhal's view that our greatest happiness is in reverie. But it is important here to recall what he wrote about the purpose of *Lucien Leuwen:* it was to be 'exact chemistry: I describe with exactitude what others indicate with a vague and eloquent phrase'. The poetry is to be in the chemistry. Love is a consciously produced effervescence; it produces its transcendant, chemical moment of '*bonheur*'; then the beautiful experiment vanishes. One returns to contemplation until the next 'moment'. And it strikes one, especially when he abruptly creates his unbelievable and preposterous scenes – in this novel the affair of a faked childbirth before witnesses – that his model for the novel was opera, the failure to invent the plausible, or perhaps a success in rising above it.

Yet a political novel like *Lucien Leuwen* is saturated in the social material it offers. It is rich in people who have been 'placed' as astutely as any in Balzac, but with more militancy. The unpopular garrison at Nancy is superbly done, for the minor characters have their own malicious concern for style and role also. They distress the hero. There are portraits of people who are drying up in futile class hatred. Stendhal is as cool – perhaps in his coolness lies the contemporary appeal – about the crude new middle class: he is exact but without the heavy hatred that is sometimes too black and white in Balzac. The following portrait of Mlle Sylvanie, the shopkeeper's daughter, is full yet compressed, poetic yet also ironically of this world. Here the chemistry is indeed exact:

A statue of June, copied from the antique by a modern artist; both subtlety and simplicity are lacking; the lines are massive, but it is a Germanic freshness. Big hands, big feet, very regular features and plenty of coyness, all of which conceals a too obvious pride. And these people are put off by the pride of ladies in good Society! Lucien was particularly struck by her backward tosses of the head, which were full of vulgar nobility, and were evidently meant to recall the dowry of a hundred thousand crowns.

His young women have tenderness and verve: their capacity for growing into their passions is extraordinary. He is always beginning again with his characters for they too are 'making themselves'. And abruptly too. This abruptness is excellent in his portraits of young men; here no novelist in any literature or period has surpassed him, not even Tolstoy. No one has so defined and botanized the fervour, uncertainty, conceit, timidity and single-mindedness of young men, their dash, their shames, their calculation for tactics and gesture. They shed self after self and a date is put to their manners. Stendhal's sense of human beings living now yet transfixed, for an affecting moment, by their future, gives the doctrine of self-invention an ironical perspective which is not often noticeable in its practitioners today.

Poor Relations

The small house on the cliff of Passy hanging like a cage between an upper and lower street, so that by a trick of relativity, the top floor of the Rue Berton is the ground floor of the Rue Raynouard, has often been taken as a symbol of the life of Balzac. The custodian of the house – now a Balzac museum with the novelist's eternal coffee-pot, his dictionary of universal knowledge and with his appalling proof sheets framed on the wall – shows one the trap-door by which Balzac escaped to the lower floor in the Rue Berton. Down it the fat breathless novelist of forty-one went stumbling and blurting, like his own prose, to the Seine. Two houses in one, a life with two front doors, dream and reality; the novelist, naïve and yet shrewd, not troubling to distinguish between one and the other. Symbol of Balzac's life, the house is a symbol of the frontier life, the trap-door life of the great artists, who have always lived between two worlds. There Balzac wrote his letters to Madame Hanska in Poland, the almost too comprehensive, explanatory and eloquent letters of a famous and experienced writer who has the art, indeed the habit of self-projection at his finger-tips; there, when the letters were posted, he went to bed with the docile housekeeper who was finally to turn round and blackmail him, and so provide him with the horrifying last chapters of *Le Cousin Pons*. At this house in the worst year of his life, the least blessed with that calm which is – quite erroneously – supposed to be essential to the novelist, Balzac wrote this book and *La Cousine Bette*, respectively the best constructed and the most fluent and subtle of his novels.

A new life of Balzac was published in Paris in 1944. It is called simply *Vie de Balzac* and is by André Billy. This biography contains nothing new, but it gathers all the immense biographical material in a couple of volumes. Its detail is as lively and exhaustive as a Balzac novel; the manner is warm but sceptical, thorough but not dry. Very rightly, M Billy looks twice and three times at everything Balzac said about his life, for he is dealing with the hallucinations of the most extraordinary egotist in the history of literature. One can imagine a less diffuse biography; one in which the picture of his time played a greater part and where every detail of a chaotic Bohemian career was not played up to the same pitch. But given the gluttony of Balzac's egotism and the fertility of his comedy, one is not inclined to complain.

Like the tones of bronze and antiques – Balzac estimated the weight and value of himself with the care of an auctioneer's valuer – with which he darkened the house he finally took for Madame Hanska when he had got his hands on some of her fortune, the novels of Balzac weigh upon the memory. The reader is exhausted as the novelist by the sheer weight of collection. One is tempted to see him as the stolid bulldozer of documentation, the quarrying and expatiating realist, sharpening his tools on some hard view of his own time. He seems to be stuck in his task. Yet this impression is a false one, as we find whenever we open a novel of his again. Balzac is certainly the novelist who most completely exemplifies the 'our time' novelist, but not by his judgements on society. He simply *is* his time. He is identified with it, by all the greedy innocence of genius. The society of rich peasants brought to power by revolution and dictatorship, pushing into business and speculation, buying up houses and antiques, founding families, grabbing at money and pleasure, haunted by their tradition of parsimony and hard work, and with the peasant's black and white ideas about everything, and above all their weakness for fixed ideas, is Balzac himself. He shares their illusions. Like them he was humble when he was poor, arrogant when he was rich. As with them, his extravagance was one side of the coin; on the other was the face of the peasant miser. The cynic lived in a world of romantic optimism. We see the dramatic phase of a century's illusions, before they have been assimilated and trodden down into the familiar hypocrisies. To us Balzac's preoccupation with money appears first to be the searching, scientific and prosaic interest of the documentary artist. On the contrary, for him money was romantic; it was hope and ideal. It was despair and evil. It was not the dreary background, but the animating and theatrical spirit.

Balzac learned about money, as M Billy says, at his printing works in the Rue du Marais. He expected to find that fallen aristocrat, the goddess Fortune of the eighteenth century; instead he found that in the nineteenth century the goddess had become a bourgeois bookkeeper. His laundry bills, his tailor's bills, his jeweller's bills were mixed with the printing accounts. The imagination of the businessman is always governable; Balzac's was not. Financially speaking, Balzac was out of date. Like his father, who also was willing to work hard enough, he sought for Fortune not for Profit; far from being an example of Balzac's realism, his attitude to money is really the earliest example of his Romantic spirit. Balzac's attitude to money was that of a man who did not understand money, who could not keep it in his hands, the plagued spendthrift and natural bankrupt. His promissory notes were a kind of poetry in his early years; later on they became articles of moral indignation; in the end – to quote M Billy's delightful euphemism, he lost all '*pudeur morale*'. The creation of debts began as exuberance; it became an appetite, one of those dominant passions which he thought occurred in all natures, but which really occur only among the most monstrous egotist. Madame Hanska's fortune did not calm him. He went on buying here and there, incurring more debts, scheming without check. And the last people he thought of paying were his wretched relations and especially his mother. To her, he behaved with the hypocrisy and meanness of a miser and the worse he treated her the more he attacked her.

At this point it is interesting to compare Balzac with Scott, whom he admired and consciously imitated. Madame Hanska's estate in Poland was for many years his visionary Abbotsford; the passion for antiques, the debts, and the crushing labour, the days and nights of writing without sleep, were Abbotsford too. Balzac saw himself as an aristocrat; Scott saw himself as a laird: they are by no means the first or last writers to provide themselves with distinguished ancestors. He went to the length of travelling to Vienna as a Marquis, with coronets on his luggage; it was ruinous, he discovered, in tips. But the honourable Scott was broken by his debts; they drove him to work as a duty; they wore out his imagination. Balzac, on the contrary, was certainly not ruined as a writer by his debts. His debts were a natural expression of a voracious imagination. One may doubt whether any of his mistresses moved his inspiration – though clearly their maternal sympathy was necessary – but one can be certain that Balzac's imagination was ignited by the romance of purchase, by the mere sensual possession of things. The moving impulse in his life was, as he said, the discovery of the 'material of civilization', the literal materials; and although he considered this a scientific discovery, it was really a mysticism of things. Every object he bought, from the famous walking-stick to the museum pieces, represented an act of self-intoxication that released the capacity – so vital to the creative artist – to become unreal.

It is easy, as M Billy says, a hundred years after, to blame Madame Hanska for delaying her marriage with Balzac and for adding the afflictions of reluctance and jealousy to his life of appalling labour, but obviously he was possessed by a kind of madness, and he would have stripped her of all her property. One understands her hesitation after reading his later and maniacal letters about money and things.

Je suis sûr qu'au poids il y aura, dans notre maison, trois mille kilogrammes de cuivres et bronzes dorés. C'est effrayant, le bronze! Cette maison est, comme je te le disais, une mine de cuivre doré, car mon ébéniste me disait qu'il y en a mille kilogrammes. A huit francs le kilo, à vendre aux chaudronniers, c'est trente-deux mille francs de valeur réelle. Juge de la valeur, en y ajoutant le valeur d'art.

Ruinous. There was no '*valeur d'art*'. His brain gave way under the strain of his schemes and combinations. Yet, *Le Cousin Pons* and *La Cousine Bette* were written in that year; and when Pons makes the fortune of his persecutors with his collection of antiques which they had despised, one sees Balzac avenging himself for the complaints of his mistress. No; he was not weighed down by debts, in the sense of having his talent ruined by them. His extravagances floated him on the vital stream of unreality. He was the Micawber for whom things were only too continously 'turning up', a Micawber who worked. Balzac and Micawber are, it is interesting to note, contemporary financiers of the period.

The ox-like groans, the animal straining and lamentation of Balzac, his boasting, his bosom-beating letters to women like Madame Carraud before whom he parades in the role of the indomitable martyr of circumstance, have created an imaginary Balzac. One sees – his own phrase – 'the galley slave of fame'. A rather different impression was formed by his contemporaries. Once he had put his pen down he was childishly gay:

Naïveté, puérilité, bonté, ces trois mots reviennent sous la plume de tous les contemporains. Le portrait de Balzac que nous a laissé le poète des Méditations se trouve confirmé en tous points par celui qu'a tracé George Sand: puéril et puissant, toujours envieux d'un bibelot et jamais jaloux d'une gloire, sincère jusqu'à la modestie, vantard jusqu'à la hâblerie, confiant en lui-même et dans les autres, très expansif, très bon et très fou, avec un sanctuaire de raison intérieure où il rentrait pour tout dominer dans son oeuvre, cynique dans la chasteté, ivre en buvant de l'eau, intempérant de travail et sobre d'autres passions, positif et romanesque avec un égal excès, crédule et sceptique, plein de contrastes et de mystères . . .

Some indeed found him grubby, ill-kempt and uncouth. Hans Andersen hardly recognized the dandy of the evening party in the touselled Bohemian of the following day. There was a Rue Raynouard and a Rue Berton in his appearance and his nature.

Instant in his admirations and schemes, Balzac was like a child for whom everything happens *now* and in a *now* that is connected with no future. Certainly with no future of incurred obligations. The burden of Balzac's life is not apparent until one sees him at work; and then we see that not debt but this method of writing was the fatal aggravation.

In a sense Balzac is a made, or rather remade writer. There were times when he rushed down to the printers at eleven o'clock at night and they took the chapter of his novel page by page as he wrote it. But such moments of inspired exhibitionism were rare. In general Balzac strikes one as being the gifted talker whose mind congests when he sits down to write what he has just spoken. No doubt he could have turned out the cheap thrillers of his early period as easily as he spoke; but with his other books the process was agonizing. There would be several versions of the text, each one smothered with erasures and additions; chapters were put into different places, more chapters were sandwiched in between. Pages and pages scrapped, more pages added. The historian of the contemporary scene had only to go out of his door to see a new thing to squeeze somewhere into the text. And this was not the end of the confusion and the struggle. Once the printers had sorted out the manuscript and had produced their galleys, the ungovernable author began a hardly less drastic process of destruction and reconstruction. Night after night, from midnight until seven – and these were merely regular hours. There were days and nights of almost continuous labour without sleep. *Il ne savait pas sa langue*, said Gautier. The time spent and the printers' costs would have eaten seriously into earnings not already mortgaged by extravagance.

Let us return to the double house in the Rue Raynouard and look once more at the two great novels Balzac wrote in that small room above the trap-door, when his brain was already breaking under the appetites he imposed on it. Open *Le Cousin Pons*. There is the expected chapter, that roughly and in a domineering way generalizes and clears a space for the characters in the Parisian scene. And then, like a blow in the face, comes the brutal sentence: '*On n'a jamais peint les exigences de la gueule.*' One stops dead. What on earth has poor Pons done that his fastidious habit of dining at the expense of his better-off relations should become a treatise on the trough? Comically treated, of course; Balzac examined the dossier of human nature with the quizzical detachment of some nail-biting, cigar-stained Chief of Police who is going rapidly up in the world; who has seen so many cases; who thanks heaven that he does not make the moral law and that a worldly Church stands between himself and the Almighty. Passion, even when it is a passion for the best food, always becomes – in the experience of the Chief of Police – a transaction; Pons trades the little errands he runs on behalf of the family for the indispensable surprises of the gourmet. In the pursuit of that appetite he is prepared to ruin himself where other men, more voluptuously equipped by nature, will wreck themselves in the capture and establishment of courtesans. Sex or food, money or penury, envy or ambition – Balzac knows all the roads to ruin. If only men and women were content with their habits instead of craving the sublimity of their appetites.

But Pons is a type. He is a poor relation. In that isolation of a type, one detects the main difference between the French and English novels. The English novel has never lived down its early association with the theatre, and has always had to wrestle with a picaresque or artificial plot. But even if this had not been so, we could never have been a nation of moralists. Our instinct is to act; our interest in morals is a practical interest in results. The French novel – and how obvious this is in Balzac – is dominated on the contrary by a sense of law. Behind the individual act lies the type, behind the act lies a law governing the act. The French novelists are the lawyers of the passions; they proceed from the prototype to the particular and then carry it back for comparison. Subtle and litigious in tactic, they conclude that human experience, however bizarre, however affecting, can never escape the deep inscription of its category or evade the ordinance of some general idea.

To an English taste there must always be something arbitrary in such a structure. Natural Protestants, we resist a determinism so Roman and so Catholic. But we must be abashed by the double reference in which French fiction is so rich. Look at the delightful Pons. His character has so many departments. He is an old man, an ugly man, an outmoded but respected musician, a dandy survived from an earlier period, a collector of antiques, a poor man, a careful man, a simple man who is not quite so simple – see his valuable collection of pictures and bric-à-brac cunningly picked up for next to nothing – a sexless man, a gourmet, a hanger-on, shrewd in his own world, lost in the society into which he has grown up. Pons is the kind of character who, inevitably, becomes fantastic in the English novel simply because no general laws pin him down. He would become a static 'character'. Instead Balzac takes all these aspects of Pons and mounts each one, so that Pons is constructed before our eyes. We have a double interest: the story or plot, which is excellent in suspense, drama and form – this is one of Balzac's well-constructed novels, as it is also one of the most moving – and the exact completion, brick by brick, of Pons and his circle. There are the historical Pons – he is an *incroyable* left-over from the Directoire – the artistic Pons, the financial Pons, the sociable Pons, the moral Pons, and in the end Pons dying, plundered, defiant, a man awakened from his simplicity and fighting back, the exquisitely humble artist turned proud, sovereign and dangerous in his debacle. Pons is a faceted stone, and part of the drama is the relation of each facet with the others. Thus his fantastic dress is related, via dandyism, to his small, esteemed, but out-of-date position in the world of art. That adjoins his love of good living – picked up in smarter days – which links up with the solitariness and social spryness of the bachelor, his timidity and his sexual innocence. We have the portrait of a man who in every trait suggests some aspect of the society in which he lives. The history of his time is explicit in him. Yet he is not a period piece. A period piece is incapable of moral development and the development of a moral theme is everything in the novels of Balzac, who facilitates it by giving every character not merely a time and place, but also an obsession. Among English novelists it is only Henry James and, on occasions, Meredith, who move their drama not from incident to incident, but from one moral situation or statement to the next. (In Meredith's *The Egoist* one recalls the tension, tightening page by page, that precedes the accusation: 'You are an egoist.') So it is with the story of Pons. He is snubbed by his ignorant relations who do not realize even the financial value of his collection of antiques and pictures. In consequence, rather than be dropped or ridiculed, he gives up his beautiful dinners and retires to taste the blessings of the concierge's motherly cooking and pure friendship with the delightful Schmucke, a man even more simple than himself. At that point an English novelist might have given up. The lesson was clear. But Balzac, like Henry James, saw that drama lies in the fact that there is no end to moral issues. For him – recomplication, further research. And so, just as Pons is getting a little tired of his landlady's cooking, society tempts him again. His relations apologize, and Pons is one of those good men who cannot bear other people to say they are in the wrong. He conceives a grandiose scheme for returning good for evil. He will find a husband for the unmarriageable daughter. He will announce the enormous value of his collection and leave it to her in his will. Result, gratitude? Not a bit of it. The family is longing to wipe out the memory of their humiliating apology by vengeance, and when the marriage scheme collapses, they finish with Pons. Once more we have come to a natural end of the novel. But once more Balzac recomplicates. Pons falls into the grip of his concierge, who has suddenly become covetous now that she has two harmless, childless, womanless old men in her power; and his downfall is ensured by the very innocence of Schmucke, who cannot believe evil of anyone.

Balzac is the novelist of our appetites, obsessions and our *idées fixes*, but his great gift – it seems to me – is his sense of the complexity of the human situation. He had both perceptions, one supposes, from his peasant origins, for among peasants, he was fond of saying, the *idée fixe* is easily started; and their sense of circumstance overpowers all other considerations in their lives. A character in Balzac is so variously situated in history, in money, in family, class and in his type to begin with; but on top of this Balzac's genius was richly inventive in the field least exploited by the mass of novelists: the field of probability. It is very hard to invent probabilities. This simply means that Balzac knew his people as few novelists ever know their characters. The marriage scene in *Le Cousin Pons* for example: there we have the rich German all set to marry the daughter of the family. The awful facts of the '*régime dotal*' – a phrase repeated in pious chorus by the family with the unction usually reserved for statements like 'God is Love' – have been accepted by him. He has merely to say the word. At this tense moment the German electrifies everyone by asking the unexpected question: Is the girl an only child? Yes, she is. Then he must withdraw. A man of forty is an idiot who marries a girl who has been spoiled in her childhood. She will use the fact that he is so much older than herself to prove she is always right. That way lies hell. The respectability of the institution of marriage is in itself no satisfaction.

But *Le Cousin Pons* moves from one surprising probability to the next, backed by the massed ranks of human circumstance. The change in the character of the charming, motherly landlady of Pons who suddenly takes on the general professional character of the concierges of her district creates another powerful situation – powerful because so isolated are we, so obsessed with possibility and hope, that the probable is unperceived by us. The last thing we care to believe is that we are governed by type and environment. Balzac believed nothing else.

I do not know that I would put anything in *Le Cousin Pons* above the first part of *La Cousine Bette*, although I like Pons better as a whole. Pons is the old bachelor. Bette is the old maid. The growth of her malevolence is less subtly presented than the course of Pons's disillusion, because Balzac had the genius to show Pons living with a man even simpler than himself. One sees two degrees of simplicity, one lighting the other, whereas Bette stands alone; indeed, it may be complained that she is gradually swamped by the other characters. She is best in her obscurity, the despised poor relation, the sullen peasant, masculine, counting her humiliations and her economies like a miser, startling people with her bizarre reflections. They laugh at her and do not conceive the monstrous fantasies of her painful virginity. And we are moved by her in these early pages when she is hiding her Polish artist, shutting him in his room like a son, driving him to work; or later, when Madame Marneffe gives Bette the shabby furniture. Bette is a wronged soul; and when her passion does break it is, as Balzac says, sublime and terrifying. Her advance to sheer wickedness and vengeance is less convincing, or, rather, less engrossing. It is a good point that she is the eager handmaiden and not the igniting cause of ruin; but one draws back, incredulously, before some of her plots and lies. Acceptable when they are naïve, they are unacceptable when they fit too efficiently the melodramatic intrigue of the second part of the book. But the genius for character and situation is here again. La Marneffe, rooted in love's new middle-class hypocrisy and growing into a sanctimonious courtesan, is nicely contrasted with the besotted Baron who had grown up in an earlier period – 'between the wars' in fact – when the fashion of love was brisker and more candid. That situation alone is a comic one. The diplomatic farce of La Marneffe's supposed pregnancy is brilliant. The lies and short repentances of the sexagenarian Baron are perfect. Only Adeline does not, to my mind, come off in this novel; and here we come upon Balzac's rather dubious advocacy of marital fidelity. He sounds as little convinced as a public speaker haranguing his way to conviction. Adeline's pathetic attempt to sell herself, in order to save her husband's fortunes, is embarrassing to read; are we to admire virtue because it is stupid? Balzac protests too much.

No one has surpassed Balzac in revealing the great part played by money in middle-class life; nor has anyone excelled him in the portraits of the parvenu. Henry James alone, coming at the zenith of middle-class power, perceived the moral corruption caused by money; but money had ripened. It glowed like a peach that is just about to fall. Balzac arrived when the new money, the new finance of the post-Napoleonic world was starting on its violent course; when money was an obsession and was putting down a foundation for middle-class morals. In these two novels about the poor relations, he made, it seems to me, his most palatable, his least acrid and most human statements about this grotesque period of middle-class history.

Flaubert

The Quotidian

Although marred by affectations of style, Professor Brombert's study of the themes and techniques of Flaubert's novels is a very full and very suggestive scrutiny of Flaubert's love-hate of realism, as it is woven into the texture of his narratives. Flaubert's own ambiguities on the subject are clear. 'I abhor what has been called realism, although they make me out to be one of its high priests,' he wrote to George Sand. He hated reality. (Or rather it disgusted him; that is also an attraction.) Art held priority over life. If so much of his work is drawn from everyday life, he forced himself to depict it (in Professor Brombert's words):

> partly out of self-imposed therapy to cure himself of his chronic idealism, partly also out of a strange and almost morbid fascination . . . Art for him was quite literally an escape . . . For hatred of reality . . . was intimately bound up with an inherent pessimism – and pessimism in turn was one of the prime conditions of his ceaseless quest for ideal forms.

In resilient moments he called himself an old *'romantique enragé'*: even, a *troubadour*.

All this is well known; we know an enormous amount about Flaubert and Professor Brombert brings all the important critics into his net. But, a good deal owing to Marxist and Christian criticism, the quite gratuitous notion has got about that Flaubert was not what he ought to have been. He ought not to have been 'an alienated bourgeois'; yet, surely, a vast number of great artists have been 'alienated' from their dispensation and especially in the nineteenth century. Alienation is a cant term for a necessary condition. The 'hatred' of Balzac, Stendhal, Zola, Flaubert or Proust are the characteristic engines of a century bemused by its own chaotic energies. The force of criticism from an outside position of Marxist, Christian or psychoanalytical neo-conformity is now fading and one is at least heartened to see Professor Brombert applying himself to 'the unique temperament and vision that determine and characterize a novelist's work as we find them in the text'.

There can be two weaknesses in this kind of criticism: first, it puritanically denies side glances at biography, social influences, etc., and rather hypocritically assumes that we have had these necessities privately at the back door. Professor Brombert is not too strict here; how could one leave out the effect of atheistic medical observation and the morgue on Flaubert's mind? Even Flaubert's obsession with style seems to have something of medical specialization in it. Secondly, the critic may find too much in the text and build top-heavy theories on images and symbols, as one finds, for example, when this kind of criticism deals with Dickens: all that talk of baptismal water! (I have only one doubt about Professor Brombert's attention to key words: this is when he catalogues the symbols of liquefaction.)

In Flaubert the danger is usually small for he was the most conscious of artists; a most ardent collector of echoes and symbols. His documentary interest in *things* is also a concern with what they tell of the imagination. Things are corrupted or corrupting. He is tortured by the fact that the century has turned mind into matter, the ideal converted into ludicrous or detestable paraphernalia.

Take the matter of the Algerian scarves in *Madame Bovary*. They were coming into fashion with the beginning of French colonization of North Africa: that is a comment both on bourgeois enterprise and greed, and on the absurdities of provincial taste. It is nearly a comment on the economy of the textile city of Rouen. The nineteenth century will colonize; so, in its fantasies, did the nineteenth-century soul. When Emma turns spendthrift and buys curtains, carpets and hangings from the draper, the information takes on something from the theme of the novel itself: the material is symbolic of the exotic, and the exotic feeds the Romantic appetite. It will lead to satiety, bankruptcy and eventually to nihilism and the final drive towards death and nothingness.

If anyone makes too much of his images, it will be Flaubert himself: for example, the snake, in the snake-like hiss of Madame Bovary's corset lace. It is a melodramatic excess, as one can tell by the eagerness with which the image was seized upon by the lurid and falsifying mind of the prosecuting lawyer when Flaubert was being charged with obscenity. The phrase could well have gone into the *Dictionnaire des idées reçues.* Flaubert's subject is the imagination and particularly of the orgiastic adolescent kind which he never outgrew and which received almost operatic support from an early reading of the Marquis de Sade and the early extremes of the Romantic movement.

How is it that – as it seems to us now – a whole century became adolescent? Is prolonged adolescence characteristic of a new class coming to power? This is not Professor Brombert's interest; but casting an eye on the ominous *Intimate Notebooks 1840–1841* – when Flaubert was eighteen and already pretending to be twenty – and proceeding though the novels, Professor Brombert is able to show how, exhaustively and like an infected pathologist Flaubert presented the hunger for the future, the course of ardent longings and violent desires that rise from the sensual, the horrible, and the sadistic. They turn into the virginal and mystical, only to become numbed by satiety. At this point pathological boredom leads to a final desire for death and nothingness – the Romantic syndrome. The *Notebooks* contain eager cries on behalf of adolescent bisexuality; moralize on the ecstatic yet soon-to-be ashy joys of narcissism; pass, without pause, into dreams of exotic travel:

Often I am in India, in the shade of banana trees, sitting on mats: bayaderes are dancing, swans are fluffing out their feathers on blue lakes, nature throbs with love.

One is struck by the drunken accomplishment of the young diarist, particularly by the precision and clarity of his ingenious self-study at a time of life when one is most likely to be turgid and blind. The son of Dr Flaubert has made notes which a psychiatrist would find useful. How perceptive to write, at that age:

Sensual pleasure is pleased with itself: it relishes itself like melancholy – both of them solitary enjoyments . . .

The style has already the élan and excessive conviction which are the startling qualities of his first novel *November*, unpublished in his lifetime. Luckily it has in Frank Jellinek a translator who responded to the youthful yet (again) accomplished puerilities of the writer. This book, above all, contains the emotional source of

Madame Bovary; it states the imaginative condition of romantic love, underlines the onanism at the heart of the fantasy of the virgin whore. The very absurdities of this first novel are moving, not only because of the afflatus but because of the fidelity to the course of an emotion that may be extravagant but is precisely recognizable. What astonishes is Flaubert's understanding of his experience at that age. Here he begins his career as the doctor who proceeds to diagnosis by catching the patient's fever first.

We meet one or two of the famous Flaubert obsessions: 'There was one word which seemed to me the most beautiful of all human words: "adultery"'; his horror of begetting a child, and passages like:

> Since I did not use existence, existence used me: my dreams wearied me more than great labours. A whole creation, motionless, unrevealed to itself, lived mute below my life: I was a sleeping chaos of a thousand fertile elements which knew not how to manifest themselves nor what to be, still seeking their form and awaiting their mould.

As Professor Brombert says, *November* is indispensable to an understanding of *Madame Bovary*, where 'the thousand fertile elements' manifested themselves in the facts of Normandy life. Life is a dream, life is bad art; only Art, the supreme reverie, can redeem it: Flaubert's pessimism is clinical and absolute. Or is it? Keeping close to the text, Professor Brombert tries to make a path through Flaubert's ingenuities, duplicities and double meanings; and taking a tip from Flaubert's own phrase that it is stupid to come to conclusions, he points out that Flaubert's pessimism is, at any rate, resilient. Style may not save us but it is a force.

There are many good things in the discussion of *Madame Bovary*. It is a novel as complex as the second part of *Don Quixote*: we shall never get to the bottom of it. For example, there is the question of how Flaubert's lyrical intention was to consort with the banal, especially in the matter of speech. In fact Flaubert's impersonality was a fraud: he contrived – since the book was a work of self-discovery and confession – all kinds of intrusion. Often openly:

> . . . it is a grave mistake not to seek candour behind worn-out language, as though fullness of soul did not at times overflow in the emptiest of metaphors.

And Professor Brombert comments:

> This feeling that human speech cannot possibly cope with our dreams and our grief goes a long way toward explaining why so often, in the work of Flaubert, the reader has the disconcerting impression that the language of banality is caricatured and at the same time transmuted into poetry.

(Yes: the comic is poetry inverted. The effect of pure comedy is poetic.)

Flaubert has the power of transmuting the trivial. He wrote:

> My book will have the ability to walk straight on a hair, suspended between the double abyss of lyricism and vulgarity.

As Professor Brombert says, one misses the charity, the 'imperceptible human tremors' in Flaubert: there is a rift between the sophistication of the author and the confusion of the characters: but it is the test of a great writer that he can turn his dilemmas to effect. Flaubert disguises the rift by:

> The telescoping of two unrelated perspectives which bestows upon the novel a unique beauty. A stereoscopic vision accounts in large part for the peculiar poetry and complexity of *Madame Bovary*.

On the subject of the death of Madame Bovary there have been wearying differences of opinion. To some she has been hounded. To others she is a silly and disreputable nonentity, her shame not worth the expense of spirit. To D.H. Lawrence she was crushed by the intellectual skill that had created her: to others no more than a cold exercise. Yet again, she has been used by Flaubert to cure himself of his own disease. In fact, as Professor Brombert shows, the theme and even something of the plot had been known to Flaubert since his youth. There are no exercises in literature. I was struck when I last read the novel – as Professor Brombert was – by the extent of the sympathy with which she is treated. She has, even when she is mocked, the honesty of an energy. Her periods of depravity do not single her out as an exceptionally deplorable being, but rather make her part of the general, glum strangeness of the people around her. She belongs to Rouen: she is what belonging to a place or a culture may mean. She is dignified by a real fate – not by the false word 'Fate', one of the clichés Flaubert derided. Delusion itself dignifies her. The comparison with *Don Quixote* imposes itself: we see

> . . . her terrible isolation, her unquenchable aspiration for some unattainable ideal. Hers are dreams that destroy. But this destructive power is also their beauty, just as Emma's greatness (the word is inappropriate to literal-minded readers) is her ability to generate such dreams . . . at the moment of her complete defeat in the face of reality, she acquires dignity, and even majesty.

And despite the clinical attentions of Flaubert, her fellow adolescent, I can see no force in the criticism that, in drawing her, Flaubert tried to turn himself into a woman: it may be said that in putting masculinity into her – as Baudelaire said – Flaubert made her perverse. But perversity is a normal sexual ingredient as well as an article in the Romantic canon. The Romantics were good psychologists.

Professor Brombert's final remarks are new. There is an apparent negation of tragic values in Flaubert! Does he suggest a new form of tragedy, the tragedy of the very absence of Tragedy, a condition familiar to contemporary writers? There is a link between him and ourselves.

> The oppressive heterogeneity of phenomena, the fragmented immediacy of experience, the constant fading or alteration of forms . . .

These are twentieth-century assumptions. Equally important, Flaubert diagnoses the crisis of language.

> The breakdown of language under the degrading impact of journalism, advertisement and political slogans parallels the breakdown of a culture over-inflated with unassimilable data.

It leads to the incoherence of *Waiting for Godot*, the triumph of the rigmarole.

My only serious criticism of Professor Brombert concerns his own use of language. It is depressing to find so good a critic of

Flaubert – of all people – scattering academic jargon and archaisms in his prose. The effect is pretentious and may, one hopes, be simply the result of thinking in French and writing in English; but it does match the present academic habit of turning literary criticism into technology. One really cannot write of Flaubert's 'dilection for monstrous forms' or of 'vertiginous proliferation of forms and gestures'; 'dizzying dilation', or 'volitation'; 'lupanar' – when all one means is 'pertaining to a brothel'. Philosophers, psychologists and scientists may, I understand, write of 'fragmentations' that suggest a 'somnambulist and oneiric state'. But who uses the pretentious 'obnuvilate'; when they mean 'dim' or 'darkened by cloud'? Imaginative writers know better than to put on this kind of learned dog. The duty of the critic is to literature, not to its surrogates. And if I were performing a textual criticism of this critic I would be tempted to build a whole theory on his compulsive repetition of the word 'velleities'. Words and phrases like these come from the ingenuous and fervent pens of *Bouvard and Pécuchet.*

Literary criticism does not add to its status by opening an intellectual hardware store.

Maupassant

When, as a young man, Maupassant sat in the talkative company of writers and was asked why he was silent, he used to say, 'I am learning my trade'; and that is what the hostile criticism of his work comes down to in the end. That he learned, and some better writers never have. He is one of the dead-sure geniuses, a hunter without a blank in his magazine. What one means by Maupassant's genius – for he was very limited in his range and depth of subject – is hard to say. The opening chapters of *Une Vie*, and many of the Seine stories, are Tolstoyan: there is the same limpid, timeless animal eye, alert without innocence to every movement, to every blink of light and shadow. There is the same crisp lick of the feathered surface by the perfect sculler. The difference is that Tolstoy is a man and Maupassant is a male; that Tolstoy is a man who can repent, Maupassant a machine that can only wear out. Or we might say, as Henry James did, that Maupassant is unable to reflect and that the existence of an inner life astonished him and struck him as being a surprising pathos. Conrad said 'such is the greatness of his talent that all his high qualities appear in the very things of which he speaks, as if they had been altogether independent of his presentation'. Life itself seems to be writing his best stories, to have inked itself upon the page; the only thing that makes one wish to qualify such a statement is that Maupassant was fly enough to say something of the kind himself in one of his letters which is quoted in the Louis Conard edition of his works. He is too consciously the successful writer to be trusted:

> No, my spirit is not decadent. I am quite unable to look inside myself; I am dominated by the unceasing, involuntary effort of penetrating the souls of others. Really it is not I who make the effort: what is around me penetrates and possesses *me*. I am impregnated by it, I give myself to it, I drown in the flow of my surroundings.

A feminine and passive analogy. It was learned from Flaubert and many writers have since professed it. One has noticed that the writers who train themselves to *be* life in this way become, in fact, less than life, that is to say to record the human wish to enlarge life (as Chekhov did), one suspects he means he is unwilling to succeed: one must limit one's objective. There, possibly, we have the hint that Maupassant's genius was not inclusive, like Tolstoy's, but selective and taught.

Like pretty well all Maupassant's work, *Une Vie* is a story from a life very close to his own. The book is his first novel. It arises from Maupassant's strongest emotion: his feeling for his mother. Jeanne, transposed into a Flaubertian key, is Laure Maupassant. Jeanne is a Madame Bovary who is not drawn to adultery by reading romances, but who is made obstinately innocent of the world by them. She receives one brutal shock after another in a life of virtue which seems touching but obtuse.

Laure Maupassant was a woman of more nerve and brain than Jeanne, who is at heart the conventional upper-class bride of the period; but Jeanne's story is Laure's in essentials. In the first place Jeanne is given a family rather more distinguished than Laure's. On both sides, the Maupassants came of moneyed mercantile families. It was Maupassant's father who quietly interposed the aristocratic *de* with its touch of the Trade Mark. Jeanne's father is, however, noticeably not a parvenu when Maupassant tells *her* story. He is the agreeable, spendthrift country gentleman whose fortunes are dissolved by the impulses of eighteenth-century philosophy. The Maupassants who moved into the chateau in Normandy were climbers who overspent on the way up; they were hard as the rich bourgeois are; they were committed to success, and were drily scornful of the aristocracy of the old régime who creaked like marionettes taken out of the cupboards of their damp and solitary houses. Maupassant, who was trained by his mother to hate his womanizing father, hated him far more for giving him no money and making him work as a poor clerk in a government office. The clerking injured Maupassant's pride, and it irked the sense of efficiency which is the strongest instinct of the self-made rich.

It is impossible to know what hardens the heart, what checks the impulse to 'look inside'. In a general way we can surmise that the broken home of the Maupassants had fixed the detachment, the watchfulness, the habit of *surveillance* in the child; hardness of heart comes, perhaps, from being forced by one's imperilled situation to be continually on the look out. When Laure left Maupassant's father, the son stepped into his place in the home, and there are instances of iron-willed impudence in his childhood which show that he was precociously aware of his powerful position as the supplanting male. Again and again (as Mr Steegmuller, an American biographer, has pointed out) his stories are of humiliated women and cuckolded men. There must have been precise scenes that remained in his memory all his life; perhaps that scene in *Garçon! Un Bock!* where a man recalls how, as a frightened child, he secretly witnessed a violent quarrel between his father and mother in which the mother is struck to the ground. Such scenes awake double emotions in a child, and they are not a pleasure to recall. They certainly fix in the child's mind a precocious, ungraduated and crude conviction that human relations are to be reduced at once to a question of animal dominance. To see life naked too young is never to observe, later on, that, characteristically, life is dressed. The animal watchfulness of Maupassant is the watchfulness of a childhood not outgrown; his cynicism is the recognition that he is like the father whom he can never cease to hate. And why should he 'look inside', in any case? Evil, the child has seen, comes from the outside. It is the outside that must be watched and, towards the end of his life, the very title of *Le Horla* – 'what is outside' – shows that the horrors come from an outside world that cannot be trusted. In the last stages of syphilis, this was Maupassant's terror: that the world would crash inwards upon a nature which, for all its assiduity, could not make itself hard, efficient, drastic, sealed off and settled enough.

Time is the subject of *Une Vie*. It is the pervasive theme of a large number of his stories. The early destruction of his moral sense – which was replaced only by an acceptance of the conventional moral sense of his class – led Maupassant to see the teeth of time eating up everything. It is disgusting of the Vicomte to betray Jeanne, but as time goes by Jeanne's virtue becomes something like stupidity. Live and let live; life will turn out to be neither as good nor as bad as we think. If we live long enough we shall see things turn into their opposites. So strong and harsh are these passive sentiments in Maupassant that it is strange that time is bungled in *Une Vie*; after the miraculous clear and truthful picture of a girl's awakening to love, at first painful and then mature, after the shock, the novel scrambles hurriedly over the years, in too great a haste to point the moral and turn the irony. There is evidence that Maupassant altered and corrected the plot many times; he was at home only in the disconnected episode. His nervous nature needed to work in a limited field; his intense feeling for time is a feeling for its minutes which became, as it were, concrete. The more slowly his narrative moves, watching dream change to love and love to desire, the more certain he is to put his finger upon the exact shiver of change. Out of this is born his wonderful awareness of the feelings of women who are more sensitive to the climatic changes of feeling than men are. Few chapters in any love story can equal Maupassant's descriptions of the marriage night and the honeymoon of Jeanne; for it is the sense of change in sexual experience, the sense of the hours or the days going by, which enables him to write of sexual experience explicitly. In his preoccupation with the sexual act in every conceivable circumstance from the brutal and the comic to the ecstatic, there is always an unruffled observation of the changes of mood that make the act possible and the changes that are part of it. To those who value sexual conquest, the stages are as important as the conquest and Maupassant, who is often hypocritically reproached for this excellence, may be compared with those sportsmen who love the creatures they kill. He has a natural sexual curiosity and he is, in consequence, freed from that obscuring zeal for personal and vicarious participation in the coupling of his characters, that ruins the descriptions of inhibited writers. There is not a woman in the sexual episodes of Maupassant's stories who does not come to life because of them.

Maupassant's open vanity in his submission to life is softened by his patient sense of time. The launch of a boat, a drink in a café, an empty afternoon anywhere, the preparations for a shoot, the enquiring hours when lovers sit side by side unable to speak, are not matters to be hurried over. He is so slow that the minutes become dramatic. Every word is an event. The most banal thoughts can be so placed that ecstatic happiness is conveyed by them: 'It seemed to her that there were only three beautiful things in the whole of creation: light, space and water.' Or again – 'They felt happy – each thinking of the other.' Time es in such simple sentences; they have the turning of the earth in them. Just as they have in innumerable minor observations in this novel. Everyone grows old in *Une Vie*, yet each in a distinctive way. The day itself and not some constructing, self-imposing author might have written a passage like this:

In the morning Jeanne would set out to meet him, with Aunt Lison and the Baron, who was gradually growing bent and who walked like a little old man with hands clasped behind his back as if to prevent himself from falling flat on his face. They went very slowly along the road, sometimes sitting down at the edge of the ditch and staring into the distance to see if the rider were not yet in sight. As soon as he appeared, a black dot on the white line, the three of them waved their handkerchiefs. Then he would break into a gallop and arrive like a hurricane, which always made Jeanne and Lison shudder with alarm and produced an enthusiastic 'Bravo' from the grandfather who cheered with all the enthusiasm of one whose active days are over.

Only one or two Russians, Tolstoy above all, have surpassed Maupassant in describing happiness, the delicious sensation of simply being alive; and it is done by fidelity to what is passing, by making concrete the sense of evanescence in ordinary things.

I have possibly been too summary in my comments on Maupassant's character and have also tended to move too speculatively between the man and his work. Let us look, as much as possible, at the work alone. What are his chief interests? Sex, animal delight, of course; more important, I think, the effect of poverty and circumstance on character. Life is made endurable by sexual love and by usage; only these relieve the meaningless and unremitting irony of circumstance. It is interesting, here, to compare Maupassant's novel *Une Vie* with Arnold Bennett's *Old Wives' Tale*, which, one recalls, was prompted by Maupassant's book and which patiently attempts the same attitude of mind. Immediately one is struck by a strain of dry triviality and perfunctoriness in Bennett's masterpiece, a connoisseur's diffidence which keeps his people at a certain distance, whereas in *Une Vie* one is struck by the nearness of Maupassant to his Jeanne, the unguarded and sincere intimacy of his observation of her as a character. He is sexually aware of her. And his picture of her sexual reserve and of how, unexpectedly, it dissolves and she becomes a woman is the mark of Maupassant's superiority to Bennett as an intuitive artist. Jeanne is an obscure woman, but she is never trivial. The pessimism of Maupassant is pitying, sympathetic and humane.

Listening to the criticisms of his stories that have been made chiefly since the rise of Chekhov, one is given the impression that he was simply a brilliant conjuror or special pleader. He has been held up as the arch-exponent of the trick plot, the cynical moral and the surprising ending. Nothing could be less true of his best work. Where is the trick in *La Maison Tellier* or in *Une Fille de Ferme*? The test of the artificial story is its end. Do you, at the end of a story, feel that the lives of the people have ended with the drama of their situation? Do you feel that their lives were, in fact, not lives, but an idea? That is the artificial story. All short-story writers produce stories like this, for, like the sonnet, the short story is liable to become a brilliant conceit. But a large number of Maupassant's tales, and especially those which deal with the lives of the Normandy peasants, do not belong to this group. The ends of these tales are, so to speak, open. The characters go on living. They are beginning to live their way into a new situation. Rosa, in *La Maison Tellier*, will not be quite the same woman after she has taken the child into her bed. The *fille de ferme* is at the beginning of a new story when she tells her husband about her illegitimate child. The triumph of custom – the custom of avarice – justifies the girl in *L'Aveu*, who sleeps with the carrier in order to save her fare, and you see her at the story's end, grown into the cramped, terrifying world of peasant poverty. It is a growth, not an end. It is true that in all these stories the characters are dominated by a strong dramatic situation; but to call this method arbitrary, when one compares it with Chekhov's, is a mistake. Chekhov's subject was life, life breaking and running like a chain of raindrops upon the window. Now the drops run and pool together, presently they part, slide off on their own and momentarily catch the light in some new, fragile and vanishing pattern. There are meetings and partings, crises and respites. For Chekhov life is an arpeggio of moments. But when Maupassant looks at the life of one of his characters he is a moralist thinking of the custom of their life. One has the sensation of seeing not merely the crises in *Boule de Suif*, but all of the lives of the people in that story. We come back to Maupassant's French respect for usage. The peasant comes out in him. There is a negative virtue in our acceptance of fate. There are certain permanent things, he seems to say: poverty, hard work, the obligations of work, the begetting of one's kind, the scheme in which a life has been set. And into this circle the heart brings its untidy animal fire, often trodden down, but never quite extinguished. Moments are a reality in that life – the *fille de ferme* will never forget the moment when, dazed by the sunlight, she lay down on the straw in the barn and woke to strike the farm hand who crept up to touch her; nor will Jeanne, in *Une Vie*, forget that time, long after her marriage, when her miserly young husband suddenly, inexplicably, became desirable to her – but these moments are part of the grave and fatal pattern of their respective lives. There is indeed an appetite for life, a robust reaching out to life in Maupassant, and especially a love of animal life, innocent and lazy in the country scene. Suppose, for a minute, that *La Maison Tellier* is a joke. I mean, suppose Maupassant did not originally intend to go beyond the farce suggested by the notice on the door of the brothel. And now look at the story again. How quickly he leaves the farce of the original idea behind. His animal spirits warm up, his heart expands; how quickly the idea ripens and becomes life itself. The description of the carriage ride through the dusty, dazzling countryside flashes with poetry; but it is an earthly poetry, written out of the heart and not twanged and tweaked on the nerves:

> *Une lumière folle emplissait les champs, une lumière miroitant aux yeux; et les roues soulevaient deux sillons de poussière qui voltigeaient longtemps derrière la voiture sur la grande route.*

La Maison Tellier dazzles one like a May morning; but in the harder story, *Une Fille de Ferme*, one also sees the same pagan love of nature. When the girl runs away from the farm before dawn, thinking to drown herself, one sees the strange, mad aspect of the countryside before sunrise. The moon appears at its unexpected and crazy slope in the sky, and the fields lie in a yellowish light, and only the warm smell of the earth in the odorous Normandy morning and the play of the leverets in the furrows remind the girl that man may be mad but the earth is not. Maupassant's feeling for nature, a feeling that went back to his childhood, is the assurance of his sanity and his heart. And nature for him is the nature of a man close to the work of the land, close to the hunter – there he reminds one of Turgenev – and close to use. How simply, too, this nature distracts and heals the human sufferers for a while: the little boy who runs away from the boys who are jeering at him, and forgets his shame in playing with a frog. And, as I said before, I think it is from his closeness to the peasant's knowledge of nature that Maupassant got his sense of the pattern of fate or necessity in life.

The morbidity, the mere ingenuity and sentimentality of Maupassant have been explained as the bad wages of the doctrine of art for art's sake, but that criticism is not very valuable. Writers write badly when they write too much; possibly Maupassant's physical disease ensured that he would write with a frenzied facility. At this second best he is still enjoyable simply because he has that gift which no theory can explain – original talent; and that quality which cannot be obtained by taking thought – sincerity, which I take to be clarity and singleness of mind. Whatever the idea of the moment, however poor or flippant, Maupassant gives himself up to it. I think this is true of a mechanical story such as the one where the man blows his brains out because he is afraid to show his fear of fighting a duel, or in that cynical story of the prostitute who attracts her customers in the cemetery by weeping at the grave of an imaginary husband. Maupassant has a wide range of character-anecdote, if not a very wide range of character or situation, because of his curiosity. And 'art for art's sake', plus curiosity, is a formidable combination. Usually, when this useful doctrine is attacked, the critic forgets that Flaubert, who was Maupassant's master, insisted that great curiosity was indispensable. The weakness of Maupassant's mind is that its atheism was cynical. It was a personal despair unsupported by any great intellectual structure – a quality in him which, oddly enough, as Mr Desmond MacCarthy has reminded me, attracted Tolstoy: 'What is truth if a man dies?' This atheism was not damaging to Maupassant when he was writing about the pagan Normandy of his childhood, but outside of that world, cynicism left him isolated and he was reduced to seeing small, ironic, moral conundrums everywhere. There are accidental resemblances to Turgenev, who was also an atheist, in Maupassant; but he has neither the feeling of the sensitive aristocrat for his people nor anything to correspond with the mystical Russian cult of the humble. And he made no political judgements about his country, as Turgenev did. Maupassant was a child of the disaster of Sedan, and that line from the opening of *Boule de Suif: 'L'angoisse de l'attente faisait désirer la venue de l'ennemi,'* reads like his epitaph, the inscription of an isolated and haunted man.

THE RUSSIAN DAY

Turgenev

What is it that attracts us to the Russian novelists of the nineteenth century? The aristocratic culture made more vivid by its twilight? The feeling, so readily understood by English readers, for *ennui*? No. The real attraction of that censored literature is its freedom – the freedom from our kind of didacticism and our plots. The characters of our novels, from Fielding to Forster, get up in the morning, wash, dress and are then drilled for their roles. They are propelled to some practical issue in morality, psychology or Fortune before the book is done. In nineteenth-century Russia, under the simpler feudal division of society, there is more room to breathe, to let the will drift, and the disparate impulses have their ancient solitary reign. In all those Russian novels we seem to hear a voice saying: 'The meaning of life? One day that will be revealed to us – probably on a Thursday.' And the day, not the insistence of the plot or the purpose, is the melodic bar. We see life again, we indeed know it, as something written in days; its dramas not directed by the superior foreknowledge of the writer, but seeming to ebb and flow among the climaxes, the anti-climaxes, the yawnings of the hours. Turgenev, who knew English literature well, used to say that he envied the English novelists their power to make plots; but, of course, he really disdained it. The surprises of life, the sudden shudders of its skin, are fresher and more astonishing than the imposed surprises of literary convention or the teacher's lesson. And in seeing people in terms of their anonymous days, the Russians achieved, by a paradox, a sense of timelessness in their books. Gogol, for example, seems to date far less than Dickens. In the Russians there is a humility before the important fact of human inertia, the half-heartedness of its wish to move and grow, its habit of returning into itself. This is true of Turgenev; obviously true of Chekhov, and I think also of Dostoevsky. His dynamism and complex narratives are the threshings and confusions of a writer who – if we consult his notebooks and letters – could never bind his mind to a settled subject or a fixed plot.

Yet the use of the eventless day could not alone give the Russian novel its curious power; indeed, it can be its weakness. No novelists are easier to parody than the Russians. Those people picking their noses at the windows or trying on their boots while they go through passion and remorse! The day is a convention like any other. What gives those novels their power, and these persons their gift of moving us, is something which comes from a profound sense of a presence haunting the day. There lies on those persons, even on the most trivial, the shadow of a fate more richly definitive than the fate of any individual human being. Their feet stand in time and history. Their fate is corporate. It is the fate of Russia itself, a fate so often adjured with eloquence and nostalgia, oftener still with that medieval humility which has been unknown to us since the Renaissance, and which the Russians sometimes mystically identify with the fate of humanity itself.

I have been reading Turgenev again and dipping occasionally into Avraham Yarmolinsky's thorough and discerning evaluation of him. It was a great advantage to the Russian novelists that they were obliged to react to the Russian question; a great advantage, too, that the Russian question was to become a universal one: the question of the rise of the masses. The consequence s that Turgenev's political novels – especially *Rudin* and even *Fathers and Children* – are less dated outside of Russia than they are inside it, for we can afford to ignore the detail of their historical context. I first read *Rudin* during the Spanish Civil War and, when he died on his foreign barricade, Rudin seemed to me (and still does seem) one of the 'heroes of our time'. At the end of all Turgenev's political stories one may detect the invisible words 'And yet . . . ' left there by his hesitant and tentative genius. He is so close to the ripple of life's process of becoming, that at the very moments of decision, departure, farewell, he seems to revise and rejuvenate. The leaf falls, but the new bud is disclosed beneath the broken stalk.

Turgenev solved the Russian problem for himself, as he solved his personal question by an ingenious psychological trick. It is rather irritating, it is a little comic when we see it in the light of his personal character, but it was serious and successful. It was the trick of assuming a premature old age. Now this device was a legacy of Byronism. One can see how it must have infuriated his younger contemporaries to hear him declare that at thirty-five his life was finished; and then to have him live another thirty years in full possession of his gracious and pertinent faculties. The trick was a kind of alibi. For behind the mist of regret, that autumnal resignation, the tenderness and the wave of the scented handker-chief in a goodbye that was never quite goodbye, there was a marksman's eye. Yarmolinsky speaks of him stalking his characters as he stalked grouse on the steppe of Orel or Kaluga. Every time he picks off his man and notes, as he does so, his place in the Russian fauna. Look at this from *A Nest of Gentlefolk*:

I want above all to know what you are like, what are your views and convictions, what you have become, what life has taught. (Mihalevitch still preserved the phraseology of 1830.)

The comic side of this adroit sense of time – so precise, so poetic and moving in his writing – comes out in Turgenev's private life. His autumnal disguise enabled him to give his large number of love affairs a protective fragility. The autumn is the hunting season.

A Sportsman's Sketches, *A Nest of Gentlefolk*, *Fathers and Children* – those are the perfect books. Turgenev is the poet of spring who eludes the exhausting decisions and fulfilments of summer and finds in the autumn a second and safer spring. He is the novelist of the moments after meetings and of the moments before partings. He watches the young heart rise the first time. He watches it fall, winged, to the common distorted The young and the old are his fullest characters: the homecoming and death of Bazarov and the mourning of his parents are among the truest and most moving things in literature. To the tenderness, this capacity to observe the growth of characters and the changes of the heart, as the slow days of the steppe change into the years that rattle by in Petersburg or Baden, there is, as I have said, a shrewd, hard-headed counterpart, the experienced shot:

In the general the good-nature innate in all Russians was intensified by that special kind of geniality which is peculiar to all people who have done something disgraceful.

Or:

> Of his wife there is scarcely anything to be said. Her name was
> Kalliopa Karlovna. There was always a tear in her left eye, on
> the strength of which Kalliopa Karlovna (she was, one must
> add, of German extraction) considered herself a woman of
> great sensibility.

Or:

> Panshin's father, a retired cavalry officer and a notorious
> gambler, was a man of insinuating eyes, a battered countenance,
> and a nervous twitch about the mouth.

Looking back over the novels, one cannot remember any
falsified character. One is taken from the dusty carriage to the
great house, one meets the landowners and the servants, and then
one watches life produce its surprises as the day goes by. Turgenev
has the perfect discretion. He refrains from knowing in advance.
In *Rudin* we are impressed by the bellows of the local Dr Johnson;
enter Rudin, and the brilliant young man demolishes the doctor,
like a young Shelley; only himself to suffer exposure as the next
day shows us more of his character. His people expose themselves,
as in life people expose themselves, fitfully and with contradiction.
The art is directed by a sense which the English novel has never had
– unless Jane Austen had something of it – the sense of a man's
character and life being divisible into subjects. Career, love,
religion, money, politics, illness and the phases of the years are in
turn isolated in a spirit which is both poetic and scientific. There is
no muddle in Turgenev. Romantic as he may be, there is always
clarity, order and economy. He writes novels as if he were not a
story teller but a biographer.

It was Edward Garnett who, in defending the disputed portrait
of Bazarov, pointed out that Bazarov ought to have been judged as
the portrait not of a political type, but of the scientific temperament.
(There is nothing wrong with Bazarov really, except that Turgenev
showed him in the country, where he was a fish out of water,
instead of in the city.) This temperament was Turgenev's, and
because of it one easily discounts the inevitable sad diminuendo of
his tales, the languid dying away which is the shadow of his own
wish in his work. The rest stands clearly and without date. But the

method has one serious weakness. It almost certainly involved drawing directly from life, and especially it meant that Turgenev was (or thought he was) stimulated to write by an interest in living persons for their own sakes. Turgenev knew his own lack of invention, his reliance on personal experience, and he studied character with the zeal of a botanist watching a flower; but, in fact, the study of character, for a novelist, means the selection or abstraction of character. What is selected is inevitably less than what is there, and since Turgenev was (as he said) governed by the actual life story which he saw, he does not add to or transform his people. They have the clarity of something a little less than life. What is missing from them is that from which he personally recoiled – fulfilment. There are spring and autumn – there is no summer. If success is described, it is by hearsay. Marriage, for Turgenev, is either scandal or rather embarrassing domesticity, something for a fond, indulgent smile, but a quick get-away. Strangely enough, it is his objectivity which leads to his limpness.

There are two qualifications to add to this criticism. One is suggested by *A Sportman's Sketches.* His people derive a certain fullness from their part in the scene of the steppe, which none described better than he. In this book, his scrupulous habit or necessity of stopping short at what he saw and heard gave his portraits a laconic power and a terrible beauty. There the Russian day brings people to life in their random moments. The shapelessness of these pieces is the powerful shapelessness of time itself. The other qualification is the one I have indicated at the beginning of this essay. If his people lack the power to realize themselves because Turgenev himself lacked it in his own life, they have their roots in the fate of Russia. You localize them in a destiny which is beyond their own – tragic, comic, whatever they are – in the destiny of their society. They may fail, Russia goes on. One remembers that startling chapter at the end of *A Nest of Gentlefolk*, where, after the bitter end of Liza's love, the novelist returns to the house. One expects the last obligatory chords of romantic sorrow, but instead, there is the cruel perennial shock of spring:

Marfa Dmitrievna's house seemed to have grown younger; its freshly painted walls gave a bright welcome; and the panes of its own windows were crimson, shining in the setting sun; from these windows the light merry sound of ringing young voices and continual laughter floated into the street.

The new generation had grown up. It is the most tragic moment of his writing, the one most burdened with the mystery of time as it flows through the empty light of our daily life.

The Hypocrite

We walk down a street in the dead hours of the afternoon, looking at the windows of the villas as we pass by. They are glass cases; they are the domestic aquarium, and what our idle eye is seeking, is a sight of the human fish within. And presently we are taken by surprise. We see a face in one of those rooms. Agape, bemused, suspended like a torpid trout, a man or woman is standing alone there, doing nothing, and sunk in the formidable pathos of human inertia, isolation and *ennui*. It is always a surprising sight and, to a novelist, always a disturbing one. We are used to the actions of human beings, not to their stillness. We are taken back suddenly to our childhood, when time went by so slowly, and when we, too, were shut in a room with some grown-up who was occupied entirely by the enormous process of sitting. How they could sit! And sit alone! And how their figures grew larger and larger in our eyes, until their solitude and silence seemed to burst the room. It was, I think, one of the first intimations of mortality in early childhood.

The Russian novelists of the nineteenth century owe everything to their response to the man or woman sitting alone in his room, to the isolation, inertia, the off-beat in human character. They are naturally aware of what André Malraux has called, in a recent book, 'the crevasse that separates us from universal life'. The chief subject of the Russian novelists – the monotonous life of the country house which is scores of miles from its neighbours – draws this response from them. And as they stand alone in the room, drumming their fingers on the window and looking out at the slow, cumbrous changes of cloud in the Russian sky over the steppe, the characters of the Russian novel fill out with the unoccupied hours of life. Loneliness intensifies character. The great personages of literature have so often been the solitary natures who overflow into the void that surrounds them, who transcend their personal lives and expand until they become prototypes. The Russian novel abounds in such figures. Oblomov is an example. Stefan Trofimovitch in *The Possessed* is another. Iudushka of *The Golovlyov Family* belongs to this category. One is tempted to say novels are important only when they create these abnormal, comprehensive people. But in saying this it is important to note one difference between the Russian figures and those of the West. Those strong-minded, bossy, tyrannical Varvara Petrovnas and Arina Petrovnas who honk their way through Russian life like so many vehement geese; those quietly mad, stagnant, frittering men who spend their time dodging these masterful women, are different from the English eccentrics. Our eccentricity or excess is a protest against the pressure of society; the Russian excessives of the nineteenth century were the normal product of a world which was so lax that it exercised no pressure at all. 'We Russians,' Shchedrin wrote, 'are not drilled, we are not trained to be champions and propagandists of this or that set of moral principles, but are simply allowed to grow as nettles grow by a fence.' Iudushka and Oblomov are natural weeds of a neglected soil. They grow by running rife and they derive their force not from private fantasy alone, as Pecksniff or Micawber do, but from the Russian situation. They are puffed out by the sluggish, forgotten hours and days of the steppe. For in the empty hours and the blank distances which separate them from their neighbours, all the fate, the history, the significance of Russia itself, is gazing back at their gaping eyes.

After reading Shchedrin's *The Golovlyov Family* one sees why a character like Iudushka, the liar and humbug, is greater than Pecksniff who is, I suppose, the nearest English parallel. Iudushka is greater, first, because he has Russia inside him, and, second, because he is encumbered with the dead weight of human dullness and vulgarity. He is greater because he is a bore. I do not mean that Iudushka is boring to read about. I mean that Dickens had no notion that Pecksniff was a boring and vulgar man; Dickens's mind was interested only in the dramatic and absurd exterior of the whited sepulchre. Shchedrin did not stop at the farce of human hypocrisy, for the tricks of hypocrisy are really too crude and blatant. Shchedrin went on collecting the evidence with the patience of one of those static realists like Richardson; and he presently came upon the really terrible thing in Iudushka's character. We can laugh (Shchedrin seems to say) at the obvious hypocrisies of Iudushka and, like his neighbours, we can grin at his eye-rolling, his genuflexions and his slimy whimsicalities; but there is something more serious. The real evil is the moral stagnation in Iudushka's character. The real evil is the muddle, the tangle of evasions, words, intrigues by which he instinctively seeks to dodge reality. We forgive his sins; what eludes forgiveness is the fact that his nature has gone bad; so that he himself does not know the difference between good and evil. He is a ghastly example of self-preservation at any price. In middle age he is befuddled by daydreams. He will pass a morning working out fantastic conundrums such as, how much money he would make out of milk if all the cows in the neighbourhood died except his own. He works out the most detailed but essentially ridiculous system of book-keeping, and imagines that he is working. Less and less is he able to face any decision, however small. He is a hive buzzing with activity – but it is the buzz of procrastination. I do not ever remember seeing such a picture of our character in any English novel; yet the humbug's art of evading an issue by confusing it is a universal one. There is one remarkable picture of Iudushka's evasion in the account of his behaviour to the servant-girl whom he has got with child. Iudushka reaches the sublimity of self-deception here. He has achieved detachment and isolation from his own actions. And the strange thing is that we begin to pity him at this point. He feels an agony and we wince with him. We share with him the agony of being driven back step by step against the wall and being brought face to face with an intolerable fact.

There is nothing notably remote from our experience in *The Golovlyov Family.* Neither the emancipation of the serfs which stupefies Arina Petrovna, nor the fact that one is reading about a remote, semi-feudal estate, makes the book seem exotic or alien to us. Our own Arina Petrovnas do not starve their sons to death, but they have driven some to alcoholism; our own Iudushkas do not publicly drive their sons to suicide. But, in the main, we must be struck by the essential closeness of Shchedrin's novel to the life of the successful middle class in England. Iudushka's prayers for guidance have a sinister echo. Walter Bagehot, I believe, said that the mind of the businessman lived in a kind of twilight, and the character of Iudushka is a remarkable example of a man whose cunning requires an atmosphere of vagueness and meaningless moral maxims. He has the stupidity of the slippery. In the end, it is not so much his wickedness that shocks his nieces, as the fact that he has become such a talker, such a vulgar babbler and bore.

Cucumbers, pickles and the mercy of God indiscriminately mix in his mind. He bores one of the girls out of the house; and one of the most terrible chapters in the book is that one towards the end when the girl comes back to his house to die and wonders whether she can bear to spend her last weeks in the house of a man who never stops drivelling on and on about trivialities. She can tolerate him only by persecuting him. This picture of the triviality of Iudushka's mind is Shchedrin's master-stroke.

The Golovlyov Family has been described as the gloomiest of the Russian novels. Certainly the characters are all wretched or unpleasant, and the reader of novels who professes that strange but common English attitude to literature: 'Would I like to meet these people?' must leave the book alone. Yet Shchedrin's book is not gloomy; it is powerful. It communicates power. It places an enormous experience in our hands. How many of the realists simply indulge in an orgy of determinism and seek only the evidence that indicates damnation. Shchedrin does this up to a point, but he is not looking for quick moral returns. His method is exhaustive and not summary. Old Arina Petrovna is a tyrant; but her lonely old age has its peculiar rewards. She enjoys guzzling with Iudushka, she adores his boring conversation; she is delighted to queer his pitch when he seduces the servant-girl. The compensations of life are not moral; they are simply more life of a different kind. Here are the last years of her life:

> She spent the greater part of the day dozing. She would sit down in her armchair in front of a table on which smelly cards were spread out, and doze. Then she would wake up with a start, glance at the window, and without any conscious thought in her mind gaze for hours at the wide expanse of fields, stretching into the distance as far as the eye could see. Pogorelka was a sad-looking place . . . But as Arina Petrovna had lived all her life in the country, hardly ever leaving it, this poor scenery did not seem dismal to her, it touched her heart, stirring the remains of feeling that still smouldered in it. The best part of her being lived in those bare, boundless fields, and her eyes instinctively turned to them at every moment. She looked intently into the distance, gazing at the villages soaked with rain that showed like black specks on the horizon, at the white churchs of the countryside, at the patches of shadow cast by the wandering clouds in the sunlit plain, at the peasant walking between the furrows, and it

seemed to her that he never moved at all. But she did not think of anything or, rather, her thoughts were so disconnected that they could dwell on nothing for any length of time. She merely gazed and gazed until the drowsiness of old age began to ring in her ears, covering with a mist the fields, the churches, the villages and the peasant walking far away.

No, Shchedrin is not gloomy because he does not soften. He undertakes to scald us with the evidence; he does not pretend that it will make vulgarity romantic or ignorance pretty. He is powerful because he remains severe. And so, at the end, when Iudushka and his niece, after their awful drunken quarrels, suddenly admit their despair to each other, and Iudushka makes the one truly heartrending cry of his life, we are moved beyond description. 'Where are they all?' he cries, thinking of the mother, the brothers, the sons he has tricked and bedevilled into the very grave. He has felt the clammy coldness of a hand touching him – and the hand is his own. His cry is like Lear's. And it is all the more appalling that he utters this cry when his broken niece is still with him; if he had cried out when he was alone we would not believe. One had indeed not grasped it until then – the total disappearance of a family, the total disappearance of all that suffering and hatred. And the force of the book is all the greater because we do not look back upon a number of dramatic intrigues capped by their scenes, but we see Russia in our mind's eye, the steppe, the little-changing sky, the distance of people from each other, the empty hours of all those lives. The English novel of family life inevitably turns from such a pessimism, but not, I think, because the English family is or was any nicer than the Golovlyovs were. The middle class, up to now, have lived in an expanding economy, which has enabled people to be independent where they could not be indulgent. If that economy becomes static or if it is put on the defensive, then a different tale will appear. The story of our money and of our religion has yet to be written.

The Great Absentee

If literature were to follow the excellent custom of the Catholic Church which adds a new saint to the calendar in every generation, and with more than half an eye on the needs of the time, it is easy to see which character in fiction is now ripe for canonization. Not the propaganding figure of Don Quixote; not the innocent Pickwick; certainly not Robinson Crusoe, that too industrious town-planner knocking up a new society. The function of the saints is to assuage the wishes of the unconscious, to appeal to that part of a man which is least apparent to himself, and today we must turn away from the heroic, the energetic, expansive and productive characters. Falstaff the coward, Oblomov the sublime sluggard and absentee, seem to me our natural candidates. Oblomov above all. In a world of planners he plans himself to sleep. In a world of action he discovers the poetry of procrastination. In a world of passion he discovers the delicacies of reluctance. And when we reject his passivity he bears our secret desire for it like a martyr. For us he sleeps, for us he lies in bed daydreaming, for us his mind goes back to the Arcadia of childhood, drinking the opiate of memory. For our sakes who live in clean rooms and who jump out of bed when the alarm clock goes, Oblomov lies among his cobwebs and his fleas, his books unread, his ink dry in the bottle, his letters unanswered. While we prosper, he is cheated. And at the end of our racketing day we see his face – the moon-like face of the obese and the slack, and with that wry kink of fret and faint madness which the moon sometimes has on it – we see his face looking upon us with the penetrating, disturbing criticism of the incurable, the mysterious reproach of the man who is in the wrong. Slowly, guiltily, his foot comes out of the bedclothes and dangles furtively above the slipper on the floor and then, with a tremor of modesty before the implications of an act so obscenely decisive, the foot is withdrawn. Who knows what valuable grains of sensibility are lost to the soul when man is persuaded to stand upright?

In all the great mad literature of nineteenth-century Russia, Goncharov's novel is, to my mind, the gentlest and most sympathetic in its feeling. Like so many great books, *Oblomov* grew beyond its author's intention. Goncharov was one of the new realists and reformers. He wrote to satirize the sluggishness of the old-fashioned landowner. The industrialization of Russia was beginning, and he wrote to praise the virtues of the new businessman. *Oblomov* is an excellent example of the ambiguous value of propagandist purpose to a novelist: in a great novelist this will stimulate the talent until it swallows the purpose. Without genius, Goncharov might have written a tract. Having genius, he has created one of the sublime comedies of all literature. After we have read this book we do not hate idleness, escapism, daydreaming: we love Oblomov. We have discovered a man, a new man whose existence we had never suspected; a ludicrous Russian nobleman who, we realize, has dwelt for a long time not in Russia but in ourselves. And so, deceptive is the relation of moral purpose and literature, we are not in the least impressed by Stolz, the busy, cheerful man of affairs, who is held up for our admiration. It is easy and natural to admire *him*; we take *him* in our stride; our sense of justice, our humanity and our sense of adventure, demand more delicate and difficult tasks. Oblomov loses Olga, Stolz marries her; but, like Olga, after her years of happy and successful marriage, we have an intuition that something was lost when Oblomov was cast away. As Goncharov wrote – and he spent many years on this book – he began to see beyond the comedy of Oblomov's condition and discern the value of it. Propaganda does not become art until it has the grace and the courage to welcome the apparent defeat of its purpose.

There is reason to regret – though such regrets are really irrelevant to criticism – that Goncharov did have a purpose, and that he took it seriously enough to create the character of the virtuous Stolz. I do not mean that Stolz is a failure as a character. Goncharov had the gift of original observation, and he was incapable of palming off on us a wooden or sentimental idealization in the manner of our Victorian novelists. He has the kind of closeness to fact which Trollope had. One's criticism of Stolz is simply that he exists at all. The book could get on quite as well, indeed it might have taken a more startling and imaginative turn, without him. And this is not pure conjecture. We now know enough about Goncharov to see that he was not merely a pedestrian realist; Russian critics had pointed out that *Oblomov* is a much more subjective book than it appears at first sight. There is more than one hint in the drawing of Oblomov's character. That he should pay for his torpor by being filthy and getting swindled we easily see. What other price is there? Ill-health, of course. But there is something more. A faint furrow comes sometimes between those bland and mooning brows; a perceptible dryness gives, once in a while, an unguarded edge to his voice. Oblomov has the horrors. Under that passivity lies a possible madness, a frantic, abysmal, screaming despair. Now, that element is neglected by the book. Goncharov's preoccupation with Stolz took his mind from it. And so, once Oblomov has retreated from his affair with Olga with all the faultless strategic skill of the neurotic, he slumps to a comfortable, though pilfered, life in the arms of his landlady. He is ill. She mothers him. She recognizes in him an innocent. This is a shock to a moral man like Stolz, who believes in self-mastery, self-knowledge, the muscular development of human character; to Stolz, Oblomov is like a man who has gone native. But benign to the end, ineffectual, happy and blessed by Fate, Oblomov dies in his sleep, protected from his enemies and wept by the few who love him.

Nothing could be more assuring. There is a transcendent gentleness, an ineffable prosaic delicacy, in the book. But we can't get away from it; the second part, although benign and moral, is dull. Suppose, for one moment, that Goncharov had not kept up his guard. Suppose that, undirected by Stolz and moral purpose, he had told much more of the truth. For Goncharov was, of course, a potential Oblomov – the fat man with the phlegmatic and malicious tongue, they called him. And Goncharov did have the horrors; he knew what they were. His life is one of those tales of mania that shadow literature, as we are said to be shadowed all our lives by our agonies at birth. Goncharov's minutely observant disposition concealed a nature eaten up by malice and jealousy. A slow, vegetating writer who wrote little, he could never forgive Turgenev for his adroitness, his skill and his success. He conceived the notion that Turgenev had stolen one of his plots and some of his characters, and even a humiliating public arbitration on the matter did not cure him. As the years went by and Turgenev's fame grew, Goncharov built up a fantastic dossier of Turgenev's supposed plagiarisms. Jealousy grew, as it will, into persecution mania. That is the drama which is missing: Oblomov's hatred of Stolz. Alternatively Oblomov's hatred of himself. Dostoevsky would have seen that; but thank heaven, Dostoevsky did not seize the character of Oblomov. He would have made him one more Russian Christ.

Looking back on that paragraph, I begin to wonder if I have not strayed into a too strenuous conception of Oblomov's character and have forgotten his humility and its complement: his immense and passive conceit. No one can say that Oblomov is a divided man, he is as perfectly integrated as a blancmange. Oblomov's relation with the swindling Zahar, his servant, is like that of wife and husband; and the master rises to feminine heights in the wonderful quarrel which takes place in the early pages. Like some inured husband Zahar watches with resignation the familiar sight of Ilya Ilyitch Oblomov building up an emotional scene:

'Then why did you talk of moving?' said Oblomov. 'Why, no man can stand it!'

'I merely thought other people are no worse than us, and if they move we can,' Zahar said.

'What? What?' Ilya Ilyitch asked in surprise. 'What did you say?'

Zahar was confused, not knowing what he could have said to cause his master's dramatic gesture and question. He was silent.

'Other people are no worse!' Ilya Ilyitch repeated with horror.

'This is what you have come to! I shall know now that I am the same as "other people" to you!'

Oblomov bowed to Zahar ironically, looking deeply insulted.

'But Ilya Ilyitch, I've never said you were the same as anyone else . . .'

'Out of my sight!' Oblomov commanded, pointing to the door. 'I can't bear to look at you. Ah, "other people"! Very well!'

The scene goes on. Oblomov calls for kvass, and begins again on an ominously quiet note:

'Well, how do you feel?' Ilya Ilyitch asked gently. 'You aren't happy, are you? Do you repent your transgression?'

'Whatever is this?' Zahar wondered bitterly. 'Something heartrending, I expect; one is bound to cry if he goes for one like this. How have I grieved you, Ilya Ilyitch?'

'How?' Oblomov repeated. 'Why, have you considered what *other people* are? Comparing me to "other people",' Oblomov said. 'Why, do I rush about or work? Don't I eat enough? Do I look thin and wretched? Do I go short of things? I should hope I have someone to wait on me and do things for me. Thank heaven I've never in my life put on my stockings myself. As though I would trouble! Why should I?'

And so he goes, pulling out all the stops, to the final words of this sublime quarrel, until Zahar is sobbing with contrition which – experience has taught him – is a necessary part of the play:

'And you,' Oblomov went on, not listening to him, 'you should be ashamed to say such things! That's the snake I've warmed in my bosom.'

'Snake!' Zahar cried, clasping his hands and setting up such a howl that it sounded exactly as though two dozen bumble-bees had flown into the room and started buzzing. 'When have I mentioned a snake?' he said amidst his sobs. 'I never even dream of the cursed thing.'

Both had ceased to understand each other and now no longer understood themselves.

Goncharov had all the comic gifts. He had the art of capping one absurdity with another yet more absurd. He is fantastic in this scene; but in the beautiful chapter which describes Oblomov's childhood and youth, he is also the master of the quieter humour of real record. The talk about the evenings drawing in, in the Oblomov drawing-room is a perfect fragment of satirical observation. Again his purely descriptive drollery is superb. There is the hour of the siesta when, the family and servants having guzzled in their plump and sunny Arcadia, all are asleep. It is a folk picture, a scene from the *Sleeping Beauty*, a fairy-tale – to those scenes Russian humour owes a profound debt:

The gardener stretched himself out under a bush in the garden beside his mattock, and the coachman was asleep in the stables. Ilya Ilyitch peeped into the servants' hall; everyone was lying down on the benches, on the floor, and in the entry; the children, left to their devices, were crawling about the yard and rummaging in the sand. The dogs retreated into the depths of their kennels, since there was no one to bark at. One could walk straight through the house and not meet anyone; one could steal everything that was about and cart it away unhindered – but there were no thieves in these parts. It was an overwhelming irresistible sleep, a true semblance of death. There was no life anywhere: only sounds of snoring of various pitch and quality came from every corner. Occasionally some sleeper would raise his head, look in senseless surprise about him and turn over or spit without opening his eyes, and munching with his lips or muttering under his breath, drop asleep once more. Another would suddenly, without any preliminaries, jump off his couch as though afraid of losing precious moments, seize the jug of kvass, blow the flies that floated in it, causing them to move violently in the hope of improving their position, take a drink, and again fall on the bed as though shot dead.

The undertone of dream and fairy-tale runs through the book like the murmur of a stream, so that to call Goncharov a realist is misleading. Oblomov himself becomes one of those transfigured characters which have grown over a long period of writing, which exist on several planes, and which go on growing in the mind after the book is put down. Now he seems to symbolize the soul, now he is the folly of idleness, now he is the accuser of success. He is an enormous character.

One other character ought to be mentioned: Olga. She is a direct descendant of Pushkin's Tatiana. In drawing her Goncharov achieved something unusual. Ever observant, he set about describing the birth and growth of a girl's personality; and especially he set out to describe what most novelists – always too much in love with their heroines – omit: the growth of their will. Goncharov showed that the apparently incalculable Olga was really quite calculable. You could show how much she would change from week to week. It is an oddly cool psychological analysis of 'the young person' and something I do not remember seeing as clearly done anywhere outside of Henry James. Much might be written about her, and much more still about a comic masterpiece which does not agitate the mind as some comedies do, but which seems to become grafted into it.

The Minor Dostoevsky

I have been reading the shorter novels of Dostoevsky. It is natural to pause before doing so for one last glance at the exalted glaciers of the major works. We stand in the sun on the modest contours of the foothills, looking up at the haggard and fog-hung precipices of Mounts Karamazov, Myshkin, Stavrogin and Raskolnikov, rather awed to think we have been up there, shuddering at the memory of it, impelled to go again, but glad of an excuse not to try it this time. We have been so lost on those heights; laughter at the wrong moments was so apt to cap the ecstasy of our expeditions. We would have periods of asking, with Tolstoy and Turgenev, whether our leader need be so shameless; and our Western natures rebelled at the notion of returning with the hangdog air of petty criminals. We conceived society to be our neighbours and their works; not a spawn of souls, half-born and without even a hour's civilization. And then, in the twenties, too heady a tradition of salvation was hung around those peaks, and it was the wrong kind of salvation. The world is not saved by novelists; and the unreason of the psychological mystics of the twenties seems to us now, I think, a rather shady attempt to get to God by the stage door. One thing scientific culture has done for us is to give us a desire for order and for intellectual propriety, and I hope we are beginning to see again that egging readers on to personal conversion is not one of the functions of the novel. In any case, the kind of salvation which Dostoevsky appeared to urge was not as private as it seemed to his adorers of twenty years ago; he did not offer a personal salvation in the form of semi-religious psychoanalysis. The people of Dostoevsky's novels are notable not for their isolation but for their gregariousness. The infection is common. They run in crowds. If they plan to commit suicide or murder they tell everyone. They are missionaries in mass-morbidity, mass-guilt, and mass-confession. Even when alone they are not absolutely alone; they have at least two selves. One hears not the private groan but the public lamentation. I can well imagine that the next time I read the great works of Dostoevsky – and we are growing nearer and nearer to his temper – I shall find he has everything to say to a Europe which is becoming a morass of broken pride, vengeance, humiliation and remorse. As a political journalist he will have a great deal to say about Christianity and Socialism, about Germany and Russia, about the criminality of Europe; as a novelist he will seem to show a profound instinct for the character of groups of people, their ideas and the common hungers that bind them.

The irrational is no longer the novelty it was, and we are consequently less struck by the madness of Dostoevsky than we used to be. A sensationalist he was; but now, whenever I open a novel of his, my first impression is one of realism and sanity. He knows the world from behind the scenes. The accent is decisive. The voice bristles with satire and expands with a capacious humour. Dostoevsky at his best writes like a hunted man who, for the moment, had fooled the bloodhounds and has time to confess and to laugh before the baying drives him on again. He is laughing hotly from the midst of experience. He is not laughing in order to forget it. The shorter novels of Dostoevsky – and in shorter works like *The Eternal Husband*, *An Unpleasant Predicament* and *Uncle's Dream*, we see the ground plan of all his greater works – are festive with experience of human society. Dostoevsky could see the terrors of our double natures, the fever in which our inner ghosts encounter each other, but he saw the raw comedy of this conjunction. It is frightful that we have so many selves and that the unconscious may wreck us; on the other hand there is something bizarre, something comic, something pitiable, in this squabbling assembly that has somehow got into one unpleasant pair of trousers. Look at *Uncle's Dream* for a moment. It is a farce; a masterful provincial lady in a scandal-mongering clique, attempts to marry off her beautiful daughter to a decrepit prince. One can picture the whole story as a very funny and quite unreal piece of theatre. But even this mechanical piece of fooling lives on several planes. One moment the Prince, with his wig, his false beard and his derelict body, is a horror; the next moment he is ridiculous. Then, suddenly, he appears as delightful. We long for him to appear again as we long for Stefan Trofimovitch in *The Possessed*. The Prince even attains a rickety dignity, and from dignity, he dwindles to a thing of pity. After all, we say, he did not really lie when he said his proposal of marriage was a dream. The conventional comic writer draws his characters to a single pattern of wit or makes the world a convenience for his joke. Dostoevsky does not do this. He is one of the great comic writers because, however satirically he may begin, he always grows into humour, and the humour is not imposed on life but arises out of it. He is aware of the collisions that take place in our natures. Somewhere – I forget where – Dostoevsky said he merely pushed things to extremes where other people went only halfway. And yet when we compare Dickens's *A Christmas Carol* with Dostoevsky's *An Unpleasant Predicament*, it is Dickens who seems to be the unreal and exaggerating artist. For Dickens exaggerated in seeing only one side of his characters. (Tony Weller's life is reduced to a reaction to widders, Barkis is merely 'willin' ', and so on.) Dostoevsky explored the whole, and the thing that is comic on one page may become tragic on the next. The profoundly humorous writers are humorous because they are responsive to the hopeless, uncouth concatenations of life.

In *An Unpleasant Predicament* we have the simple story of a pompous official who, in an access of philanthropical conceit, goes uninvited to his clerk's wedding celebrations, just to show that all men are brothers and that he is above social prejudice. Far from having a good effect, the visit ends in his total disgrace and almost succeeds in wrecking the marriage. The stages of Ivan Ilyitch's downfall, until he is carried dead drunk to the bridal bed and breaks up the wedding, are brilliantly described, and Dostoevsky, who, like all the nineteenth-century romantics, excelled in describing the moods of crowds, keeps us in uncertainty until the end. Exploring all the possibilities, that is to say raising all the mystifying issues which can be raised, as if he were writing a long novel and not a short story, he ends with justice to all. Ivan Ilyitch is not alone to blame. The poor clerk, with his pride and private quarrels with his wife, is in a muddle as well. We cannot be made responsible for the unnerving manners of our friends. No one is malignant, but everyone is to blame. It is all very well to talk about humanity and brotherhood, but be careful that in doing so you are not forgetting your own pride when you contemplate the pride of other people. Each man and woman, I warn you (says Dostoevsky, the incurable novelist), is capable of becoming a novel in himself, a novel by Dostoevsky, moreover. I warn you it is impossible to do anything whatever with any human being, unless you are fully willing to take the tumultuous consequences of his being human.

As I said before, it is odd that Dostoevsky should ever have been regarded as the novelist of the isolated soul. I can only suppose that very few readers read these comedies and do not know *The House of the Dead*, that wonderful documentary mine in which Dostoevsky describes his Siberian experiences, without hysteria or ideological puffing. In the great novels he is so blatantly the writer of spiritual headlines; in *The House of the Dead* he was content with the laconic news. No one who has read it can say that he ignored the problems of society. Like Balzac, on the contrary, he plunders society. He is acutely aware of class differences. So gregarious and populated is the unconscious, that in the typical dreams of his characters crowds of people will appear. There are, for example, the dramatic dreams in *The Eternal Husband*, Dostoevsky's most purely intellectual and accomplished comic novel. The sinister gangs of dream figures stamp up Veltchanivov's stairs and point at him with horror as he lies asleep in his guilt. In this novel it has been said that Dostoevsky parodied himself – it was written after *The Idiot* and *Crime and Punishment* – and certainly all his ideas are here: the double, the unconscious, the fantasies, dreams, persecutions, suspicions, shames and exchanges of personality. Even a child is tortured. But surely this comic masterpiece, a comedy which (as always in Dostoevsky) carries its own underworld along with it, stands completely on its own feet. In the first place the growth of Veltchaninov's sense of guilt from a vague irritation to mind and health into a definite consciousness is described with wonderful objectivity and suspense. The value of psychological analysis to the novel lay, for Dostoevsky, in its latent dramatic quality. Psychology was dramatic; for us it becomes more and more a metaphor or explanation. The farcical duel between Veltchaninov and 'the eternal husband' whom he has cuckolded, has an undertone of imaginative gravity which makes the farce more dangerous. Dostoevsky, once more, is pushing things to extremes because at the end of the extreme is the pity of human nature. Halfway – where other writers leave this kind of story – lie the conventions of melodrama and intellectual comedy; and, mad though the story is, it is full of the madness we all know about in the lives of people. The madness is the madness of life, not the madness of mind. No one will ever accuse Dostoevsky of failing to complicate a situation, and his book is a succession of superb complications. The very last one, in which 'the eternal husband' is being bullied by his new wife, and has silently to beg Veltchaninov not to cuckold him again, is one of the funniest and most moving in comic literature. The unconscious, Dostoevsky discovered, gave probability to the most bizarre situations and turned coincidence into fate. And, it is interesting to note, in the middle of this comic novel there occurs one of the very few pictures of normal, happy, family life to be found in his work.

The Eternal Husband is no doubt so refreshingly precise in its psychology, so well composed and economically written, so brilliant in its commentary because – for the time being – Dostoevsky had exhausted his anxiety for salvation. This is his one Western novel. It came from that part of him that liked to cut a social figure and was written during a rare period of equipoise and untroubled self-satisfaction. It has the genial air of a successful presumption, and it might easily have been written in our century, not his. And yet it could not have been. For the effect of psychological intuitions and discoveries upon our novel is to make it reminiscent, autobiographical, plotless; whereas in Dostoevsky's hands the novel became inventive, dramatic and far richer in plot than the rest of Russian fiction. How rich *The Eternal Husband* is in episodes; the absurd house-watching scene, the dramatic interviews, the discovery that the husband is torturing his child, the scandal at the brothel, the visit to the country, the nights which husband and lover spend together, where the husband first poses as his wife's ghost and later attempts murder! When one compares the realism of Chekhov with the romantic realism of Dostoevsky one sees how much was thrown away when novelists threw out plot. When plot went, the isolation of characters began; and though, by Dostoevsky's time, plots were stale, he showed that even the most hackneyed and novelette-like plot became rich and new when it was replenished by a new view of human nature.

An Irish Ghost

The leaves fly down, the rain spits and the clouds flow like a dirty thaw before the wind, which whines and mews in the window cracks and swings the wireless aerial with a dull tap against the sill; the House of Ussher is falling, and between now and Hogmanay, as the draughts lift the carpets, as slates shift on the roof and mice patter behind the wainscot, the ghosts, the wronged suitors of our lives, gather in the ante-rooms of the mind. It is their moment. It is also the moment to read those ghosts of all ghosts, the minor novelists who write about the supernatural. Pushed into limbo by the great novelists with their grandiose and blatant passion for normality, these minor talents flicker about plaintively on the edges of fame, often excelling the masters in a phrase or a character, but never large enough to take the centre of the stage. Such a writer is J. Sheridan Le Fanu. In mid-Victorian literature Le Fanu is crowded out by Dickens and Thackeray, talked off the floor by Lever, that supreme raconteur, surpassed or (should one say?) by-passed on his own ground by Wilkie Collins: yet he has, within his limits, an individual accent and a flawless virtuosity. At least one of his books, a collection of tales republished sixteen years ago with Ardizzone's illustrations and entitled *In a Glass Darkly*, is worth reading; it contains the well-known *Green Tea*. His other books show that, like so many talented Irishmen, he had gifts, but too many voices that raise too many echoes.

Le Fanu brought a limpid tributary to the Teutonic stream which had fed mysterious literature for so long. I do not mean that he married the Celtic banshee to the Teutonic poltergeist or the monster, in some Irish graveyard; what he did was to bring an Irish lucidity and imagination to the turgid German flow. Le Fanu's ghosts are what I take to be the most disquieting of all: the ghosts that can be justified, blobs of the unconscious that have floated up to the surface of the mind, and which are not irresponsible and perambulatory figments of family history, mooning and clanking about in fancy dress. The evil of the justified ghosts is not sportive, wilful, involuntary or extravagant. In Le Fanu the fright is that effect follows cause. Guilt patters two-legged behind its victims in the street, retribution sits adding up its account night after night, the secret doubt scratches away with malignant patience in the guarded mind. We laugh at the headless coachman or the legendary heiress grizzling her way through the centuries in her nightgown; but we pause, when we recognize that those other hands on the wardrobe, those other eyes at the window, those other steps on the landing and those small shadows that slip into the room as we open the door, are our own. It is we who are the ghosts. Those are *our* footsteps which follow us, it is *our* 'heavy body' which we hear falling in the attic above. We haunt ourselves. Let illness or strain weaken the catch which we keep fixed so tightly upon the unconscious, and out spring all the hags and animals of moral or Freudian symbolism, just as the 'Elemental' burns sharp as a diamond before our eyes when we lie relaxed and on the point of sleep.

Some such idea is behind most of Le Fanu's tales. They are presented as the cases of a psychiatrist called Dr Helvetius, whose precise theory appears to be that these fatal visitations come when the psyche is worn to rags and the interior spirit world can then make contact with the external through the holes. A touch of science, even bogus science, gives an edge to the superstitious tale. The coarse hanging judge is tracked down by the man whom he has unjustly hanged and is hanged in turn. The eupeptic sea captain on the point of marrying an Irish fortune is quietly terrorized into the grave by the sailor whom, years before, he had had flogged to death in Malta. The fashionable and handsome clergyman is driven to suicide by the persecutions of a phantom monkey who jumps into his Bible as he preaches, and waits for him at street corners, in carriages, in his very room. A very Freudian animal this. Dark and hairy with original sin and symbolism, he skips straight out of the unchaste jungle of a pious bachelor's unconscious. The vampire girl who preys on the daughter of an Austrian count appears to be displaying the now languid, now insatiate, sterility of Lesbos. I am not, however, advancing Le Fanu as an instance of the lucky moralist who finds a sermon in every spook, but as an artist in the dramatic use of the evil, the secret, and the fatal, an artist, indeed, in the domestic insinuation of the supernatural. With him it does not break the law, but extends the mysterious jurisdiction of nature.

Le Fanu might be described as the Simenon of the peculiar. There is that same limpid narrative. He is expert in screwing up tension little by little without strain, and an artist in surprise. The literature of the uncanny scores crudely by outraging our senses and our experience; but the masters stick to the simple, the *almost* natural, and let fall their more unnerving revelations as if they were all in a day's work. And they are. The clergyman in *Green Tea* is describing the course of his persecution, how it abates only to be renewed with a closer menace.

'I travelled in a chaise. I was in good spirits. I was more – I was happy and grateful. I was returning, as I thought, delivered from a dreadful hallucination, to the scene of duties which I longed to enter upon. It was a beautiful sunny evening, everything looked serene and cheerful and I was delighted. I remember looking out of the window to see the spire of my Church at Kenlis among the trees, at the point where one has the earliest view of it. It is exactly where the little stream that bounds the parish passes under the road by a culvert; and where it emerges at the roadside a stone with an old inscription is placed. As we passed this point I drew my head in and sat down, and in the corner of the chaise was the monkey.'

Again:

'It used to spring on a table, on the back of a chair, on the chimney piece, and slowly to swing itself from side to side, looking at me all the time. There is in its motion an indefinable power to dissipate thought, and to contract one's attention to that monotony, till the ideas shrink, as it were, to a point, and at last to nothing – and unless I had started up and shook off the catalepsy, I have felt as if my mind were on the point of losing itself. There are other ways,' he sighed heavily, 'thus, for instance, while I pray with my eyes closed, it comes closer and closer, and I see it. I know it is not to be accounted for physically but I do actually see it, though my lids are closed, and so it rocks my mind, as it were, and overpowers me, and I am obliged to rise from my knees. If you had ever yourself known this, you would be acquainted with desperation.'

And then, after this crisis, the tortured clergyman confides once more to his doctor and makes his most startling revelation in the mere course of conversation. The doctor has suggested that candles shall be brought. The clergyman wearily replies:

'All lights are the same to me. Except when I read or write, I care not if night were perpetual. I am going to tell you what happened about a year ago. The thing began to speak to me.'

There is Henry James's *second* turn of the screw.

We progress indeed not into vagueness and atmosphere, but into greater and greater particularity; with every line the net grows tighter. Another sign of the master is Le Fanu's equable eye for the normal. There is a sociability about his stories, a love of pleasure, a delight in human happiness, a tolerance of folly and a real psychological perception. Only in terms of the vampire legend would the Victorians have permitted a portrayal of Lesbian love, but how lightly, skilfully and justly it is told. Vigilance is a word Le Fanu often uses. We feel a vigilance of observation in all his character drawing, we are aware of a fluid and quick sensibility which responds only to the essential things in people and in the story. He is as detached as a *dompteur*; he caresses, he bribes, he laughs, he cracks the whip. It is a sinister but gracious performance.

One doesn't want to claim too much for Le Fanu. For most of his life he was a Dublin journalist and versatility got the better of him. He is known for two of his many novels: *Uncle Silas* and *The House by the Churchyard*. *Uncle Silas* has ingenious elements. Le Fanu saw the possibility of the mysterious in the beliefs and practices of the Swedenborgians, but the book goes downhill halfway through and becomes a crime puzzle. A good man dies and puts his daughter in his brother's care, knowing his brother is reputed to be a murderer. By this reckless act the good man hopes to clear his brother's name. On the contrary, it puts an idea into his head. This brother, Uncle Silas, had married beneath him, and the picture of his illiterate family has a painful rawness which is real enough; but such a sinister theme requires quiet treatment, and Le Fanu is too obviously sweating along in the footsteps of Dickens or Wilkie Collins. Lever is another echo. It is his voice, the voice of the stage Irishman which romps rather too nuttily about *The House by the Churchyard*, into which Le Fanu seems to have thrown every possible side of his talent without discrimination.

There are ghosts you shrink from, ghosts you laugh at, cold murder is set beside comic duels, wicked characters become ridiculous, ridiculous ones become solemn and we are supposed to respect them. It is all a very strange mixture, and Sterne and Thackeray, as well as Lever, seem to be adding their hand. A good deal is farcical satire of the military society in eighteenth-century Dublin, and Le Fanu is dashing and gaudy with a broad brush:

> Of late Mrs Macnamara had lost all her pluck and half her colour, and some even of her fat. She was like one of those portly dowagers in Nubernip's select society of metamorphosed turnips, who suddenly exhibited sympathetic symptoms of failure, grew yellow, flabby and wrinkled, as the parent bulb withered and went out of season.

His comic subalterns, scheming land agents and quarrelling doctors, his snoring generals and shrill army wives, are drawn close up, so close up that it is rather bewildering until you are used to the jumpy and awkward angles of his camera. One gets a confused, life-size impression, something like the impression made by a crowded picture of Rowlandson's, where so much is obviously happening that one can't be sure exactly what it is and where to begin. Le Fanu was spreading himself as Lever had done, but was too soaked in the journalist's restless habits to know how to define his narrative. He became garrulous where Lever was the raconteur. He rambles on like some rumbustious reporter who will drop into a graceful sketch of trout fishing on the Liffey or into fragments of rustic idyll and legend, and then return to his duels, his hell-fire oaths and his claret. I can see that this book has a flavour, but I could never get through it. The truth is that Le Fanu, the journalist, could not be trusted to *accumulate* a novel. You can see in *Uncle Silas* how the process bored him, and how that book is really a good short story that has unhappily got itself into the family way. His was a talent for brevity, the poetic sharpness and discipline of the short tale, for the subtleties and symbolism of the uncanny. In this form Le Fanu is a good deal more than a ghost among the ghosts.

Galdos

A Spanish Balzac

Perez Galdos is the supreme Spanish novelist of the nineteenth century. His scores of novels are rightly compared with the work of Balzac and Dickens who were his masters, and even with Tolstoy's. Why then has he been almost totally neglected by foreigners? One reason is that wherever Spanish city life had anything in common with Western European societies, it appeared to be out of date and a provincial parody; and where there was no resemblance it was interpreted by foreign collectors of the outlandish and picturesque. One of the anglicized characters in his longest novel *Fortunata and Jacinta* returns to England saying, bitterly, that all the British want from Spain is tourist junk – and this in 1873! One could read the great Russians without needing to go to Russia; their voice carried across the frontiers. To grasp Galdos – it was felt – one had to go to Spain and submit to Spanish formality, pride and claustrophobia. Few readers outside of academic life did so.

These objections no longer have the same force and it is more likely that the great achievement of Galdos can be recognized here today. A few years ago, his short novel *The Spendthrifts* (*La de Bringas*) was translated by Gerald Brenan and Gamel Woolsey and now we have Lester Clark's complete translation of the 1,100 pages of his most ambitious novel. It takes its place among those Victorian masterpieces that have presented the full-length portrait of a city.

The originality of Galdos springs, in part, from the fact that he was a silent outsider – he was brought up in the Canaries under English influences. In time he learned how to drift to the Spanish pace and then, following Balzacian prescription and energy, set out to become 'the secretary of history'. He is reported to have been a quiet and self-effacing man and this novel gets its inspiration from the years he spent listening to the voices of

Madrid. His intimacy with every social group is never the sociologist's; it is the personal intimacy of the artist, indeed it can be said he disappears as a person and *becomes* the people, streets and kitchens, cafés and churches. This total absorption has been held against him: the greatest novelists, in some way, impose – the enquirer does not. Yet this very passivity matches a quality in Spanish life; and anyway he is not the dry enquirer; his enquiry is directed by feeling and especially by tolerant worship of every motion of the heart, a tenderness for its contradictions and its dreams, for its everyday impulses and also for those that are vibrant, extreme – even insane. He is an excellent story teller, he loves the inventiveness of life itself. Preaching nothing overtly, he is a delicate and patient psychologist. It is extraordinary to find a novel written in the 1880s that documents the changes in the cloth trade, the rise and fall of certain kinds of café, the habits of usurers, politicians and catholic charities but also probes the fantasies and dreams of the characters and follows their inner thoughts. Galdos is fascinated by the psychology of imitation and the primitive unconscious. He changes the 'point of view' without regard to the rules of the novelist's game. We are as sure of the likeness of each character as we are of the figures in a Dutch painting and yet they are never set or frozen, they are always moving in space in the Tolstoyan fashion. The secret of the gift of Galdos lies, I think, in his timing, his leisurely precision and above all in his ear for dialogue; his people live in speech, either to themselves or to each other. He was a born assimilator of speech of all kinds from the rich skirling dialect of the slums or the baby-language of lovers, to the even more difficult speech of people who are trying to express or evade more complex thoughts.

The dramatic thread that runs through the panorama of life in Madrid in 1873 is the story of the love and destructive jealousy of two women. Fortunata is a beautiful and ignorant slum girl who is seduced by the idle son of rich shopkeepers before his marriage and bears him a son who dies. Jacinta becomes the young man's beautiful but pathetic wife, tormented less by her husband's love affairs than by the fact that she cannot bear children. The deserted Fortunata takes up a life of promiscuity from which a feeble and idealistic young chemist sets about rescuing her. She longs to be a respectable wife and is bullied into going into a convent for a time so that she can be reformed. But she cannot get over the love of her seducer and although she comes out of the convent and marries the chemist, she feels no affection for him. He is indeed impotent, and going from one philosophical or religious mania to another, ends by becoming insane and murderous in his jealousy of her first lover who has resumed the pursuit. It becomes a battle, therefore, between the bourgeois wife and the loose woman. Fortunata is a tragic figure of the people, a victim of her own sensual impulses who, in the end, has a second child by her seducer and regards herself as his true respectable wife because the other is barren. But her child is taken over by the rich and legitimate wife and Fortunata dies raging. The scene is overwhelming. The last time I wept over a novel was in reading *Tess* when I was eighteen. Fifty years later Fortunata has made me weep again. Not simply because of her death but because Galdos had portrayed a woman whole in all her moods. In our own nineteenth-century novels this situation would be melodramatic and morally overweighted – see George Eliot's treatment of Hetty Sorrel – but in Galdos there is no such excess. The bourgeois wife is in her limited way as attractive as Fortunata.

Among the large number of Fortunata's friends, enemies and neighbours, there are two or three portraits that are in their own way as powerful as hers. First there is Mauricia la Dura, an incorrigible, violent and drunken prostitute to whom Fortunata is drawn against her will in the convent. Mauricia attracts by the terror and melancholy of her face. She is a genuine Spanish primitive. There is a long and superb scene in which she manages to get hold of some brandy in the convent and passes from religious ecstasy to blasphemy, theft and violence. It is a mark of a great novelist that he can invent a fantastic scene like this and then, later on, take us into the mind of the violent girl after she has got over her mania. Galdos knows how to return to the norm:

'I was beside myself. I only remember I saw the Blessed Virgin and then I wanted to go into the church to get the Holy Sacrament. I dreamt I ate the Host – I've never had such a bad bout ... The things that go through your mind when the devil goes to your head. Believe me because I'm telling you. When I came to my senses I was so ashamed ... The only one I hated was that Chaplain. I'd have bitten chunks out of him. But not the nuns. I wanted to beg their forgiveness; but my dignity wouldn't let me. What upset me most was having thrown a bit of brick at Doña Guillermina, I'll never forget that – never – and I'm so afraid that when I see her coming along the street my face colours up and I go by on the other side so that she won't see me.'

Doña Guillermina, a rich woman who has given up everything for the rescue work, is another fine portrait of the practical good-humoured saint, a sort of Santa Teresa who – and this shows the acuteness of the novelist's observation – can be frightened, a shade automatic, and sometimes totally at a loss. Against her must be placed Doña Lupe, a lower-middle-class moneylender. She is a miser who shouts to her maid:

'Clean your feet on the next-door shoe-scraper . . . because the fewer people who use ours, the more we gain.'

But at the wedding of Fortunata to her nephew we recognize Doña Lupe as more than a grotesque. Galdos is superior to Balzac in not confining people to a single dominant passion:

Once back in the house, Doña Lupe seemed to have burst from her skin for she grew and multiplied remarkably . . . You would have thought there were three or four widow Jaurequis in the house, all functioning at the same time. Her mind was boiling at the possibility of the lunch not going well. But if it turned out well what a triumph! Her heart beat violently, pumping feverish heat all over her body, and even the ball of cottonwool at her breast [she had had one breast removed] seemed to be endowed with its share of life, being allowed to feel pain and worry.

The final large character is Max, the husband of Fortunata. She dislikes him, but he has 'saved' her. Puny and sexless, Max begins to seek relief in self-aggrandizement, first of all in prim and ingenuous idealism; when he realizes his marriage is null and that his 'cure' of Fortunata is a failure, he turns to experimenting with pills and hopes to find a commercial cure-all. His efforts are incompetent and dangerous. The next stage is paranoia caused by sexual jealousy. He moves on to religious mania: thinks of murder and then invites his wife to join him in a suicide pact, in order to rid the world of sin. For a while he is mad and then suddenly, he recovers and 'sees his true situation' – but recovery turns him into a blank non-being. Here we see Galdos' belief in imitative neurosis, for in a terrible scene poor Fortunata is infected with her

431

husband's discarded belief in violence. She declares she will love him utterly, if only he will go and murder her libertine lover. But Max has fallen into complete passivity: he enters a monastery where he will become a solitary mystic – and he does not realize that the monastery he has chosen is, in fact, an asylum.

It is surprising to find this Dostoevskian study in Galdos but, of course, Spanish life can offer dozens of such figures. They are examples of what Spanish writers have often noted: the tendency of the self to be obdurately as it is and yet to project itself into some universal extreme, to think of itself mystically as God or the universe. But usually – as Galdos showed in his portrait of the ivory-carving civil servant in *The Spendthrifts* – such characters are simply bizarre and finicking melancholics. Around them stand the crowd of self-dramatizers in the old cafés, the pious church-going ladies, the various types of priest, the shouters of the slums. What is more important is his ability to mount excellent scenes, and in doing so, to follow the feelings of his people with a tolerant and warm detachment. He is never sentimental. There is one fine example of his originality and total dissimilarity from other European novelists in his long account of Jacinta's honeymoon. The happy girl cannot resist acting unwisely: little by little she tries to find out about her husband's early love affair, mainly to increase the excitement of her own love. No harm comes of this dangerous love game, but we realize that here is a novelist who can describe early married life without reserves and hit upon the piquancy that is its spell. I can think of no honeymoon in literature to match this one. The fact is that Galdos accepts human nature without resentment.

Henry James

Birth of a Hermaphrodite

When the second volume of Leon Edel's life of Henry James opens, the novelist is twenty-seven. He is forty by the end, a success, 'sufficiently great', but not yet the Master. The clever book-reviewer, the nimble writer of travel sketches, is at first seen worried and restive in Boston after his 'passionate pilgramage' in Europe, fussed by the choice between American virtue and the beautiful European corruption. (In a hundred years how *that* international moral tale has changed!) He goes to his native New York and slaves for a while as a high-class hack. Travel writing once more releases him for Italy, France, Switzerland and Turgenev's Baden, but by the time he is thirty-three, his pleasant job as a sentimental traveller for the *New York Tribune* is ending and he has run through the flimsy, seasonal acquaintance of his fellow expatriates in the spas and capitals. France has disappointed in the end for he has 'seen all round' Flaubert and Zola; French social life has turned out (it always does to the foreigner) to be impenetrable. He has been thrown upon the boulevards among a lot of third-rate tourists.

Sooner or later any travelling American swallows his love-hate for the British and is subdued by the convenience of the English tongue. The strain of linguistics gives place to the pleasure of even vulgar conversation. So James comes to London and finds what he needs – tradition, the back numbers of *Punch*, speaking likenesses of Dickens's people and Thackeray's everywhere, coal fires, draughts, and a home. Looking out of his window off Piccadilly he reflects that Becky Sharp once lived round the corner in Curzon Street and that – sublime contentment – Lord Ashburton's dirty brown brick wall is across the way. James was a Londoner at last, yet not quite smoked and kippered to our condition. He indeed fell back on French in his happiness: *'Je suis absolument comme chez moi.'* The phrase preserves a nuance in his philandering relation to the city and the country he was, in the end, to adopt.

There was never anything flighty in Henry James's movements. He came to London with a prepared campaign and an inner calendar in his head. He steamed ponderously in like an engine, on time. If there is one thing that both Leon Edel's volumes have brought out it is that the Master was a major strategist as a writer and in his social life. There is – or was – no more highly trained snob than the Boston snob; he got onto the right people at once and, that done, London was easy to penetrate, for the right people were not sticklers and asked only to be amused. Their deplorable lack of 'analytical intellect' assured that they would be pleasant. London was the chosen site, a 'regular basis of mundane existence', for James's next battle: after success, the organized achievement of Greatness.

Our usual picture of James comes from the later, old Pretender period when he seems to be genuflecting, somewhere in space, before the image of Art, mysteriously sustained by an invisible private income. The young James with the glossy beard is quite a different person: dashing, shrewd about ways and means, burning with energy. There is vast confidence in his malice and his ironic laughter. He is absolutely professional. He delights to earn his living; he is tough with editors; he is prompt and clever with his pot-boilers; he has an eye to serials and commissions. He was long-headed enough to know, within six months, when he would be able to switch to greatness. He arrived in London for the publication of a work of serious criticism and of his early novels, which were unknown here. A few rapid moves and he knew everyone. At first agog, but soon he was in the clubs – a 'member' in the full soporific sense. A word from Henry Adams – the supreme Yankee snob and expert at the game – and he was staying in the best houses. The lazy, genial Thackeray had been ruined by dining out; for James it was part of the plan. In his second winter, he had dined out 140 times and in the best society – 'behold me after dinner conversing affably with Mr Gladstone'. Not always, of course, in the best. There were flops. There were shabby, literary ladies. There were dreary Oxfordish parties, shoppish and local in their eternal gossip. If he was bowled over by the handsomeness of the English men they had, he noticed, dirty hands.

Handsome himself, witty, attentive to women, especially to old ladies, James was enormously popular in mid-Victorian London. His talk was light yet serious. He pleased everyone, though he was careful not to speak his mind outright. The curse laid upon the British – it was the complaint of Taine – was their lack of that analytical mind. He never really got to the heart of the English matter. Privileged travellers, like James, tend to see any society as obligingly static and displaying the end-products of character: to the forces that make a people what they are, James was blind. It is not the business of a novelist to do so, but the novels of Henry James tell us little about *English* life beyond the relations of the rich to their servants.

There are, all the same, two Henry Jameses: the novelist with his 'beautiful contrivances' and exquisite adumbrations who confines himself, with one or two exceptions, to upper-class life; and the traveller who slums with any company. He mooched in the London streets, swallowed the fog, looked at gin-soaked squalor and so far unbuttoned as to go off with the crowd to the Derby. An unsuspected England showed itself – violent, jolly and uninhibited. He had, on the whole, a low opinion of the British female, though admittedly she did not run, after an early blossoming, to the American stringiness. The British female of the lower orders was alarming. She was 'too stout, too hot, too red, too thirsty, too boisterous, too strangely accoutred', yet (one was obliged to add) 'useful, robust and prolific'. Like Britannia, in short. In *The Princess Casamassima* he turned her to account in the fine picture of Millicent Henning, with her Cockney beauty, 'her bad grammar and good health . . . her shrewd perceptions and grotesque opinions'. (James could not bear it that English women were healthy.)

Once more in this second volume Leon Edel gracefully disposes of the notion that quiet lives, and especially the lives of writers, are uninteresting. James toiled. The hours of his life are filled up less with minutes than with words. They edge him out, phrase by phrase, from nearly all external experience except eating, flirting, walking alone at night and sleeping. The clues to the inner dramas are in his work. James's inner life – perhaps this is true of all novelists – is an affair of ghosts. The figures of father, mother and above all of William the brother and rival actively haunt him and provide their crises. No doubt all families are tyrannies of the affections, but the James family, withdrawn on principle from the contagion of participation in American life, conscientiously standing for 'being' rather than 'doing', was like some closed city state. The mother – 'too sacred' to be described by James – ruled it in what we now accept as the American habit. To think of breaking with it meant, in William's case and that of his sister, invoking the protection of illness. They are all held together by brilliance, irony, the private devices. William cannot manage to marry until he is thirty-six and is, strangely, in Europe when his child is born. Henry escapes because he is the spoiled boy, the second son, Angel as he was mockingly called, hiding his forbidding will to power and his egotism behind the mask of meekness. His deepest friendships are with elderly women, although there is one episode – his presumably platonic and prolonged and rather secret flirtation with Constance Fennimore Woolson – in which, meaning to be merely disturbing, he was himself disturbed and challenged. It led to headaches and, later, to the refinements of remorse. In art and the egotism of the artist James had found his safety and liberation.

But the ghosts could suddenly play a decisive part. They can be seen grouping and regrouping in the early stories where William and Henry grapple in disguise. When William got married the profound relation of Henry with his brother was shaken, and Mr Edel notes that one of his worst stories, *Confidence*, was written at this time: two young men fall for the same young woman who is called, of all things, Angela! The Angel has feminized himself. This might have been a fantasy of passing interest but the fraternal crisis coincided with the uproar in America about his study of Hawthorne: his deepest feelings were stirred.

Henry James, conquering London and its literary world, could be as assertive and powerful as Christopher Newman; but rejected like Newman – or pushed to the wall by his elder brother – told that he wasn't fit to play with rough boys or that his writing was full of knots and bows and ribbons, found himself reminded forcibly that he was a perpetual 'mere junior'.

Until now his novels had been about heroes. In the one seeming exception, *Daisy Miller*, the girl is seen through the eyes of a man. Henceforth they would be about heroines responding 'to their destinies in a world that jilted, denied and betrayed'. He would write *Washington Square* and *The Portrait of a Lady*. Was this a matter of imaginative dexterity, or did it come from his nature? A hermaphrodite – according to Mr Edel – discovered himself.

And in *The Portrait* Mr Edel directs us, with great perspicacity, to one of those inner dramas of compensation and confident

436

self-extending that bring a writer's powers to maturity – if they come at the right time. Who is Osmond in *The Portrait*? He is, Mr Edel says,

> the hidden side of James himself, when his snobbery prevailed over his humanity and arrogance and egotism over his urbanity and his benign view of the human comedy . . . in creating him Henry put into him his highest ambition and drive to power – the grandiose way in which he confronted his destiny . . . In the hands of a limited being, like Osmond, the drive to power ended in dilettantism and petty rages. In Henry's hands the same drive had given him unbounded creativity.

If he closely watches the ghosts in James's life, Mr Edel is not tempted into those murkier areas of the psychological limbo which have been irresistible to the reckless school of biography. We are shown James living as we might have seen him. There he goes riding every morning in the Campagna with some lady he has charmed; there he goes out for his night walks in London; there he sits reading at the Reform; watching, very shocked, the great Turgenev playing with Pauline Viardot's children on the floor; obdurately working all the afternoon in Italy while William wais impatiently for him to finish. James lived in the extremes of solitude and sociability; his is one of the most peopled lives lived by a man of genius, for the genius depended on their chatter. To have got all these people back out of literature into James's life as Mr Edel has done is remarkable in itself, but the skill with which these things are made to build up James's own life as a man is more remarkable. The short chapters, each carefully pointed, take one with alacrity along the crowded peregrinations of James's mind and person, without a moment's boredom. Mr Edel has come close to the excited spontaneous sensibility and intelligence of a man who baffles us by being enormous and yet who, in a way almost enviable, has no life at all.

By the time the fourth volume of Leon Edel's rich and searching biography of Henry James opens, the Master has had to face the shattering fact of the suicide of Miss Woolson in Venice, and is about to receive another blow in the very sanctum of his so far invulnerable egotism: in his art. His plots for success in the theatre (and as an operator James was as exhaustive here as he was in his social stratagems), his hopes of the financial magnificence of the best-sellers at a moment when he was himself becoming noticeably less saleable, are to be brutally dashed by the booing of *Guy Domville*. He took the affair as if his person had been assaulted, as if he had been mugged. The strategist, in life and in art, the addict of military memoirs, has had a public defeat, and at a truly 'awkward age'. He is fifty; a younger irreverent generation of realists, who have no interest in High Romance, has burst open the door. He is called further to account by his first humiliating attack of gout.

The next five years, in Mr Edel's diagnosis, are a period of 'nervous breakdown', and he is to be shown slowly emerging from it by his invincible belief in the therapy of his art. At his age many artists turn to easier remedies, or slacken in their vigilance, for even art has its temptations; but James (perhaps because he was a solitary and a man of puritan energy) had always known that the important thing was to increase difficulty. In his case – and I would have said for all – the temptation is to thin oneself by looking forward: the difficult task is to reconstitute oneself by looking back. And so Mr Edel's purpose is to show James performing on himself 'what Freud was busily demonstrating' – the power to heal oneself of hardening wounds by retreat to earlier experience. The process is dramatically clear: it is not a question of curing himself by work, but of divining the right work. James found it in the treacherous five years, by writing his tales of children, ghosts and phantasmagoria: it is the period of *The Pupil*, *The Awkward Age*, *What Maisie Knew*, *The Turn of the Screw* and of that mystifying search for the heart of personality, *The Sacred Fount*, before the spacious final works are attempted.

For the comedy of Jamesian anecdote Professor Edel has little use. The adroit letters (he has said before) are either recklessly discharged smoke-screens or a collection of tactical feints. They are histrionically concealing. Professor Edel notes enough of James's familiar social life at Lamb House, his meetings with Kipling and Meredith, the devastating visits of Edith Wharton, the last journey to Italy, his bicycle rides and so on, to keep the spry, practical, restless 'character' alive and to preserve his engaging momentousness. But the cure is the thing and Professor Edel studies it, until it completes itself at the end of the book, with the tremendous sight of the Master shaving off his beard. But Professor Edel relies on James's clue: 'The artist is in every page of every book from which he sought so assiduously to eliminate himself.'

The difficulty here is to avoid theory or dogmatic assertion about the meaning of echoes, symbols and images, and I don't know any writer who is so free of the vices psychology has offered to biography as Professor Edel is. He is pertinacious, but tactful, gracious and tender; indeed, this is the most moving of his four volumes. His suggestions, gathered from the novels, tend to build up a whole rather than a schematic figure, and he is aware that a writer may go far back into his past for a word or a crucial incident without consciously displaying an item of personal history. We can see Professor Edel's method at work in what he has to say about the melodramatic ending of *The Spoils of Poynton* and its possible relation to James's horrifying experience when he was booed off the stage after *Guy Domville.* Professor Edel notes that the book does not have one of James's traditional endings: why melodrama?

Perhaps because he had himself been forced to the centre of the stage, in a bit of melodrama not of his own making. His imagery went further back however than the recent disaster in the St James's. In describing Mrs Gereth's departure from Poynton and her loss of her antiques, *her* work of art, James wrote 'the amputation had been performed. Her leg had come off – she had now begun to stump along with the lovely wooden substitute and would stump for life, and what her young friend was to come and admire was the beauty of her movement . . .' Thus James had recourse in this work to one of the most personal images out of his own childhood. It suggests how vivid for all his lifetime was the memory of his father's amputation and 'the noise . . . about the house'. The father had lost a leg in a stable fire and Henry subsequently had suffered a back injury while helping to fight a stable fire at Newport. Amputation and fire: these symbols out of the past now forced themselves into the story he was telling. Poynton and its 'spoils' had to be destroyed as *Guy Domville* was destroyed.

One practical result of the failure in the theatre was that he now turned to planning his stories as scenarios. This unluckily doubled their length. We are at the beginning of the period when over and over again his stories are too long for their subject. (This is true, for the contemporary reader, of masterpieces like *The Pupil*.) Before, he never revised; now he will revise interminably; and when he takes up dictation, the manner will take on the appearance of an intricate private reverie.

So the cure has its price. But the gains are extraordinary in life and in literature. By taking his mind back to childhood, James was obliged to consider his femininity. His masculinity had been driven underground.

> To be male was to risk [in the remote fantasy of childhood] such things as amputation like his father; . . . he could escape by thinking himself a little girl.

The rivalry with the older male, William, appears in tale after tale in many forms. Lack of male conviction was the weakness of *Guy Domville*. In retreating to Lamb House and brooding on his past, James was retreating into a simulacrum of his life in the James family; and hence the buried struggles of childhood come to the surface. The feelings that arose out of the past were a 'kind of conscious nightmare'. In *The Turn of the Screw* the ghosts are the ghosts of his boyhood. Little Miles's 'rude' battle with the governess, telling her he doesn't want to be cooped up with females, is a transference of James's own conflict. Miles is defeated, and it is important to see that, told in the first person by the governess, the story is a statement of female hysteria. The femininity of Henry James is speaking. Maisie is a study of himself in boyhood – she is, I remember noting years ago, facetiously addressed as 'my dear sir' by one of her guardians. Nanda of *The Awkward Age* would be a projection of the Henry of late adolescence. The little girls – and without writing a conscious series (as Professor Edel shows) James studies them at progressive ages – emerge 'out of the personal healing' which was going on under the surface of the practical, ambitious, successful man of the world.

Professor Edel's patient and careful method makes his point; for although one can say that any author's life is buried in his work in this way, James's distinction is that he knew what he was doing: his father's faith in compensations was part of family training. Only occasionally does the reliance on verbal echoes seem to me strained. When the governess feels her 'blow in the stomach' it seems merely ingenious to trace this back to the blow in the stomach James said he had had at the St James's Theatre. And when the child Effie is murdered by drowning, I think Professor Edel is pushing matters when he links this with what James called his 'subaqueous' feelings after *Guy Domville.*

The final chapters of the volume are as moving and perceptive as those that were given to the story of Miss Woolson in the earlier volume. There, a hardness of heart and a good deal of disingenuousness appeared in James's character. He certainly feared entanglement, but the part played by a distaste that looks secretive and snobbish seems plain. That by dying our friends extinguish part of ourselves is true enough, and it is characteristic of James's truth-telling and glacial egotism to show this as an affront. In *The Beast in the Jungle* he knows remorse. The present volume contains an account of James suffering as Miss Woolson suffered, in his extraordinary passion for the young, crude and climbing Norwegian sculptor Hendrik Andersen. They saw little of each other, but the separations were agonizing and the letters are filled not only with ironical advice to the young god who was vulgarly on the make, but with physical longings. He wanted to touch the young man. He wanted to hug and embrace him: 'lean on me as a brother and a lover'. And 'I hold you close' and 'I feel my arms around you'. These expressions may be simply a well-known mode of Victorian emotionalism:

> Allowances must be made [Professor Edel says] for James's long puritan years, the confirmed habits of denial, the bachelor existence, in which erotic feeling had been channelled into hours of strenuous work and the wooing of *mon bon.* One also must remember that James had a fear of loss of masculinity . . . James was constitutionally incapable of belonging to the underworld of sex into which Oscar Wilde had drifted.

His feelings had been transferred to the intellect. His philanderings with his many women friends went to fanciful lengths, and were really utterances of High Romance. But clearly, this time, there was passion on James's part. He was still writing it at the age of seventy. He comes out of the affair with his reply to another young man who had asked him what port he had set out from as a novelist:

> The port from which I set out was, I think, that of the *essential loneliness of my life* – and it seems to me the port, in sooth, to

which again finally my course directs itself. The loneliness [since I mention it!] – what is it still but the deepest thing about one? Deeper about me, at any rate, than anything else, deeper than my 'genius', deeper than my 'discipline', deeper than any pride, deeper above all, than the deep counter-minings of art.

He wrote this while correcting the proofs of *The Sacred Fount* – that baffling and even trivial book which Professor Edel sees as the final therapeutic act that would mark his self-healing. Until now, as a novelist, he had never dealt with love in his novels, except as a 'force destructive of – or in competition with – power and aesthetic beauty'. He had now discovered that his egotism was vulnerable. Professor Edel's *Life* has not only scope and mastery of lively details and argument; it goes with bold and yet controlled insight into the labyrinth of a great creative imagination. The man and the artist have been joined – a feat that biography so rarely succeeds in.

Henry James's *The American Scene* is still one of the very few excellent books of travel by an American about his own country. He is as exact and prophetic in his own restricted way as the extraordinary and very different Tocqueville was in his. The book is unique in a genre where – strangely enough, among a foot-loose people – American literature is very poor; for penetrating observation and evocation of the land and the cities we have to turn to novels and, above all, poetry. The remarkable thing about the book is that although it was written in 1905, and in spite of the huge changes that have occurred in America since that time, it presents (as Leon Edel says in a troubled introduction) an essential America that is still recognizable.

This ought not to surprise us: great artists are always far-seeing. They easily avoid the big stumbling blocks of fact. They rely on their own simplicity and vision. It is fact-fetishism that has given us those scores and scores of American books on America, the works of sociologists, anthropologists, topical 'problem' hunters, working-parties and statisticians, which in the end leave us empty. Henry James succeeds because he rejects information. He was himself the only information he required.

It should be unfailingly proved against me that my opportunity found me incapable of imparting information, incapable alike of receiving and imparting it; for then, and then only, would it be clearly attested that I *had* cared and understood.

He was looking for a personal relationship to the scene he had left twenty years before. In so many other books on the country the sense of a relation is lacking; indeed, they leave one with an impression of a lonely continent, uncontemplated, unloved, unfelt by a people who have got so much out of it, as they move on, that they see little in it and give or leave nothing of themselves to the scene. How else to explain that sensation of things, places, even people abandoned which is so painful in the American landscape! How often one has felt what James sensed about certain American scenes, especially in New England:

> And that was doubtless, for the story-seeker, absolutely the story: the constituted blankness was the whole business, and one's opportunity was all, thereby, for a study of exquisite emptiness.

Or:

> Charming places, charming objects, languish all round, under designations that seem to leave on them the smudge of a great vulgar thumb – which is precisely a part of the pleading land appears to hint to you when it murmurs, in autumn, its intelligent refrain. If it feels itself better than so many phases of its fate, so there are spots where you see it turn at you, under some familiar tasteless inflections of this order, the plaintive eye of a creature wounded with a poisoned arrow.

Henry James knew what the poison was. It would eventually wreck the American cities – a process our planners always out of date, are eager to imitate in England today.

James was a traveller, that is to say, a story-seeker to the marrow. His novels themselves are conscious journeys into the interior. He had started writing travel sketches of things in France, Italy and Germany and England when he was young; the 'vignettes' of a sentimental traveller, meant to tease the American fancy for the Atlantic trip. *The American Scene* is a totally different matter. Perhaps at the age of sixty the returning expatriate originally promised himself one more sentimental pilgrimage. But in twenty years American life had passed through a crucial change. It could either sink him or raise him by the challenge. He was roused. Half the pleasure of the books comes from the sight of a travelling mind reinvigorated. He met the challenge with a richer and revived analytical gift. He rejected the journalistic temptation. In the twenty years since 1883 a huge immigrant invasion had changed the character of the cities; big business, the great industrial monopolies, had taken total power and had imposed the business ethos; the pursuit of money had become the engulfing and only justifying role. New York had been a rough, low-built sea port with pigs rooting in the streets of lower Manhattan when he left, Central Park was farmland. He returned to find Manhattan crammed, and the skyscrapers rising – 'simply the most piercing notes in that concert of the expensively provisional into which your supreme sense of New York resolves'.

James ignored the colossal news item. He saw that his subject was not shock and that he was not there to advertise or boost the obvious. His subject was how the consciousness of a half-repentant expatriate would be affected, and what inner meanings and sensibilities he could offer in return. Guilt there would be, but distaste: nostalgia for what was gone, but a feeling for the drama; he would have to be both personal and yet the analyst. He became the seeker. He would have to lay himself open to the full bewilderment of his situation. In his introduction to an earlier edition of this book, W.H. Auden described it as a prose poem; an excellent description. Generously evocative and labyrinthine in its tact, it also shows a man struggling with love and menace. The skyscrapers are a 'vocabulary of thrift' but there are 'uglier words' for that. With mild but deadly truth they evoke (he says):

the consciousness of the finite, the menaced, the essentially *invented* state [that] twinkles ever, to my perception, in the thousand glassy eyes of those giants of the market.

Again and again, he remarks on the 'pathos' of a civilization so exuberantly on the move, but bewildered in having to accept itself as temporary. Of the new rich he writes:

What had it been their idea to *do*, the good people . . . do that is, in affirming their wealth with such innocent emphasis and yet not at the same time affirming anything else.

They live in houses that have:

> the candid look of costing as much as they knew how. Unmistakably they all proclaimed it – they would have cost still more had the way but been shown to them; and, meanwhile, they added, as with one voice, they would take a fresh start as soon as ever it should be. 'We are only instalments, symbols, stop-gaps,' they practically admitted, and with no shade of embarrassment: 'Expensive we are, we have nothing to do with continuity, responsibility, transmission, and don't in the least care what becomes of us after we have served our present purpose.'

And the governing motive:

> To make so much money that you won't, that you don't 'mind' anything.

Not, as it has turned out, the awful sight of American cities. If you do 'mind' you can easily become an un-American activity.

For James, America was 'dancing on the thin crust of a volcano'. In personal relationships,

> the most that was as yet accomplished . . . was the air of unmitigated publicity, publicity as a condition, as a doom from which there could be no appeal.

There was the inability to communicate, which was not felt as a loss among the new immigrants, but rather as a gain; they had become American. James, the native, puts his finger on what often dismays the chatty European traveller in his casual contacts: the American chill.

To isolate James's hostile impressions as I have done or to quote his final denunciation of the reigning spirit of the time – a denunciation which did not appear in the first American edition – is to give a misleading impression of a book warm in feeling and rich in texture. Every page contains a picture or a phrase that will bring New York, Boston, the scrub forest of New Hampshire, to the eyes, but backed by his long loving knowledge of the places. He records such deeply American things as allowing the forest to come down to the edges of the innumerable lakes. The story-seeker, as he calls himself, continually questions the landscape in relation to himself and it is the self-questioning which is at the heart of his ability to create the scene in the superb chapter on New Hampshire. Why does it seem to be Arcadian? Why was he always brought back to the thought that the woods and rocks insist on referring themselves to the idyllic? Was it because they bore no burden of history? The thought charms him, but another thought makes him sceptical: perhaps he rhapsodized now, because in Europe he had been deprived:

> to excess – that is for too long – of naturalism in quantity. Here it was in such quantity as one hadn't for years to deal with; and that might itself be a luxury corrupting the judgement.

The irony is subtle; but hasn't James hit exactly upon what drifts through one's mind as one drives the scores of miles through the scrub, the brown rock and grey rock of New England, or stands by some clear cold pond in the woods – the lyrical and, at the same time, crushing quantity of Nature, stupefying the mind? How much the love of quantity, together with its inexorable, umbrageous detail, has meant to an American mind.

James spent about a year as a returned native. Business and immigration were the important themes, alien to him and to his natural nostalgias; no searching was needed as far as business was concerned. That hit one in the face. The immigrants were more difficult, but he took a lot of trouble to see what was happening on New York's lower East Side.

There, as a writer, he was as excited as he was disturbed by what would happen to the language, and to character. How long would the melting take? Then he went South, and any romantic hopes he had were pinched by the wretched weather and the general shabbiness. He is still good, but he is better on native ground. He discovered that Washington was the place where, for once, men ruled the conversation. Outside of known, friendly haunts, he had been starved of two things in America: conversation – all that was offered was talk – and privacy. He hated the open interior of the American club and house. But if, inevitably, he harks back to the times when a home was not a house, when locality existed and the tycoons were unknown, if he denounces the new age and sees it will lead to worse, he is soundly American in admiring the drama of the situation and in his feeling for the extravagant.

The search for the story, the inturned Jamesian story, is at once pertinacious and very touching. He creates an America because he creates himself in relation to it. The book is a true work of travel because it is a collaboration and with a living country that scatters a myriad unanswered questions about 'as some monstrous unnatural mother might leave a family of unfathered infants on doorsteps or in waiting-rooms'.

An Emigré

The daily evil of the emigré is his isolation. He has lost the main ground of the moral life: that we do not live until we live in others. The temptations that face him are embittering to any man capable of reflection: he can live in the past; he can become an uprooted dilettante; he can cultivate, in the words of Heyst in Joseph Conrad's *Victory*, that 'form of contempt called pity' which comes easily to the isolated man; he can regard anarchy as the ruling spirit in the world. Crime may come nearer to his fingers and, with less obstruction, to his imagination than it does to rooted people. In a world like our own, the solicitations of the police, the secret agent, the revolutionary, the traitor, are very likely under one guise or another, to come his way. No doubt these extreme enticements are evaded by most emigrés, who alleviate the sense of persecution by living in the past and keep their nostalgias and their rancours indoors; but, mild or extreme, they unite to force upon the isolated man his main addiction. He becomes pre-eminently a conscience.

Isolation and conscience are the dominant motifs in the novels of Joseph Conrad and, two of them especially, *The Secret Agent* and *Under Western Eyes*, become more and more suggestive to the contemporary reader. They attract because they are free from that sudden fogginess, that enlarged bad temper which Conrad called Destiny, and from the melodrama or rhetoric, which play tricks with the lighting and climate of many of his ambitious works. They have the compactness, the efficiency of that peculiarly modern form of writing, the thriller with a bitter moral flavour. And they put a central modern question to ourselves – what is our attitude to treachery and other moral consequences of a belief in revolution?

Conrad's terms are out of date, of course, though not as seriously as might be thought. Anarchists do not throw bombs in London; in Russia, the tyrant is not assassinated. But the essentials of European history have not changed since the eighties of the last century; what was talked about has simply come true. The revolutionary thug who has the fine art of bursting Razumov's ear drums in *Under Western Eyes* is an anthropoid forerunner of thousands who have gone one better than that in the police states. Conrad is a reactionary; for him the old despotism and the new Utopianism are complementary forms of moral anarchy. Their end is cynicism, more despotism, more destruction and to that opinion some have now reluctantly come. But Conrad was a fixed reactionary; he had never tried to tack across the revolutionary tide; he hated the Russian revolution as a Pole who was already a generation away from the hatred of his time; his hatred was glued into the past. The positive contribution of his political views is that they double the precision of our dilemmas of conscience by presenting them in reverse. The weakness – let us get it over at once. Conrad's judgement is true and untrue, but what he said of Heyst in *Victory* points out the weakness:

> The young man learned to reflect, which is a destructive process, a reckoning of the cost. It is not the clear-sighted who lead the world. Great achievements are accomplished in a blessed warm mental fog.

Conrad is an exile. He is not committed except to pessimism. He is, for private and public reasons, tortured by the danger of becoming a moral dilettante. Because he is so excruciatingly aware of all the half shades of that case, he has his authority.

Razumov in *Under Western Eyes* is a sympathetic character. He is the recurring 'lonely' being in Conrad's novels. Another Conradian theme, perhaps Slavonic and certainly Romantic: he has a 'double' in Haldin, the student assassin. 'In times of mental and political unrest', the Razumovs of the world keep:

> an instinctive hold on normal, practical everyday life. He was aware of the emotional tension of his time; he even responded to it in an indefinite way. But his main concern was with his work, his studies and with his own future.

Not a prig, not a careerist, not dull; he is intelligent and sensitive. His worst fault is a bad temper which comes from one of Stendhal's definitions of misfortune: 'Not having the evils of his age' – if we can use the word 'age' in a double sense. The irrational driving force in him comes from insecurity and loneliness; he is a bastard. Just when Razumov's good resolutions are ripe, Haldin the terrorist hides in his room and by the very contact, dooms Razumov to eternal political suspicion. There follows a scene in which Conrad's highest dramatic gifts as a novelist are brought, uncorrupted, into play: the picture of the student's room, Razumov's despairing journey through the snow at night to the inn to fetch the cab driver who will enable the exalted assassin to escape, Razumov's discovery that the man is dead drunk; and then the journey back in which, having failed, Razumov revolts against his unjust situation and his own quietism, changes his mind and betrays Haldin to the police. The scene is a very long one and also exposes Conrad's weakness – the creaking sentence, the rumble of stage scenery and some staginess of dialogue.

Conrad wrote *Under Western Eyes* perhaps to bring a harder Western focus upon a theme of Dostoevsky. There is an evident Polish contempt for the lack of fixed positions in the Russian mind; or, at any rate, an ironical wonder at its readiness for cynicism. With brilliant ingenuity he caps scene after scene with its opposite. The exalted assassin is plainly sensitive about the 'greatness' of his action. Razumov has acted from a sense of right and discovers even *that* will not be its own reward; exile alone is possible. Guilt (as always in Conrad) marks the drifter. Yet even exile is poisoned, though not by remorse; it is poisoned because the authorities can now force Razumov to become a spy on the revolutionaries as the price of concealing his act. Razumov is obliged to take on the mind of a guilty man when, by his morality, he is virtuous; in doing so, and by contact with Haldin's young sister in Geneva, he comes to see the innocent and honourable illusions that precede conversion to revolutionary action. The inevitable Russian confession follows, not because Razumov has changed his mind, but because he longs for moral freedom.

What is contemporary in this book is the response to seediness, treachery, slackness and corruption. This response is the direct product of the last words of Heyst in *Victory*:

> Woe to the man whose heart has not learned while young to hope, to love – and to put his trust in life.

Conrad himself found a strong if not lasting interest in the order and discipline of life at sea, and his scorn is softened in *Under Western Eyes* by the attempt of one kind of Slav to understand another. In *The Secret Agent* there is no such emotional entanglement; his scorn, unrestrained, now becomes almost overpoweringly rich and pungent and his irony leaves nothing standing.

The masters of Conrad's day were Meredith and Stevenson and Conrad's book about the lazy agent-provocateur who gets his feeble-minded brother-in-law killed by mistake, shows the strong influence of these writers. *The Secret Agent* is a thriller, a very artificial form of writing which realism rarely redeems from its fundamental fantasy. No thriller can be believed and even when meaning and psychological ingredients are put into it, its people and events cannot really bear the weight. *The Secret Agent* begins with the incredible character of Vladimir, the absurd highly stylized intellectual plotter, and the artifice is at odds with the truly real and powerful elements in the book: the descriptions of London, the portraits of those perfect if intellectually diagnosed Londoners, Mrs Verloc, her mother and Steve. Outside of this warm, human centre Conrad is dangerously exhibitionist. Here conscience has its sardonic comedies and he seems superbly to be showing off his obsession with the dirtiness, the shabbiness of foolish or dishonoured minds:

> His descent into the street was like the descent into a slimy aquarium from which the water has been run off.

A detail like that – and Conrad is a master of image – describes a London street and defines the book. Verloc's birth-control shop takes one down and down to the grubbiness of London's back streets and the pathetic vulgarities of cheap civilization.

Conrad's genius was for picturesque discussion rather than for narrative – he was tortured, one is told, by the difficulties of invention – and what always impresses is his rummaging about, back and forth, in the lives of his characters. Verloc, the agent, is wonderful in his laziness, his dull humour, his amorousness, his commonplaceness and his injured vanity. It was a master stroke to make this destroyer respectable and to pounce upon the isolation – once more, the Conrad theme – in which this foolish member of the French-letter trade lived. Towards the end, when the idiot Steve has been killed through Verloc's irresponsibility, it is wonderful that Verloc quite unblinkingly expects the tragedy to make no difference to his relations with his wife. After all, she has got *him*! The murder is not well done. It is, in fact, too cleverly done, with an eye for all the effects and shows Conrad at his most self-conscious. The crime is in keeping with the contrived tone of the book, the general unsavoury sapience; but the author's irony is too much with us. Mrs Verloc is as wonderful as the husband she kills. She is a simple, reserved woman, governed by the desire for security, living on two or three strong and usually concealed feelings. Her words, in the London way, rarely reveal what these are; in fact the way in which she talks off the beat of her feelings the whole time is well observed. But when she discovers that her husband is a monster, that he is a worse monster because he does not realize it or does not see why *that* should upset his domestic bliss; when she realizes he is a moral idiot and that his reply to grief is: 'Let her have her cry. I'll go to bed with her, that'll put her right,' a terrifying woman rises up with a carving-knife in her hand. Afterwards, it is perfect that she relapses into the simple resource of a feminine guile, so pathetically vain, that a crude crook can do her down as easy as winking.

Head, the police superintendent, is another sound portrait. His Assistant Commissioner belongs to the dubious higher moral reaches which thriller writers have a perennial fancy for: contact with crime and the police sows in them the desire to have everything taped: God comes to Scotland Yard. The Assistant Commissioner, one notices, has the now professional 'sense of loneliness, of evil freedom', but this is, at the last moment, made real to us by one of those sardonic afterthoughts by which Conrad saves himself from sentimentality. The Assistant Commissioner, we are told, finds 'the sense of loneliness and evil freedom *rather pleasant*'. This is indeed why he is an Assistant Commissioner: he is a hunter. (It is always, in Conrad, the small additional comment, that puts on the rounding and convincing touch.)

Conrad, the exile, the isolated man, was the master of any atmosphere. That gift comes at once to the sensibility of the emigré. Like the French novelists, like Meredith and Henry James, he moves in narrative from idea to idea, to the change in moral climate rather than from event to event. The first part of *Under Western Eyes* comes beautifully to a close on Councillor Milukin's short enquiry when Razumov says he is going to retire: 'Where to?' Obviously there is nowhere. Conrad's novels are marked by such crucial sentences, which change a whole view of life, and his dramas are the dramas of the change of view. Conrad, the dilettante, takes the soul or the conscience, and tries them now in this position, now that; a new Good means a new guilt. Heyst in *Victory* knows the reason: the son of a brilliant man who has seen through all human values, Heyst is a born exile in a world that shocks. His aim must be to avoid committal. But like the Captain in *The Secret Sharer* who has the runaway hidden in his cabin, Conrad also has the committed 'double' in his life. This dichotomy provides the drama and the rich substance of his books.

Kafka

Estranged

At the beginning of his 'Investigations of a Dog', Kafka wrote – in Willa and Edwin Muir's translation –

> When I think back and recall the time when I was still a member of the canine community, sharing in all its preoccupations, a dog among dogs, I find on closer examination that from the very beginning I sensed some discrepancy, some little maladjustment, causing a slight feeling of discomfort which not even the most decorous public functions could eliminate; more, that sometimes, no, not sometimes, but very often, the mere look of some fellow dog of my own circle that I was fond of, the mere look of him, as if I had just caught it for the first time, would fill me with helpless embarrassment and fear, even with despair.

The flat bureaucratic style strikes one as being a mask: Kafka notoriously did not know where he belonged. He was a Jew not quite in the Christian world; as a non-practising Jew – at the beginning anyway – he was not quite at home among Jews. The German critic Günther Anders, from whom I take these remarks, goes on:

> As a German-speaking Czech, [Kafka is] not quite among the Czechs; as a German-speaking Jew not quite among the Bohemian Germans. As a Bohemian he does not quite belong to Austria. As an official of a workers' insurance company, not quite to the middle class. Yet as the son of a middle-class family not quite to the working class.

In his family he wrote that he is 'more estranged than a stranger' and at the office he is alien because he is a writer. In love he is in conflict with literature. Because he was an extreme case which was exacerbated by fatally bad health, Kafka was able to enlarge, as by a microscope, the sense of exile which becomes visible as a characteristic of our experience in this century, its first martyr to 'alienation', which has become something of a cult.

When we turn from his books to his letters we have a series of self-portraits desperate and courageous, always eager and warm in feeling; the self is lit by fantasy and, of course, by drollery. His candour is of the kind that flies alongside him in the air. He was a marvellous letter writer. For these reasons alone the present translation of the *Briefe* first published in 1958 and collected by his great friend Max Brod is worth having. Richard and Clara Winston, the American translators, tell us that it is based on that volume and it is not clear to me whether 'based' means the whole thing or a selection from that volume – I fancy, the whole. (Other parts of Kafka's large correspondence have been translated, notably the important *Letters to Felice* by James Stern and Elisabeth Duckworth in 1973.) The present volume does contain now the full text of his long letter explaining his break with Julie Wohryzek to her sister, and the whole of the long letter to his parents a few days before he died in 1924 at the age of forty-one. There are also a few letters (of slight interest) to Martin Buber.

We hear the authentic Kafka when he is writing in a girl's album that words cannot carry memories because they are 'clumsy mountaineers and clumsy miners'; or to a fellow student when he is nineteen:

> When we talk together, the words are hard; we tread over them as if they were rough pavement. The most delicate things acquire awkward feet . . . When we come to things that are not exactly cobblestones or the *Kunstwart* [a cultural magazine, of Nietzschean tendency, edited by a nephew of Richard Wagner: another kind of paving], we suddenly see that we are in masquerade, acting with angular gestures (especially me, I admit), and then we suddenly become sad and bored . . . You see, we're afraid of each other, or I am.

Later on, letters are comparable to 'mere splashings of the waves on different shores: the waves do not reach one'. In 1916, quick to admit that his stories are painful, he adds proudly that he wants to be 'truly a man of his time'. In 1922 when his many illnesses have united to become the fatal tuberculosis of the larynx, he writes to Robert Klopstock, the young medical student who was often with him in his last years, that he wants no indissoluble bonds, beyond the tacit, with men or women:

> Is there anything so strange about this anxiety? A Jew, and a German besides, and sick besides, and in difficult personal circumstances besides – those are the chemical forces with which I propose to straightaway transmute gold into gravel or your letter into mine, and while doing so remain in the right.

That may sound bitter, but he is really thinking about his role as a writer of fables who reverses the classic manner of fable in order to be truly that man of his time. Again:

> The writer . . . is a scapegoat of mankind. He makes it possible for men to enjoy sin without guilt, almost without guilt.

He sways between assertion and qualification, between reaching out to the gold of friendship and retiring into defensive strategies. They are necessary, especially in his relations with women, in order to pursue literature and nothing else. Such manoeuvres have a sick man's pedantry, but in fact the self-irony, the kindness, the nimbleness, the fantasy, mask the pain. When it is certain that he is terribly ill he begs that this shall be kept from his parents and adds that his:

> earthly possessions have been on the one hand increased by the addition of tuberculosis, on the other hand somewhat diminished.

He imagines a battle of words going on between brain and lungs; talks of clinging to the disease like a child to the pleats of his mother's skirts. During a longish period at the house of his beloved sister Ottla at the village of Zürau he is plagued by country noises. A girl plays the piano across the street, children scream, men chop down trees, next comes the scream of the circular saw, then the loading of logs into an ox wagon, the noise of the oxen, the shunting of the trains going away. A tinsmith starts hammering. Noise, he says, is the scaffolding within which he works; perhaps in the end, he says, noise is a fascinating narcotic. And then the house is alive with mice and the long half-farcical, half-obsessional drama continues for many letters. The creatures race round the room – he has the fancy that he can frighten them off by making his eyes glow like a cat's. He gets a cat in, the cat shits in his slippers; when the cat quietens the mice he still sits up half the night 'to take over a portion of the cat's assignment'.

> Certainly this fear, like an insect phobia, is connected with the unexpected, uninvited, inescapable, more or less silent, persistent, secret aim of these creatures, with the sense that they have riddled the surrounding walls through and through with their tunnels and are lurking within, that the night is theirs . . . Their smallness, especially, adds another dimension to the fear they inspire.

We see by his speculations about a Mouse Sanatorium that he is on the edge of one of his breakdowns and that soon he will once more find himself in hospital.

In love, Kafka sought perfection, knowing that it was an impossibility; knowing also the ideal served as a defence as ingenious as an insurance company's refusal to admit a claim. The most honest statement of this defence is in the long letter to Julie's sister, a confessional document of pitiless and subtle self-searching and, as always, frankly expressing his guilt – elsewhere he said that guilt so easily turned to nostalgia. The sincerity, and above all the sensibility to friendship, in letters to women, give them a spontaneous grace. The self he is preserving is in no way hard but clearly expatiated. Yet it glows under the friendship he receives and also offers.

As a sick man he is, one might say, negotiating a life which he knows is diminishing. He has the patient's ironical interest in the clinical state of his condition; and when he says, for example, that there is something fundamentally childlike in the Czechs of Prague, he describes a trait many foreigners have noted in the most tormented of all European cities, and a quality he shares. There is something of Italo Svevo, who was also partly Jewish, in his exploration of his condition: illness is a kind of second self that has cleverly moved in on him.

There is scarcely anything about the 1914–18 war – illness secluded Kafka – although he does have a few incidental lines about the shortage of food and, afterwards, some anxious joking about German inflation, especially in Berlin. He is even detached about anti-Semitism: this is interesting because he shows how active anti-Semitism was in the early twenties in Germany; he makes a distinction between the Eastern European and the Western European Jews: the former were beginning to go to Palestine, to which he too was emotionally drawn and from which he withdrew: a spectator.

Kafka's most revealing things come most naturally in the letters to Max Brod, who is the strong, ever active, positive, generous and successful writer. Kafka reads Brod's latest works as they come out, comments on them with enthusiastic interest and also takes over Brod's marital troubles in the manner of a brother exhaustive in advice. There is a letter to Brod in 1923, written from Berlin-Steglitz, which shows the continuous circling of Kafka's self-awareness:

> It is true that I do not write to you, but not because I have anything to conceal (except to the extent that concealment has been my life's vocation), nor because I would not long for an intimate hour with you, the kind of hour we have not had, it sometimes seems to me, since we were staying together at the north Italian lakes. (There is a certain point in my saying this, because at the time we had truly innocent innocence – perhaps that's not worth regretting – and the evil powers, whether on good or bad assignments, were only lightly fingering the entrances through which they were going to penetrate some day, an event to which they were already looking forward with unbearable rejoicing.) So if I do not write, that is due chiefly to 'strategic' reasons as have become dominant for me in recent years. I do not trust words and letters, my words and letters; I want to share my heart with people but not with phantoms that play with the words and read the letters with slavering tongue. Especially I do not trust the letters, and it is a strange belief that all one has to do is seal the envelope in order to have the letter reach the addressee safely. In this respect, by the way, the censorship of mail during the war years, years of particular boldness and ironic frankness on the part of the phantoms, has proved instructive.
>
> I forgot to add to my remark above: It sometimes seems to me that the nature of art in general, the existence of art, is explicable solely in terms of such 'strategic considerations', of making possible the exchange of truthful words from person to person.

Letters like this take one straight across the bridge from Kafka's private life into *The Castle* and *The Trial*, both of course unfinished and published after his death. There was a great deal of Swift (whom he read attentively) in Kafka's 'mad' imagination, above all in his habit of seeing people and sensations exactly, microscopically, as objects. He was much taken by Swift's inflexible remarks on marriage and the bringing up of children. The letters to women have even something of Swift's advisory playfulness, and are all gentle to a degree one would have thought unlikely in a man so self-enclosed, alone, and perhaps even proud, with some delicacy of manner, of being incurable.

An Irish Oblomov

There is a terrifying sentence in James Stephens's account of his meeting with Joyce in Dublin that unfortunately came to my mind when I was struggling with Samuel Beckett's trilogy, *Molloy*; *Malone Dies*; *The Unnamable* – 'I looked at him,' says Stephens, 'without a word in my mouth except vocabulary.' Will someone not chart the vivid but interminable ocean of Irish garrulity for us, point out the shallows and the depths, tell us where the words are vocabulary only and where they connote ideas or things, where they are propitiatory magic, where egomania filling in time and place? Where is language used for language's sake, and where is it used as a gabble-gabble ritual to make tolerable the meaninglessness of life? It would be of practical help to know whether a writer was drowning well within his own depth or out of it; and when it would be decent to leave him to it – possibly coming back later, after a smoke, to see how he was getting on.

One does this with *Tristram Shandy*. One does it with *Finnegans Wake*. Pending necromantic guidance, with Beckett's novels, one does the same. They are lawsuits that never end, vexations, litigations joined with the tedium, the greyness, the grief, the fear, the rage, the clownishness, the physical miseries of old age where life is on the ebb, and nature stands by smiling idiotically. Why was I born, get me out of this, let me live on less and less, get me to the grave, the womb, the last door, dragging this ludicrous, feeble, windy broken old bag of pipes with me. Find me a hole. Give me deafness and blindness; chop off the gangrened leg; somewhere on this rubbish dump where I crawl there must be some final dustbin, where I can dribble, laugh, cry and maunder on the this and the that of the general mystery and occasionally give a toothless grin over an obscene word or a farcical sexual memory.

Flight, old age, and the wrangle about personal identity, these are Samuel Beckett's themes. A man is a vestige left to hop around in wearying argy-bargy after his invisible master: punishment, for the old, unremembered sin. Life is the *belle dame* with the mindless smirk and she hardly troubles to look at the victim who has been reduced to the total lethargy of compulsive speech. That is the joke: the mutilated thing can *talk*. In the first volume the man is Molloy, the tramp with crutches, a mixture of simplicity, hurt and lunatic energy. He can still spit with contempt at society:

One of us at last! Green with anguish. A real little terrestrial! Choking in the chlorophyll. Hugging the slaughterhouse walls! Paltry priests of the irrepressible ephemeral!

He bashes along on his bicycle, through the town, trying to get to his mother. He runs over a dog –

an ineptness all the more unpardonable as the dog, duly leashed, was not out on the road, but in on the pavement, docile at his mistress's heels. Precautions are like resolutions, to be taken with precaution. The lady must have thought she had left nothing to chance, so far as the safety of her dog was concerned, whereas in reality she was setting the whole system of nature at naught, no less surely than I myself with my insane demands for more light. But instead of grovelling in my turn, invoking my great age and infirmities, I made things worse by trying to run away. I was soon overtaken by a bloodthirsty mob of both sexes and all ages, for I caught a glimpse of white beards and little angel faces, and they were preparing to tear me to pieces.

– but the lady stopped them, saying she was taking the dog to the vet to be put down, in any case, and he had saved her a painful task.

This volume has all Beckett's headlong comic gift. Molloy is in the clownish state of senility, his disqualified life has the spirit of either a fairy-tale or inverted idyll; and in his pestiferous search for 'more light' on everything and nothing – mostly the latter – there is a grin half of mockery and half of frenzy on his scabby face. His sexual memories are funny because they are few, take him by surprise, and they are a mixture of the grotesque and touching, the dirty and the modest. He has dragged his body around all his life, and it follows him like some ignorant valet. There is far more to compare with *Tristram Shandy* in the caprices of this volume and its exploits in self-contradiction in order to hold the floor, than there is with Joyce.

In the second volume, *Malone Dies*, we move from the freedom of rebellion to loneliness. Malone, by the way, may be another aspect of Molloy; he doesn't know who he is. As far as I can make out the scene of the novel is a madhouse or infirmary for the old, and Beckett becomes the grammarian of solitude. The senses are dying. How does Malone know where the veils of air end and the prison walls begin? The body turns in smaller and smaller circles; the mind conjugates trifles. Here Beckett intervenes with some satirical observation of normal people, a trite couple and their favourite son, a piece which might have come out of Sartre's *Nausée*, or Nathalie Sarraute, and we are reminded that Beckett writes his novels first in French.

But we return to endless hair-splitting, metaphysical speculation sliding from association to association, and these convey that as age increases the tedium of life, so the unwearying little talker in the brain, with his lawsuit against life, bosses every half minute of it. Grief and pity hang between his words; but the book unexpectedly ends in wholesale murder, when the feeble-minded inmates of the infirmary are taken out on a picnic.

In the third volume, Molloy, Malone, Mahood, Murphy – whatever the name is now – is a lump, almost sightless, stone deaf, always weeping, mutilated, immovable, the helpless centre of a world that he can be conscious of very rarely. He is about to become Worm, all human identity gone. The archaeological kind of critic who can recover a novel from its ruins might be able to make something of this volume. I find it unreadable, in the sense that I cannot move from paragraph to paragraph, from page to page. It is all significance and no content.

The stream of consciousness, so lively and going dramatically from image to image in Joyce, is here a stream of imageless verbosity occasionally broken by a jab of obscene anger, but grey, grey, and it goes monotonously along in phrases usually about seven words long, like some regularly bumping old tram. This is, of course, not so much the stream of consciousness as the stream of solitude and provides the comedy of overhearing a man talking to himself – Bloom, one recalls, rarely talked; things 'came up' in his mind. He was in the midst of drama – a comedy that is genuine enough certainly, but not of boundless interest.

Why is Beckett interesting as a writer? As a contemporary

phenomenon, he is one more negative protest against the world going to the slaughterhouse, one more protest on behalf of privacy, a voice for myopia. He is a modern Oblomov, fretful and apathetic, enclosed in private fantasy, dropping off into words instead of sleep. They are eloquent, cunning, unremitting words.

He is far from feeble, for there is a devil-like slyness in the half grin on the faces of his old men who can hit out with their crutches. What tedium! they exclaim – speaking not only of existence and human solitude – but, we suspect, of ourselves. His imagination has the Irish cruelty and self-destructiveness that Yeats once spoke of. Beckett's anti-novels, like all anti-novels, have to deal with small areas of experience because their pretension is to evoke the whole of life, i.e. life unfixed by art; the result is that these verbose books are like long ironical, stinging footnotes in small print to some theme not formulated. But there is a flash of deep insight in the madness he evokes: it is strange that in a generation which has put all its stress on youth and achievement, he alone should have written about old age, loneliness, and decrepitude, a subject which arouses perhaps our deepest repressed guilt and fears. He is the product of a civilization which has become suddenly old. He is a considerable, muttering comic writer, and although he conveys unbearable pain, he also conveys the element of sardonic tenacity and danger that lies at the heart of the comic gift.

Graham Greene

Disloyalties

English novelists are not notable for their sense of evil. James
Hogg of *The Confessions of a Justified Sinner* has it, and so, in a
romantic way, has Stevenson, but both are Scots. Conrad, the
Pole, has it; so has Henry James, the American. Among ourselves
it is hard to find. There are signs in *Clarissa*; in Dickens evil
appears hysterically in the forms of staged melodrama. Only
Emily Brontë fully exposes her imagination to the dark spirit and
with a pagan or pantheistic exhilaration and pride which profoundly shocked her contemporaries. For Hardy evil is an aloof
and alien polity. It can hardly be called more than mischance. The
rest of the English novelists settle for a world which must be judged
in terms of right and wrong.

Against this Protestat tradition the novels of Graham Greene
are a rebellion or, rather, a series of guerrilla ambushes from a
Roman Catholic point of view. He was once said to be a Jansenist
and was certainly at variance with the accommodating Catholic
tradition on the Continent. His religion – as we see it in his early
novels – has the egocentricity, the scruple, the puritanism and
aggression present in English nonconformity, though it finds more
savour in failure than success. God is his misadventure and, for
this reason, maybe he is a religious man, i.e. he does not expect to
get anything but conflict and pain out of his religion. I must say
this is a vast relief after the optimism of the success cults. To the
spectator, it seems that Greene wishes to have an adulterer's, a
gambler's or a spy's relation with his God and Church, finding
more merit in despair than in the laborious conniving at the
goodness the ordinary hypocrite goes in for. On the other hand, a
man like Scobie, in *The Heart of the Matter*, can hardly rank with
the great sinners; he lacks the pride. His muddles and illegalities
rate official damnation but, as the priest suggests, there is still
God's mercy. His portrait has some of that sentimentality which

has come over the Channel from François Mauriac. I doubt if it is fair to Roman Catholic moralists to say that they believe the worst thing is to break the rules.

The light and serious novels of Graham Greene make their impression because of his phenomenal skill, his invention, and the edge and precision of his mind. He etches the conventional with the acid of the observable. His thrillers are not simply escapes from ordinary life, but are painful journeys into it: the agent, hunter or hunted, unveils. In *The Confidential Agent* the true subjects are pain and betrayal. He seeks the exact:

> She lay there stiff, clean and unnatural; people talked as if death were like sleep; it was like nothing but itself. He was reminded of a bird discovered at the bottom of a cage on its back, with the claws rigid as grape stalks: nothing could look more dead. He had seen people dead after an air raid; but they fell in curious humped positions – a lot of embryos in the womb. This was different – a unique position reserved for one occasion. Nobody in pain or asleep lay like this.

In one book at least, *The Power and the Glory*, he transcends his perverse and morbid tendencies and presents a whole and memorable human being; this wholeness is exceptional, for Greene is generally an impressionist, or rather a cutter of mosaics. We expect from incisive talents some kind of diagnosis, some instinctive knowledge of the human situation which we have not attended to; this Greene has had. His subjects are the contemporary loneliness, ugliness and transience. We disapprove of the ugliness of our civilization without recognizing that, for some reason, we *needed* to make it ugly. Greene makes great play with this in his novels; behind the ugliness is loneliness and betrayal. Very nearly all his characters are marked by the loneliness in our civilization, and on the simplest level – Scobie's for example – they are merely self-pitying. They fail to communicate. Scobie hates talking to his wife because of fear that she will make yet another scene; he knows that talking to his mistress will lead fatally to the re-enacting of the same stale dramas of jealousy. These people wish to be alone; yet when they are alone, the sad dialogues of nostalgia, conscience and betrayal begin in the mind; and presently each character breaks in two: the pursuer and pursued, the watcher and the watched, the hunter and the hunted. The relationship with God, if they are

Catholics, is the same. One moment it is God who will have no mercy; next it is Scobie who is torturing God. In *The End of the Affair* the narrator accuses himself of inability to do anything but hate; and Fowler in *The Quiet American* admits that he translates his personal hatred of Pyle and Pyle's dangerous political innocence into a fantastic hatred of the American continent. Loneliness, the failure to communicate in love, or rather to sustain communication, is the cause, and behind that is the first cause, the betrayal we are thought to have experienced in childhood when evil was revealed to us. This is a contemporary subject for, in Greene's rendering of the world, we are now anonymous. We are bleak, observable people in streets, on staircases, in boarding-houses, hotel rooms, cafeterias, Nissen huts, native villages, police stations – free, but disheartened and 'wanted'.

Greene's masterly power of evoking the shabby scene, whether it is Pimlico or Liberia, Mexico or Kent, is a matter of a vision true to its misanthropy and quickness of eye; but it owes something also to his sense of being an accomplice. We are guilty transients leaving our fakes and our litter. There is an odd and frequent suggestion that romantic literature misled us. China, Liberia, Mexico ought not to have looked like this. In the later books, particularly in *The Quiet American*, the mood has become rather too much the conventional habit of disillusion (assumed for self-protection) of the American school of reporting. In fact only one scene was real reporting, so I have since learned. Only the minor figures observed by the master reporter in the war scenes are individual; the rest have become types. Fowler is mere self-pity; Pyle is a flat profile. There is always a danger in Greene's novels that the stress on banality and anonymity will turn into type-casting and that he will forget that the loneliness of people, on whatever level, is only an aspect of them. In *The Heart of the Matter*, Scobie's scenes with young Mrs Rolt become typical and therefore forced. The sudden leap from pitiable youth to the jealousy of the trained virago on Mrs Rolt's part, makes Greene's point of course, but is too pat. In his honesty he is too eager to see evil doing its stuff.

In *The Power and the Glory*, Greene succeeds above all the rest. In the other tales, by quickness of cinematic cutting, by turning eveything he sees to the advantage of action, he makes circles round our doubts. The preposterous argument of *Brighton Rock* is lost in the excitement of the hunt. But in the Mexican novel no doubts arise. There is no overt resentment. There are no innuendos. There are no theological conundrums. It is actually an advantage that Greene hated Mexico and the tropical rot; he had worked the worst off in a vivid book, *The Lawless Roads*. Except for the portrait of the seedy Mr Tench, the dentist, at the beginning, and the account of the Catholic family reading their forbidden literature secretly, there is nothing to distract us from the portraits of the whisky-priest and the lieutenant, his pursuer. In this kind of drama, Mr Greene excels, but here there is meaning, not fear-fantasy; the priest is taken from depth to depth in physical suffering and spiritual humiliation. The climax is reached when he is disowned by his mistress and his child and this long scene is wonderful for the way in which the feeling is manipulated and reversed. The scene in the prison, into which he is thrown by mad misadventure, has to bear the moral burden of the story – that he is at peace with the criminals and outcasts from whom he need not hide his identity, and that he is in danger only from conventional piety. We should not forget that Greene trails his coat in order to provoke mercy and has a subtle and compassionate intelligence of unvoiced pain. As a novelist he is free of the vice of explanation in this book; we see a soul grow and recover its dignity. And the dialogue between the pursuing lieutenant and the priest at the end is a true dialogue; it is not a confrontation of two views, but of two lives. The only weakness is in the transition to the Catholic family and the inter-cutting of scenes at the end. I do not know what the intention is. Is it to take us into the starchy world of Catholic piety, into that religious respectability which Greene detests and where, indeed, right and wrong take the place of good and evil? Or is it a return to Greene's boyish love of romantic literature? The child is 'believing' in a boy's heroic adventure in defence of the Faith, as Greene himself might have 'believed' in Rider Haggard. The misanthropy of Greene often reads as if it were a resentment of the deceit of books for boys and a rancour against the loss of the richly populated solitude of childhood.

In *The Comedians* Graham Greene returns to the reporter-novelizing manner of *The Quiet American* and is in a better temper. This book has the usual self-indulgence, the usual zest in the sardonic view. A Greene character has a hard time of it. The couple whom Brown, the present narrator, saw copulating cheerfully in the hotel swimming-pool one night in Haiti could have no notion that he would make a sermon out of them later on, by placing the body of a politician with his wrists cut in the corner of the pool: later still, to ram home the text, the battered head of the same politician will confront yet another woman who kneels down in a garden to be had by a policeman. It is hard luck to be a figure in a parable of sadomasochism.

Another woman – a German whose burden is that her father had been executed for Nazi crimes and who is the mistress of the narrator – fights back against the 'dark-brown world you live in'. There is danger, you see, even in Brown's name. Having got out of bed and sworn at her suspender, she gives him a lecture.

> To you nothing exists except in your own thoughts. Not me, not Jones. We're what you choose to make us. You're a Berkeleyan. My God, what a Berkeleyan . . . My dear, try to believe we exist when you aren't there. We're independent of you. None of us is like what you fancy we are. Perhaps it wouldn't matter so much if your thoughts were not so dark, always so dark.

She is right. She has even accused him of being a novelist. And she is right again. In so many of his novels Graham Greene makes an overwhelming and literary intervention so that his people are reduced to things seen flat in the camera's eye and by the cleverest of living photographers. It is true that the author's mind is courageous, charitable and compassionate: no character can complain that he has not been enhanced in the very instant of being flattened or narrowed – and to say that is to say a great deal for Greene as an artist. If he piles it on, he does so with the inner gaiety of a great talent. But one often wishes that he were less of a contriver and would let the characters show for themselves what their meaning is. That passage about Berkeley is unlikely in the mouth of the German refugee wife of a diplomat in Haiti; it annuls her as an independent human being and breaks the novel's illusion. Not only that, one suspects the speech is there as an essayist's insurance against the suspicion that elsewhere, in the 'piled-on' incidents, Greene is parodying himself as a novelist. And perhaps as a conceit or a joke.

The theme of the novel is put by a priest preaching on the text: 'Let us go up to Jerusalem and die with him.' Indifference is to be condemned more harshly than violence. 'Violence can be the expression of love, indifference never. One is an imperfection of charity, the other the perfection of egoism.' The indifferent are the comedians, i.e. the egoists, in a tragic world. (It is odd to see indifference presented as the antithesis of violence; but I suppose we are back at that barbarous Manichean idea expressed in 'Because ye are neither hot nor cold' etc. etc.) The chief comedian is Brown himself, a lapsed Catholic speculator who has never known his father, was born in the no man's land of Monte Carlo and now runs a tourist hotel in Haiti. He has inherited it from his mother, a decent, now elderly tart, found living with her black servant: she dies – need one say – after one last fling of intercourse. The black servant is so upset he hangs himself.

Brown had left Haiti, partly because of his possessive jealousy of his mistress, the diplomat's wife; now he returns to the disgusting police state and to the murdered politician. The horrible condition of this *triste tropique* is sharply evoked. No one so powerfully burns an exotic and seedy scene on the mind. Haiti is an island run by faceless negro and mulatto crooks in sun-glasses. In Port-au-Prince arrives a farcical pair of American innocents, one-time freedom-riders, all for justice, who wish to persuade the government to open a vegetarian centre. The cranks are slow-motion slapstick, but they have their courage and dignity. They are also – in a business way – shrewd: this, and one or two adroit observations of their affectionate hypochondria, redeem them from pure caricature. They pass harmlessly from the scene – one can see that Brown's hotel had to have a least a couple of residents – to make way for a merry little spiv called Jones, self-styled hero of the Burma war, semi-secret agent, speculator, petty gambler, stoic, self-advertised Don Juan, and an instant friend of Papa Doc, the bloody dictator; selling out on him, however, he joins a Resistance group in the mountains.

Jones is a *comic* comedian – he is committed to making something of the anarchy that the deeply comic are drawn into. It turns out that he has lied about everything – he is, in fact, wanted internationally for theft – but his lies catch up with him and he is forced to lead the guerrillas in the mountains because his bluff is called. Why do the Resistance people take him on? Because he is so irresistible. He makes people laugh. He has no real notion of what he is doing, beyond perhaps being a bit awestruck by people of principle. Eventually his feet let him down in the rough country. It is a surprising weakness that one has the death of Jones by hearsay; also that of Dr Magiot, the sad, upright Marxist who has managed to survive because communists are useful political counters: they enable Papa Doc to blackmail the Americans.

In this context of secret shootings, beatings-up and dejected plotting, in which the Haitians have either the brutal or the dedicated parts, Brown and his mistress conduct their sexual comedy, in momentary beddings in the backs of cars, and in a grave-like hollow under the trees. They are nervous of discovery; Brown thinks his mistress's child may be spying on them. It is an affair constantly on edge because of his possessive nagging jealousies – Greene is always on the *qui vive* for the ironies of impotence and desire. And of betrayal. Treachery has always been one of Greene's central preoccupations as a moralist. Brown betrays Jones because he is jealous, by working cynically on his vanity; and the irony is that Jones, the liar, is the better man. His life could be construed, Brown suddenly sees, as a series of delinquent approaches to virtue. Such paradoxes fit in admirably with Greene's gift for creating suspense.

Brown is cool enough in danger, but he is a born destroyer of his own and his mistress's happiness. It is he who is really the absurd figure because all his suspicions turn out to be untrue: he has so little perception of normal feelings. Jones, the shady liar, is capable of inspiring affection. Brown, the adulterer, is so tied-up that he inspires pity. But Brown *thinks* – it is noticeable how often the heroes of the reporter's novel are Hamlets, tortured by the guilt of being outside, of having kept an escape route, as they knowingly rock their pink gin in the glass and misanthropically bitch their Ophelias – and guilt sharpens even while it perverts observation. He has one exciting episode – Greene at his best – in which he smuggles Jones out to his rendezvous. The moment in which the awful police chief – admirably called Concasseur – is shot and has his sun-glasses trodden on is very fine. That is the kind of detail that reconciles us to Greene when we are just about to cry parody again.

The end of *The Comedians* is, like the beginning, a sardonic essay. The vegetarian Americans are in San Domingo and, in their grateful and businesslike way, they get Brown a partnership in a funeral business where the drift of local politics offers growing prospects. This is a nasty but exact diagnosis; the speciousness lies in our feeling that the symbolism is being piled on and that the people are puppets in an animated disquisition. The effect is literary. We have been reading news and news leaves us with the sense of waste. But as San Domingo follows Haiti, as Nigeria distracts us from the Congo, Greene has obviously chosen an important subject; and though he is an outsider, there are moments in which he gets inside. The Voodoo scene is which we watch a sensitive man being turned by grotesque religious performance into a partisan catches a note of tropical excess.

> The priest came in from his inner room swinging a censer, but the censer which he swung in front of our faces was a trussed cock – the small stupid eyes peered into my eyes and the banner of St Lucy swayed after it. When he had completed the circle of the *tonelle* the *hougan* put the head of the cock in his mouth and crunched it cleanly off; the wings continued to flap while the head lay on the dirt-floor like part of a broken toy. Then he bent down and squeezed the neck like a tube of toothpaste and added the rusty colour of blood to the ash-grey patterns on the floor.

But I think he overcrowds with the apparatus of horror; and especially in the sexual incident, one begins to grin and even to laugh.

Greene is laughing too, but we are at cross-purposes; we are laughing at self-parody as we laugh at melodrama and he is laughing at his own pleasure in giving more and more turns to what, in both senses, is the screw. Brown is supposed to have lost his faith and to be adrift because he has found nothing to replace it. Yet in fact he *has* found something: the hotel-keeper has ostensibly written this remarkable book. That is an act of faith; certainly not an act of indifference. Or didn't Brown write the book? Is it all a game? All virtuosi are entitled to indulge their talents. But when Greene wrote *The Power and the Glory* he was not playing a game.

How many of his now huge audience know him in the very different role of the bookish man or as a literary critic and essayist? He has gone through the English mill. His *Collected Essays* contain a selection of these writings done mainly for the London weeklies or as introductions, during the last thirty years; there are also traveller's portraits of two Popes, Philby, Ho Chi Minh, Castro and others. All display the well-known concerns which have given him originality and verve as a novelist; all – or nearly all – have the final sympathy which a real curiosity about human nature deposits in an observant mind.

In the manner of English periodical criticism where the writer has to get at an essence, show his wit and his hand, and make his decisive effect with alacrity in fewer than 2,000 scrupulous words, Greene engages at once: 'A man must be judged by his enemies as well as by his friendships.' Himself he cannot resist the attractions of the enemy. He is before anything a novelist-critic, that is to say he writes to discover something for *his* purposes which might not be ours. His reviews are an artist's raids; he has the avid eye of the raider and will often pause before the corpse of his victim to note a quality or to ask what went wrong.

He has a cheerful, almost cannibal appetite for rationalists. For him, rationalists, figures like Samuel Butler and Havelock Ellis, are conceited and emotionally arid; then, among rhetoricians he cannot forgive Kipling; among sentimentalists, Barrie. Of the 'greatly gifted they are the two who have written with most falsity of human relationships'. Unresolved hatreds of infantile secrets have ruined them. Butler has the smugness of the Honest Man: 'Even Christianity would not be considered dispassionately because it is the history of a Father and a Son.' Herbert Read, who had hailed so many fashions in painting and literature, had himself supplied (in his grave books on childhood and his *Life* of Wordsworth) the 'standards of permanence by which these fashions will be condemned'. Whether they add or ruffle, Greene's opinions have an artist's necessity in them. Let the academics weigh up, be exhaustive, or build their superstructures – the artist lives as much by his pride in his own emphasis as by what he ignores; humility is a disgrace.

Greene has a marked loyalty to writers who have influenced him and to those who are out of fashion. He is free of the snobbery that pretends it has no time for the juvenile or second rate. The books of boyhood – Ballantine, Hope, Mason, Weyman, Rider Haggard and the *Viper of Milan* – were decisive for him: two or three themes, central in Greene's own writings, expand from them. Exotic, thrilling adventure, the lost childhood and its betrayal, the warnings against success, the lure of perfect evil. In the *Viper of Milan* he thinks he saw:

Perfect evil walking the world, where perfect good can never walk again, and only the pendulum ensures that after all in the end justice is done.

Life is not black and white; it is black and grey. After *The Power and the Glory, The Comedians*.

This theme was fulfilled when he confronted Henry James, Conrad – and equally important to him I would guess later on – Ford Madox Ford. Apart from anything else they are master craftsmen and, in all these reviews, we see Greene's concern for how things are done. He himself is, above all, skilled and eagerly interested in difficulty. But the importance of Henry James is the concern with supernatural evil, the nervous venture to the edge of religion; in the detection of the 'black and merciless things that lie behind great possessions'; in corruption and betrayal. This is far from being the whole of James, but the subject draws out the four most studied essays in the collection. In the thirties, Greene was allured by the James who could conceive the damned soul and who might just have become a Catholic if his father had not exhausted the subject of an organized church. But, by the fifties, looking at *Guy Domville*, he writes:

> To us today the story of Guy Domville seems . . . one more example of the not always fortunate fascination exercised on James by the Christian faith and by Catholicism.

Is there such a thing as agnostic prose? May not a rationalist be fully conscious of mental degradation or good and evil? Wasn't James?

The search for the seat of unease in his subject is Greene's point in a great many of these essays. There are eighty of them. Conrad Aiken, pushing the study of madness to its limits in *King Coffin* 'is the most satisfying of living novelists'; in Walter de la Mare's stories – now absurdly underrated or forgotten – we meet the terrified eyes of a fellow passenger 'watching the sediment of an unspeakable obsession'; of Rolfe – whose *Hadrian the Seventh* is a work of genius – he writes: 'if he could not have Heaven he would have Hell and the last footprints seem to point to the Inferno'. The unease was not always gratefully acknowledged. One would have thought his delightful and affectionate essay on Beatrix Potter's tales written in 1933 would have pleased the authoress; we imagine she would have given a thunderstruck grin when Greene's King Charles's head popped up at the climax among the bunnies and the puddle-ducks:

> Looking back over the thirty years of Miss Potter's literary career, we see that the creation of Jemima Puddle-Duck marked

the beginning of a new period. At some time between 1907 and 1909 Miss Potter must have passed through an emotional ordeal which changed the character of her genius. It would be impertinent to enquire into the nature of the ordeal. Her case is curiously similar to that of Henry James. Something happened which shook their faith in appearance. From *Portrait of a Lady* onwards, innocence deceived, the treachery of friends, became the theme of James's stories. Mme Merle, Kate Croy, Mme de Vionnet, Charlotte Stant, these tortuous, treacherous women, are paralleled through the dark period of Miss Potter's art. 'A man can smile and be a villain', that, a little altered, was her recurrent message . . . with the publication of *Mr Tod* in 1912 Miss Potter's pessimism reached its climax.

An acid letter from Miss Potter – who had become a tough sheep-farmer in Westmorland – was the reward for this grand analysis. She was, she said, suffering from no emotional disturbance when she wrote *Mr Tod*: only the after effects of flu. She said she deprecated 'the Freudian school' of criticism. Perhaps the comparison with another artist annoyed the old lady. She was certainly cross when *Little Pig Robinson* was described by Mr Greene as being her *Tempest*: he called it her last tale when it was the first written, if not the first published. But as we know now, from Margaret Lane's *Life* and the published *Journals*, there had been two extreme crises in her life and an extraordinary change of personality. Graham Greene had been an expert detective.

The collection covers a reviewer's wide field. Anthony à Wood, some Oxford eccentrics, Evelyn, Charles Churchill, Darley, Fielding, Sterne are among his subjects and done with care and point. The novelist is botanizing in human character; the traveller is absorbed by Parkman, Livingstone, Mungo Park; there is a fierce attack on J.B. Trend's book on Mexico, for though Trend was a conventional and timid Cambridge professor he was a violent anti-Catholic. (But he did write a very valuable if innocent book on Spain in the twenties.) Greene's final essay on a sentimental return to Lagos, the Scobie country, in 1968, has the nostalgia for a lost innocence which encases much of his work, nostalgia for a lost innocence never quite as innocent as it looked. In Lagos, last year (in church, one gathers),

the girl in front of me wore one of the surrealist Manchester cotton dresses which are rarely seen since the Japanese trade moved in. The word 'soupsweet' was printed on her shoulder, but I had to wait until she stood up before I could confirm another phrase: 'Fenella lak' good poke'. Father Mackie would have been amused, I thought, and what better description could there be of this poor lazy lovely coloured country than 'soupsweet'.

In all his moods, angry, serious or laughing, Greene has the patient precise eye of the connoisseur of 'brief lives'.

The Art of Koestler

Between imaginative writing and journalism the distinction is easy to make; but in some periods the critic is not required to refine on it. In the nineteenth century the readers of Dickens or Dostoevsky could see the journalism of these writers at a glance, and could without difficulty snip an editorial on the Poor Law, or a feature article on the Russian soul and its need to occupy Constantinople, from the imaginative pages. The readers of great European journalists like Herzen, Engels and, in our own time, Trotsky, were in no danger of mistaking these writers for artists in an important sense, for great artists towered above them. Today the relation has changed. It is generally agreed that the last decade has been unpropitious for the imaginative writer and that the distinguished work of our years has been fragmentary and small in compass; and as the imaginative writer has receded, so the journalist has advanced. It is he who has towered and glowered, the obstreperous, overgrown child of events; and it becomes necessary once more to mark his difference from the creative writer. The task is delicate because the distinction may be thought invidious. It is not, for many imaginative writers have been journalists in the last decade and with every advantage to the range of their interests and their talent. The digestive process of journalism is coarser than that of art, and we have lived through a period when a coarse digestion became indispensable. The journalist has had the task of accommodating violence to the private stomach and of domesticating the religious, revolutionary and national wars in the private conscience. He has been the intermediary between our private and public selves and, in doing this office, has become a hybrid and representative figure, the vacillating and tortured Hamlet expressing our common disinclinations and our private guilt. For it is typical of the contemporary journalist that his case-history goes with him. Like Hamlet, he travels with his own court of private disasters, his ghosts, his Ophelias, even his Rosencrantz and Guildenstern; and though we may often think the sight ridiculous, we must give him the credit for attempting the creation of a new kind of first person singular, a new hero, who can 'take' the assaults of decivilization, who has invented a certain style which enables him to face the spectacle of mass suffering and official medievalism, with passion, stoicism and humanity. To him the style is as important as the humanity; and eventually we may be sure that artists will collect his vestiges, as once they eagerly collected the sacred relics of Byronism.

To the journalism and the reporting of the higher kind the work of Arthur Koestler is a copious guide. He is not at the level of Malraux or Silone, for he lacks the hard self-control of the Frenchman, the brain and luminous sensibility of the Italian. Koestler's gift is bold and fresh, but it is theatrical. He is the declaiming and compelling actor. No one has known better than he when to drop what he is doing and rush to document the latest convulsion. In this fashion, he has run through the political infections of our generation; through Marxism, Leninism, anti-Stalinism; and practice has accompanied theory. He has known and documented the political prisons and torture houses. He has belonged to the class described in his book *The Scum of the Earth*, the human wreckage of the Left which Fascism scattered over Europe. How much in his writing is personal experience and how much is an intense imaginative indentification with the people he describes, is not important; or rather, only the identification is important. It is passionate, because it is moral; it is complex because it is at once theatrical and aware of itself. There are other qualities: Koestler is more than a simple reporter. He is intellectually volatile; it is second nature for him to generalize about events; he is politically trained, and likes to be politically bespattered. It is the business of the journalist to interview everything and Koestler is able to interview philosophy, science, economics, history, and to come back with a notebook full of general ideas which are put to dramatic use. For the rest, the traits of the profession are emphasized in him by his lack of roots. He was born a displaced person; half-Hungarian, half-Jew, he was educated in Vienna, worked in Germany and Palestine, lived in France. He has been created to wander without mundane allegiances. His allegiances were always to the world of ideas or myth; and when these failed, to the world of random physical events. Guilt and self-pity have been the price. With some exceptions – Strindberg is one – imaginative writers appear to allay their neuroses in works of art; but the neuroses of the journalist are exacerbated by his special opportunities for seeing life.

Yet definitions like these do not bring Koestler into the intimate scope of the English critic. He is separated from us by the education and politics of the Continent, by the vast difference between the large, stable middle class in England, and the small, precarious middle class of Central Europe. He can easily dazzle us because we have no café conversation and no café writers. We have no skill in playing poker with ideas. We are not trained to pretend that things which are entirely different may (for the pleasure of effect) be assumed to be opposites. We have no eternal students. We have no intelligentsia. These differences have led Koestler himself to as complete and conventional misreading of English life as any that have been done by Continental writers. (See *The Yogi and the Commissar.*) We must assume that our judgement of him will suffer from similar difficulties of contact.

We come nearest to him in *The Scum of the Earth.* This is partly because the book is a personal record of the events at the fall of France where, at last, English experience came close to the experience of the Continent. A second reason is that here Koestler has cleaned his slate and is putting down just what he saw and heard and, with emotion, is pulling down the curtain on a period. This report is alive; it is packed with human beings; it is resilient and almost buoyant. He is in his natural element, or rather in one of his natural elements: anarchy and disillusion. His eyes are skinned for every incident as, sombre and sardonic – but not with detachment – he notes down the fates of his friends. This book (and *The Gladiators*) contains his least opaque writing.

But we first hear of Koestler in *The Spanish Testament* and here a play is beginning, not coming to an end. We see the sullen sky over Vigo harbour glowing 'under an evil spell'. It is the Koestler spell. We are in for a melodrama. 'The constriction in the throat that affects a whole town, a whole population, like an epidemic'; as in the theatre, generalizations, simplifications. The characters wear the make-up of revolution. This writer does not appear to know Spanish history, but he knows current Marxism. He is briefed. He is in control and can switch on and off when effects are needed. Sardonic anger, raw humour and the punctures of anthropological enquiry let the wind out of his hysterical passages at the right

478

moment. All this is good journalism, but compared, say, with Brenan or Borkenau on Spain, it is slapdash. Koestler was a smatterer, and the only thing of value that emerged was personal: *The Dialogue with Death.* There have been finer, more sensitive, more humane and more objective accounts of life in Spanish prisons than Koestler's, for Koestler had to be the leading actor, and he writes with one wall of the prison down; but the attempt at a personal revelation is intellectually impressive, and precisely in the study of hysteria which elsewhere in his writing is his least attractive quality. In the end, when the curtain comes down in *The Spanish Testament* we are not entirely convinced or convicted. Perhaps because we have been over-convinced. The impression remains after other books by Koestler. Against ourselves must be put his strongest card; he has had to combat the English unwillingness to face the appalling facts of medieval atrocity on the Continent.

Yet this may not be the explanation of our uneasiness. The source may be literary; Koestler has a voice, an urgent voice, vital, voluble and lively, above all never boring – a voice, but an arid and mechanical style. On the face of it this is an unkind criticism to make of a displaced writer who is not writing in his own tongue, who has to make shift to write our own and has mastered it. But we suspect that no language is an inconvenience to him; language is a machine; not even in his own language, we feel, has he any love of words or any sense of their precision and grace. Here is a passage from *The Yogi and the Commissar*, and I think the manner itself forbids belief in the argument, that leaves us with the sensation that Koestler himself would only half-believe in it if he could express it simply, for it is only half-true:

The law of the novel-perspective prescribes that it is not enough for the author to create 'real life', he must also locate its geometrical place in the co-ordinate system, the axes of which are represented by the dominating facts, ideas and tendencies of his time; he must fix its position in an N-dimensional space-time continuum. The real Sylvia spins around the centre of a narrow family-vortex of conditioning factors, whereas the author, in promoting her to novel life, places her in the centre of a vortex formed by the great trade winds, typhoons, depressions and hurricanes of her time. Of course he need not describe or even mention them. But implicitly they must be there.

Koestler uses words as thought-saving gadgets from the iron-mongery counter, and draws especially on the vocabulary of science and economics which is paralysed by patents. Like the Latin tag, they may appeal to the vanity; and the Central European mind appears to be susceptible to technical coagulations, but neither exactitude nor illumination issues from them. The love of jargon suggests the lack of an instinct or a sense, and suggests a deaf and arbitrary nature.

The deficiency is more damaging to Koestler's reporting than to his earliest novels. Shaky as some passages in *The Gladiators* are – it was his first 'English' novel, and presumably, a translation – they are pretty free of vices of style. The jargon of Marx, Freud, Einstein, would have been grotesque in a story of ancient Rome and the Spartacus revolt. We are captured at once in this novel by the sardonic vivacity of the author, the raciness of his reporting, his light mastery of the novelist's and historian's material, even by his boyish humour. We also feel a quality which is rare in the melodramas that come after: the sense of the human tragedy and a pity that is truly pitched and moving. That feeling for tragedy is never recovered, and in my opinion *The Gladiators* is his most impressive book. No personal hatred, no extraneous obsession with persecution or guilt, clutters the running of the narrative, impedes the growth of the argument: for though the matter of the Trosky-Stalin conflict is present in the chapter on 'the law of detours' and is implicit in the main crisis of the book, Koestler has not yet projected himself into the Moscow trials. Success destroys: the revolutions that fail preserve their myth; and to Koestler faith and myth are everything. Another reason for Koestler's excellence in this book is that it has a settled subject, set in the remote past, and history has agreed on it. By gift a reporter, he is a hundred times better in recording what is given him than in contriving imaginatively what is not; with him, controversy simply brings out the 'old soldier' of the clinics.

The subject of *The Gladiators* is the rising of the slaves under Spartacus, their race to triumph; the tragic split with Crixus, and the final defeat. On the one hand the laxity and shamelessness, the experience and corruption of Rome are comically and diversely rendered with a ribaldry and a talker's scholarship that recall the early Aldous Huxley. These Roman portraits are plump and impudent medallions, cheerfully unclassical; they are the footnotes of Gibbon turned into agreeable and scabrous cartoons. On the other hand is the raw, rushing, high-voiced rebellion, tearing down the roads, laughing, shouting, guzzling, raping, killing. The wings of the traditional humane ideal raise riot above its own lusts; the brotherhood of the camp makes the spirit flesh. There is a pity for the mindless hopes and follies of simple people: this is the only book of Koestler's to show us the lowly material of revolution in the mass, the simple man who, even in his excess, does not wish to die, and whose last look, as he falls, is of surprise. (In the later books, the dying of the revolutionary leaders has lost all human quality; it has become a transaction of policy.) The masses in *The Gladiators* are incapable of salvation, and between the Gadarene downrush which Crixus will lead, and the slow, painful political course for which the mind of Spartacus is pathetically groping, they chose the former. He who cannot stand the screams of his own prisoners, is overwhelmed by the necessity of being a tyrant. He parts company with half his horde; 'objectively' he ought to have killed them.

We feel the earth under our feet in this book, and whether or not it has the developed qualities of a novel is not important. In fact, it is a collection of brilliantly placed episodes, linked by a commentary; and growing characters are not required. (This is fortunate, because it turns out in his later work that Koestler has little power to create or sustain large characters.) All that is required in this book is that his pictures of people shall have instantaneous physical reality – Spartacus himself needs very little to fix him in our mind's eye – and that the atmosphere and the feeling, shall be actual like the news. The best of Koestler is in a passage like the following one on the fate of the Praetor; and the end of the passage indicates where Koestler goes wrong:

On foot – for his horse had been left with the robbers – the bald-headed Praetor Clodius Glaber climbed down into the plain. He had been separated from his fleeing soldiers, and walked through the night, alone. He strayed from the trodden path, stumbled over the crooked, stony edge of a vineyard, looked around. The vineyard, studded with pointed stakes, looked like a graveyard by the stars' light. It was very quiet; bandits and Vesuvius dimmed to unreality, Rome and Senate were blotted out; yet one more deed asked to be done. He opened his cloak, felt the place with his fingers, gently pressed the sword-point to it.

The deed asked to be done, but it was only now he understood its full meaning. Little by little the point must be driven home; little by little it must tear through the tissue, cut tendons and muscles, splinter the ribs. Not till then the lung is reached, tender, mucuous, thinly veined; it must be ripped asunder. Now a slimy shell, and now the heart itself, a bulbous bag of blood – its touch beyond imagination. Had ever a man accomplished this? Well he might, with a sudden thrust, perhaps. But once you knew of the process and every one of its stages, you would never be able to do it.

'Death' up to now a word like any other, seemed removed into unattainable distance. All the relatives of Death, such as Honour, Shame and Duty, exist for him only who has no ken of reality. For reality, mucuous, unspeakably delicate, with its mesh of thin veins, is not made to be torn to bits with some pointed object. And now Praetor Clodius Glaber knows that dying is unutterably stupid – more stupid still than life itself.

He realizes that his shoes are full of pebbles. He sits down on a stone and empties the shoes; he observes that the pebbly discomfort had been a responsible element of his despair. As compared to the ignominious defeat of his army, the sharp little pebbles – seven in all – admittedly shrink into ridiculous insignificance. But how can you sift the important from the unimportant if both speak to your senses with equal vehemence? His tongue and palate are still covered with the stale taste of interrupted sleep; a few forgotten grapes lurk between the vines. He plucks a few, looks around; only the stars are witnessing the curious sequence of his actions, and their sight is no rebuke to him.

He feels ashamed and yet he must admit that his actions are in no way senseless; no amount of philosophy can alter the fact that grapes were made to be eaten. Besides, he has never before enjoyed grapes so much. He sips their juice together with the tears of an unexplained emotion. He smacks his lips with defiance and shame.

And night with the lights of its indifferent stars gave as a further knowledge unto Praetor Clodius Glaver: all pleasure, not only defined versions of it, and Life itself, are based on age-old, secret shamelessness.

Why can't these central Europeans learn when to stop? The

myth of 'age-old, secret shamelessness'! Not *another* myth, we exclaim, not a new thesis, a new antithesis, a new synthesis!

The real core of Koestler's thought in *The Gladiators* – it is taken up again in a moving passage towards the end of a later book *Thieves in the Night* – is in the words of the Essene to Spartacus:

> 'Prophecies are never worth anything,' said the Essene. 'I explained that before, but in the meantime you've been asleep. Prophecies do not count; he who receives them counts.'
>
> Spartacus lay in thought, his eyes open.
>
> 'He who receives them will see evil days,' he said after a while.
>
> 'Aye,' said the Essene. 'He'll have a pretty rotten time.'
>
> 'He who receives them,' said Spartacus, 'will have to run and run, on and on, until he foams at the mouth and until he has destroyed everything in his way with his great wrath. He'll run and run, and the Sign won't let go of him, and the demon of wrath will tear through his entrails.'

Spartacus listens to the Essene through the night, until the sky lightens: 'The black shadows in his eye sockets had, as it were, evaporated . . . Spartacus looked again at the glowing East and at the mountain whose everyday shape gradually broke the spell of its nightly distortion.'

Night, dawn, noon, the spell: the symbols are theatrical.

Spartacus fails, but now the dawn has come; we are moving towards the success at Noon, the darkness at Noon which is the corruption of success. This is an ancient and haunting Jewish theme. The Race, by numberless pronouncements of Jehovah, has been fated to be destroyed in success, to be searching for ever.

Darkness at Noon is a *tour de force*, a book terrifying and claustrophobic, an intellectual thriller. The efficiency, the speed, the smooth order of the narrative as it runs fast to its end, are extraordinary. Here is the story of a man arguing his way (or being argued) towards the confession of crimes he has not committed, an interpretation of the Moscow trials, a dramatized examination of the problems of ends and means. As a novelist, Koestler has a superb gift for the handling of argument in a living way; he knows when to break off, when to slip into the personal or the small incident, when to digress into the minor character, where to tighten the screw. Rubashov, the accused, makes the pace all through the story; he is an alert, intelligent man, a brain where

Spartacus was passive. And occasionally, like a sudden fragment of sunlight in this grey and horrifying book, horrifying in its grim pistol-barrel logic, glimmers of human illumination occur in Rubashov. They are moving. But when all praise is given, *Darkness at Noon* remains a melodrama. Rubashov and Gletkin are a sad pair of Jesuits consumed and dulled as human beings by their casuistry. The Communists have taken over the doctrine of original sin from the Roman Catholic Church, and have tacked the Calvinist doctrine of Predestination on to it; but they have dispelled the visionary and emotional quality of these dogmas, with the dull acrimony of the makers of company by-laws. An irredeemable dreariness surrounds the lives of Rubashov and Gletkin. They are not 'great'; they are merely committee men or chess players.

The book is not tragedy. Yet to be destroyed by your own Church or by your own beliefs ought to be tragedy. It is surely tragic for the young to destroy the old. There were (if Koestler had not been so gifted in the art of making a case) tragic springs in Rubashov's history. Somewhere in the tale, Ivanov (one of the Inquisitors who is drugging himself with drink) remarks that the murders of Raskolnikov were trivial because they served, or failed to serve, private ends; had they served the ends of the collective morality, they would have been significant. But in *Darkness at Noon* the official killing of Rubashov to serve the collective end fails to reach this high standard. It is a police act, not a tragedy, the end of a case. Koestler could reply that the casuistry of Gletkin & Co has destroyed the concept of tragedy on the collective plane; but the casuistry is, after all, Koestler's. Rubashov, who has betrayed so many people in the name of 'objectivity', has destroyed himself in advance, and is simply getting what is coming to him. By inference, the same will happen to Gletkin. The two rascals are agreed. Wolf, as the Tsarist officer says, eats wolf. Great ideas are in conflict, but in this book they are not embodied in great men.

We have to turn to the greatest of all novels about the revolutionary, Dostoevsky's *The Possessed*, to see that *Darkness at Noon* is a powerful book, but not an imaginative work of the highest kind. It has the intensity of obsession, the interest of surgery, but no largeness. It is a document, pulled up by the roots from a native soil. The revolutionaries of *The Possessed* are living people with biographies, and they are set among other living people. Russia breathes in Dostoevsky's novel, its landscape, its towns, its climate, its history, and grants them the pardon of time and place. For it is evident, from our post-war contacts with them, that the Russians are as Dostoevsky drew them; a people living by wont in a natural atmosphere of suspicion and mistrust, and consumed by fantasies. *The Possessed* is soaked in its own people, grows out of Russian soil. It is felt.

Compared with *The Possessed*, *Darkness at Noon* grows out of nowhere. It is Central European allegory. Yet even the Party is not the same in all countries, and the problem of ends and means is decided not by moralists, but by temperament, feeling, tradition. The objection to *Darkness at Noon* is not that it has overstated its case, but that it has stated only a case; the book understates its field of human, psychological and historical references. Koestler's own mind is like a prison, with its logical corridors, its dazzling but monotonous lighting, the ingenious disposition of its control towers, its traverses and walls. And there are also the judas slots through which we are led to observe the sudden, shocking, physical revelation; those cells where the dingy human being stands in his daydream; and, outside, the courtyard where the man circles, dragging his shame in his scraping feet. No selfless emotion, no love above all, can be felt there, but only the self-love and self-hatred of the prisoner. And Koestler, who occupies this prison, is like some new and enterprising prison governor, humane enough, but more and more attached to the place and infected with the growing belief that the guilty are ourselves, the free, the people outside. This is a position he shares with the Communist intellectuals of his generation. Their habit of hypnotizing and magnetizing a subject by the incantations of repetitive argument, so that it becomes rigid, is his. *Darkness at Noon* might be called a major act of literary hypnosis. And the argument is so successful and complete that we begin ceasing to believe in its human application the moment we put the book down.

After *Darkness at Noon* there is a decline. The tight organization of Koestler's gifts goes slack. Disillusion brought his power to a climax; and since then he has descended to nihilism. *Arrival and Departure* is an attack upon belief itself, due to an enterprising encounter with psychoanalysis:

If one wanted to explain why Peter had behaved as he did, one had to discard from the beginning his so-called convictions and ethical beliefs. They were mere pretexts of the mind, phantoms of a more intimate reality. It did not matter whether he was a hero of the Proletariat or a martyr of the Catholic Church; the real clue was this suspect craving for martyrdom.

More accurately, this book is Koestler's attack upon himself as a member of the small middle-class intelligentsia of the Continent, and it ends by justifying isolation. The Cause has been thrown over and humanity goes with it. Koestler appears to have had a theatrical view of faith; it was a vision, not a bond. By a really crass misreading of Freud the neuroses of the revolutionaries are made to cancel the traditions of humanism, indeed any strivings of the mind. The civilized, the believing and creating mind is dismissed. Peter solves his conflicts by refusing to recognize one side of them, and after he has exploded his beliefs goes off to fight nevertheless because 'reasons do not matter'. Intellectually a poor book, it has all the old skill in story-telling, the old lack of acceptable characters; an incapacity to describe love – love equals lust, etc. – but a terrifying power to describe torture. The effect is over-powering. One could do with the old framework of good and evil to hold this picture in, and the framework existed if Koestler had cared to recognize it. The despised liberal English and Americans of the ordinary kind were impelled to fight and destroy the nation which committed these atrocities. Koestler's atrocities appear to have been taken out of the moral scheme and to have become pornographic. He is like Ivanov in *Darkness at Noon*, who said that ever since the invention of the steam engine, there has been no normality, only war. A remark that is deeply untrue. There is always normality. *Arrival and Departure* shows those vices of style – the use of jargon – which have marked his essays, and the psychoanalysis is too schematic for words.

With *Thieves in the Night* Koestler returns to something nearer the mood of *The Gladiators*, and his ambivalent attitude to violence – and to ends and means – is almost decided. He has come full circle, i.e. he is *very nearly* prepared to justify violence; or rather he has quite decided to throw out justification. He is among the people whom he really envies and admires, the violent people, the people with grenades in their lorries. This is an old legacy from Communism; one can see it in Malraux also. If anything, Koestler is more depressed by the Zionists' capacity as colonists than by their readiness for killing; practical capacity has no Byronism. We have the suspicion that the Neanderthalers of *Darkness at Noon* are being reproduced in the Promised Land. Can it be that the inhabitants of Utopias are always dull and muttonish:

> I have watched them ever since they arrived – these stumpy, dumpy girls with their rather coarse features, big buttocks and heavy breasts, physically precocious, mentally retarded, over-ripe and immature at the same time; and these raw arse-slapping youngsters, callow, dumb and heavy with their aggressive laughter and unmodulated voices, without traditions, manners, form, style . . .
>
> Their parents were the most cosmopolitan race of the earth – they are provincial and chauvinistic. Their parents were sensitive bundles of nerves with awkward bodies – *their* nerves are whipcords and their bodies those of a horde of Hebrew Tarzans roaming in the hills of Galilee. Their parents were intense, intent, overstrung, over-spiced – they are tasteless, spiceless, unleavened and tough. Their parents were notoriously polyglot – they have been brought up in one language which had been hibernating for twenty centuries before being brought artificially back to life . . .

But the Joseph of *Thieves in the Night* has found what Peter of *Arrival and Departure* had defined as a psychological aberration: a Cause. More than a Cause: something that none of the Koestler characters has ever had – the lack is their fatal weakness in debate, a nutritional deficiency of Marxist teaching – a country. It is the embryo country, the almost theoretical country of Zionism, but still a country. In his youth, Koestler had lived for a time in the Jewish communities of Palestine, but had, for some reason, tired of them and left; now, once violence has arisen, his personal interest and his alert journalist eye for the topical story have been stirred. The truth is, of course, that he is cosmopolitan and European; that is his virtue politically; he sees the interaction and unity of European events, and this rational attitude is clearly in conflict with his new Faith, and so much so that scepticism, detachment, the yearning not to be so committed is the impression that still survives the rifle shots and the Hallelujahs. Such a conflict makes an excellent basis for Koestler's best vein: his talk, and this book has some readable passages.

Joseph looked round the terrace and sighed. The khamsin lay on people's faces like a spasm. The women were plump, heavy-chested, badly and expensively dressed. The men sat with sloping shoulders and hollow chests, thinking of their ulcers. Each couple looked as if they were carrying on a quarrel under cover of the *Merry Widow.*

'I can't blame the gentiles if they dislike us,' he said.

'That proves you are a patriot,' said Matthews. 'Since the days of your prophets, self-hatred has been the Jewish form of patriotism.'

Joseph wiped his faced. The khamsin was telling on him. He felt sick of it all: Judaism, Hebraism, the whole cramped effort to make something revive which had been dead for two thousand years.

'It is all very well for you to talk as a benevolent outsider,' he said. 'The fact is, we are a sick race. Tradition, form, style, have all gone overboard. We are a people with a history but no background ... Look around you, and you'll see the heritage of the ghetto. It is there in the wheedling lilt of the women's voices, and in the way the men hold themselves, with that frozen shrug about their shoulders.'

'I guess that shrug was their only defence. Otherwise the whole race would have gone crackers.'

The possibility that the terrorists are really Fascist or copying Fascist methods raises the old bugbear about ends and means, and these discussions are boring.

The central figure, narrator and diarist of this report is now, for the first time, English, an English half-Jew. A naïve snobbery is disclosed here; he belongs to that romantic idol of the Continent, the English country gentry. It is the Disraeli touch. When this character goes to Palestine, he has a low social opinion of those members of the British ruling class who do not come out of the top drawer. One lady – imagine it – has an official position and yet is only the wife of a sergeant! The only real 'lady' is an agreeable sketch, but women have always to be punished in Koestler's novels, and she is made to go through a boring official dinner when afflicted by her period. Koestler's attitude to sex has always been neurotic – least in *The Gladiators* – and, in one of his articles, he threatens to raise the question of the menarche, no doubt as a new myth in the space-time continuum.

Bedevilled by his journalistic habit of treating differences as opposites – it makes a brighter page – Koestler can only draw the Jewish colonists with ironical sympathy and vigour, by covering the Arabs and English with ridicule.

As we ourselves – see *Passage to India*, George Orwell, etc. – have a robust tradition of satire at the expense of our own people, Koestler's looks thin and conventional; the attack on the Arabs, since it is rarely done in English, is fresher, but historicall silly. All the same, the bias of the book works to its advantage as a piece of reporting, but only the first half, that is, say, up to the rape of the girl Dina. The narrative is brisk and dramatic, the picture of the colony is in full colour, the description of its way of living tolerant and moving. We see an Old Testament world; but debated of course, and enlivened by Koestler's short, snorting, schoolboy humour. After the rape – and rape or lust without love is a special interest of Koestler's; down to fundamentals; strip the pretences, debunk, be honest, away from liberal and *petit bourgeois* prevarications in the bedroom – after the rape, suspiciously enough, the novel disintegrates, wanders around, and Koestler's doubts appear. The story ends in 1939, which is very lucky for the Anglo-Jewish hero who, in any case, is going to be violent, not with bombs after all, but with a wireless station.

One new quality appears in *Thieves in the Night*; an interest in landscape. The descriptions of Galilee are imaginative. Koestler's talent has always been for the hard, surprising physical image that stamps a person, a crowd, a place on the mind; and now he is extending this poetic interest to places. It brings an amenity up to now uncommon in his work. We welcome it for in his intense and strung up work there have been no points of rest; the vice of the 'dynamic' conception of life is that it does not record the consolations of inertia, and never contemplates a beautiful thing. His attempts consciously to inject beauty have ended in the sentimental.

Thieves in the Night is an improvement on *Arrival and Departure*, but it represents the coarsening and mechanization of a talent. One looks back upon his novels. What is the final impression? They are not novels; they are reports, documentaries, briefs, clinical statements, animated cartoons of a pilgrim's regress from revolution. They are material, formative material: their opponents, as well as their disciples, are formed by them. The effect is hypnotic. It is a paradox that these lively and fast-moving books, at a second glance, have no motion at all, Koestler has fixed them, made them static; it is he with his 'case' who is on the move; the story and the people do not move of themselves. Our eye is following *him* and not them. The result is that, underlying the superficial excitement, a bored sensation of unbelief is built up – why read about people who merely illustrate an argument and are foils for the author? Quickly the people recede before the inevitable half-truths of a magnetizing talker with a good conceit of himself; and while he rarely makes a dull remark, he also rarely makes one that common experience does not flatly contradict. And yet the confidence with which Koestler grasps important themes makes the continued privacy of the English novel look eccentric. It commonly has been eccentric, but at any rate, except for Orwell we have no novelist of the social or public conscience who has Koestler's scope or force – no journalist or reporter either. It is the price we pay for our lack of interest in general ideas for their own sake: empiricism is not dramatic. General ideas become, however, an infatuation; for example, it may be that the Soviet runs a police State, forced labour camps, etc., because Russia has always had these things, and not because of a recent ethical lapse. It may be that Koestler has imposed a Central European efficiency upon the Russian scene in *Darkness at Noon.* Perhaps the English novelist is wise to avoid general ideas and to stick to life as it is presented to himself, and to leave what he doesn't know to the newspapers and the Blue books. For the novels of Koestler are skeletal. They are like the steel frameworks of modern buildings before the bricks go in; and up there, shaking all over with the vibration of the thing, is Koestler furiously concentrating on his pneumatic riveter. A guilty figure: he can't get over an old wish that it was a machine-gun and the principle is maddeningly similar. So guilty does he feel that presently he stops work, harangues the crowd below and the building is never completed. It remains, a stimulus, an excitement to others, a theatrical outline against the sky.

Saul Bellow

Jumbos

Saul Bellow has the most effusive intelligence of living American novelists. Even when he is only clever he has a kind of spirited intellectual vanity that enables him to take on all the facts and theories about the pathetic and comically exposed condition of civilized man and distribute them like high-class corn so that the chickens come running to them. That is the art of the novelist who can't resist an idea: to evoke, attract that 'pleasing, anxious being', the squawking, dusty, feverish human chicken. Aldous Huxley could always throw the corn but nothing alive came fluttering to it.

But immensely clever novelists have to beware of self-dispersal when they run to great length. I enjoy Saul Bellow in his spreading carnivals and wonder at his energy, but I still think he is finer in his shorter works. *The Victim* was the best novel to come out of America – or England – for a decade. *The Dangling Man* is good, but subdued; *Seize the Day* is a small grey masterpiece. If one cuts out the end, *Henderson the Rain King* is at once profound and richly diverting in its fantasy. These novels had form; their economy drove their point home. By brevity Bellow enhanced our experience. And, to a European reader – though this may be irrelevant – he seems the only American of this generation to convey the feel and detail of urban America, preserving especially what is going on at the times when nothing is going on: the distinctive native *ennui*, which is the basic nutriment of any national life.

It is when he turns to longer books, chasing the mirage of 'the great American novel', that Bellow weakens as he becomes a traveller, spreading the news and depending on the presence of a character who is something like a human hold-all, less a recognizable individual than a fantastic piece of bursting luggage. His labels, where he has been, whom he has met in his collision with America are more suggestive than his banal personal story. In

Herzog, the hero or rather the grandiose victim, is a gifted Jewish professor and polymath with a rather solemn pretension to sexual prowess. He seems a promising exemplar of the human being exposed to everything without the support of a settled society or fixed points of belief or value. This theme has offered the American novelist a chance to show his vitality for a long time now and the Jewish novelists have done strikingly well with it, for as a group they have acutely felt the sense of a missing law or covenant.

What has happened to Moses Herzog, this restless dabbler in the ideas of four centuries? He is having a breakdown because his second wife has destroyed his sexual confidence. He sees himself – and Mr Bellow sees him – prancing through one marriage and several liaisons with success and then marrying the all-time bitch; exhibitionist, hysteric, looter of his brain, spender of his money, far-seeing in matters of law and property, adulterous, glamorously second-rate but adroit with the castrating scissors. To add insult, not to mention symbolism, to injury, the man she goes off with is a one-legged radio phoney. The ruthless and learned Moses, a walking university, begins to look like a Jumboburger who has been told he has lost his mustard. His earlier women may say 'Serve him right', but neither they nor the reader are likely to think his sufferings of much importance when, in a ham ending, he solemnly shacks up with a tremendously international woman called Ramona – of all names – who is apt to come swaggering out of the bathroom with her hand on her hip like a dagger-carrying flamenco dancer, and wearing black frilly panties with saucy ribbons. Twice during the novel she clinches the entire deal by serving the gourmet the only dish, apparently, she knows how to cook: Shrimp Arnaud, washed down with a bottle of Pouilly Fuisée. His earlier ladies must have thought they had paid a high price. Why didn't they think of applying this particular nostrum to the exposed soul of modern man? One knows that the fantasy life of university professors is often surprisingly gaudy, that the minds of experts on seventeenth-century thought or the *condition humaine* often drift off to Hollywood in the evenings. If this is Mr Bellow's ironical realism it certainly describes the feeble state of contemporary erotic fancy: but I detect no irony. Yet irony and self-irony are usually Mr Bellow's strengths. What is more, the one or two love affairs in the book suggest that Moses is looking for easily punishable women without his or Mr Bellow's knowing it. In a moment of insight Moses wonders if his obsession with sex and love isn't really feminine. The reader is likely to go further and ask whether Moses is not hermaphrodite.

Structurally and in content, the story of *Herzog* is unsustaining. But what Herzog sees, the accidental details of his experience, is very impressive. Here he grows. He really has got a mind and it is hurt. It is a tribute to Mr Bellow's reserves of talent that the novel survives and over-grows its own weaknesses. The muddle Moses is in, his sense of victimization, are valuable. His paranoia is put, by Mr Bellow, to excellent use. Moses is not really exposed, but his New York and Chicago are. Mr Bellow has something like a genius for place. There is not a descriptive insinuator of what, say, a city like New York is like from minute to minute who comes anywhere near him. Some novelists stage it, others document it; he is breathing in it. He knows how to show us not only Moses but other people, moving from street to street, from room to room in their own circle of uncomprehending solitude. Grasping this essential of life in a big city he sees the place not as a confronted whole but continually askance. His senses are especially alive to *things* and he catches the sensation that the *things* have created the people or permeated them. This was the achievement of *The Victim*, and it is repeated in *Herzog*. A wanderer, he succeeds with minor characters, the many small figures in the crowd who suggest millions more. The dialogue of a Puerto Rican taxi driver, a Chicago cop, a low lawyer, a Jewish family, people brash, shady or saddened by the need of survival and whose ripeness comes out of the dirty brick that has trapped them, is really wonderful. It is far superior to Hemingway's stylized naturalism: Bellow's talk carries the speaker's life along with it. Their talk makes them move. They involve Moses with themselves and show him living, as all humans do, in a web spun by others as well as by himself.

The habit of seeing things askance or out of the corner of his eye has given Mr Bellow an even more important quality: it keeps alive a perpetual sense of comedy and feeds his originality. There is sometimes talk of a taste for elegance in his book; spoken of like that, as a sort of craving or innate possession, it sounds very nearly vulgar. But there is an implicit elegance of mind in his writing: it sharpens the comic edge and dares him to spirited invention. As far as the comedy is concerned it has all the fatality of Jewish comedy, that special comedy of human undress and nakedness of which the Jewish writers are the world's masters. The other gift of Mr Bellow is his power of fantastic invention. He has hit upon a wonderful device for conveying Herzog's nervous breakdown. How to deal with his paranoia – if that is what it is – how to make it contribute not only to the character of Herzog but also to the purpose of the book? Mr Bellow decides that Herzog's dottiness shall consist in writing unfinished letters to all kinds of people living and dead, known and unknown – to his women friends, to editors, tutors, professors, philosophers, to his dead mother, to the President. It is the habit of the mad and Moses is not mad; but he at once is comically and seriously disturbed by every kind of question. Is romanticism 'spilt religion'? 'Do the visions of genius become the canned goods of intellectuals?' He writes to Eisenhower asking him 'to make it all clear in a few words'. He begins addressing M de Jouvenal about the aims of political philosophy. The letters are really the scribbles of an exhausted mind. Travelling in the subway Moses evokes the dream figure of a Dr Shrödinger at Times Square:

It has been suggested [and why not] that reluctance to cause pain is actually an extreme form, a delicious form of sensuality, and that we increase the luxuries of pain by the injection of a moral pathos. Thus working both sides of the street. Nevertheless, there are moral realities, Herzog assured the entire world as he held his strap on the speeding car.

Since Moses is a man of intellect these addresses are often interesting in themselves; but chiefly they convey the dejected larking of a mind that has been tried by two contradictory forces: the breakdown of the public world we live in and the mess of private life. In which world does he live? He is absurd yet he is fine; he is conceited yet he is raw. He is a great man yet he is torpedoed by a woman who 'wants to live in the delirious professions' – trades in which the main instrument is your opinion of yourself and the raw material is your reputation or standing. At times he lives like a sort of high-class Leopold Bloom, the eternal Jewish clown; at others he is a Teufelsdröckh; again he is the pushing son of the bewildered Polish-Jewish immigrant and failed bootlegger, guilty about his break with the past, nagged by his relations, his ambitions punctured.

As a character Moses is physically exact – we know his domestic habits – but mentally and emotionally amorphous. Any objection to this is cancelled by his range as an observer-victim. It is a triumph that he is not a bore and does not ask our sympathy.

The outsize heroes of Bellow's long novels are essentially moral types who have been forced by the American scene to behave like clowns. They are the classic American monologue in person, elephantine chunks of ego. In *Humboldt's Gift* we meet the clown as performing poet:

> A wonderful talker, a hectic non-stop monologist and improvisator, a champion detractor: to be loused up by Humboldt was really a kind of privilege. It was like being the subject of a two-nosed portrait by Picasso or an eviscerated chicken by Soutine . . .

One recognizes the voice at once: it has the dash, the dandyism, the easy control of side-slipping metaphor and culture-freaking which gives pace to Saul Bellow's comedies. He is above all a performer, and in *Humboldt's Gift* he tells the story of performance in the person of Citrine, Humboldt's worshipper, disciple and betrayer.

As a youth Citrine had kneeled before the great manic depressive who had passed the peak of his reputation and was left, gin bottle in hand, cursing American materialism for what it does to genius and the life of the imagination. Humboldt was shrewd enough to see that the young Citrine was on the make, but was glad to have an ally among the young: everything went well, in a general alcoholic way, until Citrine did a frightful thing: he wrote a Broadway success which made him a sudden fortune. He had gone straight to the top of the tree. This was more than the crumbling, middle-aged poet could bear: he did not mind that Citrine had portrayed him as a knockabout Bohemian character; what he resented was the money going into Citrine's pocket. By this time Humboldt has become the classic American drunken genius and hospital case who shows up American philistinism. Getting out of Bellevue, Humboldt has a delightful time with the psychiatrists:

> Even the shrewd Humboldt knew what he was worth in professional New York. Endless conveyor belts of sickness or litigation poured clients and patients into these midtown offices like dreary Long Island potatoes. These dull spuds crushed psychoanalysts' hearts with boring character problems. Then

suddenly Humboldt arrived. Oh Humboldt! He was no potato! He was a papaya, a citron, a passion fruit . . . And what a repertory he had, what changes of style and tempo. He was meek at first – shy. Then he became child-like, trusting, then he confided . . . He said he knew what husbands and wives said when they quarrelled . . . People said ho-hum and looked at the ceiling when you started this. Americans! With their stupid ideas about love and their domestic tragedies. How could you bear to listen to them after the worst of wars and the most sweeping of revolutions, the destruction, the death camps, the earth soaked in blood . . . The world looked into American faces and said: 'Don't tell me these cheerful, well-to-do people are suffering . . . Anyway I'm not here to discuss adolescent American love-myths' – this was how Humboldt talked. Still, he said, I'd like you to listen to this.

And, suddenly blazing up, he howled out all the melodramas of American scandal and lust. The lawyers had heard it a thousand times – they wanted to hear it again from a man of genius. He had become what the respectable professionals long for – their pornographer.

As admirers of Saul Bellow's work know, he is a master of elaborately patterned narrative that slips back or forward in time, circulating like Sterne, like Proust even. Sterne did this because he loved human inertia: Bellow is out for every tremor of the over-electrified American ego: he is expert in making characters disappear and then reappear swollen and with palms itching for more and more instant life. Humboldt will die in an elevator, but he will haunt the novel to the end like Moby Dick: even contemporary ghosts are jumbo size. The story moves to Chicago and there, on native ground, Citrine fills out. He is Cleverness and Success in person:

It was my turn to be famous and to make money, to get heavy mail, to be recognized by influential people, to be dined at Sardis and propositioned in padded booths by women who sprayed themselves with musk, to buy Sea Island cotton underpants and leather luggage.

His troubles with the tax man, with his ex-wife's lawyers who are stripping him of everything they can get hold of, seem to excite rather than depress him. His sexual life is avid and panicky: he hopes to outsmart middle age. He has bouts of hypochondria. These are enjoyable because he is very frank about his vanity: his touchiness, as middle age comes on, is the making of him as a comic figure. Gleam as he may with success, he cherishes what his wife calls his 'cemetery bit'; he has a bent for being a victim: ironical and sentimental, he also knows he is as hardheaded as that other famous twelve-year-old charmer, David Copperfield.

Once Humboldt is dead, Citrine is without a necessary enemy, and here Mr Bellow makes a very interesting find: Rinaldo Cantabile, a small crook with the naïve notion that he can 'make' the top Mafia. Unlike Humboldt, there is nothing myth-attracting in Cantabile. He is a loud, smart, nasty smell; he understands the first lesson of gangsterdom: to humiliate your victim; but he is an ass. We remember that Citrine is out to explore the American love-hate of Culture and Genius and indeed takes us round colleges and foundations: Cantabile is introduced to suggest that the Mafia might get a foot in here. Cantabile even thinks he can terrorize Citrine into seeing that Cantabile's wife gets a PhD by fraud. My own view is that he does not make the grade as a compelling menace: he is without the extra dimension given to Bellow's strongly felt characters.

However, good comes of Cantabile, for he gets Mr Bellow back to Chicago. That city is the hero of *Humboldt's Gift*. No American novelist surpasses Bellow in the urban scene. He knows Chicago intimately from the smell of old blood in the hot nights to the rust on its fire escapes and the aluminium glint of the Lake. He knows the saunas:

the wooden posts were slowly consumed by a wonderful decay that made them soft brown. They looked like beavers' fur in the golden vapour ... The Division-Street steambathers don't look like the trim proud people downtown . . . They are vast in antique form. They stand on thick pillow legs affected with a sort of creeping verdigris or blue-cheese mottling of the ankles ... you feel these people are almost conscious of obsolescence, of a time of civilization abandoned by nature and culture. So down in the super-heated sub cellars all these Slavonic cavemen and wood demons with hanging laps of fat and legs of stone and lichen, boil themselves and splash ice-water on their heads by the bucket. Upstairs, on the television screen in the locker room,

dudes and grinning broads make smart talk or leap up and down
. . . Below, Franush, the attendant, makes steam by sloshing
water on the white-hot boulders.

The secret of Mr Bellow's success is that he talks people into life
and never stops pouring them in and out of his scenes. In his book
the women are particularly well drawn. Citrine's sexual vanity is a
help here: once satisfied, he is taken aback by the discovery that
women have other interests – the delightful delinquent Demmie is
reformed, but in sleep at night her buried life comes out in groans
and howls as she wrestles with the devil, and she wakes up next day
fresh as a daisy to get down on her knees for redemption by
scrubbing floors. Denise is the climbing wife of the climbing man.
Vassar girl, seductive and respectable – what more does she what?
The ear of top people at the White House: she wants to tell them
what she has just read in *Newsweek*! And then Renata – a fate for
more than one Bellow hero – Spanishy, flamenco-ish, vulgar,
genial, sexually voracious, knows her Ritzes, and while willing to
listen to high-class intellectual talk for a while, makes it clear that
her price is very high and her fidelity at perpetual risk. These
women are real, even likeable. Why? I think because in some clever
way Mr Bellow shows them moving through their own peculiar
American day, which is unlike the day of Citrine. One might press
the point further and say that Bellow's characters are real to us
because they are physical objects – Things. What other tenderness
can a materialist society contain?

It says a great deal for Bellow's gift that although he can raise
very boring subjects and drop names like an encyclopaedia or a
digest, he has tact and irony. He is crisp. But two-thirds of the way
through this novel he lands himself with a tangle of dramatic
situations as complex as, say, the last act of a Restoration comedy.
Here he lost me. Humboldt – it turns out – had repented of calling
Citrine a Judas and traitor; had even left him a money-making film
script – put into the hands of the right phoney director it should
make a fortune. It does. Citrine does not take the money, indeed he
behaves so well that it looks as though in saving his soul from
corruption he may lose Renata. One curious act he does perform:
he has Humboldt and his mother disinterred and reburied in a
decent cemetery. That's one thing you can do for artists.

Márquez

The Myth Makers

It has often been said of the Spanish nature and – by extension – of those who have inherited Iberian influences in South America, that the ego is apt to leap across middle ground and see itself as a universe. The leap is to an All. The generalization itself skips a great deal too, but it is a help towards beginning to understand the astonishing richness of the South American novelists of recent years. Their 'All' – I think of Vargas Llosa and Garcia Márquez among others – is fundamentally 'the people', not in the clichés of political rhetoric, but in the sense of millions of separate lives, no longer anonymous but physically visible, awash in historical memory and with identities.

After reading *Leaf Storm*, the novella written by Gabriel Garcia Márquez when he was only nineteen, but not published until 1955, one sees what a distance lies between this effort and his masterpiece *One Hundred Years of Solitude*. The young author sows the seed of a concern with memory, myth and the nature of time which bursts into lovely shameless blossom in his later book. We get our first glimpse of the forgotten town of Macondo (obviously near Cartagena), a primitive place, once a naïve colonial Eden; then blasted by the 'leaf storm' of the invading foreign banana-companies, and finally a ghost town, its founders forgotten. Shut up in a room in one of its remaining family houses is an unpleasant doctor who 'lives on grass' – a vegetarian? – whom the town hates because he once refused to treat some men wounded after a civil rising. Now, secluded for goodness knows how many years, he has hanged himself, and the question is whether the town will riot and refuse to have him buried. The thing to notice is that, like so many South American novelists, Márquez was even then drawn to the inordinate character – not necessarily a giant or saga-like hero, but someone who has exercised a right to extreme conduct or aberration. Such people fulfil a new country's need for legends. A human being is required to be a myth, his spiritual value lies in the inflating of his tale.

Far better than *Leaf Storm* are some of the short stories in the new collection, and one above all, 'The Handsomest Drowned Man in the World'. The story is an exemplary guide to the art of Márquez, for it is a celebration of the myth-making process. Somewhere on the seashore children are found playing with the body of a drowned man, burying it, digging it up again, burying it. Fishermen take the corpse to the village, and while the men go off to enquire about missing people, the women are left to prepare the body for burial. They scrape off the crust of little shells and stones and weed and mess and coral in which the body is wrapped and then they see the man within:

> They noticed that he bore his death with pride for he did not have the lonely look of other drowned men who came out of the sea or that haggard needy look of men who drowned in rivers ... he was the tallest, strongest, most virile and best built man they had ever seen ... They thought if that magnificent man had lived in the village, his house would have had the widest doors, the highest ceiling, and the strongest floor, his bedstead would have been made from a midship frame held together by iron bolts and his wife would have been the happiest woman. They thought he would have had so much authority he could have drawn fish out of the sea simply by calling their names.

The women imagine him in their houses; they see that because he is tall, the doors and ceilings of their houses would have to be higher and they tell him affectionately to 'mind his head' and so on. The dead god has liberated so much fondness and wishing that when the body is at last formally buried at sea it is not weighed down by an anchor, for the women and men too hope that the dead man will realize that he is welcome to come back at any time.

There is nothing arch or whimsical in the writing of this fable. The prose of Márquez is plain, exact, subtle and springy and easily leaps into the comical and the exuberant, as we find in *One Hundred Years of Solitude*. In that book the history of the Buendía families and their women in three or four generations is written as a hearsay report on the growth of the little Colombian town; it comes to life because it is continuously leaping out of fact into the mythical and the myth is comic. One obvious analogy is with

Rabelais. It is suggested, for example, that Aureliano Segundo's sexual orgies with his concubine are so enjoyable that his own livestock catch the fever. Animals and birds are unable to stand by and do nothing. The rancher's life is a grandiose scandal; the 'bonecrusher' in bed is a heroic glutton who attracts 'fabulous eaters' from all over the country. There is an eating duel with a lady known as 'The Elephant'. The duel lasted from a Saturday to a Tuesday, but it had its elegance:

> While Aureliano ate with great bites, overcome by the anxiety of victory, The Elephant was slicing her meat with the art of a surgeon and eating it unhurriedly and even with a certain pleasure. She was gigantic and sturdy, but over her colossal form a tenderness of femininity prevailed . . . later on when he saw her consume a side of veal without breaking a single rule of good table manners, he commented that this most delicate, fascinating and insatiable proboscidian was in a certain way the ideal woman.

The duel is beautifully described and with a dozen inventive touches, for once Márquez gets going there is no controlling his fancy. But note the sign of the master: the story is always brought back to ordinary experience in the end. Aureliano was ready to eat to the death and indeed passes out. The scene has taken place at his concubine's house. He gasps out a request to be taken to his wife's house because he had promised not to die in his concubine's bed; and she, who knows how to behave, goes and shines up his patent leather boots that he had always planned to wear in his coffin. Fortunately he survives. It is very important to this often ruthless, licentious and primitive epic that there is a deep concern for propriety and manners.

As a fable or phantasmagoria *One Hundred Years of Solitude* succeeds because of its comic animality and its huge exaggerations which somehow are never gross and indeed add a certain delicacy. Márquez seems to be sailing down the bloodstream of his people as they innocently build their town in the swamp, lose it in civil wars, go mad in the wild days of the American banana company and finally end up abandoned. The story is a social history but not as it is found in books but as it muddles its way forward or backward among the sins of family life and the accidents of trade. For example, one of the many Aurelianos has had the luck and intelligence to introduce ice to Macondo. To extend the ice business was impossible without getting the railroad in. This is how Márquez introduces the railroad:

> Aureliano Centeno, overwhelmed by the abundance of the factory, had already begun to experiment in the production of ice with a base of fruit juices instead of water, and without knowing it or thinking about it, he conceived the essential fundamentals for the invention of sherbet. In that way he planned to diversify the production of an enterprise he considered his own, because his brother showed no signs of returning after the rains had passed and the whole summer had gone by with no news of him. At the start of another winter a woman who was washing clothes in the river during the hottest time of the day ran screaming down the main street in an alarming state of commotion.
>
> 'It's coming,' she finally explained. 'Something frightful like a kitchen dragging a village behind it.'

There are scores of rippling pages that catch the slippery comedies and tragedies of daily life, at the speed of life itself: the more entangled the subject the faster the pace. Márquez is always ready to jump to extremes; it is not enough for a girl to invite two school friends to her family's house, she invites seventy horrible girls and the town has to be ransacked for seventy chamber pots. Crude or delicate an incident may be, but it is singular in the way ordinary things are. Almost every sentence is a surprise and the surprise is, in general, really an extension of our knowledge or feeling about life, and not simply a trick. Ursula, the grandmother of the Buendía tribe, the one stable character, is a repository of superstitious wisdom, i.e., superstition is a disguised psychological insight. In her old age, we see her revising her opinions, especially one about babies who 'weep in the womb'. She discusses this with her husband and he treats the idea as a joke. He says such children will become ventriloquists; she thinks that they will be prophets. But now, surveying the harsh career of a son who has grown up to be a proud and heartless fighter of civil wars, she says that 'only the unloving' weep in the womb. And those who cannot love are in need of more compassion than others. An insight? Yes, but it also brings back dozens of those talks one has had in Spain (and indeed in South America) where people kill the night by pursuing the bizarre or the extreme by-ways of human motive.

In no derogatory sense, one can regard this rapid manner of talk – non-stop, dry and yet fantastical – as characteristic of café culture: lives pouring away in long bouts of chatter. In North America its characteristic form is the droll monologue; in South America the fantasy is – in my limited reading – more agile and imaginative, richer in laughter and, of course, especially happy in its love of the outrageous antics of sexual life.

One Hundred Years of Solitude denies interpretation. One could say that a little Arcady was created but was ruined by the 'Promethian ideas' that came into the head of its daring founder. Or that little lost towns have their moment – as civilizations do – and are then obliterated. Perhaps the moral is, as Márquez says, that 'races condemned to one hundred years of solitude do not get a second chance on earth'. The notion of 'the wind passeth over it and it is gone' is rubbed in; so also is the notion Borges has used, of a hundred years or even infinite time being totally discernible in a single minute. But what Márquez retrieves from the history he has surveyed is an Homeric laughter.

Life is ephemeral but dignified by fatality: the word 'ephemeral' often crops up in *The Autumn of the Patriarch*, which has been well translated by Gregory Rabassa – the original would be beyond even those foreigners who read Spanish.

The Patriarch who gives the novel its moral theme is the elusive despot of a South American republic and we hear him in the scattered voices of his people and his own. As a young wild bull he is the traditional barefoot peasant leader; later he is the confident monster ruthlessly collecting the spoils of power, indifferent to murder and massacre, sustained by his simple peasant mother, surviving by cunning. Still later, in his old age, he is a puppet manipulated by the succeeding juntas, who are selling off the country to exploiters, a Caliban cornered but tragic, with a terrifying primitive will to survive. His unnamed republic looks out on the Caribbean from a barren coast from which the sea has receded, so that he believes, as superstitiously as his people do, that foreigners have even stolen the sea.

By the time the novel opens he is a myth to his people. Those who think they have seen him have probably seen only his double, though they may have glimpsed his hand waving from a limousine. He himself lives among the remnants of his concubines and the lepers and beggars that infest the Presidential fort. His mother is dead. He stamps round on his huge feet and is mainly concerned with milking his cows in the dairy attached to his mansion. Power is in the hands of an untrusted Minister. The President no longer leaves the place but drowses as he reads of speeches he has never made, celebrations he has never attended, applause he has never heard, in the newspaper of which only one copy is printed and solely for himself. He is, in short, an untruth; a myth in the public mind, a dangerous animal decaying in 'the solitary vice' of despotic power, fearing one more attempt at assassination and, above all, the ultimate solitude of death.

At first sight the book is a capricious mosaic of multiple narrators. We slide from voice to voice in the narrative without warning, in the course of the long streaming sentences of consciousness. But the visual, animal realism is violent and forever changing: we are swept from still moments of domestic fact to vivid fantasy, back and forth in time from, say, the arrival of the first Dutch discoverers to the old man looking at television, in the drift of hearsay and memory.

The few settled characters are like unforgettable news flashes that disturb and disappear: the richness of the novel will not be grasped in a single reading. We can complain that it does not progress but returns upon itself in widening circles. The complaint is pointless: the spell lies in the immediate force of its language and the density of narrative. We can be lost in those interminable sentences and yet once one has got the hang of the transitions from one person to the next it is all as sharp as the passing moment is because Márquez is the master weaver of the real and the conjectured. His descriptive power astounds at once, in the first forty pages where the narrator is a naïve undefined 'we', i.e. the people. They break into the fortress of the tragic monster and find their Caliban dead among the cows that have long ago broken out of the dairy and graze off the carpets in the salons of the ruined Presidencia and even have appeared, lowing like speakers, on the balconies. This is from the opening scene:

When the first vultures began to arrive, rising up from where they had dozed on the cornices of the charity hospital, they came from farther inland, they came in successive waves, out of the horizon of the sea of dust where the sea had been, for a whole day they flew in slow circles of the house of power until a king with bridal feathers and a crimson ruff gave a silent order and that breaking of glass began, that breeze of a great man dead, that in and out of vultures through the windows imaginable only in a house which lacked authority, so we dared go in too and in the deserted sanctuary we found the rubble of grandeur, the body that had been pecked at, the smooth maiden hands with the ring of power on the bone of the third finger, and his whole body was sprouting tiny lichens and parasitic animals from the depths of the sea, especially in the armpits and the groin, and he had the canvas truss of his herniated testicle which was the only thing that had escaped the vultures in spite of its being the size of an ox kidney; but even then we did not dare believe in his death because it was the second time he had been found in that office, alone and dressed and dead seemingly of natural causes during his sleep, as had been announced a long time ago in the prophetic waters of soothsayers' basins.

Only his double had been able to show him his 'untruth': that useful ignoramus died of poison intended for his master. There had been a period when the President really was of the people, the easy joker who might easily get an upland bridegroom murdered so that he himself could possess the bride. The dictator's peasant mother who carried on in his mansion, sitting at her sewing-machine as if she were still in her hut, was the only one aware of his tragedy. (Once when he was driving to a ceremonial parade she rushed after him with a basket of empties telling him to drop them at the shop when he passed. The violent book has many homely touches.) His brutal sexual assaults are not resented: – he fucks with his boots and uniform on – but when very late he comes to feel love, he is at a loss. On a Beauty Queen of the slum called the Dog District, he pours gadgets and imported rubbish, even turns the neighbourhood into a smart suburb: she is immovable and he is almost mad.

He kidnaps a Jamaican novice nun and marries her, but two years pass before he dares to go to bed with her. She spends her time bargaining for cheap toys in the market. She surrenders to him not out of love but out of pity and teaches him to read and sign his name. The market people hate her trading habits and her fox furs and set the dogs on her and her children: they are torn to pieces and eaten. There is a frightful scene where his supposedly loyal Minister organizes an insurrection. The old man's animal instinct detects a plot in the conspiracy. The Minister warns him:

505

'So things are in no shape for licking your fingers, general Sir, now we really are fucked up.' The wily President won't budge but sends down a cartload of milk for the rebels and when the orderly uncorks the first barrel there is a roar and they see the man:

floating on the ephemeral backwash of a dazzling explosion and they saw nothing else until the end of time in the volcanic heat of the mournful yellow mortar building in which no flower ever grew, whose ruins remained suspended in the air from the tremendous explosion of six barrels of dynamite. That's that, he sighed in the Presidential palace, shaken by the seismic wind that blew down four more houses around the barracks and broke the wedding crystal in cupboards all the way to the outskirts of the city.

The President turns to his dominoes and when he sees the double five turn up, he guesses that the traitor behind the rebellion is his old friend of a lifetime, the Minister. He is invited to a banquet and, at the stroke of twelve, 'the distinguished Mayor General Roderigo de Aguilar entered on a silver tray, stretched out, garnished with cauliflower and laurel, steeped with spices and oven brown – and, in all his medals, is served up roast'. The guests are forced to eat him.

Márquez is the master of a spoken prose that passes unmoved from scenes of animal disgust and horror to the lyrical evocation, opening up vistas of imagined or real sights which may be gentle or barbarous. The portrait of the mother who eventually dies of a terrible cancer is extraordinary. He has tried to get the Papal Nuncio to canonize her and, when Rome refuses, the President makes her a civil saint and has her embalmed body carried round the country. Avidly the people make up miracles for her. Once more, in his extreme old age and feeble, there is another insurrection, plotted by a smooth aristocratic adviser. The President survives. In his last night alive he wanders round the ruined house, counting his cows, searching for lost ones in rooms and closets; and he has learned that because of his incapacity for love he has tried 'to compensate for that infamous fate with the burning cultivation of the solitary vice of power' which is a fiction. 'We [the multiple narrator concludes less tritely] knew who we were while he was left never knowing it for ever . . .' the 'All' is not an extent, it is a depth.

VI · BIOGRAPHIES

Balzac

Bankruptcy and Genius

To his amazement the very independent young Balzac was brusquely pushed by Mme Balzac into hiding from his trade creditors. He hid in the flat of a young critic called Henri de Latouche, a kind if touchy young dilettante who thought there was promise in Balzac's latest novel, *Wann-Chlore*. When the scare passed off this experience of conspiracy and escape was so exciting that he lost all interest in the cause of it. He was irritated by the fact that he had to go and sign papers at the liquidators. The whole episode was an annoying interruption of his dreaming state.

When the coast was clear he left Latouche and appeared as if nothing had happened, at a little house in the Rue Cassini, near the Observatoire. In 1828 this quarter was on the outskirts of Paris almost in the country, a melancholy region of waste land, unmade roads and paths between market gardens and haunted by footpads. Creditors would have had difficulty in finding the house. A foundling hospital, a home for the deaf and dumb, a convent or two, were the only landmarks. The bells of the convents were dismal. Balzac's family had rallied to him. His mother had loaned him 200 francs, the house was taken in his brother-in-law's name: tenancies in the name of someone else or even of imaginary persons henceforth became a permanent feature of Balzac's life. Not only out of necessity; he loved mystery. For the next nine years – with intervals of flight to his sister Laure in the country, to Saché and Angoulême when Paris was too hot for him – the house in Rue Cassini was his home. He let the ground floor off to an industrious painter. He rescued what furniture he had from the printing works, including the blue muslin curtains. These he nailed up again in the new home. There was a back door, opening to stairs leading directly to his bedroom, by which Mme Berny could discreetly slip in. She was very distressed by the disaster and had taken lodgings near by in a street appropriately called the Rue d'Enfer. On the main door, in one of his fits of fantasy, he put the inscription '*L'Absolu, Marchand de Briques*'. The joke was also one more disguise.

Here Balzac's revelation of the energizing poetry of debt took one of its lasting forms. If he was a born writer, he had already shown himself to be a compulsive furnisher, a man who believed in the magic of objects bought on credit. It was part of his *gourmandise*. He began buying clocks, a candelabra, statuettes, knick-knacks, and a great deal more besides. His austere friend Latouche thought his tastes effeminate and indeed the virile Balzac seemed to nest womanishly:

> You haven't changed at all. You pick out the Rue Cassini to live in and you are never there . . . Your heart clings to carpets, mahogany chests, sumptuously bound books, superfluous clothes and copper engravings. You chase through the whole of Paris in search of candelabra that will never shed light on you, and yet you haven't even got a few sous in your pockets that would enable you to visit a sick friend. Selling yourself to a carpet-maker for two years! You deserve to be put in Charenton lunatic asylum.

The carpets were heavy, soft and blue. In time the study was in mahogany, upholstered in red leather, and there was a fine glass mahogany bookcase filled with luxuriously bound books. They bore the coat of arms of his imaginary ancestors – the device of the d'Entragues. In time his own works would stand there in a handsome edition: and next to them would be an equally expensive volume containing a collection of the bills falling due – or, for him, never falling due. He chose a sunless room for his study – he worked at night. It contained a small statue of Napoleon, to egg him on. The knick-knacks were indeed odd: a little glove, like a child's; a little white satin shoe; a rusty key which he called his talisman. The armchair was in brown silk with fringes. The work-table itself was surprisingly small and plain and was covered with green baize.

To mark the transit from reality to fiction and to invoke mystical powers, he put on a white robe when he sat down to write at night. He liked to think of himself as a monk. The robe was soon to be held by a belt of Venetian gold, and from it hung a paper knife, a pair of scissors, and a golden penknife. On his feet he wore Moroccan slippers.

Three more items stand out in this inventory: a marble bathroom 'fit for a duchess', a glass case containing a piece of silk on which were embroidered a pierced heart and an inscription, '*Une Amie Inconnue*'. He had a mistress already but there was always another, a dream-woman, in his head. The object that indicates the worker is mundane: an alarm clock. It wakes him in the evening when he settles to work all night till six in the morning by the light of four candles in the candelabra. When he finishes he goes at once to the bath. He has a mania for cleanliness and for the perfect condition of his hands. He regards his small clean hands as a sign of his aristocratic inheritance. He boasts that no ink ever stains his robe. The clean monastic austerity is at variance with the grotesque untidiness of his clothes and the greasiness of his unkempt hair, when he puts on a very old hat and goes out. But he is not always shabby. He has started to run a lifetime's account with Buisson, the fashionable tailor. There is a bill for black trousers, a white waistcoat, a chamois waistcoat. Nothing can be done about his legs which are too short; but if he remembers to do his coat buttons up he looks passably, if always a little comically, well dressed.

When she heard of his mahogany bookcase and newly bound books, Mme Balzac sent up a scream. He got his sister to intervene for him. He had been lent 200 francs, he said, 115 of which was rent. How could he be living in luxury on the remaining 85 francs! The usual evasion.

This stupid young man (he wrote to his sister) is locked in his study. He has got to kill half a ream of paper, cover it with ink. He may seem reckless to others, but he has a good heart; a hard word knocks him out. He needs, he says, large-hearted friends, people who know how to live to the full. Certainly he worked. He was doing articles, stories, sketching an historical novel – 'a volume a week'. His mother's angry letter, he says, has cost him 20 francs, the price of two nights' work.

But – the marble bathroom? Fit for a duchess? There *was* a duchess. We must go back to the drama of his venture as a publisher and printer. Whether Balzac was sexually innocent when he met Mme de Berny we do not know. Innocence is not uncommon among much-mothered, intellectual young men obsessed with their ambitions. Balzac would often say that sexual

511

restraint was indispensable to the dedicated artist and even that 'once a year' for health's sake was enough. This may have been one of his fantastic sayings. What is certain is that his affair with Mme de Berny had its roots in his desire to belong to another, more cultivated family; but having won his liberation, and however elevated he may have been by her love, he was certain now, and emboldened, to move towards other women. Ambition and new self-confidence and the Romantic stress on liberty in love would drive him and even if he had not been a Balzac he would be – like so many men of genius, conscious of rising in the world – a romantic snob. Three years after his success with Mme de Berny his head was turned, not by a young and pretty girl, but one more middle-aged woman, Laure Permon, Duchesse d'Abrantès. This affair was a stormy distraction in the life of a young man attempting to establish himself as a publisher and printer. She was the widow of General Junot, a fellow officer of Napoleon when he made his first leap towards notice at the siege of Toulon. Napoleon had made him a duke. Titles always went to the heads of the Balzacs and for Honoré – who was in the early stages of becoming 'secretary of history' – the Duchess was an irresistible history lesson. She was the intimate history of Napoleon's court in person, for she had been brought up at the Tuileries as a girl. Mme de Berny had been at the court of Versailles. He had been entranced by her stories of the *ancien régime*: in the Duchess he had met his first grand figure of Napoleon's parvenu nobility. She had been famous for her wealth, her dinners, her salon. As a young woman she had been the mistress of Metternich who was to be a haunting presence in Balzac's life.

It is thought that he met the Duchess through his sister at Saint-Cyr, near Versailles, where his touchy brother-in-law was Director of Military Studies. There is also a tale that he met her coming out of a money-lender's in Versailles. If this is true it suggests the dilapidated state of the great lady's fortunes. Extravagant and now Bohemian, she lived in a small house at Versailles with her four children and a tribe of unpaid servants and when he went there Balzac must have noticed that the house was barely furnished. She had already sold most of her fine furniture, her jewellery and her silver. A masterful and cunning woman, now in her late forties and getting stout, she saw in Balzac exactly the young man she needed: a clever ghost-writer, journalist and publisher. There was now a huge public demand for historical memoirs of the immediate past and the Duchess wanted a publishing young man to collaborate in writing hers.

He saw a small stout woman, carelessly dressed in coffee-, and even opium-stained clothes and shabby shoes; but the uncorseted aristocratic slattern with dark hair all over the place was famous for her toilette and she wore the fashionable shawl like an empress. Her voice was hard, mocking and precise. Her nose was a large and aggressive beak. She was said to be a good-natured liar but very charming with it. She was soaked in perfume. A scurrilous Versailles lawyer called Lambinet said that this was because she smelled like a polecat. But Balzac's imagination was carried away by history and her distinction. Aristocratic women (he wrote) always beguiled by their remote smiles, their manners, the value they put upon themselves, and the distance they put between themselves and the world. They flattered all the vanities in one, he said, that were halfway to love. Two active vanities, two unlikely embodiments of professional self-interest, two people unscrupulous about money had met. The Duchess showed him her manuscripts. (She was to publish sixty volumes in the end, some by his hand.) She told him about Napoleon: the young novelist had a greed for vicarious lives and, once he had got over his awe of her, he knew how to attract women of a certain age. Young girls bored him; they were sulky if not petted, he said, touchy, self-centred, and their company was unprofitable.

At first he and the Duchess were friends; but, hearing so much of the Napoleonic he determined to make her his mistress. He remembered the Napoleonic tactic of sudden assault. There was a good deal of the coxcomb in him. He began, as he had begun with Mme de Berny, with letters that are marvels of pomposity, hyperbole, and bombastic self-portraiture. She was amused and turned him down. He was annoyed but returned with a long essay comparing the characters of proud and unconquerable women with the sensitive. He dragged in Clarissa Harlowe, whose sensibility is crushed by virtue, and the fighting heroine of Maturin's *Melmoth.* And then he drifted into one of his educational excursions into entomology: like insects men and women cautiously put out feelers towards one another and the antennae of 'certain souls' recognize each other instantly. In another letter he got on to the delicate subject of the gap in age. She was in her forties.

Balzac had a sure instinct when he concentrated on the misfortunes of women for, to a woman, are not her misfortunes her romance? Balzac's success with women sprang from his compelling interest in their adventures. He went straight with bold and skilful sympathy to what was secret in their lives. The Duchess drily reminded him – and this was a mark of that jealousy which is so often the beginning of love – that she had heard he was already in 'silken fetters', a reference to Mme de Berny. Balzac knew his moment had come. It was the moment to expand and assert that he was a slave to no one. He was a man with a will of his own and not (he said) to be led by apron-strings and nurses. If he had one quality (he said), it was energy. Amid a life of misfortunes – and just as she had done in *her* misfortunes – he had known how to present 'a calm front'. As for himself, he has never told anyone about them. This was quite untrue. He had told not only Mme de Berny but everyone else. Domination was intolerable, he said. He would not be made a lackey: 'I cannot be led or governed.' And then came the exuberant outburst of the Gascon bombshell. Moralists could judge him as they wished, but they could never grasp the exceptional man:

> I have the most extraordinary character and I study it with the detachment I apply to the characters of others. In my five feet three inches I contain every possible inconsistency and contrast, and those who find me vain, extravagant, obstinate, frivolous, illogical, fatuous, negligent, idle, unpurposeful, unreflective, inconstant talkative, tactless, crude, unpolished, difficult and of uneven temper are no less right than those who would say I am economical, modest, courageous, tenacious, energetic, hard-working, constant, reserved, full of finesse, polite and always cheerful . . . In short, learned or unlearned, talented or inept, I am astonished by nothing more than myself. I conclude that I am simply an instrument played upon by circumstances . . .

The Duchess was amused. He added more gravely:

> Does this kaleidoscopic state arise out of what Chance has installed in the souls of those whose aim is to depict every condition of the human heart, to paint all feelings so that by the power of imagination they may themselves experience the feelings they paint? And is the gift of observation simply a kind of memory designed to assist the strivings of the imagination?

Exceptional herself, down on her luck, the Duchess might be hard-headed but she liked the risk of the exceptional. And, at all costs, she needed Balzac's help for her memoirs.

Balzac was soon telling her what he had years before said to Mme de Berny, now in her fifties, that life for a woman of her age was not over and the sun would rise again in her life. The Duchess reflected that the sun might just as well rise; on condition that he got down to work with her. She allowed her head to be turned once more. Soon he was calling her his beloved angel. The word 'angel' was part of his vocabulary of love; it was a fashionable word with Swedenborgian overtones. It was awkward that, like Mme de Berny, the Duchess was called Laure – it was also the name of his mother and sister – so, adroitly, he called her Marie.

Looking back on this period of his life and at a love affair that to others seemed grotesque, he wrote:

> The sudden revelation of the poetry of the senses is the powerful link which attaches young men to women older than themselves; but it is like the prisoner's chains, it leaves an ineffaceable imprint on the soul, implants a distaste for a fresh and innocent love.

Mme de Berny knew that at some time she would be replaced but she supposed it would be by a young woman of his own age. She could not have expected that he would pursue a woman a little younger than herself. On her side, the maternal tenderness had turned into a sexual passion, all the stronger because of her maturity. He was her god, her master – to this word she clung.

It is thought that Mme Balzac told Mme de Berny of the affair. There was of course anger, there were jealous scenes and misery. Balzac had behaved shamefully and ungratefully. He had 'soiled a pure love'. The Duchess had brought out the worst in his character. Balzac's defence was the defence of the artist:

> The man accustomed to make his soul a mirror reflecting the whole world must necessarily lack that particular kind of logic and obstinacy which we call 'character'. He has a touch of the strumpet . . . He longs like a child for everything that takes his fancy. He will love to idolatry and then abandon his mistress for no apparent reason . . . Men and women may without dishonour indulge in many loves – it is natural to go in pursuit of happiness. But in every life there is only one true love.

515

Mme de Berny ordered him to break with the Duchess for two years. He loved Mme de Berny, but he was indignant and embarrassed. He had sworn to the Duchess that he was not dominated. But the wretchedness of Mme de Berny moved him; he knew what he owed to her. He blustered, he lied, he evaded, but at last he gave in. The silken fetters were indeed stronger than the anecdotal embraces of the Napoleonic Duchess who sent him a contemptuous letter:

> . . . If you are so weak as to do as you are told, poor man, your state is more to be pitied than I supposed . . . Have the kindness to send me back the books which the librarian at Versailles has already asked me for ten times and were only lent to you in my name . . . I can't help laughing to see, after a few days, that my reason has completely returned to me . . . One month, no six weeks! God, it is enough to make one die laughing.

He had discovered it was inconvenient for a publisher to be harassed by three mothers but a pattern had been established.

At last the two years were up. In the Rue Cassini Mme de Berny would slip in unseen by the neighbours. Sometimes the door was locked. Often she was shut out. Was the Duchess there? Was there some other woman? Had he gone off to amuse himself in Paris? She worked on his proofs, ran messages to editors.

> If you had been kind [she wrote], you would have told me yesterday when you sent me the Review that you wouldn't be there at three o'clock. I really don't like being told by all your servants that you are not at home – so would you tell me, sun or rain, whether I may venture to the Rue Cassini at three?

She would speak to him fearlessly, she could read him clearly; but she valued the love he had made her feel and was large enough and tender enough to control her possessiveness. She knew his pride, she wrote, his outbursts of temper, his crudity, his lack of tact. She understood his lies came from timidity, pride in his independence, and fear of hurting. He was unbearably younger – that was what she had to suffer. She could tell him quietly that he had genius: but she begged him not to shout his genius from the housetops. She thought about him, longed for him, for his company, desired him every hour. And she knew and was grateful that he came to her at once when he was in trouble and that with her he worked best. The affair with the Duchess did not last long; but as with so many of his mistresses, there was never a complete break. He helped her, on and off, as a fellow writer for years. His friends, both men and women (Théophile Gautier said), were obliged to recognize that Balzac was one of those unreliable creatures who are known for their disappearances and absences. He returned as eagerly as he left.

In this first year at the Rue Cassini he was emerging from his dazed state. He must stop ghosting and collaborating under an assumed name. He must write something worthy of the secret 'de' in his imagination, a book to be signed for the first time Honoré de Balzac. The early Romantics of the eighteenth century had been philosophers; they were being followed in the 1820s and 1830s by Romantics who saw their subject, as he did, in history. Scott and James Fenimore Cooper were very present in his mind. His contemporaries, like Vigny and Victor Hugo – who was writing *Notre-Dame de Paris* – had chosen the past and they had succeeded because the public who had lived through so much bloody history wanted to read about the passions – but at a picturesque remove. Balzac was groping his way to the realization that history was not far off. It was probably now; it was certainly within living memory. He had only to look back to Tours where as a youth he had heard so much about the Royalist rising in Brittany – the *Chouannerie*. A year or two before he had started a novel called *Le Gars* on the subject. It was to be the story of a beautiful dancer, the illegitimate daughter of a nobleman who is sent by the government to get the confidence of the leader of the Royalist rebels and to lure him into betraying his troops. Balzac had made a false start, but he always kept his false starts. He had a store of them. He would begin two or three things with excitement and then, tiring of them, put them aside. Now creditors had discovered the Rue Cassini. With Scott in mind he decided on something more ambitious than *Le Gars.* He would go to the real scene. People who had been caught up in that civil war were still alive.

Balzac was an industrious exploiter of family friends. When he was a printer he had tried to raise a loan from the son of his father's old protector in Tours, General de Pommereul. The loan was refused. But now, using his wits once more, he begged the son who lived in Fougères, in the heart of the *Chouan* country, to allow him to stay for a few weeks. The son was now a general. 'The financial events', Balzac wrote, that had 'shaken the Paris business world' had brought him 'to a halt'. Honour had been saved, but at the cost of his fortune: 'I am going to start writing again and the agile pen of the crow or the goose must help me gain a living and repay my mother . . . I won't take up much room.'

The Pommereuls were delighted. They were bored in their château and knew he would entertain them. The General's young wife was a gay woman and she wrote describing his arrival:

> He was a tiny little fellow with a big head and a wide body made absurd by ill-cut clothes. His old hat was too small for his head; but once he took the hat off one forgot everything else. I could not stop looking at his head. If you haven't seen his forehead and his eyes, you won't understand the effect of them – a wide forehead that seemed to be lit by a lamp, brown eyes flecked with gold, which seemed to speak. In his gestures, his way of speaking and holding himself, he was so bursting with confidence, good nature, simplicity and frankness that it was impossible to know him without liking him at once – his humour was exuberant and contagious. In spite of his misfortunes he was not in the house more than a quarter of an hour and we hadn't even shown him his room, before he had the general and me laughing till tears came into our eyes.

Of all the accounts of Balzac's talk, hers gets exactly his manner and method. He had engaged to pay for his keep by telling the Pommereuls stories. All the people he spoke about, he said, were alive *now*. 'They love, suffer, whirl in my head, but I shall soon have them organized, classed, labelled in books – famous books.'

> He had an extremely convincing way of telling them. One was certain that what he told 'had actually happened'. He would being something like this. 'General, you must have known the X family in Lille, not the X's of Roubaix, but the ones who are connected with the Z's of Béthune? Well, something occurred in that family as dramatic as anything in the Boulevard du Crime.' Off he went and we were spellbound by his words and his imagination. When he finished one came back to earth with a start. 'But is that true?' we'd say. Balzac fixed one with his subtly dancing eyes and then with a laugh that shook the windows, as usual: 'Not a word of truth in it,' he'd say. 'It's pure Balzac.'

The Pommereuls bought him a new hat in Fougères and then took him to see the farms and the châteaux, the fields and lanes where the savage peasant war had taken place. The rebel peasants were called *Chouans* because of the weird owl-like cries by which they signalled to one another at night. His hosts noticed the extraordinary powers of absorption and self-projection which he had claimed when he was following and listening to people in the Rue Lesdiguières.

Les Chouans is a powerful study of the cruelties and deceptions of a civil war between fanatic peasants and trained soldiers, but the hand of the new Balzac is seen in the domestic detail. We have this glimpse of the scene in the home of Galope-chopine, the guerrilla:

At nightfall a dreadful uneasiness crept into Galope-chopine's cottage, where life until then had been so artlessly carefree. Barbette, carrying her heavy load of thorn-broom on her back, and her little boy with a supply of grass for the cattle, returned at the family's supper-hour. As they came in, mother and son looked vainly to see Galope-chopine, and never had this wretched room seemed so large to them, its emptiness was so pervasive. The fireless hearth, the gloom, the silence, all spoke to them of impending misfortune.

When it was quite dark, Barbette bestirred herself to light a bright fire and two *oribus*, which is the name given to resin candles inland from the coastal belt to the Upper Loire, and on the northern side of Amboise in the country round Vendôme. She moved about her preparations with the slowness of a person overwhelmed by deep feeling. She was listening for the slightest sound; and often, misled by the gusts of wind that whistled about the house, went to the door of her wretched dwelling and returned sadly again. She washed two *pichés,* filled them with cider and placed them on the long walnut table. Several times she looked at her son who was watching the cooking buckwheat cakes, but was unable to speak to him. At one point the little boy's eyes rested on the two nails that served as support for his father's fowling-piece, and Barbette shivered as she noted like him that the place was empty. The silence was broken only by the lowing of the cows or by drops of cider falling periodically from the bunghole of the cider-cask. The poor woman sighed as she prepared and filled three earthenware bowls with a kind of soup made of milk, broken pieces of buckwheat cake and boiled chestnuts.

'They were fighting in the field belonging to the Beraudière farm,' the little boy volunteered.

'Run and look,' said his mother.

The boy ran to the field, and saw the heap of corpses in the moonlight, but no sign of his father, and returned joyously whistling; he had picked up a few hundred-sou pieces that the triumphant Counter-Chouans had trampled underfoot and left forgotten in the mud. He found his mother sitting on a stool by the fireside spinning hemp, and shook his head.

Balzac wrote much of the novel at the Pommereuls' in eight weeks, and the General's wife, seeing he was thin, said he needed fattening. She was a good Catholic and a good cook.

Mme de Berny missed him: 'My precious one, it will soon be ten, take your Minette on your knee and let her put her arms round your neck . . . But you are not to fall asleep and to make sure you don't I give you one of those kisses we know so well.' But she knew, she said, that he didn't want her there. Still, she said, she was lucky in one thing: the Duchess wasn't with him.

She asked if the Pommereuls were happy. She hoped so. It would be nice to know they were as happy as he and she. 'There is so much misery in the world . . .'

When the novel appeared in 1829 it was signed Honoré de Balzac and was his *succès d'estime.* The critics praised it but said it was 'after Sir Walter Scott'. Of course. And they fell upon the careless writing. It sold only 450 copies and it brought him little money, for his way of writing was disastrously expensive and would remain so. His habit was to write as carelessly as he talked and Balzac's brilliant, sceptical discursive talking voice gave a spell to all his writings; but once he got the proofs he slaughtered them. Incidents, chapters were moved about and every passage was covered with corrections that spread like a swarm of obliterating flies over the text. He rewrote the whole book. New proofs were sent for, and the same happened, again and again, as new ideas came to him. Passages were cut out and stored, often to become the sources of other stories or even articles. Printers were tormented by the crow-pen scribble dashed off by the excited writer by candlelight. Publishers threatened because of the expense of the corrections. A notable part of Balzac's earnings was always lost in having these costs deducted. The corrections were a tribute to his exuberance and invention, but they were ruinous. He rushed on from a bit of one book to a bit of the next. He made a habit of declaring a book was finished when he had merely written down a few ideas, a few pages, and was throwing it over for a time in favour of some other work he was late in delivering.

One unlucky but eventually profitable annoyance occurred after the publication of *Les Chouans*. A few years before the publisher of *Codes* had moved on to a new idea: *Physiologies*. He had given Balzac the money in advance for a Physiology of Marriage and he had not bothered to write the book. The publisher now insisted on it.

. . .

The Price of a Dream Achieved

Her letters were rare. He had moved into the house and sat in the smell of paint and plaster among the scaffolding, like a caretaker. He had come after their quarrels to detest the place: it was a mistress, indeed an infidelity, he had tired of. Once one achieves one's desire, he had often said, it means nothing. Often he simply sat and wept about the lost child and the muddle of his life. He feared her love had gone. He tried to stir her interest in the house. He pleaded, for example, to be allowed to install a pretty and expensive water-closet, speaking of its marble, its consoles, flowers and candlesticks as if it were the most adorable little boudoir! She refused the permission. Sulkily he ventured a touch of humour! Would Her Majesty, he whimpered, permit him to buy a cheap mahogany box for his shoes – if not he'd go on keeping them in the window-boxes on the stairs. Nothing was to be bought! Even so he managed to sneak in two door-knockers for the main gate that cost more than the gate itself. Couldn't he come to the Ukraine? 'I realize that you don't want me and I fall prey to a double despair, that of not being expected and of not having written anything.'

Suddenly her mood changed; perhaps now she was in her own home she was bored. After Western Europe life in the Ukraine was dull. She told him to come.

Balzac set off as one travelling at last to the Promised Land. He was equipped like an explorer. In 1847 railways were sketchy in

France and Germany; much of the journey would be by road. He took provisions for eight days: ship's biscuit, coffee concentrate, sugar, a package of tongue, and a bottle of anisette. For a man with a bad stomach, a damaged heart, and who suffered from neuralgia, the journey was awful. He was in nothing like the sound condition he had been in on his rough expedition to the silver mines of Sardinia. The train journey to Brussels was fairly easy. But then on to Hanover he had to take the out-of-date German diligence – style 1820. Rather grand passengers were with him part of the way: an embassy man taking messages to Metternich, a collector of porcelain and a lady known as the 'queen of Hamburg'. He changed into a train at Hanover for Berlin; next day, Breslau. At every change Balzac became demented because he thought his luggage was lost or stolen. People humoured him, treating him like a drunk. On to Cracow, in a wood-burning train. At Gleiwitz, the frontier, a row with the Austrian customs. The terrible journey crawled on. At Dubno he slept for the first time for nine days. The last 100 leagues of the journey took thirty hours in a *kilitka*, a rough vehicle that hit every rut on the awful road, in clouds of dust as it crossed the cornlands of the steppe. The driver drank his anisette.

The steppe, he said, was the silent prairie of Fenimore Cooper. One more night on the road and then as the sun was setting, Wierzchownia appeared out of a fold in the ground suddenly like a mirage. The vast place looked, he said, like another Louvre or Greek temple. The month was September. He arrived with a terrible migraine.

The house was said to be the most luxurious in the Ukraine and the estate was larger than a French department. Yet inside the walls were noticeably bare except for mirrors ten feet high. There was one Carcel oil lamp for the whole patriarchal mansion. The place was heated by straw stuffed into the stoves. The night Balzac arrived a number of outlying barns and houses were burned down in a terrible fire. The estate numbered 40,000 souls and there were 300 domestic servants. He was given a suite of three luxurious rooms – the rugs and the silver amazed him and also the fact that there were five or six other suites like this. From the windows he looked out at the endless miles of corn, broken here and there by a forest of oak.

The family were excited by his arrival. He was their adored Bilboquet. He was stupefied to see the servants prostrate themselves before him, flat on their stomachs, knocking their heads three times on the floor and kissing the toe of his slipper – as he had kissed the toe of the Pope in Rome the year before. Spectacular wealth, but – it soon turned out – all the Polish landowners were up to their ears in debt; Mme Hanska's daughter, now married, had been given her share of the estate and was already spending it fast; Balzac was bewildered. But he announced proudly that he would pay off all he owed by his pen. He set to work on a novel, the last part of *L'Envers de l'Histoire Contemporaine* (The Seamy Side of Contemporary History) to show that he intended not to sponge, but to support his future wife by his own efforts. He worked by the country timetable he had followed at Saché – writing all day, coming down to dinner in the evening. In the vast drawing-room with its columns, lit by groups of candles, there was a Van Dyck, a Rembrandt and a Guercino, Balzac's own smoke-blackened portrait by Boulanger – rather gratifying – and to greet the writer in proper state, the young Mniszechs brought over from their place some miles away a Greuze, two Watteaus, and three Canalettos – every Polish landowner had his stock of Canalettos. The evening passed with the gentlemen playing chess and the ladies doing embroidery. Some biographers say that they treated Balzac as a court jester and that he did little work, but in fact he worked well and at any rate not self-destructively. He was famous in the Ukraine. He travelled. They took him to Kiev and the Governor gave a banquet for him, though in fact he had been instructed by the Russian secret police to keep him under strict vigilance: what disturbed the Russians was that this great visitor from the West was enormously popular and this might be dangerous because of the Russian-Polish tension and the semi-revolutionary peasant rising of the previous year. He was in a land where suspicion was king.

The instinctive businessman in Balzac could not be repressed. Seeing the neglected oak forests and being an investor in railways, Balzac soon saw a colossal profit in this timber. Within a month of his arrival he outlined one of his grandiose schemes in a letter to his sister: cut down all the trees and sell the timber in France for railway sleepers. Transport would be a problem. Accountancy revived. Suppose one exported 60,000 thirty-foot cords at 10 francs and allowed 20 francs for transport, at a profit of say, 20 francs, one would make 120,000 francs. Even supposing one made only 5 francs profit, one would net 420,000 francs.

Balzac told his sister to consult her husband, the engineer. He is talking, he says, only of trunks of trees, but possibly there was usable wood in the heavier branches; and there would be the profit on firewood. So he went on. But the longer he stayed the more he understood the realities of Mme Hanska's life: dealing with losses of crops, sacking dishonest managers, the ruling of an estate. He saw that he had at least two years of hard writing before he or she could disentangle themselves from their respective obligations. But life was peaceful and timeless. He felt he could stay there for ever, with only one serious care: that of keeping his mother up to scratch in supervising what was going on in the Rue Fortunée and in seeing no burglars got in to steal his treasure. He lived like a pampered but fretful sultan, but he had also seen the trials of an owner of a feudal estate. The servants might bow to the ground before one: but Mme Hanska, her son-in-law, and her effusive daughter, who addressed her parent as 'my idolized angel of a mother' were tangled in lawsuits about their inheritances. The Polish aristocracy behaved with the avarice and venom of the French petit bourgeoisie. There was little ready money; and indeed cash was rarely used in this patriarchal life. There was quite a fuss when it came to paying for the franking of letters received. As for outgoing mail, a Cossack simply rode off with it every week or so. Hailstorms destroyed the crops; fires burned down the barns; and all Mme Hanska could be certain of was an annuity of 20,000 francs. Or so she moaned. It was illegal to transfer her inheritance abroad. If she sold off her share of the estate it would have to go to her daughter who already had her own share. The money she put into railway shares and the payments on the house came from her personal savings during her marriage. As things were going, Balzac told her wryly, they would be a white-haired old couple before they married. He was intuitive enough to see she was half-hearted, even hostile; but he brushed this aside. He seems, to judge by their letters, to have had allies in the young Mniszechs. They obviously thought he was good for the mother; also the daughter was a budding spendthrift and longed to settle in Paris close to the Rue Fortunée. Their manner of writing is so ecstatic and fond that one can only conclude they had contracted the fever of their dear Bilboquet; they regarded the Ukraine as barbaric.

But a demand for payment of a new instalment on Mme Hanska's allotment of railway shares came from Paris. Bankers charged twelve per cent for transferring moneys, so Balzac left with 90,000 francs in his pocket to make the payment personally.

No more 'squandering' Mme Hanska warned him and no more bric-à-brac. In the January of 1848, when the snow was hard enough for the sleigh that would take him on the long jingling ride to Cracow, he set off wrapped up in furs on top of his overcoat. When he got to Paris in February rain was falling.

He was depressed. When he got to the Rue Fortunée he understood that he had made a mistake: he had bought the place too soon. What he had reckoned would cost him at most 125,000 francs had in fact cost 400,000. Still everything in his life had always cost more and in fact loss excited him and, in his mind, turned into heroic incidents in his struggles, forcing him to drive the work of *La Comédie Humaine* further. As he said to his sister, the situation at Wierzchownia was touch and go; the stakes were high; indeed they had reached the point of double or quits. He redoubled his campaign to maintain his fiction:

> Listen, Laure, isn't it something to have it in one's power, just for the wishing, to create a salon where only the élite of society will meet, ruled by a woman with the polish and presence of a queen, high born, educated, a woman of wit and beauty. One's position is unassailable . . . I have sought nothing less for eighteen years . . . Don't think that I am infatuated with luxury for its own sake. I love the luxury of the Rue Fortunée for what goes with it: a superb well-born woman of great family and who – putting her fortune aside for the moment – brings with her every social advantage the world can offer.

If he is defeated in this, he says, he will vanish into some hole. Indeed it will kill him.

Always on his returns from his pursuit of the mirage he was brought to earth by a shock; and this time it was from a quarter to which he had rarely paid attention. Intent as always on the details of his accountancy, he had known that Mme Hanska's railway shares had lost half their value: what he had not seen in this misfortune was its connection with politics. The railway fever in France, England, all over Europe, had overshot its mark: there were 50,000 unemployed workers in France alone, and in France this was one of the crucial items in the beginnings of the revolution of 1848. He had always been one of those sage, middle-of-the-road bourgeois who baulked at any attack on property and who took a paternalistic attitude to the working classes. They must be gently led; but since his visit to St Petersburg and the sight of the Tsar, and perhaps also because Mme Hanska shared with the Poles and himself a hero-worship of Napoleon, he leaned more and more to the mystical attractions of despotism. Domination was an idea that fascinated his mind. No one had described so intimately the lust for money and the corruption under Louis-Philippe and his minister Guizot with his famous slogan 'Get rich'; yet no one, when it came to the show-down was more suspicious of democracy, socialism, or even the new cry for an extension of the suffrage. It threatened the very basis of the profession to which he had appointed himself – to be the overworked secretary of history. Now history seemed to be saying that it had no room for secretaries: he was so self-absorbed in his task that he had not noticed that the industrial revolution had come late to France and that the disturbance was profound. He had often mocked the lethargy of Louis-Philippe; he had also seen that that lethargy had hardened into a fierce resistance to reform of any kind. He had always been a monarchist, and a Catholic too, and he now feared the call for a republic. It would lead, he believed, to anarchy. When he now walked into the centre of Paris, passing the sideshows that now lined the half-built Champs Elysées like a continuous circus, he heard nothing but the hot air of politics. The city was alive with political clubs and secret societies. Day and night there were 'banquets' at which orators declaimed this view or that, but almost all cried 'universal suffrage'. It was typical of the period that political manifestations should be gastronomic and that the habit was for the guests to stroll in procession, in a kind of peaceful gourmet demo, to the appointed place. Herzen, who was in Paris from the first riots in this rainy February to the bloody outbursts of June, described with his usual scepticism in his memoirs the play-acting that went on among the self-appointed spies and secret societies. He sat among the Reds:

> In the café Lamblin, where the desperate *citoyens* were sitting over their *petits verres* and big glasses, I learned that they had no plan, that the movement had no real centre of momentum and no programme. Inspiration was to descend upon them as the Holy Ghost once descended upon the apostles.

As for the 'conspirators':

They mysteriously invite one to extraordinarily important interviews, at night if possible, or in some inconvenient place. Meeting their friends in public, they do not like saluting them with a bow, but greet them with a significant glance. Many of them keep their address a secret, never tell one what day they are going away, never say where they are going, write in cypher in invisible ink views which are plainly printed in printers' ink in the newspapers.

This was harmless and, despite the wet weather and since Parisians lived in the streets, there was almost a quickening sense of holiday and the hope of seeing some excitement. Irony had led Herzen to underrate the explosive nature of the situation: there were hungry workless men in the family crowds that came in from the working-class quarters. If the rain appeared to damp things down, it was also an exasperation. Seeing the unfamiliar sight of ministers, generals, famous orators, dashing about, the crowd felt stirrings of importance. Balzac himself felt a growing political conceit. He had also hankered after political power and had been jealous of Lamartine's office and Victor Hugo's influence.

At last the government banned a banquet. That was enough to cause an occasional scuffle and affray in far-off streets, but when the usual procession crowded down the Boulevard des Capucines to the Madeleine and found troops there and the Garde National – by luck Balzac had not been called to duty – the first shots were fired. The crowd had been peacable and had no programme; but now, with the first dead in the street, it fled to stir up rage everywhere. That was enough. On 22 February 1848 a swarm advanced on the Tuileries. Louis-Philippe had run away; and the crowd broke into the palace. It was a mixed crowd. Some burst in merely out of curiosity and walked gaping through the corridors and royal rooms; but a wilder mob followed, made for the wine were soon drunkenly dressing up in court uniforms. The cry was 'To the throne room', where they sat on the throne and made satirical speeches. The corridors of the palace were soon deep in broken glass, people smashed the pictures and looting began. A large number of workers installed their families in the palace and ate up all the food – it took three weeks to get the last of them out.

At the Rue Fortunée the sounds of gunfire and rioting could be distantly heard and Balzac went out that night to see what was happening at the Tuileries. The destruction he saw in the palace horrified him. Not only the monarchy was destroyed; worse – furniture, bric-à-brac was being smashed as well. It was even worse at the Palais-Royal where the mob was tearing up the books in the magnificent library of the Orléans family. Always a collector, Balzac quietly picked up a few draperies and ornaments himself and took them home. He walked – the doctors had told him to walk more – and passed bodies being carried off on stretchers.

The news from abroad was bad. Germany and Italy were in disorder. In the next weeks the Paris banks closed, the bookshops closed, publication of books was stopped. Balzac saw his livelihood and his hopes of paying off his debts vanish in the next few months. The blow was devastating. For a while, always an opportunist, he tried to get into the public swim. He got scarcely any votes for the Republican Assembly; he was rejected by the Academy. (He had been rejected twice before.) He went back to the solitude of the Rue Fortunée afraid that he would be considered an *aristo* and grew a small beard so as to look like a worker.

But there was always power of recovery in him. He was to say, 'I am part of the opposition called life.' The theatres had not closed so he turned once more to writing for the theatre and wrote a play called *La Marâtre*: success for the first time in a field where he had always been defeated. He had at last discovered there is a difference between the novel and the play and he learned to be less arrogant with theatre people. But, after a splendid first night and praise from everyone, the show closed down because people were afraid to go out. The revolutionary feeling in Paris was growing more intense. There were no letters in reply to his cries of passion to Mme Hanska for a long time and then came one of her bombshells – she told him to go and find a young wife. And her sister, Aline, the one who hated her and who was always dropping in at the Rue Fortunée, and lived for making trouble, offered him her own daughter, Pauline, a girl who it turned out was dying of consumption!

He packed his bags and, unable to work in the dangerous and disturbing city, went down to Saché to write four plays. He wrote to Mme Hanska a letter of desperation:

I am doing these four plays, but as matter of conscience and if the situation in my heart and life is what it was in December, I shall give up the struggle. I shall let myself drift with the current, like a drowning man. And you'll hear no more of Bilboquet.

And again:

Mon loup chéri, life has left me. I am wretched and alone – God might have sent me these evils one at a time; together they are enough to break any human being. I am going to Saché to make one more supreme effort. After that, come what may, I shall have done all I can, everything that human strength is capable of. If I couldn't write and confide in you, as if I were uttering a prayer, there would be a hole in my life – for never, after sixteen years – have I lived so utterly in your heart as at the present moment. There is never a moment when in my thoughts I am alone. You are as much inside me, as my own sorrow, my work and my very blood. I told your sister that never at any time in my life had my soul known so much passion. It is the kind of passion one dies of. Only my wretchedness and works give me the strength to fight the apathy that undermines me in everything I feel and do. I am like the surgeon who knows what his illness is, and who in the midst of his pain follows its course with a scientific eye.

At Saché he recovered for a while. He worked and even revelled with Jean de Margonne whose glum wife had long ago died. The revelling was not good for his heart. He coughed and thought he had water on his lungs. But he worked at a play called *Mercadet* – a lost cause, the theatres were closed. It turned out to be a brilliant comedy, when it was cut down to three acts after his death. It is a play about a compulsive liar and speculator – for the farce was celebrating one of his many selves – and when he read it to the company of the Comédie-Française he became, like Dickens, a remarkable actor. He stripped garment by garment to his shirt-sleeves as he rushed about speaking all the parts to perfection. In the midst of his disasters, when everything had failed and when in fact he was breaking up, Balzac's reserves of mirth were always there. Gautier said 'he roared and cried and wept and raged and thundered in every conceivable tone of voice'. He evoked the swarm of Mercadet's creditors as if they 'stretched to the horizon'. We have to think of this Balzac, a true Bilboquet, when we see him playing – for was it more than that? – the whipped dog or furtive 'moujik' of Mme Hanska's imperium. A young novelist called Champfleury said he looked like a 'good-humoured wild boar, his paunch quivering with laughter and whose full-blooded lips exposed scattered teeth like fangs'. A caricature, but Balzac was, in many ways, a living caricature.

Safe at Saché, he missed the bloody rising in the sullen heat of the June days in Paris. The mob and the soldiers outdid one another in their savageries. There was an orgy of killing and cruelty. (One woman who cut off an officer's hands said afterwards, 'I was in a dream.') Paris had gone mad. When Balzac returned he found the city closed down. He had only one desire: to leave France for good. And, astonishingly, there were tender letters now from Mme Hanska. She had changed her tune. He managed to get a passport at last and in September 1848 he left. He was going for ever: in a year and a half he came back – to die.

It is difficult to know Mme Hanska. If by this time she was disillusioned and was not in love with him, why did she not break? One has to see her as a ruler of a small empire, unwilling to lose a subject. Considering how jealous she was of every woman he as much as spoke to, as though jealousy were her profession, an emotion stronger than love, it is astonishing at first that Balzac harks back so often to the 'cruelties' of the Marquise de Castries: cruelties, he rather dramatically said, that marked his life for ever. Dangerous words: but was he reminding Mme Hanska that in her evasions and angers she was a Marquise de Castries reborn? One can see why Balzac did not break: in her way Mme Hanska too was a cold mother-figure who never let a fault pass, who continually accused. One is left with the impression that Balzac was drawn by a childish terror of her as much as by her money. If he was such a deplorable liar and totally unreliable, why did she drop him and then take up with him again? The answer seems to be that she was lonely too and both felt the strong physical spell, but that love, on both sides, had also been an affair of minds and the mind hangs on. Hence her cruelties and his deceptions.

Cholera had broken out in Paris. He set off like an emigrant with no intention of returning. Somehow, on money from his theatre contracts and some sent by Mme Hanska for her railway shares, he raised enough for the journey – not before the 'two-legged bottle of vinegar', her sister, had reported to the Ukraine that he was carrying on with an actress. This was too much: he genuinely hated actors and actresses, for they infuriated the playwright by murdering his plays. He loaded himself with enough clothes and boots for the rest of his life, quantities of perfume for the ladies, Eau de Portugal, infallible in love, and – inevitably –

four dozen pairs of gloves for those beautiful hands. Also, remembering his shock at finding only one oil lamp in that rambling palace, he took five of the newly invented Carcel oil lamps with him to improve the premises! And he sneaked visits to the antique dealers in Mainz and Dresden on the way.

He had left his mother to manage his financial affairs and the care of the house in the Rue Fortunée and there is now a total change in the content of his correspondence. The letters to Mme Hanska – if we except those that came after his first visit to the Ukraine onwards – are the passionate self-projection of a creative imagination and of a man in prolonged headlong love. Every ounce of him – his erotic, toiling nature, his ceaseless scheming about money, property, and his collections – goes into them; they are among the strangest love letters ever written. They are done with the whole animal.

But once in the Ukraine and writing to his mother and occasionally to Laure, Balzac's letters change. He is his mother's boy once more. The creative energy has gone, his interests have narrowed to the domestic and what to do every day at the house in the Rue Fortunée. He has little to say about the Ukraine. He was of course always a man whose mind was elsewhere: in Paris, it was in the scenes of his novels and in the Ukraine; in the Ukraine his mind is on his possessions in Paris. He becomes the infinitely anxious, fussing, monotonous family meddler who worries every day about whether the floors are properly swept and the lamps spotlessly clean. Mother and son are curiously united in this. He orders and enslaves: she slaves for him, indeed the two seem closer to each other than do Balzac and Mme Hanska. One can read into this domestic surrender the decline of his health and powers. Anxiety has made him pettifogging. Mother and son are alike in their fixation on money. When he left for the Ukraine the first time she set out the story of her life in financial terms from the time she was married, the tale of exactly what losses her husband's, her son's and her own speculations had incurred. She mentions her own failures as a speculator but evading the fact – as Balzac himself did in awkward matters of his own life – that she had, as he said 'squandered' her money on the feckless and adored Henri. The Balzacs were in their peculiar way affectionate with their 'little mother', who had once been so pretty, but they were merciless in 'bringing up the past'. Vivacity – as he called it – was strong in all of them.

In these monotonous letters from a man who knows, and refuses to know, that he is at the end of his tether, Bilboquet the man of mirth has gone. The heart attack he had had at Saché was repeated; the Polish doctor at Wierzchownia said the heart was enlarged. The patient is unable to go upstairs. If he walks in the garden Mme Hanska has to help his steps on the uneven ground. He can't even raise his arms to brush his hair and he has been told he must do no work for six months. So out pour these instructions about the payment of bills, minute orders for dealing with everything in the house from the paint to the curtains.

There are two outbursts. He has made it clear that this is the great crisis of his life and everything depends on the outcome. The family must co-operate and accept what he tells them. They must not even hint at criticism of him. The essence of the situation is that Mme Hanska – who reads all his letters – must not be put off by hard-luck stories from the family: she has enough troubles of her own. She is a woman of fifty and will certainly not marry for a second time in order to run into more. In fact the lesser Balzacs will have to keep a polite distance. And it is in their interest. For – leaving money aside for the moment – he and Mme Hanska will be people of great social influence. Think of how that will help, he tells his sister, when it comes to the question of marrying *her* daughters. The family must understand they are, in turn, 'poor relations'. In other words Honoré is the only one of the family who will have 'arrived' and who can assure their happiness and security if they keep their distance.

A small mistake by the servants at the Rue Fortunée started the outburst. The servants had turned away Rothschild's messenger because he had asked for Mme Sallambier: for one of Balzac's impenetrably devious reasons he had put the power of attorney in his mother's maiden name. The servants' blunder infuriated him. His mother replied coldly excusing the mistake and addressed her son – but only in the first line of the letter – as '*vous*' instead of in the intimate second person singular. The wrongs of childhood came to the surface once more:

I don't ask you to pretend to feelings that you haven't got, for God knows – and so do you – that you haven't smothered me with kisses since the day I was born. You were quite right not to do so, for if you had loved me as you loved Henri, I'd be, no doubt, in the situation he is now in – so in that sense you have been a good mother to me. What I want from you, my dear mother, is an intelligent sense of your own interests – which in fact you've never had – and not to prejudice my future, I say nothing of my happiness.

He was so annoyed by his mother's use of '*vous*', that he wrote a long letter to his sister, begging her to knock sense into his mother's head. And he added the bitter words: 'If I don't achieve greatness by *La Comédie Humaine*, I shall at least achieve it in this [i.e. the marriage] if it comes off.' As for Laure's troubles – her husband, the canal-builder and engineer, was not doing well – Balzac told his sister that the right way to live is to cultivate useful people only, people like bankers or financiers and to drop friends who are failures and who drag one down.

The prospects of his marriage were poor. More crop fires had cost Mme Hanska 140,000 francs; he was treading on thin ice: 'Some marriages are like cream, the temperature can turn them in a moment and I look like remaining a bachelor.'

After these explosions Balzac settles down once more to his endless catalogue of requests. Always greedy, even at this stage of his financial troubles, he hankered after a small piece of land to round off the property at the Rue Fortunée and the owner kept putting the price up and then would not sell. Balzac fusses about his new bookcases and wants to know to an exact half centimetre the depth of the shelves. He indicates where the consoles are to be placed. He wants two more consoles in gilded copper for the bedroom and a red damask bedcover – everything must be perfect for Mme Hanska – and, 'remember to see the crystal candlesticks are complete'. By October he is worrying about the curtains: to protect them in his absence they should be encased in cheap calico. And don't take up the carpets: the way to treat carpets is to brush them hard and regularly. 'Pay no attention to what the carpet dealer says': he, Balzac, knows more about keeping carpets in condition than anyone in the trade and, considering his carpet buying since the days he set up house in the Rue Cassini, this is certainly true. The mother writes back that his orders about the stoves have been carried out to the letter and she has got in the coal and wood for the winter. She announces that a second coat of paint has gone on the wall. He sets out the exact duties and wages of the cook, the manservant and the maid: she must buy her fruit and vegetables from Les Halles – not from the shops – first thing in the morning. The cook will be required to cook simple meals only when he returns: two courses for lunch and four for dinner. There is a great deal about dusting and, over and over again, he reminds his mother to see that she stands over François while he cleans the lamps. He would have been a houseproud woman.

It began to strike one that there is something odd about the silent François. Mme Balzac is strict with servants and François is her special concern. Her notion is that servants must be watched and never left idle for a moment. She obviously 'kept at' François and, lest he should go round gossiping with the Italian maid called Zanella, she teaches him to read and write and to make embroidered slippers. The poor lady, in spite of her rheumatism and a worrying heart, is in a fever of attention to her son's orders: she shares his insistence on domestic order, and she loves the luxury and the power she has. Her pension has been increased – by Mme Hanska – and at the beginning of the year she comes in from her humble lodgings at Suresnes to see all is right. Eventually she establishes herself there, accepting that when he arrives with a wife, she will leave like a servant. Her day is always the same: up at six in the morning, to bed early at night to read *The Imitation of Christ* and to leave her door open in case of burglars. This is awkward because she is sometimes alarmed that François, in one 'of his fevers' will come prowling into the room.

In the Ukraine the situation was bad. Mme Hanska had still not made up her mind and Balzac's health, which revived when he got there, went to pieces. Mental and emotional distress had always had a violent effect on him. The due dates of bills, the changing figures of his accountancy whirled madly round in the head of an artist who could not achieve his dream, who had ten more volumes of *La Comédie Humaine* to write and who was forbidden to work. One guesses at a life alternating between fear and deep boredom: the Promised Land was boring. He was terrified that some catastrophe would befall his house. He kept up his spirits by announcing he would be home in a month, or two months. The fact is that he could not move. In June 1849 he had another heart attack and agonizing pains in his stomach. The doctor who lived in the house with his son, also a doctor, put him on a diet of pure lemon juice to thin the blood; but this led to frightful vomiting. Balzac liked the old doctor. He played the violin to him; but his son was sceptical about Balzac's state. The climate, with its alternations of intense heat and cruel cold, Balzac said, was destroying him; it gave him headaches that did not cease day and night. He spent most of his time in bed. Neuralgia and toothache afflicted him as they used to do when he was twenty at the Rue Lesdiguières. One tooth dropped out. He suffered also from trembling of the eyelids and then, suddenly, his sight almost went. Leeches were applied. Then the doctor took him off lemon juice and Balzac – always a believer in mysterious remedies – was put on herbal pills of a kind that were used among Polish peasants. The pills appeared to do him good, but then the Moldavian fever attacked him. It lasted for weeks, and if he coughed he brought up blood from his lungs.

Being ill like this made him childish. He made a brief recovery when Mme Hanska and her daughter presented him with a *tessomolana*, an elaborately embroidered silk dressing-gown in Persian fashion. He was ecstatic about it and walked about in it 'like a sultan'. Everyone, he says, is so good and kind to him, but Mme Hanska is not well. Her attacks of arthritis and gout have returned. The only relief for gout, which the doctor insists on, is barbarous: plunging her swollen feet into the entrails of a newly slaughtered sucking-pig, having heard its squeals as it is killed before her eyes.

It must have been plain to her that the genius she loved and the man she mistrusted was moving towards his death. His body had wasted away: the huge belly had vanished and every attack must have seemed to her to be the last. His vitality fought back for him. If only she would make up her mind. If only the Tsar would give the sanction for the transfer of the estate to the daughter and give permission for the marriage. Balzac himself wrote to the Tsar: the permission was refused. In his weariness Balzac wrote to his old friend Zulma Carraud whom he loved but whose advice he had never taken. She had frankly stated that she was quite unsuited to being the queen of an aristocratic salon.

I have been taken with terrible heart trouble brought on by fifteen years of hard labour. The treatment was interrupted by one of those terrible fevers, called Moldavian fever, which starting in the Danubian marshes, spread to Odessa and ravage the steppe . . . I never cease to think of you, to love you even here . . . How different life seems after fifty . . . What a host of things, what a world of illusions have gone by the board since then. And would you believe it, except for affection, which is ever growing,

I am not a whit further on where I am. How swiftly evil buds and blooms and how sorely happiness is baulked and hindered. It is enough to make one disgusted with life. I've been years arranging a nest here, a nest which, alas, has cost a fortune, and there are no birds in it. When will they come? The years fleet by, old age is coming on and everything will wither and decay.

And, he adds, even 'the furnishings of the nest' will wither.

The winter passed. Recklessly he went with the family on a journey to Kiev to meet the Governor and to see about a passport, an expedition that cost him weeks of bronchitis. He recovered and he was now sure that he would get well if he could only get back to France. They would have to wait now for the deep snow. Then at last in March the Tsar revoked his refusal: Mme Hanska was free. It must have been plain to her that he was a dying man, but what could she do now there was no ostensible barrier? She gave in. On 14 March 1850 they drove through the snow to the church at Berdichev, a ten-hour journey, and were married and got home ill and exhausted. Mme Hanska's feet were so swollen that she could hardly walk and Balzac's heart went badly wrong. He had to rest for twelve days against the long sixteen-day journey back to Paris.

The thaw had begun in the Ukraine, the roads were flooded and there were no bridges over the swollen rivers. The risings in Galicia had led to brigandage. An enormous amount of luggage had to be got ready. While the couple waited Balzac sent dozens of detailed orders to his mother: what flowers, for example, had to be put in the various *jardinières*, and last-minute instructions on altering the pillows in the two bedrooms, the red and the blue, for everything must be perfect for the diamond of Poland, the jewel of the ancient and illustrious Rzewuski family. His own bed was to be turned round so that it did not face the door. His mother was wildly happy – and added her petty cash account at the end of her reply. At last the travellers set off. It took them a month to get as far as Dresden. Their coach sunk again and again to the doors in the mud of the thaw and often sixteen men were needed to get it out. Hardly able to see or breathe, Balzac sat by the roadside in the rain, time and time again, watching it all. They stopped a month in Dresden where he kept having fainting fits. He was in bed most of the time, but he bought Mme Hanska a pearl necklace worth 25,000 francs: 'a necklace to drive a saint mad'. Some readers of her letters to her daughter think that, in desperation or indifference, she went on a spending spree; but if she did, she also wrote that although she had known him 'for seventeen years she had not until then fully realized what an adorable creature he was. He had a quality that was entirely new to her. If only he had his health.'

They went on by train to Paris with their enormous load of luggage and once they got into France he felt better. It had been arranged that their arrival should follow a strict protocol. Mme Balzac should leave the house she had prepared and guarded for them before the arrival: the house which she said (with a dignity that would remind him that she, too, came of a distinguished family, the Sallambiers) had enabled her to enjoy once more the luxury she had been used to before she married!

Late at night their carriage arrived in the Rue Fortunée. All the lights were on in festive welcome. But when the driver got down to open the gate, it was locked and barred. He hammered. No reply. Balzac himself got out and hammered and shouted. No reply. A crowd collected. A locksmith was at last found. When they got into the house they found wreckage everywhere: François the servant was standing there, wild and incoherent. He had turned out Zanella, the Italian maid, and was raving mad. He had to be seized and locked in his room.

In a day or two Balzac collapsed entirely. From then on he was a dying man. Injections, bleedings, diet, pills could do nothing. True, late in June he improved and, in a last reckless gesture of passion for objects, he got out in a carriage and collected some of the treasures he had brought from Dresden. No doubt the toilet set his wife had bought him. After that all hope went. Blind, unable to speak, he was a ghost, unrecognizable except, some friends said, for his large, dark, arresting and questioning eyes.

Peritonitis, kidney trouble, started. The body filled with water. Finally gangrene set in. Unable now to grasp anything, Balzac looked at his old friend Dr Nacquart, who knew the case was hopeless, and said to him suddenly, 'Send for Bianchon' – the doctor he had invented in *La Comédie Humaine.* This remark has been disputed. On 18 August 1850 he died. His face had gone almost black. His wife had gone to bed. His mother was the only person with him. He himself had written:

A man who every day for fifteen years spends his nights working, who never has a spare minute during the day, who struggles against everything, has no more time for his friends or his mistresses: I've lost many mistresses and friends because of this, without regretting it, for none of them understood my situation – the longer I live the more my work piles up . . . I foresee for myself a dark destiny. I shall die the day before I achieve my desire.

Turgenev

Childhood and Youth

I

Ivan Turgenev was born in the autumn of 1818 in Orel, a provincial capital some three hundred miles south west of Moscow and halfway to Kiev. It was, in those days, a large town of distilleries, craftsmen in stone, glass, china and timber, and the centre of a rich agricultural trade in hemp, rye, wheat and tobacco, and famous for breeding horses and cattle. The merchants lived in dull stone houses two storeys high; there was a market place stinking of rush mats and cabbage, there were bazaars which suggested the Orient. Nearby was the pillared mansion of the Governor with striped sentry boxes at the gates and the large private houses of the gentry, some of them with odd turrets on them. There was a promenade where the young trees were dying and scores of miserable taverns giving out clouds of tobacco smoke and the pervasive smells of spirits. On the outskirts were the tumbledown huts of the artisans, known by their sheepskin coats. At night most of them were drunk. Long before the industrial revolution reached Russia, Orel was reckoned to be a prosperous place. At sunrise all roads leading to Orel were crowded with long strings of wagons travelling to the market.

The Turgenevs had a fine house in Orel and another in Moscow. Ivan's mother, Varvara Petrovna, noted in French, the polite language of her class, that the new baby was twenty-one inches long. He was her second son. She was a very rich, trim but ugly young woman, in her early thirties, fond of dress, six years older than her husband, an almost penniless and handsome young cavalry officer who had been forced by his relations to marry her for her money, and after Ivan's birth he threw up his commission in the army. When the end of the thaw made travel possible the following year, he moved the family to his wife's enormous estate at Spasskoye.

The migrations of the gentry from their town houses to their estates were remarkable processions as they went from post house to post house over the bad roads of the monotonous countryside. The family coach of the Turgenevs was a heavy vehicle drawn by a team of six horses on the eighty-mile journey. A lackey sat on a mat on the rear step holding on by a rope and was either spattered with mud or choked by the clouds of dust. After the coach came a string of inferior carriages and carts carrying luggage and servants. They crossed between the low wooded hills of undulating country that opened into ravines where small rivers ran out into marshland and finally on to the endless steppe where the villages were poor. The peasant huts with their roofs of rotting straw seemed to have been trodden into the soil. In the woodland the huts were spacious and were built of fir logs and roofed by boards. From what one knows of Turgenev's father, the retired soldier who was both superstitious and a sportsman, he would have counted the magpies for luck and studied the edges of the woodlands for the first sight of snipe and woodcock and kept his eye open for pretty women. His wife would be watching the women working with long rakes in the fields, alert to see if any of her serfs were idle. For Varvara Petrovna her vast estate was a kingdom in itself; she owned all its villages and most peasants in them, every horse, cow, pig, goose, even the nightingales that sang in the trees.

What a hissing of marching geese, what a clatter in the rookeries, what barking of dogs when the coach at last arrived at her mansion. Her serf orchestra struck up a tune of welcome as the peremptory mistress got out. What kneeling to the ground, what kissing of hands for the privileged servants, what a ringing of bells from room to room as orders were given, what excited trilling from the scores of cage birds on the walls as the short, gypsyish mistress stared at her 'subjects' as she called her forty house serfs, to detect who among them had disobeyed her orders and what punishments she would award. The barking of the dogs was stopped at once. She could not bear it.

Spasskoye passed as one of the finest mansions of the province but was really large, rambling manor house. It had an iron roof and was painted white and built mostly of timber. The central part to which verandahs gave a kind of elegance was two storeys high and, inside, a gallery of stone led to the two long low wings. The place gave the impression of being some enormous white owl that had spread its wings ready to swoop and hunt over the avenue of limes and the thirty acres of garden and park and far beyond. Attached to the house were the quarters of the house serfs, the ice house, the bath house, the house for smoking meat, the tannery, the workshops, the water well and even a mill for making wall-papers and the stationery on which Varvara Petrovna wrote her innumerable orders and comments. Most of the shoes and clothes – though not of the mistress – were made on the estate: with a *belle laide*'s passion for finery she sent to Moscow and even at times to Berlin or Paris for her own clothes. The estate produced all the food and drink it needed. In addition to the waiting servants, the house serfs included her serf doctor and her office clerks; like many landowners she had her own orchestra, singers and actors and as her sons grew there were nurses and valets and a procession of French and German governesses and tutors. She ran the place efficiently. Spasskoye was less a house than a self-sufficient feudal community, the estate was an empire numbering 5,000 'souls' and extended to thousands of acres and included twenty villages which she ruled as an absolute sovereign. Her retinue were indeed divided by rank and title. There was a Chamberlain; her personal maids were ladies-in-waiting and her private office had a dais on which she sat with her portrait behind her, ringing bells – she had a mania for bells – and gave orders and received deputations. None of her serfs could marry without her permission: many she ordered to marry. They were allowed to have children, but once the child was born it was sent away from the house. The police were not permitted to come to Spasskoye although she did soften a little towards the Chief of Police because he amused her – but he had to come to the back door.

In the finest rooms at Spasskoye the furniture was luxurious. The chairs were in ebony, ornamented with bronze cupids leading lions by a chain of flowers, and were upholstered in yellow leather. There was an immense mirror – the marvel of the province. Guests were always coming and going, for Varvara Petrovna loved musical parties, masquerades and cards; and if she was giving grand dinners special food was sent for from Moscow three hundred miles away and arrived over the terrible roads by sledge in the winter or wagon in the summer, though usually in the winter the family moved to a house in Moscow until the thaw ended and travel was possible again. In the summer weeks she would go on a state progress to her villages and the long procession would take to the roads. Wagon-loads of pork and geese and other meats and drink for the journey went on ahead, followed by carriages and carts containg serving women, laundry maids, valets, butlers, clerks and the serf doctor, and finally in her own carriage the dominant Varvara Petrovna herself, with her unforgiving eye on everything.

All Ivan Turgenev's biographers and indeed Turgenev himself portray Varvara Petrovna as a domineering woman. She was governed by two passions: pride – as she admitted when she was dying – and *la rage*: the word 'anger' is not strong enough.

Her handsome husband was a cooler, more elusive figure. He was an aristocrat of long line: his wife's family were, comparatively speaking, upstarts. The pedigree of the Turgenev family hung beside the portrait of his grandfather at Spasskoye and was an index to the fancy that they had descended from a Tartar chieftain of the Golden Horde. In that remote time they had given up the Mohammedan faith and one, indeed, became a martyr of the Orthodox Church. Two were killed in the Stenka Rozin revolt in the seventeenth century, others served under Peter the Great and the Empress Anna. They were a family of ruined soldiers. A great-grandfather had been taken prisoner by the Turks and the story was that he had escaped because his charm had beguiled one of the Sultan's wives – a tale close to the tastes of the master of Spasskoye who was noted for his love affairs at home and also, when he took his family on a grand European tour in 1822, in Paris. What was deadly to women was his fashionable feminine grace of manner. He was the cool, good-looking dandy, tall and powerful, an excellent horseman, and perhaps in recording Ivan's length as a baby, Varvara Petrovna was thinking of the height of the husband whom she adored, whom she had passionately pursued, and who did not love her at all. Once he had retired, still young, from the Army he left the management of the estate to her – he himself brought only a tiny place of 130 'souls' to the marriage – and settled to hunting in the fields and among the ladies.

Whether he knew it or not, Turgenev's intelligent but half-educated father was the victim of history. Like others of his class he spoke French in the house and was shaky in his Russian spelling. But not all the Turgenev tribe had been fighting men. One kinsman was the son of a director of Moscow University, another a State official working for the Russian government in Paris, a man of liberal intellect and an important contact in the Paris embassies. It was he certainly who advised the French Marquis de Custine when the Marquis went to Russia and published his notorious account of his journey in 1839, a book which infuriated Russian readers. This Turgenev kinsman had put the Marquis in touch with a Prince Kozlowski who told him that:

Russia, in the present age, is only 400 years removed from the invasion of barbarian tribes, whilst fourteen centuries have elapsed since Western Europeans experienced the same crisis. A civilization older by one thousand years, of course, places an immeasurable distance between the manners of nations. Long before the Tartar invasion Russia had received its rulers from Scandinavia and these had received in turn their tastes, their arts and their luxuries from the emperors and patriarchs of Constantinople.

The civilization conquered by the Tartars and the saints and the rulers of the new dispensation had never heard of the chivalrous tradition of the West. The invaders remained Asiatic. Their monarchs were like Biblical Kings, they were patriarchs, and the Russian nation was not formed in the school of good faith and honour which had been so important and civilizing in the history of the European mind. Indeed –

The extreme despotism of the Russians was established in the very period when servitude ceased in Europe. Bondage became a constituent principle of society.

Turgenev's father was dead before Custine's ill-natured book appeared. He was certainly not a reading man. After his trip to France, Switzerland and Italy he returned to Spasskoye to live lazily to himself. He would have been about thirty-two when the tragic Decembrist revolt of 1825 marked the end of the hopes of reform and enlightenment which briefly followed the defeat of Napoleon. What the father thought about that revolt no one knows, but the fierce repression did paralyse the public spirit of the men of his generation. Reaction and dullness set in and he, like the rest of the gentry, was obliged to conform and to fade into private life on his estate – those little nations where inevitably women ruled and where the role of the men became futile.

In one of his very late stories, *First Love*, which tells of how a father and his young son fall in love with the same young woman, Ivan Turgenev draws a moving portrait of his father and, indeed, told friends that the story came directly from his own early youth. He had never seen, he said, a man more 'elaborately serene'.

He took scarcely any interest in my education but never hurt my feelings; he respected my freedom; he displayed – if one can put it that way – a certain courtesy . . . only he never let me come at all close to him. I loved him . . . he seemed to me the ideal man – and God knows how passionately attached to him I should have been if I had not felt constantly the presence of his restraining hand. Yet he could, whenever he wished, with a single word, a single gesture, instantly make me feel complete trust in him . . . Sometimes a mood of gaiety would come over him and at such moments he was ready to play and romp with me . . . like a boy . . . Once, and only once, he caressed me with such tenderness that I nearly cried . . . I came to the conclusion that he cared nothing for me nor for family life; it was something very different he loved . . .

From his father's sayings, Turgenev took these words:

'Take what you can yourself and don't let others get you into their hands; to belong to oneself, that is the whole thing in life' . . . On another occasion, being at that time a youthful democrat, I embarked on a discussion of liberty . . . 'Liberty,' he repeated. 'Do you know what really makes a man free?'
'What?'
'Will, your own will, and it gives power which is better than liberty. Know how to want, and you'll be free, and you'll be master too.'

Before and above everything, my father wanted to live – and did live. Perhaps he had a premonition that he would not have long in which to make use of the 'thing in life'; he died at forty-two.

And at the end of the story when the father is dying, he says to his son, words that Turgenev repeated in many of his stories throughout his life:

'My son,' he wrote, 'beware of the love of women; beware of that ecstasy – that slow poison.'

The love the boy Turgenev had most to fear was his mother's love: he was the favourite son.

Varvara Petrovna's command of the passions, in all their manifestations, was inexhaustible. She was a round-shouldered woman with large, glaring black eyes under heavy brows, her forehead was wide and low, the skin of her face was coarse and pocked, her mouth large, sensual and cruel, her manner arrogant and capricious. She was as self-willed as a child, though like many ugly women she could be fascinating and charm her friends, and was very witty. Her history is pitiable. She was the child of violence in a family who had got much of their wealth by means little short of robbery. Compared with the Turgenevs the Lutovinovs were barbarians. The portraits of one or two of them hung on the walls of Spasskoye which Varvara Petrovna had inherited. They had flogged their way forward and Turgenev has described two or three of these ancestors. In the *Freeholder Usyanikov* there is one who grabbed a parcel of land from a neighbour and flogged him into agreement when the man threatened to take the crime to court. Another was a scoundrelly young Guards Officer and a thief who stole his father's money from the family chest where his bags of coins were kept. His portrait hung beside the picture of a young woman with her hair done in the high style of the eighteenth century. Beside it was the picture of an amiable young man whom Turgenev calls Rogatchov, who has a hole in the breast: the Guards Officer had seduced the young woman who was about to be married to Rogatchov and murdered him. The true story is worse than Turgenev made it: the girl was the murderer's sister. In the story called *The Brigadier*, the mother of Varvara Petrovna appears. The old lady was paralysed, yet in a fit of temper, she knocked her page boy unconscious and, frightened by what she had done, is said to have somehow got the boy to a chair, put a cushion over him, suffocated him and had him buried secretly.

This grandmother had been twice married. In her second marriage to a widower called Somov who had grown-up children, she turned against Varvara Petrovna who was the child of the first marriage. When the mother died the drunken stepfather not only beat the young girl but attempted to rape her. She escaped from the house with a nurse and walked twenty miles to an uncle's house at Spasskoye. All this is described in *The Turgenev Family* by Mme Zhitova who, as an orphan baby, had been adopted by Varvara Petrovna in 1833. (Mysterious orphans appear again and again in the annals of the gentry families. Alexandre Zviguilsky, in *Ivan Turgenev: Nouvelle Correspondance*, dubiously suggests that Mme Zhitova was a child born of an affair between Varvara Petrovna and a doctor, Andrei Bers, the father of Leo Tolstoy's future wife.) Varvara Petrovna once took the girl to see the stepfather's house which had become an empty ruin. Pictures still hung on the wall. In the hall was the bust of her Lutovinov father. They passed down an empty corridor and came to a door that was boarded up and when the child played with the handle, Varvara Petrovna dragged her away screaming:

'Don't touch it. There is a curse on that room.'

The room was her stepfather's. When she calmed down she said to the girl:

'You don't know what it means to be an orphan: you are an orphan but you have a mother in me . . . to be an orphan without mother or father is hard, but to be orphan in the sight of your own mother is horrible: that is what I suffered, my mother hated me.'

As a young girl Varvara Petrovna had not been much happier at Spasskoye, for her uncle was irascible and stingy: she had the stubbornness of the injured and unloved and grew up to be a mannish young woman in the company of rough squires, and in his rages the uncle varied his fits of benevolence with drunken threats to throw her out of the house. He intended, she claimed, to disinherit her. His sudden death made her an heiress who, until she was thirty, was unable to get a man to look at her. Her tragedy was that when she did marry she adored the husband who had to be forced into the marriage.

Varvara Petrovna is one of those Russian Cinderellas who once they get their Prince avenge themselves for the wrongs of childhood and become tyrants. Mme Zhitova was nevertheless devoted to her, found her generous and tender, and, while not denying her tyrannies, was inclined to pity her and say that her savage rule of her serfs was common form among some women of her class in the eighteenth century and that if rage was at the heart of her nature, she was really a country eccentric.

Mme Zhitova's account of Varvara Petrovna's character begins when she was taken into the house. By then Ivan was sixteen and of the two brothers he is the peacemaker who tries to soften his mother's temper. In their boyhood she made both her sons feel the birch and indeed once when she was beating the older one she did it with such frenzy that she fainted and the naked boy had to call to the servant standing there, 'Water, for Mama.' Mme Zhitova confirms that Turgenev's story of Varvara Petrovna and the dumb servant called *Mumu* is founded on fact, although Turgenev attributes it to his grandmother. In *Punin and Baburin* there is a scene which certainly occurred; Varvara Petrovna was in the habit of going out in the park in the afternoon to see that her serfs were working and one day she noticed a half-starved unsmiling youth in rags who was gaping at her and not putting his back into his job. His name was Yermil.

'I have no need of people with scowling faces like that,' she said, for she required deferential smiles from her workers and she ordered him to be sent off at once to a 'Settlement'. She often threatened servants with Siberia or prison. The sentenced man or woman had then to be led past her drawing-room window and to bow as he or she was taken off. Turgenev writes in the story:

Yermil stood without his cap, with downcast head, barefoot, with his boots tied up with a string behind his back; his face, turned towards the seignorial mansion, expressed not despair nor grief, nor even bewilderment, a stupid smile was frozen on his colourless lips, his eyes dry and half closed, looked stubbornly on the ground. My grandmother was apprised of his presence. She got up from the sofa, went with a faint rustle of her silken skirts to the window of the study and holding her golden rimmed double eye glass on the bridge of her nose, looked at the new exile.

Her clerk, the Baburin of the story, protested and she replied:

'That is of absolutely no consequence to me – among my subjects I am sovereign and answerable to no one, only I am not accustomed to have people criticizing me in my presence and meddling in what is not their business . . . You too do not suit me. You are discharged.' And turning to her steward she told him to pay off the clerk and get rid of him by dinner time. 'Don't put me into a passion,' she said. 'What is Yermil waiting for? I have *seen* him. What more does he want?'

And, says Turgenev, she shook a handkerchief angrily out of the window.

After such a scene she would go back to her chair, her rage satisfied, and go on playing patience or reading the latest French novel. She despised Russian writing – except for a few lines of Pushkin.

Varvara Petrovna's husband seems to have behaved with formal indifference and amused himself with his love affairs or his shooting. Perhaps he too was afraid of the virago he had married, although it is said his concern was to preserve an illusion of decorum in the tormented house. He drifted into ill-health and a long illness. The two sons sat by his bedside when he died. Varvara Petrovna was away in Italy. Ivan was sixteen.

An early drawing of Turgenev in his boyhood before the tragic loss of his father – it appears in Yarmolinsky's *Life* – is of a decorous but slyly staring gnome-like creature, with a large head too big for his body. The forehead is high and fine, the eyes are intently watchful and dead-still with mischief. He sits in a trance-like state as if memorizing every inch of what he sees. He was noted for his precocious and unabashed remarks to distinguished guests which got him into trouble. He perhaps picked up banter from his mother. Children brought up under a tyranny and who are spoiled one moment and beaten the next are likely to be evasive and to lead a double life and lie their way out when in difficulty. He wandered about a large house that always had guests and hangers-on in it, and had some of the too-forward characteristics of the hotel-child of the restless European and American rich of later times. He knew very well that he and his older brother were the young masters; but in old age he said all he remembered was the birchings he got from his mother; and the cowed serfs and the severe German and French tutors. His ear for French or German was remarkable; he was a born mimic and with a gift for play-acting and fantasy. His real education, as was apt to happen to the children of the gentry, was given him by the servants. He listened to their stories, knew the barbarous wrongs his mother inflicted on them; starved of the despised Russian language in family life, he heard it continually from them.

Varvara Petrovna – who was an efficient ruler of her household – saw to it that her favourite serfs were taught to read and write, and one youth who had a taste for reading used to go off to the library secretly with Ivan to find a book. The library was not much more than a storeroom where the books were tied up in bundles that smelled of mice. They found an astonishing popular work called *Emblems and Symbols*, a sort of Russian *Iliad*, Turgenev called it, of fantastic verses about unicorns, kings, negroes, pyramids and snakes. There is a recollection of this discovery in *Punin and Baburin* when Punin:

> shouted the verses out solemnly in a flowing outpour through his nose like a man intoxicated and beside himself with ecstasy . . . In this way we went through not only Lomonosov, Sumarokov and Kantemir . . . even Kheraskov's *Rossiada* . . . There is in it, among others, a mighty Tartar woman, a gigantic heroine: I have forgotten her name now but in those days my hands and feet turned cold, as soon as it was uttered. 'Yes,' Punin would say . . . 'Kheraskov he doesn't let one off easily.'

The story of *Punin and Baburin* was one of the things Turgenev wrote in the last years of his life and one is immediately struck by the minuteness of his observation and his feeling for solitude as a boy. To the child brought up in such a place Spasskoye was a timeless, boundless country: the immense gardens and distances of the estate would seem to be Russia itself; he would know few if any children of his own class and, if any did arrive, they would seem totally outlandish. His natural affections and play were with the children of serfs among whom he would be pleased but irked by the sense of his own privilege. His childhood, as with so many rich children, was a training for the innocence of the rich who take private life to be the whole world. At a very early age and as the favourite, he found that he had two roles to play. The household was a sort of secret society containing the quarrels between a passionate mother and a cool husband and the infinite quarrels and intrigues of the hierarchy of tale-telling servants: he listened and he would try to keep the peace by charm and being funny. Watching was a necessity and an amusement. Very early he stared at faces and learned to read the moods and history that were built into them; and when, for self-preservation, he could get away he went out into the hiding places in the gardens and the woods to watch the things of nature build *their* history, from minute to differing minute: to gaze at a leaf or a bird waiting for it to move, to listen to the differing sounds of his boots as he walked over leaves, over grass, through hemp fields, to notice every change of light and shadow and the movements of cloud in the sky as the moments of the morning or the afternoon passed.

> I raised my head and saw at the end of a delicate twig one of those large flies with emerald heads and long body and four transparent wings ... For a long while, more than an hour, I did not take my eyes off her. Soaked through and through with sunshine she did not stir, only from time to time turning her head from side to side and shaking her lifted wings – and that was all.

He had the eye of a naturalist; that is to say, there is no daydreaming in it, no Wordsworthian moral content. He is already a collector of the events of the hour as it changes.

II

When they were nine or ten, the Turgenev brothers were put into a prep school in Moscow for a short time, then into a high school where they met mostly boys of their own class. At fifteen Ivan entered Moscow University, which was not much more than a secondary school to whom all, except serfs, were admitted. After a year or so there he advanced to Petersburg University with the fashionable intention of proceeding to the University of Berlin. This prosaic education was to fit young men of his class for high rank in the Tsarist civil service or life in the Army or at Court.

In Moscow Ivan drank his first draught of German idealism.

The philosophy of Hegel turned young men of his generation to metaphysics and literature. At the prep school run by a cheerful old German, the students lived *en famille* and spelled out Schiller during the week, played forfeits or charades on Sundays and went in for passionate friendships. Later on in his stories Turgenev recalled these lofty attachments: in *Yakov Pasinkov*, for example, he tells of his feeling for Yakov, the ugly duckling of the school, who had sharply pulled him up for his very Russian habit of telling lies: he told them partly out of an impetuous bent for fantasy and also from a pleasure in swaggering, but he was always quick to repent of his exaggerations. He responded to Yakov's 'goodness':

On his [Yakov's] lips the words 'goodness', 'truth', 'life', 'science', 'love', however enthusiastically uttered, never rang with a false note. Without strain, without effort he stepped into the world of the ideal: his pure soul was ready to stand before the holy shrine of beauty.

The two were soon 'soul in soul as the saying was'. The language of romantic love had become the fashion under the German influence: it was a reaction from the correct, ironical, formal language of his mother's and father's generation. When Turgenev entered Moscow University the ideals of self-perfection and the sublime absorbed the students and became grandiloquent. His own mind had turned to poetry and there is one of his early attempts in a letter to his Uncle Nikolai, an affable gentleman who had settled on the family in Spasskoye in the easy-going Russian way, and who eased the difficult moments of life there. The poem is about the annual drama of the breaking up of the ice on the Moscow river in the thaw which always drew the crowd. These ice-floes 'suddenly fly-bang!' – against the stone banks and are smashed to pieces.

They swallow each other in the wrestling of the waters
The ice-floes are born of other ice-floes
A sea is born of another sea.

Once more, one notices, his eye is moving from moment to moment.

His growing literary turn is seen in his reading. He has been 'enraptured by reading Mirabeau' and the young linguist was soon moving into English literature: Shakespeare, Shelley and above all Byron whom he knows through Pushkin. Shakespeare and Pushkin became his lasting guides. There are no evocations of Moscow's gilded Asiatic steeples and gilded domes in Turgenev's writing, but, as Gogol did, he was more likely to note oddities like the hundreds of crows perched on the crucifixes and cupolas. Life in Moscow was almost rustic. Alexander Herzen, ten years older than Turgenev, and to whom one turns again and again for close social observation, says in *My Past and Thoughts* that the houses of the gentry were all huddled together and yet the inhabitants were not of a single type: they were specimens of everything in Russian history, living unhurried and easy-going lives. There:

> was a spaciousness of their own within them which we do not find in the *petit-bourgeois* life of the West . . . the rank and file of this society was composed of landowners not in the service or serving not on their own account, but to pacify their relations, and of young literary men and professors. There was a fluidity of relationships not yet settled and of habits not reduced to a sluggish orderliness, a freedom which is not found in the more ancient life of Europe . . . the Slav laisser faire.

This Moscow lived by its dreams of Berlin and Paris. The talk went on until two in the morning and since it was dangerous to talk about politics, the subject had to be embalmed in literary and philosophical argument. The Muscovites were far from the formal Court life of Petersburg and the brisk coldness of official manners.

All the same, 'democratic' speculations were heard among the older students and the professors who had been to Berlin, and Turgenev, in his eager way, picked up one or two opinions that caused him to be mocked as 'the American'; the first sign of his private horror of serfdom.

The boys came back to Spasskoye for the holidays and at fifteen – Ivan told the Goncourts – he had his first mistress.

> I was very young. I was a virgin and with the desires one has at the age of fifteen. My mother had a pretty chambermaid who looked a little silly but, you know, a silly look lends a certain grandeur to faces. It was rather a damp day, no a rainy day: one of those erotic days that Daudet likes to describe. It began to drizzle. She took – mind you, I was her master and she was my

slave – she took hold of me by the hair at the back of my head and said to me, 'Come.' What followed was the sensations we have all experienced. But the sweet clasp of my hair accompanied by that single word – that still gives me a sensation of happiness every time I think of it.

The incident would strike his mother as normal, indeed proper; perhaps she arranged it. His inevitable love affairs would be under her control in the manner of her generation. She distinguished between sexual adventure and the far greater perils of love.

The boy had suddenly grown as tall as his father, indeed into a plumpish young giant with a long body and shortish legs which gave a sway to his walk. He had chestnut hair and large grave blue eyes, a bold nose. When his face was still the expression was of a young man self-absorbed, posing a little, and waiting. He had the fashionable lisp and he had some difficulty in getting his words out at first; the voice was gentle and caressing, but he was easily excited and then in talk and laughter the voice became high and shrill, even boisterous and he started pacing up and down the room like an actor carried away by his part.

In 1834 when he was sixteen, his mother pushed him on to Petersburg University, the proper place for a young nobleman and where she had good connections. He shared rooms with his older brother who was a cadet in the military college. His mother went off to Italy but presently there was the family tragedy. The father was dying at Spasskoye.

So much has been made of the powerful influence of his mother upon Turgenev's character that the father has come to seem a distant and negligent figure who let her run her family as she wished. This is not quite so. When he intervened his was the voice of authority and she had some awe of him. His distance had its spell. He was one of those fathers who have the disconcerting air of being a spectator in his own family. In this Ivan was very much his father's son; he too had grown into a restless spectator, his mind on his inner personal freedom. They went out shooting together: the father, though poorly educated himself, took an awkward interest in his son's education. Although he became a rationalist very early, Ivan was affected by the superstitions his father shared with the servants and one effect of seeing the agonies of his father's death was to convince Ivan for life that he would die of the disease of the bladder that killed his father.

It is tempting to trace Turgenev's life-long hypochondria to this event but when one considers the peculiar emotional conditions of life at Spasskoye, other influences pervade. Cholera moved from district to district among the peasants and the news of it besieged the minds of the landowners who shut themselves up in their houses when it was about. Varvara Petrovna feared it so much that she is said to have been borne round her grounds in a glass-enclosed chair when the plague came near. Spasskoye was a hothouse of imaginary symptoms and there was only a serf doctor living there to offer his crude remedies. Her temper brought on fainting fits and other disorders, and so strong was her will and imagination that she could act out any illness that suited her, with dramatic effect: it is not surprising that Ivan should have caught something of her morbidity.

Much more important was the effect of the father's death on Varvara Petrovna's attitude to her favourite son. She now turned greedily, almost amorously to him for the love she had not received from her husband. Her possessiveness increased and in the storms she created in the household he fell into the part of the soother, the peacemaker, the slave of her moods. When he was there – as Mme Zhitova says – Varvara Petrovna forgot her violence, but at the same time, even he had to watch and calculate the moment when he could intercede. For she was capable of punishing the servants for whom he had tactfully spoken: it was a way of punishing him.

He went back to Petersburg to the familiar Arctic Venice with its enormous palaces, its wide, windy, dusty streets down which the cold winds of the Baltic blew; and where, when they were not blowing, the fog of the marshes on which Peter the Great had built the city made the air leaden. It was a city made for hypochondriacs, dangerous to the weak chest and the throat. Its famous staring white nights were hard on the nerves of the sleepless. The capital seemed, as Herzen said, a façade, a screen, an inhuman artifice.

> One had to visualize behind the screen, soldiers under the rod, serfs under the lash, faces that betrayed a stifled moan, carts on their way to Siberia, convicts trudging in the same direction, shaven heads, branded faces, helmets, epaulettes and plumes.

What Petersburg really meant to Turgenev was that it was the stepping-stone to Berlin and Europe. In his *Reminiscences* he wrote:

> I had long dreamed of that journey. I was convinced that in Russia one could acquire only a certain amount of elementary knowledge and that the source of true knowledge was to be found abroad. In those days there was not a single man among the professors and lecturers at the University of Petersburg who could shake that conviction of mine; indeed they themselves were imbued with it . . . The aim of our young men . . . reminded me of the search by the Slavs for chieftains from the overseas Varangians.

There was no order in Russia. Everything he knew about this country disgusted him. He was for 'plunging headlong into the German sea', as soon as he could. He was ready for the Greek and German classics. And in his third year he showed Pletnyov, his professor, a laborious attempt to write a Russian *Manfred*: a play called *Steno* in iambic pentameter in the required Italian setting – 'a perfectly preposterous work'. The professor invited him to his flat and made gentle fun of it and he met a little literary society and caught sight of Pushkin, the demi-god, at the theatre.

> I remember his small, dark face, his African lips, the gleam of his large teeth, his pendent side-whiskers, his dark, jaundiced eyes beneath a high forehead, almost without eyebrows and his curly hair.

Not long after the poet was dead, killed in a duel, and he saw him lying in his coffin. He does not mention that his distant Turgenev kinsman was one of the only two persons permitted by the Tsar to escort the body by sleigh to his grave at Pakov.

The times were bad for literature. Writers were still suffering from the effects of the repression that had begun twelve years before, after the aristocratic revolt. There was no free press – indeed to start a new paper or journal was forbidden — no public opinion, no personal freedom. The only outlet lay in private conversation in small gatherings and even then conversation was restrained. Turgenev gives an account of an evening at Pletnyov's flat – most people lived in flats in Petersburg – and gives one or two exact thumbnail sketches of the forgotten writers who gathered there.

To begin with, the notorious Skobelev, author of Kremnev, afterwards commandant of the St Petersburg fortress . . . with some of his fingers missing, with a clever, somewhat crumpled, wrinkled, typical soldier's face and a soldier's far from naïve mannerisms – a man who had knocked about the world in short.

There was an editor, 'an equerry in the uniform of a gendarme', and Guber, translator of *Faust*, an officer in the Transport Department, with tousled side-whiskers which were, in those days, taken to be a mild assertion of liberal tendencies; and a shy, listening poet, dressed in a long-skirted, double-breasted frock coat, a short waistcoat with a watch chain of blue glass beads and a necktie with a bow, whose very ordinary Russian face suggested the self-educated artisan or house-serf.

At nineteen, Turgenev, with his handful of unpublished poems, was the shy listener and so conventional in his tastes that he saw nothing beyond a crude joke in Gogol's *The Government Inspector* which had been put on because it gave the Tsar himself a chance for one of his loud guffaws at lines like: 'You're taking bribes not according to your rank.'

In his years at Petersburg Turgenev read widely and showed more signs of turning to academic life than of distinction as a poet. His mind was set on enlightenment in Berlin, and where he had no difficulty in persuading his mother to let him go.

The day of departure came. The whole family went to Kazan cathedral to pray for him. With him went his valet Porfiry, a serf of his own age who was in fact his half-brother, the son of Turgenev's father by a maid at Spasskoye. There were tears at the parting. The mother made him swear not to gamble, and as she was carried back to her carriage she fainted. His brother saw him on to the steamer for Lubeck. 'I plunged,' Turgenev wrote in famous words, 'into the German sea which was to purify me and when I emerged from the waves I discovered myself a Westerner.' The first venture towards expatriation had begun.

. . .

Fathers and Sons

He was in Paris in 1861, because he was concerned about his daughter who wanted to get married but could not make up her mind about her suitors, when the Emancipation of the serfs was proclaimed and he went to the Thanksgiving Service at the Russian Church and, like many others, wept with joy. Herzen, the exile who could not return, told him that the author of *The Sportsman's Sketches* ought to be in Russia. Turgenev had, however, settled matters with his own peasants before the proclamation. He had given them a fifth of his land for nothing and at Spasskoye itself – the most intimate part of his estate and his home – he had given them the land on which their houses stood, and was soon building a small hospital, a home for the aged and had started a school.

All over Russia the peasants were bewildered by their freedom and often suspicious of the new dispensation. Many preferred the old ways to which they were accustomed. At Spasskoye they continued their traditional sport of stealing wood and, knowing Turgenev was an easy man, they grazed their horses on his flower beds. Elsewhere there were rows about the size of individual holdings and the redemption money. There were family rows between husbands and wives, and between brothers. The peasants were illiterate and often refused to put their mark on legal papers. They found they had to pay taxes and many regarded Emancipation as a landlord's trick – and among the bad landlords so it became. Many peasants sold their strips and left the land and there were not enough hands left to get in the harvest. Presently in Petersburg there were outbreaks of fire which were thought to be the work of terrorists belonging to the Land and Liberty League who, without any clear idea of policy, were calling for Revolution. The new Tsar had begun as a liberal but was now in panic; Radicals were arrested and sent into exile.

These events are in the background of the new novel Turgenev had written, *Fathers and Sons*, the tragedy of the conflict between two generations. The book set off a storm that was to last the rest of his life. It is his masterpiece. To foreign readers the savagery of the quarrel has seemed incomprehensible until recent times. In his brilliant Romanes Lectures given in Oxford in 1970 – by far the most illuminating exposition we have of Turgenev's growth and achievement as a novelist – Sir Isaiah Berlin adds an important corrective to our judgement. A book like *Fathers and Sons*, he points out, no longer seems happily remote to us in the violent conditions of our own times. His characters are not delightful Russian incurables but are now present and recognizable, now revolutionary change occurs everywhere in our own world. Turgenev was not withdrawn from disturbing realities; he was apolitical in the party sense, but he had his own commitment and could not resist his fascination with what frightened him or the duty he felt the artist had to observe and understand the types he saw dramatically opposed in his country.

The storm caused by his novel arose out of his portrait of 'its tragic hero': Bazarov. The Radicals thought it a libel on the younger generation who called for revolution or reform; the Conservatives accused him of siding with the enemies of order. In his *Reminiscences*, Turgenev is enlightening on the origins of the character and especially on his methods. Once more he says:

> I have heard it said . . . not once but many times that in my works I always 'started with an idea or developed an idea' . . . I never attempted 'to create a character' unless I had as my starting point not an idea but a living person to whom the appropriate elements were later on gradually attached and added. Not possessing a great amount of free inventive power, I always felt the need of some firm ground on which I could plant my feet.

He goes on to say that the basis of Bazarov was a young provincial doctor he had met in a train. The man had since died. The impression was still vague but in that man:

> I could watch the embodiment of the principle which had scarcely come to life but was just beginning to stir at the time which later received the name of 'nihilism'.

It is an oddity of social history that well-off Russians were in the habit of going to Ventnor in the Isle of Wight for the sea-bathing. Turgenev went there and there was talk of 'a new Russian type' – someone said he would be Rudin reborn. Walking alone on the beach, the novelist told them he had had a sudden vision of a dead man: Bazarov must be tragic. But the sources of a novelist's characters are not only parts of new persons suddenly met, but go back also to literature and literary experience. Some said that in Bazarov, Turgenev had put something of the young Radical critic Dobrolyubov who had been outrageously rude to him. Turgenev denied this, but Bazarov is famous for his rudeness – and Sir Isaiah Berlin points to the possibility of Belinsky as a source of Bazarov's brusqueness, directness, his explosions of sarcasm at hypocrisy and that there may be a link with Dobrolyubov's 'ferocious militant, anti-aestheticism'. Belinsky died tragically and the gifted Dobrolyubov died tragically young also in 1861 while the novel was being written. The random finality of death was always Turgenev's haunting preoccupation; but the hostile critics took Bazarov's untimely death at the end of the novel as a final attempt by Turgenev to make his 'hero' trivial and to punish him for his nihilism.

The moment we open the novel we understand that Turgenev is not writing the didactic work which both the Left and the Right imagined and called for in the hysteria of the time. His art rests on his ability to unself himself and to become the people he writes about. He observes and listens so that they appear to us clearly, untrammelled and living, as human beings do, in their own effortless justification. This, we say, is what they felt themselves naturally to be in the times they were living in, moving into the days that follow.

As usual the novel was carefully planned in play-like fashion in four long acts, though the scenes run with more intimacy than in his earlier work. They are less story-like and more flowing than in the manner of a European novel. In the first act we see Arkady Kirsanov, a student who has just graduated, arriving at his father's small property in the country. He brings with him his idol and friend, young Bazarov, who is coming to the end of his medical training and who is on the way to visit his own much poorer parents, fifty miles or more further on. The elder Kirsanov's property has 100 serfs – or as Nikolai Kirsanov prefers to say, for he is an enlightened man – 5,000 acres. The year is 1859. He has anticipated the Emancipation by putting his peasants on the quit-rent system and is having endless trouble with them. They are suspicious. They steal, they break his machines through incompetence. Nikolai is a warm, tender, unpractical man, a reader of the classics and a liberal of good family, but short of money and easily swindled. He is also a widower and is embarrassed to admit to his son that while the boy was away at University he has taken an innkeeper's daughter called Fenichka to live with him and that she has lately given birth to their child. Arkady tells his father that he and his friend Bazarov are above any out-of-date prejudices about marriage, so father and son are on shy good terms at once. Nikolai shares the house with his brother Pavel, once a Guards Officer, very much the Petersburg aristocrat and dandy who wears high, marble-white collars, a man of culture who affects stiff English manners. He had been famous for a long love affair with a Princess who had 'enigmatic' eyes. She had died and Pavel had given up his life in society, travelled to all the fashionable resorts and had come at last to live in correct and austere melancholy with his brother. At sight, Pavel takes against Bazarov, Arkady's lower-class 'long-haired' friend. And this first act is mostly about their growing enmity. 'This Bazarov. What is he?' Pavel asks Arkady about his friend.

He is a nihilist, Arkady says. A nihilist is a man who doesn't take any principle for granted.

> 'Indeed,' [says Pavel]. 'Well I can see this is not our cup of tea. We of the older generation think that without principles' (Pavel Petrovich pronounced the word as if it were French, whereas Arkady put the stress on the first syllable) – 'without principles taken as you say on trust one cannot move an inch or draw a single breath. *Vous avez changé tout cela*, may God grant you health and a general's rank, but we shall be content to look on and admire Messieurs les . . . what was it?'
> 'Nihilists,' said Arkady, speaking very distinctly.
> 'Yes. It used to be Hegelians, and now there are nihilists. We shall see how you manage to exist in a void, in an airless vacuum; and now please ring the bell, brother Nikolai, it is time for me to drink my cocoa.'

When Pavel forces Bazarov into the argument, Bazarov is off-hand and says he has no interest in anything outside of physics and the natural sciences. A decent chemist is twenty times more useful than a poet like Schiller or Goethe, the gods of Pavel's generation. Pavel says:

> 'I take it you do not acknowledge art then?'

'The art of making money or of advertising pills for piles!'
exclaimed Bazarov with a contemptuous laugh.

'. . . So you reject all that? Very well. So you only believe in
science?'

'I have already explained to you I don't believe in anything:
and what is science – science in the abstract? There are sciences,
as there are trades and professions, but abstract science just
doesn't exist.'

For Pavel, Bazarov is an impudent barbarian; for Bazarov,
Pavel is a ridiculous aristocrat. His fame as the unhappy pursuer of
the Princess, who has anyway been long dead, is pathetic.

'. . . a fellow who has staked his whole life on the one card of a
woman's love, and when that card fails, turns sour and lets
himself go till he's fit for nothing, is not a man, is not a male
creature . . . And what are these mysterious relations between a
man and a woman? We physiologists know what they are.'

Pavel had been taken by the 'enigmatic' eyes of the Princess.

'You study the anatomy of the eye; and where does that
enigmatic look you talk about come in? That's all romantic rot,
mouldy aesthetics.'

As for kindly old Nikolai Kirsanov's love of nature, Bazarov says:

'Nature is not a temple, it is a workshop and man is the
workman in it.'

These sarcasms lead at last to a grand quarrel in which Arkady and
Bazarov are on one side and Pavel on the other. Bazarov says that
it is useless to go on talking about Russia and social disease.
Reformers never do anything. All they talk about is art and
parliaments when the important question is getting enough to eat.
Russia is stifled by superstition, industry is a mess because the
people at the top aren't honest. Nothing is likely to come out of
this talk about emancipating the serf; the peasants will simply rob
one another and drink themselves silly. And so, says Pavel:

'[You] decided not to do anything serious yourselves.'

'And decided not to do anything serious,' Bazarov repeated grimly. He suddenly felt vexed with himself for having spoken so freely in front of this member of the upper class.

'But to confine yourself to abuse.'

'To confine ourselves to abuse.'

'And that is called nihilism?'

'And that is called nihilism,' Bazarov repeated again, this time with marked insolence.

. . .

'We destroy because we are a force,' remarked Arkady . . .

'Yes, a force, and therefore not accountable to anyone.'

To which Pavel Kirsanov replies frostily that he might as well say that the wild Kalmuk or the Mongols are a force. He and the aristocracy believe in principles and civilization and all its fruits. The proper home for Arkady and Bazarov is a Kalmuk tent.

In the second act Bazarov and Arkady leave the idyllic estate on which they have annoyed everybody and Turgenev now turns first to farce. The young men go to the provincial capital and call on a ridiculous 'advanced' young woman, Yevdoxia Kukshin, and an absurd, brash young climber, Sitnikov, who is the son of a spirit merchant and ashamed of it. Yevdoxia seems to live on champagne and cigarettes. Her room is littered with books and papers and her talk is an inconsequent litter of headlong ideas.

'Are you interested in chemistry? That is my passion. I have even invented a new sort of mastic myself.' . . . To make dolls' heads so they can't break . . . I have still got to read Liebig. Have you seen Kislyakov's article on female labour in the *Moscow News*? Do read it. You are interested in women's emancipation, I suppose. And in the schools' problem too?'

How out of date George Sand is; not to be compared to Emerson, knows nothing of physiology and hasn't even heard of embryology and in these days how can one get on without that?

Farce turns to the comedy of provincial manners when the two young men escape to the Ball the visiting panjandrum is giving. We see the grand man's struttings and snubbings. But the note changes when a beautiful and rich widow invites the young men to stay at her mansion. Bazarov, who has mocked Pavel Kirsanov for his fatal love of his 'enigmatic' Princess, finds himself snared into what he despises: romantic love for a cold, intelligent, rich woman who talks well and who is drawn to Bazarov's rebellious ideas.

Bazarov was a pursuer of women but had no time for ideal or romantic love which he regarded as an aberration: if a woman takes your fancy, he would say, 'try to gain your end and if you don't succeed – well, don't bother; there are plenty more good fish in the sea'. Mme Odintsov appealed to him; the rumours about her, the freedom and independence of her ideas, her unmistakable liking for him – all seemed to be in his favour; but he soon discovered that he would not 'gain his end', and as for turning his back on her, he found, to his own bewilderment, that it was more than he could do. His blood took fire the moment he thought of her; he could easily have mastered his blood but something else was taking possession of him . . . when he was alone he recognized with indignation a romantic strain in himself.

To rid himself of it he decides to leave and when she hears this she tries to stop him. In one last dangerous tack Bazarov cannot control himself. She is apparently tempting him too far and he angrily blurts out that he loves her and tries to embrace her. Madame Odintsov is astonished and physically frightened. She is not a conscious flirt: she is used to power and ease – her house runs like clockwork – and for her the relationship has been one of intellectual curiosity with a pleasant element of mild emotional flutter in it. She 'believes' in his gifts and that he may become a 'great man' but she would certainly not love him, a poor young man outside her own class. Bazarov sees he has made a fool of himself only too clearly and leaves. He returns to Arkady's house to pick up his luggage and his medical books and goes on to stay, as he originally intended, with his own parents. Arkady goes with him.

In the next act the two young men are seen there. The parents' place is a small farm of a hundred acres and one serf. His father, an old army doctor, and his adoring mother greet the young men with touching, overwhelming love; indeed it suffocates Bazarov and although they try to leave him alone to work they cannot bear it. They tiptoe from room to room longing to be with him. These are the most touching portraits in a book in which the conflict between the generations is most felt. The young men decide to leave but promise to come back. The parents cannot understand what they have done to offend their son as he prepares to go.

> From early morning the house was filled with depression: the plate fell out of Anfisushka's hands; even Fedka [the servant] did not know what he was doing and ended by taking off his boots.

He had worn boots especially in honour of the two young men.

> ... when Bazarov, after repeated promises to come back within a month at the latest, at last tore himself from [his parents'] clinging embraces and took his seat in the tarantass; when the horses moved off, the bells tinkled, and the wheels spun round – when there was nothing left to gaze after, the dust had settled and Timofeich, all bent and tottering, had crept back to his tiny room; when the two old people found themselves alone in the house, which suddenly seemed as shrunken and decrepit as they – then Vassily Ivanych, who a few moments before had been waving his handkerchief on the steps, slumped into a chair and let his head drop on his chest.
> 'He has gone, left us!' he faltered. 'Gone, because he found it dull here with us. I'm a lonely man now, lonely as this finger,' he repeated again and again, and each time he thrust out his hand with his forefinger pointing away from the rest.

Bazarov and Arkady return to the Kirsanovs. There is a watchful truce between Bazarov and Pavel Petrovich. Pavel even shows polite curiosity about Bazarov's microscope. But Bazarov is morose and he eventually tries to rid himself of Madame Odintsov's image by recovering his audacity with women. He sets out to see if the simple Fenichka is vulnerable. Once more the test of love appears in the story. Fenichka is an ingenuous young mother; Bazarov puts her at her ease. The only person she fears is Pavel Petrovich who keeps an eye on her. In fact, the old aristocrat sees something of his own lost Madame Odintsov, the Princess, in the blooming face of the young mother and his gazes are almost but not quite innocent; he longs for the impossible return of youth, the wild youth which Bazarov has and he guesses what Bazarov is up to. One day he sees and hears Bazarov making up to Fenichka, who is confused and does not know what to do when Bazarov suddenly kisses her. The opportunity for revenge has arrived for Pavel.

In a splendid, icy, formal scene he challenges Bazarov to a duel. Bazarov of course regards this as farcical, but the very pointlessness, the destructive aspect, makes him accept at once. He'll certainly stand up to a gentleman. (Turgenev the sportsman is excellent in duel scenes: he has one very good short story on the subject and knows that duels conceal an underlying attraction between the parties.) This one satirizes the formalities and is comical. Bazarov wounds Pavel, who falls and behaves with polite sang-froid and is obliged to let Bazarov attend to his wound. Pavel eventually recovers and realizes he has acted a good deal out of snobbery. The fact is that Turgenev is preparing, once more, a test of love for his characters: Pavel tells his brother and Fenichka that if they love each other they must marry. They overcome their nervous shyness – they were afraid of Pavel's authority.

In the final act, Bazarov packs up once more and while he does so he tells Arkady that their friendship is over. Not because of the trouble he has caused but because Arkady, he says, has changed. Arkady, who had also been sentimentally in love with Madame Odintsov, has been drawn to her younger sister whom she has dominated in her regal way. In this Turgenev shows his subtlety in showing the two sisters in another light. Madame Odintsov's idle, exalté mind veils a managing, possessive nature. Bazarov sees that Arkady has been clear-headed in love when he himself is still suffering from the romantic disease and has failed. He is not rancorous but he tells Arkady that in accepting the conventions of marriage he has lost the Nihilist spirit.

> 'There's no audacity in you; no venom . . . Your sort, the gentry, can never go farther than well-bred resignation and that's futile . . . you won't stand up and fight . . . you enjoy finding fault with yourself; but we've had enough of all that – give us fresh victims! We must smash people!

Bazarov returns to his parents. This is the moving finale of the novel. The old people realize that their son has changed and dare not ask him what is on his mind. They are relieved when they see him taking an interest in helping his father in doctoring the peasants from time to time. The father listens with admiration to his son's talk of new knowledge in medicine. The doting mother

565

restrains her effusive love and is in awe of him. But an accident occurs. Bazarov goes off to perform an autopsy on a peasant who has died of typhus and in doing so makes a small cut in his finger. He comes back asking for silver nitrate. There is none in this backward part of the country and Bazarov understands – and so does his father – that he is a dead man if he has caught the infection.

The scene of Bazarov's death is famous. It is one of the most moving and beautifully observed things that the great observer ever wrote – Chekhov admired it as a doctor and as an artist who himself was a master of recording human sorrow. The power of this narrative owes something to the hypochondria and sense of the presence of death which Turgenev felt so continuously in his own life; and in this the writing is one of those cleansings which a great artist achieves in his maturity. If the death, by such a small misadventure, may strike one as trivial and therefore not tragic – the point made by hostile critics – it has its own ironic logic: for Bazarov the Nihilist cannot object to accident or the random hostility of nature. When the death occurs, Turgenev writes, the experience of life on earth is not altogether in our hands. The last lines that describe the visit of the parents to Bazarov's grave are devastating:

> Vassily Ivanych was seized by a sudden frenzy. 'I said I would rebel,' he shouted hoarsely, his face inflamed and distorted, waving his clenched fist in the air as though threatening someone – 'And I will rebel, I will!' But Arina Vlassyevna, suffused in tears, hung her arms round his neck and both fell prone together. 'And so,' as Anfisushka related afterwards in the servants' rooms, 'side by side they bowed their poor heads like lambs in the heat of noonday . . .'

In the years that follow, the two frail old people support each other as they walk, year after year, to the cemetery, kneel at their son's grave, yearning over the silent stone.

The storm caused by *Fathers and Sons* was violent and went on rumbling for years. The Right did not enjoy the ironical portrait of Pavel Kirsanov and Turgenev's tolerance of Bazarov. The word 'nihilist' had caught on – very much as the idea of 'the superfluous man' had done years before – and the Radicals thought the portrait of Bazarov a libel on the young generation and their views. Bazarov is indeed silent on what he and his friends would do once the task of destruction was done; whereas those among the Nihilists who did think about this had a belief in some kind of Populist democracy which was too vague to become an effective Cause. Turgenev was in the impossible situation of being an apolitical man, a detached diagnostician in a period when the politically minded called for polemic and propaganda. Turgenev made matters worse by his comments. To the Conservative Countess Lambert he wrote:

> The convictions of my youth have not changed. But I never have been and never will be occupied with politics. It is alien and uninteresting to me. I pay attention to politics only in so far as a writer who is called upon to depict contemporary life must. You do wrong to demand from me in literature what I cannot give – fruits that do not grow on my tree. I have never *written for the people* . . . I have written for that class of the public to which I belong.

To others he wrote that he found himself agreeing with most of the views of Bazarov, except his views on art and literature. That sounds harmless enough but it was damaging, for under Russian despotism, with political discussion subject to censorship, art and literature had a peculiar covert political prestige. All literature was judged – as it continues to be in Russia today – by its social 'tendency'. But for Turgenev, as Sir Isaiah Berlin says, 'acts, ideas, art, literature were expressions of individuals, not of objective forces of which the actors or thinkers were merely the embodiments. The reduction of men to the function of being primarily carriers or agents was as deeply repellent to Turgenev as it had been to Herzen or, in his later phase, to his revered friend Belinsky.'

Politically Bazarov was not a revolutionary but a pre-Revolutionary; a type thrown up by a period which seemed 'on the eve' of perhaps violent change: the peasantry were eighty per cent of the population of the country. Bazarov thought them stupid. Two objections to him have some point: first, he was not, in the Nihilist sense, a true type, for he was not really an urban figure – as the active politicals inevitably were. Secondly, his ruling interest was not in politics but in natural science. Had he been a writer he could have been prophetic of Chekhov who, as a doctor, also stood outside the philosophical and literary influences which had formed the main stream of Russian novelists – including Turgenev himself.

The only weakness of the novel – it seems to me – is in the chapter on the visit to Madame Odintsov. It has some of that over-scented claustrophobic sentimentality into which Turgenev sometimes falls. She is the standard dissatisfied rich woman, but there is an embarrassing lushness in his writing when he tries to probe her mind:

> Sometimes, emerging all warm and languorous from a fragrant bath, she would fall to musing on the futility of life, its sorrow and toil and cruelty . . . Like all women who have not succeeded in falling in love she hankered after something without knowing what it was. In reality there was nothing she wanted, though it seemed to her that she wanted everything.

It is not hard to believe that Bazarov would feel the angry sensations of lust in her presence, but that he could have endured all those long, educative walks in the woods and the solemn conversations in her drawing-room is hard to believe, although we take the ironic point. We suspect Turgenev of one of his bouts of self-castigation for the long drawn out 'ideal' love for Pauline Viardot and his chats with Countess Lambert, and that here the book suffers from the blur of autobiography unassimilated.

Of course there were critics who defended Turgenev, even among the political young; but the attacks wounded him deeply. He had been looked upon as a leader by the young of his generation, now the new generation of young people despised him. They were indeed supplanted in their turn but for one who drew so much from the springs of youth as he did and who regretted the loss of his youth so bitterly – as the early pose of precocious old age shows – the blow was terrible. The effects lasted into his real old age.

As he said in *Rudin*, the young require simple answers even if they are illusory. The irony is that Tolstoy and Dostoevsky, who were hostile to radical politics, were treated with respect. The reason – apart from the fact that their range and strength as novelists was far greater – was that they were obsessed men. They had their missions which, in their different ways, were aspects of the feeling that Russia had an untainted Messianic role to play in the world; both had their religion and indeed in Dostoevsky's journalism the idea of mission was politically imperial: the

Russian right to Constantinople. Turgenev had no mission: he thought Dostoevsky's large talk of humanity mere rhetoric. Like Pavel Kirsanov, though not in his arthritic way, he stood for 'civilization' spelled out letter by letter, for what had been a long, patient, intricate growth.

. . .

Turgenev v. Dostoevsky

In August 1867, Dostoevsky and his new wife, Anna, arrived from Dresden. She was the young stenographer to whom he had dictated *The Gambler* and *Crime and Punishment* (which had not long been published), and who had rescued him from his dead brother's predatory family and from the son of his first wife who had encumbered him with debts to the tune of 20,000 roubles. With the money of her own dowry and with the help of his publisher, she had got him out of Russia and into Europe, where they were to travel for four years while he entered on his long struggle to write *The Idiot*. After the misery of his imprisonment in Siberia, the death of his first wife and his destructive affair with Polina Suslova, Dostoevsky was entering on the finest creative period of his life. He had been in Europe before and, like so many Russians, had taken to roulette at the German gambling tables. He was at the height of the gambling fever when he reached Baden-Baden, where he had come solely to play. He had lost every penny: Anna had been obliged to pawn her wedding ring and her earrings, her furs and a lot of her clothes. The couple had once or twice been obliged to live only on tea. After a short euphoric stay at an expensive hotel, they were driven to living in two cheap rooms over a blacksmith's on the outskirts of the town, where the noise of the anvil and the screams of the children were wrecking Dostoevsky's easily damaged nerves. He was soon out on the streets looking for a fellow Russian to borrow from.

He ran into Goncharov, the dour hermetic chief censor, himself afflicted with the paranoia which had caused him to accuse Turgenev of plagiarism a few years before. Goncharov lent him 'a piece of gold' and, perhaps not without malice, told Dostoevsky that Turgenev had seen him at the tables the day before but had not spoken to him because there was a convention that one must not talk to a man while he was playing. Of Dostoevsky this was certainly true: ill-luck, he always said, came to him for personal reasons. He had only to catch sight of some cool Englishman or German at play, to see the man as an evil omen, a devil personified, who would make him forget his system. The novelist drew everyone he met into a conspirator in his own drama. That, in itself, marked the ominous difference between himself and Turgenev, as artist and man. Honest Anna persuaded her husband to call on Turgenev because, on an earlier visit to Baden, he had borrowed fifty thalers from him and Turgenev would think he was ashamed of not paying back his debt. A meeting was arranged, but Dostoevsky's pride was already fermenting: he mistook the time and arrived at Turgenev's flat in the Schillerstrasse while he was eating his lunch. What happened is known from Dostoevsky's brilliant novelistic account of it in a letter to his friend, an eminent literary figure called Maikov. He wrote:

> I went to him in the morning at twelve o'clock and found him at lunch. I tell you frankly: even before this I didn't like the man personally. Most unpleasant of all, I owe him money from 1857 [in fact it was from 1863] from Wiesbaden – and have not returned it yet. Also I don't like his aristocratic, pharasaic embrace when he advances to kiss you, but presents his cheek. Terrible; as though he were a General.

Turgenev had the French manner of kissing. There sat Turgenev, the rich writer whom Dostoevsky had, as he said, 'adored' when he was young as the model aristocrat and man of genius, now waited on by a butler in a frock coat, eating a cutlet and drinking a glass of wine. Dostoevsky had read *Smoke* and disliked it and began to nettle Turgenev at once, telling him that it wasn't worth while to be as wounded by the critics as Turgenev was.

It is not easy to tell truth from fiction in what happened in the next hour. One can only say that Turgenev was apt to lose his head. It seems likely that he *did* say he was going to write an article denouncing Russophils and Slavophils. In a moment the two were at loggerheads about their convictions. Dostoevsky's hysteria was, as Solzhenitsyn has written in another connection, an evasion of his conflicts. He may not have quoted Potugin's own words from *Smoke* that the only contributions Russia had made to civilization were 'the best shoe, the shaft yoke and the knout – and hadn't even invented them', but at the height of the wrangle, with Turgenev's temper rising – Dostoevsky said he kept calm and ironical – he hit upon one of those small phrases that turn dispute into farce. If Turgenev was trying to write about Russia, he said, he had better get a telescope.

'A telescope,' said the startled Turgenev. 'What for?'

'Because Russia is a great distance from here. Train your telescope upon Russia and it will not be difficult to see us distinctly.'

On his decision to settle in Baden-Baden with the Viardots, Turgenev was sensitive. He understood Russian malice. He praised the Germans to Dostoevsky and spoke of the debt his generation owed to German philosophy. At which Dostoevsky said he had found the ordinary Germans a collection of cheats and swindlers. Turgenev denied this and said with rage:

> You insult me personally. You must know I have settled here and that I consider myself a German.

Dostoevsky said he did not know that, but if it was the case, he apologized and left, exalted by indignation. A German!

Such naked combats about convictions, as Mochulsky says in his book on Dostoevsky, rose from the endemic 'self-consciousness' in the Russian nature which, more accurately put, is a spontaneous consciousness of the self as an absolute, extended to the universal. (It resembles that capacity of the Spaniard to leap suddenly from his ego into a universal expansion of it.) Dostoevsky believed, as he often said, in going to extremes, in pushing beyond the limit in search of revelation, in going to the brink of the precipice. He was at the beginning of his vision of the Russian Christ, the mission of the Russian people to rule the whole Slav world and under the leadership of the Tsar to save mankind from the corruption of the West – even 'with rifles'. But, as Mochulsky suggests, the difference between Turgenev and Dostoevsky as artists was fundamental and irreconcilable.

> Turgenev was a fatalist lacking in will and saw history as an impersonal, predetermined process. Dostoevsky affirmed freedom of will and the power of personality. Turgenev wrote: 'Is

there a God? I don't know. But I do know the law of causality. Twice two is four.' Dostoevsky, with the frenzy of despair, fought against the law of necessity and by a volitional act 'acquired' faith in God.

Dostoevsky was the spiritual gambler: his greatness as a novelist lies in dramatizing to the limit the swaying conflict between 'knowing' and 'not knowing'.

The quarrel was part of Dostoevsky's development. He needed an imagined enemy at the roulette table to reanimate his genius. On Turgenev it had no effect but of disgust and the feeling that Dostoevsky was a sick soul. But it had a disagreeable aftermath. After his trajectory from self-abasement to exaltation, Dostoevsky often fell into cunning and double-dealing. He had his report of the quarrel copied and sent to be preserved for posterity 'in the archives'; obviously it would be publicized. Turgenev wrote to his friend Polonski in 1871:

I have been told that Dostoevsky has 'unmasked' me. Well, what of it, let him enjoy himself. He came to see me in Baden five years ago, not to pay back the money he borrowed from me, but to curse me because of *Smoke* which, according to his ideas, ought to be burned by the executioner. I listened to his philippic in silence – and what am I finding out now? That I seem to have expressed every kind of offensive opinion which he hastened to communicate to Bartenev. (Bartenev has written to me about it.) It would be out and out slander if Dostoevsky were not mad which I do not doubt in the slightest. Perhaps it came to him in a dream. But my God, what a petty dirty gossip.

Worse followed. If Turgenev had caricatured the Radicals in his portrait of Herzen's friend Ogarev in *Smoke*, Dostoevsky caricatured Turgenev in *The Devils*; he became the shrill, lisping figure of Karmazinov and a 'Red'. The portrait is spiteful. Karmazinov is an effeminate, vain, ageing celebrity who is mocked from the floor at a public reading; the Baden lunch is more fully guyed, but we learn that Turgenev did at any rate offer him a cutlet and sat with his knees under a plaid rug because, although it was August, he found Baden cold.

Turgenev is made to say, 'I still cling to honour but only from habit . . . Granted it's from timidity; you see, one must live somehow what's left of one's life.' The malice, indeed the hatred, reach their height when he parodies Karmazinov giving a reading of *Phantoms*. Karmazinov says that he has helped the town council to lay a new water pipe.

I felt in my heart that this question of water pipes in Karlsruhe was dearer and closer to my heart than all the questions of my precious Fatherland.

And then goes on to parody *Enough*, which he called *Merci*, in which Karmazinov says he is laying down his pen for good – as indeed Turgenev often did say – and if angels from heaven or the best society were to implore him, he would not change his mind. Dostoevsky's humour is broad. He underlines his jokes with a heavy hand. But when he parodies *Phantoms* as an account of Turgenev's first kiss, he is very funny indeed about the political tour of the earth. The lovers are sitting near a gorse tree – look up your nature notes – there is a touch of purple in the sky:

Suddenly they see Pompey or Cassius on the eve of battle and both are penetrated by the chill of ecstasy. Some wood nymph squeaks in the bushes. Gluck plays the violin among the reeds ... Meanwhile a fog comes down, everything disappears and the great genius is crossing the Volga in a thaw, such a fog – it was more like a million pillows than a fog. Two and a half pages are filled with the crossing and yet he falls through the ice. The genius is drowning – you imagine he was drowned? Not a bit of it: this was simply in order that when he was drowning and at his last gasp he might catch sight of a bit of ice, the size of a pea, but pure as crystal 'as a frozen tear'. And in that tear was reflected Germany, or more accurately the sky of Germany and its iridescent sparkle recalled to his mind the very tear which 'Dost thou remember fell from thine eyes when we were sitting under the emerald tree and though didst cry out joyfully "There is no crime!"' 'No,' I said through my tears, 'but if that is so there are no righteous either.' We sobbed and parted for ever.

She goes off to visit some caves down the coast and he flies off to dwell for three years under the Suharev Tower in Moscow and hears a hermit sigh. This reminds him of her first sigh thirty-seven years before, when she said:

'Why love? See ochra will cease to grow and I shall cease to love.'

Down comes the fog again, the wood nymph whistles a tune from Chopin, Aneus Marcus appears over the roofs of Rome.

A chill of ecstasy ran down our backs and we parted for ever.

This parody has its seamy side. Dostoevsky had published *Phantoms* in his own paper, *Epoca*, because he had thought Turgenev's name would draw readers: the truth is that noble as Dostoevsky seemed to his wife Anna, who passed the quarrel over lightly in the revised version of her account of him at the end of her life, he was undoubtedly a pathologically jealous man, as she knew from her own frightening experiences with him.

Turgenev wrote to a correspondent that Dostoevsky's conduct had not surprised him: 'he hated me even when we were both young', and added, 'Groundless passions are the strongest and most prolonged.' He and 'the most spiteful of Christians' did not meet again until they orated from the same platform when they were old men.

. . .

Virgin Soil

Virgin Soil is Turgenev's longest and most complex novel and it is very much written to show that he had not lost contact with the younger generation in Russia. He set out to portray the various types of educated young men and women who had thrown up the life of their class 'to go to the people', live among them, dress in the clothes of workers and peasants and to work with them and even to conspire with them. A quotation from the *Notebook of a Farmer* on the title page indicates that the novel will be a piece of practical social criticism: 'Virgin soil should be turned up not by a harrow skimming over the surfaces, but by a plough biting deep into the earth.' The Populists were skimmers, but there were many extremists among them. To Stassyulevich, his publisher, he wrote that he expected the novel would be as violently abused in Russia as *Fathers and Sons* had been.

Hitherto the younger generation has been presented in our

literature either as a crew of crooks and scoundrels . . . or as much as possible idealized . . . I decided to choose the middle course and to get closer to the truth – to take the young people who are, for the most part, good and honest and show that despite their honesty their very course is so false and impractical that it cannot fail to lead them to complete fiasco.

Whether he succeeded or not, he said, the young would at any rate sense his sympathy if not for their aims, then for their personalities.

Turgenev feared the censor and indeed reluctantly suppressed things that might too obviously offend. The novel was published in two parts and having passed the first, the censor's Committee were in a difficulty about the more disturbing second part. One faction wanted to burn it and insist on the 'correction' of the first part. The Chairman gave an embarrassed casting vote in its favour, but said if he had known the whole book in the first place he would have banned it. In the end, as Turgenev expected, the novel was damned by both sides who were swayed by party feeling. The Conservatives, the official classes, said Turgenev was a dangerous Radical who himself was personally involved with conspiracy – and indeed he did give money to the paper of the Populist leader, Lavrov, but simply because he hoped it would take the place of Herzen's *The Bell* as a forum for political discussion. He knew enough about political opinion to know that its phases do not last long. The Populists were a moral replacement of the Nihilists whose policy of rejection had soon spent itself. The Conservatives, especially, derided the idea that one of his characters, a girl called Marianna of the gentry class, would involve herself with the movement. No young woman would join it. The Radical critics ranged from those who said he was an old man libelling the young to those who said he knew nothing about the genuine revolutionaries and that, in any case, his absence from Russia made him out of date. Turgenev proved to be more accurate than either party in his diagnosis, as he had been in the case of Bazarov in *Fathers and Sons*: almost immediately after the publication of his novel eighteen women out of fifty-two conspirators were arrested and put on trial. The world's press reported the sensation and *Virgin Soil* was translated into many languages and became a best-seller in France, Great Britain and the United States.

Turgenev was easily affected by hostile criticism. Once more he said he was finished and, once more, that he would never write again. But presently he recovered and stood by what he had written and, like many gentle men who are bullied, he had his malice and a sharp, firm pride. Indeed, the novel itself had a satirical harshness which is exceptional in his works. He repeated one or two stinging epigrammatic judgements, one particularly on the notorious Oriental love of lying which so many Westerners have complained of in Russians:

A truthful man . . . that was the great thing! That was what touched her! It is a well-known fact, though by no means easy to understand, that Russians are the greatest liars on the face of the earth and yet there is nothing they respect like the truth – nothing attracts them so much.

In its opening pages, we are pushed abruptly into a dirty attic and see a slovenly young man and a young woman with coarse lips and teeth. Both are smoking and paying no attention to each other; nevertheless, we note their air of honesty, stoicism and serious commitment. From this moment we see how Turgenev's familiar world and manner has changed. The style is harder, more photographic; the grace has been replaced by the instant, the summary and the laconic. He is now attempting a larger number of characters from a wider canvas of life and is about to involve them in an elaborate plot and to grip us with a long story of imposed suspense which he had said earlier was outside his instinct and competence. We remember that Tolstoy and Dostoevsky have overtaken him, in this sense, and have given the Russian novel a density where before it had only surface and extent. We remember that what he admired in Dickens was the variety of mood – indeed he wondered, after the book was done, if he had not taken too much of the caricaturist from him. We have certainly an impression of cartoon and in that the book has something in common with, say, Dostoevsky's *The Devils*.

Both Turgenev's conspirators and his innocents who 'go to the people', strike one as living in a vacuum. Conspiracy is an urban matter and Turgenev is not by nature an urban novelist, although for once he does give us a picture of a Russian town, probably Orel, for its own sake. It is well photographed:

It was Saturday night; there were no people on the street, but the taverns were still crowded. Hoarse voices broke from them, drunken songs and the nasal notes of the concertina; from doors suddenly opened streamed the filthy warmth, the acrid smell of alcohol, the red glare of lights. Before almost every tavern were standing little peasant carts, harnessed to shaggy, pot-bellied nags; they stood with their unkempt heads hanging down submissively, and seemed asleep.

Or:

The coach crossed a wide market place, positively stinking of rush mats and cabbages, passed the governor's house with striped sentry boxes at the gates, a private house with a turret, a promenade set with trees recently planted and already dying, a bazaar filled with the barking of dogs and the clinking of chains, and gradually reaching the boundaries of the town overtook a long long train of wagons, which had set off late for the sake of the cool of the night.

An un-Turgenevean scene, brutally observed, but it must be said, well placed. For Nezhdanov, the young poet and idealist and, so to say, political guinea-pig of the novel, is getting a first sight of the Russia he has vowed to 'go to', live with and understand. But what one suspects already is, as Richard Freeborn says in his study of Turgenev, that *Virgin Soil* is going to be a forerunner of the crude, black and white, schematic works of the Socialist Realists of our time and that:

The distinctions Turgenev makes between the aims of the Populists and their persons was artificial, especially for a writer who had been used to accepting both the man and his ideas.

This change is certainly felt and although one can say that Turgenev's effort of will in keeping in touch with Russian realities has some of the guilt of the absentee in it – a matter that was, as he put it, his fate – we know that he judged rightly when he said that the Populist movement was a pathos, that no root and branch change would take place for another twenty years at least. The central characters are nevertheless representative. The aristocratic young Nezhdanov has traits of Turgenev's character: like the young Turgenev, he is handsome and has chestnut hair (but he is an illegitimate son). He has a double nature: he is secretly a poet but ashamed of his poetry, his real interest is political activity. He is an idealist, passionate, chaste, timid; ashamed of these qualities, he even tries to be coarse in his language: 'Life did not come easily to him.' His feelings push him forward, but beyond his power of performance. He is the Turgenevean mixture of Don Quixote and Hamlet, a throwback to 'the superfluous man'. When he 'goes to the people' and solemnly dresses up in workman's clothes, the workmen see through him at once and make him drunk on raw vodka. Another time he is 'beaten up' and makes a mess of everything.

Marianna, the brusque upper-class girl whom he falls in love with when he is tutoring in the grand house of the wordy liberal Sipyagin, is as innocent as he, but she is the new kind of young girl. She is a rebel who has cropped her hair and (interesting when one remembers Turgenev's old-fashioned habits), she belongs to the generation who have also given up hand-kissing. When she boldly runs off with Nezhdanov to 'go to the people' with him, she refuses to be married and they live together in chastity. Marianna is a rebel not a revolutionary – a rebel eager to leave her class, to be useful and to sacrifice herself. The real revolutionary is Mashurina, the unkempt, plain and awkward girl who silently loves Nezhdanov. She is quietly efficient in secret work, alert for traitors, spies and mistrustful of some of the hangers-on of the movement, for example of Palkin, a cripple, a foolish yet far-seeing man, but a danger to the cause because he is an unstable and excitable chatterbox, easily flattered. It is Mashurina who will disappear deeper into conspiracy when Palkin's foolishness and swank give the group away.

The 'hero' in Turgenev's eyes – although Palkin makes Turgenev's point in a prophetic speech about the dull, immovable men who will eventually rule Russia – is Solomin. Turgenev calls him an American type – he knew no Americans but America had provided a Utopian dream for early revolutionaries (except Herzen who called Americans 'elderly children'). Turgenev rejected the traditional Russian respect for Germans as the practical race; he looked back on the Germans as the guiding philosophers of his youth; so he turned to the English and made Solomin, the son of the despised priesthood, a man who had learned his trade in the cotton factories of Manchester and his politics from the English reformers of the industrial revolution and who may have a touch of Engels in him. Solomin is sympathetic to the conspirators, protects them loyally but advises caution and gradualism to the headstrong. He is strong, healthy, hard-working, generous, sober and resourceful, a man of sense. Inevitably he strikes one as being too good to be true; as a still portrait he is well enough done, but Turgenev can't make him move except in small helpful ways. Markelov, a retired artillery officer and landowner, is the dour type cantankerous conspirator, a lonely, unhappy man who can't farm his land effectively because he tries to run everything by giving orders in a military way. He is the same in conspiracy – too aggressive, given to acting independently and openly like a fanatical officer. He is certain to be arrested and to go grimly silent and still determined to Siberia.

These figures are well enough done in the first volume of the novel which deceived the censors, for they are seen in the setting that Turgenev can always do well: the still, timeless scene of the great country house where the family and the guests dine and talk, when Sipyagin, the host, is mellifluous at the table, where his pretty wife flirts with the tutor in her boudoir, where the rebel girl gazes at Nezhdanov and sulks before her aunt, where people walk in the gardens and the carriages come and go. It is the same sort of Paradise from the past as one finds in *A Nest of Gentlefolk*, in *Fathers and Sons* – but the characters are now hardened. Turgenev shows his contempt for the gentry openly, especially for the conceited and pompous young Kammerjunker, Kallomyetsov, who is an active 'Red' hunter, vain of his certainty in spotting revolutionaries. He is far cruder than Pavel in *Fathers and Sons* or the other comical Frenchified asses of earlier novels. And Sipyagin, the bland, sporting landowner with his skin-deep liberalism is also ridiculed. The drawing-room quarrels become edgy when the egregious Kallomyetsov says Sipyagin should be President of a Commission that would decide everything.

Madame Sipyagin laughed more than ever.

'You must take care: Boris Andreivitch is sometimes such a Jacobin . . .'

'Jacko, Jacko, Jacko,' called the parrot.

Valentine Mihalovna shook her handkerchief at him.

'Don't prevent sensible people from talking! Marianna, tell him to be quiet.'

Marianna turned to the cage and began scratching the parrot's neck which he offered her at once.

'Yes,' Madame said, 'Boris Andreivitch sometimes astonishes me. He has something . . . something of the tribune.'

'*C'est parce qu'il est orateur,*' Kallomyetsov interposed hotly. 'Your husband has the gift of words, as no one else has; he's accustomed to success, too . . . *ses propres paroles le grisent* . . . But he's a little off that, isn't he? *Il boude* – eh?'

'I haven't noticed it,' she replied after a brief silence.

'Yes,' Kallomyetsov pursued in a pensive tone, 'he has been overlooked a little.'

It is all drifting to a row about Marianna being a Nihilist because at this time, before she runs off with Nezhdanov, she teaches in a village school.

The things we rely on Turgenev for are here: the naturalness of all kinds of talk and the silences in it – with him it is a pianist's gift – and his ear is just as fine when we get to the drunken and confused talk of the Radicals in the second volume. His summary penetration into character does not fail. Madame Sipyagin for example, is excellent.

> She was clever, not ill-natured – rather good-natured of the two, fundamentally cold and indifferent – and she could not tolerate the thought of anyone remaining indifferent to her . . . Only, these charming egoists must not be thwarted: they are fond of power and will not tolerate independence in others. Women like Sipyagina excite and work upon inexperienced and passionate natures; for themselves they like regularity and a peaceful life . . . Flirtation cost Sipyagina little; she was well aware that there was no danger for her and never could be . . . With what a happy smile she retired into herself, into the consciousness of her inaccessibility, her impregnable virtue and with what gracious condescension she submitted to the lawful embrace of her well-bred spouse.

Not until we get to the second volume does Turgenev break out of talk into dramatic scenes. Madame Sipyagin seems to be a development of Madame Odintsov in *Fathers and Sons* but done in acid. She spies on her niece, intercepts letters and exposes the girl's love for Nezhdanov to Markelov who had hoped to marry her. The point of this jealous intrigue is to show the extremes to which the apparently gracious Sipyagins will go to preserve the unity of their class. At the moment when the defiant Markelov dashes to support a local riot of the peasants and the conspiracy is betrayed, the hypocrisy of Sipyagin's liberalism comes out. He is smoother than the violent Kallomyetsov and, in masterly fashion, Turgenev as the novelist of personal relationships shows these relationships being undermined politically. There has been an excellent scene at the end of the first part of the novel in which Markelov begins to have the force of a tragic figure. As a man of honour, reckless and incapable of spite or jealousy, indifferent to enemies, determined as an analyst and not deceived, Markelov does not spare his host:

'If we wait for the moment when everything, absolutely everything is ready, we shall never begin. If one weighs *all* the consequences beforehand, it is certain there will be some evil ones. For instance, when our predecessors organized the emancipation of the peasants, could they foresee that one result of this emancipation would be the rise of a whole class of money-lending landowners who would lend the peasant a quarter of mouldy rye for six roubles and extort from him (here Markelov crooked one finger) first the full six roubles in labour and besides that (Markelov crooked another finger), a whole quarter of good rye and then (Markelov crooked a third), interest on top of that – in fact squeeze the peasant to the last drop. Our emancipators couldn't have foreseen that. And yet even if they had done, it was right to free the peasants and not to weigh all the consequences. And so I've made up my mind!'

And when Markelov is arrested at the end of the book he is obdurate and does not repent. It is one of Turgenev's excellences that he is true to the basic character of people. Markelov is the incurable soldier when he reflects on his betrayal:

It is I who am to blame, I didn't understand, I didn't say the right thing, I didn't go the right way to work. I ought simply to have given orders and if anyone had tried to hinder or resist, put a bullet through his head! What's the use of explanations here. Anyone not with us has no right to live . . . spies are killed like dogs, worse than dogs.

Turgenev is hard to follow in the facts of the conspiracy: there are too many hints and shadow figures, but one is well done. This is Palkin, the vain, chattering and comic exhibitionist, the born mysterious contact-man longing to be trusted and knowing he cannot be; he is burdened by the knowledge of his own muddle-headedness. The scene in which Sipyagin flatters him, inflates his conceit, snubs him and slyly worms everything he wants out of him and dismisses him with contempt when Palkin is out to impress the Governor, is good. Into the mouth of this walking calamity, Turgenev puts shrewd prophecy. He defends Solomin to whom the intellectual revolutionaries are now cool: Russia needs sturdy, rough, dull men of the people.

> Just look at Solomin: his brain is clear as daylight, and he's as healthy as a fish . . . Isn't that a wonder! Why do we Russians always have the idea that to be a man of feeling and conscience, you've got to be an invalid?

There are two more characters to whom a complete scene is given, who on the face of it have no relevance to the theme of the novel and who in fact seem to belong to a short story thrown in for relief. Turgenev was inclined to cut them out but was persuaded to let them stay. They are an elderly, childless pair of innocent, doll-like, eccentric creatures, called Fomushka and Fimushka, the oldest inhabitants of the town, who have preserved themselves and their house as untouched models of the life of lesser gentry in the eighteenth century. They blissfully ignore everything that has happened since that time. They still drink chocolate because tea had not come in, they play duets, look at old albums and sing sweet and old-fashioned songs about hopeless love in their cracked voices. They have one unbroken rule: they have never allowed their house serfs to be flogged and if a servant turned out to be drunken and intolerable they bore with him, but after a while passed him on to a neighbour saying, 'Let others take their turn with him.'

> But such a disaster rarely befell them, so rarely that it made an epoch in their lives and they would say for instance, 'That was very long ago, it happened when we had that rascal Aldoshka,' or, 'When we had grandfather's fur cap with the fox tail stolen.' They still had such caps.

The interesting thing is that this dream of an Arcadia in the past is often found in the Russian novel: in Oblomov's dream, for example; even in the talk of the senile Iudushka in Shchedrin's *The Golovlyov Family*. In Turgenev, it is more than one of his 'old portraits', reminiscences; it is not antiquarian; it is really an incipient fairy-tale or a fable without meaning which is budding in the depths of a people's mind. It is also a relief after the vulgar scene at the merchant's house that has preceded it, a holiday of the mind from the yearning for the future which rules the whole novel – the burden of Russia which the other characters bear. Fomushka and Fimushka bear no burden.

If *Virgin Soil* has not the sustained serenity of *Fathers and Sons* because the people in the right and the people in the wrong are too blatantly stated, it is an impressive attempt to have a final say. It can hardly be called an old man's book, for Turgenev was in his late fifties when he wrote it. The strain, we feel, comes from trying to pack too much into it and not without artifice. To the critics who said that he was out of touch with the new Russia, Turgenev replied that he was closely in touch with the dozens of young people who came to seem him in Paris; but although they may have revealed themselves to him they did not really bring their Russia with them and were more likely to present him with arguments than with intimacy. If we are to go by what we read in Anna Dostoevsky's diary of her life with her husband and, of course, in Dostoevsky's novels, the quality that was missing in Turgenev's young visitors was the fact that at home they lived in crowds, above all in one another's lives: their very homes, in whatever class, were normally crowded, public to their relations and their friends. It is in the nature of Dostoevsky's genius to show that when one of his characters appears his whole life and all his relatives seem to be hanging out of his talking mouth. When Russians soliloquize they are never alone. Turgenev himself said that in Russia writing was easy for the novelist: the stories and people spring up around him and crowd in on him at once.

The political perspicacity of Turgenev is astonishing and now the state of our world has changed it seems closer to our political experience than it was to English admirers of Turgenev in 1900 who saw in him something close to the experience of an English country gentleman of sensitive tastes. The only thing that really shocks in *Virgin Soil* is Nezhdanov's suicide: the 'superfluous man', whom Turgenev invented, seems to die as a convenience in the interests of early Romanticism and Turgenev's preoccupation with death.

THE NAMING OF ELIZA QUINN

Cork, 1969. In the hollow of an ancient tree, beyond Darby's house, Beatrice Conrad finds some tiny bones. A thirty-something American, she has come to claim the derelict cottage left to her by her Granma Lizzie. She finds a low grey cottage, a door and two windows like a picture a child might draw. There was a stone wall out front, and the ghosts of old potato ridges running up the hill behind.

Beatrice's discovery harks back to the great potato famine of the mid 1800s and that is where this extraordinary story leads. To the Quinns. And to the Verseys. And to a feud that begins in the time of the famine, and has repercussions that will affect generations to come.

This is a wonderful, absorbing, epic novel about families and neighbours; about physical and emotional hunger; about love and long memories.

THE NAMING OF ELIZA QUINN

Carol Birch

WINDSOR
PARAGON

First published 2005
by
Virago
This Large Print edition published 2006
by
BBC Audiobooks Ltd by arrangement with
Little, Brown

Hardcover ISBN 10: 1 4056 1332 7
           ISBN 13: 978 1 405 61332 3
Softcover ISBN 10: 1 4056 1333 5
           ISBN 13: 978 1 405 61333 0

British Library Cataloguing in Publication Data available

Printed and bound in Great Britain by
Antony Rowe Ltd., Chippenham, Wiltshire

For Diana Scarth

ACKNOWLEDGEMENTS

I am grateful to the Author's Foundation for a bursary, which assisted in the writing of this book.

Thanks to Martin Butler, Emily Atherton, Nina and Dave Bleasdale, Charles Root, Donal Mac Neamhabhnaigh, Somhairle, Mic Cheetham and Lennie Goodings.

The following books were invaluable:

Letters from Ireland during the Famine of 1847 by Alexander Somerville
Famine Echoes by Cathal Poirteir
The Great Irish Potato Famine by James S. Donnelly Jr
The End of Hidden Ireland: Rebellion, Famine and Emigration by Robert James Scally
Black '47 and Beyond: the Great Irish Famine in History, Economy and Memory by Cormac O'Grada

PART ONE

1969—early summer

1

'. . . but do not put your hand down to see . . .'

Last night I saw a light high up on the mountain. It was as if a door was open in the rock, letting out light from within; and there was a shadow in front, like a man smoking, gently rocking to and fro as you might if you were just standing there in the cool of the night, looking out over the sea and having a last pipe before going to bed.

My front door is like a stable door; I had the top half open and I was leaning out to get some more of the summer night air, when I saw it on the hillside. I pulled in the shutter and locked and bolted, and then I didn't think about it any more. Here, as soon as the dark comes down, I draw the curtains, taking care to leave not a crack anywhere for an eye to peep in.

Everything around here is named. Darby's House is what my house is called. Who's Darby? That was the first thing I asked. Oh, he was before my time, that's what they say, these stocky Irish farmers I encounter in the lane. I've been here three weeks. I like to sit and feel my silent presence in the room, with the miles of darkness pressing in, and the sea singing very far below; it sounds distant at the moment, though I know that when I step out of my front door in daylight it will hit me in the face, and for a second I'll reel with vertigo. Though really, to fall into the sea you'd have to walk about half a mile down a rocky path then clamber over three or four grass ridges.

My house sits solitary in a stony hollow in a hillside high above the Atlantic Ocean. It has no electricity and I draw my water up from a hole in the ground surrounded by a tumbled stone wall. Three nights ago when I looked out, I saw the tip of a lit cigarette. Someone was standing down at the end of my track in the pitch black. There was no moon that night. I saw the light move up, brilliant as someone took a drag, then move back down again. But that was nothing, just old Pierce O'Donnell from down below. Nothing at all to what happened this morning, that thing I found, my hand upon the sudden something.

I was standing beside the old hollow tree out back, looking into the dank earthy hole that went down like a tunnel inside, like Alice's rabbit-hole; it made me remember a poem my Granma Lizzie used to scare me with when I was a child, a poem about the stump of an old dead tree. '*But do not put your hand down to see*' runs the refrain—

> *but do not put your hand down to see,*
> *because*
>
> *in the stumps of old trees, where the hearts*
> *have rotted out, there are holes the length of a*
> *man's arm, and dank pools at the bottom*
> *where the rain gathers and old leaves turn to*
> *lace, and the beak of a dead bird gapes like a*
> *trap. But do not put your hand down to see,*
> *because*

—and there it was, this hole for me to put my hand down to see, in fascination; so I did and what I found there was a dead baby.

4

She was just bones. I knew she was a she straight away, I don't know how. I had to walk all the way down to the village to telephone, it took me half an hour and I didn't see another soul on the way. I didn't know who to call, so I dialled the police. The switchboard lady said there was no one there. I mean, *no one* there. Can you imagine calling the cops in New York and finding no one there. She said she'd transfer me, and I stood and waited in the booth in the village street, listening to all the clicks and hums on the line, watching the way the tall grasses on the wall outside were quivering very finely, as if they could sense something, as if they were straining and listening with everything stretched. A feeling of weeping was coming up inside me thinking of the shock of the bones, but I swallowed it down into my chest. I didn't let it get to my eyes.

A voice came on the line. 'I found some bones,' I said. 'I think it's a child.'

There was a long pause, then, 'You say you found some bones,' the man repeated, as if he were writing it down very slowly, as if I'd reported a lost purse.

'Bones,' I said emphatically. 'Little bones. A child.' A shudder seized me, a blast of cold. 'In a tree at the back of my house.'

I heard him sighing in a weary kind of way. 'Your name?' he asked.

I told him my name was Beatrice Conrad, and he said at once: 'Darby's House.'

Everyone knows everything about me. I don't

know him but he knows me.

'Must be rough living up there, I'd say?' he remarked pleasantly.

*　　　*　　　*

I had a wanderlust in my thirty-seventh year. It was the tail-end of the sixties and I'd had to get out of New York. I had a nice apartment on the Upper West Side, but it was full of people I hardly even knew. I had money and I was an easy mark.

Granma Lizzie's the reason I'm here. The day I learned she'd left me a ruin in Ireland I tasted the taste of the strawberry sodas she used to buy me, and the past came flooding back in a Proustian leap. I knew her well as a child. I stayed with her a lot at her house in Nyack, I was her unabashed favourite, and it was me she left the house to, not my brother. It's not worth much but none of us even knew she had it. She never spoke of it, and though she loved her country, she never wanted to go back. Soon as I saw the address written down on the deed, I knew I would come here. I fell in love with it on paper: Darby's House, Kildarragh, Lissadoon, Boolavoe, County Kerry, Ireland. There was a map with my boundaries marked in red. Ireland, whose praises had been sung in my ears since the day I was born, arose in my mind. I used to be a total sucker for all the old shamrock bullshit when I was a kid, the St Patrick's Day Parade and all that. My mother used to take me and my brother every year. I'd been to Hawaii with my parents, and Mexico a couple of times, but never Ireland, though I'd always meant to. And now I had a house there, a ruin.

There I was thinking of change, and Ireland just kind of jumped up and grabbed me. It came at a funny time. I was working in Stack's Music Store, bored; I'd been thinking of going away for a while. I'd turned thirty-seven in the spring and I'd barely spent a day alone in my life. It's like I was something getting used up, a bar of soap infinitesimally shrinking day by day.

I wrote to my mother's cousin Dec in Lissadoon, with whom, out of a sense of duty, I'd been exchanging Christmas cards religiously since she died. I asked him what kind of a state the house was in, and he wrote back immediately. It had been used for cows for the past twenty or so years, but was reasonably sound. Said it had a tin roof that leaked a bit, the doors and windows were boarded up. There was a spring. The spring did it. Something happened when I heard about the spring. The sound of clear water rising out of the ground joined the taste of strawberry soda, and that sealed it. All I can say is it was a kind of hunger, but it wasn't a hunger for anything I had or had once had. I didn't miss any of my old beaux. I was independent, doing OK. I'd never had to work at anything I didn't want to do. I didn't know what it was I wanted. But it was simple really. For the first time in my life I was just hungry for quiet. And I was curious too. I'd heard so much about this place from both my mother and my grandmother, yet they'd never taken me there. For all their misty-eyed longing, neither one had ever wanted to return.

I thought I'd go over and camp in the house for the summer, see about fixing it up, maybe use it now and then and perhaps rent it out. I arranged it all with Dec, sent money over for someone to go in there and clean it out before my arrival, give me a window or two, put the doors back in. I had an idea of Ireland, all green and soft and lovely. You can't imagine though till you see for real these houses in the old abandoned villages: ruined, their ownership lost in time, whole families gone overseas. Kildarragh's all but gone, whatever it was. My house is standing, and old Pierce O'Donnell's, but between us lie the remains of a dozen or so dwellings, all tumbled long since. The grass grows over their fallen stones. When I first saw Darby's House I fell in love, it was just so beautiful. A low grey cottage, a door and two windows like a picture a child might draw. The roof shone. The hollow in which it nestled on the side of the mountain was purple with foxgloves. There was a stone wall out front, and the ghosts of old potato ridges running up the hill behind, left over from before the great famine.

There was a rainbow that day. It seemed to come down in the little patch of earth at the back of the house. But then as I walked further up the track I thought it was on the other side of the mountain, by Lissadoon, the pretty village of pink, green and blue houses I'd come through that morning.

In the stumps of old trees with rotten hearts,
where the rain gathers and the laced leaves
and the dead bird like a trap, there are holes
the length of a man's arm, and in every
crevice of the rotten wood grow weasel's eyes
like molluscs, their lids open and shut with
the tide. But do not put your hand down to
see, because

8

The bones were making me shudder through the wall.

I couldn't stay there in the house waiting for them to come and take her away. She was coming through the walls at me. I went out and stood on the track looking down towards the sea over those lost famine lands, those lost crowded dwellings, smoking a cigarette. The track meanders up from the low road that rounds the cliff, looks in at my gate then snakes its way higher and higher through house-high rocks and running streams. There are hares and wild goats up there. The mountain too is named. They call it Quilty's Door. I'm living on Quilty's doorstep. A black car comes beetling along the lower road and turns up my track, the stocky strut of old Pierce O'Donnell following after. No show without Punch, as my mother used to say. The car grinds to a dusty halt and stands sighing and creaking and clicking, cocked at a weird angle on the uneven track. Father Lynch and the garda and the doctor and Matthew Kelly from the village store slowly and solemnly emerge.

'It's this way,' I call, leading them round the back and up the hill a way, head bent, hands shoved up my sleeves.

I'd laid her skull and a couple of bones on the grass by the old tree. The rest of her was still down there with the weasel's eyes. In my mind, I see them give a synchronised slow reptilian blink, and a shot of fear goes through me. I'll never put my hand down to see again. How am I going to stay here tonight all on my own? How can I not? I have builders coming to look over the place Tuesday. I have this gilded silence I've been nurturing. I'm

9

one with the big sea. What's fear anyway? Only fear.

Her skull, the eye sockets black and huge, and two tiny bones lie at our feet.

'Hrrm,' says the garda, a sweet uncertain young boy with a mop of chestnut hair, 'these look like human remains to me all right.'

'These are very old bones,' says Father Lynch, who smiles habitually, whose eyes revert to humour in repose, 'very, very old indeed. Wouldn't you say, Matty?'

'Jesus, Father, how would I know?' says boxer-faced Kelly, shaking his head. He has taken off his brimmed hat and it dangles by the knees of his baggy black suit.

'The older the better,' says the doctor, a gingery-bearded man with the look of a seaman. I don't know why he's here. He can't do a whole lot for her now, can he?

Father Lynch is unsmiling. Strange to see him serious, his mouth a straight line. 'Well, boys,' he says, and hoiks up his sleeve and steps forward.

'No no, I'll do it, Father,' the sweet young policeman protests, but the priest waves him aside with his free arm, the other plunging down and reaching, feeling about amongst the weasel's eyes and laced leaves. 'Stand there, Barry, I'll pass them out to you.' His face is plump and firm.

There's something so moving about the way they bring her out, piece by piece, very gently, the priest's big soft hands coaxing her from the sticky bowels of the tree, handling her like porcelain, handing her on to the waiting boy, who lays each little pale stick of her side by side in the grass. They're so careful. Other men from the village and

10

round about turn up. One of them is my uncle, Dec Vesey, a rotund old man with a red face and cropped grey hair. They know all about me, all of them, or think they do, and I know nothing about any of them apart from Uncle Dec, who isn't really my uncle but my mother's cousin; and all I know about him is ancient stuff my mother used to tell me, about what a fine strapping hunk of a boy he'd been. I can't relate that to this stout shambling farmer, nodding to me from the little crowd that's gathered on the hillside around the fragile haul of bones.

I step over to him while they're wrapping them in sacking.

'Hello, Beatrice,' he says gruffly.

'Hello, Dec.'

'Strange business.'

I've asked him before but try again. 'Dec, do you know much about this house? Who lived here?'

He shakes his head. 'No one's lived in that house for years.'

'But someone lived here at some time.'

'Oh, sure.' He shrugs affably, smiles, rubbing the back of his neck. 'Will you be all right here on your own now, Beatrice?' he asks kindly. 'You know where we are.'

'Oh, I'm OK,' I say very firmly, smiling to prove it.

People are moving away. The bones are in the car. No one seems to know what will happen to them now.

'You will let me know,' I ask the young garda, 'you will let me know if you find out anything about them?'

'I will indeed.' He's in the car, leaning out. 'Don't

you go getting upset about this, Miss Conrad,' he says. 'Those are very old bones. God knows how long they'd been in there. Long before your people, I'm sure. It's just some old story, nothing for you to worry about.'

'I'm OK,' I say, 'Thanks.'

'Come down for your tea, Beatrice,' Dec says shyly, 'Rosemary might know something about this old place. She has more of a memory for that sort of thing.'

I watch them go, and when I am alone I do cry at last, sitting on the high stool in the bare downstairs room where a manger still adorns one wall. Dec and his boys have made good use of the money I sent over, to bring in a stove, a table, a couple of chairs, the essentials. They have whitewashed the walls and cleaned out the chimney and fixed me a fire in the grate with a bellows and fire-irons. The high stool must have come from a bar. Sometimes I sit on it and am just the right height then to look out of the small slit window that faces the sea, like an arrow vent in a castle wall; at sundown it frames a painting of vivid hue, a blood-red globe sinking slowly into the horizon, the rim of which is indigo under a luminous sky daubed and streaked with peach and pink and viridian. Tonight the picture is blurred and smeared by my tears. I feel so sorry for her all alone in the tree, all those years, her bones unburied for so long. I am actually trembling a little. I feel as if all the people who ever lived in this house are somewhere absorbed into the walls, all in there looking out at me. This won't do. I can't be chased away, not when I was getting used to the peace, to not being wanted for something all the time. The solitary condition is a good thing, I

12

have decided; I was coming round to it, getting it licked; there's a way I found, a way to let the silence slip all over me like a new silk dress, something to savour. It was scary, of course, but all the best things are. You just sit still and let it happen, and it comes good in the end. I feel like a lone explorer at the North Pole. Waiting for the Northern Lights, which will make everything clear. So I'm just fine here on my own with all the ghosts of the lost village till the end of summer. After all, they're invisible. I don't want this thing to chase me away. I have old Pierce O'Donnell a mile or two down the track, Kelly and the nice people in the village store, all the people in the lanes who stop and talk, and the countless Veseys, my mother's people, who always say to me, 'You're Johanna's girl.'

But at night, no one comes calling.

*   *   *

As I walk over the high track with my back to the sea, going for tea with Dec and Rosemary in the evening, there's a rain that's so fine it's like a faint sensation of pins and needles all over my face. It's more of a climb than a walk. Sometimes I stop, breathless, and look back down and feel the dizzying drop. It's hot, and the rain is refreshing. I sit down on a rock and consider my situation; I cannot shake this sense of unreality. My friends are very far away beyond that great water. Already the letters from home come strangely into my hands, and all those people, all the jangle of life, the rumble of the New York streets—all a dream. It seems to me now that I was fated to come all this

13

way to that particular moment when I put my hand down to see, and touched someone who had not been touched for—how long? Fifty years? A hundred? How can that not be momentous?

When I get to cousin Dec's farmhouse, a strong square building set back from a winding lane of high dripping fuchsia hedges that runs between Lissadoon and Boolavoe, I feel myself to be such an alien that at first I can hardly talk. I hardly know Dec and Rosemary, I've only met them once or twice since I arrived just a week ago, and so far they've been very good to me. The room is bright and many-patterned, the busy wallpaper on the walls, the tablecloth, the curtains, the pictures hanging from the picture rails, of wildly crashing turquoise seas and blue horses, and the soulful eyes of Jesus sadly watching in pride of place from above the cast-iron fireplace, a classical riot of columns and chalices and trailing laurels. A million small ornaments adorning every surface, and everything immaculately clean and very bright. Rosemary, a child-sized crone with a magnificent head of white and grey ringlets, bustles forward and kisses me heartily, then plonks me down on a fat red couch. 'Oh the child,' she says, 'look at her! Now sit you down and make yourself comfy. Will you have tea?' Her legs are little sticks in dark brown lisle stockings, her shiny black brogues as ugly and heavy as can be.

They speak so quietly, Dec and Rosemary, such rippling little snufflings of sound, I can scarcely hear them, and whenever I open my mouth I am too loud. And they're small. And me, well I'm a sizeable piece of a lass as my mother used to say, God knows where you get it from, Beatrice. My

14

mother wasn't tall, and Granma Lizzie was tiny. I stand six foot, near as damn it, in stockinged feet. My face is large and peculiar, my mouth too big, my eyes too small. My hair would not shame an Amazon, black and plentiful, my lovers have always enjoyed filling their hands with it. But I don't hunker over, I never hunker over, I stand up straight and tall. The air is thick with good smells of savoury food, and the turf fire, smoking gently in spite of the warmth of the evening, gives out a sweet aroma, a taste that settles in the back of the throat.

Rosemary seems slightly offended when I follow her into the kitchen and offer a hand making dinner, so I return to my chair beside the riotous fireplace. Cousin Dec, baby-faced and smiling, sits opposite me with his hands on his knees as she comes and goes. *He was eleven*, I hear my mother say, *and I was eight*. We had a house in Mineola. I'd come home from school and my mother would talk, her voice throaty because she chain-smoked. I see her standing by the window with a cigarette, looking out towards the turnpike. She was a hard woman, but Ireland she was sentimental about; a bone of a woman, tall, too thin and jerky, with shanks like a cat and all these memories of before she came to America, how Granma Lizzie took her to stay with her cousins in Lissadoon when she was a little girl living in England. 'Oh that boy!' she croaks. 'A golden Adonis! And I was only eight years old.' Strange she never went back. Maybe she was afraid it would disappoint her. And look at him now sitting there with his feet in brown tartan slippers on the fender, thick yellow fingers cupping a cigarette with a curious delicacy. His red face is

15

double-chinned, his gut hangs over his belt. His eyebrows are terribly heavy and whiter than the tufty hair on his scalp.

'Do you remember my mother, Uncle Dec?' I ask.

'Oh now, Beatrice,' he replies, clearing his throat and leaning forward, 'I do, of course, remember little Johanna, but you know it must be more than sixty years ago. I remember her getting out of the cart with her mammy. My father went for them to Kenmare. Of course that was a very big journey to make in those days.'

I have to smile. She remembered individual cats and dogs and cows on the farm, buttermilk licked from a spoon, and the big boy Dec who hung upside down from trees and could row a boat on the sea.

'She remembered you,' I say. 'She had such a crush on you, Uncle Dec. She never forgot it.'

He smiles a shy inturned smile. 'I'm sure I don't know why,' he whispers, reaching for the tea Rosemary has placed beside him. 'She was with her mammy most of the time.' He looks sideways into the fire, stirring his tea with a tiny silver spoon, then shakes his head as if at a great marvel. 'Your grandmother—now *she* was a fine-looking woman. A very fine-looking woman indeed.'

'Granma Lizzie was a beauty,' I say. 'She was a beauty into old age.'

She had good bones. I never saw a picture of her when she was young, but you could tell she must have been something. She was some great age, ninety-two, ninety-four I think, something like that when she died last year; all bent over and a mass of wrinkles and liver spots, but she still had big eyes

16

and thick white hair, and she'd kept her Irish accent till the end, very soft and sweet, with the sibilant t's.

Rosemary comes in with a dish of steaming floury potatoes. 'Sit up now,' she says, and we do. Pork chops with cabbage and potatoes, the gravy thick and red and salty. The first half of the meal we while away with small talk, then I weasel the conversation back to my house and who lived there in the past.

'It was your Uncle Pats had it,' says Rosemary to Dec. 'Pats had it,' she repeats, and turns her steady gaze on me. Her face is seamed and scored, there are white hairs growing out of her chin and her mouth is weathered and grown thin. There is something both fierce and calm in her face, and she speaks slowly, precisely. 'But this was a very long time ago, oh, fifty years or more; then his Martin had it; and after that, it fell empty, and then there were strangers living up there for a while.'

'I wonder how long ago it happened,' I say, 'when the child was put in the tree . . .' trying to make connections.

'Terrible thing.' She shakes her head. Dec, shaking his, agrees. 'Not in our time anyway.' She lays down her knife and fork and sits back, folding her arms across her cardigan. 'I'm sure it was not in our time.'

*   *   *

Dec drops me off at the foot of the track, turning the car and waiting to see me safely in with the lamp lit, honking the horn in a friendly way as he

17

drives off, headlights sweeping the hillside. The sound of the engine hums fainter and fainter as I bolt the door and let the place settle around me. Rain whispers on the corrugated roof. I take my lamp and go straight upstairs and light the candle beside the rickety iron bed with the ticking mattress Dec's sons hauled up for me by tractor and trailer. The candle burns bravely in a saucer standing on a large flat stone about two inches thick and as wide as a dinner plate. I found this stone under a thorny bush by the gate in the garden, and was taken by its perfect oval and the thin seam of something delicately green running straight across the middle like a ruled diameter. Then I found there was a whole beach of them if you struggled south from here along a meandering spine of rock that peaks suddenly on an unforgiving windy plateau. It's like the Grand Canyon or seeing the rings of Saturn through a telescope, one of those things that reduces you to nothing. God knows how they got it from there if that's where it came from, I think, letting down my hair. It falls heavily. There are caves there too, lonely caves far above the sea, and somewhere beyond, I know, an old famine grave. I'll take another walk over there tomorrow.

The room is pleasant by candlelight and dim lamplight. I get undressed and crawl naked into my sleeping bag, extinguish the lamp, put my arms behind my head and take stock of the day. The mountainside, running with rain, sings.

Something is different outside. She's gone from where she's been so long, and surely the mountain misses her. In stories, the disturbance of bones is often the prelude to a haunting. My mind's eye sees the light on the rock. But I'm not afraid, or if I am, I'm enjoying it. I have always loved a challenge. I find myself smiling, while the hairs on my nape prick up beneath the heavy weight of hair. I shouldn't be here now. I should have gone into town and checked into the hotel. I'd have been in bed, reading a book. There'd have been the sound of other people in other rooms, people downstairs in the bar. Instead I'm here all alone with the dark outside too big—oh God, *far* too big!—and that tree at my back, the tree where I put my hand down to see. The feeling grows that the finding of the bones in some way ties me to this child, for I have touched her, and she lived once and ran about and played and prattled, and some fateful line drew me to stand just there just then, to think of a certain poem and not heed its advice.

That's the trouble with me. I always put my hand down to see.

I fall asleep while the rain patters on the roof.

*   *   *

'God, it's awful clever how they know these things, isn't it?'

I am in the post office in Lissadoon talking to some distant relation of mine. Kate and I have been reading in the local paper that the bones may date back to the famine, because it was not a baby after all, but a child of three or four, which means she must have been very badly undernourished. In any case, her bones are now so old that no matter what happened, even murder, it was all too long ago, and they are to be given a decent Christian burial in Boolavoe churchyard.

19

'God, the poor wee soul,' Kate says. 'Wait, Beatrice, there's something I want to tell you.'

She buys a bag of Taytos for her little girl, a stout sage in a green coat, then takes me firmly by the arm as we leave. Her basket bangs between us. Arm in arm down the dead centre of the main street of Lissadoon we walk, the three of us graded by size, like steps, openly watched by three long-haired boys of about eighteen who loiter with cigarettes by the water fountain. Kate comes up to my shoulder.

'Are you OK up there?' she asks cheerfully. For a moment I think she's referring to my height. 'I'd hate it. All the empty houses.'

'I love it,' I say. 'The carpenter and builders have been, you know.'

Lissadoon is supernaturally quaint; reminds me of a little old town in a Wild West movie, except for the Coca-Cola sign hanging outside Burke's Butchers. A donkey stands patiently, rhythmically twitching one ear, between the shafts of a yellow cart.

'So you're staying put?'

'For the summer.'

'Brave girl.'

We stop by her car, parked next to a yellow wall where an alleyway leaks out into the street. The back window of the muddy car is rolled down and a coop of chickens croons on the back seat. My sort-of cousin adjusts a polka dot headscarf round her shiny brown bangs. 'Listen, Beatrice,' she says, 'I just thought of this. Why don't you go see old Tiernan in Boolavoe? He's a local history man, does little books about round about here, you know. If you're after the gen on your old place he's worth a look.'

'That's terrific, Kate,' I say, 'I'll do that.'

She lets go of my arm and shakes out her car keys. 'Bill Tiernan,' she says, 'on the back road. You ask anyone in Boolavoe. Want a lift?'

I'm about to accept when it crosses my mind that it's Thursday and the minibus from the shop will be leaving for Boolavoe in about half an hour.

'Thanks, Kate,' I say, 'but I think I'll hang around and wait for the bus.'

A dog with a black lion's mane lies panting outside Murphy's Bar across the road, with its Sweet Afton signs, and the signs for Cork Dry Gin and 7-Up; inside it's brown and dim, cosy with a crackling fire, empty apart from two old men in caps, one at either end of the bar like bookends, a fuggy blue mist between them from their pipes.

'Now, Beatrice Conrad, what can I get you?'

It still shocks me how everyone knows my name.

Mrs Murphy, I suppose, a tall dark spiky woman with a gentle air, gets up from the fire and steps briskly behind the bar. I get a Guinness, chat the obligatory chat, then go sit under the frosted window to read the letter I picked up at the post office. Betty writes everyone's still living in my apartment. The heat is atrocious. She has to meet Benedetti at Penn Station at four, they're going up to his dad's place at Ocean Grove for the weekend. Imagine stifling to death in Ocean Grove. Still, it'll be nice to get out of the city, she says. The club had a great weekend, she says twenty-eight turned up. Everyone's asking about me. They had a party afterwards back at someone's place and she can't remember how she got home.

The names of the people she mentions echo in

21

my skull. Real life, far away, not just the measure of an ocean but light years of space, stars and galaxies and black holes.

The old man on the right of the bar addresses something unintelligible to me in a high singsong voice, and Mrs Murphy laughs. 'Now, Pats!' she says softly, 'don't be scaring the poor girl!'

I look at the old man and see for the first time how very ancient he is. His white, stark, prickled jaw reminds me of a cactus.

'I'm sorry,' I say, 'I didn't catch that.'

'Twasn't worth catching,' smiles Mrs Murphy.

The silent old man on the left chuckles into his stout.

'I said, did ye hear the ghostie yet?' barks Pats, hale and hearty, sucking vigorously at his pipe.

'Oh, please,' I say, 'don't tell me about the ghostie,' and a second later, 'Yes, please, tell me about the ghostie,' thinking of Rosemary Vesey saying to Dec: your Uncle Pats had it. There could be a million Pats around here. There are many ancient men. This one's eyes are pale blue and wet, full of a kind of mad humour.

'It's just a little voice,' he says, and his own is high and reedy and cracked.

'Now, Pats!' says Mrs Murphy sharply.

'What does it say?' I ask. 'What kind of a voice is it?

'It says: *Is feidir liom thu a chloisteail. Teigh a chodladh.*'

There is a silence while we ponder this, broken only by the peaceful ticking of the clock and the crackle of the fire.

'And that means?' I ask.

A grin, absolutely toothless. *'I can hear you. You*

22

go to sleep.'

I'm cold.

'And this was after a couple or five of these, I'll betcha,' says Mrs Murphy lightly, grinning and tapping the side of the old man's pint glass.

He pulls a strange face, an ancient baby grimace. 'Not at all, Maureen,' he says, sitting up straight-backed, turning to look at me. His eyes have an intense, dancing quality. 'I was just up out of my bed in the morning, first light, blowing up the fire, it was winter it was, and this little voice said as clear as day: *Is feidir liom thu a chloisteail. Teigh a chodladh.'*

Mrs Murphy winks at me.

He lived there. He's Uncle Pats. He's Granma Lizzie's actual brother. I don't believe it.

'You don't want to take a blind bit of notice of anything he says,' she tells me, smoothing her skirt down as she walks back to her nook by the fire, 'he's an old eejit.'

I stand. 'Uncle Pats,' I say, 'I'm very pleased to meet you.' I shake his small, cold hand.

There's a bus to catch, and nothing more to be had from him that day.

*   *   *

Of course Bill Tiernan has heard about the bones. He is a dignified, handsome old man with a massive moustache like a white scrubbing brush wedged in under his nose. His hands are huge and rough and gesture constantly when he talks. And God, can he talk. Fortunately he's a raconteur, a teller of tales proliferating out of tales; unfortunately, he's the slowest person on the planet in speech and movement, a smiling, chuckling rambler of sidetracks that have nothing at all to do with the matter in hand—such as how to make perfect porridge, or the naming in sequence of every shop on the main street of Boolavoe, along with the names of all the people who'd had the shops before them. He tells me the history of a dozen families, none of them anything to do with me, charts the road to desolation of many a forgotten village, and finally, when I am mesmerised by the tight-stretched leather mask of his face and the persistent sonorous tolling of a bell from the Christian Brothers' schoolyard next door, he imparts to me that Kildarragh once consisted of fifteen dwellings, possibly more, most of them down on the more even ground closer to sea level. Looking at it now you'd never be able to count the houses. From the top of the hill it looks as if they've all been kicked around by a giant careless foot. My house, Darby's House, is away from and just out of sight of the others, higher, its plot of land running steeply up the side of the mountain.

Bill Tiernan consults his filing system, a bizarre arrangement consisting of about ten cardboard boxes with the tops cut off, all lined up around two of the walls of his plain square living room. Behind him, the window looks out over a row of bicycles tethered like ponies all along a wall. I envy him his slowness. Time must be different for him, I think. He acts as if he has aeons of it still before him. I never feel like that, I feel time running like sand through an hourglass. At last he shows me a document, a copy of a will. My house, he informs me, was left on her death in 1917 by Margaret

Vesey of Lissadoon, widow of James Vesey of Lissadoon, in the joint ownership of her two youngest children, Mr Michael Vesey of Manchester, England, and Mrs Eliza Jakey of the Bronx, New York.

Such a lot of Veseys.

'Eliza Jakey was my grandmother,' I say, and think of Granma Lizzie. 'Her maiden name was Vesey.'

Two days later I got a letter in a shaky hand: *Dear Miss Conrad, I have been checking my files again and discovered that the Vesey family first took over the lease of your house in Kildarragh in 1848. Before then it was in the hands of a Darby Quinn. The only Quinn I know of in these parts is Luke Quinn at the saw mill. Trusting this is of interest to you. I have the relevant documents if you are interested in seeing them. Yours Sincerely, William J. Tiernan.*

So I am going to see this Luke Quinn at the saw mill.

I ask directions at the garage in Boolavoe and the man there says sure thing, my love, you just keep on the Lissadoon road till it goes over the bridge where all the trees start, then go left instead of straight on home. 'You after timber?'

'I'm looking for Luke Quinn.'

'Luke,' the man says, and smiles. 'He'll be there or up at the house, you'll see.'

I turn to go.

'You'll know him,' he calls after me, 'Your man's got funny eyes.'

25

2

I hear the saw mill first, a harsh silver voice coming through the trees, then I smell it, sharp and sappy. The woods hang out great vertical mats of rhododendron, past their best but still gorgeous, great purple blooms all crumpled and faded like hungover showgirls after a heavy night. Just off the road the whole area gets wild and tangled, impenetrable, like the forest around Sleeping Beauty's castle. Everywhere, the shiny green swords of earlier bluebells are growing limp. The saw mill appears, a massive shed in a huge clearing, open at either end, surrounded on all sides by stacks and piles and towers of wood, cut, uncut, higgledy-piggledy. The ground underfoot is shaggy, like the bark of a redwood.

Two men, rough friendly types, sit smoking on a great log in front of an orange truck. I have to shout to be heard.

'Luke's up at the house,' one of the men shouts back, and points me the way further along the road. 'Can't miss it,' he yells, 'it's the only house you'll come to.'

The lane winds steeply upwards, high-sided, cascading with yellow and blood-red flowers, little bleeding hearts everywhere. At the side of the road there's a wide metal gate that clangs as I open it, setting a dog barking somewhere inside. A stone path leads through a rampant jungle of nettles and foxgloves and high-necked raggedy pink flowers to the solid grey house, high and beetle-browed, its front door standing open to a damp-smelling porch with a filthy doormat and shelves full of clutter. High overhead, the forest hangs long arms that wave infinitesimally. The sound of the mill is less alarming here.

I rap on the inner door.

The dog's barking grows louder and someone appears behind the cloudy glass, cursing at the dog and pushing it back, then the door opens and an unearthly boy in a powder-blue sweater looks out, saying nothing.

'Hello,' I say, startled, 'I'm looking for Luke Quinn.'

His eyes are too far apart in his head. The irises are a subtle dove-grey and the pupils are strange, elongated. They are rather beautiful but scare me in an immediate physical way so that I feel a pulse begin to throb in my throat. Of course you never show it when a face makes your heart jump.

'I'm Luke Quinn,' he says, staring.

The dog, a Jack Russell, yaps round his feet and he kicks out automatically.

'Geddown!' he snarls, flickering his goat eyes. His face looks six years old but he's nearly up to my shoulder, or he would be if he wasn't all hunched up. Something changes in his face when he curls his cupid's bow lip at the dog, a wrinkling of the sides of his nose, a flash of baboon-like savagery, fascinatingly ugly and gone in a second.

'Beatrice Conrad.' I hold out my hand. He looks down at it, as if no one ever shook him by the hand before, hesitates for an awkward moment then takes it. We shake. 'I'm staying up at Kildarragh, near Lissadoon. I don't know if you heard about the bones that were found?'

'The bones,' he says, coughing. He takes his hand

back and looks at it intently for a second as if it just appeared on the end of his arm. A little jolt of déjà vu kicks in from somewhere and ticks alongside.

'It was in the newspaper.'

'Hm,' he says, folding his arms again, sticking both hands under his armpits and staring. All seen before. His eyes produce a feeling akin to panic so I have to keep looking away. Come now, I scold myself like Alice, don't forget your manners.

'Well,' I press on, 'I found out that a man by the name of Darby Quinn used to own my house a long time ago, and I wondered if there might be a connection with your family? I'm trying to find out about the house, you see.'

'Why?' he asks.

What a funny thing to ask.

'Luke,' comes a deep voice from inside the house, breaking the déjà vu, which has been oddly exhilarating, although I'm relieved it's gone, 'Who are you talking to?'

'It's a woman, Ma!' he calls.

She comes on two canes and pushes him aside with one of them. 'What do you want?' she says rudely, greying hair severely scraped back from a faded face.

'I'm researching the history of my house,' I say, 'and there's a Quinn connection. There was a man named Darby Quinn living there till 1848. I just wondered.'

'Well, I don't know,' she says anxiously, 'I've never heard of that.'

The boy fidgets manically behind her, looking down and grinning wildly to himself.

'Could we talk for a few minutes?' I ask as nicely as I can.

She draws in a long breath through her large hooked nose, licks her lips and sighs before saying unwillingly, 'Come on in then.'

The boy makes tea while she and I sit down by the range. The dog mooches up wanting to be petted. Mrs Quinn, a thin stick of a woman with baggy brown skin, stashes her canes, seizes the dog and holds it before her on her lap like a shield.

'What a lovely house this is!' I say.

It is, or could be if it wasn't for the decor. The pictures on the pink floral wallpaper are of holy scenes and gruesome sad clowns with wistful tear-filled eyes. The drapes are startlingly op art, full of strident brown and yellow squares and circles. Everything's dusty. Trees crowd the windows, looking in. Turning my head I can see through an open door: Luke Quinn fiddling about with cups and saucers in a dingy kitchen, fingers effete, shoulders round and frail under the powder-blue sweater a size too small. I look around. 'What a lot of books you've got!' The wall going upstairs is entirely covered with a hotch-potch of home-made shelves crammed with books.

Her bony fingers drum on the dog's head. 'My late husband's,' she says. She has a man's voice.

Luke Quinn drops a spoon in the kitchen.

'And you are . . . .?'

'Oh, I'm sorry, I haven't introduced myself. My name's Beatrice Conrad. And you are Mrs Quinn?'

'I am.'

'My grandmother left me a house in Kildarragh,' I say, 'and I'm staying there for the summer. It needs a lot of work.'

'Sure, you're mad,' she says.

I laugh. 'Probably.'

She doesn't laugh. She looks as if she never laughs.

Luke emerges from the kitchen with a tray, his strange eyes cast down, elbows held stiffly out to the sides. He could be anything between twenty and thirty, I've no idea. He sets the tray down on the range next to his mother and retreats to perch on a stool by the window and looks at me with open, childlike rudeness. Both of them stare, waiting for me to speak.

'Well,' I say, 'I found some old bones in a tree at the back of my house.'

'I heard about that,' she says, pouring the tea.

'I'm just interested in the history of the place. Bill Tiernan on the back road told me it was owned by someone called Darby Quinn till 1847, as I mentioned earlier. You don't think it could have been your husband's family, do you?'

'I never heard of any Quinns up at Kildarragh,' she says, handing me a cup and saucer. She doesn't look interested.

'Oh, well!' I sip my tea. 'It might have been different Quinns.'

She sits forward. 'Biscuits, Luke,' she says.

All this time I've been aware of him from the corner of my eye, watching me.

'They think the bones are from then,' I say, kind of performing. 'It was the famine time, wasn't it?'

She twitches her mouth. 'Would have been.'

'It's just my curiosity,' I say, shrugging and wondering suddenly why I am here. I laugh at myself silently. 'Sorry, I guess I had some idea that it would all just fall into place like in a book, and I'd come here and you'd have some marvellous old family story to tell that would solve the mystery of

30

who's the poor baby in the tree.'

'Biscuits, Luke.'

Luke jerks to his feet and goes into the kitchen, returns with a caddy he hands to his ma like a good boy.

'On a plate,' she says.

'Oh that's OK.' I smile at him.

'On a plate,' she insists.

Poor boy, off he droops.

'The Quinns are mostly round Eskean or around here,' she says, sucking her tea, 'I never heard of any up at Kildarragh.'

'Oh, well. It was worth a try.' I sip. 'Sorry if I've been a nuisance. This is nice tea, Luke. Thank you.'

He smiles shyly, bringing biscuits on a small flowered plate. 'Judith would know,' he says, glancing quickly at his mother before retreating once more to his perch by the window and pulling a cigarette pack from a pocket.

'What?' She turns her head, irritated.

'Judith would know.'

'Judith's senile,' Ma says.

'She's not senile, Ma.' He puts a cigarette in his mouth then takes it out, jumps up awkwardly and jerks across the room, remembering his manners. 'Would you like one?' he asks me.

'Who's Judith?' I accept.

'My auntie,' he says, back on the stool, lighting his own cigarette but forgetting about mine.

'She's not your auntie,' Ma says.

'My dad's auntie,' he says.

'She's senile.'

'You would say that,' he replies gently, turning his beautiful misshapen eyes full on me. 'She's in

31

the Cloverhill Home,' he says. 'You'll have seen their minivan. And she isn't senile, Ma,' he turns to her, 'no more of that.' But he keeps his voice soft.

'Your father's aunt,' I say. 'Is she also a Quinn?'

'Was,' Ma answers for him. 'She married a Rochford.'

'Do you think she'd talk to me?' I still address him. 'Would she mind, do you think?'

'You won't get sense out of Judith,' Ma replies quickly, slamming her cup down in the saucer, 'she's in her dotage.'

He makes a move as if to speak but subsides immediately, thinking better of it.

'I'd love to talk to Judith,' I say. 'It's amazing what old people can remember.'

She looks scornful.

'Ma,' Luke says, crossing one leg over the other and twisting his arms together in a painfully awkward knot, 'What was Aunt Judith's daddy called?'

'How would I know?' Ma turns her malicious old face towards him. 'Give her that William Tiernan thing if it's history she's after. Maybe that'll do her.'

He blushes at her lack of manners, unwinding himself; going to the stairs, reaches up to the top shelf for a book.

'Bill Tiernan's the man who gave me all the information,' I say, but no one replies and the silence is awkward. It's time to go.

'Well, thank you so much for tea,' I say, getting up, 'I hope I haven't been too much trouble.'

She feeds a sugary biscuit to the dog, ignoring me.

'Here.' Luke hands me a thin, very battered book

32

and steps back quickly. 'Local history.'

Boolavoe and Beyond by William Tiernan. The line drawing on the cover is of Lissadoon Bay, with the Skelligs in the far distance.

'Thanks so much. Mind if I keep it a little while?'

He looks at Ma.

'She can have it as far as I'm concerned,' she says without looking round, 'I never look in it anyway.'

I like behaving extra nice and sunny to rude people, it drives them mad. 'Thank you so much,' I say graciously, 'I'll let you know if I find out anything.' And I smile at Luke, who grins and looks away. He walks after me into the porch. 'If you're in town next fair day and I chance on you,' he says under his breath, 'I could take you to see my Aunt Judith if you like.'

The wood round the window frames is rotting. Slug trails glisten on the threshold. I open the door on the sound of the mill.

'I'll keep an eye open for you,' I say. When I look round, he's gone.

*   *   *

Boolavoe on Fair Day. Weavergate, the main street, is blocked with sheep. I stroll among their soft brown eyes to the big square on the southern edge of town, packed with stalls and teeming with people: inscrutable farmers, women in headscarves, scruffy little kids in rubber boots. Country music plays around the stalls. There are cattle with wild, rolling eyes and dripping pink noses, muddy sheepdogs trotting through dirty puddles rutted with cart tracks. My eyes are peeled for the funny eyes. He's been on my mind: that

33

boyman, a faun of the woods, a Puck, living in the tangled forest with the Old Hag of Beare. As well as him, I'm looking out for Uncle Pats, who heard the ghostly voice. I meet a lot of other Veseys but not him, and finally some other old one tells me Pats has been having trouble with his chest and has gone off to stay with his daughter in Limerick. No one seems to know when he'll be back, and I guess at his age it could well be never.

Old Pierce O'Donnell is going into Finn's Bar on the corner of the square, so I figure I might as well follow him in; and of course who's sitting there but Luke Quinn himself, leaning on the bar and looking straight ahead through a fuggy cloud, obviously drunk. Finn's is packed, the air boils with smoke, thick beams of light stream in through the clear panes like heaven piercing the cloak of hell. A fog lies over the gold-leafed windows and mirrors. Layer upon layer, the voices go hubble-bubble, hubble-bubble as I squeeze up to the bar and order a Guinness. Luke sees me but pretends not to, covering one side of his face with a hand.

'Luke!' I call loudly.

The poor creature blanches.

I move around to his side of the bar and edge up beside him.

'Hello, Luke.'

He nods.

'So, did you mean it?' I say. 'About taking me to see Aunt Judith?'

He speaks but his voice is too quiet for the babble. I lean in. His collar's frayed but he's clean, smells of aftershave.

'Yes,' he says, too loud.

'Is she expecting me?'

He shakes his head. 'You could tell her,' he says, 'but she wouldn't remember.'

'The other day,' I ask him, 'did I offend your mother in some way?'

That makes him smirk. 'Oh, no. She's always like that.'

'Well, she was good enough to give me Bill Tiernan's book. I've been reading it but there's nothing at all in it about Kildarragh. Interesting though.' I drink. 'Your father had a lot of books,' I say. 'Have you read all those books?'

'Some.' Luke's face is flushed. He's not making eye contact at all, reminds me of a big hunting dog that belonged to a friend of mine. This dog would sit at the other end of the couch and take sly little glances at me, but whenever I looked at him he'd turn his head away, bashful. A terror in the field but shy as a maiden in the house.

'How old are you, Luke?'

His eyes dart quickly towards me then away. The colour, like you dipped your brush in violet and just touched it to the white, the merest tinge, then grey again. 'Twenty-five,' he says.

'Ah, a man then,' I say. I am twelve years older than him.

He's finished his drink and is folding his hands neurotically up into his armpits.

'So is it just you and your ma up at the house?' I ask. 'Just the two of you?'

'It is now.'

I think: Psycho, and in the space between draining my glass and setting it down on the bar, understand his unease. The whole place is watching us, including old Pierce O'Donnell who's taken up a position by my left elbow; and I am the only woman in here, larger than life with my hair all over the place. I feel it growing, coiling out from my head into the mists of the bar, climbing up the walls like a creeper. I am embarrassing him horribly.

'Shall we go, Luke?' I say quietly. 'Shall we go and see Aunt Judith?'

He looks at me, his weird wide eyes from the gloom. 'OK.' He stands and pushes through the crowd to the door. Everyone has a nod or a word for him, and for me as I follow after, towering over him. I wish I was in a big city, anonymous. We walk along through the sheep pens, past the bars and shops. The raw beast smell is in the air. He lopes along in a high-collared grey jacket and corduroy trousers, a consistent three feet away from me, out of town, up the lane.

Poor awkward creature. I suppose he never thought I'd go in there; I suppose he was hiding, thinking he was safe.

'It's not far,' he says.

We walk along without speaking, striding out at a good pace. After ten minutes we come to a sign in the beech foliage: Cloverhill Retirement Home, tall gates standing open, a curving drive leading up through bushes.

'What was it like finding the bones?' he asks suddenly.

The house where the old folk live is large and red and square, surrounded by a big lawn on three sides, with trees and a few benches in the shade. A long glass extension has been made into a conservatory, and the old folk can be seen scattered all around it in various stages of catatonia.

'I've thought about that. And I can't find a simple answer for how it made me feel. I just put my hand down and there was this little skull. I can't get it out of my mind that she was a real child once.'

There is a long pause.

'That must have been a shock for you,' Luke says.

'You can't imagine.'

The Cloverhill Retirement Home is part hospital. We pass the reception room and walk straight through the hall. Everyone knows Luke, all the attendants and all the old people who are capable of noticing anything at all. A nurse leads us past open wards full of old women in ancient beds of pale institution-green bars, speckled dark where the paint's flaked off. Boxes of Kleenex spit out their contents. Bottles of Lucozade make rings on narrow bedside cabinets. Beyond this is a corridor with squeaky linoleum, then a very large rusty twilit interior with long curtained windows at one end and a wide-screen TV at the centre front. Ancient men and women sit immovably in small groups of easy chairs, and a woozy somnolence weighs down the air.

'Now, Judith,' the nurse is saying loudly, 'there's someone to see you, darlin'.'

We have stopped before a harpie, a death's-head. Her great age inspires dread and awe. Her tiny size beggars belief. Her legs stick straight out in front of her like a child's.

'My good boy,' she says fondly, putting up her monkey paws to Luke. The crisp intelligence in her voice shocks me. I'd been getting ready for gaga. Ashamed, I wait to be introduced.

'Howya, Aunt Judith.' Luke stoops to kiss the thick, cracked leather of her cheek. She smiles alarmingly, showing a full set of horsey yellow teeth.

'This is Beatrice, Aunt Judith,' he says. 'Aunt Judith, Beatrice is over from America on a visit and I've brought her to see you.'

'How are the girls?' she asks me, seizing my hand and holding onto it.

'It's not Briege,' he tells her, 'It's Beatrice, not Briege.'

'How are the girls?' she repeats, still taking me for whoever Briege is.

We sit one on either side of her. 'They're absolutely fine,' I assure her.

'And the little one?'

'Fine, too.'

'My husband was a schoolteacher, you know,' she says, 'and a very good one.'

'Was he?'

'You've grown your hair.'

'That's right. How did I have it before?'

'Up on top,' she says, wiggling her finger about over her head, then turns to Luke and says crisply, 'How's your ma? Batty as ever?' She smiles and her lip folds like a leaf.

He gives a little snort, biting his nails.

'Do I know you?' she asks me.

'I'm Beatrice. I wondered if you could tell me anything about my house at Kildarragh.'

'She pretends to be ill, you know,' she says. 'Mind you, I'm glad poor Luke has my husband's books to look at. We brought him up as a reader, you know.'

'Luke?'

'Of course not.'

'She's talking about my dad,' Luke says.

Her lids of mottled lilac droop and flicker.

Luke takes out his cigarettes. 'She's falling asleep,' he says.

But she opens her eyes and looks right at me. 'My brother Tom, you know,' she says, 'now he never read a book in his life. He drowned, you know. Went over the cliff at Kildarragh.'

'At Kildarragh?'

'Was it at Kildarragh?' Luke asks, 'I never knew that.'

'Now he was a lovely boy.'

'My grandfather,' Luke tells me.

'Girls all right?' she asks me.

'Fine.'

'Oh, that's good. And the little one?'

'The little one's fine too.'

'Aunt Judith,' Luke says, 'Beatrice is staying up at Kildarragh.'

'Who's Beatrice?'

'This is Beatrice.'

'My grandmother came from here,' I tell her. 'Lizzie Vesey. Vesey was her maiden name.'

Something happens in her face. She is looking at me but she is looking in at herself, wheels turning, cranking.

'We don't like the Veseys,' she frowns.

'I'm Johanna's girl,' I say. That always seems to place me, but I am unprepared for the remarkable effect it has on her. She wriggles, thrusts her turtle neck forward, peering at me as if she would lean toward me in her chair, though being so frail she cannot.

'Little Johanna,' she says in a tone of wonder and

39

sadness, 'little Johanna.' Then: 'Is she happy?'

'Did you know her?' I say, amazed.

'Know who, dear?'

'My mother.'

She frowns. 'Well, I don't know, dear,' she says, 'what was your mother's name?'

'Johanna. And my granma was Lizzie Vesey.'

She sucks her teeth noisily. 'She's one of ours,' she murmurs.

'Aunt Judith,' Luke says. 'Did you know something odd was found over in Kildarragh? In a tree at Beatrice's house. Aunt Judith, do you know if any Quinns ever lived at Kildarragh?'

She looks perplexed.

'You don't have to tell her about the bones,' I whisper, but she picks up the word, God knows, her ears are sharper than her wits.

'What bones?'

It seems wrong to talk about death to someone so close to it, but Luke puts it straight: 'There's been some bones found, Aunt Judith,' he says, 'in a tree near Beatrice's house. The bones of a little girl, they think it is.'

'I knew your granma,' Judith says. 'Lizzy Vesey. Oh yes, she was a Vesey, you see. We didn't have anything to do with those ones.'

'Why not?' asks Luke.

Her head tips over and she starts to snore softly. We sit for several minutes.

'I guess that's it for today,' I say, but she revives and looks at Luke. 'They used to play in that tree,' she says.

'Who did?'

'My daddy did.'

Her eyes droop.

'My tree,' I whisper, a kick of excitement inside. Her father played in my bone tree. Her brother Tom drowned in Kildarragh.

'Is she happy?' she snaps suddenly, opening her eyes.

'She's very happy,' Luke assures her.

'Aunt Judith,' I say, 'Johanna did OK. She went to live in America with her mother and father and sisters. She got married and had a nice place to live and a lot of friends, and she had me and my brother.' I could add that Johanna died nine years ago in Manhatten State Hospital from secondary pneumonia after a very bad bout of influenza, but I don't. I feel oddly displaced, here in this overheated room full of people as gnarled and withered as ancient trees, people grown back to babyhood, people with proud necks stuck high out of their crocheted shells, reeking softly of curdling bodies. No one knows me at all, I could be anyone, I could be this Briege she takes me for. I could be anyone I wanted.

'He gave her the one chair,' she says. 'Our Tom. A lovely boy. He made it. He was good like that, that's where *you* get it from.' She places her trembling leaf of a hand on Luke's knee.

'Aunt Judith,' I say gently, 'how do you know my mother and my grandmother?'

'Are you a Vesey?' she asks me, putting up her tiny paws to get a grip on the yellow ribbons threaded round the neckline of the odd garment she is wearing, something like an overgrown baby shawl, 'We Quinns never had nothing to do with those ones.'

41

Luke is peculiarly persistent and persistently shy.

He appears early one evening on a rock above my house, and thereafter every night. He sits on the rock until I take notice of him and wave; then, surprisingly nimble-footed and graceful on the mountainside, down he comes through the old potato ridges and sits by my fireside, where he blushes furiously and chews his nails. Poor baby. Tying himself in knots. He hardly speaks, but listens to me ramble; in a way it's like talking to myself. I try to make sense of whatever it is that's emerging, coming through static, appearing like the pattern on wallpaper persisting through several coats of paint, like the marks of the famine coming through the landscape.

He came this evening while I was lounging in the deck-chair in the yard I'm making out back, trying to write a letter home. I'd written two or three sentences in half an hour. The idea was to clear my head by getting something down on paper but all I ended up doing was gazing at the horizon, chewing the pen and drifting. This place induces a whole host of sensations, peculiar and disconcerting, that I used to but no longer have. Three or four times in the past two weeks I've been nudged by déjà vu. I used to get stuff like that when I was a child and in my teens, but I can't even remember the last time it happened. I thought they'd gone with youth. Why've they come back? Because this is like another youth in a way, everything quite new?

Luke sits in front of my bone tree. His thin neck

sticks out from his too-big collar; his Adam's apple lurches up and down when he swallows.

'Of course, to some extent,' I say, 'all this stuff about my mother and grandmother has taken my mind off that poor child in the tree. I suppose I feel that story's so far back I could never reach it now. But there's a link between the Veseys and the Quinns. And this house is the link.'

Something about the Veseys in the scrambled brain of that ancient woman, something she holds against poor old Granma Lizzie; and that I *can* reach, I think, given time.

Luke coughs asthmatically. 'Aunt Judith gets things wrong,' he says.

'It must have been sixty years ago when she used to know my mother and Granma Lizzie, because the one time in her life my mother was here was when she was eight years old and she was smitten with Dec. Now, let's see. How old is your Aunt Judith?'

'Old,' he shrugs.

'Just trying to get my bearings,' I say. I look around. I went to town and brought packets of seeds: nasturtiums and lovage, which I've sown close to the cottage. I don't know what'll grow this high up and so close to the sea. In the ditch round the side I found a big iron cauldron with a handle and three short legs, wonderful old thing, and now it sits by the door, planted up with some periwinkles Rosemary gave me. Maybe it was Pats' old cooking pot. Maybe it hung on a chain over the fire. Maybe it's older than that, maybe the Quinns boiled their potatoes in it before the famine.

'What do you think of my garden?' I ask him.

'It's very nice,' Luke says politely, 'what are you

43

going to do with the tree?'

'Cover it with flowers,' I say. 'What else?'

He smiles, twisting his fingers together and lapsing into silence.

'So, what do you think? Are you making sense of it? Judith's ramblings?'

'Only that her father came from Kildarragh.'

'He played in my tree. Her brother Tom drowned somewhere near here. Your grandfather.'

He gets up and walks over to the tree, stands with his long hand resting on its bark, looking up at the mountain's rising levels. His forehead is extremely pale and thin-skinned, blue-veined. I don't know why he keeps coming up here. If he was older I'd think he was after me, but I don't think it's that. Maybe it's the place pulling him up here, the place where his—what?—great-grandfather played in the tree? I need to write it down. Let's see: Luke's father was brought up by the childless Aunt Judith and her schoolteacher husband after his own father drowned, so . . .

'We should make you a family tree.' I say to Luke, and he laughs as if I've made a very funny joke.

'I found all kinds of things while I was digging the ground.' I rise and head inside. 'Come and see.'

On the window sill I've placed a rusty spoon, a long green glass earring, some old accounts carefully written in a neat sloping hand, and a small bottle clogged full of what looks like human hair.

'I feel like an archaeologist with one of those little brushes they use,' I say, 'delicately exposing some buried artefact.'

He picks up the bottle. 'This is a pishogue,' he

says.

'A what?'

'A spell.'

'A spell? How fantastic. How does it work?'

'I wouldn't know. I don't believe in all that.'

'Me neither. Still, it's a rare thing, isn't it?' I walk over and stand next to him and he sways disconcertingly towards me then jerks back in a peculiar way.

'What should I do with it?' I say.

'Leave it where it was.'

I am at work on two excavations: one for a lost, possibly even murdered child, through layers and layers of silted time and memory; the other excavation, completely separate and all in my mind, down into Luke Quinn. I'm getting used to him. What's odd about his eyes is not the colour or the indigo rims, nor the strange wide placing in his head; what's odd is their mutability, and the speed with which they change. Sometimes they're blank marble, sometimes beast intense.

We go outside and look down the sloping track to where the old ruins of Kildarragh slumber above the sea.

'Imagine all the people moving around down there,' he says, quite unprompted, 'all the people who ever lived here.'

A bird skims over the Atlantic Ocean.

We lapse into silence and I take the cigarette he offers.

*   *   *

When he's gone, just before dark, I bury the pishogue where I found it, then go inside, light the

45

tilly lamp and sit down by the fire to finish my letter. Still, I keep drifting. I think of New York, all the poets and posers and phoneys. *Say hello to everyone for me*, I write, then get a sudden flash of Granma Lizzie in those last years when she was living with my aunt, tiny, with hunched shoulders and big wide watery eyes, straight white hair, lively, aged face. She kept cats and her smoker's voice was gravelly, deep and from the chest, but quiet. She was a cotton throstle-spinner in Salford when she gave birth to my mother. A cotton throstle spinner—I love the sound of that. She never talked about Ireland, though I knew she'd grown up there. My mother was always putting her down, hiding her away whenever any of her la-di-da friends were going to be around.

The people are nice to me here because they know me, I write, *I am Johanna's girl, of the Veseys.* There's a Vesey Street in New York, in the Financial District. That's nice, they'd like that, my new Vesey kin. They like to hear of the ones that made good over there. So when they ask about my mother I tell them yes, Johanna did well, and she did too. She was a clever girl, she married my dad and had a beautiful house and made a garden that was her pride and joy, probably the greatest achievement of her life. People were paying to see that garden by 1958. All that I tell them, but I leave out any bad bits because they don't want any of that, they want the eight-year-old she was when she last appeared in these parts, hanging onto the hand of her handsome mammy.

'Which one are you?' Aunt Judith asks, frowning.

In the few weeks I've known her, the texture of her face has yellowed and thickened everywhere except the sharp bridge of her nose, where the skin is so thin it seems the bone must break through at any moment.

'I'm Beatrice.'

She's not placing me. I've come alone today.

'Johanna's girl,' I say.

'You're too big.'

I laugh. 'I know.'

'I remember Lizzie Vesey,' she says. 'I saw her that time with the little girl. And God forgive me for what I said to her, for the poor child was upset and jumped up and put her arms around her mammy's neck.'

'What was she upset about, Aunt Judith?'

'I always blamed her, you know,' she says, 'because she got him drinking. He was a lovely boy, Tom, a lovely sweet creature and he wouldn't have hurt a fly, but he was downright stupid about *her*. And she was up and off without a word to him after all she put him through, and it was after that that he went wrong.'

I sweat in the heat of the hushed conservatory.

'She never dared show her face till he was dead,' she says.

'Who, Aunt Judith?'

'Which one are you? Briege?'

Then—

*'Bold as brass she says to me—this is my little girl, Judith. This is my Johanna. And I look down and see this child she's got with her, and the child's got just our Tom's face—*just *his face—and, and I says to her, I says—'*

And Aunt Judith says very coldly and distinctly, looking into my eyes:

'You killed him, you whore. You killed my brother sure as if you stuck the knife in his heart, you brazen bitch.'

'Well, she bursts into tears. And little Johanna bursts into tears too, and she stands up on her tiptoes and gives her mother a big big hug. And that was wrong of me—very wrong—for it upset the child.'

And if that's true—

*   *   *

Straight from there I went to the saw mill.

Luke's working in the big shed with the men but he comes out when he sees me.

'You're my cousin,' I say.

He looks worried. 'What?'

'You're my cousin. Well, sort of. Second cousin, half cousin, something like that.'

'I don't understand what you mean.'

Aunt Judith believes my granma, Lizzie Vesey, and her brother Tom Quinn were sweet on each other, and that my mother was their lovechild. I tell him but he says nothing. I write him a family tree on the back of an envelope.

'Aren't you pleased?' I say, 'don't you want to

welcome me into the family?'

He laughs uncertainly, scratches his head in a buffoonish way and laughs again. 'That's really funny,' he says.

'Shall I tell your ma?'

'Sooner you than me.' He starts backing away. 'I have to go back to work.'

'Won't she like it?'

'She likes things to stay the same,' he says, 'she doesn't like things to change.'

'Will I see you later? Want to talk about all this?'

'Maybe.' He hovers. 'Maybe.'

'Aren't you impressed at all, Luke? Not at all?'

He just grins, inneffable.

On Weavergate, Uncle Dec pulls up alongside me at the kerb and offers me a lift. I start babbling away about my findings: Tom Quinn and Granma Lizzie, and what does he think? Thank God for Dec and good sense. 'I have absolutely no idea,' he says like a rock, 'it's all long before my time. I recall seeing your granma that one time when I was only a boy. She was a beautiful woman.' He drives stolidly. 'Tom Quinn—I have no idea—no idea at all.'

I ask him to drop me in Lissadoon. I'll walk from here, I need to think. The churchyard calls me. Wandering among the graves, I find a whole host of Veseys but no Quinns. The older stones are all weathered and lichened, their letters here and there fading to tantalising ripplings on the stones. The stately building with its clocktower and cross looms like a sphynx above me. A railed path runs back up the hill to the front of the church. I walk slowly, my head spinning with Veseys. They are a liability, these Veseys, this long trail winding

49

behind me. They're too much to take. I get mixed up with all the greats and great-greats and great-great-greats. They could all go lie still if they hadn't left me their cabin with the child in the tree. I never asked for that. I should just go back home and forget all about them.

*   *   *

I'd thought Luke Quinn would come and talk to me. Surely he's curious. First I thought I must have missed him. Surely he must have wanted to know?

A day or two go by, and I tidy the place, change the flowers, bring down the seamed stone from upstairs and place it on the window sill, and on top of it a small glass jar containing two yellow flag irises. What a weight that stone is. Everything's clean and fresh. I've brought in driftwood from the shore, polished smooth and white by the tides. The turves are neatly stacked by the fire, an Indian cloth with a swirling purple and green design is thrown over the table. I sit quietly, taking stock, reading Bill Tiernan's book, waiting for Luke Quinn to come, but he doesn't. I think about getting some of my friends over here maybe. I imagine us sitting outside with a bottle of red wine, lighting cigarettes and joints to keep the midges away.

The builders come in September. I'll be home by then. The floor needs fixing, the roof mending, new doors, new windows. A pump to bring the water into the house. A flush toilet, septic tank. Electricity's more of a problem but not impossible. What do I *do* with this house now it's mine?

I go over the options again: sell it, rent it, live in

it, leave it to the rain.

Live in it. Stay. Collect shells. The sand on the strand is shells, a million tons of mother-of-pearl. There's worse things to do with your life.

Leave it to the rain. To the mist and the wind and the bright sun and salt air, all the soft days and starry nights. Let it sink into the lap of the mountain. Quilty's Door.

The first visitor I do get, on the third day, is Pats Vesey. I'm in the front garden trimming the grass between the stones on the path when I look up and see a tall thin old man in a flat cap and baggy grey clothes approaching from below at a remarkable pace, the sea at his back. Before he reaches the gate I recognise him. He's taller than I'd imagined. In Murphy's Bar I'd never have credited him with being able to move so fast. I stand up and go to meet him.

'Beatrice Conrad,' he says, a spiky man coming through the gate, 'put the kettle on.'

'So you're back from Limerick?' I say. 'How are you?'

'Fair.'

'Back for good?'

He laughs. 'Who knows?' His toothless mouth is an absolute cavern. 'I hear you've been looking for me.' His voice a cracked reed.

'That's right. I want to pick your brain, Uncle Pats.'

He seems incurious about his old house. Once inside, he only glances about once, quickly. His eyes are gummy and shrunken, but somewhere in their narrow slits a slightly crazy humour dances.

'Tea, Uncle Pats? What can I offer you? I have some cake. Would you like some cake?'

51

I keep, for just such occasions as this, Battenberg cake and Dundee cake from the shop in Lissadoon. I feel deeply honoured to have old Pats sitting by my fireside in my one good chair, ('he gave her the one good chair,' I remember Aunt Judith saying) filling up his pipe while I slice the cake nicely and let the tea brew. His back is very straight.

'What do you think of your old place?' I say.

He waves a hand. 'Ah, she's sound enough still.'

'I've got the builders coming in in September. It's a lovely old house and it's so beautiful up here. I don't know what to do. What do you think I should do with it, Uncle Pats? I don't want to sell it. I couldn't live here all the time but I'd like to be able to keep coming back. Do you think I'd find a tenant for a place like this?'

'Not these days.'

'You don't think so?'

He grins, looks sideways. 'Who'd want to live in this lonely old hole?'

'You did.'

He lights his pipe with a reedy sucking. 'That's right, but I wouldn't live here now.'

'Granma Lizzie was your sister,' I say. 'What was she like when she was young?'

He smiles. How old is this man? He has a long gnarled jaw, peppered white with stubble. Older than Judith, older than Granma Lizzie; I can't get my mind back to where he started. Look at him, puffing away there on that black tobacco, no wonder he has a bad chest. The air all around us reeks with its strength. I can taste it in my chest, black tobacco, turf, seaweed, tea made with spring water.

'Lovely,' he says, 'she was lovely.'

52

After a while, he lays down the pipe and dips his slice of Battenberg in his tea. 'That stone,' he says, pointing to the window sill, 'Did you find that down by the gate?'

'Yes. Under a bush.'

'Our old dog lay under that.'

'Really?'

'Died of old age,' he says. 'Nice dog.'

'What was he called?'

He thinks, his face cracking up into that odd grimace I remember from before. Baby to baby he's gone, full circle. The effort of remembering is too much.

'It doesn't matter, Uncle Pats.'

'Oh Jesus, what was that dog called? What was that dog called?'

'The Quinns used to live here, didn't they?' I say, and he chews his tongue in an avid, slightly obscene way.

'Long before my time,' he says.

'I've been talking to an old lady in the Cloverhill Home. She says she used to know Granma Lizzie.'

He doesn't respond to this.

'That old dog,' he says, 'it'll drive me mad now.'

'It'll come to you,' I say, 'in the middle of the night. That's what happens. Did you know Tom Quinn?'

An ancient person puts so much energy into the act of thinking. It becomes a heroic deed, a retrieval.

'Tom Quinn,' he says eventually. 'I remember Tom Quinn.'

'What was he like?'

Pursed lips and puckered brow. 'Decent enough,' he says.

'Did he know my grandmother?'

I have to tread carefully. After all, it's his sister I'm talking about.

'Ah, I suppose. Everyone knew everyone else. Did your granma not tell you?'

I shake my head.

'She didn't talk about us?'

I make a vague, negative gesture. 'This old lady in the Cloverhill Home,' I say, 'She says Tom Quinn was her brother. She says he died falling over a cliff.'

He thinks again, consciously, for two whole minutes, then says: 'He brought it up from the stone strand.'

'He did what?'

'He brought that stone up here from the stone strand.'

'Where the caves are?'

'Near there.'

'Tom Quinn brought that stone up here?'

Pats puts down his mug and reaches for his pipe. He nods, relighting, stands up. I wish he'd stay and talk a little more.

'Are you walking back, Uncle Pats? Will you get there before dark?'

'No trouble, Beatrice,' he says with his gaping smile, 'I've walked that road many a night.'

I go down the track with him as far as the lane. The sun's turning red, going down west, towards America.

'Will I see you in Murphy's bar?' I ask him.

'Sometimes I'm there' he says.

'I've heard no ghostly voices,' I say.

'*Is feidir liom thu a chloisteail.*' He smiles, '*Teigh a chodladh.*'

'Do you think my house is haunted?'

'If it's a ghostie,' he says, as we part, 'it's only a very little ghostie.'

Why does this reassurance prick the hairs at my nape?

'How do you think those bones got in the tree, Uncle Pats?' I ask.

'Before my time anyway,' he says equably.

A few steps on, he turns back. 'Captain,' he says. 'The dog was called Captain.'

*   *   *

More and more I feel a part of this place. I'm alone up here so much, and now it no longer seems a condition to be feared or endured. There are times when I am sitting like this at my door watching a silver downpour and the sea shining, and I feel utterly happy. This is a very full solitude. When the skies teem and all you can hear is the rushing of water, there could be a million small voices hidden under that white noise, and it seems the place is alive, throbbing with Veseys and Quinns. The Quinns were here before the Veseys. Where are they now? Bill Tiernan's book hasn't told me much; it scarcely mentions small places like Kildarragh. The land around here, it says, was owned by a Lord Tarlton, who died a very old man in Dublin, of gout of the stomach, which sounds horrible.

Some places, it says, suffered far worse than others during the famine years. My famine images are all of Africa and India, thin brown people, ragged, naked, in a land where nothing grows and no rain falls, where flies have won the day. Strange

55

to think it was here in this place, its leavings beneath my feet. The abandoned potato ridges ripple here and there all over Quilty's Door; one lies, a patch of corrugated green, at the side of my cottage. My little corpse girl knew hunger. Was she a Quinn or was she a Vesey? Was she neither, just a dumped dead child, forever to be nameless? If Judith is right I have the blood of both Veseys and Quinns in me, and so did my mother. What if I'm related to the tree child—what if she's in the family? Does it make a difference if there's a line of blood between her and me? I think of imaginary invisible bloodlines, spreading out behind me like a peacock's tail, every eye a story.

The rain that drummed on the roof for the past half hour has stilled to a gentle fall that shimmers in the bright air. Outlines are clear and sharp. The mountain whispers. Luke Quinn is walking slowly up the track. He comes and sits with me at the door and neither of us says a word, though we smile in greeting, a peculiar piercing smile that passes between us like the clashing of teeth. He's wearing a high-collared grey jacket and a pair of jeans.

'You haven't called by for ages,' I say. 'Did she keep you from coming?'

He keeps smiling, looking nervously at me. 'She can't stop me from doing anything if I want to do it,' he says.

'Well, you're a funny person,' I say, 'first you're up here all the time, then I go and see your mother and she shouts at me, then I see neither hide nor hair of you for days on end.'

'Her nerves are bad,' he says, 'Sometimes she can't be left.'

'She said *your* nerves were bad.'

'Well, she would,' he says. 'She thinks everyone's nerves are bad. It's really her own.'

He's an odd-looking boy. He takes out his cigarettes and offers one.

Cigarettes are flirty things. 'OK.' May as well go along with this. I accept his light, trying to catch his eye. Then the rain comes down steadily again, turning the sky above the rocks a beautiful sodden blue-grey; and it turns a little cold, but not unpleasantly so. I have a bottle of red wine I was keeping for something like this. I consider getting it out, but the silence between us grows so pure it seems a shame to break it. After ten minutes or so, he moves his head and locks eyes with me. His face has taken on a fixed, goblinish appearance, glazed, and he doesn't blink. I have known him all this time as shy, and now he does this, turns scary on a pin. I don't blink. We stare each other out for so long the world makes a change around us, infinitesimal.

'At night you close your curtains very tight,' he says.

It was him. The cigarette glowing in the dark down at the end of the garden.

'Tonight,' he says, 'leave your curtain a little bit open.'

He stands and walks quickly away, through the gate, down the track, out of sight. I sit on for a while, watching the way the light dances in tiny spots in the air before my eyes. I sit and sit and the mountain chuckles and croons, rushy water all around me, a silvery cadence in my ears. Being here is a dream. I fell asleep in my apartment and dreamed I was here. It's two hours till dark.

I fill up every container with water from the rain barrel and get a bathload on the stove for later, lock all the doors and windows, pull the drapes, leaving the smallest chink, just enough for an eye. Then I go upstairs and light all the candles. Those cigarettes in the dark, sometimes they were at two, three a.m. He knows how to hang around. I open a bottle of red wine and make some strong black coffee, then pull out the tin tub and position it carefully, making believe it's Cleopatra's barge, before the open fire. When the bath's ready I take off all my clothes and bathe by fire and candlelight.

*   *   *

Things were different there, then, on that isolated hillside. I didn't know how I'd got into this. I didn't care. Every night for the next five nights I left the smallest little gap in the curtain. I didn't know if he was there outside. It didn't matter. He didn't come by in the days at all. I found myself thinking about him. Has he ever been touched? Ever been kissed? On the sixth night I left the curtain closed and took a break.

It was so quiet I could hear the mountainside yawn, then tap tap tap at the door.

The lamp flickers. I rise and flit to the door silently, put my ear there and listen.

Luke says, 'Beatrice, it's me.'

My fingers slide back the bolt. Everything's bright, the moon very nearly full. He grins, awkward as ever.

'Come on in, Luke,' I say. 'I'll make you some coffee.'

I let him in.

And, of course, he turned out to be the wolf. He fell upon me clumsily, frightened by himself, and I took him straight to bed. His hair was very tangled, as if he'd been hanging around on the mountain for hours. We had a fierce, sweet night of it and somehow fell asleep in the end, towards morning.

We'd drowsed no more than an hour when he sat up abruptly, as if called. His ghostly eyes were open but he was fast asleep.

He said: 'There are three children playing on the tree.'

PART TWO

1900—
about seventy years ago

5

The Vesey house, solid and square, stood a little back from the main Boolavoe—Lissadoon road. Lizzie was out in the yard with her mending when she saw a cart coming along the road driven by a man who was not one of her brothers. She didn't get up from the stool but did several things almost unconsciously: bit her lips all over, licked them, tilted back her head, straightened her back and flexed her shoulders; so that when the old green cart drew to a creaking halt just beyond the gate she was ready. She was seventeen and bold. A lean young man dressed in old clothes, a blackened clay pipe in his mouth, sat up front with a dog. A bony brown horse snorted between the shafts. On the back of the cart were a couple of baskets, three or four buckets and a large barrel with a tap.

'Would you be wanting any water?' the man called over the wall.

'Don't you see the pump there?' she said, nodding towards the dairy.

'I'll tell you what.' He got down from the cart and leaned over the gate. He had long brown hair, a straight mouth and a fine-boned jaw. 'I've got some beautiful apples. All the way from America.'

'You'd have to see my brother,' she replied.

'Well, where's your brother?'

'He's beyond,' she said, and suddenly smiled at him. She had big teeth and full lips, and her neck and shoulders were graceful. Smiling was something she practised in front of the mirror. He didn't smile back. She indicated with her thumb, somewhere that way, past the outlying cluster of thatched sheds.

'I can deliver apples,' he said, 'any time you want. I go this way regular to Tadhg O'Donnell's.'

Lizzie got up and came to the gate, still with the mending in her hands. A thick grey stocking hung down. 'Does Norah buy apples from you?'

'Yes, she does,' he said, his elbow over the gate, 'and plenty more. I can get things for you. What do you want?'

'Nothing. You'd have to see my brother.'

'Tell you what I have got,' he said, 'a good pup.' He turned, went round the cart and returned with a basket in his arms. He was handsome in a spiky boyish kind of way, she thought. She leaned over the gate. A very young brown pup was asleep in some straw at the bottom of the basket.

'That's a runt,' she said.

'Don't you be hasty.'

'I know a runt when I see one,' she said, 'poor scrap.' She reached and lifted it out to look at its belly. 'Boy,' she said. It mewed pathetically. Its breath smelt of onions. 'We have two dogs as it is,' she said. 'What happened to his ma?'

'In the sea,' he said.

'Drowned?'

'All but this one. This one fell out the bottom of the bag. He's got the luck with him.'

'Has he, now?' She was watching the hawker to see what effect she was having on him. There was always an effect, always had been.

'He's grand.' The hawker said everything in the same serious way. 'He can lap. Feed himself. Look.' He stowed his basket on the cart, came into the yard without being invited and took the pup

64

from Lizzie, setting it down next to a metal bowl in the dogs' corner. Its legs squashed out sideways.

'He's got very short legs,' Lizzie said.

'He's just tired.'

'No,' she said, 'no dogs, no apples, no water. Not today thank you. I'd have to ask my father and I'm not waking him. You might see one of my brothers if you're going over the top. They might want something you could get, I don't know.'

A slight smile hovered on his face but only for a second. He scooped up the dog. 'I wouldn't get the cart over the top,' he said.

'Come to think of it, you wouldn't. You're better by road.'

'Tadhg was in a very bad way last time I was here.'

'Still is,' she said.

The man ran his finger under the frayed neck of his wilted flannel shirt. 'That's a good dog, I guarantee,' he said. 'I won't take any money for him, he's yours. I'd have him myself, only this one I have here would kill him if he got out of the basket.'

Lizzie looked at the black and white dog sitting quite still and calm on the cart, gazing down the road as if deep in thought. 'That one doesn't look fierce,' she said.

'Oh, no, he doesn't look it, does he, but he's got a nasty nature on him, that dog. He can't live alongside of another creature.'

'I don't believe a word of it,' she said. 'Now take the poor desperate creature away with you.'

She followed him to the gate.

'Wait,' she said, 'Can you get me some ducks?'

'You want ducks?'

65

'I've had a hankering to keep a few ducks.'

'I can get you ducks.'

'I'd rather geese,' she said, 'but my father won't have them about the place.'

'Geese are fierce creatures,' he said.

'I have a hankering for geese.'

'I can get you geese,' he said, 'I can get you geese, I can get you ducks, I can get you whatever you want.'

'Get me ducks,' she said. 'Two. White ones.'

He grinned. 'Done.' He began climbing back onto the cart with the pup held in one fist but then turned back. 'I couldn't just trouble you for a bit of bread, could I?' he said, 'I'm famished.'

She sighed and went into the house, stood blinking for a moment in the gloom.

'God bless you,' he said when she returned with a hunk of soda cake, ate it down in two great bites and wiped his mouth with the back of his hand. She watched him get up on the cart. He put his hand in his pocket and brought out a small wooden whistle. 'I got this for the baby,' he said, 'Tadhg's grandbaby.'

'The baby can't play that!' She laughed.

Two clay pipes followed. 'For the little girls,' he said, 'for blowing bubbles.' He stashed his presents away again and fixed a navy blue cap on his head. 'What have they named the wee man?' he asked.

'Pierce.'

'Well,' he said, *there's* a name for the gentry,' and grinned. He gave the reins a shake. 'I'll have you your white ducks on the next Fair Day,' he said, 'I'll be in the square.' The horse moved wearily forward. 'Or shall I bring them up to you?'

'Bring them up.'

Only after the sound of the cart had faded away did she realise the pup was still in the yard, nosing around in the turf mould on its stumpy legs, wagging its bit of tail. She sighed, looking at the stocking dangling from one hand. This was one mild day come suddenly from nowhere, early in the year. Tomorrow in all likelihood it would be cold again. The cats were sleeping on the roof of the dairy, the hens scratching contentedly. There was still a lot to do before the family started drifting home and she didn't feel like doing any of it. The pup, realising all at once that it had been set down free in a paradise of smells, tottered rapturously this way and that on the stones before squatting to pee, then darting wildly at a thin black hen that was scratching about near the puddle under the pump. The hen was a fierce old harridan that was having none. She flew forward, screeching. The stupid pup yelped and the cock flew up onto the turf pile.

'Ssh! Don't you go waking him up!' Lizzie grabbed the pup and shook it in front of her face. Her father, who was very bad with his head and stomach, had gone to bed at two o'clock this afternoon after a dreadful night of groanings and wanderings. 'Not a sound or I'll skin you,' she said, dumping the thing down and letting it stumble round after her as she brought in an armload of sods for the hearth, topped up the kettle and hung it back over the fire. She closed the bottom half of the door against the hens, but left the top open for the steam. A pudding in a cloth bubbled in a pan on one side of the chimney. On the other, a foul scum had risen to the top of the ancient vat in which her father's handkerchiefs had been steeping in simmering water for the best part of a couple of hours and now needed slopping out and rinsing. Leave it, she thought, and played with the dog instead, rolling it over and over on the rug till it was frantic, then sitting down on the floor in front of the fire and letting it suck her fingers; only when it continued to whine and fret did she realise it might be hungry. She put it outside to finish the old stirabout in the dogs' bowls. It was an ugly, undistinguished creature with a smug face, but at least it could feed itself. Enough, she thought, leave it outside; but it whined and she let it in so as not to waken her father, and in keeping it calm and quiet, fell sleepy and passed into an idle state, just sitting and thinking about the way that tinker had fooled her. The cheek of it, she thought. And look at me with the holes in my apron. I'd like him to see me swanked up going into town, buckle shoes, lace collar. Bet he's not seen anything like me in a long time. Fellow like him knows he's no chance. He was much nicer looking than bold Robert Emmet though, her mother's hero, whose portrait hung above the table. Robert Emmet was grandly dressed with sword and epaulettes, but she liked the face on this tinker much more.

Her oldest brother Henry came in, reeking of sweat, threw a spade down in one corner, grabbed a bucket from the stack by the fire and went out again, acknowledging her with a silent nod. It was time to get up, drain hankies, peel potatoes, make tea. When she put it down under the cane chair, the pup yawned, showed fine white needle teeth and fell asleep immediately. Lizzie got the potatoes and turnips on low, checked the pudding, took down the tea caddy and enamel mugs from the corner shelf and spooned tea into the teapot. By the time she heard the cart draw up and the voices of her mother and Hanna, the whole kitchen was steamy. She looked out and saw the white donkey in the yard, front legs black to the knees, tearing with its teeth at the shrubs that grew along the dairy wall. Henry was unhitching the cart. Her mother swept towards the door, Hanna following with the market bag.

'Shilling a yard!' her mother exclaimed. 'Look at this, Lizzie,' throwing back her hood and unfurling a length of blue cotton over the table.

Hanna unbuttoned her jacket. 'What is *that*?' she cried, spying the dog at once.

Her mother had taken off her cloak and hung it on the door, and was already tying on her pinny, a great voluminous thing that went over all and made her look stouter than ever. 'Not another dog!' she moaned.

'That's the ugliest dog I've ever seen,' said Hanna.

'A hawker left him.' Lizzie held the cloth against herself.

'Where's your father?'

'Still sleeping.'

'What's it doing in the house?' Hanna asked.

'It made too much noise in the yard. I didn't want it to wake Daddy.'

Her mother came and took the blue cloth from her. 'Later,' she said. 'Now, where in the world is Mike? Lizzie, go and call. Hanna, go and see after your father.' Margaret Vesey rolled up her sleeves and starting taking down the plates from the dresser, sighing and muttering to herself. 'Lizzie, you could have seen to your father's handkerchiefs at least, couldn't you? What have you been doing all day? Take that creature outside, you know your father won't have a dog in the house. Off with you! Out you go!'

'Youse are all heartless,' Lizzie said as the pup was chased scuttling out the door. Following, she scooped him up in one hand, opened a gate between the pigsty and the dairy and strode up the mound to stand and call as loudly as she could for Mike from the top. She could hear the dogs barking, and the sound of a bell very far away.

Lizzie was the youngest and last. Ever since she could remember, she'd been given to understand that she was the most beautiful and remarkable person in the world. Oh, what a lovely baby! they'd said. Then: oh, what a lovely little girl! Now, it was looks they gave her more than words. I'm going to keep the pup, she thought, and I'll get my ducks too. She always got what she wanted. Why can't I have my geese anyway? I will, one day. Everything comes in the end.

The dogs' waving white tails came in sight in the valley, then Mike's white shirt. She waved to Mike and he raised a hand.

Her father was up when she got back in the house, standing at the foot of the stairs tying his paisley handkerchief round his neck, and she walked straight up to him and held the dog up right in his face. 'Daddy,' she said, 'can I keep him?'

'Let the poor man catch his breath!' her mother said, turning from the pot she was draining. 'Now, Jamie, don't let the little'un softsoap you.'

'*Please*, Daddy.'

Her father's serious bloodshot eyes softened.

'No, Lorelei,' he said, 'absolutely not.'

'I hope you didn't pay good money for that, Lizzie,' her mother said.

'I didn't pay a farthing. The hawker man just left him. He was selling apples and I said I didn't want any and I gave him a drink and when he'd gone he'd left the dog. What was I supposed to do?'

'No, Lorelei,' her father said gently, 'no dog,' putting his hands on her shoulders. He smiled fondly. The fact that he was a big man and she very small made her feel more than ever like a child. A horseshoe-shaped scar puckered his left cheek, just under his eye, from where a cat had bitten him when he was three or so. Since the beginning, it was a story: your daddy was bitten by a cat. Ripped his cheek out when he was a tot.

'Well, what am I supposed to do with him, Daddy?' she shouted, 'drown him?'

'Lorelei, you remember who it is you're talking to!' He pushed her away and she threw herself down onto a chair and sulked, still holding the pup.

'Put the poor thing out, Lizzie,' her mother said, 'you know he's going to have to get used to it.'

She pushed the tears out over the rims of her eyes.

'No, no,' her father said more kindly, 'let the littl'un carry it round with her for the night if it makes her happy. In the morning she can take it over to Kildarragh. Pats's Lady's on her way out, maybe he'll want to train this one up.'

'*That* one?' snorted Hanna.

It was the best she was going to get. Lizzie raised her eyes but didn't smile. She sat up straight and stared coldly at them all. The dogs were barking in the yard. Mike came in.

71

'Lizzie's been codded by a tinker,' Hanna told him, 'he's left her with a runt.' She was beating the potatoes, grinning, her thin brown face crooked in the firelight.

Mike grinned, strolled over and poked at the dog. 'Ugly thing,' he said pleasantly.

Lizzie ignored him.

'What's up with her?' he asked.

'Lizzie, get up,' her mother said, 'stop acting the princess.' Her mother went to the fire, pulled out the kettle on its chain and poured boiling water onto the tea. 'Run and see if Henry's coming for his supper.'

Lizzie got up with a loud sigh and sauntered out, swaying her hips, the dog cradled ostentatiously in the crook of her neck. Her oldest brother was in the shed, in the dying light, surrounded by tools and the plough on its side.

'Ma says do you want your tea,' she called from the door.

There was a long pause, then his quiet voice from the gloom: 'Bring me a lamp, honey, I have to finish this off. Tell her to leave it on the side.' He was a gaunt scarecrow under a ceiling of hanging shadows, strings of onions, dried fish, bundles of rolled beef. Lizzie went back to the kitchen and wouldn't do anything but slouch against the wall playing with the dog, despite all entreaties to put it outside; while Mike scrubbed up and her mother and Hanna dished up the food. The ridiculous bundle ran up her shoulder, like a tic. Her father limped over and stood looking at her. An old man now, silver-haired, stout and tall. His thumbs were hooked in the lapels of his waistcoat, from which a button hung loose. 'Now now, Miss,' he said, 'none of this.'

'Tell her to stop sulking, Daddy,' Hanna said.

'Now now, Miss,' her father repeated, 'sit up to the table and eat. All's settled.'

'What was on you to take a whelp like that, Lizzie?' Mike said, appearing in the doorway as she crossed the floor, 'He must have been a talker, this tinker.'

'He wasn't a tinker.'

'He was a robber,' her mother said, 'asking money for that. It won't last the week.'

'I didn't pay money!'

Mike sat to eat.

'He was a bit of a charmer then, this tinker?'

'Mike!'

His mother clouted his head and turned to Hanna. 'Take your brother's on a tray. Poor Henry working away! For pity's sake, Lizzie, change your face!'

But Lizzie kept it up till the lamps were lit and everything cleared away and washed up, and all the work of the place over. She wasn't even sure why. It wasn't the pup. She'd never thought she could keep it in the first place. It was just a feeling, as if they were all of them laughing at her in a way she hated; as if everything she did and said were no more than the mewlings of a pup. Well, if that was it, if they laughed at everything she said, well, she just wouldn't say anything any more, so there. But she got so sleepy again; sitting there with the pup asleep in her lap because her father said she could; and the blanket she was making spilling in folds to the floor. And everything peaceful again, the firelight flickering up in the rafters on the hooks and on the horseshoe her father had hung there, and the lamplight reflected in the steel hook poised in her mother's hand. A strip of lace hung down. Hanna and Mike were at the table, talking in stifled bursts of laughter; they were close in age. Her father was smoking his pipe and gazing into the flames, frowning.

Sometimes at these moments a terrible sadness would come over her, a kind of mourning for the moment as it passed. Such things as her mother's pleated black cloak hanging on the door would fill her with a terrible sweet rush of love. Tears would prick her eyes and her nose would start to run. It was happening now.

'Now come on, Lizzie,' her mother said, 'be a good girl now.'

'Oh, she's grand now.' Her father smiled at her. His teeth were missing at the side. 'She's a good girl now, aren't you, girlie?'

But the tears rolled out.

'Girl, what is the matter with you?' he asked. 'You know there's nothing to cry about, Lorelei. What a silly girl you are.'

'I know,' she said, sniffing.

I don't want you all to die, she was thinking. She didn't know where the thought came from and it frightened her: as if the thought itself might strike them down. They smiled at her kindly. A bobbin was under her mother's arm. A mug of tea was handed to her.

It's just the little'un bawling again, they were thinking. She's always been like this. Cries easily.

'Come on, Lizzie.' Hanna got up and shifted her chair. 'Let's comb your hair, it's all over the place.' Hanna's brisk fingers took out the pins and set to with the tortoiseshell comb. Let down, Lizzie's

74

straight fair-brown hair was startling. Hanna parted it neatly in the middle. Mike came and sat on the floor by Lizzie's chair, chafing her bare feet tenderly.

'There now,' Hanna said, and she combed and combed, lightly and smoothly and rhythmically till Lizzie stopped crying.

* * *

Every night the two girls argued about the window. Lizzie always wanted it open for the fresh air; Hanna liked it shut. They shared their bedroom with a few sacks of meal that had nowhere else to go. Lizzie hated the smell of them, subtle as it was; she said it was like dirty babies. But that night Hanna didn't care about the window. Lizzie had kept the dog in the room with them because it howled, and Hanna said the dog stank. She said she'd rather freeze to death than have to smell that dog.

After the candle had been blown out and darkness fell sudden as a scythe, Lizzie was glad of the faint scent of hedge coming in, and the soft onion breath of the dog faintly upon her face. It lay fat and warm across the pillow, snoring gently. Drifting, she tried to guess the age of the tinker. How could she know? Twenty-four? Twenty-three? Young enough. She couldn't quite remember his face. She heard the jingling of her parents' iron bed as her father tossed and turned. Terrible nights he was having. Hanna turned over. Lizzie made her hawker walk into the yard all over again. This time she took him into the house and let him sit at the table. The kettle was boiling. 'A cup,' he said, 'no more,' but when she rose to get it for him, he reached out and took hold of her hand and stood staring down at it as if he had no idea how it had come to be there.

She heard her father's heavy footsteps descend the stairs, heard his muted groan in the kitchen, saw the ghostly candlelight appear in the crack of the door, and realised she was awake. He was poking about amongst the canisters on the high shelf by the chimney breast. Maybe he was making himself a cup of tea.

*   *   *

Next day she walked over the mountain to Kildarragh with the dog in a basket. A snappy wind was blowing, clouds flying. Far out to sea there were fishing boats with red and brown sails. At the top she let the pup out of the basket and chased about with it for a while, across the rath where, according to the old people, the fairies lived; where the white bog cotton grew tall, down the slope that dipped steeply to where the cliffs went on for miles and miles, pink with thrift, white with birds. There were caves here, safely high and dry above the sea line and easily reached, where she had liked to hide when she was younger, to sit and look out towards the Skelligs and be soothed by the hollow booming of the sea and know that no one could find her. A little further and you could look down on the stone strand where seals sometimes rested. But there were none today.

Kildarragh from above was a scattering of grey houses, mostly ruined, one or two inhabited further down the track towards the sea. After that there was nothing till you got to where the track ran into the crossroads a mile or more beyond the townland, where Tadhg O'Donnell's long low shebeen with hens roosting in the thatch nestled in a crook of land above a small shingle beach. A little away and above from the main cluster was Darby's House, where her brother Pats lived with his new wife Minnie. God alone knew why Pats wanted to make something of that place is what Lizzie's father said, grumbling over his pipe of an evening. There was no good land up there. But Pats had whitewashed the cabin and thatched it neatly, and though the ground was steep and stony, there was room for twelve rows of potatoes on a wide sloping patch beside the house. A white goat was tethered to an old twisted tree at the back. Minnie came out and stood with folded arms, headscarf flapping, watching as Lizzie came down.

'Well, look at you,' she said, 'don't you look nice.'

'I've brought you a dog, Minnie,' Lizzie said, as the mutt galloped clumsily forward. 'I got him from a hawker but they won't let me keep him. Daddy said you needed a dog.'

Minnie picked up the dog. 'The dote,' she said gravely, 'we'll have him.' She was a firm, handsome, steady woman who almost never smiled. 'Patsy!' she called, 'come see what your little sister's dumped on us!'

'He was going to be drowned,' Lizzie told Minnie.

'Come along in, Lizzie.'

It was dim inside. There was a clunking noise and Pats came stumbling down the ladder from the loft. 'Is it Lizzie?' he cried. 'Well, this is nice!'

The hearth was ashy, the floor a mess. Tadhg

O'Donnell's ginger-haired grand-daughters, in identical gingham dresses, sat on the settle blowing soap bubbles through short clay pipes.

'Here, girls,' Minnie said, 'now you can run outside for a bit and play with the puppy.'

'Jesus, is that ours?' Pats sat down by the fire, picking up the tongs and rearranging a few sods of turf to make the fire draw. 'Tea, Lizzie? That's a pathetic creature you've brought us.'

'Shoo!' Minnie clapped her hands, 'shoo! Take him to Lady, girls, he'll be grand. Old Lady, she'll sort that one out.'

'The Young Pretender.' Pats grinned, striking a match against the chimney breast.

'What way is Tadhg?' Lizzie asked.

'A bad way.' Pats lit a cigarette, picked up the shovel and stood.

'The priest is down below,' said Minnie, scooping a dipperful of milk from the churn.

'He can't piss,' Pats added, lowering his voice so the little girls beyond the half-open door wouldn't hear.

Lizzie's eyes fell on the clay pipes discarded on the settle, a few dribbles of soapy water leaking from them.

'I'd sooner go quick than linger,' Minnie said.

'I was sweet-talked into that runt,' Lizzie said.

'By a hawker?'

'Well, no, he tried to, only I wasn't such a fool. "Take it with you," I said, but he left it in the yard and I only saw it after he was away. Did he not come here?'

'Tom Quinn was here,' Minnie said.

'Tom Quinn?'

'He's your hawker. Bit of a rascal.'

'Said he was going to see old Tadhg.'

'That's right. They used to go fishing together out of Dingle.'

Pats dribbled turf shreds over the fire. Minnie poured tea.

'He's going to get me some ducks.'

'She's mad,' said Pats to Minnie, 'the old man hates ducks.' He laughed, coughing out smoke. 'He'll wring their necks.'

Minnie handed Lizzie a mug. 'Tom Quinn was in my school,' she said. She pulled off her headscarf and scratched her curly head. 'He was a nice lad,' she said.

Lizzie left the pup living in the shed with Lady. She looked back once when she was halfway up the hill, and once more at the top. There was barking, and the high voices of Tadhg O'Donnell's grandchildren. The white goat had wound itself in on its rope and was feeding on the long lush grass from which the tree's trunk coiled, snake-like, throwing up its old tree arms in anguish. On top, the breeze blew ripples across the wide rath and her hair whipped about. Twenty minutes in the cave, she thought guiltily, and found herself running down the tracks above the sea, turning sideways once or twice, jumping here and there over the crumbly bits, till she reached the best cave, the one that was always dry and sheltered from the wind, well above the water line where no one else came. Its overhung, thrift-grown mouth was the size of a door, its floor a rock. The space it made was like a large cupboard, the back blocked up with rocks. She liked to sit here and do nothing at all but watch the sea. Sometimes a fishing boat far out would slowly cross her line of vision. So his name was Tom Quinn. So what if he was only a hawker? He had a nice face. He looked at her in the same way as Bob Jakey did, as if seeing her more deeply than everything else around her. Bob Jakey was a townie who'd slept in their barn for a week last summer, over from Salford with her sister's husband on a walking tour. Lizzie couldn't even remember her sister, she'd lived in England since before Lizzie was born. So, there were these two Manchester men in the barn, Bob Jakey a coach driver, and Cathy's husband a shipping something. The two men were strange and wealthy in their wing-collared shirts, full of loud laughter and an odd kind of energy. Bob Jakey was much too old, probably even older than Henry, but he'd taken a real fancy to Lizzie, and she was only sixteen at the time. Anyway, all she got was teased. Mike and Hanna went mad over it. She got used to Bob Jakey following her around like a dog, house to dairy, dairy to shed, shed to house, slick black hair carefully parted in the middle. His customary stance was hands behind his back, a smile on his kind, large-featured face.

He was nice, you could tell by his eyes, but he wasn't a patch on Tom Quinn.

*   *   *

Next Fair Day, late, she went into town with Henry. She wore button boots and a flounced blue skirt and one of her mother's lace collars, with a five-pointed yoke that set off the navy of her blouse. Henry left her down on the pavement at the top of Weavergate and headed off for the sawmill. The square was packed with carts with horses between the shafts, clusters of cattle hanging their heavy heads to the puddled ground. Around the edge of the square were the poultry sellers and their crates, pens for sheep, the occasional pig. If Tom Quinn had ever been there he'd gone, so she walked down Weavergate where it was cleaner underfoot, and bought oranges from an old woman in a white cap. She needed castor oil for her father, soap, a new covered dish to replace the one Mike had knocked onto the stone floor of the dairy with his big clumsy elbow the other day. Weavergate was crowded, loud with the crying of wares. She kept her basket held out in front of her as a buffer against the press.

'Lizzie!'

It was Norah O'Donnell, Tadhg's daughter-in-law, with the baby screaming in a creel on her back and a huge basket pulling down one arm. God, she looked awful. Her fierce brown face was wrinkled and old, though she was only thirty-five. 'I'm worn out, Lizzie,' she said. 'Come on in here with me till I set this lot down,' seizing her arm and steering her into a place where a few people were sitting on benches. A woman ladled lemonade and ginger beer from two iron pots on a counter that was a plank over two barrels. 'Fetch me a ginger beer, darlin',' Norah said, dropping her basket and flopping down, 'while I sort this one out. Here, there's money, and you can get one for yourself too, darlin', I'm dead if I don't get a drink down me this minute. I was up all last night again.'

'With Tadhg?'

'*And* this one.'

Pierce was all worked up into a frenzy and purple in the face. Norah pushed him under her shawl to let him feed, stifling a yawn.

Lizzie fetched two ginger beers and sat to hear the news.

'He's had a Mass said in his room,' Norah reported.

'Ah,' said Lizzie.

The ginger beer was good. The door stood open and all Lizzie could do was keep her eyes on the street, looking out for Tom Quinn and her ducks. Men with sticks passed the door, women in shawls, boys in caps, dapper gents in bowler hats. A sheep was tied to a drainpipe. A horse with its head in a nosebag deposited steaming droppings onto the cobbles. Norah leaned forward and put her long brown fingers on Lizzie's arm. 'Tadhg's ranting, Lizzie,' she said softly. 'He's talking to someone who isn't there.'

Lizzie looked at Norah with sympathy. How must it be in the shebeen, one dying, one just born?

'That's how it was with Granda,' Lizzie said. 'They do that.'

'Quite unsettling.' Norah placed the child on her shoulder. 'The way Tadhg's like a baby.'

'Granda was the same.'

'He says some strange things. He started crying this morning. Said, "Sal's screaming for her baby". I tell you, it makes my blood run cold sometimes.'

'Sal's screaming for her baby,' Lizzie repeated in a tone of wonder.

'He has some story no doubt. You'd never get it out of him in sense though.'

A cart laden with loaded sacks rumbled by on the cobbles. A man in a long black buttoned coat with a cape sat up front.

'Was there a man called Tom Quinn out to see

Tadhg?' Lizzie asked.

'Tom Quinn's a rogue,' said Norah.

'Why? He was supposed to be getting me some ducks.'

'Oh well, I dare say he'll get you your ducks. He's had money out of Tadhg, I know that. He's a gambler.' She shifted the baby to the other arm. 'Tadhg likes him.'

'Have you seen him today?'

'Not today.'

'I should go,' Lizzie said vaguely. She rose, giving her finger to the baby to hold. The grip of life, not like the cold weak hold of the dying old. She left Norah sitting on a while, talking to some woman she knew, and went out into the street.

How dare he do that, she thought, what is he? No one. First he gets the laugh on me with the dog, now he doesn't turn up with my ducks. She walked along as far as the station. A few post-cars were drawn up waiting for passengers. A man was selling papers and comics, so she bought a newspaper for her father. There was a haze on the hills over the trees and rooftops. The stalls had run out and there was nothing much beyond the station but cabins with dogs lying in front of the doors and a few women sitting on stools, so she turned and walked quickly back down Weavergate, the angry feeling swelling, went into a shop and looked at the plates and dishes. Her mother wanted something plain. The man behind the counter tried to sell her something with a cherry pattern.

'I don't want that!' she snapped.

These people would swindle the hair off your head. How could she be so stupid as get taken in by a tinker? If he wasn't a tinker he wasn't much more.

She bought a plain covered dish and walked back up the town, looking at all the stalls on the way. She kept meeting people she knew. Everyone was there but Tom Quinn. She filled up the market bag, treated herself to a slice of apple cake and ate it while watching the soldiers exercising their horses in the barracks yard, then it was time to meet Henry by the square. Already the lamps were being lit and it was getting chilly. The cart was there, loaded up, but no Henry. Lizzie sat up on the seat and hugged her shawl about her, shivering, breathing in the sweet reek of the horses. Perhaps they'd come too late. Perhaps he'd been here in the morning with her ducks and couldn't stay. Maybe he'd thought she wasn't coming and sold them to someone else.

Then there was Henry walking towards her in his big coat with the collar raised.

'Did you not get what you wanted?' he asked.

'No.'

He smiled. 'Never mind. Ducks, was it? Daddy would never have let you keep them.'

'Yes, he would. Once I'd got them, he would.'

He shook his head. They rode sleepily home, hardly speaking. Henry's presence rocking beside her was solid, enduring. His hair was going grey already and it didn't seem he'd ever marry now. He'd be here for ever. Mike would go soon, she thought. His America money was steadily growing. And her? What would become of her? She was so sunk in thought she hardly saw a thing of the passing countryside in the gathering dark, till the slate roof of their house appeared suddenly, shining wet against the lowest shoulder of the mountain.

Her father stepped forward to hand her down from the cart.

'Why the long face, Lorelei?'

'She was after buying ducks, but there were no ducks to be had,' said Henry, jumping down.

'God in heaven! You don't want ducks *or* a goose. We had all this with the geese. Your hens are destroying the thatch as it is.'

'Don't you vex yourself.' Lofty, Lizzie swept into the house. 'I won't be getting any ducks.'

Her father followed, muttering, 'Dirty creatures!'

Her mother was putting the irons to heat. 'What are?'

'Geese. Dirty things.'

'Ah, well. What have you got there, Lizzie?' She laid the tongs in the ashes.

Lizzie showed her mother what she'd bought.

'What were you getting ducks with anyway?' Hanna asked, turning from hauling a piece of bacon from the pot oven.

'My egg money.'

She put the oranges in a bowl.

'*Your* egg money?' Hanna smirked.

'*My* egg money.'

'Enough!' said their father.

'I saw Norah O'Donnell.' Lizzie sat down and started rolling down her stockings and her father turned away. 'Tadhg's had a Mass said in his room. He's talking to people who aren't there.'

'Like Granda,' said Hanna.

Mike came in all scrubbed up from the pump.

'Take those potatoes out now, Lizzie,' her mother said.

'I'm only just in!'

'So you are. Now, take those potatoes out, there's the girl.'

Lizzie put on a clean pinny and did as she was told. I'm not feeling bad about *him*, she thought, and smiled at her mother and was pleasant to everyone; and after tea swept the floor, packed turf on the lids of the ovens and filled up all the lamps without being told. Then she sat down by the fire with her father and read to him a little from the daily paper she'd bought in Boolavoe that day; and the white cat came and sat on his lap and purred loudly along with the ticking of the clock. He didn't mind cats. He stroked this one on the side of its face with his rough old finger. Once she'd seen it put up its paw, claws sheathed, velvet-soft and loving, stroking the yellow-red cat-scar under his eye.

A rap came on the door and Mike opened. It was one of Henry's men after his wages. He came in and stood waiting. 'Tadhg O'Donnell is dead,' he said, making the sign of the cross, 'God rest him.'

*　　　*　　　*

Her parents weren't going to Tadhg O'Donnell's wake. They didn't go about so much these days since her father was so weak, and he didn't approve of wakes anyway, he said they were barbarous. Henry brought the big sidecar to the front of the house. Lizzie had done her hair with papers and fluffed it out. She'd tied a ribbon around her neck. She hadn't had a good dance in ages, and there would be a lot of boys there, maybe even Tom Quinn. Hanna came out and hauled herself up beside her, adjusting her hat, then came

Mike, smelling of soap and raw under the chin from where she'd shaved him that afternoon.

'Ladies,' he said with mock gallantry, handing them up a blanket, 'for later when it's cold.'

'Up with you, Mike,' called Henry over his shoulder, and Mike got on the other side. The big mare danced a little, Lizzie clutched the rail, Henry clicked his tongue and they were off.

For upwards of fifty years, Tadhg O'Donnell had presided over the shebeen at the crossroads. Now he lay in his coffin in the parlour there, under a crucifix, candlelight flickering on the rosary between his fingers. His youngest son and daughter-in-law sat by to receive the guests. Lizzie looked down at the face of the old man who'd been such a friend of her grandfather's, a square, corpulent face, putty-grey, with massive grey whiskers that all but covered his cheeks. She kneeled and prayed, then stood and touched Jack's hand, then Norah's. 'I'm sorry for your trouble,' she whispered, 'I shall miss seeing him.'

Norah nodded and smiled. 'He's better now,' she said.

'He is indeed.'

Lizzie went through into the crowded smoky house. The table had been pushed against the wall. Tom Quinn was with a group of men taking snuff by the open door. Minnie, handsome with her dark hair piled up, called her over to sit by her on a bench against the wall. Marty Blake was there, the one her sister Hanna would probably take if she ever got down from her high horse.

'That's a very pretty frock, Lizzie,' Minnie said.

One of the little girls brought Lizzie some punch and she drank deeply.

'You'll never guess,' said Minnie, 'Pats has it that we're haunted.'

'Don't say that.' Lizzie crossed herself.

'No, he does, he says he heard a tiny voice.'

'What did it say?'

'Something in Irish.'

'Now don't go scaring me, Min.'

Minnie leaned forward, 'It said: *Is feidir liom thu a chloisteail. Teigh a chodladh.*'

'*I can hear you,*' Lizzie said softly. '*Go to sleep.*'

An ancient with a big wooden rosary and a shawl thrown over her bonnet seized Lizzie by the shoulder. 'What way is your father, Lizzie?' she demanded.

'Only very middling, Alma.'

'God be with the good days,' the old woman said portentously, 'the old ones are fading away.'

The daughters were bringing things out of the pot ovens. There was a stew made of chicken and turnips, a soda cake too big to go on any of the plates, buttery cabbage and potatoes. Drink flowed. An old man named Scanlon remembered how well Tadhg O'Donnell had played hurley when he was only a slip of a lad.

'Didn't he play for the county?' Minnie asked.

'That he did, Ma'am. When he was only sixteen.'

'You should have seen him,' old Alma Sheehan said, 'and wasn't he the handsome boy? They were all after him, you know. There was hearts broke when he married Curly Callanan.'

Norah was taking things from the ovens still, setting them out on the table. 'Eat up now, everyone,' she said, 'Come on now, there's plenty.'

After the food the fiddlers arrived, along with a boy of about twelve carrying a melodeon. They set up outside on the flat triangle of land above the shebeen, an upended barrel making a table for their drinks. People spilled outside. When the dancing began, Lizzie walked straight over to Tom Quinn, who was drinking whiskey and smoking a short clay pipe, and punched him on the arm. 'You rap, where were you with my ducks?' she said.

He grinned sheepishly. 'I swear there were none to be had. How is the great little dog?'

'Great little dog? The runt, you mean. They called him Captain. Grand name for a runt. He thrives. I gave him to my brother, him over there.'

He peered through the smoke.

'Do you still want the ducks?'

'My father won't let me have them.'

'I know who you are,' he said, 'you're Lizzie Vesey. Your brother Pats lives above.'

Norah went by with Pierce screaming on her shoulder. 'He's mad for his supper,' she said, smiling.

The people were clapping the rhythm, slow at first then faster and faster.

Hanna danced with Marty Blake, Henry with Minnie. The night drew on, fine with a full moon. A piper turned up. The old ones sat indoors and the children started running about playing games, pushing each other on the swing that hung from the elm tree. Tom Quinn had a thin, comfortable smile. 'Will you dance with me, Lizzie?' he said. It didn't matter. So much dancing, with everyone, with old men and women, children, brothers, sisters, sweet young men who'd drunk too much, sweet young men who didn't know where to put themselves. So she danced, simple-headed, with Tom Quinn and anyone else who would. So much was drunk and still so much more that the glasses were never empty. Lizzie must have had more than she'd ever had before. The moon shone bright on the sea and all the land was lit up. She danced as she never had, as free as if this was some dream and anything at all could happen, things that never happened in real life, laughing uproariously, losing all her family in the crowds. She felt she'd gone into a place she'd never gone to before, and after that, everything happened outside the real, everyday world. Like the cave: that was outside the real. So was this place she came to after drinking so much at Tadhg O'Donnell's wake.

Early in the morning when things were quieter and the children had mostly gone asleep; when the old people, who could outlast any of the young, were still mumbling and yarning and ruminating by the fire, a whole bunch of them went up the mountain to the rath to scare themselves witless. Pats and Minnie were there, and Mike, and Tom Quinn. It was so light they could see each others' faces. The white of the bog cotton was sprinkled all over like fine snow. They ran about in the big circle and shouted and whooped, silly people, young and drunk, daring whatever lived there; moonshine. They came together at last, ten or twelve of them sitting in a huddle in the centre, giggling. Minnie said there was a whistling seal came and laid on the stone strand of a full moon and they should all keep quiet and listen. But there was nothing but the whooshing of the sea in its holes.

'Let's go down by the stair,' said Pats, 'past our house and through Kildarragh, 'tis quicker now.'

But no sooner had they set off than they all started telling stories about the fairies, and Tom

Quinn stood still and hung back, turning his head and looking towards the cliffs.

'Tom!' called Minnie, 'come on now, they'll get you.'

He held up a hand as if to silence her.

'What?' asked Lizzie.

'I hear it,' he said.

'Oh, dear God,' Lizzie said, 'he hears something.'

'Ssh!'

The others were going on. Lizzie and Minnie lingered, arm in arm.

'Listen.'

Nothing.

'I'm going to look,' he said and set off towards the cliff that overlooked the stone strand.

'Ach, the man's mad,' said Minnie, setting off after Pats, who waited ahead. Lizzie giggled and ran after him.

'Lizzie!'

After waiting a minute or so and Lizzie not returning, Minnie walked on.

Lizzie caught him up on the other side of the rath, coming alongside reckless. 'I want to see a ghost!' she said. 'My head's spinning! Tom! My head's spinning!'

'You're very drunk,' he said, taking her arm to steady her.

They drew near to the edge, to a place from which they could see the moonlight gleaming on the rock striations under the caves.

'Did you really hear something?' she whispered.

'Whistling,' he said, 'very faint.' His arm went round her waist.

She slid her arm under his jacket. 'There's nothing to you,' she said, 'I can feel your ribs.'

'Feel them,' he said.

They kissed clumsily. Tom Quinn had a smooth chin, though his whiskers had encroached a long way onto his cheeks. She felt the kiss in her armpits and the soles of her feet.

'Lizzie!' came the voices, 'Lizzie!'

They stood apart.

The strand was bright. Three fat grey seals lay on the shingle.

'They'll have my hide,' he said.

She took his arm. 'I can do what I like.'

'Lizzie!'

She was very silly, that much she remembered afterwards. She laughed every time she fell down. He walked her back across the rath and half carried her down the mountainside to where Pats and Minnie waited below. Lizzie couldn't care about a thing, she had her arms round his boyish neck and was smiling madly. The feeling of his kiss was still in her armpits. She looked down. Something white was going round the tree at the back of Pats and Minnie's house. For a second her blood chilled, but then she realised it was the goat.

'What are you doing to the poor man, Lizzie?' called up Pats.

She laughed. She didn't care. 'I'm chasing him!' she shouted. 'I've chased him all around the rath.'

There was a wall to get over. Everything seemed funny to her, she couldn't stop laughing. Tom lifted her off her feet. 'You're only a wheeshy little thing,' he said, striding over the wall, whirling her round and depositing her on the other side. She staggered. For a moment she thought she was going to fall over, but then he righted her and she breathed very deeply till things stopped whirling.

'Are you all right?' His voice. 'Lizzie? Are you all right?'

The others were all there, around the ruins. The dogs were barking, old Lady and Captain. Pats had brought a bottle of whiskey from his house and it was being passed around as they ambled back along to Tadhg's.

Tom stopped suddenly and looked back at the ruins. 'Which of those is Darby's House?' he asked.

'Our Pats' house is,' Lizzie told him.

'Is it now? Back there?' He walked backwards.

Ahead they were singing sporadically, a ragged rolling sound, straggling back to Tadhg's. There were the lights. A mist, rolling up from the sea, gave them a slight haze. They walked separately now, smiling at each other with no need for words from either side of the track.

'There you are, Lizzylie,' Mike said, 'did you find the whistling seal?'

'We did,' she replied, 'three.'

*   *   *

'You know what I'd like? I'd like one of those big flat stones from the stone strand,' Lizzie said. 'For the dairy. To put on top of the cheese.'

They were sitting on the cliffs, looking out at the sea. Six or seven of them. Inland the fiddle's thin sweet whine. Tom peeled away and started running towards the shingle where the boats were shored.

'The man's a raging lunatic,' said Mike.

He didn't come back. Time passed and they went back inside where it was bright and warm. She kept looking for him whenever anyone came in the door. He'd said not a word, just off like that, was he mad? Another hour passed. The lamp was turned down and Alma Sheehan started berating the young ones for going up to the rath. She said they had no respect for the Gentry, that's what she called the fairies she truly believed lived there. 'Many a one's lived to regret that kind of disrespect.'

Alma's husband was there, old Matty, completely drunk.

'Matty,' she said, 'tell them about your lady.'

They pulled nearer to the fire.

'I used to be drilling with the Fenians up by the rath,' he said, 'this was after terrible times, after the hunger. And we looked across and a woman was walking from beyond the rath towards us with a basket on her back. We knew at once she was not a woman of the townland. She was the most comeliest thing I ever saw, very tall and long in the face. When she came near, it was as if something made us stop, afterwards not a one of us could tell how it happened, only that we were waiting and she drew close and put down the basket from off her shoulders onto the earth and says, says she, "Let your eyes take a glimpse of that good food." I saw great fat strawberries and pancakes and figs and soda bread. And she had wine too, in a leather bottle; she said it came from the Indies. But she put the fear in all of us and there was some fell down in a faint and remembered nothing. So we all turned away, and Cathal Buckley who was our captain called us back to attention and she went on down in the direction of the cliffs over there where you can look down onto the stone strand.'

Then Pats told the story of the small voice as he was blowing up the warm sods in the morning—'*Is feidir liom thu a chloisteail. Teigh a chodladh'*—and Lizzie felt the hairs prick up on the nape of her neck because she knew that Pats was not the kind of man who would lie.

*   *   *

Pats called round next day. He said Tom Quinn had come back with a big stone for her after she'd gone. He'd taken a boat from the jetty below Tadhg's and rowed round to the stone shore. Later he'd hauled it all the way up to Darby's House and left it at the gate. Pats laughed. 'There's devotion,' he said, and Lizzie turned away and smiled.

'Ha!' she said, 'he did that?'

'He did. You want me to bring it down for you?'

She thought for a moment. 'Not really. Leave it where it is.'

Every day she expected him.

He left it a week and then turned up while she was in the dairy beating the butter into rolls. She heard boots heavy on the stone steps and thought it was Henry but when she looked up it was him.

'Hello, Tom,' she said lightly, looking away and dipping the wooden bats in water.

He said he'd been in Mallow. Mallow was a grand place, he said, setting a heavy bundle down on the stone floor. There was a jug of buttermilk on the table, and she gave him a tumbler and told him to help himself. When he drank he threw back his head and gulped hungrily. Fascinated, she watched the movements of his pale throat.

'That was a wild thing you did,' she said, 'running off like that and taking Tadhg's boat.'

He set down the tumbler, half full.

95

'Were the seals still there?' she asked.

'The seals took no notice of me at all,' he said. 'They were like dogs. Three wild dogs. I was not too near them. I walked about for a while finding the right stone. Was it the right stone?'

'It was the very one,' she said, and laid down her bats to take a drink. The buttermilk was bitter cold and sharp to taste.

'See what I got in Mallow.' He stooped and opened the bundle. Out came long scarves made of gauzy material, yellow, green, orange. 'Which one for you?' he said.

'Oh, the green.'

'The green it is.'

He put it round her neck.

'I have to do the butter,' she said.

They kissed quickly.

'Where are your brothers?' he asked. 'Your mother and father?'

'Working. My mother's in the village. I don't know where Hanna is. Is she in the house? Did you see her?'

'No.'

They kissed again, more furtively.

'Will you come for a walk with me, Lizzie?' he said.

'Not now.' She laughed. 'How can I?'

The sound of boots in the yard. It was horrible and sudden and made her laugh recklessly. She put her wet lips very close to his ear and was going to whisper something, but no words came, so she stuck her tongue deep into his ear and licked. It tasted salty and dark and he squirmed in her arms, arching his neck and ducking his face into her throat, then pulled sharply away as footsteps clattered down into the dairy. Lizzie turned briskly and set about wrapping the butter in muslin, but she couldn't keep the outlandish smile off her face, even when she saw her father standing in the room with a face of thunder.

'Hello, Daddy,' she said.

Her father's eyes darted to Tom Quinn then back to her.

'Who's this?'

'His name's Tom Quinn, Daddy. He has things to sell.'

Her father was in one of his rare states of quiet anger. Once more he glanced at Tom Quinn, but his worst look was for her. 'What are you wearing?' he asked.

'Oh!' She pulled off the green scarf. 'I was just trying it on, Daddy. It's nice, isn't it? Here.' She handed it back to Tom. 'I don't have money for such things.'

Tom stuffed the scarves back in his bundle. 'So I'll be on my way,' he said, drawing the neck of the bundle tight and hauling it onto his shoulder. He moved towards the steps.

Her father was not a man for losing his temper. When he suddenly shrieked, 'You will leave my house!' in a voice unaturally shrill, Lizzie jumped visibly and burst into tears. His reaction, so extreme and unexpected, as if a soft old dog had suddenly turned, terrified her. 'You will leave my house and never show your face here again!' he shrieked, trembling.

Tom Quinn had gone pale. 'Sir . . .' he said. Lizzie's father blocked his way to the door.

'You'd cheat the girl. It's bad blood. Everyone knows. Bad blood from way back! Get out or I'll kick you out!'

'Sir, I am not a cheater.'

'All your dirty tribe are cheaters! Away! I'll have the polis on you!'

'Sir, I am not a cheater.' He spoke steadily. She saw how young and callow he was, how very shabby.

'What's the matter, Daddy?' she cried, running to him and seizing him by the arms. He wouldn't look at her. The look in his eyes was something other than pure anger, a complicated look of profound hurt, of sheer embarrassment at the ferocity and nakedness of his emotion.

'So this is the wind-up of it!' he gasped, and stood aside.

'Daddy!'

Tom walked up the steps, shifting the bundle on his shoulder. Her father shook her away and followed after, coughing with rage and crying out: 'Filthy set! Beggars and cheaters! Bad cess to the whole lot of ye!' Then came Lizzie, crying in bewilderment. Her father aimed a kick at Tom but missed. Henry, coming round the side of the house and knowing nothing of what was going on but seeing that his father was chucking a tinker out, put down the bucket he was carrying and strode forward, squaring his shoulders. The dogs barked. Tom's dog barked, quivering, up on the cart. Hanna appeared at the door in a white pinafore.

Tom got out into the lane and climbed up onto the cart and shook the reins and was off in the direction of Boolavoe, his dog looking back fearless now they were on the move, hurling challenges.

'What's up?' Hanna came out.

Henry was laughing. 'Well, he'll not be back. What did he do, Da?'

Her father turned on Lizzie and roared. 'Bad, Lorelei! Bad! Bad bad bad!' and stormed away into the lower pasture with the dogs slinking at his heels.

'What was all that about?' asked Hanna.

'I don't know,' sobbed Lizzie, 'I was just in the dairy and he was showing me some scarves he had for sale. What have I done?'

*　　　*　　　*

That night at supper her father, chewing furiously, denounced the Quinns. 'They've not shown their faces round these parts in years,' he sneered, 'You'd think they'd know better, they was always a bad lot.'

No one spoke. Lizzie's mouth was sullen. Her mother sighed. Mike caught Lizzie's eye and raised a brow. She stared coldly back. He knew, of course, that she'd been up on the rath with Tom at Tadhg O'Donnell's wake. Tell him then, her look said, just see if I care.

'Vagabonds,' her father said. 'Scum. If my mother had not been so kind to them she'd have lived to see her grandchildren.'

'Jamie . . .' her mother said, covering her father's hand with her own.

'Why?' Lizzie put down her knife and looked at her father.

'Don't be bold,' said her mother, and her father leaned forward, stared gravely at Lizzie. 'Because, girl,' he said, 'your grandmother, Eliza Vesey, died of the fever that came with the famine. She caught

99

it from walking up to Kildarragh, to Darby's House, every blessed day with food for the Quinn children. That's what a good woman my mother was, and she caught the fever off the Quinns.'

There was a long silence. All Lizzie knew was that her grandmother was a saint who'd died years and years before any of them were born, when her father was a child himself.

'It wasn't their fault though, was it?' she said.

'Why do you think you know everything, Miss?' he asked evenly.

'I don't.'

'I tell you the Quinns are bad in the blood. Do you think I don't know what I'm talking about?'

She said nothing.

He pushed back his plate. 'Kindness itself she was, and the Quinns run away with her character in return, putting it about that she spent time with the fairies. That's the kind of thing we're talking about. That's the kind of fools will put a bad name on a good woman.' He spoke quickly and gravely. 'They are nothing but badness and they've come to no good ever since those days and they never will, and if a daughter of mine ever thought to simper and smirk at the likes of one of them—' He turned his tumbler upside down, stood up so abruptly his chair fell over, and walked out.

For a moment no one spoke. Hanna righted the chair. Then her mother, seeing that Lizzie was stretching her face in a peculiar manner and sniffing, hissed, 'Pull yourself together, girl! See how you've vexed your father.'

'How was I to know all that?' retorted Lizzie.

'You should have known better than to bring a strange man into the dairy.'

100

'I didn't bring him in, he just walked in.'

'Even worse. Of course your father's annoyed. Someone like that an' all!'

'Like what? He was at Tadhg's wake. He knows Pats. He was at Minnie's school.'

'He's still a bogtrotter,' Hanna said.

Lizzie beat her fist on the table. Mike laughed, pounced sideways and tickled her. 'Lizzylie's got a sweetheart again!' he crowed. Lizzie screamed.

'Stop it, the pair of you!' Her mother got up. 'Mike, stop teasing her, Lizzie, clear the table, Hanna, pour some water.'

'Youse are all horrible,' Lizzie said.

Sometimes she could have killed Mike and Hanna. She was sick of being the baby, the little'un, the one they spoiled and teased. She couldn't ever have an admirer, she thought, not with Mike and Hanna. It was like the Bob Jakey thing all over again only much worse, because then she hadn't cared at all, and now she did. They teased her about Tom Quinn all night long, on and off, till she could have screamed. Crying made it worse. They tried to coddle her then, as if she was a baby who'd lost its rattle. A weight was on her. Her father's fury had seriously frightened her. Nothing seemed to account for it, but it made seeing Tom again an impossibility.

Hanna started again when they went to bed. It was the same old argument about the window. Lizzie said she felt sick with the smell of the meal sacks stacked against the wall, but Hanna flatly refused to open the window even an inch. 'I'll say one thing, Lizzie,' she said, thumping her pillow happily and nodding towards it, 'you wouldn't want for fresh air with the likes of him. You'd be under a hedge.'

Lizzie turned over and refused to speak. How stupid, she thought. Anger gritted her teeth. How can my father blame a man for things before he was born? It's not fair. It's not *fair*!

* * *

It was months before she saw him again. It was after the GAA sports that were held in the big field on the edge of Boolavoe, out past the sawmill. She and Minnie had been to the hurling and then to listen to the music in the square. It was getting late. On the stalls that had been set up all around the perimeter of the field, the traders were lighting candles and placing them in bottles. She was wearing her straw hat with the little blue feather and showing a good bit of leg above her buttoned boot, and they were counting out the pennies and farthings between them, seeing what was left, when she noticed the thin brown horse with its nosebag, and the solemn dog sitting up there waiting as patiently as ever on the cart.

'Look,' she said to Minnie, 'there's Tom Quinn's cart.'

'And there's himself,' said Minnie.

The cart was drawn up with some others by a fire of sticks on the edge of the green, where a fat woman with bare feet and a black cape was dishing up tins of stew for the traders.

'Where?'

He turned from talking to a man in a grey tweed suit and she saw his face, blank-eyed and thin-jawed, not seeing her.

'Tom!' she called.

102

'Lizzie, you be careful,' Minnie said. 'Your ma and everyone'll be along any second.'

'I'm doing no harm.' She walked over to speak to him. Minnie stood and waited.

'Hello, Tom.'

'Hello, Lizzie.'

'What are you selling?'

He smiled. 'Nothing,' he said.

'Nothing?'

'Nothing.'

Not a word came. They stood awkwardly.

'I'm sorry for my father,' she said.

'What's he say about me?'

'Tom,' she said, 'it's all ancient history. Whatever he's on about it's nothing to do with you.'

He looked sideways, always smiling, slightly shifty.

'Your people lived in our Pats's house,' she said.

'Only it was our house then.' He looked back at her. 'My grandfather built it.'

'Lizzie!' Minnie called.

'Really? Your grandfather did?'

'So I'm told.'

'Who tells you?'

'My father told me. He was born there. They lost it in the famine.'

'*My* father was on about the famine.'

'Lizzie!'

'There's Minnie,' she said. 'You went to school with Minnie.'

'True.'

'In Eskean.'

'In Eskean.'

'God, but you're a lovely girl,' Tom said, very fast and low and clumsy.

Minnie came up and took her firmly by the arm. 'Hello, Tom,' she said.

'Minnie.' He dipped his head.

'Here's your ma, Lizzie,' Minnie said softly, 'we must be going.'

There was Hanna's striped skirt and her mother's bonnet, coming along through the stragglers. Lizzie became aware at the same time of a tall heavy-laden woman who had been standing off to one side all this time watching them. Tom retreated into the shadows before the fire glow.

'What are you doing, Lizzie,' came her mother's harsh voice.

'Goodbye, Tom!' Lizzie said clearly.

'Bye,' he said, turning and walking quickly to his cart.

'Where have you two been?' Hanna cried, 'We're dead looking for you.'

'We watched the dancing,' said Minnie.

'Minnie, you should know better,' her mother scolded, 'letting her talk to that man when you know how upset her daddy was about it all before.'

'I was there all the time,' Minnie said, 'they were only saying hello.' She squeezed Lizzie's arm.

Henry and Mike were already up on the cart. Mike got down to help his mother up.

'It's not fair,' Lizzie said.

'Not another word! You know what your father said. No more!'

'Am I not even to be civil to people any more?' Lizzie hauled herself up lightly on the other side.

'Not to him.'

'Ah, come on, Lizzylie.' Hanna plumped down beside her. Mike tied the rope across. 'You don't

104

want to waste your time on him. There's better fish in the sea.'

Like Marty Blake? she wanted to say but didn't.

They stood in line to get out of the field with all the other carts waiting along the hedge. Tom Quinn's cart was a little ahead and to one side. She could see stray strands of brown hair coming out from under his cap at the back. His dog's ears were pricked up. Lizzie felt an urge to do something ridiculous, pull down the rope and jump down, hit Hanna or something. A handsome young woman with a big creel on her back and a basket over one arm walked by and stopped a little further along the line.

'Is there any room up there for me, Tom?' she asked. She wore a tattered coat, a man's cap and boots, and her face was brown. Her right hand, clutching the ropes of the creel, was long and graceful and strong. It was the woman who'd watched as they talked.

'Room and to spare, Marie,' he said, and up she got and set down her load and settled beside him, taking out a pipe and lighting it. The carts began to sway forward. Ahead of them, the woman's tousled black hair, the tender back of Tom's boyish neck, swaying. Hanna settled a blanket over both their knees. 'There!' she said comfortingly. It was cold. Lizzie shivered and felt a sinking in the pit of her stomach. She was being ridiculous. Of course her mother and Hanna were right. How could she possibly contemplate a man who had friends like that? Look at that woman sitting up on the cart with him so familiar. And the rags he wears. No pride. Anyway, it always goes hard with those divided by money.

'I've told your father.' Her mother sounded upset but defiant.

'Told him what?'

'About you and Quinn.'

Lizzie was hanging up her cloak, her mother had just come in the back door and was bustling about the room. Hanna looked up from the fire.

'Mother!' Lizzie's hands flew up to her face. 'You haven't!'

'I had to!' her mother hissed. 'Better from me than from some other! Standing there for all to see!'

'Doing what? Doing what? Just talking!' Her father and Mike came in. 'What's this, what's this?' her father said in his deadly quiet voice.

'She has a grah for Tom Quinn,' said her mother bluntly.

'I have not!'

Henry came in. All of them, looking at her, waiting for the flood. She wouldn't cry though, not this time. 'I have done nothing wrong,' she said with what she hoped was dignity. Her father looked around at them all. For a terrible second she thought she was going to laugh. His eyes! As if there'd been murder and death, and all she'd done was say hello to Tom Quinn.

'Hanna,' he said fraily, 'you, my girl, tell me.'

Hanna glanced at Lizzie. 'I don't know, Da,' she said. 'She was just standing there talking to him and Minnie when we came up. He went off when he saw us.'

He shook his head from side to side slowly,

moving across the room and feeling for the back of his chair as if he was blind or in pain or much older that he really was.

'What?' Lizzie laughed. 'What?'

'Lizzie!' said her mother.

'What have I done?'

Her father sat down and covered his eyes as if he'd just received a terrible blow.

She picked up a pot of blackberry jam that stood open on the table and hurled it against the wall, where it shattered in an explosion of flying jam and glass shards. Everyone leapt back. Her father jumped up. Her mother took one stride and struck her hard across the face.

'How dare you!' her mother cried.

Lizzie stood horrified, one hand on her burning cheek.

'You clean that mess up now!'

'I'm sorry.'

'Lorelei,' her father said gently, putting his arms out to her, 'come and sit on Daddy's knee.'

Then she really did start crying. 'No!' she shouted, 'No, it's not fair! I haven't done anything.'

He came towards her and she flinched. 'I'm sorry about the jam.'

'Lorelei,' he said, with eyes of mournful reproach, 'you know I never laid a finger on you.'

There was a moment of stillness. Hanna coughed.

'I'll clear the jam up,' Lizzie said.

That was when her father slammed the wall with his fist rather than hit her, knocking some of the whitewash off. He did that once, then sat down forcefully in his chair, breathing heavily down his nostrils. 'I'll do away with him myself,' he said, 'true as God's above me, I'll do away with him if she so much as looks at him again.'

*　　　*　　　*

They were all wrong, she told herself. What matters? She asked. That he's a nice boy or that he's got a rough edge or two? No one mentioned Tom at all after that night. It was all over, the scenes, the long faces, her father's discomfort with the effort of strong emotion. Things were back to normal in every way but in her mind. Every night lying in bed she burned with the injustice of it all, that something good and innocent could be seized on and made shameful. He'd brought that rock all the way up from the stone strand. That must mean something. And he'd been so dignified when her father shouted at him, though he must have been shocked.

She should have let it go, she knew. She'd already faced the fact of impossibility before her mother betrayed her so atrociously by telling her father. And there was that big hard woman sitting up there on the wagon with him. What did that mean? Was she just a neighbour? A sister, even, or a cousin? I have to find out, she thought. So I can let it go. He can't come here so it's up to me. Because if he really wants to see me, I'll go against my father, I'll go against them all.

She would have written but she was sure he'd not be able to read it. So she cadged a ride into town one day with Jack and Norah O'Donnell, saying she needed wool, and when they'd set her down and arranged a time to meet, lost no time at all in setting off. She was carrying a basket of eggs. A rising wind rippled the grass growing between the slates on the rooftops across the way as she passed the barracks and the forge, walking very fast, then the sawmill loomed up. Two miles further on a plank bridge crossed the river to Eskean.

The village was one long terrace. Outlying cabins were dotted here and there.

'Which way to the Quinns?' she asked a boy with a stick who was driving a bullock down the road.

He jerked his thumb. 'Go to the crossroads,' he said, 'take the left fork and go on to where the wood's on your right then you'll see a stile and you go over and up the boreen and it's on your left. It's got a lady scarecrow in a red frock.'

It was a tiny mud-walled cabin with scraggy thatch. The lady scarecrow did nothing to keep off a horde of crows that strutted here and there over the lazy beds at the back. The house opened straight onto the boreen and Tom was sitting on a creepie outside the door, having his eyes bathed by a barefoot girl of about fourteen in a filthy pinafore. When Lizzie appeared in front of the cabin, he could not see her because of the water streaming down his face. A dirty child pushed another in a wheelbarrow. Seeing her, the girl stepped back. 'Tom,' she said, 'there's a lady.'

Tom straightened up and shook the water from his eyes.

'Hello, Tom,' said Lizzie.

He stood, flustered, looking around at the squalor as if he'd never seen it before.

'What's this?' he said, 'why are you here, Lizzie?'

'I brought you some eggs,' she said, 'we had so many. How are you, Tom?'

He wiped his face with a dirty handkerchief. 'I'm

well,' he said, 'and yourself?'

'Very well.' She smiled at the bony-faced girl, who did not smile back.

'This is my sister Judith,' he said.

Lizzie still smiled. 'What's that you're putting on his eyes?' she asked pleasantly.

'Some herbs I got,' said Judith. 'From McGrane.'

'Do you have sore eyes?' she asked him.

'Sometimes I do.'

She thrust the basket at him.

'Thank you,' he said stiffly. 'Have we something to put these in, Judith?'

'Of course we have.'

'Very kind, Lizzie,' he said, 'very kind. Will you come in and have some tea?'

'Don't put yourself to any trouble.'

'No trouble, no trouble at all. Is there hot water, Judith?'

'Of course there is.'

'Make a pot of tea, there's a good girl,' he said.

It was dark inside. A girl of ten or so turned from stirring a pot on the fire. The floor was scattered with crumbs and ash. A bashed old fiddle hung on a peg on the wall. Tom showed Lizzie to the one chair, while he sat down on a box, twining his long fingers and looking at her. The children came in.

'Do you play, Tom?' Lizzie asked, indicating the fiddle.

He shook his head. 'It was my father's,' he said.

Judith made tea. All of them stared openly at her as if she was a strange animal. She had not worn her best by any means but even so she felt like a queen in a hovel. She looked about at the dinginess. 'What a pretty cat,' she said. The animal sat on a window sill, blue-eyed with wild black hair.

110

A little boy went and got it for her and placed it in her lap, but its fur stood on end and it scratched, leapt down and flew out of the door.

'It's wild,' said Tom.

A thin red line appeared across the back of Lizzie's hand.

'You're scratched,' he said, perplexed.

'Oh, it's nothing.' She licked the scratch, took out her handkerchief and dabbed at it briskly, smiling. Judith gave the pot a stir and poured out the tea, strong and dark and bracing.

'That's a lovely cup of tea, Judith,' Lizzie said sincerely.

Judith, sitting on the table swinging her legs, ignored her.

'Have we any soda cake?' he asked awkwardly.

'No.'

'She could have a saucer of stew,' said the child at the fire.

'No, no.' Lizzie sipped her tea. 'Nothing for me, thank you very much, I've had something not long ago. I'll just finish my tea.'

There was an awkard silence, then Tom said again, 'Thank you very much for the eggs. It's kind of you.'

'Not at all,' she said, and knew that she must go now, there was nothing more to be said here with all these Quinns sitting around watching her every move, and him there with his misty eyes and his bare toes braced against the dirt floor saying nothing. She took the empty egg basket from the bench and stood. 'Well, thank you for the tea,' she said politely, 'I really must be going now.'

Tom stood up so quickly his box fell over. He saw her to the door.

Hens pecked about on the stones outside. 'Bye so,' she said softly, and set off, straight-backed, smiling triumphantly. A little way down the boreen, she heard, as she'd known she would, his footsteps behind her. He came alongside. 'I'll walk you back to the bridge,' he said.

They walked in silence till they were leaving the wood behind, coming to the crossroads.

'I hope your hand is not too bad,' he said. 'The cat's a terror.'

'It's nothing,' she said.

'That was a long way for you to bring the eggs.'

'Yes.'

They walked on. A couple of women passing looked at them curiously. A sense of danger crept through her. When they reached the bridge she stopped and faced him.

'Well,' she said.

He grinned nervously. They were standing on the bridge looking down at the water flowing under. 'May I say, Lizzie,' he said, 'that you are a lovely girl, much too lovely for me. That you have walked all this way to see me—'

'Do you still want to go for a walk with me?' she asked.

He clasped his hands on the parapet and bowed his head down till his forehead touched his knuckles. 'I don't think your father would like that,' he said.

'No.' She said it resignedly but with a faint edge of surprise.

They stood for a long time. The sound of the river running over stones combined with the rustling of leaves into a hypnotic, low-throated music. I must be going, she thought frantically, I must be going, but she said, 'I do what I like.'

He raised his head and looked at her. 'Want to go for a walk?' he said. 'Now?'

Then she was all briskness. 'Not now, no time,' she said, shifting her basket to the other arm, 'I have to go and buy some wool, I must have been away hours. Come up to the rath above Kildarragh if you want to see me. I'll go up Sunday after Mass on the way to see my brother. Where we saw the seals? It's safe enough up there. We can go for a little walk. Yes?' She smiled brightly.

'Yes.'

'Good.' And she walked off across the bridge without a backward look, rubbing at her scratched hand.

*   *   *

That whole summer was like a falling drop, flashing for one second. Every Sunday they'd meet on the cliff top; every week waited for Sunday. The path down the cliff was safe but took a sure foot, so they'd hold hands and go down slowly to the cave, crawl in and sit at the back where the booming of the ocean and the cackling of the sea birds was muted, out of the way of the wind. It was like being in a mouth.

Though he was her first, Lizzie was no innocent. She knew as soon as she told him to meet her on the rath that she would take him there. Inside, with the sea shining in the cave's mouth, framed by wild grasses, they were out of the world. This had been her solitude since she was twelve or so. She'd never found anyone else there, never taken anyone there. He was greatly honoured, but that first time

113

she didn't think he appreciated it so she didn't allow him to touch her. She knew all about what went on. It wasn't wrong. You saw it all the time, the cattle and sheep and cats and dogs. She'd been exploring her own body furtively for years and had noted how much it had changed this past year. She was small but her breasts were bigger than Hanna's. She smiled at herself in the mirror a great deal these days, or simply looked, occasionally stunned by her own face. He was right, she was lovely. She was some wonderful thing, full of power. *She* would say when, and she'd only relent when she was sure he was fully aware of the extent of his luck. She was a prize.

The first four weeks she let him kiss her but no more. Each time that was only after an interval of decorous conversation which both of them knew as a prelude. They talked about everyday things. He went away a lot, he said, working here and there; he'd been in England two years ago. In September, he said, he thought he might be able to get a start with a road gang in north Wales.

She smiled mysteriously, trying to keep her feelings secret. In fact she had no idea what her feelings were, only that she was mad in the head with the whole thing. 'Will you come back?' she asked.

'Oh, yes,' he said, 'I always come back.'

This gave her a premonition of tears.

'Why do you have to go away? Why can't you just stay here like everybody else? My brothers don't go away all the time.'

'Money,' he said, smiling, 'I don't have the land.'

And there it lay between them.

For three months they played a game. She

thought about getting a nice painted wagon like the gypsies and going on the road for a while with him. She told him and it became another thing they did: lying side by side on his coat in the dim belly of the cave, talking about the wagon, where they'd go, what they would eat and drink, and how in the evenings they'd make camp somewhere tranquil and light a fire. Only, of course, you couldn't really come back from a thing like that. It was just another part of the bigger game, the one that went on changing all the time, because you could do anything in the cave. It was not in the world. You could play.

6

After Christmas

Silly things, Minnie said, when Lizzie tried to explain all this. She'd come over the top and started crying passing the rath. It was mid-October and Tom had been in Wales or Dublin, she wasn't sure which, six weeks. His cousin had sent word there was work on the road gang, and if not, then he was bound to get taken on at Jacob's biscuit factory over Christmas and he could be back in the New Year. She had not been prepared for his distress when he told her this. He'd buried his face in her lap and mumbled things she couldn't understand. She thought he was weeping, and stroked his head.

By the time she reached Darby's House she'd fallen over and skinned her hands on the stones.

115

'What happened?' asked Minnie, pouring water over her hands.

'I fell,' she sniffed. The icy water brought tears back to her eyes.

The dog Captain sat upon the path, scratching for fleas. Still a runt, bandier than ever.

'You fell.' Minnie's voice was flat. 'What's wrong with you? You're always ill.'

'I'm getting a weakness.'

Minnie looked closely into her face, her eyes solemn; and then Lizzie had told her everything in a great outpouring. She'd thought about talking to Hanna but simply couldn't; she'd even tried, but couldn't say a thing at all, at confession. She hadn't known till she got here that this was why she'd come out today, because somehow someone had to be told.

'Are you pregnant, Lizzie?'

'No!'

'Are you sure?'

'I can't be,' she whispered. 'He was very careful.'

'Dear God,' said Minnie, 'you are.'

'I don't know, Min, I pray God I'm not. I don't know what to do.'

Minnie put her stiff arms around Lizzie's shoulders, but Lizzie was tearless now. 'Maybe it will be nothing,' she said. It was a clear day, the sea and sky bright blue, everything outlined with a clear edge. She felt pure suddenly, untroubled. There was a baby or there was not. It would be or not. The sun would go down, the moon would come up. 'I feel,' she said, 'I feel—' but couldn't say what, and anyway Pats was coming up the track and she couldn't say anything to him. She looked around.

116

'Don't say anything, Min,' she said, and knew with absolute certainty in her soul in that moment that she was going away. The goat that was tethered, the old hollow tree, the big green-striped stone resting up against the wall of the house, the dog nosing its nether parts on the path—all of these things she would see no more. That time was near. It was a little death.

*   *   *

Minnie went with her to see Doctor Gildea at the dispensary in Boolavoe. Later, all she could remember of the room was that he had a blind on his window, with a lacy edge to it that could be pulled down by a little tassle; and she remembered the thin sympathetic smile with which he confirmed her worst fear, and the way both he and Minnie seemed to expect something more of her than what she showed, which was what she felt, which was nothing.

Still later, much later, she would remember how serene she had been when she stood with Minnie, and listened to Minnie tell her mother the truth; how her mother had not wept or shouted or scolded but simply sat down and said nothing for half an hour or so then gone to find her father; and how terrified she'd been. How he'd walked through the door with his killing eyes, come straight over to her and pulled her into a long and dreadful embrace, breathing heavily, and it had made her cry and want to break away though she didn't dare to.

Then all of them knew.

Not a word against her from any of them.

It was horrible. A kind of mourning fell on the family, and the household was sombre. Lizzie carried herself through it all, erect and calm, like someone very bravely bearing a terrible illness. The worst of it was her father's eyes, which she felt burning upon her sometimes as she sat in the evening with her sewing. Of course, she had to go away, that was understood. Before Christmas, before he came back. She didn't fight it. Everyone was being so kind and making a path for her. It all happened very fast. They wrote to her sister Cathy in Salford and it was arranged that she'd go there to have the child, and it would be given out that she was recently widowed. And then when she came back with the child it would be given out here that she had a husband over there.

It was too much to think about. Her father didn't speak much. Once, in the middle of a meal, he stopped eating and said darkly to no one and everyone: 'If it were not for the Quinns, I would not have lost my own mother.'

A silence followed.

Her mother told her he'd said he'd die before she'd marry Tom Quinn, not that she'd ever seriously expected to. Everyone knew Tom Quinn would never make money and Lizzie Vesey would never go and live in a hovel. These things didn't happen and there'd be no happy ending. So now, when she thought about him and the things they'd done in the cave, she felt slightly sick and refused to see his face.

No sooner had the forms been filled in at the post office and the money found for the passage than a letter arrived from England addressed to Lizzie alone. Something about the firm script jogged something in her memory. Miss Lizzie Vesey was in larger letters than the address. It was from Bob Jakey, the English coach driver who'd stayed in their barn with Cathy's husband, the one who'd taken such a fancy to her. Bob Jakey wrote that he had discovered her situation from his very close friend, that he realised this might sound precipitate but would she accept his sincere offer of marriage. He had often thought of writing to her before but had not found the courage. He said that she must believe him to be absolutely serious about this, and that he would wait her reply. *PS: I will never cast it up at you and will raise the child as my own.*

*   *   *

Her trunk was sent on to Manchester.

The night before she left, though it was cold, she went out and walked about the yard and the sheds while the others were all inside. Familiar things held a kind of wonder, simple things shone: the bits of rock that hung from the pigsty roof, the puddle under the pump. She could smell her mother's cooking, listen to the soft crooning of her chickens settling down for the night. When she went in, her mother was chopping cauliflower and Hanna was slicing the pig's cheek. Everyone was coming for a farewell meal. They wouldn't let her cook or do anything at all.

It was a wonderful meal. Everyone came, and later, her father got down the whiskey for the men. Mike sat and stroked her feet and Hanna combed her hair, and Minnie had brought some little cakes she'd made. Her father said very little and hardly

119

looked at her; her mother smiled bravely every time she caught her eye. Lizzie laughed and was very charming, and when they toasted her with wine, drank hers down in one quick gulp and laughed more, and said wildly, 'I can't believe it! I can't believe it!'

She couldn't remember Cathy's leaving. She couldn't even remember Cathy, even though she was going to be living with her and her husband and their five children. She couldn't imagine it, any of it, couldn't imagine Bob Jakey either. She hadn't said yes and she hadn't said no. She couldn't stop laughing, it ran away with her, trying to remember what he looked like and seeing only his hair with the dead straight parting in the middle, but no real face under it, only an impression of something good-natured but not particularly marvellous.

It was all so bright: the candlesticks, the bottles and canisters on the ledge above the chimney breast, the glasses and egg-cups on the top shelf of the dresser, the long-handled slane resting by the fire, the font at the foot of the stairs. And the pictures of poor Robert Emmet who was hanged, and Parnell and the Blessed Virgin Mary, all made strange with leaving.

Hanna gave her a beautiful rosary carved out of bog oak. Her mother threw her apron over her head and wept. 'Oh, Jamie!' she sobbed, 'Oh, Jamie!'

'Hush!' said her father, 'She'll be back.'

'I'll be back, Mammy.'

'Of course you will, of course you will.' Her mother blew her nose and wiped her eyes.

120

Her father did not come into Bantry with her. He
didn't like to travel far, and Bantry was as far as
he'd ever been. It was a gloomy grey morning three
weeks before Christmas, a faint rumble of thunder
grumbling over the distant ridge of mountains that
ran down the Cork and Kerry border. He came as
far as the gate, to the sidecar which Henry was
driving, and reached up to where she was sitting
with her mother and took her hand.

He smiled. The scar beneath his eye was white,
tight-looking. 'Well, it's seldom we'll see you now,
Lorelei,' he said softly, 'whatever way things work
out. So you be a good girl in your life now, won't
you, Lorelei,' and then the tears came spouting out
of his eyes, shocking.

'I'm coming back, Daddy,' she said.

He wiped his face with one great swipe of his
palm, stood back and raised his hand to wave
solemnly as the cart swayed forward into the road.
It was freezing. Henry had a sack over his
shoulders. Lizzie wore two petticoats under her
skirt, and the thick stockings her mother had
knitted. But the rain kept off till Bantry, beginning
in a soft silvery fall through the sun-motes falling
through the dark clouds over the bay.

There was not much time before the post-car
left, thank God. Now they were curiously formal.

'Well, Lizzie,' Henry said, hugging her swiftly,
'safe journey.'

'Bless you, Henry.'

'God bless.'

Her mother kissed her. 'Here,' she said, shoving
a small bundle into her bag, 'for if you get hungry.'

121

She climbed on board in her tight black button boots and sat as elegantly as she could. Opposite her sat a small boy with a big white collar and a corpulent man in a thick tweed coat. A woman with a tightly-rolled umbrella and smart kid gloves got on. Then it was all rattling and movement and waving and smiling, and her mother and Henry were gone. Soon after, everything she'd ever known was gone too.

Only when she was standing at the rail watching the lights of Cork City moving in the darkness as the ship sailed past Blackrock Castle and Spike Island, did she suddenly recall, clear in every detail, Tom Quinn's face; and then the whole unutterable vanished sweetness of the thing poured through her in a great torrent, along with the mournful lowing of cattle in the hold; and she cried at last, bitterly and drainingly, and finally, standing there on the deck. And after that she never cried for him again.

PART THREE

THE VESEYS
AND THE QUINNS
1845—late summer

7

Now what is he about bringing that child home with his cheek damaged? He didn't have to go up there anyway, he could have sent a boy; he didn't have to take the child at all, and if he did he should have made sure he was safe and not running around with those rough little bodies. Said they were playing on the tree, the three of them. Blood pouring down his cheek, my poor baby. Brave lad.

'Jamie, what have they done to you!' I cried.

'S'alright Mamma,' he said, 'I didn't cry.' Though the tear streaks were like stripes on his dirty face.

'You mustn't play on that horrible tree!'

Phelim standing there like a lump. 'It's not that bad, Eliza,' he says.

Child with a hole in his face, scarred for life, and he says that.

'What would you know?' I say, dabbing away at the bite with a bit of cloth. The blood still flowing. There can be deep poison in a cat's bite. And a cat up there in that place.

'Twas only a kitten,' says Phelim.

Fool. I'd have killed it. One smash of the loy.

'Why weren't you watching him?'

He scratches his head like an imbecile. 'He was with the boys,' he says, 'they were all together. And I was only inside with Darby after tying the pig.'

'He's only four. You should have watched him.'

'It's not bad, is it?' He leans down with a frown, big dirty fingers stretching towards the child's face.

'Don't touch it! Your hand's filthy.'

The hand darts back as if stung.

'I'm sorry, Eliza.'

'It's not me you should be apologising to, it's him, he's marked for life.'

'No!'

'He is,' I say.

He is. The boy sits on my knees, dirty legs dangling. Mrs Vesey, they used to say, when I took him into town, what a beautiful baby. What a beautiful child, Eliza. Everyone said it. Everyone. Now look at his poor face.

'You must never, never play on that tree,' I say, 'It's a bad tree.'

'It wasn't the tree, Ma,' he says, 'It was the cat.'

'Then the cat will die.'

'He was with the children,' says Phelim again.

I left the boy with his granda the next evening and off I went. I had to wait but I don't mind. I sat absolutely still above and looked down like the eye of the Lord on Kildarragh and saw Darby Quinn walking between the lazy beds at the side of his cabin. There are seventeen houses in Kildarragh and not a shoe between them. Darby built his the highest, away from the rest and out of sight of them. He stands and surveys his patch as if it was great lands. He works for us and he works for others. Those Quinn boys had fixed up a plank of wood and were playing seesaw next to the old dead tree at the back, and the cat, a skinny black thing, was on the window sill. Both bigger than him, the Quinn boys, and they let my Jamie get hurt.

I can wait and wait. I can move and make no sound. I can get out of bed at night and go out of the house without waking a soul. I'm invisible. I hold a raven's feather between my fingers. I have some words in my mind from nowhere, saying, the circular web. That's all it says, the circular web, over and over again. It happens like that, words in my mind. I don't mind.

Darby Quinn walks around to the front of his cabin and his wife, that one Sal, comes out of the house with the babe toddling at her skirts and her belly pushing at its apron with the next one on its way. He used to be a traveller. He carried a loy and went about between here and Kenmare for work, digging, booleying, whatever presented, but he settled down with Sal. He comes behind her, even with the child there at her skirts, and puts both of his hands under her enormous breasts and squeezes them like fruit, and she sticks her arse into his stomach. Around her black hair she wears a red kerchief as bright as poppies.

Then it smites me in my soul that I hate Sal Quinn.

I wait.

When the light was fading, and they were all inside, and the little ones eating their stirabout, I came down; came so slow and silent, invisible. The cat was on the sill. I killed it with one touch, without a sound. Little puss, little puss, I whispered in the darling's ear. There was blood and slime from pussy's mouth and nose.

I crouch beneath the window. They're talking in Irish.

*   *   *

Phelim is a shy man who hardly knows himself because he's spent his whole life standing back, stilling his wants because of the tidiness of his soul. This man would have stayed in the womb if he

127

could, it was all so easy in there. My heart went out to him as soon as I saw him, a childish youth when he first came to our house with my father. A bad fairy had touched him in the cradle so he'd grown with a bent nose, long, jagged teeth, pale freckled skin, hairy nostrils, huge ears and a large Adam's apple. And he's always had a silly smiling amiability that makes people think he's simple, but he's not simple at all, not Phelim.

I fell in love with him because of a dream I had when I was thirteen years old. In this dream I'm a small child in a downstairs room in a very old dark house, and there are grown-ups talking over my head as if I can't understand. An old woman like my grandmother, but not her, says, 'She's not to go, she'd only get upset.' But I sneak out anyway and go up a staircase that runs right up the middle of the house. I push open a door and there's a boy of about sixteen lying dying all alone on a narrow bed in the middle of a very large, very dark room. He seems to be in a lot of fear and pain. A long beam of pure white light shines out of his right eye, going straight up to the ceiling. He's my brother and I'm stricken with grief. That's it. Actually I never had a brother. But when I saw Phelim I recognised at once the silly pale awkward dying brother in the dream and that was that. I was nineteen then. I had the choice of the two of them, him or Tadhg. I chose him because he was soft. He wanted to please. Tadhg was a bit wild. He was in with those Ribbonmen running round making trouble for the landlords. I could have had better than Phelim as far as money went, and far, far better for the looks. But I do love him. I brought him six more acres, glass for his windows and a feather bed.

He never asks where I've been. He knows I go walking.

Jamie mo chree
Pussy's in the tree . . .

My little boy lies sleeping with his hands thrown above his head. His bloody cheek is staunched with cobweb.

'I'll take the pig to Lomas's tomorrow then,' says Phelim as we get into bed.

He's getting none of me tonight. Last night he was down at the shebeen. She goes there, Sal Quinn, with her husband. It's like her that she would. She's been everyone's fancy at one time or another, even Phelim's, but that was years ago, before me. There's a great deal of nonsense goes on when it comes to all that. She never had a chance with him, she was not his kind. They can sing their songs about it but there's never been a good match between high and low. And if Phelim's low to some, she's lower still. We are not living in the Middle Kingdom with the fairies, the place where stories happen. We live here on this ground. In the Middle Kingdom a king is not like a king here and a queen is not like a queen here, not like that fat queen over the sea. In the Middle Kingdom a king can fall in love with a beggarmaid and turn her into a queen. But not here. Anyway, let's hope the one in the belly's not as sickly as the last, the peery one. I delivered her. I delivered all her lot. She's a brood mare, and all the doors were open, but that was a poor weak thing she had, a little girl baby all pale and quiet like a stillborn but

129

with a shocking smile on its face and its strange eyes wide open. And that's the creature she has to go and name after me, would you believe? Oh, you're so good, Eliza! You bring all my babies into the world. Still, a girl. I'd have liked a little girl, but after Jamie came the long bleed. It went on for thirty-six weeks, four days and six hours. I thought it would go on forever. I put an iron knife under my pillow for the strength. My mother used to say it was our power over men, that blood. My mother had only me and I have only Jamie. She died when I was twelve. Her belly swelled up very, very big and then she died. Then there was only me and father, and the land. We have twelve acres now. The Quinns have only two of conacre, and that's scattered everywhere. But they have those two big healthy boys, and the girl that's not right with my name, and now another. It isn't fair when those that can't look after them get them, and those with the means don't. But my boy's the best of them all, the best boy in all the worlds, the best of all those I ever held in my arms all slimy from the womb. And there's been a good few. How many? It's all the same, every babe's a blessing when it comes, every poor tiny scrap. Doesn't matter if it's a hovel or a glebe house. It's when I look at the mothers I worry. All these bonny babes born to become what I see walking around me every day, for human beings can be very ugly. Surely life's terrible to do that to us, to start us pure and twist us as we grow? Then again, sometimes I am so stroked with wonder at these times that I feel like a nun seeing Christ in the face.

*   *   *

130

This has been an awful rainy season. Phelim says the crop's been bad upcountry. There's maybe the taint, he says, and we're not yet through the meal months. Hey-ho. Last time we had a hunger was when my ma was alive; she and I used to go down on the strand for kelp. My ma could always get us something. We did fine. Well, the earlies are pitted and safe anyway, and there's plenty of oats, so we'll do.

I was shaving my father, he was all suds, when a girl came and called me up to Kildarragh to look at Scanlon's child that was ailing, and while I was up there I met with Sal Quinn in her red kerchief like a Queenstown whore. She's got the two boys with her, proper little spalpeens they'll make, and the queer girl wrapped in a blanket slung round her body. That child must be one now and it's still completely bald. I don't like it, it has no hair anywhere. I don't like its eyes because I don't know what it is about them. I wonder was she up there on the rath about the time she fell? Now that I'd like to know.

Sal looks wild, her eyes all a-stare. Have I seen Darby down the way? I have not.

'Oh,' she says, 'I need him here, he's got to come!'

'Why, whatever is it?'

'There's an awful crying,' she says then, and those poor scared boys looking up at her with their dirty scrubby faces, 'I can't stay there,' she says, 'It's like a voice in the ground.'

She doesn't even think to ask after the little one.

'Come,' I said, 'I'll walk up with you, there's nothing frightens me.'

So we all trail up there and the sound, coming the louder as we approach the cabin, would curdle your blood in your veins.

'Holy Mother of God!' she whispers. 'It's a soul in torment.'

'It's the cat,' I say, and up I go to the old tree and throw down stones and sods till it stops.

'It's dead now,' I tell her.

'Down there?'

'Must have fallen in and got stuck. Never mind, it's out of its misery now.'

'Oh the poor thing!' she says, and then she remembers. 'How is Jamie's cheek?'

'Mending. He'll have a scar.'

'Oh, surely not!'

'Oh, surely.'

'Oh, poor little man, and he's such a brave boy.'

'He is so.'

Then Darby Quinn arrives on the scene. Well, he's a handsome enough man, fair, too squat for my liking, but a hard-built, strong man. 'What is it, allanna?' and he's straight to her and she's all soft and silly with him.

'The cat's dead,' I say. 'It fell in the tree.'

Those two boys are peering down there.

'You'll see nothing,' says I.

'How is the little boy, Eliza?' asks Darby kindly. He has a nice soft voice. Picks up his little girl and rubs his long soft hair against her pate.

'Mending.'

'She says he'll be scarred,' Sal tells him.

He looks closely into my eyes. 'I am very sorry for it, Eliza,' he says, 'I am very very sorry it happened here.'

I nod.

132

The baby holds out its arms to me.

'There, she's giving you a love,' says Sal, 'she does it with everyone.'

Look at their foolishly smiling faces. Darby is one of those soft-eyed souls, transparent. They see no flaw in that child. All of them, the boys as well, they bow down around her like the sheaves of corn in the dream in the story of Joseph and his brothers. It's always baby Eliza this and baby Eliza that, and look at what she's doing now, as if there'd never been a baby before. Well, she'll get her nose put out of joint when this new one comes along, won't she? I reach out and touch her hands. Same chubby hands as any child. Her eyes flash red for a second. Dark wine red.

*   *   *

It's funny how the boy knows the way I'm feeling. I've said nothing and I thought I showed nothing on my face but he came up and put his hand on my knee. 'What's the matter, Mamma,' he said.

'Oh nothing nothing, my sweet baby.'

I'm known as a woman of knowledge. I have always known that if you do this thing and that thing—certain actions which must be taken at the appropriate times—good will follow. I have a very strong will and nothing yet has defeated me. But I know too when a time comes that topples the old rules. When you do this at the right time and that at the right time, exactly as you have always done, and it's all been right before; but now it isn't. Like a cold stream in the blood, all those sure things are gone. Like a falling in the blood. That's how it was when my mother died.

133

How did he know I was feeling like that?

'Never mind, Mamma,' he says and puts his arms round my neck and hugs.

So we hug and kiss and rock and make everything good again.

It'll be hard. It's been hard before. We don't know what it is. It's not the taint and it's not curl. I've not seen it like this before. The look on Phelim's face when he came in from digging the potatoes told me. 'Come and see this,' he said. I know all the expressions of his face, and this was like nothing I'd ever seen. I didn't want to go and look. I don't know why, but it made me feel as if I was suddenly dreaming, a bad dream I wanted to wake up from. I didn't want to follow him, but I did. We went out to the pit. It was pouring down. The spade stuck out of the pit, and when Phelim shifted it, it raised a stink like a rotting sheep. The spade came out from the potatoes with a sucking noise, all covered in black muck. 'Oh, Jesus!' I covered my mouth and nose with my apron. God, it was like breathing poison.

'The whole bloody lot,' he said. 'Rotten. Rotten rotten rotten.' He threw down the spade.

We stepped back and took in fresh air and rain. My mouth had filled with spit. Our eyes watered.

'That is sheer rotten,' I said, 'Are you sure it's the lot?'

'As far down as I've gone with the spade. I couldn't go down more, I was nearly sick.'

Jamie came running.

'Jamie darling, don't go near!'

Summer was the lean time. Always so, summer lean, then the harvest. I looked at the slimy pit and was angry.

'But it was a good crop,' I said, 'they've turned in the pit. It must be how you put them in. What did you do?'

'What I always do,' he replied tetchily. 'What I've been doing for years. They're all gone, Eliza. Do you know what this means?'

'It means we'll get heartily sick of stirabout before we're through. Here, Phelim, go down to Bob Neary's and see if they've got the same. Sniff around. Come in, Jamie, you're getting soaked.'

I took him in and played trit-trot-trit with him on my knee. I remembered the last time. There were some died in the uplands, but we saw nothing of it. The beggars multiplied. There was a little cove where you could go for the mussels, and we waded in up to our thighs. I used to love wading there with my mother. She always knew what to do. She had a smile that never quite left her face, she even died with it on. I have a nervous feeling in my chest, a peculiar thing like the string on a fiddle vibrating very high. There must be within my inner soul a girding, a hardening, a rock wall of being that will not fall, let all the seas wash over it for a million years. I am iron.

He comes back and says it is not so at Kildarragh but it is so at Neary's and Gilhooley's and all along the strand beyond Lissadoon village. Jamie has fallen asleep sprawled across my lap. Phelim sits forlornly on the stool with his thin-fingered, gentle hands loosely clasping one another. 'It's going to be a bad winter, Queen Eliza,' he says.

He worries. Always has. Even when there isn't anything to worry about he can't be easy. I'll have to pull him through another bad winter. I'll pull us all through. I put my hand on his knee. 'We'll not

135

go short,' I say, and smile.

My poor heron looks into the fire and his eyes are black. 'I know that, love,' he says, 'it's the debt I'm worried about. I told Lomas I'd bring the debt down come November.'

'Well, we can't do the impossible. Have sense.'

'Oh, I'll have sense,' he says, 'I'll have sense alright, but will he? Anyway, it's not Lomas that counts.'

Not Lomas, not even Cloverhill in his big house. Tarlton's the man. We are all in his pocket. Tarlton is a big lord, lives in Dublin, owns everything between here and Kildoran, which lies beyond Boolavoe. Owns us and owns Kildarragh, owns Lomas, owns even Cloverhill. Cloverhill's his middleman and Lomas is Cloverhill's agent. Everyone's got his master.

'There'll be folks put out,' Phelim says darkly.

It won't be us. The Quinns come into my mind, and all at Kildarragh. But their crop's not touched, he says.

*   *   *

Phelim and me have plenty, with the oats and the barley. As for the debt, it's older than the two of us, it'll wait a while more. Lomas can bring in Kildarragh's rents, we can't do the impossible. Theirs have rotted now like ours, and the late crop's got the mould under the leaves. It's all the talk and there's people crying. People do love to cry and wail. I was up there seeing Becky Scanlon again, and there was Alma Sheehan and Nan Fox both after me wanting to know what way things are with Lomas. Phelim's seen him, I told them, as far

136

as I know there's no cause for alarm. Well, he has seen him, but they'd never tell you anything. Well, we can't do the impossible, can't keep carrying others too, not necessarily, not if Cloverhill gets nasty. I said as much to Phelim, and he says: 'We'll do what we can, Eliza. It won't come to that.' Well, of course. But you ought to see the prices in town. Doesn't take the hawksters long to take advantage of misfortune. I said to that woman in Moran's store, 'What's this?' I said. 'What d'you think people are made of? I paid the same last Thursday week here for a loaf and it was twice that size.' She just says, 'I know, 'tis terrible, it's what they're going for.' And as for those awful lumpers, God knows where they're getting them from, three times the cost and they turn to mush in the pot.

I get home and my da's up stomping around in the yard like an old turkey cock, stirring up the chickens. Pathetic whingeing old thing, takes more looking after than Jamie. Says his legs are bad but he's getting about, isn't he? When he wants to.

'Eliza,' he says, puffing and blowing as if the next breath's all too much, 'there's been a fellow looking for Phelim.'

'What's he want?'

'I donno. Says there's papers from the government. I told him he was working for Cloverhill today and surely he'd just come from that way. He must have seen him there. He's gone back looking for him.' He has a wheedling miserable way about his speech.

Papers from the government. What's all that?

'Get back inside, you old rep,' I say. 'What are you doing out?'

God, the man gets under my feet.

'Just getting a breath of fresh air, Eliza,' he says.

'Well, it's going to tip it down any minute,' I say, shooing him, 'go on in,' and I take Jamie's hand and we start off down the lane to see if we can see his daddy coming, but no sooner do we reach the cross than we hear the sound of a cart; then it's round the bend with a little brown pony trotting smartly, and sitting up there with two government men in their good warm coats and high hats, looking strange and grey in his old working clothes, is Phelim. The man driving pulls on the pony's mouth and they stop and Jamie wants lifting to stroke the creature's nose. One of them says to me, nice as can be, 'Would you climb up and ride with your husband now, madam, you'll be getting soaked.' And in fact it is starting to come down now, the clouds over west are like cow's udders desperate for milking.

'A ride in a cart, Jamie!' Phelim says, and jumps down to hand me in like a lady. There's nothing wrong here, I can tell by his manner and the way he smiles at me over Jamie's head. We're home in a trice, hedges and ditches flying by, and me and Jamie snuggled up with my shawl wrapped round us. Jamie says nothing, but his face is a picture. They're nice men. The one who isn't driving has a jolly demeanour and pretends to steal Jamie's nose off his face. My father's all agog, hanging round the door. I could bet you ten shillings he's got the place in an awful state being up and alone all afternoon, and of course he has. The dust's like grey sand round the fire, and the table's covered in slops. I have to clean it up quick so they can spread out their important papers. They're not real government men, they're only from Boolavoe. The papers are instructions telling us what to do with our rotten potatoes, and they want Phelim to give them out in Kildarragh.

'They have a schoolteacher up there,' I say, 'he can read it out to them.'

When they've gone Phelim goes through the whole thing very slowly, stumbling over some of the words. It says you can cut out the bad bits and eat the good bits quick before they rot, as long as you boil them well.

'What good bits? Ours were rotten through and through. God knows what eating slime would do to you. What good bits? That's what I want to know.'

'Eliza,' he says, 'let me read.'

If they stink it's too late. You have to break them up then—

'—imagine the stench—break them up in my good pot?'

You'd be scared to use it again.

Break them up, he says, and get the starch and mix it up with flour and make bread. Couldn't you just retch at the idea? I wouldn't eat it.

We ate well that night. I killed a chicken yesterday and we had the broth with some of the meat and some bread. Next day, when Phelim went up to Kildarragh I went with him. I took some broth in a can for Becky and found her running about again, so all's well there for now. There was a bit of a gathering in the house of O'Carroll, the schoolmaster, a tiny beaky man with straw for hair. He has some very nice things. Over his fireplace hangs a white carved pipe, very long, made out of ivory. I was looking at it and he came over and told me it came from very far away, and named a place I'd never heard of. He was very civil. He has a

139

clock on his shelf. Matty Sheehan and Darby Quinn were there, and old Nan Fox with Peader, her long streel of a husband. And Tadhg was there. When O'Carroll read out the bit about how vital it was to separate the good from the bad as soon as possible, Tadhg laughed loudly and said it reminded him of in the Scriptures where the Lord separates the wheat from the chaff and throws the chaff into everlasting fire, and we all know damn well who the chaff is, don't we?

Tadhg'll be fine, thank God, with his boat and the shebeen and his bit of carpentry. I could've been there at the crossroads instead of Curly Callanan. Now his daddy's dead, he's the man. See me, mistress of the shebeen. Not that I'd have wanted that, not like some, larking and wasting time when there's work to be done. He and me would not have made a pair. They're all wild, those Ribbonmen. Guns and pikes and lurking about in the dark. Good luck to them, I say, but don't marry one. I look at Tadhg sometimes and wonder what my life would have been like if I'd had him. I imagine sleeping with him in our feather bed, waking up with his dark square face and the big side whiskers that grow on his face like bushes on the side of a rock. Didn't choose the handsome one, did I? I still think I got the better bargain.

Make sure it's all dry, O'Carroll's telling us. Don't pit them any more, they have to be ventilated.

'It's the wet,' Darby says. 'God willing, we have a drier season coming.'

Tadhg laughs again. 'And what'll we plant?' he says. Tadhg always laughs when there's nothing to laugh at.

140

Nan Fox snorts and picks at her peeling nail, the end all broken off and crooked. Man, woman and child, the cottiers all have a long spike of a thumbnail for peeling spuds; not that they'll be needing them now, not for a while anyway.

We walk back over the top past Darby's house. Darby walks along with us as far as there, him and Tadhg. Now we're out of the general company, Tadhg's face is grim. Cloverhill and Lomas have it coming, he says. He says there's ships of grain sailing out of Cork Harbour and people going hungry.

'Whisht,' says Darby in a weary way, as if he's heard it all before.

Sal's at the front of her cabin, with the girl. She waves. She's showing now. Looks like another girl to me, I have a feel for these things. Two boys and two girls she'll have. Tadhg stops and says, 'Well now, my little lady!' to the child, who holds out both her arms to him and crows in a weird breathy little voice as he scoops her up in his arms and kisses her cheek. She croons delighted nonsense, and he carries her on into the house as if he lives there. Sal gives him a smile as he's going in the door. I feel ashamed for her, giving a man who isn't her husband a smile like that, but no one seems to notice. The brightness about Sal is the thing. Her eyes are dark and glittery, her big red lips shine, her teeth shine, her hair springs vital from her head. Mine doesn't. Mine is plain and straight and thin, and I have no red kerchief or a single ribbon about me. Yet still I have something. I can sit and sit and it grows and grows. And I know I really could have had either of them, Phelim or Tadhg, because there is something very

141

strong in me that gets what it wants, even though I'm very, very small, and very, very thin with no breasts; even though my face is dark and narrow.

'I want to do right,' Phelim says as we pass by the rath.

Phelim is a weak man. We're going to want every penny we can get.

'You will,' I say, 'you always do.'

'I'll talk to Lomas tomorrow.'

Phelim is a good man and nothing wrong with that. But he's a soft man in a hard life. Rent day's coming up, and no word yet from Lomas about Cloverhill's decision. If he insists on the lot, he'll get it but we can't carry our labourers this year, the Quinns and the Foxes, the Sheehans and the Scanlons. They give us work, we pay their rents, that's how it's always been, but not this year surely. Of course it's hard but they'll not starve. There's plenty of meal. And Tadhg's still out there with his nets and his boat.

I haven't got Phelim to agree to this yet but he'll have to. What can we do? How many years we've seen them through with Lomas, even when there's not been the work. No good comes to them if we go down. And next year things will be better. Even they can see the reason in that.

8

I have always had another person inside my head. She even has a name. She's called Juliander and she comes from the Middle Kingdom, the place where things not real live. She has accompanied me throughout my life and been a great comfort, though she hasn't always had her name. First I used to play with her, then I realised that she was not outside but inside myself, that she was in fact me, though she had another name from me; it came to her about that time. But this is all a very long time ago.

She's like me but different. She's always the same age. She has a history, her own life and beginnings that I have discovered. No one knows her origins, she was left as a newborn outside the cabin of poor cottiers but they all died in one of the hungers. All of this happened somewhere up the coast from here. She left behind everything she'd ever known and walked the roads of Ireland till she came to Dublin City, where she had many adventures. She'd never worn a shoe till she came to Dublin City. Now she is rich beyond your dreams and her life is full of adventures. Everyone loves her. She knows everyone I have ever wanted to know and all of them admire her. Not only is she beautiful, but even though her life has always been one of tragedy, she's wise and brave and clever and full of love for all things. Nothing changes this. She is bereaved many times, suffers terrible sorrows, grieves deeply and never forgets, but grows still wiser and somehow more pure in spirit, though she is a woman of the flesh. Of her many lovers, none has survived. Her lovers are strange, dangerous, fiery men, lonely and intense; her love affairs are holy passions.

When I first met her she was a little girl playing with acorns. She became my best friend. Thereafter she came every night of my life, through all my growing years, and she still comes. She's small and light, like me; in fact she's exactly the same size as me, but with a finer bosom. Her hair is black as the raven's wing, her eyes the blue of deep twilight. She comes when all is over, at the moment when you turn over and know it's the final slide into sleep, she comes and plays out her life in my head, a little at a time. Her life, like mine, is a gradual thing. It changes.

Wherever in the world she goes, someone will love Juliander. There is something about her that demands it.

*   *   *

Lomas says Cloverhill's prepared to stand for half and we can make it up when things are better. I knew. We won't take anything from Kildarragh. We'll carry them.

It was a terrible winter. Terrible. Nothing worked. They said it was a fungus. They said it was the wet. I suppose it's like toadstools, they love the wet. First you heard of places not touched, then it was everywhere: up the mountains, down by the shore, everywhere. And all that about how to store them with the little turf roofs on for the ventilation, all that came to nothing. They still turned to mush.

144

Sal Quinn sent for me up to Kildarragh because she was feeling scared about the child she's carrying. I was taking her up milk. Her place was in an awful mess. They're a dirty couple, that's what it comes down to. The pink-eye's still a baldie. She'd spread her stirabout all over herself, and the mother was letting her totter about like that any old way. She's at the falling over stage, and the two little ruffians in their raggy breeches were there, Young Darby and Mal, following after her like faithful servants ready to catch her at a moment's notice, or pick her up off the filthy floor and set her upright again.

'Oh, she's the clever girl,' says Young Darby, 'she's the clever, clever girl.'

They see something in that child I don't. They see a darling thing. I think she's like a maggot. I remember a dream. There was a creature wrapped in swaddling clothes like the baby Jesus, and it had a white face like a seal pup but without the big eyes, because its eyes were closed and it was scarcely even aware. I think it was very ill. There were thin white whiskers all over it, but when I leaned over it to see if it was wanting anything, it didn't have nice fur like a seal pup. It had skin of a kind of horrid white creamy consistency that made me shudder. I decided I couldn't have the thing about the place any more because it was turning my stomach, even though it hadn't done anything wrong. So, quick and spry, as you would if you were cleaning away a maggoty lump of something found in the drain, over I goes to it with cloths on my hands, and picks it up firm. But then it opens it mouth and screams at me in dreadful distress, and the feel of it, even through the cloth, is so hideous

145

it sends shudders all through me. I dropped it and it lay on the floor crying very piteously, a poor thing in pain, absolutely helpless, and I wanted to stamp it away as you would a grub, but instead I took it out and put it down at the end of our long field and just left it out there because I couldn't have it inside, it was making a terrible noise. And then I felt awful. It was a fearful cold windy rainy night, and I remember I was looking out of the window all the time down towards the thick hedge, thinking of the helpless thing suffering out there.

I gave Sal a potion. I'd say she'll not have a problem with the milk. Her bubs have swollen up like bladders and the blue veins stand out on them like roads. She's sitting on a stool by the fire, and she's not her normal self. She's a vain woman. She has a penny looking-glass on the ridge above the chimney stack. She has high round cheeks and she never looks drawn. Now she's pale. There are dark rings under her eyes. Black hair straggles out from its pins. Her soft lower lip juts out and the light shines on it. I like to see her looking dull.

'Are you sure you can spare this, Eliza?' she says of the can of milk. 'This is awful good of you.'

I shrug. 'It's necessary.'

She gets up and stretches her back and groans. She's very big for her time, God spare us twins.

'Ach, what a world, Eliza,' she says, stifling a yawn, 'this one'll have to be dainty. A girl, I hope. Not a great big boy that could eat a whole horse, like these ones. God, I'd give anything for a good watery lumper! Melting in the pan.'

'It's a girl,' I say, 'set your mind at rest.' Though God knows it looks like an eater.

'Well,' she says, 'you've never been wrong

before.'

Look at her. I don't know who she thinks she is, the Queen of Sheba maybe. There's none like her round this way; there was that Bridget one that rubbed soot on her eyebrows but she's gone now, married into Eskean. People talk about Sal, they've said things to me. Nan Fox said, she holds herself in high esteem, that one. That's what Nan Fox said to me. And they don't like it when someone sets themselves above, why would they? Phelim brought me a green ribbon once, it was given him by a lady who was staying at the House, for your wife, she said, because he took up eggs and beastings. Well, I've never worn it out. They'd think I was putting on airs. It's very pretty, hangs above the bedroom door.

'God willing,' she says, 'next year will be better. I have to have a lie-down.' She's a very lazy woman. Others have to keep going. 'Boys, take baby out and play. Keep an eye on her, give your poor mother a little time. I'm heavy, Eliza. It's lying like a stone.'

Going back over the track I look down and see the boys walking the baby down into Kildarragh, slowly, a hand each. All the little fields run in a muddle over the hill towards the sea.

I have said in my heart that I hate Sal Quinn because when I look at her I'm angered and grieved. She's never wanted for anything. It's not that I like hating her, I wish I didn't. And because I know I should not hate her, I must do good to her. It's a grim seam.

*   *   *

147

Christmas came and went and for fear of fever they were whitewashing the back lanes in Boolavoe. Sal Quinn got bigger and bigger all over till she was like a big seal cow lying on a rock. Her ankles swelled up terrible. I have graceful ankles. One of the things Phelim's always liked about me is my daintiness. He's a man of nice words. Once he said to me you move across the grass leaving no trace, as if there's no weight of you on the ground. Queen Eliza. He used to carry me when we first married, pick me up and carry me about like a child. My arms round his neck, my eyes close to his pimply neck. I liked to rest my head there and he would kiss my hair. Here's the strange thing. I know my face is wrong. I know it's too narrow and a little twisted but I can make it the only face in the world he wishes to see. I think it so. What he sees then when he looks at me, though he doesn't know it, is Juliander. Not her features but the tincture of her as it were. And no man can resist Juliander.

The weather goes on foul, rain, rain, endlessly splashing in the yard, making mud. The sky so low it sits below the tops of the mountains. The air swirls. Everything streams, the earth sings and gurgles through January into February. And on a dragging day as foul and dark and cold as any other, I put Jamie down for his afternoon sleep in our big feather bed with his granda, who's taken it over for the day and is lying flat complaining of backache, and find myself quiet and restless and mad to be out of this damp-smelling house; so I put on shawl and cloak and boots and all and walk out as far as the end of the cow's grass, look down over the wall past the mound at the land, the small fields in a hotchpotch and our own bits and pieces of it scattered here and there, and see a man come running over the ups and downs from the long strand as if his life depended on it. Sometimes he stumbles. Then I see the dark green uniforms of two peelers running along about a half mile behind in pursuit. Well now, what's this? One of our good boys running from the law. The little man zigzags across the boggy land, towards me. It's Tadhg. My heart gives a lurch. The fool, didn't we always know this could happen? What's he done? They'll shoot him. I get down below the wall and watch. Poor Tadhg slithers and slides down into the big hollow leaving long scorch marks through the muddy earth, hares across it and comes pounding and scrambling up the rough gorsy hillside towards me. Now I hear his breath, scraping itself out of his chest like a knife. It hurts. I scuttle back down the length of the cow's grass and wait, quivering.

Here he comes, clearing the wall with a great leap and pounding on. He sees me. His eyes, never timid, are deadly scared, scalded and beat and miserable, like a child's. For that one second, his eyes like that meeting mine, it's as if he and I are naked together.

He sobs, can hardly speak. 'For God's sake, Eliza—' his knees give way and it's as if he's begging me to have him, '—help me, I'm dead.'

No time. I'm standing aside watching myself, exulting in some strange way. I think my eyes are cool.

I say nothing, grip his arm and haul him along after me as if he was Jamie, take him in the house and through to the room where the two of them are in our feather bed. Jamie's well away but my da's awake, sour-faced and flat on his bad back.

149

His eyes show only mild annoyance when we burst in, as if we're an irritating draught coming in the window.

'Move over!' I command.

'Get in!' to Tadhg.

And they're lovely, all tucked in together the three of them, Jamie still sleeping rosily at the wall, Granda outraged in the middle, Tadhg squeezed in at the side heaving like a bellows with what I think is now a kind of laughter.

'Be still!' I hit him through the quilt and glare at my father. 'Ssh!' And in another second am outside going for water with a pail over my arm when the two peelers land like bullocks in my yard, red-faced and bristling with their bayonets and carbines. One carries a sword.

It's starting to spit rain.

'Is it the man you're after?' I whine. 'The one that was running?'

One's stout, his chest heaving. The other, a weed of a man, says in a high voice: 'You saw him?'

'Oh, I did,' I say, 'he went over the wall beyond as if it was the devil after him. What's he done?'

'Which way?'

'That way.' I point towards Lissadoon. 'What's he done?'

'Do you know him? His name?'

'Oh, sir, I never saw him before.'

The stout one with the moustache and wide arse heads for my door.

'Oh, sir!' I run. 'Please be quiet, sir, my baby's asleep and my father's not at all well!'

I trail him in while he stalks about my house. He throws back the curtain. There's my poor father with his watery old eyes staring. There's Jamie, sweetly sleeping with his red cheeks and surprised eyebrows, all hot and sweaty. There's no movement under the covers. The polis turns away and makes up the ladder, but there's nothing up there, only a few stores and my father's old chaff bed. Then he's off after his friend. Puff, puff, puff with their load down the lane towards Lissadoon. I'm back inside.

'Not a word from a soul!' I say in a terrible deep voice.

And make them stay there. It's no hardship for the child, he knows nothing. What's he dreaming? Where's he gone? I wonder if a child goes back to where he came from when he sleeps? When he's there, does he understand everything? And when he wakes, it's gone like the morning mist that sits so low upon the land. There's nothing from the man all squashed and sweated up in his boots against my father's side. Perhaps he's fallen asleep too. Perhaps he's back in mammy's womb. Perhaps his killing breaths have finished him off. My father's piercing eyes stare like an aggravated baby. God, look at him. He's not a man, he's hideous. 'Eliza,' he says, as if he had any say in anything, 'what, for the love of God, are you doing?'

'Not a word till I say so!' I make a fist and show it him. You dare, you old fool. I pull the curtain across fiercely.

He'll not stir. Neither will any one of them, they'll stay so still and quiet as little mice knowing puss is there, till I come and set them free. Ha. The rain's pounding it down now. Oh, I do love this moment. By the back door looking out when the rain's just setting in good and proper and making

151

the back wall drip and gleam and everything like a cascade of silver music, all smelling so fresh and new. Times like this I wish I was learned and could make a poem.

I'll leave them a while. Serves them right. Except for my little boy, who's done no wrong but he knows nothing of all this anyway. I sit by the door on the creepie and watch the rain and wait and wait and wait until I'm as sure they'll not come back as I am sure of anything; how much time that is I do not know; and then I stand, as if waking up from a lovely dream, go back inside and put back the curtain and say softly, 'Up now, Tadhg.'

Meek as a lamb he follows me. The door stands open.

'You'll not stay here,' I say.

He has tears in his eyes. 'God save you, Eliza,' he says, 'you're a grand woman,' and hugs me up off my feet in his turf and sweat embrace. His whiskers scratch my cheek. I struggle down. 'Go now,' I say, 'you can't stay here. What have you done?'

'We went for Lomas's oyster beds.'

'You didn't!'

'We did.'

'You and who else?'

He's still pale but he smiles. As if he'd tell me that. 'The keeper fired on us.'

'Why?'

'Why! Because of the oysters!'

'You must have done something.'

'We threw stones.'

'Ah!'

'Eliza,' he says, and pulls a pistol out from his clothes, 'take this for me, I daren't be abroad with it. Please, Eliza.'

'You fool!'

'Bury it for me, Eliza.'

'Take it away from here!'

'They won't come. You're Phelim's wife.'

'So?'

'Eliza,' and his voice cracks and falls, 'if I'm caught with that I'm dead.'

I've known Tadhg O'Donnell since I was five. 'No, you're not,' I say, 'you're transported.'

His eyes cloud over with misery. I look at him for a second then grab the gun and put it in my apron. 'Oh, go on, Tadhg O'Donnell,' I scold, 'out of my sight, you bad man!'

'Eliza!' he leans forward and grips my arms. His thumbs dig in. 'Eliza,' he says bitterly, 'they're going short in Kildarragh and Carraroe and Malahies and Scarran. When times call for it, you do what you can.'

'Would you rob *us* then?'

'Never!' he chops the air angrily, then he's off at a lick in the rain along the lane towards the gap.

That was stupid of them, I think. Lomas's oyster beds. If you were going to go for anyone, you should go for Cloverhill at least.

*   *   *

I'm not one to panic. I thought about burying the pistol. I kept it safe in my apron, it lay at my navel very heavy as if I was bearing it like a baby. I walked through to where my father still lay, grumbling and mumbling. Jamie was sitting up.

'Jamie, my love,' I say, sitting down on the bed, 'your Uncle Tadhg was here but you missed him. Now up and play. Granda's getting up too, he'll

153

take you and show you where the snowdrops are beginning to push through at the side of the ditch. Won't you, Pa? Take him for a walk while I get these sheets washed.'

My father's had enough. 'You remember who you're talking to, girl,' he splutters, a vain attempt at the kind of authority he may once have had twenty years ago.

I pick up Jamie.

'Up, Daddy,' I say.

'I have a bad back!'

'A walk will do you good.'

'It's foul!'

'No, no!' and I run to the open door. 'It's stopping, see? Go and look for the rainbow.'

I go back and pull and push him from the bed, him groaning all the while.

'What nonsense is this with Tadhg O'Donnell?' he complains.

'Not a word, Pa. Not to anyone or I'll skin you. Not to Phelim, whatever you do. Do you understand, Pa? Do you? Do you understand?' I am staring into his eyes in that way that scares him. I bring my face to his, my eyes very close to his, till both of us are squinting, and I stare and stare and never give up. 'Do as I say. You saw nothing. Nothing happened. Unless you want that man shot by the peelers, and you carried him on your shoulders when he was a gossoon.'

'Eliza,' he says, 'you're an awful bold girl, you'll be in trouble yet.' He's pulling on his breeches over his long flannels.

'Maybe so, Da,' I say.

Finally I get him up and staggering out with his collar turned up and a tremendous air of injured

154

dignity. Jamie runs ahead. Look at the state of these sheets, full of mud from that man's big boots, I say to myself. They'll need a good soak. Never mind. I work steadily, build up the fire, put the water to heat. Soon I know what I must do. The pistol lies hard against my belly. They transport you for bearing arms. I must get it off our land.

*   *   *

Nine at night going up to Sal Quinn's, called there by the eldest wee boy, I meet Tadhg going over the rath. He must have known I'd be coming, he's been waiting for me; he jumps down from the bank on the other side and runs across to me. 'Eliza,' he smiles, 'my saviour and my queen.'

He's a terrible man. He married Curly Callanan but he puts those eyes all over me still.

'I destroyed it,' I say, 'if that's what you want to know.'

He looks at me, his eyes bright and playful. 'Now how did a little scrap like you destroy a big gun like that?'

'It's at the bottom of the sea. I threw it over by the stone strand.'

He laughs. 'Tell me you're joking me, Eliza. Do you know how much a gun like that costs?'

'I do not,' I say.

He walks crabwise alongside me. 'Twenty eight shillings for a gun like that.'

'Fancy.'

'You know, you're wasted on Phelim,' he says. 'I have not thanked you. Is your father safe, you think? Will he talk?'

'He hardly sees a soul. He wouldn't talk.'

155

'Have you told your jackeen?'

'Don't call Phelim a jackeen.'

'But he is. Thinks he's a cut above the rest of us, doesn't he?'

'That's because of me.'

'Exactly.'

'I *am* a cut above,' I say. '*You* couldn't have me.' I say it, it comes out of my mouth. He looks startled, even scared, opens his lips as if to speak but falls dumb. We walk on, side by side, silent. On the descent, he turns now and then and offers me his hand like a gentleman, and I take it like a lady, all very nice. But we don't speak, and I sense he's gone shy. At the bottom, in sight of the Quinn house, he says suddenly, 'Don't tease me, Eliza, you didn't throw it in the sea, did you?'

'Yes.'

'No.'

'I did, Tadhg,' I lie, 'I really did throw it in the sea.'

He gives a great exasperated sigh and closes his eyes for a second. 'You shouldn't have done that.'

'Why? So you can kill a man and get hung?'

He breathes heavily down his nose. 'Oh, Eliza,' he croons softly, 'Oh, Eliza.'

The gun is in the tree. It's lying on top of the pussy cat. I came over when the night was quite black. I see well in the dark. I sing as I come, to lighten the way, a thin high song that no one can hear, a gnat-like sound in the low place just beneath speech. I came over in the pitch black when they were all asleep, and dropped the weary burden of my apron down the tree. Now no one'll find it, and if they did, it's not on my land. I don't like guns. Too hard and heavy. They're better kept away from hands like Tadhg's.

'Did you shoot at the keeper?' I ask him.

'No.' His lips press inwards and I believe him. 'I had the gun and I didn't even use it.'

I smile, seeing the tree from here, ugly misshapen thing scragging its long witchy fingers out across the green hillside. I wouldn't have it reaching at my house like that. I wouldn't live there. I like the idea that I know something no one else knows. It gives me a little power, though I'm not sure over what or whom.

'I don't care what you've done with the damn gun,' Tadhg says earnestly, 'I thank you from the bottom of my heart and I can't say more than that. I'll never forget what you've done for me.'

I won't let you, thinks me. There's a thin wisp of smoke from the chimney. 'Well,' I say, stopping, 'there'll be hard work here tonight. She's not a coper.'

'She's strong though.'

'Not with pain she's not.'

Sal screamed the place down when the girl was born. I remember clearly, Eliza Quinn was born with a caul. I still have it.

'Poor Sal!' he says.

You too, Tadhg O'Donnell. I'd like to meet a man who was unmoved by Sal. I remember even when we were little girls, five or six, her swanking it like a Dublin whore even then, hand on hip, rolling gait. And the lads, even then, with their google eyes.

'She'll weather it,' I say.

She will. She was made to bear babies, she was made to hate pain. She's a screamer.

'Birth,' I say, 'is a great leveller. Like death.'

157

Tadhg watches the cabin, grey and peaceful with its wisp of smoke, as if there were no mighty struggle within. 'I have more cause to have thought of death than most recently,' he says throatily.

I laugh. 'Listen to him! More cause than most! As if there weren't poor people much worse off than you starving.'

He was ashamed at once, his mouth dropping weakly. 'Forgive me, that was stupid,' he says.

'And there's been deaths they're saying. Where? Up in Clare?'

'So they say.'

I breathe in very deeply, girding up for the task ahead. 'It's exaggerated. There's always deaths this time of year. There'll be more, of course.'

'Well,' he says, 'no more talk of death tonight. Look after our lovely Sal, Eliza.'

Our lovely Sal, is it?

Here's Darby coming, tight-faced and haggard. 'Nan's with her,' he says, 'she's desperate for you, Eliza. It's been all day since a little before noon.' He has a chubby strong face by nature, but there are long bags hanging down under his doggy eyes. I'd guess he's not slept.

'Where are the children?' I ask.

'Below at Scanlons.' He rubs a square hand over his face and gives a great yawn. His fingernails are chewed to the quick. 'God bless you, Eliza,' he says, smiling wearily down at me, 'she'll be better now you're here.'

I'm a woman greatly blessed. If I had a penny for every time I've been blessed I'd be rich as the Queen of Sheba.

It's dark in the cabin, though the fire's burning and the candles are lit. Sal lies on her side in her nightdress with one arm trailing down to the floor, her black hair free of its pins and hanging from the bed to the ground. Her knees are wide apart. Nan Fox is holding a hot turf wrapped in sack onto her belly low down.

'I'm such a scaredy, Eliza,' Sal gasps, starting to cry when she sees me, clutching the black and red shawl that covers the bed. 'You'd think I'd be getting used to it by now, wouldn't you?'

'You're grand, honey,' Nan says, 'you're faring just grand.'

'Let's take a look,' I say.

She smears her face with her hands and sniffs, hoiks up her nightie. Coming on nicely but the head's still a bit high. Water runs down her leg, her breasts are leaking too. She's a bag of water, a seal of the ocean. A pain takes her. 'Oh, Jesus!' Her knuckles are like hen's claws, fingertips biting down hard on Nan's long brown hand. 'There now, there now,' Nan says steadily, her gaunt old face stern. I count. A minute, more. Sal draws in a long breath as it fades, closes her eyes gratefully.

'It's a while yet,' I say. 'Put the kettle on, Nan. We'll have some tea.' Then around I go loosening the ropes of the creel, the knots that tie Sal's shawl on the door, the string that keeps the bundle of herbs above the fireplace. Nan's put a sheet and a clean flannel nightie to air in front of the fire. She's already got the rags steaming in hot water in the red ashes.

'Did you see Darby?' Sal asks.

'He's gone down with Tadhg.'

'Tadhg's been on at him to join up.'

'Darby with the Ribbonmen? Ha!'

'Oh, he has more sense,' she says.

159

I rub her back. The pains come and go. Scrawny Nan lights her pipe. We drink tea, the three of us, me and Nan on either side of her. When the pain comes, we rub her down, Nan at her back, me at her front, and she weeps and groans and whimpers and says she can't stand it. She cries on God. When the pain fades we wipe her face and tidy her hair and tell her she's a good girl. She wants to get up, but when she tries, her knees wobble and she has to bend down over the bed with her hands in fists on the old red and black shawl, panting like a horse. 'I can't stand it,' she says over and over again, 'I can't stand it,' in disbelief, endlessly, and I say, 'But you are standing it, Sal, you're standing it even as you say you can't stand it.' She hates me for that. I grip her hand and she grips mine as hard as she can and both our hands shake.

Three hours pass like this, till she crawls to the edge of the bed and calls for a bowl. Nan runs with one just in time. We clean her up and rub her down. Then she gets a bad one and starts screaming. This one goes on and on, and she screams all the way through it, jerking her head back as if she's in a fit. I hold her head. 'Enough now,' I say, 'you're fine now, not much longer,' which may or may not be true. There's a break. I grab the minute or two to look below. All's well. 'Oh, that's lovely now,' I say, 'that's coming along nicely, she'll be here in no time.'

'You, Eliza Vesey, you are amazing,' she says, smiling as best she can in the sudden lull. 'You have me convinced she's a girl. Have you ever been wrong?'

'Never. What name'll she go by?'

'Margarita,' she says proudly.

160

I snort mildly but smile too. Margarita indeed. Fancy. Hah, she'll only end up as Peg.

'Oh, Jesus!' She screams piercingly right down my ear.

Nan jumps up and grabs a hot cloth from the pot, stands wringing it out with her long hands held stupidly high. She looks like a hare. 'Ow!' she cries as it burns her hands, runs clumsily and lays it on Sal's stomach.

Sal screams and swears, pushes us both away with surprising strength, lurches from the bed and squats like a fat frog for a second or two before falling over onto her front.

'Come on, now, love,' I say, 'hold on to me.'

We have her, she's on her knees, sobbing.

I put my finger down and feel. 'Nearly there,' I tell her. We hold her hands and pray, all three of us in murmurous harmony. Suddenly she hauls herself upright and gives a great shriek. Nan gets behind her and holds her under the arms, and we start her pushing. This is the bit I like. This is when it's all up close, death and birth together like twins. I'm pushing it down with my hands. I'm pushing it out of Sal Quinn's body, and though I have said in my heart that I hate Sal Quinn, at this moment I feel like God dealing with her, and I almost love her in that passionless, indifferent way God must have for his creatures. Her belly is clay from which I'm moulding a new being.

'Now,' I say, 'lay her back very gently, Nan, and open that door,' and while Nan's at the door and the cold air creeps in, I give her a little shake to shake the baby down. A great gush of water comes, and a very strong pain that has her groaning like a soul in hell; I get between her legs and see the

161

slimy head push against pot-bellied skin.

'Stop pushing.'

Nan's back. She holds her. It's going to tear.

'Don't push, love.' I put my hand there to steady it, the big wet head, black-haired, pressing up at me. 'Not so fast,' I whisper, 'not so fast.'

Beast. You'd tear your poor mother to bits.

'Now,' I say. 'Now. Easy.' Patting the head like a nervous animal. Steady now. And close my eyes and wait until I know it's good and time, then tell her softly in the ear, 'push.'

It comes. It takes a good few more pushes then out she sails, Margarita on a tidal gush, a bonny blue girl covered in cream. No caul on this one. Her eyes are wide open, shocked. Sal reaches down for the child between her legs, scoops it up into her arms and holds it fiercely against her breast. It cries once, sharply. 'Oh, a girl, a lovely little girl,' Nan croons, throwing a bit of warm blanket over the slippery thing, and Sal stares intently into its face. It won't suck, but after that first cry doesn't make a sound, only wants to look around with its wide open eyes. Alive and pulsing, the cord loops down from under the blanket into Sal. She starts to laugh weakly. 'Oh, I'm such a silly, such a silly,' she says. Nan puts her arms round mother and babe and laughs with her.

I build up the fire.

'More tea, Nan,'

Life goes on, whatever you think, life does go on. I have thought very often of the end. At every birth, I think of the end, and I think of Phelim. I think of all the things that have ended. My childhood. My mother. The doll that used to sleep in my oxter. Things are taken away, things are

162

constantly taken away. I feel very lonely, sitting by the fire far away from the three of them, Nan and she and the babe, the Margarita, all cuddled up together there.

'It's coming,' she says.

No rush. Let it come.

'Yes, yes,' say I, 'coming, coming.'

'Eliza!' Nan calls, scared, 'Oh, Eliza, I don't know what to do!'

I feel very tired, not at all like getting up and going to that woman I don't like. I should be at home in bed, there's bad times coming. I feel them in my bones. I should be with my own. We're just poor stupid creatures, how are we to proceed? I've closed my eyes and am whispering a prayer: My God, my God, tell me what to do, when Nan says, 'Eliza, what shall I do?'

Cut the cord.

'Here it is,' I say. 'Here.'

'Now?'

'Time enough.'

Always, always, time enough. I think of them, far down there below in the darkness of tonight, Phelim and Jamie. Fifteen minutes later the afterbirth comes. I cut the cord with my birthing knife and drop it in a bucket.

'Go and tell Darby he's got another daughter,' I say.

Nan goes.

'She's not sucking,' says Sal.

I sit by her. 'Time enough.'

'Eliza,' she says softly, sitting up with the baby in her arms, thick lips smiling, 'will you come up here and see me sometimes? I don't feel very strong, Eliza.'

163

'You're stronger than you know,' I say.

'Not as strong as you.' Her eyes brim tears and look unnaturally large. 'Nowhere near as strong as you.'

'Look at you.' I reach for the pipe Nan's left. 'You're twice my size.'

'Will you?' she insists, 'Will you just keep an eye on me, Eliza? Just drop by once in a while?'

'Of course,' I say.

I take the baby and wash her then hand her back to ma, take a fist of salt for my pocket and pick up the bucket with its bloody smell, nearly colliding with Darby at the door, rushing in, bringing the cold air. She hurries the shawl around the babe.

Oh, look at this, he's down on his knees, she's his love. Throws his arms around her and weeps. Such a fuss for a fourth child.

Outside is a rare clear night about three in the morning, and a neighbour woman's coming up the road bringing something in a big pot that she struggles to carry. Behind her the high bright moon, nearly full, makes its path across the calm sea. I slip round the back. The ground's hard but a place has already been prepared, into which I tip the big jellyfish with its knotted cord, the knots my own hands made. I sprinkle the salt and cover all, murmuring a prayer. I need to sit out here a while in the dark and cold, while the neighbours stir, bearing gifts. I yawn and rub my eyes. The see-saw the Quinn boys made is still there, next to the dead tree. I yawn hugely. I'd like to be lying next to Phelim, he asleep, deeply breathing and far gone in dreamland.

I'm chilled.

Tadhg's arrived. He's brought a sprig of thyme

164

and he's smiling and a little staggery with drink. Because he's a special friend, he's allowed to lean over the mother and babe to place the scraggy herb gently in the baby's grip. Darby's turned into a pure fool. There's Nan, towering over the little neighbour woman, the two of them tidying up and making yet more tea. I'll wait a while in case she needs me, then I'll go down and sleep, and then I'll kill one of our precious chickens and bring her some meat, and the broth. I sit by the fire getting warm. Nan hands me a pipe.

Tadhg hadn't noticed when I came in. His eyes are all for Sal. Even like that, all of a sweat with her great udders sticking out, she takes his eyes.

9

1846

You heard terrible things, rumours to catch your breath, that a woman had set off to walk to her people in Westport, County Mayo, and had died with her children on the road and a cart ran over them in the dark. That a man in Dingle saw the devil pissing on a shrine.

Then I'd go out back and stand up on the mound, even on a foul day—so many foul days we seem to have now—and see the creamy hush of the waves far away and think inside myself that life is wonderful and God is kind. He's been good to *me* anyway. We have the grass of five cow's scattered here and there. We got eightpence the stone for our oats in town. Me and Jamie go down to the strand and we collect dulse and the big mussels, like I used to with my mother when I was no bigger than he is now. They do say we'll be fine if we can get a dry harvest, but for now the wet seeps in everywhere and the house stinks with it. The sky sits there wanting to burst.

My mother used to say to me, 'Do just what you want. Do it for me.' She had the most amazing eyes, bright piercing blue like a spring sky, and I always remember her smiling. I never knew what she meant because she never told me, even though I asked. She used to say funny things. But now I think I do know what she meant. She wasn't a good speaker; she was good with her hands and at doing things, but she couldn't talk well at all. I think she meant get what you want because life is very short; get what you want like she did, she always got what she wanted. She took a man like my father to do as he was told, and I took Phelim because he was butter in my hands. Him and me and Jamie, we'll sit here till it's all over and we'll do fine because I'm blessed—I've been blessed so many times by so many people—and I carry my protection around my neck in a small blue cloth bag next to my skin. My mother put it there when I was three. She sewed it up herself with tiny black stitches. I have no idea what's in it, for to open it would be to remove its efficacy. So we won't suffer, but there's some will suffer. God knows what Kildarragh will do. There's a miserable look up there, though there always is this time of year. I took them milk. The way word flies around, everyone's hearing things. Alma Sheehan came up to me and she says, 'I'd sooner die than go in the workhouse, Eliza.'

'What are you talking about the workhouse for?'

I asked her, 'You're not going in the workhouse.'

'I couldn't stand it.'

Then it's Cliona Scanlon crying about the bellyache and Becky with the runs and thinking it's fever, which I soon put her right about. She's a sickly child but she's not got fever.

Lomas himself turned up on a terrible wet night. The sky had just burst like a bladder over the house when he came squelching through our yard, his horse tied at the gate. I peeped out of the shutters and told Phelim, who met him at the door. Lomas is a squat red-faced man with a wispy ginger beard. 'God save all here,' he says brusquely, whipping off his dripping hat and planting it down on the table to drip on to the floor. 'Is there room by the fire there, Phelim?'

Phelim indicates the chair and takes the stool for himself. 'Some tea would be nice, Eliza,' he says.

'Now let's not mince words.' Lomas shakes his head and sends raindrops spinning into the turves. 'Tarlton has three years of poor rates due, and there's not a chance in hell of him getting his rents. He has Cloverhill by the throat and Cloverhill tells *me* to bring them in. Now, Phelim, what would you do in my position?'

He sits forward, a hand on either knee, his stomach sitting on his thighs. Phelim frowns. Never a one to speak quickly, he puts his face in his hand, sighs and considers. After a time he says with slow deliberation, 'I don't know.'

Lomas laughs. 'Ah, Phelim,' he says, 'a man of firm decisiveness.'

Phelim smiles faintly. 'You can't get what isn't there,' he says.

'Quite.'

'You can tell Cloverhill we'll bear the fines for our labourers as we always do.'

I stop what I'm doing. He'll have us dead before he'll see sense. Sense is often unkind.

'As for the rest, I can't say.'

Lomas is clearly relieved. His dancing blue eyes smile up at me as I solemnly hand him his tea. 'Thank you, Eliza.' He takes a long slurp of it, hot as it is. 'Well, I'm very glad to hear that, Phelim. Very glad indeed.'

Then they sit and yarn there by the fire like two old fools, as if nothing were happening and the world not tightening its heart around them, steeling itself. The very sky is telling them. I leave them, slip through the curtain and sit by sleeping Jamie. Beneath the golden down there's a flush on his cheek, but when I put my hand on his forehead there's no heat. This is the healthy flush of a boy asleep. His dreams are serene as the rain beats on the shutters and the roof. Looking at him I cannot feel helpless, though I should. All I know is that as long as there is a will in my body no harm shall come to him, even if a million perish. What can I do? I'm not God, but I have a will. No one takes the food out of this boy's mouth while I'm alive, not Tarlton nor the Quinn brood nor Jesus himself if he came crawling at the door. I'm charged with the keeping of one only.

I say as much to Phelim while Lomas is hauling himself like a bloated sack, dropping heavily onto his poor streaming horse's back.

'I'd not see anyone starve,' I say at his shoulder, 'but our own child comes first.'

'What do you want me to do, Eliza,' he says snappishly, 'we've had a year's labour out of them.'

'Shut the door, for God's sake, the rain's driving in.'

He all but slams it, walks ponderously to the fire and sits down in a rare state. 'What do you want me to do, Eliza?' he says again in a loud voice, peculiar for him, and turns his head from side to side as if there's something down his ears.

'Do?' I say gently, 'All I want is for you to be a good father and look after your child.'

He looks pained. 'I *am* a good father. Eliza, you're unfair. We are not so badly off. There's others far, far worse. We'll not starve, we can tighten our belts a bit and get through, even paying for our cottiers. It's what we've always done.' And then he looks so miserably into the fire, his pale grey eyes glistening with moisture, that I soften and sigh and put my hand on top of his head.

'All right, Phelim,' I say, 'all right, all right, we'll say no more.'

*   *   *

Christ, but this is a bloody awful summer. I've never seen anything like it, this weather going on and on. They're all getting sick and calling for me. That Doctor Carmody's been up there and sat a while yarning with O'Carroll in his house. O'Carroll told him some have had nothing but turnips since Christmas. That's not true. I know for a fact they've been bringing in cockles and mussels by the basketload, and now there's this Indian meal stuff coming in from America. And how wonderful that is. Bright yellow, spits up out of the pot and fills them up with nothing but gas. Phelim went down to the new depot in Boolavoe with John

169

Scanlon and Matty Sheehan, and hauled back three sacks, up to Kildarragh. Everyone got the colics. I had a family down towards Carraroe ate it practically raw and near killed themselves, six of them all doubled up and retching, the ma and pa too sick to tend the little ones. Nothing much you can do for them, it just has to work its way through. It's the kind of stuff you can cook for hours and it'll never be done. You get all these little hard bits that just about break your teeth and scratch your throat going down. Some places there's been people bled to death from getting their insides pierced.

'You've got to soak it,' I tell poor old Nan, 'stands to reason.'

Nan's bad with diarrhoea, I'm feeding her a nice powdered tea, a spoonful now and then, but it's coming out both ends, she's bringing up blood, and her lips are turning creamy and making me feel sick. I look at her as little as possible. I haven't told her how worried I am. I like Nan. She never had any babies and I'm sorry for her for that. We've had no deaths near here. Don't be my first, Nan, I'm thinking. Carmody's been told but he's half dead himself running here and there and hasn't showed up, so I've stayed by her all night so Peader can get some sleep. He's been bringing his guts up all day too but he's just got on with it. Looks like a ghost but he's through the worst. And no one can look quite so like a ghost as long grey Peader, thin as a hound, even when he's well. I've heard people say the reason they couldn't have children was because they were both so tall and skinny but I've never given it any credence.

By morning there's no blood. The moans have

170

stopped and she's fallen asleep. The air's foul. I go outside for a breath of air and look over and see Tadhg's boat tacking over the grey choppy sea and he a black hump at the oars. Nan and Peader's old dog comes over and sits beside me, scratching, his fur all wet and matted. Grey rain pours steadily down in thin rods. I wouldn't want Phelim out there. The weather could turn worse any moment. The fish are far from shore. I think of Tadhg and how he has always admired me and been so nice, how he had looked in that one scared moment when the peelers were after him with their guns, and how when I was picking along the shore with my mother, sometimes I'd see him bringing in the nets with his father and big brothers when he was just a little thing. He was different then. He was at ease. He's tight as a fiddle string now. Suddenly, a small revelation, I realise I love him. It doesn't make any difference, doesn't tear my heart or anything like that. I think: this is interesting. Then the feeling pushes itself out from me, like some invisible bubble blowing itself outwards all over the world, rolling over everything in its path. For one thrilling moment, I think it must be possible to love every creature in the world. Even Nan, draining her bile into the bowl. Tadhg's little boat rides the waves like a seal. Foolish, but then he is. Blackened his face with two or three others of them Ribbonmen and off to Cloverhill's and cut the tails off the cattle. I saw Cloverhill going through town a day or two after. All his guards round him bristling with pistols. *I* wouldn't like to be him in these days. He's a handsome man, with soft waving brown hair that bushes out around his ears, and he wears a very fine waistcoat. His mouth is large and red and curly. I could imagine kissing him.

Trudging up from below comes Sal Quinn with her baby tied on behind, 4 months old, a black-haired girl like her ma. She has little Eliza by the hand. Well, that one's had her nose put out of joint for sure. Look at her. Two years old and tottering along over the rocks drizzling like a miserable sky.

'You're abroad early,' I say.

She looks a wreck. 'It's her,' she says wearily, jerking her chin back over her shoulder at the gently snoring baby. That child looks sickly to me. Not like the pink-eye. 'She only sleeps when I walk about outside. Soon as I set foot over the threshold she'll be off again, howling the place down. How's Nan?'

'Still bad, but she'll mend.'

Sal yawns in her pretty way. 'And my little shadow here, of course, she never lets me out of sight for a minute.'

'Jealous.'

Slowly, Eliza Quinn turns her face up to me and what I see there sends a panic thrill up my spine. Her face is dirty, smeared with tears and snot, but she smiles at me in a sudden ingratiating way. She has an odd little face. She's not bald any more but what she's got is wispy and colourless, so you can see the shape of her head, a pale nut shaped like an elongated onion. It's a vegetable head. I would not be surprised to see a bug creep from its ear. Why has she got my name? The panic is not that she is so repulsive to me, but that her eyes themselves frighten me. What looks back is not human, nor is it animal. It's sly and dangerous and full of fun.

'She's been a good girl,' says her mother fondly, smiling down at her, 'and now she's a very very tired girl who should have stayed in her nice warm bed.'

In the Middle Kingdom, there is beauty beyond human beauty, and there is also, of course, wickedness and abomination. The thing I recognise looking out of the child's eyes is of this last kind. Juliander has her origins in the Middle Kingdom also, but she is noble and true and brave. It's not that she can't feel fear. She wouldn't be so brave if she didn't feel fear. She gets terribly scared, so scared that she cries and weeps and falls all the way down to the very darkest depths of the well. But she always gets up again. Finger's length by finger's length, she pulls herself back up to the light.

'Are you all right, Eliza?' Sal says, breaking in on me. 'You look a bit queer.'

'I've had no sleep,' I say, blinking. 'Neither have you. We're both in some half land.'

They go slowly on up the hill to their cabin. Eliza Quinn turns her head once as she walks, looking back at me over her left shoulder. She should not have my name. She can see Juliander. Creatures of the Middle Kingdom always recognise each other.

*   *   *

They were pitifully small, those green-tops we planted, the tiny poreens soft and watery, not fit to eat. I tried cooking them but they turned to black slime in the pot, so we set them in good hope and they've come through for us. This morning I walked between the ridges below our house. The potato's a handsome plant. Its flower is a white spiky star with a rude yellow tongue, and it clusters like bells in a belfry, many bells in many belfries rising up all along the ridges, pretty as anything. The flowers stand tall, the stalks are sturdy and green. There's a good few planted between here and Kildarragh. Not long now and there'll be a great lifting, and then, oh, won't we all be going mad for a lovely buttery potato with salt?

It's as if the long dry spell we had never happened. The downpour is dreadful, endless, and the seeping damp everywhere, and those poor people out there on this new government scheme, they don't stop for any weather. I don't suppose they ever get dry. They're shoring up pure bog, and everything they clear in a day is flooded by morning. They're walking in from as far as Sneem and Cahirciveen for six in the morning to stand up to their waists in freezing water every day. There'll be all kinds of fever and grippe, you'll see.

It's harsh, but they're like that, these Whigs. Peel's gone. Peel wasn't so bad, at least he brought in the yellow meal. We cursed him for it too. Peel's bloody brimstone. At least they don't die from it any more. The millers learnt how to grind it, and the word came round on what to do with the damned stuff: which is simple: soak, soak, soak, boil, boil, boil, and don't take any chances. Whatever you do, don't say, oh, God, that'll surely do, let's just eat the stuff. Throw in some oatmeal if you've got it, makes it more digestible. Of course they haven't at Kildarragh, so naturally there's Phelim off up there with a big bag of the stuff hoisted on his back and his big heart pumping him along. God love him. I wouldn't have him out there

174

on the Scheme in all this; thank God we're not reduced to that. They're all up there now, Peader Fox and Darby Quinn, John Scanlon, Matty Sheehan. They get sixpence a day to buy India buck. There's women there too, Nan's up with Peader, she gets fourpence a day. And children. They're making a road across Clunagarthy. Why they don't make one over to Kildarragh, I don't know, not many use the Clunagarthy track. Still, they're glad of the work, I suppose. Good luck to them, I should say, but they've left us in a pickle. We've got no one to lime the land. How can they expect Phelim to pay them a wage as well as clear them with Lomas and Cloverhill? Don't they know how good he's been? Of course it'll be a different story when the rents next fall due. I suppose they think we're made of money. I suppose they think we've had a fat winter and a full summer and don't drool sometimes at the thought of all we're missing. If they could see me walking between the ridges praying God and the Holy Mother and all the Saints to bless these potato plants and bring us in a decent harvest at last. There were so many potatoes before, they were dumping them in the ditches. They were using them as manure. And now look, these beds are so precious. Sometimes I have to stop and attend to this great weight in my chest. And yet sometimes, thinking of this foul year and how it's fared with so many, I know that the worst is past and I think of that good time of year that's coming—the pulling down of autumn and the settling in of winter is cheering, when everything's in and the meal months are behind us all again and we can breathe easy. Then I'm so lightened with hope it's like a fountain bursting up inside me, and I know again that the terror times are necessary in order for the fountain to renew.

Tonight there's a gap in the weather. We stand at the gate, Jamie and me, looking down the lane at the growing dusk. The earth is poised. Everything's damp and breathing, and a dark figure wades through the fog that is creeping up from the sea, lying low on the land. From the walk it's Phelim coming up from Lissadoon.

'Daddy!' I say, and Jamie runs. Phelim lifts him and carries him back on his arm, and smiles at me as he comes near. I think that I am very lucky.

'Do you smell that strange smell?' says Phelim.

There is something in the air, now he mentions it, faint yet distinct.

'It's in the fog,' he says.

'In the fog?'

'Well, it seemed to come on with it. The smell and the fog at the same time. Didn't you notice?'

'I didn't notice anything till you said.'

We stand, the three of us in the foggy lane, sniffing the air. Now I can't smell anything but dew and mist and sweating plants.

'Maybe we're in for a storm,' he says, 'it's very still all of a sudden.'

We can hear the murmuring of water in the hillside and in the ditches, the dim far howl of the sea.

'I want a storm,' Jamie says, pulling his father's face round towards him with rough affection.

'You may well get one, Jamie,' replies Phelim and we go in and close the door and all the shutters against the fog.

All night it seeps in. In the morning the storms begin and rage for three days. It's nigh impossible to get out of the house, you open the door and the weather drives you back in and follows you. It's always trying to get in. If you do go out you can't see a thing. We're using up too much fuel, I know, but what is there to do but sit in by the fire and keep out of it? Poor Jamie, grizzling and griping away because he wants to go out and play, wants to be off with his da seeing to the beasts, but Phelim won't let him. You could die out there, it's winter in summer, on and on and on, howling and banging around your head till you could scream.

Till suddenly on the fourth day we wake to a quiet morning.

'Thank God for that,' says Phelim, getting up groggily and sitting on the side of the bed with his shoulders rounded. 'It's not raining.' He stands and stretches, yawning loudly before going into the room and blowing up the fire. I get up, dress quickly in the first morning chill and get started on the stirabout. Jamie's up but my father's still snoring vigorously. It's when Phelim throws open the door to the yard to let in what seems the first clear morning in an age that I know, with a hollow and terrible certainty in the pit of my stomach, that the catastrophe has struck. I have known it since the moment in the lane when I felt lucky and Phelim said, 'Do you smell that strange smell?'

What comes in is rotten in the nose and throat. Phelim turns back from the door and looks at me. Our eyes hold for a long time. I wonder what he sees in mine.

'Pooh!' says Jamie.

'I'll go and see,' Phelim says.

'Can I come now? The storm's gone.'

Phelim hesitates for a moment then takes his

hand. 'Yes, you come,' he says gently, 'I think we'll find the potatoes have gone bad again, Jamie.'

'Oh no!' cries Jamie, holding his nose, but he has no idea what this means.

The three of us walk down together and stand in the field, just stand and gawp. Last night the stalks were upright and green, I walked among them in the rain. A dragon has come and breathed on them while we slept. They've fallen sideways and laid down their burned black heads, ridge upon ridge of them felled at one stroke. We don't speak. Phelim gets down on one knee and takes a handful of withered rot. The stench is wicked.

'Don't!' I say, and Jamie covers his nose and mouth.

Phelim heaves a great sigh. 'Oh Jesus,' he says, an appeal, not a curse.

A faint rainbow has its tail in the meadows beyond Lissadoon. The air shimmers over the sea. It's a soft warm morning and my father's up wanting his breakfast. I don't know what we're going to do. Maybe it's just ours. This can't be happening again. I got that child through the whole of the last year without a hungry day, and now what am I going to do? Oh, God! I'm not giving that child yellow meal, I'm not watching him cry with the wind. They'll have to reduce the cost of bread, they'll have to. We've still got oats. No, no, no, we'll get by, we will if we keep calm. There's a horrible wriggling of unease rearing its wormy head in my gut. Down, down. The rainbow in the warm meadows beyond Lissadoon has deepened. Distinct, I see the seven colours.

'You take Jamie in for his breakfast,' Phelim says quietly, 'I'll see to this.'

I could laugh. See to this?

'Go on.' He nods his head towards the house, its grey spiral of smoke climbing into the sky.

When I break the news to my father, his grey old face makes me sad. Poor soul, I think, he should have had a bit of peace in his dotage, not this again. He's seen it all before. He subsides by the hearth with his knotty old hands linked and his lower lip hanging stupidly. He'll endure. Funny that he survived all those hard years when my mother, who was so much stronger than him, did not. She had a thing in her stomach that swelled her up till she died. There's nothing you can do for a thing like that, she knew that and she told me. She was a very proud woman who always spoke straight to the mark, and she taught me to be brave. 'Eliza,' she said, 'I'm going to die and you're not to worry, you're to be a good girl and look after your father.'

'No,' I said, 'you're not really going to die.'

'Yes, I am,' she replied simply, with the smile I see always when I remember her, 'It's going to happen.'

She was always right.

I wonder what she would have done. We sit by the fire and wait, my father and I, while Jamie runs about in the yard kicking his ball, glad to be out and about in spite of the smell. The news comes in in darts from here and there, from Phelim coming and going, from Father Buckley who's making the rounds, from Tadhg who always knows everything, from Darby Quinn, pale-faced at my door and wanting help for Sal. The blight is total. Everywhere.

'She's very nervous, Eliza,' Darby Quinn says,

pushing a thick-fingered hand through his springy fair hair.

'I should think she is,' I say unsympathetically, 'I should think we all are.'

'No, no, you don't understand,' he says patiently, 'I mean, she's ill. She keeps on crying all the time and it's upsetting the children. She says she can't stop.' As he speaks he grows agitated. 'I don't know what to do, Eliza. I don't know what to say to her. She won't get out of her bed in the morning.'

'Well, I can give her something for her nerves,' I say, 'but she'll have to wait till tomorrow.'

There's enough to do here. They think I can run to them whenever they want me.

'That's grand, Eliza.' Darby turns ponderously. 'I'll tell her you're coming. That'll cheer her up a treat.'

Tadhg brings me a fish. He's not on the Scheme, he's still got a business and his nets and goes out whenever he can, which has been precious little with this weather, but he got out first thing this morning before light, as soon as the weather cleared. He could smell it from out there in his boat. He knew, he says. He drifted in his boat, and he knew.

'People will die,' he says.

Like my mother. Simple.

I do not contradict him.

*   *   *

We cut down the stalks near the ground. You couldn't lift that mush. Here and there are one or two little poreens not worth saving, even smaller than the last lot. How could we ever have expected anything from them? Still, they put on a good show for us for a while, a very pretty show.

Kildarragh's in despair. I got up there late the next day with some milk and bitters for Sal Quinn. She has a pot of water over the fire simmering, waiting for Darby to come home with the meal. It'll be a good hour yet, then up they'll all come trudging from Clunagarthy with their sacks on their backs. God, they work them hard. Wait till they get over towards Corrabreac, it's covered in rocks.

'How are you, Sal?' I set down the can of milk.

She bursts into tears.

'I'm not good, Eliza,' she sniffs. She's lying on her bed against the wall, her children gathered about her, made solemn by the state of her. The baby's sucking fretfully.

I sit down.

'I've not enough milk,' she says.

'You will have. Drink this.'

'You're very good,' she says. 'I feel so scared, Eliza.'

'You're a strong woman. You'll do well enough.'

She drinks and makes a face.

'Nan's very good,' she says. 'She brings me some of her share every day, for the babies.'

'Nan loves babies,' I say, looking at my namesake who's squatting on the bed beside her mother's tousled head. 'You must calm down, Sal, you're upsetting them.'

'We thought we'd have the potatoes again,' she says.

'You have a husband who's working,' I say, 'and food in your belly. There's plenty worse off.'

'I know! But it's not enough. They're hungry

181

every night and it's not enough for a man to work on and poor Darby's worn out.'

'There, that's going down nicely. You run out and play for a bit,' I order the boys, 'I'm talking to your mother. Go on, the rain's stopped. Go on,' and I shoo them unwilling out and close the door. The elf Eliza sits on her mother's pillow, watching me with her uncanny eyes. One hand rests on the shoulder of her baby sister. For the first time I notice how long her fingers are, long and pale. They look as if they could lift up their blind heads, wormlike.

'You know what scares me?' Sal asks with another gush of tears. 'You know what really, really scares me?'

'Tell me then.'

'The workhouse,' she says. 'I'd rather die than go in the workhouse.'

'What are you talking about the workhouse for?' I ask, amazed. 'Who said anything about the workhouse? You've got a husband in work.'

But she just cries.

'Some more,' I say, pouring from the can. 'This is doing you good.'

'Oh God, not the workhouse!' She throws back her head on the pillow. 'Please God, not that! They'd separate me from the boys. If my boys were dying they'd keep them away from me. Children want their mothers. But all the little boys are taken away from their mothers. Oh, that's cruel! And the husband from the wife. Not even an eye to look at you in the way that it knows you.'

Her daughter croons, an odd small keening, leans over and tries to cradle her mother's head and the sucking baby both together.

'Sal!' She needs a slap and she'll get one in a minute if she carries on. 'Why are you upsetting the children with all this? Stop it at once and drink your milk.'

She blinks and sits up, pulls both her girls to her. 'You'd need someone with an eye that knows you, wouldn't you, if you was getting near the end?' she says. 'Don't you think?'

'You would,' I reply, 'but it won't come to that. Drink.'

I didn't go back over the top that night, I went along the low track along past Tadhg's shebeen and back along the road. It was as I was passing the lime kiln I noticed the queer light over the sea. It was dark. This dark summer is fading away into a dark winter. I'd love to see a blue sky again. The mizzle soaks me, and the queer light says another storm is coming in. Something has closed over the world like a tunnel raised above our heads. I have one of my moments where I must stop and stand. My blood thrills. This storm will be bigger than the last. It's coming in like blood in the sky. Below me I see men, women and children walking home along the shore with their measures of meal, heads down. They don't seem to see something rising over the sea, they just want to get home and get warm and eat. They've worked a twelve hour stretch. The men dig, the women pull box-barrows, the children load them. All in their own little worlds, they are, while the storm that is right for the times is coming in as sure as the blight settled from above. And they'll work through that too or they'll get no pay.

It comes with thunder and lightning and a heavy downpour in the middle of the night. It comes with a vicious, moaning voice that cries about the house. Many a time it strikes with a big crack over the great stones towards the coast. The ground shakes. The sea's up in fury. No one can sleep.

It goes on for days. No one can expect me to go slogging up to Kildarragh or down to Lissadoon in all this. They can leave me alone. We have enough fuel if we're careful, we have enough food. The weather has wrapped us up in our nest. My father stays in his bed. Phelim darts in and out when things need doing. I keep by the fire with Jamie, telling him stories and fashioning games and singing songs. I make up my own. 'Pussy's In The Tree' and 'Old Sow Got Caught In The Fence Last Spring'. He laughs. The fire's glow exaggerates the scar that will always mark his pretty face.

After a while, with the sky dark in the day as well as the night, with no one coming near, with the noise always howling and the wind pounding our house with angry fists; day after day, night after night of this, awake or asleep, I go into a strange state of calm. I become the eye of it all. It's a peaceful place to be and perfectly safe. At night the three of us huddle together in the big feather bed, Jamie warm in the middle. I throw an extra blanket on Father. He needs it more than we do.

The gales howl us into winter at last. It's never clear when summer ends. Some people are got down with the weather but not me. They call it a curse. All this palaver about the devil and God's wrath, it's all just a load of old dung. It's not God, it's stupidity and greed and politics, that's what Tadhg says. That's where ruin comes from, not the weather. That's what he said. But when the weather goes on and on and on, maybe even he

184

wonders.

There was no way a man could go out on that sea, and the fish were all miles off anyway.

So he pawned his nets and sold his boat. He had to. He went on the Scheme. Now, there's a man growing bitter. Sold his boat! I can't believe he'd do that. But he's sold his boat and seethes and boils as he works on the road. He says the ganger's a bastard, he'll dock you half a day if you're a second late.

*　　　*　　　*

Phelim told me he'd been to see Lomas to say the people couldn't meet their rents this season, and Lomas had said that as far as he knew Mr Cloverhill didn't appear inclined to make any concessions come November. The cutting of his cattles' tails hadn't helped, Lomas said, though of course all that might change if anyone decided to come forward with information about any subversive activity they knew of in the district.

'So, what are we to do, Eliza?' Phelim asked but not as if he seriously expected an answer.

'We'll meet our commitments,' I said. 'What other people will do I don't know. That's for them to work out with Lomas, it's not our concern any more.'

He sighed.

'We can't pay for work we haven't had,' I pointed out. 'If they're working on the Scheme they can't work for us, it's as simple as that; and if they're not working for us we don't owe them anything. We'll pay our own way but no one else's. Face facts, things have changed.'

185

Another long sigh. 'I suppose you're right,' he said sadly.

I lay wide awake that night thinking hard for a good long spell. It was time for me to act. I didn't know at first what I would do, but I knew it would be something bold. The demons of the weather were still whistling outside. Let them. Sound, that's all it was. Sound.

*   *   *

I know how Phelim talks when he talks to Samuel Cloverhill, like a lackey. It's all your honour this and your honour that: yes, your honour, no, your honour, three bags full, your honour. That's the way everyone talks to Cloverhill.

Not me.

I march straight up the road from Boolavoe to his big gates, pull on the bell and stand there in the wind and the rain looking through the bars. After a while a surly old man with pointed ears and a threadbare black jacket and high collar comes trotting along the muddy path, stands a little distant and asks me what I want.

'Tell Mr Cloverhill that Phelim Vesey's wife requests a word or two with him if he would be so kind as to spare the time.'

He goes away and leaves me standing, getting soaked for ten minutes before coming back and unlocking the gate without a word, motioning for me to follow him. Phelim's done a lot of work for Cloverhill, so I'm admitted, up the rutted track through dripping shrubs and old beeches festooned with ivy, to the house; ugly, red and square in its circle of trees. It's very fine in its way,

186

but I wouldn't want to live in it. I think it's gloomy. He takes me in a side door and puts me standing in a hall at the bottom of some stairs, listening to the soft ticking of a large clock somewhere, smelling dust and polish and a strange, almost mouldy atmosphere that evades the senses. The wood is very dark and the stair carpet has a pattern of green roses. You don't get green roses in real life. Juliander has lived in houses like this, well, very much finer than this one actually. I wonder what she would make of Samuel Cloverhill. For myself, I'm not sure. I've only seen him once or twice and I can't make my mind up. The picture of him in my head can go either way. The door to a room opposite is open and I go over and look in carefully. It's a lovely but stern room, full of books, and on the wall above the mantelpiece is a painting of a fine young lady I recognise as Samuel Cloverhill's daughter, only looking much prettier than the real thing, at least as I remember her. We don't see much of her in these parts nowadays, he sent her to school in Cobh in Cork City. Opposite her on the other wall is another picture, of a woman completely naked, lying down on a sofa with her legs wide open and her hand draped over her private parts.

I hear footsteps and move away, shocked.

A woman called Martha Colgan comes out of a room on my right and tells me to come this way. I know all about her, everyone does, she comes from Kildoran and she's a widow and his housekeeper; everyone says she sleeps with him but I can't see it myself, she's old enough to be his mother and she hasn't even worn particularly well. Very broad in the beam she is.

187

He receives me in a small study at the front of the house, where he sits scratching away at some papers at a small wooden table that has been polished up to a yellowish shine. The room smells of snuff and tobacco and he appears as a dark shape with the window behind him. I can't see his face.

'Do sit down, Mrs Vesey,' he says.

'I'll stand, sir, if you don't mind.'

I can't see his face to tell if he's surprised or not. He gets up too, and comes round the desk to stand facing me and say, 'Now, what can I do for you?' as if he were a shopkeeper.

I'll bet Martha Colgan's got her ear to the door.

I can see him now, no longer a silhouette. His mouth is sweet and soft but his nose is cruel. A serious man, disappointed. Trouble in his eyes. I am in no hurry. I would oblige him to look at me as closely as I am looking at him. Easier then to make him listen. 'Sir,' I say, 'I'm sure you're aware of the bad state of things.'

'Oh, indeed I am, Mrs Vesey.'

'I thought you should know, sir,' I went on, respectful, 'that the cottiers cannot pay any rent this season. None at all, sir, just in case there were any doubt. Not that they will not, they *can* not.'

He looks stern but says nothing.

'For myself and my husband,' I say, 'we will settle our own affairs but I want to inform you that we will be unable to carry any of the debt for Kildarragh as we have not been able to hire any help from there this year on account of they're all on the Scheme. It's been a very bad year, sir, and after last year, sir.'

He starts coughing, deep in his throat and

188

phlegmy, sounding like a much older man. His eyes stay fixed on me all the time, still stern as they grow moist. When the coughing fit is over he wipes his mouth with the palm of his right hand and says, 'Mrs Vesey—Mrs Vesey—to the best of my knowledge there are two private charities operating in Boolavoe at this moment.'

'I wouldn't know about that, sir.'

He nods and looks away, thoughtfully gazing into a corner of the room. I know what he's thinking—he's thinking: they cut off the tails of my cattle and expect leniency. I think he's maybe quite a good man at heart, not like Lomas, who just wants life easy for himself. That man reminds me of a bladder. You should get out while you still can, I feel like telling Cloverhill. See if old Tarlton can get himself another fool to get shot. Suddenly he looks back at me sharply as if he knows what I'm thinking, and smiles faintly. 'You can't get blood out of a stone,' he says. 'I know the situation.'

'Mr Lomas has told my husband he thought there were to be no concessions come November and it's what people are saying, and a lot of them are very worried. It's not that they wouldn't pay it if they had it, sir, it's that they can't because they haven't.'

'I am completely aware of the situation, Mrs Vesey, and I'm dealing with it.'

That seems to be that.

I smile at him. 'Thank you for listening to me, sir, and I'm sure you are.' It sounds insolent but not quite enough to anger him.

He blinks at me for a while very rapidly. The poor man's eyes are dark and hopeless. 'I'll speak to Mr Lomas,' he says, 'No one will be put out,

189

Mrs Vesey. You can tell them that. No one who is honest has anything to fear.'

*   *   *

Lomas puts out that some rents are exempt till the first of May. So there you have it. We, though we're sick to death of turnips and cabbage and the scrapings of the oat barrel, *we* have to pay our share; and all that lot up there don't pay a penny. They have me to thank for that. They do because he was impressed, he must have been impressed that I'd just go marching up and say my piece like that. The one thing I can do is look a man in the eye. I've probably saved his life. Suppose I had not gone up there and impressed him with the truth, he'd have exacted his rents and there'd be weeping and wailing and gnashing of teeth, and one of Tadhg's Ribbonmen would go up and shoot him. I did a good thing, I saved a good man, two good men—him and Tadhg—because maybe it would be Tadhg himself to go and kill him and then get hung on a gallows. My mother saw a man hanged once when she was a very small child. She watched his face every moment of it, she told me. It went on for a very long time and his legs were kicking all the time. She says she knew the precise moment the life went out.

Well, I'll get no thanks and no one knows I spoke at all except Cloverhill himself.

At last the weather stops and silver shines in the puddles along the lane. I couldn't wait to get up and about and into town, so off we go, me and Jamie. Set free, Jamie's wild, running along the tops of the ditches. There's no rain, not even a

190

drizzle, not even a fine mist you can feel but not see. It's clear and still, and the sea washes on the shore far away with its old gentle hushing sound. I've been cooped up so long and I have no money so I don't know why we're going, it's just for the sake of it. My father's crying out for a scoop of sugar to put on his stirabout. Well, we can get that at Neary's, then we can see if there's any stalls in the Square, and walk about the river bank for a bit and be home to get supper. It's still very cold though. The nip in the air whets knives on your cheeks, making them burn and flake. Your eyes water continually. But the sun's as bright as high summer, and the hedges are full of dark leaves and growths of bright bitter yellow fungi. The fact we're out makes us festive. The fact is we're getting through these terrible times, and Jamie's in high style, cocking it all along the ridges.

Coming out onto the high road down into Boolavoe, we meet with a tall old man like a grey wraith, hand in hand with a tiny hobbling old woman.

'The man's legs,' Jamie says, 'look at his legs, Ma.'

'Shh, I know. I know, Jamie, don't say anything. Don't stare, it's not polite.'

The man's naked legs are obscene white sticks covered in fat red boils. His head is much too big for his body. He strikes us dumb because he looks so strange, like a ghost, like whatever it is that wails in the wind. The old woman looks half daft but she doesn't scare me like the man; she's just a bent ugly old ball of rags, the kind you'd see anywhere.

'God save you,' says the ghost, wild-eyed.

191

'God save you,' I reply.

'Save you,' whispers the old woman.

'Is it far now to Boolavoe, ma'am?' the ghost asks. He has a fine strident voice and his thick grey hair is tangled and matted into a barbarous mane. His coat, all torn and filthy, is pinned tightly in three or four places for lack of buttons. Holes gape at the sides and under both arms, and it looks as if the hem's been hacked off hurriedly, so that it ends some three or so inches above his knobbly knees. Barefoot, he's striding out as best he can with his ridiculous thin shanks exposed so. I believe he has nothing underneath. Yes he has, an apron, a sack maybe, tied round his middle. But there's nothing up top. His sickly old flesh and the ribs that ripple under his skin, all's visible through the rents in the coat.

'Two more miles at most,' I reply. 'Have you come a long way?'

Sobered, Jamie walks holding my hand, peering round me at the spectral pair.

'From Portmagee, ma'am,' says the man.

'But that's miles away!'

'It's surprising what you can do,' he says, 'when you put yourself to it,' and smiles at me, a grinning skull with unnaturally brilliant blue eyes, fierce and intelligent. His wife turns her face away from me into his arm, like a shy child. She hums a soft high hum into the raggy sleeve, a sound like a little fly dying on a window sill. 'Not far now, Jess!' he says cheerfully. 'And is it true, ma'am, that they have a boiler in Boolavoe?'

'I believe so. Have you been out in all that weather?'

'We took shelter,' he says, 'we managed to stay

out of the worst of it.'

Even so, they must have taken something of a battering. And us all snug in our house.

'It must be bad where you've come from?' I say.

His eyes sharpen. 'Bad? It's terrible. Terrible, ma'am!'

We shuffle on for a while. He says his name is Michael Byrne. His poor addled wife is called Susan. She never speaks, just totters along beside him with an idiotic smile on her face. He says they've not eaten since yesterday and hope to get soup at Boolavoe. There was fever on the way, he says, so they come away before it. If they can get to Cork they'll be fine, his wife has a cousin in Cork.

'No point in waiting to meet it,' he says, 'no point at all.'

I look at the boils on his legs, pustules with sore wet heads. I don't think that is the fever we've heard of. It doesn't have the fever smell. No, this is something else, perhaps he's being bitten by something, eaten away. There's poison in his blood. But it's not the fever, definitely not the fever. I would know a thing like that.

He says his son had looked after them, he'd been a labourer but there was no work and now he's gone and listed and they have no one. We've always had bad times. There's always been beggars and there always will be. We have accepted this destroying season that never ends because we know that there *is* an end if we just keep walking on through it, sensible, steady as she goes. But I've never seen anything like these two along any road I ever walked upon before. It takes my heart into a lower place and gives me a fear I had not imagined.

'Jamie,' I say, quiet in his ear, 'don't be afraid. These are people just like your mammy and daddy, only a bit older and they haven't got any money. They're souls like you and me. Don't ever you forget that when you see poor people, wherever you may be, always remember they are the children of God like you and me.'

'He looks like Peader Fox,' he whispers, 'only more so.'

'He's had a harder time than Peader.'

He has to understand these things. This is an awful time to have to rear a child up, poor scraps having to learn these terrible things for which there's no comfort.

'That's a fine lad you have there,' Michael Byrne says, rolling his unnatural eye Jamie's way.

'He *is* fine,' I say, 'the finest boy in the world.'

The crone turns her perished mushroom of a face to Jamie, smiling her fatal smile. Her eyes are slits, nothing of them visible. She frightens me now more than him. They are death, both of them. Death and the cold fear, walking down the same old road to Boolavoe. Begone! I would say if I could, away from me, but it's not possible to do so because they are too real, too apparent with their streaming noses continually wiped with genteel scraps of cloth kept handy for the purpose somewhere in their lousy rags. They are hungry souls on the road, the poor to whom the good Christian must always attend; and they are also death, smiling into my son's soft face.

We meet a woman with a wooden can on her head, coming back from town, who tells us there's no soup, only Indian meal stirabout in a big boiler in Fallon's Yard. As we walk on we keep passing them, more and more people on the road with cans on their heads taking home the meal. None are as ragged or hideous as my old pair, none so liable to cause thought of death. He reminds me, this tall bony old man, of a picture I saw on a wall once, it might have been in the schoolhouse, of Old Man Death with his scythe and his grinning skull peeking out from a loose black hood.

Things are hopping on the old woman's neck. We keep our distance. In town, they dither and dander, and in the end I take them to Fallon's Yard myself because it's easier than leaving them standing there. But my God, when we get there it's madness. It's so long since I've been into town, things have got worse, infinitely worse. I don't know where all these people are from, they must be coming in from all around, you don't see anything like this even on a Fair Day. At the back of Fallon's Yard there is a metal cauldron as wide across as our bedroom, and two big men stirring away with sticks; and there's Father Buckley and Father Dolan measuring out thin stirabout from a tap on the side of the pot, a pint into each can, and all the people lining up.

I'm not waiting with this lot. Jesus Christ, they're all bloody lousy, look at the wee black bugs thick on them, jumping round their filthy grey collars. I can't have Jamie in there. 'Stay here and don't move,' I tell him, and go in to where the old couple are standing uselessly at the back with everyone pushing in front of them.

'Here!' I say loudly, 'let these people through! They're old and they've walked all the way from Portmagee and they've had nothing since yesterday.'

195

'Have you a ticket?' a man asks. 'You have to have a ticket.'

'It's not for me, it's for them. Look at them, man, they're dropping. Come through, Mr Byrne, come through, Mrs Byrne dear,' and officiously I shoo them through the crowd towards Father Buckley.

Father Buckley knows me; he knew my mother and knows my father. 'These people are hungry, Father Buckley.' I say.

'A lot of people are hungry, Eliza,' he says, hard-faced.

'They're dropping, Father. Look at them. They've walked from Portmagee with nothing in their bellies since yesterday morning.'

'Have they tickets?'

'Where can we get tickets?' Michael Byrne asks.

'You have to go to Mr Lomas at Malahies,' Father Buckley replies. 'He's head of the committee. He'll give you a ticket.'

That's when I lose my temper.

'Oh, for God's sake, man,' I shout at him, 'they've just walked all the way from Portmagee and they're old and they're starving. Let them first eat and then get the ticket. Tell you what, you give them something to eat now while I go and get the tickets for them. They'll not make it there and back unless they're fed in any case.'

Father Buckley looks vexed. 'Oh, come up,' he says impatiently in their direction, 'come up and get a tin can from Sean. But you'll have to get a ticket for the next time, you know, or I'm not supposed to serve you. And you, Eliza, you can't go for them, they have to see Mr Lomas in person. It's the rule.'

What a fate for human beings, I think, getting

196

out of that place as Michael and Susan Byrne are having their pints doled out. What a thing to come to at their age. I swear, if it ever gets like that for me and Phelim and Jamie, I'll go and get that gun from the tree and I'll finish us all off. I swear it.

*　　　*　　　*

Ah, but that was only the beginning. Something turned in me that day in Boolavoe. Because I've known Boolavoe all my life and it was changed, full of creatures I could scarcely bear to think of as human beings because they were ugly and mad-looking, strangers to me. They were from other places, and with them came fear and starving and the end of everything as it had been. I passed back along Weavergate and into the Square, where a post-carriage was loading up for Limerick, and a couple of gentlemen onboard surveying the crowd with troubled eyes. The windows through which their anxious faces peered were mobbed.

'Think of the childer, sir!' a wild-faced woman cried, holding up her filthy baby, its loose-skinned legs dangling from a tatter of rags.

Where are they all coming from? We can't help them. We have nothing of our own.

10

Sal thought the room seemed very plain without her mother's old red and black shawl lying across the bed as it had done for years. She'd sold it in the town. So many nice things you could get there

197

these days if you'd only had the money. People were selling everything they didn't absolutely need: caps and bonnets, stockings and blankets, gewgaws that had stood for as long as anyone could remember on shelves and chimney pieces. As for the shawl, her mother had made it when Sal herself was only about eight and she could remember the making of it, her mother's big rough hands working away by firelight. She sold it in Boolavoe along with her mirror and a bunch of ribbons she'd had for best. She kept her red handkerchief though, folded and stowed away, but that would have to go too if things didn't improve next season. They said it was far worse up-country. Here life went on somehow. Darby brought home the meal.

And one day Tadhg, God bless him, brought a hare he'd killed up to the house, saying it'll make a meal for the children anyhow. He gave it to Darby on the path.

'Christ Almighty, man.' Darby's voice broke. He was a soft man, Darby, and these days often close to tears. 'This must be the last bloody hare on the mountain.'

'Not quite.' Tadhg smiled.

'What about you and Curly?'

'When we've mouths to feed,' Tadhg said, 'you'll be helping us out.'

Darby's eyes were big and swimming as he presented the hare to Sal. Of course it should have been hung, but who could wait? It was meat. 'It'll do if we stew it a long time,' he said.

'I'll make a pudding with the blood.' Sal was already grabbing the sharp knife, reaching for a bucket, 'I'll make a pudding with the blood and—' She set the baby down on the floor to crawl.

'If I could get a couple of turnips—' he said.

'Go and tell John and Cliona—'

Margarita started whining. Sal slit the hare's belly and the innards slithered into the bucket. A rank smell rose up, making their tongues sting.

'I will, and the Sheehans.'

The Scanlons and Sheehans were their nearest neighbours. Between the three families there were nine children.

They came together in the Quinn house very late. The children were asleep except for Margarita, who was being passed around the circle of adults, picked up and set down onto her feet from time to time, to totter and gimble on her toes while they held her hands. There was a little tobacco, which they passed around in a pipe, its fug mingling with the smoke of the fire, and the steam from the hare that simmered gently over the turves in a thin stew with a bit of wild cabbage and nettle and a handful of meal. The hare was young and had bled profusely into the bucket when Sal opened it up. Now she was mixing a blood pudding with her hands. All of them were wet about the mouth but they'd all had a good feed of stirabout and could wait. The men talked half-heartedly about stealing turnips.

'You have to be careful,' said Matty, a tall, fair-faced man with curly hair, 'wasn't I nearly caught with my arse hanging out of a shed window one night over toward Kildoran.'

'You would,' Alma said, appealing to the room at large. 'He'll take one chance too many one of these days.'

'You were glad of the turnips,' he said, smiling.

'I wouldn't be glad of you getting transported,'

she snapped, 'then again maybe I would.'

Everyone laughed.

John Scanlon said nothing but sat there solidly with his mouth smug, puffing on the pipe. Everyone knew he had a knack for stealing. Of the three men, Darby was the only one who had not stolen turnips. Sal wouldn't let him, not because she thought it was wrong—you could steal; God made a special dispensation for the poor at times like these, everybody knew that. What could you do? What other way could you live?—but because she didn't want him getting caught, and Darby was just the kind of man who *would* get caught. He wasn't a careful sort. Clumsy and genial, he'd always stumbled and bluffed his way through life, taking very little seriously and getting by on his humour and good nature.

'How long you reckon that'll be?' He nodded at the pot.

'Two hours to do right by it,' Sal said, yawning, 'but I can't see us holding off that long.'

The boys, Young Darby and Mal, aroused by the ineffably sweet smell of slowly cooking meat, crept up to the fire and were scolded for getting out of bed before time. Eliza came and leaned against her mother's legs, sucking her thumb and drooling, slumbering on and off. Darby watched his daughter's skimpy-haired head droop against her mother. Her thumb, festooned in saliva, slid from her slackening mouth.

He stood up. 'Hold off till I'm back,' he said. 'I'll get us a few turnips.'

'No, Darby,' Sal said sternly.

'No risks,' John Scanlon said mildly, too comfortable to move, 'not now.'

A peculiar smile crept over Darby's face.

Matty gave one of his deep scattershot laughs. 'Not you, Darby!'

Darby just went to the door, shrugging into his coat, taking a sack.

'Darby!' shouted Sal, and Eliza woke and started up with a little shriek.

'Give me two hours,' he said, and was gone.

'Oh, go with him, Matty,' cried Sal, jumping up.

'You will not indeed,' said Alma.

'He's such a big fool, he'll get caught!'

'He's a big boy, Sal,' Matty said, leaning back suddenly philosophical and poking at the pipe just passed to him by Cliona.

Sal ran to the door and stood shouting into the darkness, 'Darby, you come back here!' and Eliza ran after and peered round her legs.

But he was off.

*   *   *

He went to Mr Cloverhill's because he knew it, he and Phelim Vesey once having worked alongside each other there, digging ditches. No other reason. He knew Cloverhill had mantraps set around the place and had belled his cattle after their tails were cut, and he knew there was a guard on the shed where he kept the turnips, and a guard on the perimeter. Everyone knew these things, and that only a fool would go near Cloverhill because of them. Still Darby went there. He had actually thought about this many times and decided that if he ever did it, against her wishes, then he must do it daringly or not at all, and now that he'd decided, nothing in the world could have turned him

201

around. He walked with a huge smile on his face, every now and again laughing to himself at his own boldness.

It took him half an hour's brisk walk across scrubby mountain and low-lying boggy fields made treacherous by the heavy rains, but it was land he had good knowledge of and he saw well in the dark. He approached the wall of the house slowly, under cover of darkness and light rain. The perimeter guard could not be everywhere at once. Dogs were worse. A dog charging you in the dark, snarling like a demon, was unpleasant. But Darby was a strong, stocky man and he carried a big stick, a long cudgel with which he felt his way ahead like a blind man, checking every inch of the ground before he stepped on it.

It was alarmingly easy. He scaled the wall, putting his faith in his coat which he doubled over on top of the shards of broken glass on top, and dropped down in the shade of trees and sombre rhododendrons.

He could be shot. They'd have guns. Luck of the draw, if you got a frisky guard or not. They could send him to jail or Van Diemen's Land. Still, he smiled and walked on, elated by the danger. Sal didn't think he could do this, but he knew he could. And when he came home there would be glory. The smile never left him.

He skirted a large mantrap, a wide patch of bramble into which his stick suddenly sank down with a sucking sound; moving on, slower and slower and ever more cautious, he reached the edge of the trees and saw the side of the house, with the stable off to the left, and the shed and the lean-to round the side, in which everyone knew the turnips were stored. He edged round towards it, keeping under cover. The rain fell more insistently now, pitter-patter in the leaves. Darby shivered. He had a clear view of the side of the lean-to with its narrow window high up. In front he could see a boy of about sixteen, his gun on his back, slouched in the deep doorway, keeping out of the mizzle, looking as if he'd rather be anywhere else in the world than shivering there. The yawn that stretched his already long face and practically wrung out his body was so palpable it brought tears to Darby's own eyes. It was followed by a deep sighing exhalation that settled inexorably into a long shallow snore, followed by three or four others. Propped up by the corner of the doorway, he was sleeping on his feet.

Darby stood for five more minutes before creeping past the sleeping boy, round to the side where the narrow window was. It was a stretch. You'd need Peader Fox for the height. He looked around. Nothing. Then he saw the arms of a barrow sticking out from round the back of the shed. It was an old rotten thing, slippery with rain, but he carried it round and deposited it under the window with its arms pressing into the sloppy earth and its one wheel facing the sky. He was completely calm now he was underway, sure what to do. He had to be careful not to catch the wheel with his foot as he stood up on the barrow's underside. The wood squelched and the whole thing tilted, but he was able to grab the sill and balance there till everything had stopped rocking. The few inches made all the difference. His hair dripped into his eyes.

Standing on tiptoe on top of the barrow,

clutching with his toes, sticking his arm as far as it would go through the window and feeling around, he resisted an incredible urge to laugh out loud. He couldn't feel a damned thing. He'd have to knock the boy on the head.

'What are you doing?' a man's voice asked.

Darby froze. Everything went through his head, a gunshot and terrible pain, a prison boat leaving Cork Harbour, Matty Sheehan hanging out of a window in Kildoran, laughter in Kildarragh. There was a sound of snuffling and hawking and general pulling together, then a boy's high voice said, 'Was I asleep, Mr Cloverhill?'

'Of course you were asleep, Ted, you know damn well you were asleep.'

Slowly and silently, Darby breathed out.

'Sorry, Mr Cloverhill, I swear I was only out for a second.'

There was a shifting of feet.

'This is a bloody awful night again,' Cloverhill said.

'You shouldn't be out in it, sir.'

Darby's arm, held at an awkward angle through the slit of the window, was beginning to ache.

'And let you sleep? Have you seen Martin?'

'Not this while.'

'Damn.' More stamping and shuffling. 'Go up to the house and ask Martha to make you a drink.'

'That's kind of you, sir, oh, yes, yes, I'll do that . . .'

'Go on, Ted, for God's sake. If you see Martin send him down here.'

After the heavy footsteps of Ted had squelched away into silence, there was a long pause full of the dripping of leaves, then Cloverhill said, 'Come out of that,' stepping round the side of the shed, 'I have my pistol on you. Who are you?'

'Darby Quinn,' said Darby, unthinking, pulling out his arm and looking into the muzzle of the gun. He dropped the cudgel.

'What the hell are you doing?'

'It's to make the pot go further for the children, sir,' he replied, hangdog, dropping his eyes. No point saying anything else.

Cloverhill sighed. He was silent for an uncomfortable time, studying Darby moodily.

'I'm very sorry, sir.' Eyes down, head down, a dog.

'Oh, for God's sake,' Cloverhill snapped, 'don't you know you could be shot? I know who you are. You were on the drains.'

'Yes, sir.'

'What have you got there?'

'It's a bag, sir. For the turnips.'

'Do you *want* to be shot?'

'No, sir.'

Cloverhill snorted and was taken with a fit of coughing that made the gun quiver in his hand. He hawked and spat. 'I told Mrs Vesey when she came to see me,' he said, vexed, 'no one would be put out at Kildarragh and in the townships beyond. I said it, and I've kept to my word. There is a relief committee. There are two private charities. There is a board of works. What are you doing here?'

'Yes, sir.'

'For God's sake, man!'

There was a trembling in Darby's hands and eyes.

'Are you armed?' demanded Cloverhill.

'Oh no. No, I'm not armed, sir, truly I'm not, sir,

I swear I'm not. Sir, I have four children.'

'What about that?' He motioned with the gun at the cudgel Darby had thrown down on the ground.

'My stick, sir. For feeling my way. I was 'feard of traps.'

'Damn you!' Cloverhill holstered his gun furiously and pulled out a bunch of keys. 'Come here!' He turned and strode back to the front of the shed and set about opening the door. Darby followed. 'Quick,' said Cloverhill, 'take a few quick and go, and if I catch you here again I'll shoot you for sure. Do you understand?'

Darby gawped at him.

'Quick!'

Darby ventured into the dark of the shed. He was trembling severely now and couldn't see a thing, but he groped and groped and got a dozen or so turnips in the bag before a cold sweat broke over him.

'Quick! Quick!' Cloverhill was at the door. When Darby emerged he slammed it shut, locking it smartly. 'That way.' He pointed. 'Quickly. If you meet a guard, you're a dead man.' Then he turned on his heel and stamped away through the rain.

Darby fled as silently and swiftly as he could, but he'd left his stick behind and kept catching his feet and lurching into bushes, and most of the time had no idea where he was. Any moment a shot would explode in his head. He'd fall headfirst into a mantrap. His breath sounded very loud in his ears, and the bag bounced about on his back and thumped him every time he stumbled. Finally he hit the wall and scrambled up and over, careless of the glass which slashed hard in one or two places and caused hot blood to trickle down inside his

206

clothes as he fell on the other side. There was a moon. Once the house was back on his left he ran. The cuts on his knees and arms throbbed and his muscles ached but he was pushed on by a wild elation, and as he ran and marched by turns, up and up into higher ground, he laughed aloud to himself and even spoke in ragged bursts. 'Just take a few, he says, just take a few . . . well, well, fancy the man . . . ha! . . . I know who you are, he says . . . oh, Jesus, he can't go back on it now, can he, he can't go back on it now? . . . they'll never believe! . . . they'll never . . . Jesus! When I open up the bag . . .' and he saw them, their good familiar faces in the fire glow when he spilled out his haul, all radiant with appreciation for what he'd done.

Sal was cuddling Darby's old hat to her breast when he burst in, a big comical smile on his face. She threw it down and jumped up. 'How dare you!' she cried, taking three quick steps towards him, her neck thrust forward. 'How dare you frighten me like that! I thought you were dead.'

He stepped across the room and opened the neck of the bag, letting the turnips roll out onto the table. Sal screamed.

Matty Sheehan roared. 'You did it!'

Then they were all over him, slapping him on the back and telling him what a good man he was, and he started to laugh and laugh and laugh. 'I just did it,' he spluttered, 'I just put my arm in the window and kept feeling about and I took them one by one. The guard was standing round the front with his gun at the ready and he didn't know a thing about it!'

His coat was all torn from the glass on the wall, and when Sal tugged it off him and saw the blood running down into his palms, she paled visibly and shuddered.

'It's my knees too,' he said proudly.

'God, Darby, and you're soaking wet.'

He was dried and fussed and petted, his wounds tenderly dabbed clean and dressed with cobwebs and strips of torn up sheet. Only the gash under his right knee was deep and troublesome and would leave a long scar.

'Jesus, Darby, I never thought you'd do it,' Matty said, chuckling and shaking his head.

'She's been a wreck,' Alma scolded, walking up and down and patting the baby's back, 'a complete wreck.'

Cliona scrubbed the turnips. 'Your father is a very brave man,' she told Young Darby and Mal.

'No, really,' Darby said, still plastered with a mad smile, 'it wasn't hard really. There's just this young lad having a nap in the doorway.' He hooted a fleeting relief-filled laugh. 'Honestly, it was so easy, all I had to do was stroll up and stick my arm in. Anyone could've done the same.'

'Ah, no, that's where you're wrong.' John Scanlon handed him a freshly filled pipe. 'You had to keep your head. You had to have the nerve. Not many would have done that. You did well, Darby.'

Darby shook his head, unable to believe his own bravery. His body was still trembling but in a good way now. Warmth seeped into his frozen bones and the aroma from the strong meat juices was almost unbearable. Young Becky chopped the turnips very small so they'd cook fast, and it was scarcely any time at all till everything was ready and the children of the three households were awakened for the feast and sitting blinking in the smoky

208

glare.

Nine children got the lion's share. The adults had the broth thickened with meal, and plenty of turnips.

*   *   *

Later that night Sal began to cry. She couldn't tell why. Everyone had left and the children were fast asleep and she was lying in bed with the blanket pulled up over her head.

'What is it?' asked Darby, getting in and finally blowing out the candle.

She could only say she didn't know, it had been so awful thinking he was dead and now she couldn't stop the feeling.

He laughed. 'I was never in any danger,' he said.

'You were.' She blew her nose. 'Of course you were. They could take you away. They could hang you, Darby. What would I do then?'

He laughed again. 'What would *I* do?'

'Promise me,' she said, sitting up and looking down at him in the darkness, 'promise me you'll never ever do such a stupid thing again. Promise.'

But even when he swore on his own mother's soul that he would not, she didn't stop crying.

'What is it?' he sighed, desperate now for sleep. The wind was getting up again in fits and starts and tomorrow was another day of digging.

'I don't know,' she said miserably, 'I don't know, Darby, I really don't know. I feel so sad.'

He put his arms round her and drifted to sleep against her restlessness. 'I wish I hadn't sold my mother's old shawl,' she said, but he didn't hear. She started thinking about the red and black shawl again, how she'd sold it to a woman from Kildoran in the square. Her mother's hands were in every stitch of that shawl. She bought a loaf with the money. Six years since her mother died. I'm glad she's dead, Sal thought, she'd have hated these times. The sound of breathing filled the air around her and the wind blustered outside. The more and longer she cried into the dark, the more alert she became, till she felt as if she'd never been so wide awake and alive in her whole life. The crying settled into a rhythm, becoming luxurious, enjoyable. She drifted in and out of sleep, in and out of worry. Her stomach hurt.

A woman called Annie Porter had gone down with the fever on the other side of Lissadoon. They said it was terrible up-country. If it got here what could you do? Perhaps, Sal thought, drifting, she should stop going to town and keep the children in. Eliza Vesey might know of something, she'd been away with the fairies like her mother before. I'll go and get a charm, she thought, and something for Darby to carry with him when he goes out because he'll want to do that all over again now he's done it once and everyone making a great palaver over it. Hail the conquering hero indeed.

Margarita grizzled in her sleep in the crib next to the bed. Sal put out her hand. The only sleep her mother got that night was bad sleep. She was still awake when Darby dragged himself from the bed and started shivering his way into his breeches, grumbling and belching to himself in front of the smouldering fire.

Sal sat up. 'I think I'll go and see Eliza Vesey,' she said.

'You awake?'

'I've not slept.'

'Ah, go back to sleep, love.'

The rain swept the roof.

'I've not *slept*.'

'Too rough to go out.'

She flopped back down again. 'You have me worried sick,' she said pettishly.

They were whispering so as not to wake the baby. 'Me?'

'You? You? Hear the innocent. After last night. Darby, you have me worried sick.'

'Oh,' he said, smiling, 'did you not enjoy the feast then?'

'You know what I mean!' She was up again. 'I don't want to lose you, Darby.' This hissed in a vexed and scolding way.

He went and sat on the side of the bed, grinning. 'Poor Sal,' he said, 'you're stuck with me a while yet, I'm afraid.'

'I'm going to see Eliza Vesey,' she said, '*She's* got a head on her shoulders. *She'll* give me something to keep you at home.'

Darby laughed. 'That old sourmug,' he said, '*she* doesn't know anything. She was up seeing Samuel Cloverhill, you know.'

'Who was?'

'Eliza Vesey.'

'Was she? How do you know?'

He stood up and went to mess about with the fire, squatting with his back to her.

'Darby? Who told you that?'

'Martha Colgan,' he said quickly.

'You saw Martha Colgan?'

'The housekeeper, you know.' He turned from the fire.

'I know who she is. When did you see her?'

'I met her on the road.'

'When?'

'Last night.'

'What? At that time of night? You were stealing their turnips and you stopped for a chat with the housekeeper?'

'Well—she didn't know anything about it, it was on the high road, nothing wrong with that.'

'Oh, Darby! Didn't she think it was funny you being out and about in all the wet at that time of night?'

'Oh,' he said, imperturbable, 'I said I'd been looking for work and was late coming home.'

'What was *she* doing?'

'She'd been to see someone who was sick,' he said, standing and looking about as if searching for something with his eyes. 'A relative, I suppose.'

Sal was quiet for a moment, looking distant and thoughtful, then she said, 'Well, I hope you didn't get too close to her then, Darby.'

'No, no, no, the colic was all it was, she said. No fever.' He was pleased with himself. This was easy.

She thought for a while. 'You never mentioned seeing Martha Colgan last night,' she frowned.

'Did I not?'

'No.'

'Oh, well now,' he shrugged, 'I met her on the way there, you see, and I thought it best just to chat as if everything was normal; so I just said I was back from looking for work, and, and she said, I think she said, she was off seeing someone sick. I think her niece it was, and then she said that Eliza Vesey had been up to see Mr Cloverhill.'

'What for?'

'She didn't say.'

'Didn't you ask her?'

'She didn't know. I don't suppose she stands there with her ear to the door.' He sat briefly on the side of the bed, peering down at the sleeping Margarita.

'Do you think she looks flushed?' Sal whispered.

'No, no,' he said, 'she looks fine.'

He looked in on the children.

'They'll sleep awhile,' he said, 'you go back to sleep, love.'

'I haven't *been* to sleep.' Sal flung herself down again, sticking out her lower lip.

But after he'd gone, she finally did drift off, briefly and deeply, waking only when the boys started yelling at one another outside. They'd been up and heated the stirabout and fed little Eliza, and there was a horrible mess all over the floor where they'd eaten. Now they'd gone out and left the back door open and it was freezing cold in the house and her head was aching. It had stopped raining though, and the wind had died down. She blinked and scraped sleep from the corners of her eyes with her fingernails. Through the open door she could see Young Darby, Mal and little Eliza playing on the old tree.

She sat up and shouted, 'Close the door!' and the sound woke Margarita, who was sleeping late. The boys stopped and looked towards her, but Eliza went on walking round and round the tree in her shabby white dress. So young and dirty the boys were, poor big-eared vagabonds, muddy bare feet hard on the knuckles of the tree. Were they mad not to feel the cold?

'Come in here!' she called.

Young Darby jumped down, splashing into the mire below. The earth under the slope from which the tree writhed out was boggy, heaving beneath his heels, and he tavered and smiled, the spit of his dad but thinner in the face. Setting her feet on the floor, Sal felt the cold about her ankles. 'Come in and close the door, all of you! Now!' she fairly shrieked this time. Margarita, who'd been frowning perplexedly at the light for some time, set up a surprisingly deep, throbbing kind of a wail and had to be picked up and stuck on the breast with no more ado. She snuffled and squalled at the teat, red-faced and angry. Sal stared fiercely into her face, looking for signs of illness.

'Blow up the fire,' she told Young Darby, who skulked in the threshold with a silly grin like his father's, Mal in tow. 'Eliza! In now!'

That girl was getting naughty.

'Scrub yourselves up a bit,' she told them when they were in and the door closed. 'We're going to see Eliza Vesey.'

'Do we have to?'

'Can I stay here?'

'And nearly set fire to the place like last time? Away and scratch. Darby, you wash you sister's hands and face.'

There was nothing left in the pot but she didn't care, she couldn't have eaten much anyway, her stomach still felt uncomfortable from last night when she'd had too much. What a laugh. She washed her face and scrubbed her neck, then wrapped them all up severely and tied Margarita on with her shawl and set off with them up and over the top, telling them the walk would do them good. It wasn't too bad today, the worst of it had blown out in the night but little squalls still sprang up out of nowhere every now and then, racing visibly across the billowing hillside, which seemed alive like the skin of a horse. She was going to Eliza Vesey to get a charm if she could, or something at least to make her feel she was heading off the fever.

When she reached the Vesey house, the first thing she saw was Phelim clearing up around the dung-heap. His boy was with him, shovelling with a little spade.

'Hello, Phelim,' she called over the wall.

His head shot up and for a moment he looked confused.

'Oh, Sal,' he said, 'how are you keeping these days?'

'Never better.' She smiled very widely.

He gave a nervous laugh. She thought he was sweet, poor thing. He was looking grey and washed-out. He still liked her, she knew by the bashful sideways looks he kept sliding over her.

'Eliza at home?'

'She's inside, just go on in, Sal.'

But she lingered a moment or two. 'And how's the wee sweet boy?' she asked Jamie.

He looked away.

'He's grand,' said Phelim, 'say hello, Jamie one.'

Jamie mumbled.

'Not talking to me today, Jamie?' Sal put her hands on her knees and leaned down to smile in his face.

He looked at his shovel.

'Ach, he's a vagabond.' Phelim gave the side of his head a fond swipe.

The two big rough boys, Young Darby and Mal,

215

ran off round the back. He wasn't to play with them. His mother called them hooligans. He and little Eliza stood looking at one another. The baby was awake and wide-eyed, quietly gazing over her mother's shoulder at Phelim.

'Look at her,' said Phelim, smiling, reaching out one long finger and stroking it swiftly down the baby's cheek, 'anyone can see where her mother gets her eyes.'

Sal laughed. 'You've got that the wrong way round, Phelim,' she said.

'No, I haven't.' His eyes threw her a quick humorous look and he laughed the nervous laugh again, which made her smile even more.

11

Look at her out there flirting with him. She doesn't even know she's doing it. She'd flirt with a donkey, that one. Not so round in the face any more, is she? Anyway, she can flash her eyes at him as often as she likes, he knows his place. That would have been a terrible match, that would. She's too good-looking for him, he's too nice and soft-bred for her.

Those boys are making a terrible din out the back there. That older one should be on the Scheme. Tuppence they're paying the children. But they've always spoiled theirs, the Quinns. Here she comes now. So what's she after this time? I meet her at the door.

'What do you want?' I fold my arms and lean on the doorpost. I'm not pleased she's here, why

216

should I pretend?

'Hello, Eliza,' she says, pleasantly enough.

'Oh, well, come in.'

It's cold. We're going very easy on the fuel. She sits at the table and her baby looks over her shoulder. The pink-eye sucks its thumb. In comes Jamie and stands gawping at it.

'Close the door, love,' I tell him.

'This woman, Annie Porter,' she says. 'Have you heard?'

'Course I've heard.'

'Is it the fever, do you think?'

'How would I know? I've not seen the woman.'

She looks at me closely, frowning. 'Are you all right, Eliza?'

I sigh. I'm not discussing this in front of Jamie. 'Run up to Granda, love,' I tell him. 'Away!'

But he doesn't want to go, gets as far as the ladder and stands there kicking his toes against the lowest rung.

'Take little Eliza with you, sweet boy,' says Sal, giving her child a push.

'Don' wanna,' growls the elf. Her voice is soft grey and furry like a catkin.

'Oh, Eliza!'

The child's thin white face crumples, then straightens out into a savage glare, directed at the floor. Her mother grabs and hugs her fiercely, her threadbare cloak falling open. 'What am I to do with you at all, my little funny one?' she cries. 'Go on and play now with Jamie and Granda. Go on!'

The child shrugs angrily.

'She never used to be like this,' Sal says wearily, looking at me with desolate dark eyes. 'I don't know, I can't seem to do right with her any more.

They've got me run ragged, this lot.'

I can see it. She's got dirt in the corners of her eyes, and a big grey tidemark round her throat. 'Of course you can,' I say. 'This is how you do it.' And I put on my voice of authority: 'Eliza, do as your mother tells you.'

That's all I have to say for her to go, slouching sullenly across the floor to the ladder's foot. It's the same with dogs and horses. If you know you're the boss, they know it too. Sal Quinn's the weak one. And here's me, a brown small thing, got all the strength.

'It's the new one,' I say when she's gone, 'her nose is out of joint.'

'I suppose so.' She puts her hair back.

'You look tired.'

'Ha! I didn't get a wink last night. Not a wink.'

'She's not sleeping?' I nod at the baby, which has fallen asleep with its head on one side.

'Oh, she sleeps. It's me doesn't.'

'They're all cranky these days,' I say. 'What can I do for you?'

'I'm wanting something to keep away the fever, Eliza,' she says, 'if there is any such thing. This woman Annie Porter's at no distance.'

I sit down with her at the table, clasping my hands before me and giving a long sigh. What does she want from me? She starts to speak again but I hold up my hand for silence, and close my eyes. I need to think. She has a superstitious regard for my silence, she thinks I'm doing some magic, but I'm letting my sleepiness have its five minutes while I think what to do.

And what if there were fever at Kildarragh? What if it were at Boolavoe and Lissadoon and

Kildoran and every little townland between here and Kenmare? What do they want me to do? Am I God? Do I have the power of life and death? Can I think the world well, make the potatoes flourish again? Because I have the secret for myself, they all want it. Through the worst of times, my mother kept the fever away from us all, and she always found food. She had something very strong. What killed her was not a fever or a chill, it was some great malignancy inside, too powerful for any charm. Before she died she gave me the strong bag that lies always against my chest bone, the size of half my thumb and tightly sewn shut, never to be opened. I have no idea what's inside but it feels like powder and smells of must and faint spice, and because of this, all in this household are protected, even that old fool upstairs. But I have nothing like this to give anyone. I open my eyes.

Sal Quinn belittles me with her very presence. I am weakened, and that is a thing I cannot have and that is why I do not like her. This seems a great realisation. I also realise it's not her fault. She means me no harm, at least not more than she means to any. I hate her because she is as she is and I am as I am, and that is that. Such a hate is not proper and therefore I must, with all my might, do right by Sal Quinn.

I smile. 'What will I do, Sal,' I say, 'if the fever comes here? What will *I* do!'

She just looks at me.

'Do you think I have power over life and death?'

'No, Eliza,' she replies pertly, 'but I do think you're very clever.'

'Don't I have enough on my hands without having to nurse people through more sickness?' I

219

say testily. 'Can I work miracles?'

'Only our Lord ever worked miracles on this earth, Eliza.' This is said in no pious way. She dares—she actually dares—to put her still cold hand on mine. If she knew how my innards cringed. I dislike to be touched, unless I specifically invite it, but I do not withdraw my hand even though it wants to curl up and creep away from her.

'Eat ramsons,' I say. 'Pierce an orange if you can get hold of one—ha!—put an onion under the bed, maybe it'll work, maybe not. I'm not God. I can't change the world.'

'I know that,' she says quietly, looking down.

I draw my hand away.

'I thought a pishogue,' she says, 'it's better than nothing.'

'I can give you a pishogue.' I stand, the fire needs blowing up. 'Come back tomorrow.'

I can give her any number of pishogues. But if the fever comes, it comes.

'You're an angel, Eliza,' she says warmly with her sudden big-toothed smile.

They'll all be after me. And then when a number have died, they'll stop.

'There's another thing,' she says, 'I'm a bit worried about Darby.'

I turn with the bellows in my hand, raising my eyebrows.

'I don't want him getting in any trouble. I don't know, I worry about him, not that he's a . . .' she trails off as if she thinks she might have said too much.

So what's he been up to? Come to that, when is it Tadhg ends up on a gibbet? No, no, don't think

220

that. Never, never, never, not Tadhg.

'I don't know,' she sighs, 'just some small thing, something to keep him safe or to stop him coming down with something, some . . .' she trails off again, looking sideways towards me at the fire. She has a sly look, or is it me imagining things? I'll pick her some centaury from up on the rath, steep it well. If she pours the water over him she'll feel better. I can't say it will protect him, not if he's determined to be a fool. I can't say anything will. But if he's a good boy it might just help him, I suppose.

'Come back tomorrow,' I say, pumping on the bellows and blowing up a cloud of dust. 'I'll have you something. Jamie! Come down now and bring little Eliza. Careful on the ladder, the pair of you.'

Like pale spiders, their thin grey legs, their curling toes coming down the ladder. Oh, my Jamie. Where have I been all this time? My blood runs cold. He is a thin young thing not getting enough, his belly gurgles all day. Those old knee breeches he has on, ragged, like a gypsy. What is happening to you, Eliza? Where are you while this unfolds? Come back. Come back from wherever you've gone. A year ago it wasn't like this.

'Well, then,' Sal Quinn says, standing at the foot of the ladder to greet the white-legged grub. She holds out her open, welcoming arms, and the girl jumps from the third rung straight into them. My teeth clench.

'I'd worry about that one if I were you, Sal.' It's out before I know I've said it, before I even know I've thought it. Her head swings round and she glares at me, a child on the front, a babe on the back.

221

'What do you mean?' she says in a low voice, covering the child's ears with her hands.

'Don't look at me like that,' I say, 'anyone can see she's sickly. Oh, don't worry! I'm not talking about the fever, I'm talking about the look of her. When did you last see her laugh? There's a spark gone.'

Sal is studying her daughter's face anxiously. The child, like a cat washing itself, is fussing its hand about its ear. 'It was me told you she'd changed,' she says.

'Of course. You'd be the first to know. That's all I meant. She's been put out by the new one, that's all. Give her time. I'll give her a tonic.' I sigh. 'So that's my work cut out for me till tomorrow.'

Sal puts the child down and hoists the baby higher on her back. 'Well, if you're too busy, Eliza,' she says, a touch huffy.

'Not at all. But don't come before noon.'

I could have said more. I could have said what a scowling joyless creature the child's becoming.

'Keep her spirits up if you can,' I say. 'Don't you be standing for her moods.'

She walks out and stands in the yard, calling her boys to her like a hawker. She has another word or two for Phelim while she's leaving, another bright smile. Watching from the window I see him nod and grin, hear the murmured soft tones of him but not the words. Jamie comes up behind me. 'I didn't talk to her,' he says.

'What?'

'Granda tickled her. He called her a bonnie little gossun, but I didn't talk to her.'

Sal Quinn is walking away with a weary tread, the girl whingeing round her while she shifts Margarita to the front, to give her back a rest, I suppose. Young Darby takes his sister's hand but she shrugs him off. Mal tramps hunch-shouldered along the top of the ditch.

'I'm not talking to her any more,' he says, 'because you don't like her.'

Now, how does he know that? He picks things up, that boy.

'What do you think of her, Jamie?' I ask him, as if he were the same age as me.

'She's not nice.' He shrugs. 'She smells stinky.'

'Well, they're not as clean as us, love. Come on, let's get you all cleaned up nice, shall we?'

The water's only lukewarm but it'll do. I take a cloth and rub it all over his face and behind his ears, down his neck inside his collar; he complains it's running down inside. 'Never mind,' I say, 'never mind that,' and think that now I've started I may as well go the whole hog, and tell him to get his clothes off and we'll shake them out and air them a bit, he can put his nightie on for now and sit by the fire, it'll be up and roaring in a while. Jamie doesn't want to do this. He says it's too early for his nightie, so I tell him if he's a good boy and does what I say I'll wrap him up in my shawl and we'll have a little session, just the two of us by the fire, with singing and talking. That's when Phelim comes lumbering in from the yard bringing in the cold, and spoils everything.

'Gah, it's freezing,' he says, going to the fire and leaning over holding out his hands. 'What did Sal want?'

'The usual. Something for nothing.'

'Well, don't let her take advantage, love,' he says mildly, turning and smiling down at Jamie.

223

'There's worse off than them.'

'I know. She's scared of the fever.' I whisper this last not to upset the boy.

'Aye, well . . .' He lights his pipe.

'Well, the Quinns are no more likely to get it than anyone else. I don't know why she thinks she should be special, what if the whole lot of them come wanting stuff? I've told her, I can't do the impossible.'

'Of course you can't. She doesn't expect you to.'

'You'd be surprised what they expect.'

'Ah, she knows what's what, Sal does.'

'Are you in now or out?' I ask him.

'Out again in a minute after a warm and a smoke.' He stands smiling with his hands behind his back in front of the fire. 'Very cheerful, isn't she?' he says.

'Who?'

'Sal.'

'Is she? I thought she was looking rather miserable.'

'Did you?'

Very familiar, it seems to me, the way he talks of her.

'What do you mean by cheerful?' I ask.

'Cheerful. You know, cheerful. The way she is. Smiling and so on, you know.'

She was run ragged, fed up, tired. All smiles for him, of course, a man. She's one of those.

'Well, she didn't look cheerful to me. Go on, Jamie! We're airing Jamie's clothes.' I lower my voice, adding in a whisper, 'I'm checking for lice.'

Phelim knocks his pipe against the chimney breast.

'And we'll wash your hair, Jamie,' I call. 'Phelim,

224

can you fill the big bucket?'

Yes, let's make the most of it. As I am rolling up my sleeves, I am unsure whether it's the fire or something in me that is making my face burn so; then I realise it's a variety of fury, something unaccountable for the present but which must have its way. It's so big it tightens my chest and blocks my ears and turns the world before my eyes red for a moment. Ah, but that's only the fire, burning and popping now, sizzling and darting on the small sticks I placed on top to entice the flames. Yes, let's make the most of it, my unaccountable hatred.

Phelim goes out for the water, humming happily to himself. Bucked him up a treat, she has.

'Jamie! Hurry!' I call up. Times when I've sat for ages gazing into the fire, chewing my lips and the skin inside my cheeks, hating Sal Quinn. A feeling like that doesn't listen to reason. Strangely, it is enjoyable, though it shakes my soul and sickens me. No, not enjoyable: necessary, as if suddenly the veil that is normally drawn between me and my true feelings is rent like the veil of the temple. Then I know that for most of the time I am lost, though safe enough, behind the veil. Now in my anger I am real. And an image comes strongly into my head, the picture of the woman on Samuel Cloverhill's wall, reclining open-legged on a couch, staring back at me. She makes me think of Juliander, who can do anything, even that. Even that. She can lie back slowly upon the couch, completely naked, and she can stare you out while she does it. Juliander lives on the other side of the veil from me but I can call her up. Come through to me, Juliander, I can say, I am too safe here without you.

A sudden clear day. The village is a single line under the mountain. Everything is blue and still, many blues, the mountainline vibrating, too bright to look at directly. It's such a lovely day I have to go for a walk, I must, I can't bear this house any longer. After all you have to take your chances.

Me and Jamie walk down to the strand. It's so strange. People are up and about, walking the lanes. We keep meeting others, and we always smile and nod and reassure one another, saying: this is the change coming, God bless and protect us all. Surely the bad weather can't last forever. Then we'll get the crop back and all those poor people up-country will stop dying. We've had our deaths here now of course. There's always deaths. In Lissadoon I meet Nan Fox just coming out of the shop with her ashplant and a wild grey look about her. More and more like a witch she looks. She's suffering on the Scheme, poor old Nan.

'Did you hear Annie Porter died?' she says. 'They've boarded the place up and the people are passing food in through the window.'

Nan's one of those who loves to be the first to tell you anything. She's enjoying this, I can tell, though her face shows no sign.

'So it *was* the fever,' I say.

It's here. We must all walk carefully. I look across to where Jamie's climbing about on the wall, making sure he can't hear.

'It's the others in the house I can't get out of my mind,' she says. 'Imagine. There's three in there.'

'Is she buried?'

226

'Oh yes. It's the typhus. They took her out straight away, they had to, they brought her out on a hurdle and buried her in the cemetery, but the others had to stay in. Please God it won't spread.'

'How many in there? Three?'

'One's only nine. Nine years old! Poor baby!' Barren Nan was always a weeper over children. She starts now, her watery grey eyes turning pink and small. I wouldn't have her with me at a birthing if there was a chance of a death. She'd be stupid. You can't be stupid at a time like that, it doesn't do. 'He's in there with the sister and the aunt. The sister's sick, they say.'

'It's hard on them.'

What can you say? It could be me, me and Jamie. Under my cloak, my palm is enclosing the little blue bag that rests upon my breast bone. It seems a small warm heart is beating within; my own heart, quite separate, beats a different rhythm beneath.

'They're putting the food in on a long shovel,' Nan says. 'Isn't it horrible?'

I shake my head. 'Horrible.'

She goes home towards Kildarragh, and we go on through the village. I'm frightened. I have had fear many, many times. I know what to do. I open up my soul and let the fear have its way, as with the anger. It is another twitch of the veil. And this fear is very strong, rolling in like the ocean, the last wave, the one that finishes you. I'm coming, I'm coming, I'm coming, fear says. Standing where the village begins, I'm made a statue by fear.

'Horrible times,' I whisper.

Jamie is a child in horrible times.

I'll walk no further. The fear is in the village. I turn my back on it and make for home. If we sit

227

tight at home we'll do well, if they don't all start coming to me, wanting this, wanting that, as if I can do anything when the great wave comes. Walking in. Hello, Eliza! Just marching into my house the way they do. I've got this awful runny eye, Eliza. I've got this big toe that throbs. This ache here. This itch there. This funny kind of feeling in my jaw.

The fear's in me all the way home. It's not for me, or even for Jamie alone, it's for everything I've ever known, Boolavoe and Lissadoon and Kildarragh and all the little townlands beyond. It's for all the faces I've ever seen. Still, there's nothing to be done. Aren't we only weak creatures after all, waiting like the spider for some hand to brush the web? Everyone dies. Some die worse than others. My mother had a very hard death, a lot of pain, and she was granted the time to know it. And she was a good woman. If that's what's waiting for you, there's no trick in the world will help.

Phelim's cleared a space at the side of the yard. 'That's where I'm going to put the dairy,' he says, turning his head as we come in at the gate. 'It'll be a lot of digging.'

'Annie Porter died,' I say, walk in the house and hang up my cloak.

12

Fever makes you lock the door. I never used to. First I started doing it because of all the theft there is nowadays—they'll come in and take your food out of the pot while it's cooking, and run away. It's not happened to us, but it's happened to plenty. I don't want to lock my door against hungry people. I've never done it in my life, and I've always given where it was needed. But what can you do?

Let them knock and I can decide whether or not they get into my house. You can't give to everyone; it's just not possible, there's too many now.

I don't go into Boolavoe any more. I was sickened the last time I went. I could never take Jamie there now, and he used to love coming into town with me.

'When can we go into town, Ma?' he says. 'You said we could.'

Seven next birthday, poor mite, and stuck here with my father all the time, and *he's* up and about and getting under my feet again all the time, wouldn't you just know it; they're dropping like flies and *he's* getting better. It's a mad world. How could I let Jamie see those children who don't do what children do, don't run or smile or play or even cry very much, who just stand there with their tin cans empty and their eyes dull as dust? All these people losing their cabins, running before sickness. There's middlemen less soft than Cloverhill putting them out by the dozen not thirty miles north of here. And in amongst them, standing around outside Fallon's Yard, I see faces from round here, faces I've known, ones who've dug alongside Phelim for Lomas, who've tipped their hats at me in the lane and sometimes come walking all day to see me and get a potion. And there they are queueing to get into Fallon's Yard with all the strangers, and when their eyes meet mine there is a terrible joining and a quick veiling, and then all goes blank because now everything is different.

The weather continues foul, even worse than last winter, I think, or at least it feels that way but maybe it's because this day and night battering has gone on for so long. It accompanies our work and our rest. We've grown quiet, beaten into submission. Life has diminished to a small round of necessary actions. I remember summer days. Hot days. But most I miss the spring and autumn, certain days that could be either. We've had no spring, summer, autumn. Only winter. It's as if winter has won and will never lift again. We are sometimes very cold, and this worries me more than hunger. We always have turnips and meal, but sometimes there's no more than a wisp to warm us because we have decided to ration, and we know it's wise. But it's hard. We'll cut turf next year. They say the Scheme's coming to an end so there'll be labour if they don't all die first. We had to sell our big eiderdown too, though that's a small thing compared to what other's are having to put up with. We can do without it. Last thing every night I throw Phelim's big coat over the other two coverlets, the big blue one and the lumpy quilty one we've still got. They're fine. It did look nice though, our big eiderdown. It had a pattern of purple flowers and came down from Phelim's parents who died of the pneumonia together under it. Fancy that, and now it's gone to strangers. Phelim took it into town and sold it to a hawker, and he brought home with him a newspaper that said they were thinking of finishing off the Scheme, that there's been people rioting over food in Cork, and that in some areas the famine's completely out of control. I don't want to read about it. The word famine makes me think of the famine in Pharoah's time, in the Bible, where Joseph's brothers come and beg him for food. And he says go back and get my father, or something like that, doesn't he? He could save his own family but he couldn't save the whole of Israel, could he? No one could.

*   *   *

There've been fevers over towards Kildoran, the relapsing fever that comes and goes in waves. They've been eating such rubbish, you see. Worms. Crab apples. Mice. It's getting like that here too. Nan came to me crying because Peader slaughtered their old dog Mick that used to be always sitting panting by the door with the ticks all round its eyes. I had to laugh at that, after she'd gone, of course. Poor old Mick must have been tough as old leather. I'll bet they were picking him out of their teeth for days.

'Ma,' says Jamie, swinging listlessly on the doorframe, 'I want to go out.'

'Run out onto the mounds, Jamie. See if you can see a hare.'

But there are no hares.

We used to see a lot of hares, they used to box on the mound. When do you see a hare these days, or even a rabbit? Pretty things, they are. I wish they'd come back.

People pass by our house, coming back from town with bags of meal on their backs. This twilight, strangely, is quite beautiful, the wind has died down and there's just a gentle steady rain catching the last of the light. I'm out in the yard watching a family go by, a father and mother and

231

four scrubby lads, all barefoot, each with a precious tin can. Their heads are bowed against the rain and they plod on at a steady pace, getting wet, enduring like horses pulling a plough, or sheep standing against a wall in the blast. They too are beautiful, their shadows through the rain becoming softer and more ghostly as they walk. I love a moment like that, when all is well though all is not.

When I turn there is another ghost, close to me in the yard, but I don't jump or scream. I have no fear of ghosts.

'Tadhg.' Tadhg walks past here regular on his way back from work to the shebeen. Curly's pregnant! What a time for it. She'll have to have more milk. We're grand for milk, we've been very careful, so I told him: Bring a can and I'll fill it up for you.

'Nan Fox is down with the fever,' he says.

'Nan!'

'She's down. Peader came to work on his own. Said she'd caught a bad cold and was feeling too weak to walk over. And then he gets home and finds her raving. Burning hot.'

'Oh, not poor old Nan again. Were you up there?'

'Just come from there.'

'Did you see her?'

'Jesus, Eliza, I wouldn't go in. I was in Darby's and they were full of it.'

'I'll have to go up.'

Then Tadhg does a very strange thing. 'Jesus, Eliza,' he says again, and takes me into his arms and hugs me very hard and slowly, 'You're such a little thing, you're nothing but bones. You've got

232

yourself to think of, love, you have to take care of your sweet little self.' I feel like a child, held there against his broad chest, my ear flattened and his heartbeat thumping away in it like an army on a brisk march. He lifts me high off my feet and then puts me down.

'Oh, I'm all right, Tadhg,' I say, 'It can't touch me.'

He shakes his head. 'You're not invincible, Eliza.'

Neither of us mentions what has just happened. His bear's embrace has quickened me and I laugh. 'I am.'

He smiles. 'No, you're not.'

'Don't worry about me, Tadhg,' I say lightly, 'you worry about yourself.'

'I do.' He turns out of the gate and sighs deeply, looking down the lane. 'What a time to be bringing a mouth into the world. Know how many deaths now, Eliza?' He sighs. 'Six in Carraroe, eight or nine in Malahies, Barney Kelly's child in Scarran last night, and God knows how many in Kildoran and Boolavoe. What's happening, Eliza? What's happening?'

'There were a lot of deaths when I was little,' I say, 'my mother used to talk about it. We went round all the houses, she always took me with her, and not a thing touched us. Don't you worry about me, Tadhg.'

'But I do.'

I laugh and shrug. 'Worry then.'

Next morning I go up to Kildarragh for the first time in ages. It was bracing going over the top, over the old rath, with the sea all whipped up and the air a mist. I looked down on the Quinns' house. I'd call there first, get the lie of the land. Sal must

233

have seen me coming because she's out waiting for me when I arrive, so eager to talk that she's bustling towards me up the track before I'm even over the stile.

'Have you heard anything from Cloverhill about the May rents?' she says.

Well, that's nice, isn't it? No time for a how nice to see you after all this time, Eliza. Nothing about poor Nan.

'Of course I haven't. Why would I?'

'Oh, I just thought you might have heard something.'

'Well, I haven't.'

She stands there frowning at me. 'Because Alma heard he was short of money and he might . . .'

'Of course he's short of money. Who isn't? So? He was short of money last year too.'

'She was talking to Martha Colgan's niece. He owes a lot apparently. His daughter's got to leave her school.'

I laugh. 'Oh, the hardship!'

Sal laughs too. 'I know, but . . .'

'What do you think, Sal? Think he's on the turn? He's not put anyone out yet.'

'I don't trust any of them!' she says, suddenly vicious.

'It doesn't really depend on Cloverhill anyway. It depends on Tarlton.' Which is, of course, true, though none of us ever think it.

'Nan's sick,' she says.

'I know. I'm going to see her.'

'Are you and Phelim sowing this year?'

'Darby after work, is he?'

I look at her hard in the eye but she hasn't got the grace to blush. That's it then. Soon as the

Scheme ends they'll all come crawling back.

'He will be,' she says.

'We'll sow a few turnips,' I say, 'I don't know what help we'll be wanting, you'd have to ask Phelim.'

She nods, compressing her lips. We'll try the potatoes again too, even though Father Buckley's giving it out that no one should sow them any more. Anyway, Phelim wants to have another go with the poreens. We split them yesterday, but there's more eye than flesh about them. She offers me a cup of tea and I go in and stand looking around, speechless for a minute. It's disgusting. Look at the *state* of this place. The queer girl sits dribbling and drooly-eyed, wailing listlessly in the middle of the bare floor. The boys are just squatting with their dirty toes splayed in the dust, idle. That boy Mal never closes his mouth. Adenoids. The baby's asleep on a pile of rags.

'You need to clean this place up, Sal,' I say. 'What's it like? What's it like for Darby getting home from work?'

'He doesn't mind.' She sulks as she makes tea. 'Eliza, do shut up,' she says to her daughter, her whole face wincing.

They must have sold everything. Or pawned it. There's nowhere to sit down but on the flat straw mattress, full of bugs probably. Oh, well. I sit. What I should do, what I *would* do if it were any other child, I would pick that whining girl up from the floor and walk about jollying her and shushing her up for her poor tired mother.

'What's the matter with her?' I ask.

'She's hungry,' Sal says.

The tea is weak but very hot and surprisingly

refreshing. She sits there sullen-faced with her hair uncombed and hanging, just sits, saying nothing, doing nothing.

'So how are things with Nan?' I ask.

'Bad, it seems.'

'Any sign of a rash?'

'He didn't say. Peader told Matty she was rambling in her mind and sweating like a pig. I daren't go down there. I didn't want Darby to go to work today. He said Peader seemed fine yesterday, just the way he always is.'

'He probably is fine. It's the way of it. Some get it, some don't. The devil knows why.'

I can't take my eyes off the girl. There's nothing to her, no substance. Her mouth gapes, gummy like a crone; her milk teeth are falling out and nothing's coming to replace them. And that awful endless droning whine. I should take a good look at her but I can't.

'Oh, come on,' says Sal, reaching down and suddenly scooping her up into her lap. 'Come on, my little kitten.' The child moans into her mother's chest, and Sal croons, stroking down her wispy fair hair and rubbing her cheek. And there they rock together, crooning and moaning softly, till Margarita stirs on the floor and gives out a few sharp coughing little yelps, and Sal hands the girl over to Young Darby. 'Well, well, well,' she whispers, puckering her lips and seizing the baby under the oxters, 'you've had a lovely, lovely sleep, haven't you, my love?'

Little Eliza goes quiet, cramming her thumb in and slumping against Young Darby. I leave them to it. There's milk in my basket but that's for Nan. I put something in it to do her good if she can get it

236

down. We'll see. Sal hardly glances up as I leave. The fine mist still shimmers in the air before my eyes, and the waves dance, and the bright white clouds run towards the sun. I shiver. I don't suppose it could be that the weather's on the turn, but something's different. Something in my nostrils and my bones. There's no one about. I stand still for a while at the turn of the bend, with the Quinn house above me and the cluster of dwellings below. There's no movement between the cabins, not a dog or a cat, and no creature stirring on the mountainside. The people are all inside, hiding from the spores of the air. I stride down, breathing deeply.

I knock and walk in. I can smell it at once. Poor Peader's sitting in the corner with his sharp pointed knees sticking straight up out of his britches and his great bony wrists up on either side of his face. He's been crying. 'Oh God in heaven, Eliza,' he says, 'thank God you're here.'

Here's the good wise woman come to set all to rights.

'Any rash?' I say.

Nan's a smelly heap on the mattress, twitching and mumbling in a fever sleep.

'I don't think so, Eliza.'

'What do you mean, you don't think so? There is or there isn't. Haven't you looked?'

'She won't eat anything!' he complains, 'She won't talk sense!'

Useless.

'Has she had a pee?'

'Not since . . . I don't know.'

I sit down beside her and say kindly, 'Now then, how goes it, my Nanny?'

237

She opens her eyes, blinking as if there's a very bright light, snorts and sniffles like an infant. Her lips, thin, white and wormy, champ and burble. There's blood on them. Gingerly I lift her upper lip as if she's a dog. It's the gums, they're rotten.

Peader's got up and is hovering behind me uncertainly.

'There's no rash,' I say. 'It's not the typhus anyway.'

'Oh thank you, thank you, thank you, thank you, Eliza!' he rants, as if it were anything to do with me.

'Are you managing for food?'

'Oh, we're coping, Eliza, coping you know. They're good people, they'll not let us starve.' He grins pathetically.

'She doesn't need to eat. Just keep giving her sips of this. I'll bring you some more in a couple of days. It's just thin whey milk with a few herbs in it.'

'God bless you, Eliza.'

'Oh, He does,' I say, and smile, and then he falls down beside me and blurts: 'they'll not have me back on the Scheme.'

'That's the way of it, Peader,' I say.

Nothing else I can do.

I leave, stand out in the cold and look at the sea. It may actually turn out a nice day. Still not a soul abroad. It's not the typhus, so she might pull through though I doubt it. If she were younger or stronger perhaps, but not Nan. I suppose it's a good thing she has no children. No orphans to worry about. Peader though, it'll go hard with him.

I go back via the shebeen but there's no life there either, and it's not a time for paying calls. I'll go back and wash myself all over and wash everything

238

I have on.

13

The world's gone mad. They're putting things in to Peader through the window. Food. Water. I just walk in, I walk in wherever I want. There are others down with it now in Kildarragh but they've left me alone. They know I'll only tend our old cottiers, the Sheehans and the Scanlons and the Quinns and the Foxes. You have to draw the line somewhere. The Sheehans are a terrible family for diarrhoea. Too many greens. The Scanlons all seem to be fine, even young Becky, and as for the Quinns, I don't know why they don't put that boy of theirs on the Scheme while they still can, buy a bit of flour. Margarita's a healthy baby, I wonder if they're giving it all to her and letting the others go hungry. Sal wants to be careful. She wants to be careful of that girl. I'm thinking there is a thing up there I dare not name, in the house of the Quinns. Now more than ever I'm realising the truth, I've been lying and thinking about it, just lying and thinking about it all night long unable to drop off. Phelim keeps twitching in his sleep. She's come from out there, up high, the reeds and starry pools and rocks. But she doesn't scare me. I'm not scared of any of them, they don't scare me at all, and they never scared my ma. There's only one world and we have to share it with them, as long as you remember that, you'll not go wrong. And these things from out there come and look at us sometimes, and they have a certain look, a certain steadiness of gaze that cuts you to the bone just like the butcher's knife; and they have a certain smile. And that's one up there in Darby's house as sure as I can be.

But Nan though. Poor old Nan died hard, and was the first of ours to go at Kildarragh. There'd been three more down below towards the shebeen, people I did not know well, but Nan was the first of ours. We kept her going for three weeks, me and Peader between us. She did well for a while and got her senses back, but then she starts lapsing and being sick again. She'd been dead three days before I found out, and Peader was in there with her and no one would let him out and no one would go in. Last time I saw her she was sitting up. She'd had some milk with a sop of bread and she kept it down. I couldn't say there was any colour in her face but then there never was with Nan. She looked as if she was at death's door even when she was well. But she was sitting up and talking sense, and she even laughed. 'Eliza,' she said, 'it's a good job you're half gentry,' and she laughed. She meant because I couldn't catch the fever. By gentry she meant the other people that live in the Middle Kingdom. I didn't laugh with her because you shouldn't make light about things like that, but she meant no harm. She asked after Phelim and Jamie and my father.

I really wasn't worried about Nan, not to any great extent, I don't think I gave her much of a thought over the next day or so, and then we got some very bad winds that lifted the corner of the roof of the shed where we'd had the turnips, so that was a lot of trouble; and it was Sunday when Phelim came in and said he'd heard from Darby

Quinn that she was dead but still in the house and no one doing anything about it because they were all scared.

'Peader can take her to Lissadoon,' I said.

'They won't let him out.'

'Who won't?'

'The ones nearest. They've built turf up over the door. They say the house smells of fever. They're still putting food through though.'

'The house smells of Nan,' I said. 'What do they expect? She can't stay there.'

I was for going straight up and sorting it out, but for the first time Phelim showed doubt. 'You're not your mother,' he says to me, but I don't think he was seriously worried. He knows me well enough by now. Still, we had an argument of sorts, I suppose. It was my da stuck up for me strangely enough.

'Give it up, Phelim,' he says, 'she knows what she's doing.'

Then Phelim says an unforgivable thing: 'Think of Jamie.'

As if I'm not thinking of him day and night!

'Do you think,' I said, 'that if there was even the slightest shadow of a threat to that boy I'd take the risk? Do you think I'd even step out of that door? They could be dying in their droves and I'd not lift a finger.'

He looked at me with his serious grey eyes searching, and I stared right back as firm as rock.

'I believe you,' he said faintly after a time.

'It's you that brings him home with his cheek ripped open,' I muttered as I went out to call Jamie to me. There he is on top of the mound, turning and looking back at me with his small surly face. He gets cross with me nowadays: I no longer take him to town, I leave him behind when I visit the townlands. Last time he thumped me in the back. But he's all right with his daddy, and this cannot be put off.

'That's not fair.' Phelim speaks at my ear. 'That was years ago. That wasn't my fault.'

I turn round and give him a kiss. 'That's enough now, Phelim. There's plenty of stirabout in the big pot. Don't let the old man grab it all.'

And I'm off to Kildarragh.

They're all in their houses and it's a lovely day at last, smoke curling up thinly here and there from the odd chimney. The silence chills me. I've thrown back my hood. How long is it since I've been able to throw back my hood and feel the air? When I get to Nan's house I stand and look. Beyond is Flynn's and John Michael's and Bat Sheehan's, Matty's cousin. The door of Nan's house is all stuffed up with sods, and all the windows apart from one small one on the end. I stand there with my wet feet growing cold on the rocky ground, staring at Nan and Peader's barricaded house, and can't believe what's happening. I never saw anything like this in my life before. How long I stand and stare I do not know, but suddenly my temper's gone.

I run and knock on Flynn's door. The door opens and Mary Flynn's face peers fiercely through the gap.

'I want the Fox's cabin opening up now,' I say, imperious, 'tell Larry.'

I go on and call out the Sheehans and John Michael and Tim Felix and his crew, and they all come out shamefaced and stand at a safe distance,

242

making excuses.

'It's all right for you, Mrs Vesey,' Bat Sheehan says, 'you don't have to live alongside; now that makes all the difference.'

'We all know it doesn't touch you, Eliza,' says Mary Flynn in an aggrieved voice, 'but there's children living here, you know.'

'I have a child,' I say.

'So you do,' says she, 'and he doesn't have to live next door to a fever house, does he?'

I shout at them. 'No one's asking you to go in or touch anything. You let that man out now to bury his wife and get himself to the fever hospital if that's what he has to do. You think it's healthy to leave corpses lying around?'

'It's not exactly something we like, Mrs Vesey,' says John Michael, a shy, ugly man with a shock of ginger hair.

'Here,' I say, 'who'll go down to Tadhg O'Donnell's and ask him to knock up a coffin as fast as he can and bring it up here?'

John Michael twists his lip. 'I'll go,' he says.

'Tell him it's not a work of art. It's a box big enough for Nan, and it's needed now.'

I don't think even then they would have made a move to pull down the wall of sods if I had not put them to shame and started doing it with my own hands. Then one by one the men set to.

'That's enough, Mrs Vesey,' Tim Felix says gently, touching my arm, 'this is no work for you. You go and have a sup of tea now while we clear this. But we'll not do any more than clear the door.'

'That's all you have to do.'

When the door's clear they all vanish. I feel as if I

am at the mouth of the tomb of Lazarus, and have a sudden impulse to lean forward and call in a sonorous voice: 'Lazarus, come forth!' This I do, and I giggle as I go in. It is very dark inside and the smell from Nan is sickly sweet and evil though not as strong as I had feared. Nevertheless, it forces bile up through my gullet. I stand in the bit of light from the doorway. 'Peader!' I call softly, 'Peader!'

There's nothing, but then as my eyes are somewhat adjusting I hear a scuffling like the sound of mice and he looms towards me through the shadows. 'I'm not sick, Eliza,' he says in a high quivering voice, 'you mustn't be afraid, I'll not hurt you.'

'Out of this bad air,' I say, 'come on now,' and out we go.

He's very dizzy from the light and the fresh air. His eyes and mouth screw up like a baby's, and his knees give way till he sinks down on the ground with a faint moan, head in hands.

'Take your time now, Peader.' My hand on his shoulder, whispering. 'Take your time, there's all the time you want.'

Slowly he eases down till he's lying on his face against the earth. He's not hot, he's tranced.

'She took bad again, Eliza,' he says, eyes closed, fingers fiddling with the earth.

'Aye, she did.'

He coughs. They're all watching.

'We're going to get her buried now,' I tell him. 'Tadhg O'Donnell's bringing her a coffin.'

He starts to cry, a gentle steady rain. For ten minutes he lies like that, then falls silent. John Michael returns and stands a way off from us, calling out that Tadhg's started on the coffin and

Curly's raising the roof saying she won't let him come up to Kildarragh any more. 'If there's anything more I could do, Mrs Vesey,' he says respectfully, then stops abruptly, struggling with some emotion.

'A wheelbarrow,' I tell him. 'You're very decent, John Michael.'

He nods sharply. 'I'll leave it about here,' he says, looking down at his feet.

'Get up, Peader,' I say, when he's gone, 'show them you're alive.'

After another moment or two Peader sits up and squats there in front of his door with his head held precariously erect. His eyes are red and squinty and he blinks frantically, as if they'll never again be clear, but I'd swear he's not catching. He's been sitting in that stench for three days and nothing's fixed on him. 'There, Peader,' I say, 'you're going to live a long time,' but he isn't capable of talk.

I sit on the hillside in front of Nan and Peader's old house and think how strange the world is; that I used to sit here a long time ago when I was a little girl with my mother, before all of this, and then, though there was always want and sickness—which is simply the way of life—there was never anything to touch this. And now she's gone and here am I. And there is dear Nan's body in there making the darkness in the cabin smell foul.

Peader will be an old man now Nan's gone. Sure as sure. If I were a poet or a shanachie or a maker of songs, I'd make a song or a tale that would make you bleed, knowing of Peader and Nan and all that they were. I have not got the words, so Nan will not be sung. I know only that Nan was Nan, not a bad woman, and Peader's an old man. That's all. It's

245

not new.

Tadhg brings up the coffin, a terrible rough affair, after time elapses. How long? Who knows? Time itself stands back.

'Look,' I say. He won't come close, he's scared of Peader. 'When all this is over, you must not go back into your house till you've got some clean clothes left out ready and you've washed yourself thoroughly all over, then you take off the old clothes and burn them, and then you put the new ones on and go in. Do you understand?'

He gives the merest hint of a shrug.

'It's all right, Tadhg,' I promise him, 'it really is all right. Would I set you at risk, boy? Come now, would I? Would I?'

Smiling at him, I can put him at rest.

He's very serious of face, very scared. He's been drinking.

'Are you scared, Tadhg?' I ask him.

'I am, Eliza. This scares me more than anything.'

He smiles like someone who needs to vomit and is putting it off.

Peader and I put her in the coffin. It wasn't Nan, it was matter. Just matter that putrefied and smelt, though not as bad as it might have done. After all, this was not the height of summer. This was a dead creature left for longer than it should have been, and by now things were moving. Things lived in Nan. Her flesh bred new life. My God, my God, I prayed, oh, my blessed saviour, you too are in these wrigglers. As I writhe in spirit, so writhe they in her. As my spirit fails, so are you made strong. Uphold me, my Upholder.

We carried the coffin into the house. In the dark we felt for her, we placed her gently in the home-made box.

Tadhg had John Michael's wheelbarrow. We lifted the coffin on at an odd angle, and I couldn't help but think of poor Nan's thin bones getting bashed about in there, rattling and subsiding into one another like dropped beads.

I watched him wheel her away, with Peader.

14

Gawky, wide-eyed Peader became the Kildarragh corpse-shifter. It made sense. Nan was gone and he had no children. What else was there for him? He was a lovely man, Peader, and he came to his rightful place after Nan died and he was left to his occupation. Some of us there were who could not be touched, and I was one and so was he. And whenever we met after that, united over a burial, eye-locked over a corpse to be moved, something would occur. It was the strange love like a drink you've drunk, a deep potion, knowing no limits, so that I could love Phelim and Tadhg and Jamie and Peader all in their own ways that were theirs alone, and none could diminish another and there was no end. I never really knew Peader before Nan died. After, he was a long gentle thing that shifted corpses and lived all alone in a scraping in the side of the hill with a thatch cover. Everyone loved him. Everyone.

We're hard people, we've had to be.

We've all heard the stories; how our fathers and our mothers suffered. From that they grew, spawned in a bog of chance. Chance set us down

247

here in these times, spawned of our chance-spawned parents. Walk through it, I tell myself. You are not God. Set down here, walk through it.

When the Scheme ended, there was work digging graves, but not enough. I don't know why the Scheme ended, it's not as if they even finished the road, it just stops in the middle of a field in the middle of nowhere. When I think about it, I don't know what any of it was all about, why some things happened at certain times and others didn't. I know there came a time when things didn't work any more, things we'd always had. Fear was always in my mouth like cobwebs, in my throat like coming illness. Nan started it. I knew things were seriously adrift when Tadhg returned and told me how they'd got her to Lissadoon and were redirected because the cemetery was full. They'd opened up a new place out on some headland called Briggan two miles further west, and that's where they wheeled her in John Michael's wheelbarrow, and tipped her in that old knocked-up coffin into a long trench for the outraged dead, caught surprised as they went about the endless palaver of living. There weren't enough coffins. Our Nan had one because of Tadhg, but they were tipping them in without, he said, from the townlands down the peninsular, all soft and soilable as they were, just throwing down the dirt on them however they lay. I wonder the souls didn't rise up crying out in anguish for their mothers and fathers. I wonder the mothers and fathers didn't throw off their immortal dreams and scream out the names of their children through eternity.

In bed I touched Phelim all night long. My hand

248

was on him. I didn't sleep. He lay breathing steadily under my hand, and the night passed peacefully with me whispering my charms and prayers and saying in my mind: good man, you are safe, safe under my hand. When the morning came I fell asleep and dreamed of an eagle flying from the crest of Lissadoon Point out over the sea, a very beautiful bird both fierce and desirable, but then it was time to get up and start another day, and the endless bloody stirabout.

*   *   *

It's been mild and dry and I've been into town. They've turned the old bakery into a fever hospital and the Quakers have taken over a house on Weavergate and are dishing out soup. Cloverhill's daughter was giving out old clothes from a cart in the Square. A very plain girl, I thought, doesn't take after her da, but tall and graceful; I suppose it's the dancing and the deportment and all these things they learn at those fancy places. I feel sorry for her, she doesn't look easy in herself and I don't think she catches one half of what's being spoken to her, but I'll say this for her, she's got guts. I'm surprised her father lets her do it. I'm surprised he even let her come back here at all, but then I suppose she's a young lady now and does what she wants. She must know the Commissioner got the fever from talking to the people outside the poorhouse, and there was a clergyman and his wife at Kildoran both went down with it and died. And who should I see there standing in line for the clothes but Alma Sheehan and her three, and ragged little vagabonds indeed they do look. I didn't let on I'd seen her; she'd have been shamed. But I saw that she saw me, and she turned away.

Some of the men marched up to Cloverhill's house and made a protest against the May rents at his gates. Martha Colgan came down and said he wasn't there. 'He's in Dublin,' she told them, 'seeing Lord Tarlton.' Then as she turned to go back to the house she spoke over her shoulder: 'I don't know why you don't just let him alone, you lot. He's only trying to live the same as everyone else.'

Father Buckley was there, and O'Carroll the schoolmaster, who shouted out: 'That's true, Martha, but some live harder than others.'

Then Miss Belinda came down with her scarf wrapped round her head and opened the gates and came out. 'My father isn't here,' she said gravely, 'but you can say anything you have to say to me.'

But no one wanted to talk to Miss Belinda, and soon after, everyone drifted away.

'You have to admit,' Darby said later to his wife, 'Sam Cloverhill's daughter, she's no coward.'

'Why?' Sal asked. 'What harm's she going to come to with a big crowd of witnesses and O'Carroll there, and Father Buckley and all. What's going to happen to her?'

'Still. There's a few been shot.'

'Not young ladies, there's not.'

'True.'

'I'd go for Lomas myself,' Sal said, 'I hate the man.'

'Anyway, he's got to be back for the meeting, Tadhg says. There's going to be a hooley in the Square.'

'Well, you don't have to go. I don't want *you* in

250

any trouble.'

'Why? Would you miss me if I was hanged?' He grinned.

'Oh stop it!' Sal was tipping the last of some whey into Margarita's mouth, around them the heavy triple breathing of Young Darby, Mal and little Eliza. 'No, she's not that brave. I'll tell you who's brave. Eliza Vesey's brave.'

It was Eliza Vesey who'd brought up the whey. A kind of awe was attaching to her after Nan's death. She was the only one who'd go into Peader's shelter. It was terrible the way Peader was living like a wild man in that hole in the ground and his good house there all shut up.

'She's turned out strange, Eliza Vesey,' Sal said. 'You have to admire her.'

Darby thought, leaning over to stroke the hair on the baby's head. 'I can't say I like the woman myself.'

Sal nodded. She knew what he meant. Eliza Vesey was hard to like. You felt it was terribly bad not to like her because she was so good, and yet. And yet. 'Sometimes I like her,' Sal said.

'Certainly she's a godsend.'

'You know, she was always sweet on Tadhg O'Donnell.'

Darby smiled. 'They don't suit.'

'I did a bad thing once,' Sal said suddenly, looking down into the ashy grate, 'really wicked.'

'What was that?'

She chewed the inside of her lip and shook her head.

'Ah, go on now, you have to tell me,' he said, and she turned her head slowly and gave a great sigh. 'It keeps coming back to me now she's being so

251

kind to us. She must be a very kind woman, mustn't she? And fearless.'

Darby licked his dry lips and steepled his fingers.

'We was both at a dance once, me and her. A big dance on Cully's Field. Everyone was there, Phelim Vesey and Tadhg O'Donnell and all the boys from Lissadoon and Kildoran had come in and it was wild. Do you know what she was like then? She hadn't the courage she has now. She was an awkward stiff creature, and she used to stand there with a look on her as if she thought badly about everything. She was like a little old woman. And I went up to her and said, aren't you going to dance, Eliza? She looked at me and said, "I *may* dance. I *may* dance."'

Sal put into her voice and tone everything she could of disdain.

'It was,' she spoke haltingly, 'as if—as if she was far too grand for foolery such as the rest of us might get up to. She could make you feel very small. I've just said she hadn't the courage then, but now I'm speaking I don't know: maybe she did have—she'd look at you and not blink, just look at you. When I say she had no courage I mean, it was so clear, I *think* it was, that she wasn't easy at all in herself about being with other people, with all the rest of us, and yet she was always there at everything going; whenever anything was on she was there, as if she just had to make herself go, even though it was all beneath her.'

'Go on,' said Darby, taking the baby from her. Thank God they were all asleep at last.

'Oh, I don't know,' she said, 'it wasn't really anything.'

'Go on.'

252

'We were all so young. We were fifteen or so. Well, I was, I don't know, we were all thereabouts. Very young. And there was a man from Killarney had come, I don't know who he was, he was one of the pipers, and he got up on a barrel and said there was to be a competition as to who, out of all the boys, could box the best; and who could sing best out of the girls. And the winners were to lead the dancing and get a prize. And then he called on the boys all to come up and give it their best, and of course Tadhg O'Donnell goes up there, with John Scanlon and Tim Felix and Dinny Buckley and a few more, and they do knockouts till there's only Tadhg left, wouldn't you know, victorious. And then the man says that there's to be another competition, for the girls, as to who could sing the best; and the winner was to dance with the winner from the boys, which of course was Tadhg. Well, four or five sang and none of them was too bad, and then I was amazed because there's Eliza Domican, as she was then, getting up and singing *The Green Linnet*. Eliza, who never joins in with anything at all. I wonder now I haven't ever told you this before, Darby.'

He laid down the baby between them on the bed.

'*The Green Linnet*!' she whispered wonderingly. 'You know what that's like, Darby. It's full of tricks. It goes everywhere. You need a damn good lilter now for that song.'

'Was she good?' Darby's eyes shone brightly in the very faint light from the candle stub.

'Blow out the candle, love,' she said.

He did.

'What about you?' he asked, 'What did you sing?'

'Me? I didn't sing. You know me, I have no voice

at all for singing. And if I had I'd never have chosen something like *The Green Linnet*. I'd have chosen something easy.'

'So was she good? Did she win?'

Sal was silent for a moment then pushed her hand to her mouth to stifle laughter.

'She was terrible. *Terrible*. It was the most—oh, it was the most!—it was agony. It went on for *ages* and *ages* and not one single note of it was right. She had an awful, weak, cracky voice, and she made that beautiful song sound as if it had no tune to it at all; just one long dirge she made of it, and it made you wince, it really did, it was like your ears were curling up and trying to close themselves. It hurt.'

'Oh God, poor Eliza!'

'I've never heard the like. I don't want to ever again.'

'Did she not realise?'

'Now, that was the funny thing. She did. You could see it in her face all the while she was singing. She knew exactly how awful it was but she didn't stop, she just went on and on with her face getting redder and redder; she was just burning up and dying of shame with every single note, but there it was. She sang it right the way through to the bitter end, and we all stood there with our mouths open listening as if she was as good as anyone. No one said a word. No jeering. No laughing. We were struck dumb, I think. And when she finished there was this little silence and then everyone clapped just like they had for all the others, and she got down and went and stood away from everyone the way she was before. You could never read Eliza's face. Have you noticed that?

You can never read her.'

'Whatever made her do a thing like that, do you suppose?'

'God alone knows.'

'But that wasn't your fault, was it? What was this wicked thing you're supposed to have done?'

Sal sighed. 'Well, then, you see, when a couple more had sung their bits this man from Killarney said that because Tadhg was the winner of the boys he had to choose a winner from the girls. And Tadhg chooses Eliza. He gets up on the barrel and says, the winner is Eliza Domican, and the man calls her up and she still has that blank face of hers, and everyone calling: Well done! And she gets a bunch of lovely purple ribbons, and Tadhg gets a hurley stick, and then they both get down and they're supposed to lead the dancing like the man said. And that's when I did it.'

'What? What did you do, Sal?'

'I felt cross,' she said. 'He only chose her because he felt sorry for her making such a fool of herself like that, and no one said anything about it because they all felt sorry for her too, and you could see that she knew that. But no one was going to say anything at all. And what about all those other girls who sang so much better than she did and gave it their best? What about them? I don't know, she bothered me, she did, in those days. She was so bloody serious. And Tadhg had been pestering me for a dance all night long, he was very taken with me at that time, you know, and I'd been saying no just because, just for the fun of it because he wanted me to. She was so bloody serious and because of that everybody always took her so seriously as if she was something different and

255

nothing applied to her that applied to common people, no one else would have got away with singing like that, but because it was her, somehow—anyway. I was standing next to her when she came down, and the dancing was about to begin. I remember it as clear as when it happened. We were standing by the punch tub and she gets in front of me, between me and Tadhg and her nose up in the air, and I, God forgive me, there was something of a hurley-burley all around at the time and I bent down and picked up the hem of her skirt at the back and tucked it into her waist. Oh, it was terrible, just on a whim, you know, it happened before I could stop myself, and I'm sure I was saying to myself as I did it, no, no, no, you mustn't do this, this is wrong, Sal, this is wrong, but I did it anyway. And next thing she's off in the dance with Tadhg, up and down as merry as can be—she was even smiling—and her showing her scrawny arse in calico drawers to the whole country for miles around, and her thin little legs stepping and kicking away and a big hole in her stockings at the back.' She covers her face but she's laughing. 'Oh, couldn't you just die? Couldn't you just die?'

'Well, it was bad, Sal,' Darby replies slowly, 'but you were very young.'

'That's neither here nor there. I've felt sick about it ever since. I felt sick about it then, but I did it. Aren't I bad?'

'No no no no no,' says Darby. 'How could my Sal be bad?'

'I am though, I am. It was very bad.'

'No.'

'What a spiteful thing to do to someone. Poor Eliza! And now she's so good to us.'

'Did she know?'

'Of course she did! Don't you think as soon as she finished that dance and she turned off the floor, they were queueing up to tell her. And she knew it was me too. Someone of them told her, I know. I know because of how she looked at me ever since, after that night. She's always known, and yet she's always been so good. And I feel so bad about it, Darby, I feel so bad!'

Darby put his arm across her shoulders. 'Hush now,' he said, 'it was all a very long time ago and you're older now and everything's forgiven. She's forgotten all about it.'

'No one forgets a thing like that, Darby,' Sal said, 'I know *I* wouldn't. Not in a million million years. Can you still love me? Oh, what a cruel thing to do!'

'I still love you.' She could feel the bulge of Darby's cheek smiling against her forehead. 'I'll always love you, Sal, you don't know what you are to me. You're not a bad woman. You're good! How could my Sal not be good?'

'I'm glad I told you that,' she said, 'glad.'

Margarita between them slept deeply, at peace.

'Ssh!' he said.

*   *   *

Then there was the riot in Boolavoe. How it fared with other places no one really knew, but for Boolavoe this was the big riot that people would pass down and tell to their grandchildren. Eliza Vesey was there, alone, which caused some comment.

They all gathered around the barracks where the

257

meeting of the relief committee was being held, and all the big people were there, Cloverhill and Lomas and others. Tadhg was in the crowd along with all the wild boys, and many of the small farmers from round about, and the people of five townlands. Father Buckley stood on the steps and addressed the crowd while the meeting went on inside.

'We are not unreasonable in our requests,' he said. 'All we are asking is a simple commitment to life and health for the majority, something which cannot occur without yet another waiving of the rents. All we are asking is that facts be squarely faced. The poor have no decision to make. It is not that they wilfully withhold their rightful dues, it is a matter of no choice at all. If they desired with all their hearts and every nerve in their bodies to pay every single penny owing, if they vowed to sweat and toil to the last gasp of their bodies, it would make no odds. Blood cannot be got from a stone, and rents cannot be paid by those whose only concern is putting a sop of gruel in the mouth of the child who will not live the night without it. Tell me, my friends, what matters more to God? The life blood of Mammon bled from the poor to succour those in grand houses? Or a mouthful of thin stirabout to keep a child from death? Who is there here so inhumane that he would satisfy his landlord and deprive his dying child of comfort? Who? Who, my friends?'

A roar rose from the throats of the crowd. They became so restless that six gentlemen from the meeting came out and stood at the top of the steps, Cloverhill and Lomas among them. Cloverhill stood forward.

'The meeting is not yet concluded,' he announced in a strong voice that rang above the crowd with the conviction of authority. 'Your concerns are being addressed at this very moment. I can tell you that no decision has yet been made as to the collection of rents immediately pending. However—' and here he paused and let his gaze slowly rake the crowd, 'I can assure every one of you standing here this evening that our sole purpose here tonight is to find a way forward for us all—every one of us; man, woman and child, no matter what his station. Upon this I pledge my word.'

'That means nothing!' a voice cried from the crowd. Someone threw a clod of dirt and it hit Lomas on the left arm and left a dirty mark. That upset Cloverhill. You could see him flinch and the anger and fear flit across his face. After all, there could have been a gun. The crowd tensed and the six men turned stiffly and marched back inside, Lomas scowling and dusting earth off the sleeve of his jacket. And then the peelers turned up with their truncheons drawn at the ready and the dispersement began; but a few of the wilder lads, including Tadhg, turned over one of the gentlemen's carriages on the edge of the Square, and there was a fight on the steps of the cross. A few heads were bloodied.

Whether it was the hostility of the crowd that night or the prospect of his own eviction by Tarlton if he didn't get the rents in, something must have hardened in Cloverhill, because he put out at a meeting a few nights later that this issue of arrears could no longer be ignored. Last year the tenants should have paid half-rent but none had paid any.

259

This year the May rents would be let go because of the continuing hardship, but come November all outstanding debts must be settled. And he called on all the farmers of the area to provide work wherever possible. People needed to get back into work, he said, that was the best way forward, and he himself would take the lead. A massive programme of planting must be implemented now that the weather was looking more favourable, and they must all pull together. But there must be no more non-payment of rents.

*   *   *

Well, Phelim is no saint. So much we've done, we can do no more. For their time they'll get a fair wage, but we can't pay their rent. Not this year, not next year. Not this year, Lord, anyway. Lord, this year, you pay the rent, you're able surely if anyone can, we're not. Hear me, Lord, we're just not. I have a child. Lord, Lord, Lord, didn't you ever have a child? You who know everything? Of course you had a child, every child that ever was born is yours, so you know, you know how it is for me and Jamie. You know.

I am afraid. Not of the fever, which nibbles and hounds away at the district, spreading like mould on bread. It's *want* I'm afraid of. Of course Cloverhill's a fool to talk of a big planting. What are they to plant? The funny thing is, those silly little poreens we cut up, me and Phelim, it looks as if they're going to yield; no sign yet of any blight there. But there's only enough for us, and as for those others who never planted because they'd got no seed from last year, what can *they* do? We can't

260

feed them all. And now there's this new law, this quarter acre law. I don't know what that means. Everyone thinks it's bad. It was all the talk when I was up at Darby's house. I'm there again often these days, taking her whey. Tadhg and Darby, they're thick as thieves. I often see Tadhg there. And sometimes there's Matty Sheehan with his ridiculous grin and clever talk, or one of the Scanlons. Tadhg thinks it's lovely, the way I look after everyone. And so it is. They can say what they like, I'm a good woman, I've made sure of that. I know the things to do and I've done them, and maybe that will atone for the hatred in my heart.

They were saying you'd have to give up your land to get relief. You couldn't have more than a quarter of an acre or you wouldn't get anything. We've got twelve so we'd never qualify.

Tadhg was furious, I've never seen him like that. He had his mouth hard closed in a line and he was breathing heavily, in fact at one moment I was convinced he might burst into tears. 'There's a weapon to beat the poor man with,' he says bitterly. 'Starve or be landless. Whose land is it anyway? They'll have it all.'

'All but your last quarter acre,' Darby points out.

Darby has a single acre and most of it's mountain scrub. Now he's off the Scheme he takes in his ticket and gets meal in town. He won't be able to do that now.

'What will you do?' I ask him.

He gives a crooked mirthless smile. He's sitting on the mattress. They only have the one blanket now it seems, but that serves for the time because it's summer.

'What choice is there?' Tadhg spits. 'Starve or go

261

in the poorhouse.'

'I'm not going in that poorhouse,' Sal says quickly, 'I'd rather die in my own house.'

The Scanlons and the Sheehans are in the same boat. So is just about everybody else in Kildarragh.

'They work you like a dog in the poorhouse,' Sal says, 'even the children.'

'They've all got the fever in there,' Matty Sheehan says.

'You'd not survive,' says Sal.

Matty sucks his big square teeth. 'They're not making me give up *my* wee patch, I'm telling you that.'

I don't know why they're bothering. They'll do what they have to do to stay alive because that's what you do. What good's an acre with nothing to plant on it? I think they're all mad. There's only the meal. They'll give up the land when the babies cry.

But not yet.

For now Darby Quinn goes out roaming. He goes past our house every day, he always gives us a wave but he doesn't usually stop, he's in too much of a hurry. He never begs from us. Why would he? He knows we do what we can anyway. He goes down to the main road and begs, and he gets what work he can. I suppose he steals too, I don't know, but I know he wouldn't steal from us. I shouldn't think he gets much. There's no pigs and sheep any more. There's scarcely a chicken between here and Kenmare. You can walk all day and not see so much as a rabbit. It's been change, change now, for so long, and never a change for the better it seems, though it must be coming, it must; nothing in this world ever lasted forever. Walk on. Every day

262

another change. The last time I was up above, O'Carroll's house was all closed up. They said he'd gone away. Scared, I suppose. We went over and looked in the windows. He'd locked up so we couldn't get in, but there's nothing in there. All his nice things have gone, went ages ago, sold for food for Kildarragh. Why should the poor man stay and starve? So how will the children get their schooling? I said this to Phelim. And what about Jamie? Shouldn't he be out now playing with other young ones? Shouldn't I be taking him into Lissadoon? But there's no school there now either, because the mistress is sick; and no one dares send their children out to sit among others.

Phelim has fear too, I think, but it's hard to tell with him. He never lets on. His face is heavy with something though, some deep trouble he's trying not to show. When I tell him the things I've seen, he shakes his head and sometimes closes his eyes as if struck, and says, 'I don't know if I wanted to hear that, Queen Eliza.' But he never gets angry, like Tadhg, and he never shows despair. His shoulders hunch though. He stands sometimes, stick-like in the yard, leaning on his shovel and just gazing down the lane, but he's looking at nothing.

*   *   *

We have potatoes. Those silly little poreens we split so carefully and planted with so little hope and against Father Buckley's advice all came up a treat.

This is a muddle. How do these things happen? Poor Phelim's bewildered as to what to do. There's us and the very few who planted that have a yield, and no disease in sight so far and the weather fair; and if we're very, very careful and keep a few back for seed—and God knows that's going to be well nigh impossible the way things are—then we may, we just may—no, we will, we will, because we have to—we will get through.

God bless us. God's given this crop to us, then please God, we will be safe and I'll see Jamie grow up. Of course I will.

But there goes Phelim again, sitting with his long arms hanging from his knees and his eyes like all sorrow staring in the empty fire like he's daft, worrying about everybody else. I said we'll do what we can and we can't do more than that. First I feed my child. The rest is for God. We'll plant, my God, be it ever such a small patch, and we'll guard it day and night and we'll do what we can.

I made boxty. There are some scallions growing in the field and I mashed a few in. They talk about nectar and manna and food of the gods but there was never anything since time began to rival that boxty all mashed up with a few scallions and a splash of two-milk whey. My mouth fairly dripped as I smelt the white potato smell begin to rise from the pot with the steam, and by the time I had the bowl and was whipping it into cream there were tears of joy in my eyes. It had been so long. And their eyes, Phelim and Jamie and the old man, their eyes by the fire. We were very happy that night. It sounds funny but I think I can truthfully say that that was one of the happiest times of my life. Things have not always gone well with me. But that night even my father was not in a mood to complain, and when we had finally eaten there was a deep and sleepy silence between us all, and everything was good.

We have them stored and hid. Phelim goes up by night and scatters a few around Kildarragh where people will find them; he says it's fairer that way rather than having to choose who gets them. What would you do, he says, going up there and looking them all in their eyes and having to decide who got them? You couldn't do it, that's what he says. And he wants to pay their rents for them come November because we haven't done too bad with what he sold in Kenmare. That's where he had to go, all the way to Kenmare to sell them. He'd have got a price in Boolavoe but he wouldn't dare go there and have to face our own people and them all knowing what we'd got. So the way he sees it, it's no sin to sell a few potatoes for a good price in Kenmare and use what we get to pay the rents for our old labourers come November, the Sheehans and the Scanlons and the Foxes and the Quinns.

Or what's left of them, I say under my breath.

I'm easier in my mind now when I lie in bed. Now I know we'll manage. I've been very scared, perhaps I did not realise how much so at the time, but now I know that I've come through a kind of fear that rots the soul without you even knowing.

One night I wake in the dark and hear soft male voices and realise Phelim's side of the bed is empty. Half asleep I listen for a while until I'm sure of who it is, Phelim and Tadhg sitting up late and yarning pleasantly together for some reason. Unlike these two to sit so late and so companionably. Then Tadhg begins to sing, so I turn my head and draw back the curtain just enough to see the two of them in the light of a single candle, Tadhg singing softly and quietly because he doesn't wish to wake the household, a song about a girl little more than a child, a girl so beautiful that the small wild flowers open up as her bare feet pass by and the stars lean down from the heavens to sigh. He sings that she is his little dew-wet flower, whose song puts to shame the nightingale and thrush, more graceful in her movement than a fawn. A lovely singer, Tadhg, he brings tears into my eyes. Of course they're drunk.

Where he gets it from we'll never know but he still gets it even in these awful times, a strong sweet poteen that has you mellow as a summer moon.

They don't see me looking. A bottle passes back and forth between them.

'Oh, she was,' he says, 'the dew-wet flower.'

However he's to get home I do not know.

Phelim's bony hand shakes a little as he takes the shiny bottle, puts back his head and drinks.

'The most beautiful thing I ever saw,' says Tadhg, leaning back and looking at the ceiling, 'was Sal when she was only fifteen, washing her feet in a tub at her ma's back door.'

Phelim laughs softly. 'I used to walk by that way deliberate.'

'We all did.'

Mellow as a full summer moon, the two of them drinking, thinking soft thoughts of Sal Quinn. There is a feeling in me I cannot name, a toiling, moiling restlessness that never lets go, that lives constantly in the whole of me, body and soul. Because of Sal Quinn. What am I to do about it?

'Phelim Vesey,' I say from the bed, 'that's plenty you've had.'

They jump to, laughing.

'Come out and join us, Eliza,' Tadhg calls.

266

'I will not.'

'Ah, do!'

But I let fall the curtain and turn over on my side, and soon after hear Tadhg leave. I have no idea what time it is. Phelim sits on for a bit, silent, thinking God alone knows what thoughts, till he gets up and puts back the curtain and stands with the candle looking down at me. I'm stiff as a board. He sits, touches my shoulder. 'You're not angry, are you, love?' he asks softly.

'No. But it's time you came to bed.'

'It's not that late.' He puts the candle on the shelf. 'Wasn't that good of Tadhg to think of us? He's left us a half bottle.'

'Well, you'd better hide it well,' I say, 'if my da gets his hands on it, it'll last all of two minutes.'

He chuckles. 'Will you have a drop?'

'A sip.' I sit up and he hands me the bottle. The liquor burns its way down.

'It's a bit of fun in hard times,' he smiles, leaning towards me to rest his face against the front of my nightdress.

'You'll have a bad head in the morning,' I say, capping the bottle.

But he only laughs, and when he's in bed and the candle blown out, huddles up hot against me and wriggles like a child. 'Queen Eliza,' he murmurs, 'Queen, Queen Eliza,' and falls heavily asleep, snoring faintly. I can't sleep though. I can't even close my eyes. My body's as tight as a fiddle string in spite of the drink that warms my stomach. Why should he be asleep when I'm not? I push him. He rolls over and catches his breath. I hate him for smiling so stupidly in his cups over Sal Quinn. I wish she'd die. Why can't she take the fever? Why

267

poor Nan and not her? Why is it misfortune never comes to the right ones? Not fair, not fair, not fair, I cry in the night, and after an hour and another hour and then another of night crawling over and around me, I give up and lie on my back with my eyes wide open, summoning Juliander.

She's alone by candlelight, plainly dressed in a blue skirt and black shawl. Her hair hangs long, combed out, and her eyes glow. She's thinking very deeply about life and its endless turnings, contemplating the next step. The world's put distance between her and her lovers, but they are still there, strong presences within. Death has crept up close to the cottage in which she sits, death rubs itself all over the roof and every wall, obscenely amorous. A woman of supreme courage, she is acquainted with abominable fear. It has, she sometimes thinks, accompanied her every step of the way, she cannot even remember a time when it was not. And so it should be, so it must be, for there's nothing else that moves her on, keeps her walking through and through this madness the world has become. The strength of Juliander is that she transforms fear. It becomes the food of life, sustaining all. Beyond the glow of the candle, lighting her simple beauty, is a darkness full of death, and in it, the faces of the dead are clear. These are not times for play, they are times of testing. So what, in these times, does a woman like her do? She takes up her invisible staff and binds about her an impossible armour of humankindness, tempered in a fire she can no longer endure. What else is there now? She goes through the darkness to see what there is to see. And when she gets to the top of the hill, she looks

268

down on the townland of Kildarragh so still and peaceful in the pale rising dusk of a new morning.

*　　*　　*

I have to keep returning to that miserable house in Kildarragh where the Quinns are starving. She keeps sending for me and it's driving me mad. If it's not one thing it's another. Poor little Eliza was coughing so bad last night. I'm a bit worried about Darby, do you think he looks a funny colour? And what about these lovely big lads, little broad men's faces, slit-eyed and callow, self-conscious. I suppose she loves them like I love Jamie. I suppose it's all the same, there's people all around loving each other like me and Jamie love each other. What a terrible weight that is, when so many are dying and we're all jumpy. I'll not let him pay their rent. There are soup kitchens, that's fair. The food's there if they want it. It's us or them. I've been sitting here gnawing my nails bloody all day. My da's up. He's off for a walk, he says he'll catch the good weather while he can. And Phelim, Jamie with him, is doing something necessary in the lower field down under the mound. They leave me to think here, looking out and biting on my raw hands and thinking what should I be doing? What should I be doing? I'm going to bash up some neeps tonight. I'll make them into little cakes with a few greens. I don't know, I daren't think what's happening above. There's far worse down below on those lower slopes. Our people aren't so bad, not amongst the worst. I keep thinking about Juliander and what she did last night. But then, she has no husband or child, she can do what she

269

wants. She's outside of all that. She went through the night of cool breezes over the mountain by the light of a mellow full summer moon, she looked down on the sleeping townland. Then down, down, down, with small wild flowers springing at her feet, the small pink stars I make into a potion to protect; and the stars out, and the sea so many bright small silver-tipped black waves. It is easy to be drunk on the beauty of a night like this, whether or not you've had a drink of Tadhg O'Donnell's strong poteen. And being who she was she was suffused with joy, drifting down through those low cabins. There was a smile on her face. The night was indeed very lovely. She stood on a rock and looked out at the sea. Far away, somewhere down the coast, where the caves were and the long shingle where the seals come in, something strange called, a long, high, quivering call.

Then she walked down into the very depths, till she came to a cottage on the extreme edge of the settlement, under a high ridge that kept off the worst of the wind from the sea, with two or three faint ghosts of potato ridges rippling out the back and a bit of rope tethered to a tree, dangling forlorn. The doors and windows were silted up with earth. With her cold hands she pulled it all down, scratched and scrabbled a way through, a small voiceless mole woman burrowing with strong claws. And when she gets in and the light's come though the door again and a window is clear, what does she find?

I didn't know the names of those people. They were not ours. The mother was dead in her bed, and a child lying beside her, a boy of about two. Who knows? He could have been older, he was starved small, a poor sweet monkey boy, still alive.

I'd seen them in town by Fallon's Yard, these monkey girls and boys and babies, but here? They grow hair. I heard about it and didn't believe it but it's true. They grow hair on their faces when they're starving. There was no fever smell, this was hunger alone. I'd heard of the hunger deaths, they were all the far side of Lissadoon, thirteen or fourteen I heard. But this was here, a walk away. A faint but foul smell rose from the mother. Her eyes were closed, her mouth was open, she looked as used and pointless as an old cloth screwed up and thrown out in the rubbish. There was no man. A girl of about thirteen lay across the floor, and a boy of ten or so on a sop of straw. They were horrible, not dead but no longer alive, dirty things with claws like mine, and sad flickering eyes. The place needed whitewash. I picked up the little one from his mother's side, and he lay across my arms with all his limbs dangling. He wouldn't stop crying. He couldn't keep up his head, and his eyes glittered black. He didn't weigh a thing. One arm came up at me, a rag on a pole, and I caught it in my hand and began to cry.

That was how Peader found me, crying with the little one in my arms.

'Nothing I have will do them any good,' I say.

'Of course not, Eliza,' he says, 'of course not.'

I am bewildered.

Peader says, 'you go, Eliza, these are beyond us.'

Nothing to be done but walk out into the air with the rag boy and watch the light go out in him as the dawn comes up fully, big and bright over the mountain. I sit for a while and study his face. The eyes of the dead are magnets, the shadow of

271

the soul is there, a mere phantom. Peader comes out and touches my shoulder. 'I'll bring a hurdle,' he says. 'Leave it to me now, Eliza.'

I lay down the monkey boy.

Juliander sits with the dying night after night. There's nothing she can do but sit by their sides and hold their hands and watch them leave the world, and give them gentle words as they go: 'there now, my darling, soon better, soon all better now, soon, soon better.'

*   *   *

But here, as bright and loud as can be, are the Quinns. God, that woman is selfish. She thinks she's the only one in the world. Would you believe, she's wearing her red kerchief? It's like a slap in the face.

'You should have put that big lad there on the Scheme,' I tell her.

We're at her gate.

'He's only eleven,' she says, 'I wouldn't have had him killing himself like a man out there for tuppence and the ganger standing there doing nothing for four times as much.'

'He's a big lad and the times are not just bad, Sal,' I say, 'they're desperate. You should have let him go.'

'Well, that's what you think, Eliza,' she says. She's looking haggard.

'I would have gone,' says Young Darby.

'I know you would, my love,' she says, touching his head as he passes; then to me: 'Now you're here, would you mind very much just taking a quick look at little Eliza? She's got that cough still

272

and it keeps her awake.'

'It keeps us all awake,' Young Darby says.

I suppose one day there'll be rest for me.

I go in. The girl sits in the middle of the floor, whining and ugly.

'What colour's her pee?'

'Normal.'

I'm not touching her. I sit and wait and she coughs, a rough liquid grumbling pulled up from the chest. I sigh. 'It's no worse than before. Get her hot water to sip. Give it time. Where's Darby?'

'He'll be back today.'

Begging. I don't suppose it's anything much to him, he's done it before. Well, I think, I'm not waiting around here after a night like that, I need my own rest now. She gives me a funny look as I'm leaving, suspicious I think, though what it's for I don't know. Little enough any of them have to reproach me with. What do they want from me? To use me all up, every bit, till there's no more left of me? That's more or less what Phelim said when I got back. Of course he did have a bad head but I thought there's no need for that, taking it out on me.

'You can't just keep going off like this in the middle of the night,' he says. 'Not at a time like this. What about Jamie?'

'Jamie's safer here.'

He's listening to all this, the boy.

'So? What about you?'

'Oh, you needn't worry about me. If I was going to get anything I'd have had it by now.'

'It's not that, it's the wear and tear. Can't you see it? Look how tired you are.'

'I'll have a bit of a rest.'

'It's not fair on us, Eliza. On your own family. You don't belong to everyone, you belong to us.' He threw down the rag he'd been wiping his neck with, just hurled it to the floor.

'Well, that's nice, isn't it?' I say. 'Shall I tell you what I've seen last night, Phelim? And to have to come home to this.'

'I don't want to know,' he says, and walks out.

I pull a face at Jamie. Like, isn't your da an old silly, making such a big fuss.

'Don't go there again, Ma,' he says.

'Oh, I'm all right, Jamie.'

'Dad says they're wearing you out.'

'Oh, yes? Who's wearing me out?'

'The Quinns.'

'I wasn't with the Quinns last night.'

But he's right, I suppose. She calls on me more than anyone, she does, and they haven't even got the sickness or anything. They've got off lightly. And there's a wearing out that's nothing to do with walking over the mountain in the middle of the night, there's the kind that comes from having a thing go round and round in your mind till it's like a tune on the brain, one you get to hate. I can't get it from me that my life would have been better if Sal Quinn had never been born. And there's that creature. I've been very good with putting her away at the back of my thoughts, but now as I lay on my bed in the morning with the curtain drawn against the light, she comes forward in my wandering half awake dreams. She's an abominable thing. She's walking along a mountain track near the sea, over by the caves. I never noticed before how bowed her legs have become. She's always in that dirty grey dress with her thumb in her mouth. She smiles a thin smile at me, and her face is all curving lines, the slits of her eyes and mouth, curls that go on curling up and up and up like grubs that clench at a touch. Her nose is a mere tweak of the clay. What is she? A cuckoo, a mooncalf. There's nothing of the human in her, and what is there has its origins under the ground. She has the earth about her. Her substance is worm-holed, cracked and ancient, muddy at the core. Looking at her gives me an ill feeling.

Then I wake with a start and a dreadful headache. God save me from this feeling I have about the child. I won't go again, I'll do as Phelim says, and I'll stay home like before and let Juliander do her wandering alone. I toss in the bed and fall back soon into the netherlands of sleep, but just before I take the plunge over that final sharp edge into oblivion, a clear small voice says: Why else were you put here at this time if not to see it all? What other purpose?

*   *   *

And for all my fine resolutions, I was pulled in when the Quinns got sick, sucked back in as if by a sinking sand.

I was dreaming about them every night, and I was waking up, frightening myself with a curse aloud on my lips. Twice I woke Phelim. 'You were shouting,' he said, and stroked me with his hand. After all they were my nearest neighbours and they were all sick, all the children but the strange one in differing degrees. And who else was there to see to them? They don't call on each other any more, the Scanlons and Sheehans and Quinns. There's very

275

little flitting between cabins now. Tadhg told us they were sick and I went up. Should I not have done that? Phelim cried last night. He says he's so heartsick and tired at the way things are going. He never shows it and now he's showing it, and I can't have him breaking. Not him. But there's something strange goes on when he's unmanned, a baby of a thing; there's something of a thrill that makes me strong. I sit him by the fire and cuddle his big stupid head and let him cry into my apron for a bit, then I sit on his knee and give him one of my big strong kisses that makes him well.

'Now when have I ever told you false?' I say. 'I'll not go further than Darby's house, the worst of it's down below. It doesn't touch me and you know it.'

I touch my hand to my mother's charm, and tell him to stay in today with his sniffly nose and sad eyes, stay in and keep himself warm and put two potatoes to bake in the red ashes. When I come home the house will be full of the aroma. I take some soup in a bottle, a big lumper and a pint of milk. It's such a beautiful day, early autumn, a little cold and the scent of the seasons changing. I swear this mountain on such a day is the seat of the gods. There's nothing in all the stories and great tales, nothing anywhere in the world to compare with it for beauty. For a time I sit among the heather and gorse looking out over the bay and the distant blue line of Lissadoon village shimmering in the softness of the day. This is a lovely land. When we're all dead it still will be.

The Quinns are in a bad way. There's no fire because she's got no fuel. She's on her own, he's been on the road nearly a week and she's scared stiff he's dead. I told her not to be so stupid. Why

276

him rather than another? Can you blame him staying away? I thought, but I didn't say it. Who'd want to wait around here to die? Look at you, Sal Quinn, just look at you, this hunger's a great leveller, you can say that for it. That brightness of the eye has gone, that was always one of her great things. I used to think she put something in her eyes to make them like that, it irked me because it was a secret I didn't have, and I have many secrets but not that one. But now look at you, Sal Quinn. And look at me. Serene and sure I go about my business in this reeking hovel with you traipsing, clumsy and big-shouldered after me with your frightened face all haggard and wild. You've cried into the soup, thin poor stuff, because of my kindness. 'If we had a morsel of turf,' you've said, 'we could soften the potatoes,' and I've promised I'll bring you some when I can, because the last time you ate raw potato it gave you the most horrible pains and you were up all night.

All the food in the house before I came was a ladle of yellow meal with maggots in. You don't know what you'd do without me, do you?

Young Darby and Mal are raging hot and vomiting. Margarita's limp. She'll not last but I'll not tell her mother, she'll turn on me. They do that, as if it's your fault. The other one's quiet, just sits and watches the boys and sucks her thumb, the only thing about her that's clean. As for Sal—well, she's poorly herself and she's not coping.

'I'll not let him go again,' she says, picking at her knuckles.

'Right enough.'

'I need him here.'

'Of course you do.'

'He could get me some wood.'

'Phelim'll bring you some. He'll leave it over by the stile.'

'Oh, you are good, Eliza. You've been a true friend to us.'

I smile and send her for more water. These need cooling down. She takes little Eliza with her.

'Up, my fine lad.'

Mal's hair is drenched. He whimpers like a dog.

'Soon better now,' I say, holding his head and keeping back his hair. 'That's it, let it go, the more the better, good boy.'

A child can be miserable in a fuller way than a grown person. If he's well enough to cry, that's good. That baby's quiet as a mouse. Young Darby is a little still for my liking too, but when I go over and look at him, his eyelids flicker and he puts his hands up to me in a peculiar grasping way. How fine his hands are, long-fingered and with a gentleness in the way they touch the air. He gulps noisily and whispers, 'Where's Ma?' never opening his eyes.

'Ma's coming,' I say, 'she's just bringing you some lovely cold water.'

'Want Ma.' His voice a high wheeze.

'Ma's here.'

'Mammy's here, my big boy,' she says, sinking to her knees with a cold rag.

'He'll be fine, Sal, don't you worry.' I can say it as one who knows, reassuring her. And it's true, he will be fine and so will his brother, they're tough little tykes, but the baby's going to die. She breathes scarcely at all. She's hot but her hands are freezing cold, and there's no power at all left to hold the life in. Just nothing there. But when I pick her up and bring her close against my breast, I feel that she is suffering somewhere beneath the stillness, as if a mirror-calm pool concealed a boiling bed of mud.

I remember her birth a year and a half ago, when things were bad but not so bad; how her eyes were wide open from the first, and very bright. She had strength, all sparkle and shine like her mother, and her black hair glistening wet too.

She was wet now too, but dull.

'Margarita,' I whisper, blowing gently on her forehead, 'Margarita.'

Someone should be holding her all the time from now on. It's wrong for a baby to die unheld. She should have her mother. Even closed, you can see how large her eyes are, they bulge and stare behind the almost transparent eyelids, which are crazed, leaf-like, with thin lilac veins. The way I'm holding her, I can feel her heart running into mine, pouring in like a flood. The way it's going, there will be nothing left in her by the time death takes her, she'll be all in me, whatever she was. She hurts me, coming in.

'Sal,' I say, 'Sal.'

She turns from swabbing down Mal's scrawny chest. The child's ribs ripple like the sand on the beach.

'You should take her, Sal,' I say, and her face begins to collapse, but then in from the side runs the girl crying: 'Mamma, Mamma, Mamma!'

Sal shakes herself and seizes her elder daughter, lifts her high onto her shoulder and pats her back. 'It's all right, my baby, Mamma's here, Mamma's here,' and she swings her slowly from side to side.

That's when I feel Margarita go. She bleeds the

rest of herself into me and, empty, dies with a slight shudder. Now, though I may put her down, I'll have to carry her forever. Dear me, it is getting crowded in here. Already we were Legion.

I count. They'd been forty-two in Kildarragh, I think. There was eleven gone now with Margarita. Peader would bring a box, very rough. There'd be no more wood after this; in fact, is there wood enough for Margarita? She's only very small. Forty-two take away eleven is—

'She's gone, Sal,' I say.

—thirty-one.

*   *   *

We can get that little bit of land. Some must live through this. That little bit of land would be ours. It would be easy. I could go see Cloverhill. Not that it's such a great little bit of land, but there's the cabin and the spring. Something for Jamie. Land anyway.

'So, you have your quarter acre and your cabin,' this is Tadhg in his cups, 'you can go in the poorhouse, get fed, come back in better times.'

The good stuff's gone. I've told them, this'll rot you from the inside out, but will they listen?

'Aha though, but can you?' he continues, waving the bottle, and answers himself: 'you cannot! Of course not. You know what happened over the way?' He jerks his thumb as if an event twenty miles away were just in the next hollow. 'Soon as you leave the house, they torch it. Tumble the whole blamed thing in! If the poor man once gives up his plot he's ruined. He can *never* come back.' He's slurring his words, waving his arms about.

'The peelers and the soldiers out in all their glory. Oh yes, it's a fine thing for the landlords, this mess, and we all know whose pocket the peelers and the soldiers are in, don't we? Don't we?'

'We do indeed, Tadhg,' Phelim says mildly, waving away the bottle's neck and turning away from the fire, 'we do indeed.'

I'm sitting by quietly, listening and watching Tadhg. He's grown shaggier and rougher, this past year. There's no business at the shebeen any more, and he sold his boat and his nets, for which he curses, but Curly's da helps out. He's a daddy himself now, Tadhg. It was a girl, Sorcha they named her. Hasn't stopped him going about, he gets a bit of wood here and there for the coffins, but there's not enough now, what with the demand from Boolavoe and Kildoran as well. It's been very bad at Kildoran, he says. They're using the same coffin over and over there, they're tipping them out of the coffin into the trench then taking it back to use again. I think that's terrible. I wouldn't allow it if it were one of mine. They're bad enough anyway, the new graves up over Briggan, you can't tell who's who. That's where they took Margarita. It's just lots of big mounds on those bleak cliffs by the sea and they're all put in together. You could be lying in there face to face with anyone, all rotting away into each other, a lively business, one imagines, but it's only matter. She was buried already by the time Darby came back two days later with a bag of meal on his back.

Now here's a surprise. Since her baby died, Sal Quinn hasn't cried once. I thought she'd have screamed the place down but she just went stupid. She let me and Peader take care of everything, and

281

didn't say a word even when we lifted the child out of her arms to take her away. Poor Darby did all the crying. He was still at it when I went up on the Sunday, his big boyish face with a wrung-out look though the skin was very red. But then he's always been a weepy sort of a man. Sal now, she's gone like a doll. She just does what she has to do, empty-faced, and when there's nothing to be done sits useless with her mouth open, clinging onto her one well child, the one who stole her little sister's death moment. That one. Look at her sitting there in the corner of the room looking at me. Smiling.

I had a dream last night, very like the ones I keep having, where I'm always alone and wandering somewhere. Last night I was just walking through some small town like Boolavoe only it wasn't Boolavoe. I was a stranger there, that was the whole point of it. At first I was inside, in a large, light, warm place where there were many other people. There were stalls selling ginger beer and apple cake and a thin lumpy snow-white broth made out of fish; lots of sweet things I can remember. Everything looked lovely, but whenever I tried to choose something from one of the stalls something went wrong. Either there was no money or the woman serving couldn't see me, or else when I looked closely at the thing I wanted I realised it was actually completely unappetising. Nothing had any taste. Well, anyway, somehow I had to leave that place, and this seemed to be an act of bravado. I knew no one well enough to stay there with, and there was no one with whom I could leave. Outside I found myself in the night-time streets of a strange town. Here and there was a light but it was all very quiet, and no

282

one at all was about. It must be very late indeed, and I had nowhere to go, nowhere to be, no one anywhere waiting, so I just kept walking because there was nothing else to do. If I just keep walking, inescapably I'll walk into my future, I thought. It was beginning to rain but it wasn't really cold. Well, yes; a little, but in fact it was quite pleasant.

'Look at her,' Phelim says, 'where in this world has she gone to.'

Oh, I've not gone anywhere. It's all one. I can be in two places at once. Maybe I should go and see Cloverhill again, but what's the use? It's not him that makes the laws, is it? You'd have to go all the way to the Parliament in England, wouldn't you? Even the Queen of England, she can't make the laws on her own, it's the Parliament that does it. How do you go to a Parliament's door and ask for a word?

'Wait and see,' Tadhg says, 'we've seen nothing yet. There'll be such a vicious sweeping of the land, we won't recognise it after. They'll not stop now. Oh Lord, no, they'll not stop now.'

A grand sweeping of the land. I was thinking of his words the next time I was up on the ridge and looking down on Kildarragh, and I imagined a huge besom coming down out of the sky and rattling about in all the lanes and gaps between the cottages, clearing everything out the way you'd sweep all the woodlice from the crannies of a shed. I imagined it was me wielding it, God's charwoman, making all the bugs run for their lives. This idea pleased me, so I was smiling as I descended like the wolf on the fold, the delivering angel, being Legion. I have to pay a visit to the Scanlons. Becky's sick again, wouldn't you know it,

283

but then whenever wasn't she? She'll always be like that, one of those that takes everything going. I'm amazed the fever didn't sniff her out months ago. Still, some of those sicklies can be remarkably tough. I wouldn't be at all surprised if she just floated straight through and out the other side. As for the Sheehans, the whole lot of them are right as rain, hungry of course but then aren't we all? She's good with food, Alma; she'll make a pudding out of anything, God knows what she's giving them. I don't ask and she's very close is Alma.

I look in on the Quinns as I'm passing. The boys are rallying. The big boy smiles at me. They remember me being there when they were sick. Sal's still dull, but Darby gets up and greets me gratefully. 'How nice to see you, Eliza,' he says, grinning, his big blue eyes shining brightly, 'you're a breath of fresh air.'

I smile on him graciously, the good lady, the lady who is always clean and fresh and serene, bringing comfort no matter how small. Darby Quinn suits hunger, I have to say it. He looks lovely now he's thinned down, his face is showing its shape. There was something of the lump about him before but that's gone altogether, and a queer quick thrill happens to me when he turns and ushers me to the hearth, where straw is strewn about and the ashes neatly cleared away. He's been home since Margarita died. They're making the meal stretch, and I must say the place is looking the better for his presence. He's the woman here, she's just a drab. The muscles in his back move under his thin shirt. Ragged suits him too.

'How are you, Darby?' I say.

'I'm keeping.' He smiles.

284

She doesn't deserve him. Hunger doesn't serve her so well, she needs the flesh on her cheeks. She looks awful. 'Hello, Eliza,' she says, not smiling, 'is that a drop of milk? That's kind.'

'I'd give it the girl if I were you.'

Little Eliza. I don't like to look. I can feel something coming off her I've never known before, some new foe in whose presence I'm wary.

'And how are you, Eliza?' I ask her.

She gabbles nonsense.

'Come here, *allanna*,' Sal says, holding out one arm, 'come for a nice drink of milk.'

Nothing at all under that rag, her private parts showing, the girl sits in the corner with her bare knees up about her face. Two perfect curves of deep brown skin, rough and pimpled, have been gouged out under her watchful eyes. I can see the taint under her skin. Something walks across the back of my neck, a louse no doubt. When I scratch, it cracks under my nail. Little Eliza crawls like one much younger to her mother and is hauled up onto the lap. Sal smiles. Very pretty, Madonna and Child; till slowly the child turns its head and smiles its goblin smile at me, and I know for sure what my bones have always sensed: that she is the only one that can bring me down. She is my doom.

She jumps down suddenly from her mother's knee and scampers towards me.

'Look how strong she is!' Darby cries and at the same moment I scream.

'What's the matter, what's the matter?' Sal gets up heavily, eyes wide. The boys are watching.

'Eliza!' Darby has my elbow. 'It's all right now, Eliza, soft now, you're all right.'

The child has stopped still, looking up at me.

285

'What is it?' says Sal. 'Did you see something?'

I shake my head.

Sal's lips have gone white. 'You scared me!' she says accusingly, 'I thought you'd seen something.'

The child touches my hem and I jerk back in mortal terror.

'What's the matter, Eliza?' says Darby.

'I won't touch her.'

'What?'

I take my arm away from his grip. I have been badly frightened, it's not like me. My heart pounds, making me sick, knock knock knock old thing, bang bang bang on my gullet. 'I won't touch her, Sal,' I say.

They're all looking at me.

'Why not?' she asks.

'I can't touch her. Don't you know what that child is?'

I meant to say: Don't you know what that child has? Don't you see the fever under her skin? But it came out wrong.

Sal began to scream at me. 'She's just a little girl!' she shrieked, 'she's just a little girl, what are you suggesting?'

They wouldn't understand. A little girl with my name and the fever marked for me. When she moves, I flinch.

'How dare you!' Sal screams, flying at me and shaking me by the shoulders. Little Eliza starts to cry. 'How dare you! How dare you, you old witch!'

'Sal!' Darby says, pulling her away from me. 'Sal! Easy, Sal.'

'I will not be easy! How dare she be afraid of my daughter. How dare she!'

'I'm sure she didn't mean—'

286

'There, Darby,' I say, 'give her the milk.'

Sal's still screaming as I walk on down the hill to see Becky Scanlon. I'm shaking. Well, if she wants it like that she can have it. I've been good to that family. I feel something bitter rise in my throat and my eyes burn, but I will not have it, I will not have it. Becky's not too bad. Coughing up phlegm and scratching herself silly, that's all, but she'll do. I say to John and Cliona, 'What is it about Sal Quinn these days?' I say. 'Do you think she's getting very nervy?'

'She's always been a nervous type,' John says.

'It's the loss of the child,' says Cliona.

'She just flew at me,' I say, 'flew at me like a frighted hen, screaming.'

Cliona looks closely at me. I suppose I'm still shaking from my fright.

'Are you all right, Eliza?' she says.

'I'm a bit upset,' I say, but my heart's still much too fast. 'I don't know why she went for me like that.'

Tears start up in my eyes. I will not have it.

'Ah, pay it no mind. She's not herself.'

'I'll not go back,' I say, 'I was trying to help. The other little girl's coming down. I was trying to help, and she just flies at me.'

Their faces are kind. 'Sit a while,' John says, but I can't. I have to keep moving. I rush home. The tears keep coming like silly waves washed in but I won't take any notice of them at all. I will keep on walking and walking ever onwards into the future. Every footfall of mine along this path over the rath is a heartbeat. The sea is pounding in on the stone strand, booming under my feet. Another heartbeat, down in the earth, in the Middle

287

Kingdom.

When I get home, the lights are on. Jamie's asleep, so's my da. Once I'm by my own hearth again the tears flow freely. Phelim is distraught.

'He cried for you,' Phelim says. 'He wanted his ma. We want you here, Eliza. Look at you, look at the state of you. Please don't go any more, don't go, don't go, Eliza. Oh, *please* stop crying.'

'She shouted at me,' I sob, 'she shouted at me and called me a witch, and I was only trying to help.'

He puts his arms around me and crushes me. 'They don't deserve you,' he says stoutly.

*   *   *

I'm staying at home now. I'm no fool. They're putting it about that I spent time with the fairies. Well, that's the Quinns for you. What nonsense these people talk about the fairies. They don't know anything and they have no respect. Well, they'll find out. They'll find out. As for me, *I* never saw a fairy in my life and I never spent time under the earth. I'll have none of that madness. They ought to take a look at themselves. The only thing that was of the Middle Kingdom I ever saw outside of my own head was Eliza Quinn.

Of course no one's taking any notice of them. I heard it from Alma Sheehan. She says she thinks Sal's lost her mind since the baby died, and I'm not to worry about anything she says. I don't know what they all think. I don't know what Sal's told them. I only meant little Eliza was coming down with some really bad thing, something I have no power over. What do they think I am? Immortal?

Anyway I've been so good. I never said a bad word about that child to anyone. They can draw their own conclusions, they can do without me. I've been sitting here by the back door now for ever so long biting my nails. I didn't mean to be so scared of her. I can't help it. I haven't been as nervous as this for years, not since my mother died I don't suppose. I put my hand to the little blue charm bag as I do a hundred times a day, and there's nothing there. Oh my God! It's gone. I feel sick. Where did I lose it? It's gone. I'll not be able to take another step without it. It's always been there, always hanging there between my breasts, always a comfort. It's like my mother's died all over again. How is it possible I didn't feel it go? When did its weight leave me, it's small, sure, secure weight, the difference between the dark and the light?

Then I truly despair. I throw my apron over my head the way I've seen the old ones do, and I weep and howl and groan my despair.

When I put down my apron, Jamie's standing there.

'It's all right, Mamma,' he says. 'If those Quinns come round here I'll chase them off with the loy.'

That makes me laugh, and I grab him and hug him fiercely, and he hugs back.

'I'm staying with you now, my love,' I say, wiping my eyes on his narrow shoulder, 'I won't be running off again. Not any more.'

'Good, Ma!' he says, 'Good!'

It's a black omen. I don't know what I'm going to do. If I was scared before, what is this? I pray with my bones. I don't need to say the words, I put the prayers singing in my bones and they pray all the time like chimes while I do other things. While I

289

smile for Jamie the whole world perishes. But he needs this smiling mother face more than I need to scream out loud. 'I'm sad, Jamie, because I lost my little charm bag your granny gave me,' I say. 'Will you help me to look for it?'

'*I'll* find it,' he says.

My father comes rambling out of the house in his underwear, scratching his belly. Everything's going to seed. 'Get in!' I order him. 'Get in!' and he does it at once like a stupid dog. Everything's going mad. I can't lose control. I must keep calm and keep upright.

'Come on, Jamie, we'll have a look.'

I take his hand and we go on the hunt, trying to make it a game for him, poor little thing's not got much fun with no other young ones around, and God knows he must get sick of his granda. God knows I do. I don't know where the hell Phelim's got to. He's off at Tadhg's maybe, I don't know what goes on down there. I've not been. I don't know, I wouldn't feel welcome somehow, even though Tadhg himself has always been very thick with me one way or the other. I've not even seen the baby. Do you know—oh my God, I'm stopped in my tracks, what is happening to me?—I cannot even remember whether it's a boy or a girl. Was it a boy? A boy? What name had it?

We look everywhere. All over the house and all over the mounds at the back where I might have gone and sat, and up and down the lane, and up towards Kildarragh and all that way, but there's no point going too far. I had it yesterday certainly so it can only be about here somewhere. What else have I lost? I've lost time, that's what I've lost. I have no idea how much time passes. I think I remember feeling it there this morning, surely I must have done, because surely I always do. But I don't think I know my own mind so well at this minute. I think I remember feeling it there quite recently. But I'm not sure. Phelim stops me as I'm attacking the dung heap and weeping.

He says, 'Hush now, my precious, my lovely little Queen Eliza, it's hard times for us all but we're getting by. We're getting by, love. We're getting by.'

'Did Tadhg have a boy or a girl?' I ask him.

He looks at me strangely. 'A girl,' he says.

'What's her name?'

'Sorcha.'

'Where's Jamie gone? Where is he? When did I last see him? I want Jamie.'

'Oh, he's around somewhere. Don't you worry about him, he's fine.'

'I lost my mother's charm bag,' I say, breaking down.

'Ah! Your nice little charm thing. So *that's* what it is. Of course you're upset. Come in here, come in here, Eliza.'

He takes me in and we go behind the curtain and lie down together on the bed, rocking each other for comfort. I nearly fall asleep. Wouldn't you think there'd be time for a little peace, just a little time at least? If we don't even have time, what *do* we have? But someone's coming. Phelim gets up and goes to the door. It's Tadhg. I'm not getting up, I don't look my best. But I listen, sitting up and wiping my eyes and smoothing down my hair, as Tadhg rumbles on in his ranting, rambling way. He says Lomas has been keeping back some of the meal for the distribution and giving it to his cronies, people north of here by the name of Terence. They're using it to fatten up pigs. Lomas owes these people apparently. It's true you don't see Lomas getting thin, and he's not the only one. They say they're feeding meal and turnips to the cattle inland. That's the way of it, says Tadhg. You don't see many a thin Protestant or a strong farmer, do you?

Swish, swish goes the big besom from out of the sky. Into the sea they all go, flying out like specks of dust towards the sunset. Blow them all the way to Amerikay. What will they do with the empty land? Tadhg'll not go willing, that's for sure. Tadhg'll get him another gun, he thinks his other's in the sea. He was mad about that, the cost of a gun's not to be sneezed at. It's all wet and rotten and useless by now. I'll get one anyway, he said. You can't save me, Eliza. When did he say that and why is my mind going? What have I done wrong? Where's Jamie?

I jump up and run out past them, looking for him.

'Jamie!' I shout hoarsely in the lane. 'Jamie!'

Phelim comes up behind me and puts his arm round me, saying, 'There he is, see.'

He's coming down from the top. He went searching.

Tadhg walks by, nods at me, serious-faced.

I'm fine now. Fine

'Tadhg,' I say. 'Baby well?'

'Grand.'

'And Curly?'

'Grand, too.'

He's very grave.

'Don't you go getting in any trouble now,' I say as

292

he goes.

In the lane, passing Jamie, he puts out a large square hand and ruffles his hair. I wonder, has he heard anything about me? These fools of men are all soft on Sal, they'd listen maybe to her rubbish. She's never liked me, I know that. Never. I don't know what I ever did to her, why she thought she could always get the laugh on me. Well, I've gone up and she's gone down; she has no bed any more, only a sop of straw. It's all gone, all her nice things; anything she had could raise a penny. The mighty are now fallen and she knows it and she's biting back, that's all, and I'm to take no notice.

'I didn't find anything,' says Jamie, coming in the gate. 'I've been up nearly to the top.'

'You're a good boy.' I bend to kiss him and see my feet are bleeding, both of them, between the toes. Now when did that happen?

'Could be anywhere,' Phelim says. 'Leave it and let it come back if it will.'

But I hate thinking of it lying lost somewhere all through the winter.

'It's like the story,' he says as we go in and he blows up the fire. There's broth in the cauldron, and a little steam rising. 'Where the ring turns up in the fish's belly. If it's meant to be, nothing will stop it. And if it isn't—' but here he breaks off, smiling. 'Your poor feet,' he says.

'Are you feeling better, Ma?' asks Jamie.'

'Ma's fine now,' I say.

They were so sweet. They washed my feet by the fire, and we laughed and it was like old times. Even my old da comes and sits with us, he's put his breeches on at least, but his frontage gapes and we have to look at his freckly white chest. Even so,

293

something calm has settled against all the odds, something from Phelim. Jamie creeps up to me. His hand slides into mine. I keep thinking about the gun I put in the tree, and that night when I sleep, Juliander comes along and takes it out and stands looking down at it in her hands in a thoughtful way. Now, what will she do? When I awake it's deep in the night and I sniff winter coming in the air. I put up my hand to curl my fingers on nothing. Omens are no more than tides in the blood. It isn't the occurrence, the losing of the charm, the calling of the bird, the crawling of the snail; it's the turning of the tide in the blood. I've sat out there on the rocks at the moment when the sea tide turns, and it's just the same, the strangest sensation. A moment of perfect poise comes, like the moment between the drawing in and the sending out of God's breath, and for that moment there is the silence of a great change. This is to know something of what it must be like in that moment after the final breath, when the soul realises there's no more to come. I've seen that in others.

Sometimes, everything in the world echoes my great perception. The tide in my blood turned today.

15

There are soldiers bristling with their big guns and bayonets down below Corrabreac. They have swords by their sides, and the swords are freshly sharpened every day. Me and Cliona Scanlon saw them from the heights, the soldiers walking with the peelers, bringing three carts of meal over Corrabreac down into Boolavoe, armed for a war with their carbines at the ready and their pouches full. They must be brave or mad the lads who go for them these days. I wonder, does Tadhg still play that game? He says they're all in England's hand; well, of course. And Lomas is in Cloverhill's and Cloverhill's in Tarlton's and Tarlton's in England's. Tadhg says the landlords want nothing more than to lick John Bull's arse, but John Bull hates the landlords and doesn't care a fig, and now that they're all whingeing and whining and begging for mercy he's left them high and dry.

I couldn't care less about the landlords going under, serve 'em right's what I'd say, if it weren't that we're all going down with them.

We have a curfew now, if you don't mind, on account of someone taking a shot at Cloverhill. That's what they do, they make us all pay. Well, they're not keeping me in. Nobody tells me not to walk about at night in my own country.

No one knows what happened. Someone must have let them in, one of the guards must have been in on it or something, or someone's just turned a blind eye. It was eleven o'clock at night and he was just going up to bed with his candle when someone shot him through the window. They said whoever it was must have got past all the guards to get over the outer wall and across the fence, then past the big dog with the fierce bite. Did someone know the dog? Like one of the guards? Someone familiar, a regular visitor? All kinds of things people are saying. Even Martha Colgan's fallen under suspicion in some quarters, but she wouldn't have

295

the cleverness to do a thing like that and act the way she did that night, running about in her nightgown in the mud screaming for the guards. No. She would never willingly lose her dignity like that, she's a stolid woman. Anyway she's in love with him, the pathetic old sow. But then again, some say—but some always would—that perhaps it was a jealous conflagration. But I doubt it. No, it was one of those wild boys for sure though not Tadhg since he's become a father.

Cloverhill's not dead. His left shoulder took the force. Doctor Carmody tended to him in his own house so it can't have been that bad, but he's not gone out since. His daughter's up there with him, and Martha Colgan of course, so he's not too badly off, but I bet he's scared. I bet they all are. I bet they run. If they run, what happens to his big house and all the things in it? I'd like to go up there and get that picture he's got on his wall of the girl on the sofa. What would I do with it though? It makes me laugh to think of that picture hanging up on the wall in our house. How could you have it there with Phelim and my da and Jamie? You couldn't. So why do people like Cloverhill have things like that in their houses? I wonder what his daughter thinks of it?

So everyone's scared and here we are with a board across the door. It's not fair on us having to be scared like this, having to keep the child in. I used to roam all over when I was his age. We've not done anything wrong. Well, I'm not keeping in. From now on I will not be pulled about by everyone, picked at like bones. I will do exactly as I want. I'll go out if I want. And if I don't want to I won't. I'll stay in bed if I want. I'll not talk to

296

anyone unless I want to. And if anyone wants me and I don't want to go, I just won't.

So when Darby Quinn comes into the yard, I run and put the board across.

Phelim looks up sharply. 'What's the matter?'

I've scared him. He thinks it's the bayonets.

I grin. 'It's Darby Quinn,' I say. 'I don't want to see him.'

He looks relieved. Only Darby. We haven't seen him for so long and he used to be a friend of sorts. Darby raps on the door.

'You don't have to see him if you don't want,' says Phelim, 'but we should ask what he wants at least.'

'Why?'

I know what he wants: another bite of me. These people are sapping my strength. Then it occurs to me that maybe my mother's charm was lost in their house that terrible day when Sal Quinn screamed at me and called me a witch. It gives me a sick feeling, thinking of it being up there in that place with that creature.

Darby raps again and calls, 'Phelim!'

'What is it, Darby?' I lean against the door.

'Eliza,' he says, 'Sal's asking for you.'

I laugh. 'Is she now?'

'Please, Eliza.' The voice pleads through my door. 'Let bygones be bygones. She says things without thinking sometimes and then she's sorry. She didn't mean any harm. Our little one's sick and she's out of her mind with worry.'

I look at Phelim and our eyes talk. He's saying, I don't want you to go but God, isn't this awful? I'm saying, watch me now, see how it is to be strong. I raise my voice. 'No, Darby,' I tell him, 'I'm all

297

through with that now.' I don't take my eyes off Phelim, whose face is taking on that distant echo of a plain child with a trembling lip that means he's holding down tears.

'At least tell me what to do!' shouts Darby.

I'm silent.

'Eliza! What should we do?'

'I don't know, Darby. What do you want me to do?'

'How am I to know!'

'How am I to know, Darby!' I shout. 'Why am I the one? I don't know any more than I know, and you've had all that already. Go home!'

'She wants *you*, Eliza! She wants *you*!'

'She can't have me.'

'Eliza!'

'Nothing I can do, nothing you can do, nothing anyone can do.'

'Eliza!'

'No!'

Phelim comes.

Darby cries out very loudly: 'You've always held us in contempt, Eliza Vesey! But not anywhere near as much as we hold you!'

'Leave her!' Phelim says darkly.

'Eliza!'

'Go away! I'll not open this door!'

'Leave her, Darby!'

'Our little girl's going,' he sobs. 'She's going! Eliza, Eliza, what can we do?'

'You can't do anything. Nothing at all in this world.'

'You helped the others!' he cries.

'There's what can be done and what can't. I can't help you.'

'Why?'

'I can't.'

'Because you won't!'

I sense him weeping.

'Only because you won't,' he says.

I suppose he's right, after all. If it were Jamie, if it were me, I'd do anything, step out of any door. But I'll not for her, not for Sal Quinn and her weird daughter; not for them. I'll put myself out for a complete stranger, but no more for her and hers. Why should I do a thing for that woman? She has not the wrinkles I have. She has not the blood vessels that have burst under the skin and in the whites of the eye; she has not the small hairs growing out of her nostrils, or the furrow between her eyes. She has never had bad breath.

'Your daughter,' I speak it clearly through a crack in the door, 'will go where she is going.'

'What?'

'Home.'

'What?'

'Home.'

'What do you mean?'

'Leave her alone, Darby,' Phelim says firmly, his hands on my shoulders. 'Take yourself away from here now and leave her alone.'

'You could help her,' Darby says, quieter, through the door. 'Eliza, you could help her if you wanted to.'

'But I don't want to,' I shout very loudly, 'I don't want to. Do you understand? I don't want to help her, Darby Quinn! I do not.'

Phelim puts his hand over my mouth gently. 'Queen Eliza,' he whispers against my neck.

'This door is locked and bolted,' I call out, 'you'll

never get in,' and fall to my knees with Phelim, a swoon, altogether silly and wrong. Sometime in the swoon, Darby must have given up and gone away, because when I come back to the real world Phelim is caressing me. Such is life. My boy was sleeping an hour ago. Did the shouting wake him? My old dad's in a drunken snore, he found Tadhg's poteen we'd hidden away and so were the mighty vanquished. Ha! So, undisturbed we lay, I don't know how long, on the cold floor. Phelim falls asleep because he always does. Wherever love deposits us, it's me has to rouse him and lead him to bed.

*   *   *

I'm a little laughing rocking lady, rocking all the time. I rock into the future. I have seen the ones who rock, the old ones with their aprons thrown over their heads, the poor ugly children like Eliza Quinn with slimy thumbs in sticky mouths. A whole night I sit and rock before deciding what to do.

In the early morning, a little before light, I set out and walk to Samuel Cloverhill's house. I love this time of day, the beautiful silence full of the wash of waves on the distant shore. No one about. Curfew, ha! So what if I meet a group of soldiery? They have no power over me. As the light comes up and the line of the roofs of Lissadoon appears, purple in the dawn, and the blue falls off the mountains beyond, it's as if the last three years have fallen away and none of it ever happened, and the day will soon begin with all the people getting up and going about their daily tasks, the opening of doors and stirring of pots and coaxing of beasts and emptying of bowels and bladders. Nothing's changed. There was a bad dream in the night, no more of it remembered than the sense it's left me with, the patch of shadow in some closed place, but now the light's up again and life goes on and I'm off on a message. This is the place I've always known, the twists and turns in the lane as familiar to me as the feel of my own breath going in and out of my lungs.

Moisture grows, teeming and drifting in the air. At Cloverhill's gate I pull heartily on the bell and wait. A man with a gun comes out from the trees and asks me what I want.

'A word with someone. Martha Colgan, she'll do.'

I'd not get near him now, Samuel Cloverhill, whose lips I remember, full and red.

The man slopes away and leaves me waiting long enough to sing myself all the way through *The Green Linnet* and *Paudeen* and *Carlingford Lough*, till the broad solid figure of Martha Colgan comes bustling down the path with her hands shoved up her sleeves. There's no accounting for tastes. She doesn't speak, just stands there looking at me through the tall locked gate with her mouth like a trap and her eyes nasty.

'The gun's in the tree,' I say, 'at the back of Darby's house in Kildarragh.'

Which is simple and true and makes no claims. I don't wait to watch her face or hear her questions, I just turn and walk away home along the lanes with my back to the sea. I feel so light. I swear I'll leave the earth in a second. During the night when I was a little rocking lady, I believed I was thinking; but now I don't believe I was. Now I think I was just passing away the time in a whirlpool of words that flew and swooped and chased and rose and dropped like nothing more than a few blown leaves. Blown brown leaves are lovely, but they come to nothing. It's like words. They are pushed about like bottles and in the end you do what you do anyway, and after, you feel right or wrong as the case may be. I feel right. I feel sonorous with import. I smile, walking. My lips are dry and I know I'm not very well. It's only later that afternoon when the whole world is stiff with sameness that the voice begins, going, Why? Why? Why?

The voice a high whining in my head, a horrid child that needs a slap.

Why? Why? Why? Why? Why?

By this time I'm back in my bed. Phelim's sitting beside me wiping my face with a cold cloth.

'What's happened?' I ask.

'Nothing,' he says, 'nothing at all has happened.'

'Why? Why, why, why?'

'You've got yourself a little bit upset,' he says, 'now hush, there's nothing wrong, you're right as rain.'

'Where's Jamie?'

'Gone for wood with your da.'

'Did he see me?' I say, rising up, 'did he see me coming back?'

He pushes me back down. 'Not at all.'

'Did you know,' I say, 'that there are things that suck the breath out of living creatures? Not human things.'

'Hush!'

'Yes, there are.'

He'd never understand. A single basilisk can

poison an entire nest. There's nothing to be done, you have to burn out the lot. It's a dangerous game. I am a dragon-slayer. Sometimes in the struggle, others are scorched. But someone has to take on the dragon or it delivers the whole land to desolation.

I stayed in bed and waited for news. Jamie and my da came and looked at me.

'Is she ill?' I hear Jamie say.

'Only a little bit,' Phelim says, 'she'll be up and about in no time.'

'Oh, certainly,' Dada says.

'Hello, Dada.' I put up my hand.

'Hello, Eliza allanna,' he says. He smells of smoke.

'Have you a pipe, Dada?'

He smiles. 'I still have my pipe,' he says.

'Will you light it up for me, Da? I could really fancy a little smoke.'

'Of course, lamb.'

I stayed in bed and waited for news. They were all so kind to me. Even my stupid da, he could do nothing but light up his pipe for me and give me a smoke now and then. At night I was too hot for Phelim to sleep with, I burnt him up, he said. He came to me three or four times every night and wiped my forehead with the cold cloth. The water smelt funny. They had no idea what to do, the only one who could have helped was me; and I, of course, knew exactly what to do, or at least I would have done if only I hadn't been so damnably hard to reach.

Then, after some time, I don't know how long, but I do know Christmas came and went, the news came, but it wasn't what I'd thought, not crisp and

303

clear like a cut. It was Phelim told me. 'Eliza,' he said, with me sitting up against his arm. I'd had a drink and was feeling better and wondering if soon I could get up and walk about again. 'They've arrested Darby Quinn. They've taken him to Clonmel.'

Clonmel. That's on the other side of the country.

'They found a gun on their place.'

'The Quinns had nothing to do with guns,' I say.

'We don't know,' Phelim says.

'I do. I know everything.'

He chuckles. 'I'm sure you do, Queen Eliza,' he says. 'You're pulling yourself through. There is such strength in you,' he says.

Then he tells me they found the gun and took Darby away, soldiers and police in all their glory, and Sal screaming blue murder and the boys trying to kick the shins of the peelers and getting themselves a whack of the head for it. I hadn't thought it would happen like that. I thought they'd just go, swept out by the big broom. I thought they'd be gone from my sight overnight and I wouldn't have to think about them any more. They'd put them out and they'd go and it would all be over. It's happened to hundreds of others, and they were moving that way anyway. All I did was give them a little push. The gun, after all, was an old thing. But that's not what happened; what happened was they took Darby away for trial at the next assizes, but *she* remained, she and those poor boys, and that thing with my name.

I'd thought she'd die, but she didn't die, she was much too crafty for that. She was up again, running about. Everyone was so pleased about that. Let's be thankful anyway, people were saying, at least the little one's thriving again, we'd thought the poor mite was going the way of her little sister. Blessed Jesus, what times we're living in!

And shouldn't she have been grateful she had her children, all three of them safe and sound in these times? But did that stop her with the weeping and wailing? Not at all. I wouldn't be up there listening to her for a pound of gold. He's so far away and she can't get to him.

'What'll happen to him?' I ask Phelim.

Now I think I'm well enough to get up and go out and about again.

Phelim licks his lips and shakes his head. 'It doesn't seem—' he didn't finish.

'Surely not!' I say, 'Surely you're not saying.'

'I don't know, Eliza,' he says, 'it all depends.'

'They wouldn't hang him. Oh God, no, they wouldn't hang Darby Quinn, would they? That's brutal! Oh, not poor Darby!'

'Well, no one knows what'll happen,' he says, 'but they'll not let him off a thing like that, will they?'

I burst into tears with my face in my hands, and my shoulders shake with laughing and crying.

'Now now now,' says Phelim, 'it's a sad thing but it's happened. Let's hope for the best.'

'I'm going back to sleep now.' I lie down again and he leans over to kiss me.

'That's right,' he says, 'you get a little more rest. You're much better than you were.'

I am, I feel it. I could get up tomorrow. But now I'm going to put the blanket over my head and lie here away from them all and think about this. I want to know exactly what I've done.

I didn't tell any lies. I didn't intend harm to Darby Quinn, he's a nice enough man. The worst thing he ever did was take up with that Sal. Now that was stupid, a woman like that was bound to bring a man down. But he shouldn't die for it. No, no, they won't do that, not for the one old waterlogged gun. Far more likely he'll go to Van Diemens Land. So he'd have his life, and where he's got that there's a brand new story. Now see it thus: that the best thing that ever happens to him, looking at his life as a whole, is getting free of Sal and everything that binds him to this ditch his life's become. Who knows? He's a young man still. He might make something of himself, find himself a wife who won't give birth to creatures of the Middle Kingdom. Who's to say I'm not the kind hand of fate that seems to deliver a blow but really offers a great blessing? It needs a wiser eye than mine, and I know one thing for sure (yes, the more I think of it the more I realise how fortunate this may conclude) that if Darby Quinn stays in this country the best there is for him is turning a capstan mill or breaking stones in the poorhouse, where he'd be separated from her anyway; and the worst that could befall him is death. Perhaps I'm saving him from death. Who knows? Perhaps in twenty years time he'll bless the day he left Ireland.

And then there's her. She'll not suffer. She'll get another man in no time, but not here. She'll have to go in the poorhouse for a time. Well. Think about that. It'll not kill her, she'll get out again, a young strong woman like that; though she's not strong in the mind. Still, that's not my fault. The boys now. The boys. I'll say a prayer for them, a serious one, and I'll send Juliander to their father tonight whatever cell he's lying in. She can sit on his chest and kiss him and bring him dreams of reassurance. Courage, my good boy, she'll say, don't cry—and oh, what a cry-baby that man is—courage, I'll give you a kiss. Hunger's made you sweet. The times have given you a wild gaunt look that was never there before, and I do find it very becoming.

In the night I wake again, refreshed, with a burning urge to get out of my bed and go up and see how things fare with Sal Quinn. Did I say the middle of the night? I don't know, time has become so strange lately. I have no idea what the real time was.

It seems there's a smell almost of spring in the air. But then the weather's so strange, who knows? Then it occurs to me, what if Martha Colgan, that ridiculous plodding woman who gets to share Samuel Cloverhill's bed, what if she told on me? What if she tells it was me who told about the gun? Oh God, what would they think of me? What have I done? I'd have to go away. How could I face a soul after that? How could I say it wasn't me? I never told a lie. I said one small thing, a fact, not an untruth. Others took it up, but that wasn't me. I said a fact. How did I know? Why haven't they come for me with guns? Soldiers with bayonets and guns, asking why. Why, why, why, why did I know there was a gun in the tree? Who told me? Who put it there? Me? No! I had a gun but I threw it over the cliffs near the caves, it's long gone. That's what I told Tadhg but of course it was a lie. It was me who put the gun in the tree and that's all of it. Has it occurred to him? A gun lost and now a gun found. Isn't it funny and terrible? It would seem as if I planned it, but I never planned a thing in my life. What if Tadhg thought I was an informer?

Imagine, Tadhg sent with a big gun to shoot me. Fear comes at me like a burning in the gut.

*   *   *

But she's said nothing. Martha Colgan's said nothing. Like a cow she goes about her business, as she always did. Bovine, she sways her graceless swathe. A peasant woman, she says—I heard it was said in Boolavoe and Lissadoon: a peasant woman in a shawl, a starved thing, who called through the mist as she passed the gate. That was me. That was what I looked like to her. And now another night falls and I'm still here lying on my back looking up at our ceiling, and Phelim sleeping peacefully quiet next to me.

I've got away with it. A thin cold tear trickles into my ear. It makes you wonder, doesn't it, just what you can get away with in this life?

I rise up from my bed as I have always done, and walk across the floor barefoot, making no sound. I don't dress but I put on my shawl and my cloak and my boots and get out of the house without anyone knowing I even woke up. It's dark, but there's a nice big moon, not quite full. As long as I've been alive I've walked at night. Who can stop me? Those who loved me never tried. Curfew. Ha! Sometimes, I think when I die it won't matter as much to me as to others. I'm only half in this world as it is. I love this time of night, this time when there is no known hour. When I'm alone with the great sounding swell of the night, and cannot doubt that the swell is in my blood as well as out there in the sea and the sky and the earth. Sometimes in the night my joy is bigger than this world alone, this small world of valley and mountain and sea and road shining and misty looming heads of flowers and nodding reeds; than all this, and even than the night sky with all its stars and beckonings. Bigger than my own heart beating in the middle of it. Big enough to kill me with its fierceness.

I walk in delight through the beautiful moony night. Why is it they say a sunny day but never a moony night? This is a moony night. It settles on the wild mountain in soft shawls of silver-grey. On the hillside I am not the only thing alive. I think not of the little running, creeping, hunting, busy things, I think of those living things that have always hung between us, between the worlds, between every comfortable restful place. I think of the things wild beyond my understanding, that have always lived on the mountainside.

But no time to stand. Up across the rath, as bright as, no, not day, as bright as the rath in silver moonlight with the sea presenting small sabres to the sky. This is a brilliant madness, one not to be missed.

I know there are people say I'm mad, since I was small and very easily hurt they have said those things. But I've been given mad moments on raths in timeless parts of the night, wanderings I could never have lived without. I wouldn't have missed them for the world. Tell me this, if we are to be born, are we not born to drink as deep as we can from the cup we're given? This is my given cup. Mad raths in moonlight. And over the crest above the bright sea, and down to a small light in a small window, the small apologetic light of Darby's house.

It will be nothing to me when I am forced to be a ghost.

(I suppose I will be. I suppose I have not been good enough to be released from the earth. No, certainly I have not been good enough.)

When I am a ghost, I'll feel I've already had plenty of practice. I have the gift of it. I can haunt. Yes, I can, and here I come. Why should I be afraid of anything on this mountain when I'm here with them, the same substance, a substance not of the life of broad day? Not of the true midday, the fully awakened real of day. When I'm a ghost I'll float all over this mountain. Shall I wail? Like the banshee? To see the desolation! The empty hearths and the places where the children used to play, grown over with weeds; and the places where the young people went courting, those too. The broad patches beaten flat by the beating of many dancing feet. I could wail so beautifully. Someone surely must wail in the wind for these things, and if not me, who is filled with so much, then who?

Under the window I listen.

'Bring him back to me,' she croons in Irish, the poor sad rocking lady. 'Bring him back to me, blessed Mother of God, he's not a bad man, bring him back to me.'

Being good never saved a man.

She'll make me weep soon, this woman in the night, crooning by her hearth with her hand on the horrible child, the poor little grub there, sick again I see now, sick again—they must draw it to them, these creatures—that thing I can't touch, savouring its every breath upon her broad lap. The sights you see are the sights for you. The things befalling are for you. My life joined to hers.

I open the door and run in and throw my arms about her and let her sob.

'Sal, ssh!' I sigh, 'Sal, don't fret, my pet, I've come.'

Her eyes are slitty red and pouring water, her mouth agape, her upper lip shiny with snot. 'What will they do to him, Eliza?' she pleads, as if I have a say in these matters, 'they won't hurt him, will they?'

'No, no, no,' I comfort.

'He's never had a gun in his life! He wouldn't touch a thing like that. He got a turnip or two once upon a time but they can't take him for that, can they? Cloverhill will speak for him, won't he?'

'I don't know what Cloverhill will do. Darby's not a bad man, he'll do fine.'

'He's not a bad man! No, he's not! Why should they hurt him? They won't hurt him, will they? Please don't let them hurt him!'

As if I'm God.

'I won't let them hurt him,' I say, 'There! How long's she been like this?'

She looks down at her sick child. 'You wouldn't come,' she says, 'I sent for you.'

'Well, I'm here now. How long has she been like this?'

'Since Sunday this bad.'

This is the child's first relapse. Shall I give her her own caul? Her lips are white, and a caul's a powerful thing, particularly hers. Lusmore would help too, I can get that. She smells bad. There's a greyness on her leg, spreading from her toes. This is not the fever I've seen in others, this is not even the fever she had under the skin the time she scared me so. I have lost my luck so I'll take no chances. I won't touch her but I'll bring her lusmore, then no one can say I'm not a good woman.

'Tomorrow,' I say, 'I'll bring her something to help.'

'Will you? Oh, please, Eliza, will you? I don't know what I'm to do.'

'You're to get some sleep,' I say, standing up and looking round. The boys are in a huddle under a blanket, a sleeping heap in the straw. She lies down where she is with the girl, wrapping her shawl about them both. I can't spare her any more turf. What does she think, I'm to give her my own cloak?

'I'll come tomorrow,' I say.

She nods, dull, wriggling for a little comfort. Little Eliza gives a thin sharp cry like some unknown bird you might hear close by in the dark as you're walking.

'Hush, baby,' Sal whispers, suckling her goblin. Away from here, shuddering over the top as the light begins to threaten. I thought I'd get away with it, but he's already there in the yard, watching me down the mountain.

'Where've you been, Eliza?' Phelim says.

'To see Sal Quinn.'

'And why was that?'

'You know why.'

He sighs. 'Do I have to lock you in to keep you home?' he says, and we both laugh at the very idea.

'I want to help her because of what's happened to Darby,' I say, 'she's off her head about it.' I walk into my house, where it's warm enough, and safe enough, because we still have a bit of turf for the fire and a morsel in the pot. I sit down, suddenly weary. 'She's very lonely up there,' I say, watching the hot small flames lick around the wiry fibres of the turf. 'If it wasn't for the smell of the sickness, she'd have a man with her in no time.'

He sits opposite me, hugging his knees. 'What am I to do with you?' he asks, forlorn yet amused. 'Is there anything I can say to keep you home? Does it matter that we all want you home?'

'It's all right, Phelim,' I say, smiling. In spite of it all, everything, we've kept our home nice. I feel so tired in the warmth. The idea of taking myself back up there is outrageous. I've been trying too hard for too long and I should give up the ghost. 'I only have to go back up there one more time and that's that. I said I'd take her some lusmore.'

'No,' he says.

I close my eyes and feel the fire gentle on my eyelids. Jamie's waking up. My da, he'll sleep on for a while.

'Enough's enough, Eliza. You've got Jamie to think about.'

I open my eyes and the curtain parts around Jamie's round face, yawning in the early light, his poor damaged cheek. The brown pucker of his skin has grown with him, and is now part of his charm. When he's a man, I think, some woman will fall in love with him because of that. He opens his eyes, sees me and grins. His bare feet pad across the floor and he gets on to my knee, not even knowing I've been gone.

*   *   *

Then, as if to side with Phelim and keep me in, the weather turned. Suddenly we were battered again,

313

and the sea came right up as far as Scarran. It went on bad then, and the four of us went under like small animals in their shelter, for a long time. So there could be no getting about, and secretly I was glad. I kept saying, guilty and in comfort by my own fireside, 'As soon as this clears, I must take some lusmore up for Eliza Quinn.' But it didn't clear enough, so she couldn't have been expecting me really; and soon we were into another time, with trouble abroad on the roads again, so I couldn't go out. I thought, I'll just sit here in my house and let the times move on outside; I'll be just fine and sweet in here. I took out the old caul, Eliza Quinn's caul, and I made a little bag for it out of a bit of blue cloth, as near as I could get in colour to my Ma's old charm bag. Oh, Ma! I thought, I wish you were here. What d'you want to go dying so young for? Leaving me so half made. I always felt like that, Ma. Half made. And you seemed finished somehow, the strongest thing in the world.

So, trouble abroad again. Not here but near enough, Malahies, one of the guards at the manse knocked over and his ears cut off. That's a foul thing, I don't hold with it at all. There's no need for us to be butchers. I'd rather you killed him clean actually than cut his ears off. My God, how cruel we are to one another, how truly vile we are. I went into one of my places, one of my times, when all the others are out there looking in, going about the house smiling and being nice and saying the things to be said and doing it all so well. What are we coming to? Tell me that. No one, no one can make it make sense. Outside the flies are beginning to gather in blurry clusters, like dots

314

before a fevered eye, in clots above the stagnant pools in our yard. The walls drip. Every now and again I go out and throw something on the dung heap. Inside my head are such lonely thoughts. Such fearful thoughts I dare not think. Sometimes everything runs into one and I forget who is my enemy and who is my friend and it all seems silly. Sometimes I feel I'm falling into fragments that are spreading out all over these fields and mounds and bogs and raths and all the houses and cabins and even the low turf-covered hole with the buttercups beginning to spring on top where Peader Fox lives. And all the while I walk about and talk in the world as if everything were normal.

There's a hardening. Cloverhill's shut up in his house with Martha Colgan and sees no one. His girl's gone to Dublin. Soon be the gales. Rent day. I hang Eliza Quinn's caul in the blue bag on a knotted string around Jamie's neck under his nightshirt. No harm will come to him now, I know, it's a thing was passed to me when the time was right and now it's leaving me and going into him. It's the way it moves on. And then the news comes, the news awaited one way or the other, as the news always does come, as things must move on whether you want them to or not. The one thing you can have no power over is time's revelation. And he's who the caul's for, not she. I had not seen her. It wouldn't have made any difference anyway, the lusmore. She was beyond me, that child, she always was. I don't know what she was. I know it was from her I got whatever it was I got, that stopped my reign. But I did not know it then, when the news came in. First, that Darby Quinn was to be transported. Then, within a day or two, that the rents were to be collected in full. Enough's enough, they said, Lomas in his house with the soldiers all around, Cloverhill in his, with his mantraps and ditches and guard dogs and endless circular patrols. I suppose Tarlton clapped his hands. Bring in those rents, boys, he said.

Those who can't pay must go. They've got till the end of the month.

I'm staying in again. I've had enough. I'm not slipping and sliding over to Kildarragh in all this. The potatoes we lifted are stored upstairs where no one can get at them; we'll do nicely, and enough to keep back for the next planting if we're careful. We can't pay all. They'd never put us out, would they? Tenants-at-will? Surely. But things are happening that haven't before. I asked Phelim, he said we'd be all right because we have the one cow still and she's not a bad little thing even though we've bled her. They'll take her. We managed to keep her all this time. They'll take the cow and they can have all we get from the oats too. Will that do? Surely that'll do.

Evening. As if to remind us that the roads will be hard, it starts to rain. But we're still cosy in our house. Phelim stands at the door looking out at the rain, one leg crossed over the other. I know what he's thinking of: Darby Quinn being taken all the way to Cork City and put on a sailing ship and setting out on that terrible long voyage to the other side of the world. No one ever comes back from there. If it were America or Canada I could imagine that, but where he's going to is very wild, I believe. Still, he's got his life, which is more than can be said for many another. I imagine him riding into Cork City, down to the quay where the prison ship lies. I could envy him. Like Juliander when she walks on and on and on, forever brave, now *he* must guide his steps up the gangplank into a new life.

To sail away forever on that great shining ocean! To a wild place. Well, there's hundreds gone before him so who knows what he'll find?

Phelim turns his head and smiles at me. I married the right man. 'Come here and look at this,' he says quietly.

It's nothing, just our hedge dripping wet, but he's standing smiling at it as if it's a thing he's never seen before.

'What?' I say.

He snorts a laugh. 'Nothing. Only, doesn't it look nice?'

It's wet and covered with cobwebs that have turned golden in the light from the setting sun. Evening sun and rain.

'Yes,' I say, 'it does,' and all of a sudden my teeth begin to chatter.

$$*\qquad*\qquad*$$

I'm coming down with a fever, I know it. It started with that rush of cold as I stood at the back door. I had a fever before, a small one, but not like this. This one speaks to me deep inside, a dark something coiling in the base of my womb. This is something that has come to live in me. I've been aware of it from that moment when my teeth lost all control and rattled madly, when I felt such cold at the heart of me it was a silver dagger of ice that made me yawn and forced water from my eyes.

Then we went in and got warm and drank some

of Tadhg's poteen (not the best) and I was very bright and gay and full of laughter because of the chills striking here and there and now and then, because that's the best thing to do when it's that or scream and frighten them all, and the child just gone off to sleep. But I'm not stupid and I understood that something new had got inside me. When I stood up it set my knees to knocking under my petticoat.

I felt very light, almost as if I could have made some game of these knocking bones and flown away dancing out through the window or up the chimney. Phelim put his arm round my waist and rubbed his face against my side, and we were very happy. I suppose the drinking helped. I don't really remember going to bed. But here I am once more awake alone, the dark, the breathing all around me in cadences all over the house. Everything is as it should be. Soft rain on the roof. Soft ticking of the turves, the sweet smoky tang of it, and my eyes wide open in the dark. My mouth is very dry. Slowly, very slowly, my organs begin to heat. They quiver like jelly. There's a hot slick drying on the ice-cold of my brow, and a fat and nauseous worm runs up my gullet. I have to get out of bed, it's the thing to do. But my head is spinning and boiling. I get down and lie on the floor. Everybody sleeps on. This is it. It's the fever, one thing or another, they call it the fever but there's a hundred fevers, they're swarming in the air, invisible, crawling in and out of us like grubs in apples. It's one thing to be brave, it's another to die. I don't know how to do this. I know what my ma did. She just carried on the same as usual, but that was a different thing. That was something big that grew strong inside her. This came from out there. Eliza Quinn put it in me when I was there that night, even though I never touched her. I can't remember how long ago that was now. It seems like only last night, but there have been so many rainy nights, so much rain I've been worrying for the crop again. So it must be some time. She put something in me then, an egg that lay there in the warm, another baby, how disgusting, a baby thing that cracked its shell as I stood at the back door with Phelim looking at the shiny webs in the hedge. And now it unfurls its cold little wings in me.

The sickness passes and I fall asleep on the floor, waking up very cold. It takes me about five minutes to sit up, but by the time I've done it I think I probably will not be sick now. It's still pitch black, I have no idea at all how far away is morning. I know what happens, give or take it's never quite the same. I have time, there'll be ups and downs. I have to get away so Jamie doesn't get it. Thank God I gave him the caul. This is a strong one, it came at me with its teeth bared: that's what Eliza Quinn was for, she's the vessel for my deposer. I'll not be the vessel for his. If I go now, quickly enough, and if I say a prayer in my every waking moment for him, and if the caul does its work, he'll be spared. The caul is of her substance so it will be proof against her, and there's something else in with it too, something very pure and powerful I put there. I won't even look at him, I'll just go. I've done this so many times, you could say I'm practised. I dress warmly, silently. I feel in the dark, slow and careful, thinking myself a ghost and letting my eyes get used to the darkness, which now seems only very slightly less thick than before.

I take a cake of bread and a couple of pennies, and walk as far as Tadhg O'Donnell's shebeen at the crossroads.

The moon's come out and is making a reddish ring about itself. I'd say it's maybe four in the morning. I stand outside and the dog barks. I don't want to wake the baby but I knock on the door. After a while I see a light in the house, then the voice of Tadhg comes gruffly through the door: 'Who is it?'

'Eliza Vesey.'

The baby doesn't seem to have woken. Tadhg's quietened the dog, and I can hear him breathing heavily as he shifts the bolts. I walk back as far as the gate and stand just beyond it.

There he is with a lantern, peering about. 'Eliza?'

'Tadhg, I have an illness,' I say clearly, 'so I'm standing over here.'

'Oh God, Eliza, not you!'

There is such despair in it, quiet as it is. I suppose Curly can hear every word. He starts towards me.

'No!' I back off.

He stops a few steps away, and the wall between us. 'Not you, Eliza,' he whispers miserably.

'Listen, Tadhg,' I say, 'I can't have Jamie catching anything so I'm going away. I want you to go and tell Phelim for me.'

'What!'

I laugh. 'Don't look so shocked. I couldn't tell him myself or he'd have stopped me from going. Let him sleep the night out, God knows he needs it.'

'You should have told him, Eliza. Does he know

320

you're not well?'

'I don't think so.'

'What shall I tell him? Where are you going, Eliza? The hospital?'

I laugh again. You'd have to be a fool to go in there, it's full of sick people. I have absolutely no idea where I'm going, it will come to me. I'm just taking the demon as far away from Jamie as I can get it.

'Yes,' I say, 'I'll go into Boolavoe.'

'You go straight to the hospital now, Eliza,' he says, 'straight there, do you hear? They can help you there.'

'Yes, Tadhg.'

Some do come out of that place, now and then, but I'd rather anything else than go in there. I'll seek my fortune.

We stand a while, awkward and stupid.

'If I could, Eliza,' he says, 'I'd step right over that wall and give you a big squeeze.'

I smile and blow him a kiss. 'Tell Phelim,' I say, and away I go, walking briskly and never looking back.

16

'Am I just to be kept worried all the time?'

Jamie had never seen his father so angry, but here he was, breathing hard with it. He said, 'I'll have no more of it. Jamie, keep inside!'

Jamie retreated as far as the door and stood there listening.

'No, no, no,' he heard Tadhg O'Donnell say to

his father, 'it's not that way, man, she's ill.'

'Of course she's ill! Going up and down the bloody hillside in all weathers and at all times of night. What does she expect?'

Tadhg O'Donnell looked very serious. He said he was just going to repeat the message she gave him and say no more. She'd said she was not well and did not want to pass on whatever it was she had to the family, so she was going to the fever hospital at Boolavoe.

'I told her!' Phelim burst out. 'I told her not to keep going up there to the Quinns. What did she expect? Anyway, what good did it do? They're all going to be put out now, and poor Darby might as well be dead. Jamie, get in!'

Jamie, who knew a lot about sitting quietly and watching, retreated to the dark corner beyond the hearth and stood completely still. For a while his father's voice went back and forth with Tadhg O'Donnell's, then his father came in bringing the cold, gnawing away at his lips and the skin inside his mouth, the sockets of his eyes brown but the rest of his face long and pale and hunted.

'Patrick!' his father yelled, 'Get you down here!'

His grandfather came on the third shout, his face all screwed up with the indignity of the morning light, his hairy bare legs, knock-kneed, groping down the ladder like those of some peculiarly ungainly wading bird.

'She's gone again,' his father said grimly. 'I've got to go into Boolavoe and get her back. She's taken herself off to the fever hospital, the stupid woman, but if I'm quick enough I can catch her up before she gets there.' He was pulling on his lumpy jacket, throwing his sack over his shoulder as he always did. 'I'm not having her in there,' he said. 'Jamie, you stay with your granda,' and throwing open the door, he set off at a fine pace down the lane towards town.

*   *   *

It was very late when he got back. Jamie was used to being left with his granda but not usually for this long, and by the time he heard his father's footsteps in the yard he was thoroughly scared. His granda, who scarcely spoke a word to anyone else, was a great talker when he was alone with Jamie. He'd given him a smoke of his pipe and let him sit up late while he told him all about the banshee and the weird washing woman over at Corrabreac, and the seal that came out of the sea near Briggan and said to a man fishing from the rocks, 'Seven more years and I'll come for you.' And the man vanished seven years later to the day. Then his grandfather had gone quiet and just sat there stupefied looking into the fire and using too much fuel. Jamie knew his mother would be angry when she saw how much fuel he'd burned away. She'd call him an old rap. Hours passed. Jamie fell half asleep on the floor, but woke up and clearly heard his grandfather say in a tone of great awe, 'I don't think she's coming back, Jamie.'

His mother always told him not to worry. Not to worry, she and he'd be fine. She'd told him so many times it must be true, and it was true. She always came back. He'd fall asleep and when he woke up she'd be there, just as it always happened. But the next time he woke up there was only the firelight still, and his grandfather snoring behind

323

the curtain on his mother and father's bed. Jamie lay on the floor covered with a blanket his granda had thrown over him. He listened to the darkness outside and waited, and fell asleep again. Next time he woke, the door was grating open, and his father coming in.

He sat up. His father strode across and took him up in a great bear hug, smelling of the cold in the yard. 'Not in bed?' his father said.

'Where's Ma?' Jamie asked.

'I can't find her, Jamie.' His father's voice was no longer angry—his anger never lasted very long—just puzzled.

'When's she coming back?'

'Oh, soon, very soon, I'm sure. You know your ma, she always turns up.'

'But she's been gone ages and she never said anything to *me* about it.'

'No, well, I think she was in a big hurry.' His father picked him up and carried him across the room. 'Patrick,' he said, pushing back the curtain, 'get up to your own bed now.'

Granda rose grunting and yawning and groaning. 'Where's Eliza?'

'I don't know.'

'You don't know? You don't know?'

Jamie had not heard a note like that in his grandfather's voice before. But his father hushed everything and put him into the big bed, where he lay awake behind the curtain listening to his father stirring up the fire as quietly as he could and putting some water on for tea. The pillow smelt of his mother. Then he heard his father say, 'The hospital knows nothing about her, she never went there. It's as if she's vanished into thin air. No one's seen her.'

His grandfather's voice then, a horrible low keening like an old dog they used to have that ululated in the night. 'Oh, Eliza, my daughter,' his grandfather mourned. 'I'll never see you again.'

Jamie curled up tight and screwed his eyes closed. If he only waited long enough his mother would come and pick him up and put him on her knee like she used to, singing some silly old song that made no sense straight out of her head. But he could still hear the high keen of his grandfather, and his father's sober voice going, 'Hush. Hush, Patrick, let him sleep.' And then he did sleep.

When he woke up it was morning, his grandfather was asleep upstairs, and his father was out again looking for his mother. He didn't know what to do. It was so long since he'd been out and about and seen any other children that he'd become a great stander and starer, and for a long time he just walked up and down the lane, every now and then stopping and looking at something or other, a patch of grass or a pattern on the wall or a particularly mesmerising, murmuring cloud of small darting things hovering on the air. Sometimes he cried and rubbed his face, making a dreadful mask of smeared dirt, through which his blue eyes peered fiercely. Then it occurred to him that he might as well go look for her himself, since he was doing no good at all hanging round here, and he set off with a great sense of purpose that gave him sudden energy and sent him right down to the shore, and all over the land between here and the back of Lissadoon. Shyness made him avoid people. He kept thinking he'd see her familiar shape walking ahead of him at every turn in the road, but it was never her; and when finally he returned to his house it was getting dark and his grandfather was lighting the lamp and grumbling about where was his da gone off to now, was the whole world just going to up and vanish on him? The old man flung a handful of meal in the pot, swearing.

They'd eaten by the time his father came back, looking very tired and sad. Granda dished up the stirabout.

'You lazy old devil,' his father said. 'Could you not at least have thrown in a few greens?'

A tear dripped down Granda's face.

'Come on, Jamie,' said his dad, 'come and sit on your old man's knee.'

When he was settled, his father put his sharp chin on the top of his head and his jaws worked. 'I didn't find her,' he said. There didn't seem to be anything to add to that. Jamie sat on his father's knee all night, even while he was eating his supper. Once or twice he thought his father had fallen asleep, but whenever he stirred, his father's hand would cover his forehead and stay there for a few minutes. Much later, Phelim spoke. 'That's what her goodness brought her,' he said wearily. 'If she'd stayed away from the Quinns like I told her these past few weeks—'

Then he stopped and from the sound of wet blinking and tiny catches in the throat, Jamie knew that he was crying.

Later still, his father said, 'What do we do now?'

Over the next two days, Jamie continued looking for his mother, even after his father had given up. His father sat at home all day, staring into the back of the fire and thinking hard. He'd never seen his father lost for what to do and it scared him more than anything else. A knot of unease sat low in his guts. He wandered this way and that way over the foothills of the mountain, as if she may be hiding somewhere, behind a bush, in a fox's hole. Sometimes he even called out as if she might be in earshot. In bed on the third night, his fingers touched the pouch she'd put on a bit of string round his neck. She'd made it. He thought of all the other times he'd watched her small hands, no bigger than his own, making and mixing and measuring deftly, and the thought popped into his head that she'd taken lusmore up to that horrible girl. Of course. It seemed obvious now. She'd mentioned it several times over those last few days before she left, when she was so restless and kept walking backwards and forwards in the house. How many times had she muttered to herself, I must take lusmore up to the Quinns? She'd gone over to Kildarragh, that's what she'd done. Surely that's where she was. But then surely his dad would have looked there? And why hadn't she come back by now? Maybe she'd taken ill there?

It was very dark and he had no idea just how much of the night had passed. It didn't matter. A small smoky blur on his wall showed that there was some light outside to see by. He got up, just as he knew that she had done herself so many times, not making a sound; crept across the floor, put on his coat and tied a muffler round his neck, and went out into the night. Before these bad times she used to let him go with her, sometimes at night. He hadn't been this way for a long time now but he knew the way and found just the right track, the one that forked up and off to the right, to the rath.

327

Seeing in the dark was easy once you got used to it and sometimes when the moon showed through a hole in the thick bustling cloud, the sea lit up and shone on the land. He could hear it whush-whushing away in the caves below the rath, which was very wide, so far he could hardly see the other side. Daring anything to come, he set off right across the middle. He wasn't scared. Nothing had ever frightened his mother, nothing but the girl, the bad one, the one she crossed herself against. 'I don't want you playing with her,' she'd said to him once. 'She can't help being the way she is, but you don't want to get too near. She's—' here she had paused and thought. She was very wise. '—not right. She's not right.'

He wasn't scared of a little girl like that. She couldn't do anything to him, he could knock her over if he wanted to. He'd done it once, a long time ago, and his dad had slapped him for it. She was unsteady on her pins and he'd only had to give her a little nudge and over she went. She'd frowned but she didn't cry.

'She's of a different substance,' his mother had said another time. 'She's from the Middle Kingdom.' This was a place under the mountain, with the rath on top like a stopper in a bottle. His mother was scared of it but he wasn't. He whistled softly through his teeth as he went over the ridge and down towards Kildarragh. Near the bottom, he turned silent. There were no dogs any more in Kildarragh, no goose to rise up and hiss his approach. He went round the back of Darby's house, stood on tiptoe and looked in the window. There was a bit of light from a wispy fire in the grate. Sal Quinn was sitting on the floor with her

328

knees apart and one hand resting on the girl, who lay sleeping next to her on a bit of straw. There was no sign of his mother. As he watched he saw movements in the lumpy darkness. It was the boys, Young Darby and Mal, pushing each other about and whispering when they should have been quiet.

'*Is feidir liom thu a chloisteail*,' Sal said, '*Teigh a chodladh.*'

I can hear you. You go to sleep.

He went round to the other window and looked in there too, but there was still no sign of his mother. Perhaps he ought to go in and ask, but now that he was here he felt too shy. His mother and father had both forbidden this place to him. Supposing Sal Quinn told on him? He walked away from the cabin a short distance down the hill in the direction of the other houses, stood irresolute looking at the ragged rows of dark humped cabins, smelling faint smoke, sickly-sweet, rotten dung, and the sea. He felt funny out here all on his own and everyone else in their houses. He picked up a stick and walked up and down between the cabins with an odd feeling of power. After a while, he went back to Darby's house and looked in the windows again. Sal had lain down on the floor and closed her eyes. Everything was still.

Jamie pushed open the door and went in. In the weak light of the smouldering fire he saw at once that his mother was not there, not hiding in any of the corners. Everyone was asleep. He went over and looked at Eliza Quinn. She lay on her side with her knees drawn up, mouth and eyes open, face resting on one hand, which was small and wrinkled as the paws of a monkey he'd once seen on the shoulders of a gleeman on fair day in

329

Boolavoe. The stillness of her was final. Her eyes were glossed over, and the lice were walking boldly on her neck. Then with a shock he saw a braided ribbon against her throat, put down his hand and pulled on it, and found locked in her other paw his mother's lost charm. This made him look round wildly as if his mother might be watching. Then he thought his mother was in the little blue bag and he had to get her back off this girl, but when he tried to prise the tiny fingers from the charm they wouldn't move; he even thought they tightened a jot, and the icy wrinkled feel of them sent a shiver to the roots of his hair. He sat back on his heels and wondered. The firelight, flickering, prepared to die. Why had she got his ma's charm that she'd always had, that she went mad without? She'd killed his ma.

His face crumpled up. He shoved a filthy fist into his mouth and bit down on it hard. Then he picked up Eliza Quinn, stiff and cold in her raggy old dress. It was like picking up a rabbit, the lightness of her bones. She was nothing. He took her out through the door and closed it carefully behind him, making no sound. He stood listening. No one stirred. He couldn't see a thing, the moon had gone in. Black clouds moved swiftly above. Then it cleared a little and he saw the winding black arms of the wicked old tree where the cat bit him, reaching out and throwing into sudden relief a swollen indigo sky. Far away a bird called out on the mountain, sweet and quivering. Then a hole appeared in the sky, lined with silver and red, and the moon looked through and lit up the abomination in his arms.

He dashed nimbly, bare-toed, up the bank. He

330

had to stand on tiptoe to reach the hole in the tree where his mother put the cat. She thought he didn't know, but he knew everything because he followed her sometimes, watching the things she did, and he'd seen the cat go in. Down, down, down, far, far below. He tipped her in. A soft crunching sound followed, like the soft grinding of teeth. The earth from which she'd come took her back where she belonged.

It seemed to take a long time to get back up the hill. He kept stumbling, and his knees scraped against the rocks and bled. He fell in a pool up to his knee. By the time he was nearing the top the light was up: ahead of him the sun's sloppy yellow gaudily rising, behind him the moon going down. He turned and looked back.

From here he could see most of Kildarragh, from the tiny hovels by the edge of the cliffs, to Darby's house on Quilty's doorstep. Morning was bringing the people out, but they were not behaving in the usual way. Some of the men and a few boys were gathering in the fields along the lower path, congregating here and there in clusters and talking very seriously. Father Buckley was there, and Peader Fox standing a little distance apart on his own. He saw Alma Sheehan come out of her door at the same time as Cliona Scanlon, the pair of them meet in the middle between their two houses and put their heads together and talk.

Then two strange things happened simultaneously, as if someone had given a signal. A band of soldiers came marching round the bend of the road from the shebeen; and Sal Quinn came tearing out of her door in a terrible state, with her heavy white breasts hanging out and her hair wild, shouting, 'Eliza! Eliza!' in a sore voice. The boys came running after her, all dishevelled. She was mad, screeching, and Cliona Scanlon put out her arms to catch her. After the soldiers came dragoons, six of them, two abreast, and constables on foot. Some of the men in the fields started shouting. Father Buckley strode out in front of them and faced the soldiers, and a sergeant on a white horse rode out before the bailiff and the men with the big ram and all the tackle. Then the priest and the sergeant spoke together for a few minutes. Jamie could hear Father Buckley's high voice but not the words, because Sal Quinn was making so much noise as she ran from house to house, in and out, round all the walls, searching for her daughter.

'She's gone! She's gone! Someone's taken her. She couldn't have walked on her own, someone's taken her. Where is she? Eliza! Eliza!'

The boys ran here and there with her, but Cliona and Alma had realised something was starting up below, and they set off running down through the cabins. A voice in the crowd reached him where he stood, crying, 'Shame! Shame!' Sal fell down on her knees and covered up her face.

'Eliza!' the boys called helplessly here and there.

More people were emerging from their cabins. Jamie saw the sergeant ride forward into the crowd and address the people directly, but he still couldn't catch the words. The big white horse rode here and there; bit by bit, the edge of the crowd fragmented. A neighbour woman he didn't know ran up and put a shawl round Sal's shoulders, covering her breasts. Sal sat down on a rock, called the boys to her and pulled them in under the

332

shawl.

Jamie counted.

Eight houses down below nearer the sea, just hovels really. Three further up the village, and Darby's house. Twelve then. He didn't really know any of the people except the Quinns. The houses by the sea went down easily: the people came out of them and stood watching while the bailiff's men set up the ram and tumbled them all in. They were just dry sod and went: Poof! Dust. Eight heaps of dust. You wouldn't have known they'd been homes with people living in them.

The whole village was out watching by now, standing here and there on rocks to see better. There was no more shouting. Whatever the man on the white horse had said had quietened things down. Those who had to go were gathered all together where the track to the crossroads began, some with bundles, some with nothing. So many people had come out of those eight cabins, Jamie tried to count, but the children wouldn't keep still. Then the dragoons formed up on guard, at attention, and the bailiff's men went further up the hill and got the people out of another three houses, this time bigger buildings made of stone.

Cliona Scanlon came running back up the hill.

'Have you got everything you're taking now, Sal? They're here.'

Sal looked blankly at her. 'Where's Eliza gone?' she asked.

'Sal, *allanna*,' Cliona said, 'she must be dead.'

'We can't leave her!'

Sixteen people, seven of them children. He had time to count this time. These three houses didn't go down like the others. Instead, the bailiff's men boarded up the windows and drove big metal hasps over the doors, then bashed the thatch in on the roofs while the people stood watching with their hands in their pockets and their bundles on the ground. When they came up to Darby's house, Sal jumped down from her rock and ran desperately towards them.

'My little girl's gone missing,' she cried.

A man with a pale blue waistcoat, who seemed to be in charge, turned a sad, cold face towards her, then talked to Cliona Scanlon. Jamie couldn't make anything out. Sal gave a little scream and ran back to the house, crying her little girl was gone, her little girl was gone, she couldn't just go and leave her. Everyone thought she was mad, even Cliona Scanlon did, you could tell by the way she was looking at her.

'I don't know,' Cliona said to one of the men, 'I didn't see the child this last week at all. She was very ill, I do know that.'

So many had died, they must have lost track.

Sal ran about like a panicked hen, the boys trailing after her, then she flopped down exhausted out on the stony track. She didn't look round to see them banging in the staples, but she screamed when the roof fell in, as if the child was still in there, with the thatch and heavy roof beams falling on her. A man hammered something on the door, a sheet of paper. Another came and spoke to her rapidly, and another, then they got Cliona to sit and comfort her for a while before they took her down the hill to where all the others were gathered. She walked with her head down, flanked by her boys, each holding a hand.

Everyone came out, the women with the

children round them, and stood in the fields on either side of the road with the men and Father Buckley, saluting those who passed out of the townland, even those they'd had very little to do with.

17

Don't ever think you can get away with it. Whatever you do goes with you for ever, wherever you go. Remember that, Eliza, I think as I walk on along this road that winds up and down and everywhere and takes me nowhere. I'd call it running mad if it were not me, but I am not running and I'm certainly not mad. I'm seeking my fortune. Everything's coming with me, my home in my head. I've never gone far before. None of us has, except for Darby Quinn and the men who go on the fishing. When all this is over and the fever's gone and the crops back, and when my feet have walked enough steps, then I'll go home.

I took ten pence from the sideboard. I hate to leave them short but it's better than giving them this thing I have. This is for me alone.

I had a piece of bread but I ate it a long time ago. How long? Oh, I don't know. Long, long. Long since I saw anything familiar. These lanes all look the same to me. It's not as pretty here as home. I walked as far as I could after Boolavoe, till I had to sit down. I have to be very careful and preserve my strength. I felt tired as soon as I stopped and could have just lain down right there at the side of the road and had a nap, but I didn't want to make a spectacle of myself. I pulled my cloak about me because it was chilly. It's not rained at least, but there's something in the air says it will. I thought I was getting weaker as I sat there, so I thought I'd better keep on, and now I can't remember how long I've been on the road. There was a night, very long and cold, when I just kept going. Very slow progress I think, because I was getting dizzy. It was the dark making me dizzy. It seemed full of lights that came out of nowhere and pricked my eye, voices shouting loudly from a place in the centre of my skull, blasting outwards. The country is haunted, for sure. Why wouldn't it be? Some of the time I sat under a bridge by a stream. It was nice there. I could hear small night-time things moving in the dark. The stream made a soft singing sound.

This day that's passed since then has been very strange. Long as a lifetime, yet a mere flicker. I went alongside a forest that went on for miles, and there was a farm where they sent out a girl with a dish of thick gruel that lay like a lump of stone in my stomach, but it kept me going.

There was a man followed me and asked me questions once, but I wouldn't speak to him.

And now it's starting to get dark again and I've not got to anywhere. There've been cabins here and there, and the odd cluster of buildings, but nothing like a town, nothing even as big as Lissadoon. If I can get to a town I can buy food. I haven't touched my money yet. I'm not my mother's daughter for nothing; she always knew what to do. You put one foot in front of the other, that's what you do. Even in the dark I can do that. In some ways it's easier, no one to see you in the dark, but it gets colder, and the cold sends quarrelling scurries of wind round my ankles, waking me up and giving me hope. I'm getting on, and if you get on, eventually you reach somewhere. Actually I'm not feeling too bad. I was awfully low yesterday, so bad I had to go off away from myself, get right out and look over my own shoulder. The right one, always the right one I look over, because the left's where I throw salt at the devil, and who wants a faceful of salt? Oh, look, I thought, she's sitting on the bit of rock because she doesn't want to wet and muddy her clothes, and it isn't pleasant to think of all the worms in that loamy earth. If she lay down on there, they might come up in the night and walk all over her. So she keeps going.

That's what yesterday was like, but now I'm back. I'm all here. The night's a beauty. I have enough air in my lungs and the only things hurting are the soles of my feet. I've never quite known this before, this onward push. I feel like a small sliver of something caught in the swell, borne abreast, landward. I might as well sing, softly in respect of the night. *Sleep, oh babe, for the red bee hums, the silent twilight falls. Aoithal from the grey rock comes to wrap the world in thrall.*

I knock at a house along a winding lane and stand far back. A woman comes out.

'What is it you're wanting?' she asks.

'A lodging in your cart shed till the morning,' I say.

She looks thoughtfully at me.

'It's going to be a wet night.' I look at the sky. At that moment it begins, just a few small drops for now, and a gust of wind.

'Oh, go on then,' she says. 'You can get up on the cart, you should keep dry up there.'

'Thank you,' I say graciously, 'it's very kind of you.'

'Go on with you.' She shoos some children back inside. 'I'll fetch you a sup.'

The cart fills the shed, which smells of damp turf and mould and old dung. But it has a wooden door hanging crooked on its hinges, which you can pull across to keep out the worst of the wind, and the roof appears to be sound. It's dry up on the cart anyway, away from the ground chills nipping my feet. I pull my toes in under my skirt and petticoat. I'm glad of my cloak. I wonder what Phelim, who is here in my head, would say if he could see me now? But I can't think of him, it doesn't work. I can't see him unless I see him just as he is and was and always will be, the long grey man sitting between me and my cloak hanging on the wall. And Jamie.

Jamie. Leave it. Some day you'll see him again and you'll explain.

The woman comes and sets aside the door and leans into the darkness. 'I'm putting you something here on the end of the cart,' she says. 'Now don't knock it off.'

This is good of her. She'll probably want to wash the cart down with something strong when I've gone, certainly before she'll let the children ride in it again. I wonder is there a man about?

'God bless you,' I tell her.

God bless you, God bless you, the voices say, *God bless you, Eliza Vesey*. If I had a penny for every blessing of God called down upon me, I'd not be on this road. But then again—

'Here,' she says, putting the warm bowl to my groping hand, careful not to touch me.

'Thank you.' I wrap my two hands around the bowl and lift it towards my nostrils: a faint savoury aroma makes the juices spurt in my mouth. Look how God has blessed me.

'Come far?' she asks.

'Boolavoe.'

'Boolavoe! You're the first from there.'

'Is there a town if I keep going east?'

'Where are you heading?'

'Cork.'

'I wouldn't go to Cork. Everyone's going to Cork. Got people there?'

I shake my head but I don't think she can see me.

'You keep on this way and you'll reach Closheen. Eight mile away. There's a depot there. After that it's Macroom.'

'Macroom,' I say. Well, now I am going to see the world. I'd rather it were Mallow, I'd like to see Mallow.

'Can I get to Mallow?' I ask.

'That's a fair way north.'

We shall see.

'You watch out for yourself.' She pulls the door across. Her footsteps retreat and I hear her closing up for the night and wonder what it's like for her in there with her four children. She has a light; it's what drew me through the darkness. But I'm snug in the dark, out of the wind and rain, eating my supper, broth with boiled cabbage lying at the bottom of the bowl. I feel well, better than when I left home. I feel very strong in my mind.

*   *   *

Early morning when I left, the rain was over and

there were some very bright stars out, low in the sky. I thought I'd get into Closheen before it was mobbed, but by the time I got there it must have been getting on for midday, and for the past couple of hours there'd been more and more people on the road: things I never thought I'd see, horrible sights to look away from, then look back furtively till your eyes get used to it. Then look and look and look because you must see; ghostly women, aged children, ancient madmen, their bellies swelling up and their mouths green. Closheen is a grand place, with a big church and a poorhouse and a dispensary, but it's all overrun with these people. I couldn't get near the depot. I didn't know what to do. I thought, if I buy some food now with some of my money, I can take it with me and eat along the way. Then I'll get to Macroom or Mallow and maybe I can find a place, a lodging somewhere, and I'll keep some money back.

The way I feel, this thing may not after all be such a death's-head and I'll weather it out. So I walk up and down in Closheen, looking for a shop, keeping away from the scurvied lot sprawling round the poorhouse with no chance at all of getting in. I don't know why they do it. I'd rather take my chances in a field alone than sit down with that lot, at least you'd have a chance, 'stead of breathing the air of someone bringing up their guts and coughing all over you. They don't cover their mouths.

But after I've spent four pence on bread and found it stale, and walked on out of Closheen into some wild, mist-ridden highland that goes on throwing itself higher, I begin to wonder. The fine mist covers me and turns the bits of my hair I can see pearly. The sides of the road are bare and run with rivulets. Anywhere you sat for a rest you'd get wet, no hedges, no walls, only ditches, deep ones like shallow gullies. Pray God it doesn't go on like this till night. What am I to do? What for the love of God am I to do? Suddenly my head races. Pulses hammer. Here in the mist, coming up from below, falling down from above, thick white clouds, flowing and billowing down the mountainside, this strange mountain, not the old mountain I walked over a million times. This one's much bigger. A real mountain, I suppose. I suppose wherever you go there'll always be a bigger mountain, if you keep on marching forward and forward and ever forward in the world till they shoot you down in your tracks, and that's what they'll have to do with me because I am immortal, the only one; I created Juliander, who has materialised on the very top of nowhere and stands in front of me now in the mist in her plain black shawl, completely unadorned, yet far, far more beautiful than I could ever be.

She trails me all down the other side in the rain, sometimes behind, sometimes before. She doesn't scare me. She's the gentlest thing ever born, she wouldn't hurt a fly let alone me. And she's on my side. Thank God, we're lower down now, and the mist is more kind. This is a beautiful valley. A flat dish with a lake and walls all round, and the sweet small cluster of whitewashed cabins there ahead. Oh God though, but it's very poor past Closheen.

I'm stopped in my tracks by the grey pillar of a gate post. Someone's taken a lot of care with the wall by the house, the stones have been lovingly placed. There's a goat, white-eyed, very high up, watching me, but no one in any of the houses. Not

341

even a skinny cat. I don't know what this place is. I walk on. When I look back I see the eyes of the houses watching me, dark and hollow.

Sing, Queen Eliza, to shorten the road. *Sleep, oh babe, for the red bee hums, the silent twilight falls.* I have a beautiful voice. The road keeps forking and I never know which way to go, and there's no one to ask, so I guess. But then the land evens out and goes this way and that, a pretty, sweet kind of a prospect, with a stream where I see a heron and wonder why no one's killed it. You used to see herons under Briggan. Wonderful to see a heron take flight close by. Wonderful big long-legged bird. I don't know what call a heron has. Reed beds line one side of the road. Where am I coming to now? There are people. Faces along the road. I don't think anyone can see me. I'm walking. I was always a walker. I love to sing as I walk but not too loud. *The pale moon has drained her cup of dew.* I think the whole country must be on the move. *And weeps to hear the sad sweet song I sing, oh love, to you.* That so unnatural a mass of us are on the move makes me afraid more than anything yet. This is death, isn't it? The death of something very big. It's like throwing a log on the fire in the old days and seeing all the woodlice run this way and that, hopeless. Here we are, running this way and that, woodlice. Dying under the hedges, under the stairs, in the drains and in the boreens, lying on our insect backs kicking our frantic insect legs.

I passed a roof of sods over a ditch. A white face peeped out, a child, girl or boy I couldn't tell. I smiled and the face smiled back. I gave a little wave, as you do to a child. I kept on and met a man and a woman from Limerick making for Cork and hoping to get on a boat. She was pregnant and said she didn't want her baby born in this country. America for me, she said cheerfully. This country's finished for me. The man's small and shy. They wonder about me, a woman alone. I say I'm going to meet my husband, he's working in Cork and has a place for me, and we keep each other company as far as Macroom, where we split up at the gate of the union poorhouse. A foul crowd waits in the cold there. Their eyes look blank, as if they've waited for days. The pair say they'll wait and try for a place. He can get eight pence a day in there, he says, but God, the work, it's killing. Still, for a few days, and you're fed; and the money will see them through till they're on their way.

Well, it's no use to me. I'd never be strong enough, and anyway you wouldn't get me inside that place in a million years; so we wish each other luck and part.

Macroom's full of lost raggedy people, wandering here and there trying to find someone to beg from, but everyone's just as hopeless as they are. No one bothers me. I'm just another one of them, lost and raggedy, I suppose. Looking down I see how the hem of my skirt is muddy and decaying, the dirt spreading upwards through the fibre. That's just how the dark shadow spreads through the skin, starting at the feet, at the cold, cold ground; sucking up the badness and pulling it up through the body. I've given up avoiding people though; there are too many about, too many of us, and half of them are far worse than me. What can you do? We'll all wash around in this and some'll sink and some'll swim.

I'd never have gone out looking this dirty before.

343

Look at *her*, Juliander standing looking in a window at things she can't have, her white face sideways against the dark lining of her hood. She's dirty too but dirt becomes her.

*　　*　　*

'Wait a while,' the man says.

'What?'

I hope he's not going to stick to me.

'Hold back,' he says.

We're in a barn, waiting in line for stirabout. I've been here two or three hours, I'd say, and I'm scared they'll run out. It's got dark while I've been waiting but they've lit lamps next to the boiler.

'What are you on about?' I ask him.

'Give it another ten minutes,' he says, putting his face, small and deeply seamed, loose-skinned, too close to mine and speaking confidentially. He's being too familiar with his eyes. His breath smells of meat. 'Honestly, Miss,' he says, 'if you can wait another ten minutes, the screb from the bottom of the pot's much, much better. Here.' He takes my arm. 'Stand just here, you'll not lose your place.'

He's short and slight, I hardly have to look up to him at all. I saw he had his eye on me from way back in the queue. This could be good or bad, I think, he may have his uses. He's some rough spalpeen from nowhere, the kind used to dig for us in the old days.

'What's your name, Miss?'

'Juliander.'

'That's a funny name. I've never heard that one before. Julie-what?'

'Juliander. It's a very old name.'

'Is it now?'

'What about you?'

'Me?'

'Your name?'

'Cornelius Dunne.'

There's no harm in him and he's younger than he looks, going by his voice.

'Where you from?' I ask.

'Fermoy.'

'Why d'you leave Fermoy, Cornelius?'

He grins and shrugs, liking my familiarity. 'Now,' he says, 'move forward a little now, Miss. We'll be just in time. I'm famished.'

He's right. By the time we're there with our cans they're down to the crust, prising it from the bottom and the sides with knives so it comes up in great big chunks, nice and thick and burnt on one side. The old woman at the boiler packs it down in my can.

'That'll put a lining on your belly,' Cornelius Dunne says.

'It will, my dear,' the old woman says kindly.

The burnt bits are lovely. It's like eating bread. We take our cans and I walk away and find a place where I can sit and eat, not too close to anyone else. All around, the ground is filling up with the filth of us. And here comes Cornelius Dunne following Juliander. He says nothing, just sits alongside, companionable but not too close, eating screb from the tin with his fingers.

'You going to Cork?' he asks me.

I nod. Everyone's going there, we're on a tide. You can get a lodging in Cork, and there's work.

'You eat very dainty, don't you?' he says.

'Just because it's hard times doesn't mean we're

pigs,' I reply.

He cocks an eyebrow. It's his teeth put me off, they look worm-eaten. They must pain him. Another wave of fear is rising in me. Very like a sickness, the moment rushing on unbearable, the moment before your body forsakes you. Oh, forsake me not, not here, not now. I think I sway. A rushing in my head and my eyes blank out for a second or two, but it passes and I'm back, just.

'It's the food,' he says, 'too quick. Lie down for a bit, you can keep the rest for later.'

God, don't let me, don't let me, not here. I hand him my can, still with a fair amount in it, and down I sink very, very slowly to my stomach, till my cheek is against the cool earth floor. Sweat breaks on my forehead, hot but freezing at once. My teeth give that vile skeleton chatter, that mad clatter, insane. 'Look away!' I say before my teeth clack again.

I don't know whether he looks away or not, I don't care any more, I close my eyes and welcome the darkness. If I can just stay still and quiet and not get too hot. Leave me alone. Oh God, this is hell. How long can hell last? Walk a straight line. Give up. Thank God for the cold coming up through the earth.

Then I remember what this is: it's nothing but fear flexing its slow wing over me. Let the earth seep in, purifying, drawing heat down into the underworld, into the Middle Kingdom, which has gone to ground.

So I slept, I suppose. Since I left home it's become so hard to tell the difference between sleeping and waking. But now here I am waking up on the ground. It's dark and very cold. I'm not sick any more. I'm fine, in spite of the rotten smell in this place. Still, it would be wise to do everything very slowly. Sickness is like a hawk, it can drop like that. I sit up and look around. Light comes in through the gaps in the barn walls. Attempting sleep, the shadowy humps reek steadily all around me, as far as the eye can see. If I open my mouth the tainted air will get in, already it's coating the insides of my nasal passages. I must be mad to have come in here, but I needed to eat, and I need to keep something by for Cork. I got a ticket for this, it cost me a ha'penny. I can stay one night and in the morning I get to fill my can again before I go. That's not too bad.

Three or four feet away, Cornelius Dunne is sleeping gracelessly. Where's my can? I'll need it. I start feeling about for it. These people don't sleep easy and quiet. They whisper and groan and mumble, quietly sob into soft things to muffle the sound. A baby's restless, its mother's desperately trying to keep it quiet. Of course it'll cry, poor thing, it's hungry. She's got no milk for it. I can hear it, champing away frantically at her empty teat, every now and again spluttering with frustration.

He sits up. 'How are you, Juliander?'

'I'm better now.'

'Got your stirabout here,' he says, leaning forward to place the can in my hand.

'Good man,' I say.

'Shall I stay with you?' Cornelius Dunne asks.

How should I say? Cornelius Dunne, you are a sweet good man, but I don't want to be saddled with you. How I say it I don't know, but I do say it.

'Juliander,' he says, 'you don't have to explain a

thing to me. How if I stick by you while it suits us both?'

We sit close, heads together, and talk quietly through the night. I have a husband and a son. He has a mother and a father and a wife who's dead. It's fallen to me to be his comfort.

We stayed together next day, then there was a lane, darkness, a night of stars. A hedge. His wife was called Mary. Well, I'll be Mary, said I. You'll be Tadhg and Phelim and Jamie.

I lost him somewhere the next day.

My cloak is lost too. I have been dizzy, wandering. I wish I could get a ride on a cart but I haven't even seen one since Closheen. The road to Cork's too crowded. Truth to say, I don't know where I've been, I don't know anything. God's pitched me in with this lot. So many faces here next to me looking at me in the crowd. I'm hungry. I go on. Moment to moment, I have no idea beyond moment to moment. Old man, face of a saint in a window. But people are ugly, all told, and where are *my* people? My people are far far away, gone, back there where they knew my name.

Roads. Lights. Rain.

I hear of food. Shelter.

I learnt a thing or two on the road to Cork. I learnt: Wait if you can before you eat, give it time to thicken up. I learnt: let yourself go, like falling in a pit, let go, let go, let it happen. I learnt: Wait and see. Wait and see.

*   *   *

I always had a feeling one day I would see Cork City. Beyond it, there is the whole world. Seeing

348

the dove-grey of its spires springing up on the skyline, I say: Stay with me, Lord, I've made many a mistake but I'm still trying. Take me somewhere. Show me the next sight.

A long river approaches the city. I cling to its side as closely as I can, for a river is always a good thing to keep near, and this is a great one, the size of which I've never seen before. At home we just had little streams running down everywhere to the shore, but no real big river like this, with the other bank very far away. I feel strangely joyful. The marshlands are full of poor people, all of us flowing into the city along with the river. Tall-masted boats accompany our progress. Sometimes a carriage goes by with high-stepping horses. The meadows roll on, up and down, and the road is good, graced by tall trees. Here and there on the hills I see beautiful houses with sweeping gardens, willows, lawns sloping down to the water's edge.

*   *   *

Cork is really very beautiful, with its houses so large and clean and sombre. I find myself walking through an area of long streets with terraces and crescents. The wild hurricane could blow all night long and nothing would touch these houses. The streets are paved on either side.

I drift on, further on. The buildings become grander, great stone frontages and doors wider than any doors I've ever seen. I have to stop and just gape. No one takes any notice of me. When I turn the corner there are raggy boys whipping their tops on the pavement, sweet, barefoot babes, dirty, silly and proud. I have to stand and smile at them,

349

but one of them says, 'You're silly in the head, missus,' and another picks up a stone, so I walk on, tears coming into my eyes. I haven't a clue where I'm going. I just wash about here and there, tossed like a bit of wood on the surf. My feet are killing me but I can't stop and sit down, not here. The streets are just too fine in this quarter. A whiskered gentleman in a fine silk waistcoat walks from his front door to a high black carriage waiting at the kerb. I've never seen such lovely horses, they look as if they've been polished.

I watch people very closely, following anyone who looks poor, who might lead me to somewhere more suited to my condition. At last I come to a bridge with a whole road going over the river, with pavements and people teeming upon it, and carriages and carts pulled by great snorting horses, and I see shops on the other side with bright crowded windows, and people with money to spend going in and out of them. Downriver there's another vast stone bridge reflecting in the water, three massive legs and wide shallow arches. A heavily laden boat is passing underneath.

But when I've crossed the river, I can't get over the road to the shops because there are too many horses and so much shouting, and I start to feel weak and peculiar. So I stick near the wall and walk back across the other bridge, letting myself be carried along just anywhere the tide goes. I soon discover that Cork is full of bridges. Wherever I go there's one to cross. The river is everywhere. There must be more than one river, I decide. Tired out at last, I lean on the wall. Looking one way I see wharves and warehouses, factories. The other way there are buildings like palaces, with columns

350

and great flights of steps and stone people carved above the doors. The river is as busy as Weavergate on fair day. Boats line the walls, three deep in places. Men shout to one another, hauling bales and pallets up and down the high walls of the quay.

I close my eyes. It's too big, all of it. Why did I come here? I don't know what to do. Think. Think. First, am I ill? That's important. Stand still and consider. What is there of pain, sickness, weakness, unease, disease? I know I'm not well, but am I ill? Where's the brooding thing I felt within?

Yes, it's there, like a dragon sleeping in a cave underground. Ssh! Let sleeping dragons lie. Tiptoe.

After I time I swallow the thing in my throat, sickness or fear or both in a clot. I open my eyes and look around. On a corner across the road a coarse-faced woman is begging from passers-by, her apron very dirty, the flounce of her skirt all fouled with muck and dung. She'll know, I think. I wait till some other people are crossing, then run over in their wake and approach her. She sees at once I'm no good for money and looks through me, but I walk right up and ask her where's the food depot.

'Adelaide Street,' she says.

'Is it soup?'

'You can get soup,' she says, 'but you need a ticket.'

'Where can I get one?'

Another beggar woman has appeared from nowhere, this one with a big mole on her face and a couple of dirty little scrubs dancing attendance. 'Go to the Society of Friends,' she says, 'they'll give you a ticket.'

The paving slabs are flat and smooth and even, so my feet don't trip up; I can see them walking on beneath me, flap, flap, flap, with the last bits of the soles of my shoes just about falling off. I'm going round in circles. I listened very hard, but I can't find the Society of Friends and I can't find Adelaide Street and I can't keep going either, so when I see some steps I stop and sit down and lean my head against the wall, my hands keeping hold of the iron railings. That'll keep me fixed to the earth. I close my eyes. I shall wait now. Just wait here quietly and see what happens.

After some time—who knows?—a shadow falls across me. I look up. An old gentleman with a round pink face, watery eyes and a moustache is leaning down kindly towards me. 'Are you after the depot, Miss?' he asks.

I nod.

'Well now, isn't it just around the corner from here,' he says cheerfully, 'Come on now, I'll show you.'

He puts out his arm to me but I'm afraid to take it because he is so scrubbed and shiny and I'm so dirty.

'Oh, come now!' he says, 'Come, come, come.'

I stand unsteadily, take his arm and walk along with him. I feel so strange. So dizzy.

'I haven't got a ticket,' I say.

'Well now, we can fix that,' he says, and walks me round the corner and through another street, and down a lane that comes out at the side of a building where a great mass of people are queuing on the pavement, some standing, some sitting, some even lying, so it looks as if no one's moved in a long time. 'Now, Miss,' he says, 'you take your place here and if you wait you'll get your soup.'

I sit down on the pavement at the end of the line. He stands, looking this way and that. I suppose he thinks I'm silly in the head. I can't help it. It's just that I'm so tired I have to put my head down on my knees at once. It's so rude, I haven't even thanked him and he's being so kind. How many of them would want to touch you, let alone give you their arm? I can't keep my eyes open, not even for a second, even the burning in my feet won't keep me here.

Next thing I know, I've slept; maybe for a long time, because I'm numb from the pavement and the lamps across the street have been lit.

'Miss! Miss!' Someone shaking my arm.

All around me the people have hemmed me in. I'm packed up tight against the wall.

'Miss!'

It's him, my deliverer, his kind eyes pale and wet, his grey moustache sticking to his lip and getting in his mouth. 'I've got your ticket, Miss,' he says, 'you'll be all right now.'

I take it.

'Keep it safe now.' He folds it into my fingers, enfolding my hand with his two big warm ones, squeezing briefly. A quick smile, a firm pat on the shoulder, and he's gone.

I look down at the ticket between my fingers. How small and dirty my hands are, like a child's that's been playing out all day. The ticket has three numbers on it but they swim before my eyes. I try to see down the street, but the kind old gentleman is long gone; tears spring into my eyes, hot and sudden. Taking out my hankie, I blow my nose,

353

hold my bundle close and wait.

There's no movement, just more and more people coming.

Waiting for soup in that endless line I think of all the songs I ever learnt about Cork City.

When I was on horseback wasn't I pretty?

Me. Straight-backed on a horse. I never rode on a horse in my life, and I never was pretty. When I was a child we had a book on the shelf: *The Songs of Sweet Cork*.

When I was on horseback, wasn't I gay?
Wasn't I pretty when I entered Cork City,
And met with my downfall on the fourteenth
  of May.

Some of the people around me have got spoons tied to their cans. They're all families by the looks of them. Awful, plucked-looking families, their colours all greyed over by the dust of the road. Down the line there's a baby that cries all the time. A little girl, missing her two front teeth, smiles at me. A man down the line has a big boil on the side of his neck and a wide trap of a mouth, loose and dripping like a broken gutter. Thank God, some of these people look worse than me. Ah well, I suppose I fit in nicely. I've fallen down a drain, found my place. I haven't got a spoon. Poor me, all alone. Where can I get a spoon? Will they give one inside? Should I ask?

Some sleep, some sit and stare. Two women chat quietly as if by their own firesides.

So very icy cold it gets in the night, and worse towards morning; I thought I couldn't bear it, kept thinking, shall I die soon? Now?

I wanted to sleep, I tried and tried but couldn't. Then something terrible happened.

I wanted to pee, it got worse and worse, a sharp pain that had me doubling over, but I was scared to move and lose my place, so I stayed and stayed till there was a sweat all over me, and then it just went—a great pain, stabbing—and I peed myself under my skirt and petticoat. I pretended to be asleep. No one said anything. It was such a relief I could have cried, and all the sweat dried up in a second and I felt much better. Then after, as the wet turned cold and clamped against my skin, I shivered and my teeth were set click-clacking again, old chattering skull that I am. It brought back drifting cobwebs of memory of a time when this feeling was familiar. But then someone would come and whip off my sopping drawers and sit me by the fire. That was the first fire of my life, with the straw and turves burning yellow; and the round cauldron steaming on the chain, and my mother and father there. There've been other fires since, fires I coaxed up of a morning, tamped down last thing at night; I've set potatoes roasting in the amber glow of the soft live ashes.

But now I feel as if every fire in the world has gone out and I'll never be warm again.

Morning at last. The cold lifts a little. Sluggish, my blood begins to flow again.

As if at a signal, a lifting comes. A long wave movement all along the line, and we are standing at last and shuffling forward. Standing makes my head spin. Sweat pops out. If the light gets any brighter it'll split my eyes open. Really, I'm only slightly here. A breath could take me. I'm the first-gone, the not-strong, the poor one, the weak one,

355

the giver-up, the one you look away from. People are walking past now on the other pavement, normal people who don't want to see us. The only ones who look are those like us. If Phelim were here searching for me, would he see me, I wonder? Don't look for me among the ordinary people, you'll have to go down for me, down among the doomed things. I see that a dark rivulet of pee has run down across the pavement and into the gutter from where I was sitting.

A man asks me where I'm from but I don't answer.

Someone else is talking behind my back.

'Skibbereen,' a voice says. 'And your people?'

'Dunmanway.'

A woman puts an arm round my waist. 'Come along now, bonny,' she says in my ear, 'keep moving.'

I start. There are pains in my ears.

'Have you got your can?' she asks.

I have my can.

Slowly we troop forward. Dogs bark somewhere in the city. Under my breath to keep me moving I sing *When I Was On Horseback*, a pretty song about a dreadful thing. Funny. That a young man dying of the clap could make such a lovely song. He had a terrific funeral though and a great wake, I dare say. We're not getting our proper funerals these days. Briggan they were putting them in the ground any old how all on top of one another. How would you find your people, all this being over? Then it strikes me that if I die, Phelim and Jamie won't be able to find me, they won't be able to come and see me in the earth. I'll be in a paupers' grave with a lot of strangers. How vile. I must go back, if only for that. I will, as soon as I've eaten. I still have some money kept back for lodgings, I wonder if it's possible to get on a coach from a place like this?

I'm inside, in a dark hallway, and the smell of us all packed in is atrocious. The babies loose their full-throated morning howls. We stay in the hall for a long time, looking at the brown walls. Over the smell of our bodies another settles, something good and thick and heavy, government soup. I feel sick. My knuckles have gone white on my can, which has become to me like Phelim and Jamie and my da and ma all rolled into one. It's mine, my only one, it's been with me ever so long. Since—when did I pick it up? When?—I don't know, I can't remember. A long time ago, and it's gone everywhere with me from far back, very far back, when there was a place to return to. My stomach's all knotted and cramped, I must eat and then I'll be able to think straight again.

It took another hour to get into a big room with a very high ceiling and people sitting all over the place, on the floor and on benches round the walls, drinking their soup. I don't know how long I waited in there. I slept, I think. I lost my place twice and was scared the soup would all be gone before I got there. My God, I thought, I'll never be so stupid again, I'll buy some bread and make it last. I'll make it so there's always just a little bit left in my pocket. The strong smell of the soup was making me feel sick but I wanted it. Oh God, how I slavered for that smell even as taking it in made me retch. I kept my breathing very shallow but it was like drowning. All the lines moved forward at a snail's pace. You were supposed to wait for your

357

number to be called but any system had gone long ago, and as long as you showed your ticket you got something. Every now and then one or other of the lines would slow down completely and stop while they topped up the pot. It happened with mine just before I got to the long table, where grim-faced men and women, too rushed to bother with talk and palaver, ladled green-yellow soup as fast as they could. Sweat greased their foreheads. I'd have preferred the stuff from the bottom, but what can you do?

At last the man fills up my can and I go to the side and blow on it. I drink, burning my lip. Tears fill my eyes. The soup's just water, hot, coloured water. A few bits in it, pooh! Cabbage. I can't do this. I can't do this any more, I need to be home in my bed; oh God, more than anything in the world I need to be home lying in my own bed. I need a spoon. Where can I get a spoon? How stupid, if I'd known I could have brought a spoon with me from home. You live and learn. I get a sudden vivid picture in my mind, the open drawer in our kitchen with the knives and forks and spoons all thrown in any old way. I could almost pick up that apostle spoon we have. And Jamie's old teething ring. But it doesn't really matter. You don't really need a spoon for this watery stuff, there's nothing to it really. It goes straight down, scalding my throat, too quick I know but I can't help it. It's nowhere near enough. I want more, something solid. I've never been so hungry in my life.

All those hours waiting, I thought I was hungry, and now I've eaten it's worse than ever. My tongue bleeds, which seems appropriate. I think I must have bitten it while I was eating. I'll have to go for another ticket. I'm swallowing blood. Will I spend eternity in a line, waiting my turn? Now what? Live on my blood till I get my hands on a loaf, that's what I'll do. Buy a loaf, it's more important than rent money.

First, buy a loaf.

My ticket's gone and I can't stay here, so I'm out with my stomach churning, into bright sunshine and a white sky. What a fool I am, I drank that much too fast, you'd think I'd know better by now, wouldn't you? I walk along for a while, dizzy in the sudden sunshine, nowhere to go, and I wonder what they're doing at home at this exact moment. I have to sit down. Where? All these big buildings and so many people. Get away from the main thoroughfare. An alley. A doorway. The waves of sickness are rising, jostling each other. Something comes up and I swallow it down, an effort that makes my throat sore. I waited so long for that, I'm not letting it go all over this filthy ground, rubbish strewn everywhere. I bet there's rats. I sit on the ground and my head goes down between my knees. I wait, fighting with all my might, trembling, till the spasm has abated; then wipe my forehead with the edge of my shawl and look about me.

I'm not so bad now it's passed, I'll do for a while. This is a narrow mean sort of an alley, with three or four dirty-fronted shops and scruffy people standing about the doorways and staircases. No one seems to think it at all funny that I'm sitting here in the gutter with the rubbish. Maybe there'll be a room here somewhere, where I can go and lie down for a while. That's what I could do with, a place to lie down till I'm feeling stronger. When I feel a bit better I'll ask.

359

I give myself a few more minutes then slowly get up. Could be steadier but I'll do.

First, get a loaf.

I must have left that place, though I can't remember it. There are holes in time. I'm in a slow dream of a walk. The city's too tall and I can't get across the wide streets—a brewer's horse nearly knocked me down when I tried. Everywhere I go there's people, more people than I've ever seen. I have no idea where I am or where I'm going, I'm just wandering about. Now I see stalls, a few barrows in a side street. A woman's selling soda farls. But when I walk towards her, suddenly I'm so light I might lift off the ground and float away. This becomes a real fear, so that every few steps I have to stop and touch the wall. I know what this is, it's one of those dreams where you know you're dreaming—at least, you're sure you are, but then again you might be wrong. You have to get a hold on these dreams and anchor them, refuse the next soaring step that will carry you higher and ever impossibly higher than anyone could ever go and live. Keep one foot always on the ground. One then the other, one then the other, one foot always on the ground. Keep an eye on them, they're very important.

If I want to look around me I have to stand still because I can't do that and control my feet at the same time.

When I reach the barrow I say, 'How much for one of those?'

'Wait your turn,' says a woman's voice, not the barrow woman's.

The barrow woman is rushed off her feet, you can see. Her mouth moves all the time as if she's talking to herself.

'I'm sorry,' I say. I hang my head and look only at the pavement and hot tears pour from my eyes and splash on the ground.

'Oh for heaven's sakes, let her go,' someone else says.

'What do you want, dear? Buck up now.'

'One of those.' I point.

'A farthing,' she says and hands me the soda farl.

I'm wiser now, I won't rush. I'll wait a while before I even start nibbling it. I put it in my bundle and walk away, feeling better knowing it's there. I can smell the river. That's where I go, to stand on one of the bridges and nibble slowly at one torn off corner of my bread while watching all the activity. A great ship is being loaded up. I'll eat a tiny bit now and save the rest. It occurs to me I could get on a boat like that and sail away. I wonder how much is a passage to America?

The sky is light and I have no idea of the time, and though the sun's bright it's still cold. I turn to walk away and a woman no bigger than me pushes her beak into mine. She looks like a blackbird, bright brown eyes on the sides of her head. 'Hello, my dear,' she says, blotting out everything else. 'Are you not so well then?'

She has a scarf tied under her chin, dark hair on her forehead. 'All on your own, are you?' she asks.

'I'm looking for a lodging,' I say, my voice floating out startlingly from a place on the crown of my skull.

'What is it, dear?' Her voice is crude but steady. 'Looking for a lodging? How are you off for money, love?'

I'm no fool. I'm not telling her how much I've got

361

left.

'How much is a lodging?' I ask.

'Tuppence a week,' she says, 'sharing.'

I can get two weeks with what's left after the soda farl. I can get off the streets, rest, get better.

'I can pay,' I say. 'Is it near?'

She puts a hand on my shoulder to steady me as I rise.

'Come with me.'

I walk beside her, nearly running to keep up with her even strides, like a child walking with its mother, though she's no size. She's wearing a dress cut high above her ankles, all patched and tattered in many different shades of blue, and her mouth is set in a natural upturn that is not a smile. She's carrying a three-legged stool. 'I have to hawk this,' she says, shaking it by one of its legs. 'I'll be a while.'

We stop on the corner of a street wider than any I've yet seen. It takes my breath away.

'Straight up there,' she says, pointing a thin downward-bending finger with a long black nail as thick and ridged as a ram's horn. 'Follow the curve round. Near the top, ask for Harper's Row, just off Paul Street. Number nine, top floor. Just knock and go in and say Margaret Foley sent you. I'll be along within the hour. What's your name, dear?'

'Eliza Vesey.'

She repeats it, nodding once, conclusively. 'Go on now, Eliza,' she says, blinks her bird's eyes sharply and leaves me there dazzled.

You could fit a score of Weavergates in this street. Smart carriages line the kerb, the horses snorting in their nosebags. The men are dandies and wear top hats. Surely she doesn't mean down here, this can't be right. Look at me. Oh God, just look at me. No one does, but I stare at them. A lady is getting helped from a gig, her foot reaching down from the step to the pavement, pointed and dainty in its tight black boot, the leather old but shined up beautifully. I can smell food, delicious, unbearable. A boy is shouting, selling something, and a carriage rumbles by, the sound of the horses' hooves bright and smart in the road. I look up and see grand bay-fronted houses and shops. The street is a magnificent curving highway of great pillared buildings, with columns, turrets, graceful arched windows and doors, here and there a dome. In my dream, knowing once more that I'm asleep and wandering in that other world where a second changes everything if you let it, I drift up this bright highway.

I have somewhere to go to: Number nine, Harper's Row. First thing I'll do in my lodging is get rid of my stiff clinging drawers and let the air to my skin under my skirt. I'm dry now, but they feel terrible. How can my lodging be near here? I walk past a building with semi-circular steps running up to an arched doorway wider than a barn. A man in uniform stands bent-kneed at the top. A beautiful blue gown flashes at me like a kingfisher from a window high above the street. Heads and plants and figures and bunches of grapes are carved in stone.

'Harper's Row?' I ask a little boy selling papers on a corner.

He points me down to Paul Street, a narrower, flatter and altogether more modest and rambling kind of a lane, down around a corner and off to the side.

363

I'm back in the alleys, and yet so close to that marvellous thoroughfare. An old woman points me deeper into the warren. It teems. So much for sweet Cork, it stinks to high heaven too. No one sees me. Men in doorways, women walking here and there, the crying of children incessant, sad and unlusty. Blood pounds insistent in my ears, the steady pound of the surf washing in. Well, Eliza, my mother's voice says encouragingly, now you *are* having adventures. We are insects, we are too many, the great besom in the sky is sweeping us all before. These people look like goblins, all of them, an old woman swallowing her nose, a woman with cheeks of scalded red, eyes blackened holes. She laughs in my face. Of course, it's still a dream. They can't all be goblins. Unless, here in the city, at last I have wandered into the Middle Kingdom.

Harper's Row is a narrow high-walled court you have to go under an arch to get into. The front door of number nine stands open onto a dark hall. I can't see anything inside, so I call out, and a young woman opens a door, sticks her head out and says, 'Yes?'

'Margaret Foley sent me.'

She twists brown hair in and out of her fingers. 'Ma!' she calls back over her shoulder, 'which one's Margaret Foley?'

'Top right,' says a deep voice.

'Upstairs,' the girl says.

'Where am I to go to?'

'Top floor.' She turns back into the room, stifling a yawn, 'door on the right for Margaret Foley.'

I stand a while till my eyes are used to the dark. The stairs are narrow and smell like damp rags forgotten for months. On the first floor landing a small window is open to the calls of the yard and the nip of the cold. Four more doors, another staircase, bare, groaning as I walk up it. There are two doors at the top, left and right. The left is not really a door, just a wine-red curtain hanging over an empty door frame; the right has four green panels, on one of which is neatly written the single word: *here*.

I knock.

A small pale man with long straight hair and the look of a noble rodent opens and stares at me: Lord Rat.

'Margaret Foley sent me,' I say.

His lips part on broken teeth. 'For what?'

'For a lodging.'

He sniffs and blinks, throws wide the door. 'Oh yes, yes,' he says, stepping back, 'come in, of course.'

The room's small, with a sloping ceiling and a fire smouldering in the grate. The corners have beds, three straw, the fourth a raised truckle bed where a woman with dark tousled hair lies snoring lightly. On one of the straw beds, a little girl is on her side with her knees drawn up to her chest. Two young boys and a girl with a poor froggy face lurk in other corners.

'Have you money?' asks Lord Rat, and it occurs to me that I've been sent here to be murdered.

'Who am I to see about the rent?' I ask cautiously.

There's no floor space, no room for anything. The rag smell is on everything, and another smell under it, darker and even more dirty.

'Margaret herself,' he says, 'she'll be here soon, I suppose,' then sticks out his hand. 'John

Cullinane,' he says, 'from Fermoy.'

I shake his hand.

'Have you money?'

'I'll pay my way.'

'That's good.'

'And where am I to sleep?'

I hoped he might say, over there across the landing, beyond the curtain; and I'd go over and find a tiny room, a garret, with nothing in it at all as long as it's mine and I can take off my drawers at last and get a jug of water and drink half of it and throw the rest over my private parts. But he smiles apologetically and says, 'It's as you see. The boy'll move over and sleep closer to his ma and sister,' and I see that this is it, my lodging, and I'm to sleep on the straw where those dirty little boys slapped their fleas last night.

Pale Lord Rat has a rapid blink. 'Let the lady rest, gossuns,' he says, 'move,' and the young ones rise like flies and reassemble elsewhere. He indicates the corner to the right of the fireplace for me.

'What name do we call you by?' he asks pleasantly enough as I sit down slowly with my back against the wall and my bundle on my knee.

'Eliza.'

'It's better you keep to this side of the room, Eliza. My wife and little girl are not very well.'

I nod. I understand. I am so tired and stiff I can't help but lie down and close my eyes.

I drift. I'm home at last, in the old feather bed we hung onto through all the bad times. I'm wandering along the great curving street, looking sideways down the narrow lanes where rain beats on the awnings of the stalls selling red apples.

366

What I'd like is some of those apples made into red juice. I feel I've done wrong and must be paying for something but I can't think what it is. I think it has something to do with that slimy seal thing I put out under the hedge in the rain. I never should have done that, even though it had me all ashudder. It had a mouth that cried wide for help, straight into my face, poor ugly thing no one wanted. Now it's got into my dreams, and once a thing gets into your dreams you're stuck with it. Not a thing you can do.

A sound wakes me.

Margaret Foley is sitting by me, still wearing her headscarf. What a peculiar thing she is, eyes bright black droplets with the candlelight in them. 'How are you feeling, honey?' she asks.

I swallow. My throat's bone dry.

'Sissy,' says Margaret Foley, 'get us a drop of water.'

Sissy is the froggy girl. She comes with a baby's cup, which Margaret Foley holds to my mouth. The water is blessedly cold.

'Would you like to sit up now, honey?' Margaret Foley says, then leans close and whispers, 'I've took your old stuff for washing, and your petticoat, but you're fine with what you have on now.'

I'm wearing a strange shift. It's not clean. I rub my spiky hands down it and a shudder follows my fingers, a great icy convulsion.

'Up now, honey,' she says, her hands under my armpits, raising me. My head whirls round and then the room settles, and I'm sitting up.

'Cold,' I manage to stutter, my teeth going mad again.

'Sip,' she says.

367

One candle lights the darkness.

I look at faces looking back. Two pointed boys' faces, white and ghostly; Lord Rat turning toward me from where he bends over the woman in the truckle bed, who was sleeping before but now is moaning and tossing. 'Oh God!' she cries, her white arm a bone ending in his strong fist. 'Oh Francy!'

Her head is thrown back. Her legs kick, her nightgown reveals her nakedness, and her nakedness is plucked and raw and florid as a game bird hanging by the neck.

I can hear someone else in here, out of my sight, in pain. A child it is, groaning like the devil.

From the handsome white blur of Lord Rat, my eyes pass across Margaret Foley and the Frog Princess. I have sunk into the Middle Kingdom. I am attended by a bird, a frog and a rat. No doubt there is some meaning in this.

'Sip,' says Margaret Foley.

If I was home I could give that child something for the pain. I can't see her, she's in the alcove on the other side of the fireplace. Sissy's gone to her.

'Bread and a quart of soup,' Margaret Foley is saying, 'a pennyworth.'

I nod as if I know what she's talking about.

'Sip.'

Cold soup, watery. The other smell, the dark smell, is our insides, seeping out of us.

'Good,' she says, 'now you've eaten you'll be better.'

My skin is tight on my hands.

Like the tide washing out, I'm gone again.

It's dark. Aha, I think, I still have my bread, and I feel for it in my pocket but my pockets are gone, all my clothes are gone, everything is gone. All I have is someone else's shift. How can I go for a walk along that lovely street? I'd like to get a peek at the shops just once, I didn't see them properly before, didn't take the time to stroll, just dandering along and looking. I'll go when I feel a little bit stronger. But then I'm stronger than I think, I always was stronger than anyone thought, strong enough to get up and float away down those brown stairs made narrow by the thin moaning of the damned behind every closed door. On the street my head is weighed down, so that I can only look at the pavement, the black flagstones my shadow slowly crosses. Till it leaps up bright, the street of promenading people, the lanterns lit, the sky pale above the darkened rooftops, and Juliander walking towards me in a peacock-blue dress, low-cut to reveal her pale shoulders and the plump rise of her breasts. Her black hair hangs in ringlets about her throat. She smiles at me very warmly, then slips her arm through mine, and we walk along together looking in the shop windows. But we don't go far. She wants to take me across the road, but I can't do it, it's too wide, and when I look at the other side I feel weak.

A big wagon flies past and I step back. Her little fingers are very pale and graceful in my rough brown ones.

'Shall we take the stairs?' she says. The stairs are through a featureless door in the wall, between two grand buildings. Up and up and round and round they go, through the wild dance of spiralling dust through which she ascends before me, lit by some unearthly light. At the top there are two rooms and she goes into the one on the left, the one with the

369

wine-red curtain, turning as she lifts it and looking back at me with a smile of such sweet, clear-eyed goodness that she scares me. I follow her into the darkness. Her hand seizes mine, pulling me along with a sense of excitement, as if we are children on a bold adventure.

'Look,' she says.

We're in a room, both of us very small, holding hands and looking down. The slimy seal thing is dying on straw, it has nothing about it of a human but the mouth that wails. It's an eyeless, noseless, sticky thing you'd never want to touch. God! Wouldn't a thing like that contaminate a saint? I draw back from its stink with a gasp. But Juliander croons somewhere above my head. She's grown very tall, a high soaring tree of a woman in a grey dress, unadorned, a sorrowing queen of the olden times, beauty sharpened and purified by grief. From her parted lips comes an ancient sound. As everything she does is fully done, she's weeping fully, from the soul. When I wake I still hear her for a moment, then I realise that what I've woken into is just another part of the dream, that she's gone and that I'm still here in the room behind the curtain, this time alone. I stand for a moment absorbing the darkness and the soft pale moonlight pouring in on this quite glorious mid of night, settling into an ashy wash over things which are becoming distinguishable by discernible stages. Something ripe and foul is on the air.

Someone's in bed under the window. I go closer and see it's an old man and a boy. They remind me of Jamie and my da in our big feather bed at home, the two of them that afternoon when Tadhg ran from the peelers, and the thought makes me smile.

370

Then a cloud moves, and the moon shows me the stillness and the blue skin, telling me they're dead.

*   *   *

A little boy is looking at me, his fresh face sweet and dirty.

'What's your name?' I ask him.

'Tommy Cullinane.'

I turn my head on one side and see Margaret Foley and John Cullinane turning the sick woman over in her bed on the other side of the room.

'Tommy, come away from there,' someone says.

The sick woman's nightdress rides up again and she screams. She's all sores on her back and backside, from the straw. I can feel her pain. It's in the room, in the shadows, in the high parts where I can't see, outside in the air, there on the stairs. She screams, then her daughter, the one I can't see, groans even more deeply than before, a sound you shouldn't hear from a child. It's as if something inhuman has come, the voice of some passing demon that's lodged low in her chest.

'Mamma!' shouts Sissy, 'the little woman's being sick.'

Tommy Cullinane's face goes away and Margaret Foley's pinched and withered one appears, smiling benignly down at me, a kerchief that once was white wrapped round her head. Her bird transformation is almost complete.

'Is she a little girl, Dad?' Tommy Cullinane high up on his father's shoulder asks Lord Rat.

'No,' Lord Rat replies. 'She's a little lady.'

Margaret Foley bends over me, smiling down warmly and stroking my face. I know nothing of time any more. I've been away. In pain. 'Poor little creature!' she says with infinite love, 'you're fading all away from us, aren't you?'

The child in the alcove keeps moaning very softly.

My mother puts her hand on my forehead. 'Let's see,' she says. 'There, close your eyes.'

I close my eyes and see Juliander walking on the quay among the crowds that wash around a great ship bound for America. Her shawl is blue, the hood thrown back. The mass of her hair is soft and clean. She's smiling, even though she's scared. Now she's on the gangway. She turns for a moment and looks straight at me, straight at all she's leaving though she loves it painfully. Her eyes glitter. What she is going to she cannot imagine. She looks her fill then turns and walks on up the gangway, and never looks back again. I watch her till she vanishes into the crowd of people milling about on deck. Sailors cry their wild, rough cries.

I hear the striking of a match. It lights the Frog Princess, whose odd wide-mouthed face is curiously beautiful, as if she was begotten of a frog and a fairy in the reeds at new moon. She looks over her mother's shoulder. The light hurts my eyes.

'Look, Sissy,' Margaret Foley says, 'just like with Jojo and your dada. She's going.'

I have to close my eyes now.

18

1850

When they redivided Kildarragh, Phelim, who was working off his debt clearing drains for Lomas, had put in a bid for the top land, which included Darby's old house. He was going to put sheep there. Tadhg was now working the lower reaches of the townland, putting in fences and planning for cattle, no longer such a foolhardy proposition now that the land was so empty and quiet.

Phelim's last cow had been bled to death one night down by the shore. He'd cried about the cow. 'Poor bloody creature,' he kept saying, 'poor bloody creature.' But when Jamie said something about wanting to kill whoever it was that bled her, he shook his head. He looked very old, Jamie realised, and sad about life.

'They were poor people,' his father said, fingering a tear from the corner of his eye, 'they'll have made a pudding.'

Sometimes Jamie rambled for hours on the mountains with his dogs and his gun. At ten he was already taller than his mother had ever been, a lean but sturdy boy with a broadness of face that was neither hers nor his father's but from his grandfather, who sat by the chimney corner more and more now, hardly ever going out even into the yard. Jamie's wanderings often took him over the top, across the rath, down into Kildarragh. It was very different there from the days when he used to trail over with his ma and go in and out of the cabins and play with the children of the cottiers.

All of that was so distant. Walking down towards Kildarragh now with the dogs' white-tipped tails waving before him, he felt only a sense of dislike for its dreariness, the bare and flattened places, the grassy heaps of rubbled stone now hosting a comfortable growth of vetch and thrift, and the open-mouthed, hollow-eyed houses with their tumbled roofs. A few families had hung onto their places here and there. There was smoke from three or four chimneys but there weren't many young people left, and no lads of his own age any more. They'd all gone, drained away by the bad times: first the rains that caused the sheep to have liver-fluke, then the crops unbelievably all rotten and mouldy again, and the familiar smell rising up from the earth so that once more people took to walking about with cloths over their faces.

That was when the Scanlons took ship. The Sheehans and a whole other gang were put out when the Gregory clause came in, but they only moved as far as Carraroe. His father said it was cruel and hard. And the Quinns, they were well and truly gone—Darby to Australia, Sal and the boys to Eskean, according to Tadhg O'Donnell, where she had people who took her in. The only person still here that Jamie really remembered clearly was old Peader Fox, who'd moved into one of the empty cabins and was managing to pay the rent by booleying for Samuel Cloverhill. And of course Tadhg O'Donnell, who sometimes came knocking at the door with a bottle late at night and would sit and talk politics with his father till the early hours. The Terences who'd fattened their pigs on Indian meal were better off now than ever before, Tadhg told his father. He said they'd get a shock one day. Memories were long, and there was all the time in the world.

'No, Tadhg,' his father replied, 'you've lost the fire, and why wouldn't you with a family to raise up?'

Then when Tadhg had gone he'd said to Granda, 'Anyway, hasn't Tadhg done well enough himself, when all's said and done? He can't look askance at us.'

There were no sounds in Kildarragh.

Jamie sat on the cliff tops, his dogs panting on their bellies in the grass, looking out to sea. He thought about his mother. Great feelings surged inside him, too much to understand. What became of her? He remembered her, he always would. She was a saint gone to heaven, his father said. But one night lying in bed he heard his grandfather say she was in a famine grave somewhere. His grandfather said that was the worst of it, that she was lying somewhere in a famine grave with no one taking her flowers.

'She did it for the boy,' Jamie's father replied.

PART FOUR

LUKE
1970—late Summer

19

It's not often I get a letter, and now two. Bill Tiernan the history man came up to me outside the post office in Weavergate. 'Here,' he says, 'this came quite some time ago, but I've been bad with the flu,' and he had two letters for me from America, one dated a couple of months ago, one only last week. Sent care of him. What did she want to do that for? God knows what he thinks. I suppose it's all over the place by now. He looked embarrassed. I acted casual-like. I went into Finn's and sat in the far corner with a pint. Her handwriting on the envelopes was not as I would have expected; it was round and looked like a child's. It came back to me how I used to wait till Ma was asleep and then creep out and go over the mountain all those nights, four weeks or so of it, and the quietness and the tap-tap-tap on the door and the drawing back of the bolt, and seeing how much I unsettled her. I was always away again before six, back in time to get Ma's breakfast.

There was nothing particular doing and no one taking any notice, so I opened the oldest letter first, the fat envelope. There was a letter and a photograph of a baby in a red baby suit lying on a striped blanket.

'*I send this by Bill Tiernan,*' she says, '*because I think the other two letters I wrote you didn't make it. Your mother maybe? I have news, which if you did not get those first two, will come as big news. You have a daughter. Her name is Eliza Quinn Conrad, which I think is a very good name. She's extremely* beautiful, as you can see. I've thrown everyone out of my apartment except for one or two good friends, so there is plenty of room now and you are welcome here whenever you want to come. Do whatever you want to do though, not just whatever reason says or what duty demands. No pressure, Luke. No strings. Things are fine. I don't know if I'll come back to Ireland. Sometimes in the wee small hours me and my friends talk about it, going over when Eliza's a bit older, living in Darby's house and planting vegetables. But to be honest I doubt it. I wouldn't stay there too long with a child. Too lonely. Still, I do like the idea of the house being full of children again, to think of them climbing about on the old dead tree, just like your great-grandfather used to do. I imagine the little townlands rising up again. I would never have the tree cut down. I filled it up with earth on my last day and planted forget-me-nots. Go over there, if you would, and take a look for me. Tell me, how are the forget-me-nots? Last week a couple wrote me from Dublin and asked if they could rent the house. Back-to-the-land types, I suppose. Of course, I said yes. It's in pretty good shape now. Dec's fixing up a bunch of men to even up the track.

About the name. The name's important. When she's older I'll tell her where it came from. Eliza from my grandma Lizzie, because that was her real name. That's from the Veseys. Quinn, of course, from you. I'm having her christened at Corpus Christi on the Upper West Side, the whole works. For some reason I've invited my aunts and my brother and his wife and kids, and I'm not normally a family and fuss person. I don't know why I did such a thing. I seem to think she's significant, the way she brings the two sides together, like the ending of the Wars of the Roses

380

or something like that. Anyway. It would be so nice if you could be there. If money's a problem, don't even think about it. I have money, just you let me know.'

The baby in the picture was lying with its head on one side looking straight at me, its hands raised up in the air. It was a nice enough baby, not that I knew anything about them. I looked at the picture for a while waiting for something to happen. I didn't know what to make of it. I felt as if I should do something but didn't know what. The baby had a serious face and looked as if it knew more than I did.

I put the photograph back in the envelope and took a drink. There was a sweat on my forehead. Who does she think she is, I thought. *I have money, it's not a problem, just ask.* As if I'm lower than her. She thought she knew it all, but she didn't. She said to me once, this is just the flare of a match, this thing with me and you, it's like rain, it just happens.

No, it doesn't, though. I planned it, everything. If you wait long enough, things come to you, you don't have to go anywhere. *She* came. I can't say I knew she would, but I knew exactly what to do when she did. She liked it with me. It was good. She couldn't hide that, the last time I saw her, when they buried the bones. She's one of those people who has it all there in the eyes to see, unlike me. It was in the churchyard in Boolavoe, pouring with rain, and everyone was there from miles around, the local press and one or two reporters from the nationals. She was standing with the Veseys. She was looking at me and I was looking at her and I suppose people noticed, people always notice. Father Lynch said when he

381

put down his hand and felt the little skull he experienced a sense of profound grief that the remains of this fledgeling soul should have lain uncared for so long, while the world and all its changes passed on above. And at the same time, he said, there was a sense of humility and wonder. None of us standing here today will ever know the story of this child's life.

There was a silence while we all stood and thought about it.

Nevertheless, he said, God who sees everything saw fit to raise her up at this precise time. Truly, nothing and no one is ever forgotten by God. And he spoke some more about her soul being at peace now and far beyond all suffering, before they lowered down the very small coffin into the earth. The rain was running in on top off the mud.

I met her on the path outside the church. She was going away in a few days.

'Hello, Beatrice,' I said.

She had tears in her eyes. 'Luke,' she said, 'how are you?'

'I'm OK.'

What I liked about her, she was like those women in the old stories, big fierce warrior women with heavy hair. What I liked, she acted big and tough, but under it all she was shaky.

'When do you leave?' I asked.

'Sunday.'

She leaned towards me as if she'd put her arms round me in spite of them all.

'You'll be back,' I said.

She laughed. 'Who knows?'

'Beatrice,' I said, low, 'am I to come up to you one last time? Am I?'

She laughed again. 'OK, sweetheart,' she said, 'one last time.'

The night after she'd gone I went back up there in the middle of the night. It had become a habit. It was very quiet, not a breath. Little moth-things hovered round the tree. I thought about how I used to sometimes watch her when she thought she was alone, she'd be roaming around and around the ruins, and I'd appear without warning right next to her and scare her with my eyes. I thought she was brave to live there alone. I sat on the rock outside her house and lifted my muzzle up to the full moon and howled, and the sound made me think of packs of wolves pacing the tundra, of snow whirling, blinding.

I finished my pint.

Who does she think she is? Why should I go? Let it be her that comes back over here. She will. She will. Nothing's more sure.

Then I opened up the second, the flat envelope dated only last week. There was just one thin sheet. It said: *Eliza Quinn Conrad christened today. Family should be here. You're a grown man. Get yourself a passport and fly.*